E ldo ✓✓

A New World of Love

Emerald trembled in Joe Scanlon's arms, afraid of what she sensed he was about to say, and even more afraid of the feelings welling up within her.

"I've known you six weeks, it seems like a lifetime," Joe Scanlon said. "I love your laugh, Emerald, and the lilt of your voice. I love your cool head, the fire that I know burns beneath the calm. I love the way you move your hips when you walk, the shape of your breasts. I love you as a whole woman, the woman I want to spend my life with."

Emerald tried to reply, but Joe lifted his finger to her lips. "I know I'm lonely and vulnerable. So are you. But woman, I'd have wanted you even if that wasn't so. Come with me back to America, Emerald. You've taken chances before, take one more. . . ."

Emerald knew too well what it meant to love and lose. Now she was being asked to risk it all again—by this handsome stranger from America who demanded she share not only his desire, but also his overwhelming drive for more wealth and power than she had ever dreamed existed. . . .

EMERALD'S HOPE

SIGNET Bestsellers

EMERALD'S HOPE

by

Joyce Carlow

A SIGNET BOOK

NEW AMERICAN LIBRARY

TIMES MIRROR

PUBLISHER'S NOTE

This novel is a work of fiction. Names, characters, places, and incidents are either the product of the author's imagination or, if real, are used fictitiously.

NAL BOOKS ARE AVAILABLE AT QUANTITY DISCOUNTS WHEN USED TO PROMOTE PRODUCTS OR SERVICES. FOR INFORMATION PLEASE WRITE TO PREMIUM MARKETING DIVISION, THE NEW AMERICAN LIBRARY, INC., 1633 BROADWAY, NEW YORK, NEW YORK 10019.

This book was created and produced by Larry and Helene Hoffman, Authors' Marketing Services Ltd.

SIGNET TRADEMARK REG. U.S. PAT. OFF. AND FOREIGN COUNTRIES
REGISTERED TRADEMARK—MARCA REGISTRADA
HECHO EN CHICAGO, U.S.A.

SIGNET, SIGNET CLASSICS, MENTOR, PLUME, MERIDIAN AND NAL BOOKS are published by The New American Library, Inc., 1633 Broadway, New York, New York 10019

First Printing, June, 1983

1 2 3 4 5 6 7 8 9

PRINTED IN THE UNITED STATES OF AMERICA

*To the children
of the troubles*

Book I

1

Belfast 1900

It began with the *tuatha*, the independent kingdoms which, one by one, combined to form larger and more powerful kingdoms until they were five in number and known across the land as the Five Fifths. There was Ulster (Ulaid), Meath (Midhe), Leinster (Laigin), Munster (Muma), and Connaught (Connacht).

Of the Five Fifths, Ulster was the first to dominate, but when Ulster lost its dominance, it brooded and smoldered like a bubbling caldron of evil witch's brew, till once again it rose, demanding to be known, to be recognized, to rule.

That was the beginning of a longer account, a tale that nestled in Emerald's memory and mingled with the remnants of a hundred others. There was beautiful *Connla and the Fairy Maiden*, legends about the fall of the gods, myths galore about the hero Finn, and narratives about wars with the giants. A wealth of Celtic lore combined with religious teachings about the great silver cross, about Jesus and his sainted Mother, Mary. But were Jesus and Mary little people? Did they live behind the great silver cross the way the fairies hid behind great blades of grass in the early morning? Emerald could not quite remember all the stories or the way in which they related to one another. Still, she retreated to her recollections of the tales, repeating them to herself over and over, though the details grew vague and she never repeated them to herself in quite the same way her mother had related them to her.

"Don't call me 'Mother'!" Mrs. McArthur instructed Emerald.

Mrs. McArthur—yes, that was her name. Or at least Emerald thought that was her name. Emerald had to strain to listen and to understand the conversation that day. Perhaps, she thought, the vicar, Mr. Macauley, would say the lady's name again and then she would be certain if the woman was called "Mrs. McArthur." But at the moment Emerald was distracted and confused. Why would Mrs. McArthur think that Emerald would call her "Mother"?

"Call me 'Auntie Elizabeth'—that sounds right and respectful," Mrs. McArthur intoned.

Emerald, who was only three and a half feet tall, looked up at Mrs. McArthur. From her vantage point she saw two large chins, a small mouth above them, a great large head covered with a frenzy of hair, then a short squat neck, and below, a large stomach which seemed to extend into two legs both swollen by some mysterious malady.

Once Emerald's mother had taken her for a walk in the park, and there, under the trees on a trim lawn, old men played a game. They rolled a hard round ball across the smooth grass and attempted to knock over carefully arranged wooden pins. It occurred to Emerald that Mrs. McArthur looked rather like one of those pins. She smiled a little, and Mrs. McArthur noticed.

"Is that child silly?" Mrs. McArthur asked, arching one of her dark eyebrows. "She's grinning like a silly child. Has she got all her parts upstairs? It'll be difficult enough if she's got normal sense, impossible if she's silly."

"She's not silly," the vicar replied. His eyes were darting around the room as if he were trying to memorize everything in it. His eyes flitted from the overstuffed furniture and odd end tables to the mantel, where a dusty collection of small glass animals was lined up as if they were part of a parade.

Emerald's eyes fastened on a picture in a tarnished gilt frame over the mantel. It depicted a woman dressed in black. She wore a white lace collar and some sort of net or bit of lace in her hair. Dead center, at her throat, was a large brooch. But it was her facial expression that puzzled Emerald. She looked for all the world as if she had just eaten a barrel full of prunes.

As if she were a mind reader, Mrs. McArthur pointed to the picture. "I ought to get a new frame for Queen Victoria," she offered as she looked from the painting to the vicar. "In fact, there are many new things I ought to get. But times are hard. And now that there's going to be another mouth to feed, well, you understand."

"You're a fine generous woman," the vicar replied solemnly.

"How old is she?" Mrs. McArthur asked, pointing to Emerald.

"About five," the vicar replied. "But you know how it is, we found no birth records, so we can't be entirely sure."

"I don't suppose she can pronounce 'Auntie Elizabeth,' then?"

Mrs. McArthur bent down, and Emerald observed that she did, *after all*, have eyes buried in the fleshy folds of her face. They were pale blue eyes, eyes with red circles surrounding them.

"Can you say 'Elizabeth'?" Mrs. McArthur queried.

Emerald frowned. "Isabet," she answered, displaying a great gap where her front teeth would have been had they not mysteriously fallen out some weeks before.

Mrs. McArthur looked miffed. Or at least Emerald thought she looked miffed. "Call me 'Auntie Bess,' then. Can you say that? Come on, say 'Auntie Bess.' "

"Auntie Bess," Emerald stuttered, still wondering why this woman thought she might call her "Mother" in the first place. The woman was not her mother. And as quickly as Emerald thought about her mother, her small freckled face clouded over and tears filled her large green eyes.

Mrs. McArthur motioned to the vicar to sit down, and she herself flopped into a worn velvet chair, stuffing her excess between its plump arms. She peered directly into little Emerald's face. "Don't blubber, child!"

"I expect she's overcome with your kindness," the vicar suggested.

Mrs. McArthur turned her faded blue eyes away from Emerald and grunted. Then she forced a smile at the vicar. "Tea?" she offered.

"Oh, that would be delightful," the vicar enthused. He was in fact eager, since he had been unseemly busy. He had not taken lunch, and though it was a trifle early for tea, his stomach grumbled.

The Vicar Macauley was a man of slight build, wiry and nervous. He weighed little more than nine stone, his poundage stretched out over a five-foot-eight-inch frame. This gave him a skeletal appearance that excited the motherly instincts of his female parishioners and was in keeping with his own desire to appear religiously abstemious. Ulster was full of fat overfed clergymen, but somehow the Vicar Macauley did not believe that a fat clergyman presented quite the right image. Therefore, he had good cause to give thanks to the Lord that he had inherited the ability to eat, and eat well, without gaining so much as one pound, and that his very build encouraged the women of his church to feed him at almost every opportunity, as if he were a starving cat or small pitiful bird. Thus did he save considerable money from his meager salary.

Mrs. McArthur pulled herself out of the velvet chair, leaving a vast impression where her immense bottom had been. She disappeared into the kitchen and returned carrying a great tray to the tea table. A pot of tea steamed, and on one plate there was an arrangement of neatly prepared brown-bread sandwiches with watercress peeking through the side of the thickly buttered bread. On the other plate was a pile of round light brown objects, which Emerald knew must be sweets of some sort. Unconsciously Emerald ran her tongue around her lips. The memory of her breakfast bowl of watery porridge, served promptly at six A.M., had entirely vanished.

"Sit over there, girl," Mrs. McArthur commanded. She pointed to a straight-backed chair opposite the settee.

"Her name is Emma," the vicar put in, "Emma O'Hearn."

Emerald frowned. Nobody had ever called her "Emma." Her mother had always called her "Emerald"—"For the color of your eyes, for our Emerald Isle," she had once told her. Not even her older brothers had ever called her "Emma," though they called her other names. "Baby Plump Rump" was one she recalled, just as she remembered them tickling her, her giggles filling the room.

"Do have a sandwich," Mrs. McArthur pressed the vicar, "or some of my sweet biscuits. I made them just for you."

The vicar smiled and tilted his head. His teeth were a bit yellowed and his breath smelled like a room that had been closed for a long time. But perhaps I am the only one who notices, Emerald thought. The vicar was, in fact, always leaning over her and looking directly into her face. Somehow he seemed to feel that if he didn't confront her eyes directly, she would not understand him.

Mrs. McArthur poured some tea into two fine china cups, passing one to the vicar. She also poured tea for Emerald, though not into so fine a cup, but rather into a quite ordinary tin mug. She poured with great flourish, and when she had finished, she pushed the plates of food toward the vicar.

"Do not spill your tea," Mrs. McArthur told Emerald when she turned to her. "I'll have no tea stains on the carpet."

Emerald felt her hand shake a little, but she took a sip of the dark brew. It was hot, and it burned her mouth a little, but it tasted warm and wonderful. It had been a long time since she had last sipped tea, and thinking about it made her want to cry again.

It must have been nearly a year ago, before her mother got sick. The image of her mother moved across Emerald's mind and she could almost see her mother smiling. Katie O'Hearn had intense green eyes ringed with gold around her black pupils. Her eyes could twinkle, and did when she told Emerald the old stories. But more often than not, Katie O'Hearn's eyes were distant and sad, as if she were trying to recapture a moment lost. Emerald also remembered her mother's hair. It was golden red and cut short, allowing a hundred ringlets to frame her face. In the summer her mother's curls grew even tighter, and they clung to her forehead. There was always a soft-spoken quietness about

Katie O'Hearn, and Emerald remembered her mother's kisses as well as the tiny lines of worry around her mouth. She could, if she tried very hard, recall falling asleep on her mother's white breast. It was fearful how her memories were slipping away, and even the last cup of tea was a partial blur.

"It's our last portion," Katie O'Hearn had told her young daughter. "So we'll share it, and let's drink it properly and pretend we're grand ladies." Her mother had set the little table and she brewed the tea in a tin pot, and together they drank the tea and shared some bread. "This is fine cake," Katie O'Hearn told her young daughter. And Emerald had smiled at her mother. Somehow the bread did not taste as stale as it had in the beginning.

Unconsciously Emerald reached across the distance between where she was sitting and where the tempting plates of food were placed. Her small fingers reached for one of the sweet biscuits.

Mrs. McArthur's flat palm came down on Emerald's hand, delivering a swift, stinging slap. "Those aren't for the likes of you! Those are for the Vicar Macauley!"

Emerald's hand withdrew instantly and she blinked uncomprehendingly at Mrs. McArthur, even as the tears that always came so easily flooded her eyes.

"I doubt she's ever had a sweet biscuit," the Vicar Macauley said without emotion.

"Well, there's no need for her to develop such tastes," Mrs. McArthur concluded. With that comment, and ignoring Emerald's tears, Mrs. McArthur passed Emerald one of the dark bread sandwiches. "Take one," she instructed. "Just one."

Emerald's eyes moved swiftly from Vicar Macauley to Mrs. McArthur and back. She took the sandwich quickly, fearing it too would be withdrawn and then she would have nothing.

"And have you nothing to say?" Vicar Macauley questioned.

Emerald lifted her eyes, "Thank you," she said, looking at Mrs. McArthur.

Mrs. McArthur scowled. "Thank you who?"

"Thank you, Auntie Bess," Emerald repeated.

"You are a truly charitable woman," the Vicar Macauley praised. And Emerald noticed that his left hand, the hand that didn't hold his teacup, slipped to Mrs. McArthur's knee and patted it gently. "It's not every woman who would raise her own fine brood and then take in a foundling girl." He paused and turned toward Emerald, who quickly moved her eyes away and concentrated on her sandwich. He lowered his voice, causing

Emerald to strain all the more in order to catch his words. "Especially a wee Catholic girl."

The Vicar Macauley was not Irish. He came from Yorkshire, though he did his best to hide it. He always used Irish phrases; he thought such affectations would make him more acceptable.

"And how are your sons?" the vicar added.

Mrs. McArthur sighed, sounding rather like air escaping from a balloon. "Working extremely hard, they are. I never thought I'd have sons who'd turn out to be farmers, leastways not in some country filled with heathens! Did you know they have to make women cover themselves, their tops you know. Imagine walking about bare-breasted and brazen as can be! I tell you, from the letters I get, I can't imagine Rhodesia. I can't see how it'll ever be fit for God-fearing people."

Emerald stared at her tea and tried hard to imagine half-naked women running about. She was afraid to look up at all, and somehow sensed that it would be better if the Vicar Macauley and Mrs. McArthur thought she wasn't listening.

"They're brave lads to go forth and tame the wilderness." The vicar was shaking his head. "I've heard Rhodesia is a hard country, but the land is good and there are real possibilities, once you get started."

"I trust you're right," Mrs. McArthur replied, "though I hate to think of my grandchildren being born in a heathen land."

"As long as they're not born to heathens," the vicar quickly answered, once again squeezing Mrs. McArthur's knee. "Your sons are married to good women. I'm certain you have nothing to fear."

Again Mrs. McArthur grunted. She would not complain to the vicar, but in truth she did not like the women her sons had chosen to marry, nor was she pleased that they had packed up and gone off to what seemed the other end of the earth. In the back of Mrs. McArthur's mind was the conviction that they should have stayed in Belfast and looked after her.

"And what have we here?" Emerald lifted her large green eyes to try to take in the stranger who entered the room. He was even fleshier than Mrs. McArthur, and since Emerald was sitting down, rather than looking up at him, she could clearly see his swollen red nose and round red cheeks. He was, Emerald thought, a man without a neck. His face simply dissolved into his great barrel chest, which in turn melted into a perfectly round fat belly. But unlike Mrs. McArthur's, his legs were not all fat. They were, in contrast to his body, quite spindly, giving him the appearance of a large red balloon standing on two toothpicks.

"The Vicar Macauley has brought the child," Mrs. McArthur said by way of explanation.

"I was just saying how charitable you are, how very charitable!"

Mr. McArthur did not reply. He simply reached across the tea table and took two sweet biscuits. He stuffed one in his mouth and held out the other to Emerald. "Here," he said, extending the biscuit.

Emerald looked up, but she did not reach out to take the biscuit, remembering all too clearly Mrs. McArthur's slap.

"Here, take it!" Mr. McArthur sounded gruff.

"I told her she wasn't to have them," Mrs. McArthur explained.

"Oh, why not? You know you're a stingy one." He turned and grinned at the vicar. "She can squeeze half a crown until old Victoria smiles!"

Mrs. McArthur's face went beet red, and the vicar looked faintly embarrassed too.

"All right, have it," Mrs. McArthur said to Emerald, "but don't think this house is made of sweets or that cakes and cookies will be your regular fare."

Emerald nodded politely. "Thank you, Auntie Bess," she mouthed, reaching for the sweet biscuit.

"Tell us what you can about her," Mrs. McArthur pressed. "Does she thieve?"

The vicar shook his head. "She's been very quiet in the home," he informed her. "Of course, we haven't had her all that long. But she appears to be a good girl."

Emerald sucked her lower lip, but she didn't raise her eyes, not wanting to look at any of them. She took another gulp of tea and savored the taste of the sweet biscuit. I must listen, Emerald thought to herself. I must listen and try to remember everything.

"Apparently," the vicar began, "her mother was Catholic. But the records indicate her father was Protestant. Killed last year in South Africa fighting with the Boers."

"Fighting against the Empire!" Mr. McArthur said in a sharp tone.

"And in this, the queen's sixty-third year of rule!" Mrs. McArthur added. She ran her hand through her electrified hair and turned on Emerald. "You should be ashamed, little girl. Deeply ashamed. Your father was a traitor!"

Emerald blinked. She had no idea what they were talking about and she didn't feel one bit ashamed.

"The sins of the fathers . . ." Mr. McArthur mumbled.

"Any brothers or sisters?" Mrs. McArthur pressed, still shaking her head.

"None that can be located, though she had spoken of brothers. I suspect they were older and had left home already. Her mother died of consumption, and the wee girl was with her when she passed on."

The vicar paused to stuff his mouth with yet another sweet biscuit. He chewed it rapidly and swallowed. "But she's healthy enough. 'Twas neighbors who called us. They heard the child crying, and they told us her father was Protestant and the child should be taken into our foundling home or sent to a good Protestant family."

"Her mother didn't live in the papist part of town?" Mr. McArthur questioned.

"No," the vicar responded. "But they were as poor as church mice. We didn't find a scrap of food in their room."

Mr. McArthur slapped his belly. "What does it matter where she came from? She's too young to remember much anyway. She'll be brought up in a good God-fearing home, and there'll be no more of the papist mumbo jumbo for her."

"Graven images and beads," Mrs. McArthur muttered.

But I'm Catholic, Emerald silently protested. Mama said I was, she told me a hundred times. Emerald imagined her rosary, the silver-and-ebony-beaded rosary that had been taken away from her at the foundling home. *Hail Mary, Full of Grace.* Emerald repeated the words to herself and moved her fingers just a tiny bit, allowing her imaginary beads to fall through her fingers. *Blessed Art Thou Among Women, Blessed Is the Fruit of Thy Womb* . . . Emerald paused in her silent litany because she had never understood that part. She imagined a womb as something inside her stomach, way down her throat, near where the brown-bread sandwich and the sweet biscuit had gone. But did it grow fruit? And if it did, why was she always hungry? Emerald lifted her eyes and looked at the McArthurs and Vicar Macauley, and she wisely decided not to ask about the fruit of the womb.

"You say she has brothers, they could come back for her," Mrs. McArthur suggested.

"I doubt that," Vicar Macauley replied confidently. "Sent off to earn their living at a young age, I imagine. Working in the bogs, I suspect. They'll only be concerned with their own stomachs, they'll not be looking for another one to feed."

Oh, let them come looking for me, Emerald prayed silently. Don't let them take me away from the foundling home. Let my brothers find me. Oh, please . . .

"I'd hate to take her in and spend months and months training her, just to have her brothers come and take her away,'' Mrs. McArthur announced.

Was she to stay with these people? Emerald quickly looked up, then away again at the floor. That was what the vicar was saying; that must be why she was all dressed up in the only dress she possessed.

"Have no fear." The vicar smiled. "They'll not come back. This girl will be brought up Protestant, and she'll be a real daughter to you, I promise you that."

Emerald ran her small hand over her dress. It was heavy, stiff and gray like the walls of the foundling home. It hung well below her small dimpled knees, as it was several sizes too big. "That way you can wear it longer," the matron at the home had told her. "That's the trouble with children your age, they keep growing like weeds and it's all we can do to keep them in clothes."

Below her dress, Emerald wore long heavy stockings and plain brown oxford shoes. The shoes, like the dress, were too large, and in spite of the tissue paper that had been stuffed into the toes, she could move her toes about, and even make the paper crinkle. For a long time, ever since the matron took away her rosary, Emerald had said the words of the "Hail Mary" and simply used her fingers. Now it occurred to her that she could also use her toes. And, she decided, it might even be safer, because her toes were hidden inside her shoes and then no one would guess what she was doing.

"She's a pretty child," Mr. McArthur commented.

Emerald did not feel pretty, but perhaps that was because her dress made her skin itch, and it didn't seem possible to be pretty if you were always scratching. Now, the fairy princess her mother used to tell her stories about was truly pretty. And Emerald was sure fairy princesses never itched. That thought brought a question into Emerald's mind.

"Well, do you have anything to say for yourself?" Mr. McArthur asked.

"Do fairies itch?" Emerald asked, looking at him with her large green eyes.

"What kind of question is that?" Mrs. McArthur blurted. "Is this child quite all right in the head? You said she wasn't silly or daft. Are you sure?"

The vicar shook his head. "No, the matron at the home said she was quite quick."

"As long as she's smart enough to help out with the chores," Mr. McArthur asserted.

Mr. McArthur smiled at Emerald, and Emerald thought he seemed a bit nicer than Mrs. McArthur. Still, no one answered her question. But that was the way it had been since they took her to the foundling home. Nobody ever answered her questions. People were forever asking her things, and they expected answers, but they didn't seem to hear her when she asked a question.

Emerald ran her finger around the neckline of her dress and shook her short red curls. She was suddenly consumed with the desire to look at the large freckle that was on the very tip of her nose. It was a desire that seemed to come over her at least once a day. She always looked just to make certain it was still there. Emerald crossed her green eyes and stole a glance at it. Yes, there it was!

"Are you making a face?" Mrs. McArthur demanded. "If you make fun of us or make faces around this house, you'll get a good cuffing!"

Emerald's eyes returned to their normal position and she looked up at Mrs. McArthur with a somewhat startled expression. "No . . . no, ma'am, I wasn't making a face," she stammered, aware that her face suddenly felt warm and flushed.

"Well, what were you doing with your eyes, then? Speak up!" Mrs. McArthur's tone was quite different from the one she used when she spoke to the vicar.

Emerald looked down at the floor. "I was . . . was . . . I was just making sure that my freckle is still there." Emerald lifted her finger and pointed to the freckle on the end of her nose.

Mr. McArthur broke into a raucous laughter, and the vicar snickered under his breath.

"Why would you do a thing like that?" Mrs. McArthur asked, unamused.

"Because my mother said I would be grown-up when it disappeared."

Mrs. McArthur shook her head. "Daft," she mumbled. Then, turning to the men, "One wonders what other nonsense her mother put into her head. The things these people tell their children!"

"I'm certain you'll get the nonsense out of her head," Mr. McArthur concluded. "I'm sure you'll turn her into a model of good manners and decorum."

Mrs. McArthur ignored the tone of resignation in her husband's voice. "Be assured, I intend to do my best with her," she responded with a toss of her frazzled hair.

"Well, you can't imagine what it will mean to the little tyke in the long run," the vicar said solicitously. "To be well fed, to

live under a good Christian roof, to have the privilege of
helping you around the house. Such a charitable family! She's a
lucky one, I can tell you, a very lucky one!''

Emerald's eyes traveled quickly around the room. Here and
there were small objects encrusted with dust and colorless with
age. The furniture was massive, like its owners, and the room
was cluttered. Emerald looked at the portrait of Queen Victoria
over the fireplace and shuddered. Then her eyes moved from Mr.
McArthur to Mrs. McArthur, whom she was to call "Auntie
Bess." Somehow, Emerald did not feel so lucky. She sighed
quietly to herself, and above all, she wished for the freckle on
the end of her nose to disappear.

The Vicar Macauley stood up and smoothed out his trousers.
He leaned over into Emerald's face, and his foul breath momentarily engulfed her. He smiled with his yellow teeth. "You be a
good little girl. You do exactly as the McArthurs wish, and I
shall see you each and every Sunday in church. And tonight,
before you go to sleep, you pray to God, as you were taught in
the home, to forgive you your sins, and you thank him for giving
you such a fine home. Do you understand?''

Emerald nodded her head, willing to agree to almost anything if
only he would stand up straight and leave her alone. "Yes, Vicar
Macauley,'' she said, making a quick little curtsy. The vicar
smiled and stood up. He extended his hand to Mr. McArthur and
shook it firmly. "A pleasure to see you, and my heartfelt thanks
on behalf of the child.''

Mr. McArthur only nodded. The vicar then turned to Mrs.
McArthur. He took her plump hand in his. "I enjoyed the
tea and refreshments ever so much. You are, without a doubt,
the most charitable woman in my parish. May God bless
you.''

Mrs. McArthur smiled and showed the vicar to the door,
returning in a few minutes' time. "Now,'' she said, looking at
Emerald, "I must get you settled. Come along. These are the
front stairs,'' she said, pointing to the narrow staircase. "You'll
not use the front stairs. This way.'' They moved down a long
corridor. "This is the kitchen, and out there is the toilet. Now,
here are the back stairs. You'll use these.'' Mrs. McArthur
climbed the stairs, grasping the railing and panting. Once at the
top, she took a deep, deep breath and expelled the air noisily.
"That's my bedroom and Mr. McArthur's. You'll never, do you
understand, never, come into any room without knocking.''

Emerald murmured, "Yes, ma'am.''

"Auntie Bess," Mrs. McArthur quickly corrected. "And this is the room that once belonged to my sons. I like to keep it the way it is, in case one of them comes home." Mrs. McArthur opened a door, and behind the door was a narrow ladder that led upward. "That's the attic. That's where you'll sleep. I can't climb the ladder, but you can go up and have a look now. We'll give you some blankets so you can make a bed."

Emerald bit her lip and looked at the ladder and the small opening above. Clearly neither of the McArthurs could fit through it. Gingerly Emerald climbed the ladder and peered into the unfinished attic. A bit of light filtered through a vent near the back, but otherwise it was musty and dark. There were some trunks and some old dresses strewn about. "It's dark," Emerald said, realizing that it would be much darker when the light of day was no longer filtering through the vent.

"We'll give you a lamp, but you'll have to learn to use it first. Oil lamps can be dangerous, you know."

"Yes, Auntie Bess," Emerald replied.

"Come down now," Mrs. McArthur instructed. "I'll have you do the tea dishes first and help put on supper. Then I'll give you some blankets and you can come back up and fix your bed."

2

And the wee fairy squeezed through the tiny, tiny opening at the bottom of the great tree, and inside she discovered a sweet-smelling room with just enough light to see by. "I'll be safe here," the fairy said aloud to herself. "And I'll make it into the nicest house in the forest, nicer even than Mr. Squirrel's." And so the fairy used a large bit of moss for her thick rich carpet, a great flat stone for a table, a pile of soft green leaves for a bed, and two bits of wood for chairs. The little fairy bathed in dew drops just outside her door, and for decoration she had mistress spider spin her a magical web that sparkled like jewels in the half-light.

Emerald crouched in the corner of her attic refuge and thought that it was not quite as secure as a tree stump. "But I'll make it a magical place," she whispered to herself. She arranged the attic to her liking. She used the top of the great old steamer trunk as a table, covering it with a faded blue gown. On it she placed the small gas lamp which Mrs. McArthur taught her to use, cautioning her to take the greatest care lest she set the house on fire.

She made her bedroll near the great stone chimney so she would be warmer in the winter. But it was in the far corner of the attic, as far away from the opening as possible, that Emerald constructed her treasure, comforted by the fact that it was hidden from view even if someone poked a head through the opening.

On a small carton, Emerald laid a white cloth she had found lying about. And from two pieces of wood she made a cross. "And each night," she whispered to herself, "I will say my rosary on my fingers and pray for the souls of my parents and that my brothers will find me." Emerald pressed her lips together and clenched her fists. "I am a Catholic," she whispered. "I am a Catholic. I will not forget my mother or my name. I will not forget the stories and I will not forget that I am a Catholic because the Catholics are like the fairies, and the Protestants must be like the evil giants." And I will understand all of this, she told herself, when the freckle disappears and I am grown.

3

The days passed and grew into weeks. Mr. McArthur, Emerald soon learned, was not always so slovenly as he appeared around the house. Each weekday morning he stuffed his bulk into a dull conservative black suit and a stiff-collared white shirt. In this costume, Emerald thought, he looked like a great huge turtle.

Mr. McArthur worked at the Commercial Bank of Belfast, where he was the assistant manager. The McArthurs were far from rich, though they enjoyed a comfortable economic position. The ancient brownstone in which they lived was located on Ulsterville Avenue in a middle-class area solidly populated with good Protestant families. Like all houses on the street, it was joined to the house next door, resulting in the fact that no daylight ever entered the house from the sides, but only from the back and front. The house had been purchased with Mrs. McArthur's inheritance, a fact that was mentioned regularly, especially when Mr. and Mrs. McArthur were at odds.

The small backyard was big enough only for the sagging clothesline and the outhouse. When Emerald stood on the chair to hang the Monday-morning wash, she could see all the way down to the end of the street. All the little yards were identical, save the one on the immediate right. It lacked an outhouse because, as Mrs. McArthur explained, her affluent neighbor had installed an indoor toilet.

Emerald could not imagine what such a fixture looked like, but she had been at the McArthurs' only a short time when she learned what it sounded like. Through the common wall that joined the houses, there was a sudden thundering sound followed by a rush of water and the gurgling sound of a great river. Emerald had cried out in fear when she first heard the sound. But Mr. McArthur just laughed at her, explaining that it was the neighbor's toilet being flushed.

But to Emerald it sounded for all the world like a fierce animal inside the wall. In spite of Mr. McArthur's explanation, she continued to regard the toilet as a pent-up spirit of some wild beast who had been captured and now held prisoner within the very structure of the house. Not unlike myself, she thought. I too am a prisoner.

"For now, Emma," Mrs. McArthur intoned, "you will do the breakfast dishes, wipe them and put them away. And you'll do them carefully. I'll punish you if you break any, do you understand?"

Emerald shook her head and repeated the phrase "Yes, Auntie Bess."

"Then you'll make all the beds—changing the linen on Fridays—and sweep and dust the whole house. You'll also do the tea dishes and the supper dishes and help with the wash on Monday by hanging it out. Do you know how to do all those things?"

Emerald bowed her head. "Yes, Auntie Bess. But I can't reach the sink."

"You will stand on that stool, then." Mrs. McArthur rolled her eyes. "You'll take your meals in the kitchen and eat only what you're given. If I ever catch you stealing food, I'll strap you, do you understand?"

"Yes, Auntie Bess."

Mr. McArthur hovered in the doorway watching as his wife gave forth with endless instructions. "I suppose this means you're ready to retire." His voice was heavy with sarcasm and his eyes traveled his wife's body from head to toe. "You'll be getting even fatter."

Mrs. McArthur turned from Emerald to her husband. Her pale blue eyes snapped and her hair flew in all directions at once, or so it seemed to Emerald. "See to the dishes, Emma!" Mrs.

McArthur gave the command without even turning to face her.
"Don't talk to me like that in front of the girl. How do you
expect her to respect me!"

Mr. McArthur turned and went into the parlor; Mrs. McArthur
followed on his heels. "You know my legs pain me. You know I
need help around here . . . little as I ever get from you! Little as
I ever got from our sons, who up and married and went off to
some heathen land! And it was me who paid for this house,
Donald McArthur, me whose father got you the job with Commercial Bank that you could live in such comfort all these years!
'Twas me who gave you my body when I was young and pretty!
You're full of gratitude, you are!" Her voice was reaching a
crescendo of emotion. Emerald strained to listen and to try to
understand the words being said.

"Oh, shut up, woman! That child is only five years old, going
on six maybe. You're treating her like a slave! I agree she has to
work for her board, but not doing everything for you!"

"She's not doing everything, only what she can do!"

Mr. McArthur made a face at his wife. "You're lazy!" he
accused.

"And you're not?" Mrs. McArthur snapped back. "Look at
you, you haven't had a promotion in ten years, you ought to be
manager by now, but no. Not you. You're going to be assistant
till you die. All you do, all you want to do, is drink beer and sit!
Except of course when you want to partake of the sins of the
flesh!"

Mr. McArthur suddenly roared with laughter. "To sleep with
you is no sin, it's a damned ordeal! Sin is something to be
enjoyed, the way I understand it!"

Emerald heard Mrs. McArthur let out an anguished wail, and
then she heard the corpulent woman's footsteps as she clambered
up the staircase. Next Emerald heard the door of the upstairs
bedroom slam shut.

"Dishes done?"

Emerald turned to look up at Mr. McArthur. "Yes, sir."

Mr. McArthur smiled broadly and walked over to her. He
leaned over and pinched her cheeks so hard that Emerald nearly
winced. "You're a good lass," he said; then, frowning, "But be
respectful with Mrs. McArthur. I'm the only one who can talk to
her that way, understand?"

Emerald nodded and Mr. McArthur fished into his pants pocket
and withdrew a large orange candy wrapped in paper. "It's a
boiled sweet," he said, extending the candy to her. "Picked it
up on the way home for you."

Emerald smiled and bowed her head. "Thank you, sir."

"That's a good lass, run along now, go on up to bed." With that, Mr. McArthur slapped Emerald playfully across her small round bottom.

Emerald hurried up the narrow back staircase and up her ladder to the safety of her attic. She lit the lamp and went to the far end of the attic and knelt before her altar. Rapidly, on her fingers, Emerald said three "Hail Marys" and an "Our Father." Then she sat cross-legged and stared at her makeshift wooden cross. "I am Catholic," she repeated. "My name is Emerald O'Hearn. I have two brothers, one named Padraic, one named Seamus. My father was killed in Africa, my mother died of consumption. My name is Emerald O'Hearn, I am Catholic."

When she stopped, Emerald stared at her little altar. If I don't keep saying it over and over, I will forget. I must not forget, she told herself. Then Emerald went to her bedroll and turned out the oil lamp, snuggling down under the blanket. She stared into the blackness and began retelling herself a story.

The fairy princess nestled under her leaf blanket and snuggled into her moss carpet. All the creatures of the forest kept saying bad things about her, but the fairy knew. "I'm a good fairy, I'm Catholic like all the fairies, and one day I'll find those who love me. One day I'll find my brothers." Emerald stopped. Did fairies have brothers? I'll have to ask, she thought. Sometime.

The next morning was wash day, and Emerald was perched on her high chair, adjacent to the basket of clothes that rested precariously on the railing junction of the back porch. She shook out a pair of Mr. McArthur's underpants and pegged them to the line. Then she moved the pulley the way Mrs. McArthur had showed her, and hung a shirt—upside down, so the peg marks can't be seen, Mrs. McArthur had told her.

"Pssst. Little girl! Yoo-hoo, little girl!"

Emerald stood on her tiptoes and looked over the clothesline. There, on the other side of the straight fence that divided the two yards, stood a little old lady. She was as thin as Mrs. McArthur was fat and she wore a pair of spectacles that rested on the end of her somewhat sharp nose. She was dressed entirely in black—much as Queen Victoria was dressed in her portrait.

"Come here, don't be afraid." The woman beckoned her with a crooked finger. "Just for a moment."

Emerald climbed down from her perch and went over to the fence, glancing behind her furtively. Mrs. McArthur, she knew, was worn out from doing the wash and was lying down upstairs.

"I have to hang out the wash for Mrs. McArthur," Emerald said to the two bespectacled eyes that peered over the fence.

"Here, here's a biscuit." The woman passed Emerald a cookie and then said abruptly, "Mrs. McArthur goes to the market on Tuesday—that's tomorrow. Come out and talk to me then. I'll give you another biscuit."

Emerald didn't answer because she wasn't quite sure what to say. The woman had walked away quickly and had disappeared into her house, closing the door behind her.

Emerald slipped the cookie into her apron pocket and returned to hanging out the clothes. The woman who gave her the cookie was surely the owner of the animal imprisoned in the wall. Perhaps the cookie was poisoned, and if she ate it, she too would be imprisoned in the wall. But then, Emerald thought, I won't have to work and I can make horrible noises.

Later, while Mrs. McArthur was preparing supper and Emerald was cleaning out a cupboard, Emerald ventured to ask a question. "I saw the lady who lives next door today," she explained. "She spoke to me when I was hanging up the clothes."

Mrs. McArthur turned abruptly from what she was doing, displaying avid interest in Emerald's statement. "Mrs. Higgins? My word, Mrs. Higgins spoke to you? What did she look like?"

"Small," Emerald said, using the first adjective that came to mind. "With gray hair and spectacles." Then, deciding to tell a rare lie, she added, "She just said hello."

"She's a recluse, she never comes out. They say she's the richest woman in the neighborhood—the only one with an indoor toilet. But she never comes out, never speaks to anyone, and, God help her, never goes to church."

"A recluse?" Emerald repeated the strange word, wondering if a recluse were something like a witch. Perhaps the cookie was enchanted.

"It is someone who is mad, someone who never leaves the house and never talks to anyone."

"Is she a witch?" Emerald asked.

Mrs. McArthur snorted and made a rude face. "Certainly not! Where do you get such ideas? There's no such thing. She's just a loony, a person who is not . . . not quite all there."

Emerald frowned and thought about Mrs. Higgins. She had arms and legs, hair and eyes, and a nose. She looked all there, though of course she was not as all there as Mrs. McArthur, who was so very fat. Which was to say there was not so much of her to be all there.

Mrs. McArthur plopped a mixture of meat and vegetables into a pan and put it into the oven. "I'll be going off to market tomorrow," she told Emerald. "You'll stay here and do your chores."

Emerald nodded. "Yes, Auntie Bess." And she silently decided that she would talk again to Mrs. Higgins. Perhaps, Emerald thought, she is a witch and will turn me into a wild beast and I can run away.

1

Spring 1900

The sun shone through a haze of smoke, and a light warm breeze stirred the grass. Emerald followed Mrs. Higgins' silent motions, moving down to the end of the fence that separated the two houses. "Here!" old Mrs. Higgins said with delight. She lifted one of the planks right away from the fence, creating an opening no more than nine inches across. "It's been loose and just standing in place forever," Mrs. Higgins imparted. "Now, just squeeze yourself through . . . there, that's it, there you are." Mrs. Higgins replaced the fence board.

"Mrs. McArthur will beat me if she comes back and finds me gone," Emerald said nervously.

"I've lived next door to that woman for twenty years. I know when she goes to market and when she comes back. I'll send you home in plenty of time, no need to worry."

Emerald followed Mrs. Higgins up the rickety steps that led to her back door. "The other children in the neighborhood are dreadful little creatures," Mrs. Higgins told her. "They run up at all hours of the day and night knocking on my door and then run away. They say I'm a witch, you know." Suddenly Mrs. Higgins turned. "But you've never knocked on my door and run away, you've never called me a witch."

Emerald looked up at old Mrs. Higgins. It was true that she wore a black dress as a witch might, but her dress was trimmed in ivory-colored lace, and down her front there were a hundred tiny white buttons. Her skin looked to Emerald like tissue paper. It was pale and almost transparent, and on her hands one could clearly see blue veins beneath her skin. But in spite of her skin, Mrs. Higgins' eyes were bright and seemed to twinkle with friendliness. They were a warm brown, soft and kind.

"You're a nice lady," Emerald said softly. "And I want to thank you for the biscuit."

"What a lovely polite child," Mrs. Higgins praised. "Come in, come in. There, slip off your shoes, will you? I don't want outside germs all over the house."

Emerald didn't ask what a germ was, she simply slipped out of her oxfords, which were too big and easy to get on and off without actually untying the laces. Mrs. Higgins smiled and led Emerald into the kitchen.

It was much like the McArthurs' kitchen, though the table was finer and the curtains brighter. Mrs. Higgins didn't pause. "We'll get the cookie on the way out," she told Emerald, leading her deeper into the bowels of the house. "That's my flush toilet," she remarked, swinging open a door and revealing a strange white object with a great tank above it, from which hung a chain. "It's the only one on the street," Mrs. Higgins informed. "A gift from one of my sons, who lives in America. I have good sons."

"I've heard it flush," Emerald said in a small voice. "I thought it was a spirit in the wall."

Mrs. Higgins did not answer, but only laughed. They entered the parlor, and though it was the same shape as Mrs. McArthur's parlor, it was completely different. The furniture was almost new, and along the mantel were rows and rows of pictures. Emerald stood on her tiptoes and looked up at them, her eyes settling on one of what could only be a fairy princess. She wore a snow-white dress that fell to the floor around her, and her long dark hair was piled high on her head, except for some that fell over her shoulders. "It's a fairy princess!" Emerald said excitedly. "Oh, I never saw one before!"

Again Mrs. Higgins laughed. " 'Tis me when I was young, on my wedding day. Can you believe that I was ever young? Can you believe that I married such a handsome man?" Mrs. Higgins indicated a mustached, dignified-looking man in another picture. He stood behind a stately chair in which the fairy princess sat.

"You look like a fairy princess," Emerald observed, and of course one couldn't be certain, no matter what Mrs. Higgins said. After all, fairy princesses probably did get old; then too, they never told people they were fairy princesses.

"And that is my son Charles Higgins and his wife, Amy, and here . . . here are my four grandchildren. They're all grown now, of course. They live in Boston."

"Boston?" Emerald repeated the strange name.

"It's far across the sea." Mrs. Higgins sighed. "I don't see them now. Charles came once, a few years ago, but not the children."

Emerald thought she saw Mrs. Higgins' eyes mist over.

"I don't have a family," she replied. "That is, I have brothers, but I don't know where they are."

Mrs. Higgins seemed not to hear her. Instead, she put her arm around Emerald's shoulder and squeezed her. "You look like the tintype of my little granddaughter. They say she has red-gold hair and green eyes. They say she's bright as a button." Mrs. Higgins bit her lip and inhaled, "They're better off in America, of course. They can afford to go to the seashore every single year, and there's money to be made easily. And out west . . . out west, they say you can take gold nuggets right out of the ground. And all the houses look new. Oh, I tell you, child, America is a wondrous place."

Emerald had never heard of America and she wasn't at all sure what Mrs. Higgins was talking about, save the fact that it sounded like someplace where people were not hungry. "No one is hungry in America?" Emerald asked, seeking to confirm her own understanding of what Mrs. Higgins was saying.

"Not a soul!" Mrs. Higgins told her. "Oh, but you must go now. Mrs. McArthur will be home soon." Emerald stood up, and Mrs. Higgins took her small hand. "Come back next Tuesday, and mind you don't tell her about us meeting. Yes, come back and I'll show you some pictures of America—hand-painted postcards they are, and we can look at them through my stereoscope. It's wonderful! It makes the people look alive!"

"I should like that," Emerald said politely; then, bowing, "I have liked our visit."

"What a lovely child," Mrs. Higgins replied, patting her on the head. "Now, hurry along." She led her back through the kitchen and gave her the promised cookie, having taken it out of a great jar. She took Emerald back into the garden and moved the board so Emerald could squeeze back through the fence. "Next Tuesday," Mrs. Higgins said. "I'll be waiting."

Emerald hurried inside the house. Mrs. McArthur was not back, and she scurried about finishing her assigned chores. When Mrs. McArthur returned, she looked about, and seemingly satisfied, slumped into a chair and ordered Emerald to bring her a cup of tea.

"I've bought you a churchgoing dress," Mrs. McArthur said, opening a brown paper sack and withdrawing a plain gray wool dress with a small white lace collar. "You can wear it with your oxfords. Of course, it isn't new, but it ought to last a good long time. You're to wear it only on Sundays, do you understand?"

"Yes, Auntie Bess. Thank you, Auntie Bess." Emerald did her little curtsy, aware that it pleased Mrs. McArthur, insofar as Mrs. McArthur could be pleased.

"You've been here three weeks, and the vicar is asking after you, so I suppose you'll have to go to church with us next

Sunday.'' Mrs. McArthur paused and took a big gulp of tea. "I
won't be enrolling you in the Sunday school because that would
mean getting up earlier in the morning. You'll go at eleven with
us, and with God's help you might absorb some religion. Now,
when we sing the hymns, I want to hear your voice, do you
understand? And when the Psalms are recited, I want to hear you
speak good and clear."

"Yes, Auntie Bess."

Mrs. McArthur twitched her nose. And almost at the same
time, Mrs. Higgins next door flushed her toilet and the wall
shook as the water rushed from the tank into the bowl below.
Emerald could imagine the whole thing: she could see Mrs.
Higgins pulling the chain in her mind's eye.

"The loony has relieved herself again!" Mrs. McArthur mumbled blackly. "I hate the sound of that thing, hate it!"

Emerald turned her head so Mrs. McArthur would not see her
smile. "I ought to peel the potatoes now," Emerald suggested.

"You do that," Mrs. McArthur replied. "And see to it that all
the peels go into the soup stock."

Seamus O'Hearn had his full growth at the age of fifteen. He
was a solid five feet, eight inches, and well-muscled. His chest
was wide and well-developed, as were his arms. His waist was a
trifle thick, his butt broad, and his legs strong but short. The top
half of his body would have suited a man six feet; the lower half
suited the height God had given him.

Padraic O'Hearn, by contrast, was only thirteen and nearly as
tall as Seamus. But he was lean, a wiry boy with a ready smile
and an infectious laugh.

"Good boys, those," Mike Flannery commented a he watched
Padraic and Seamus disappear in the distance.

"They're doing men's work," Colin Ryan answered without
looking up. "How long have they been here, then? It's over a
year, isn't it?"

Mike Flannery nodded. "The one's fifteen and a man, the
other is still a lad of thirteen, his voice is just beginning to
crack."

"But they get along." Colin was resolute. He'd worked the
peat bogs for over twenty years. He'd seen a lot of young lads;
he himself had come when he was only nine.

"It's not right," Flannery said, sticking his forefinger into his
nose on an expedition into its inner recesses. "One day lads will
have time to be lads. No time for the Irish—that's the trouble,
you know. We have no childhood, no time for anything but

work. And look at these lads, near a year without the softness of a woman, bunking with men, working with men, listening to the jokes and drinking beer and wallowing in the filth. It's not right! It's not right!''

"Mike Flannery, social reformer." Colin beamed and shook his head. "You've looked after those lads, seen to it that they didn't get into any trouble, seen to it they weren't molested. What more can you do? You can't change the way things are. You can't change the way of oppression. Ah, no wonder the grass is always green, it's from the tears, it is.''

"I went to Belfast, I looked for their mother." Mike shook his head. "I don't know what to tell them, or how to tell them. What do I say, 'Well, lads, while you were gone trying to earn enough to buy bread, your mother up and died and your sister is missing. Now you've got no family, that's what. Now back to work with you.' Is that what I'm to say?''

"You're too softhearted."

"Damn right," Mike retorted. "Too softhearted indeed."

"Then go to the priest and tell him. Have him tell the boys about their mother. He'll have the words, you know. He'll have God's words.''

Mike nodded. "Seems cowardly. I ought to tell them myself."

"They're not your sons," Colin said with a shrug.

Mike nodded silently. "Not my sons . . ." he repeated in a near-whisper. Of course not. If he had any sons, he didn't know about them. For certain they were born to a whore, because he'd not had any other woman but Flatboat Fanny, whose body was known to near half the men in the peat bog. She was a woman about whom jokes abounded. "Her hold can take a two-ton cargo" and other obscenities were to be heard whenever payday came round.

It wasn't right, no one ever said it was, but the priests were silent during the confessions, they had heard it all before. A man couldn't hope to marry before he was forty. Some men, like himself, would never marry at all. There wasn't enough to support a wife and children; jobs for the illiterate were hard to find.

"You're sentimental in your brew, Mike Flannery." Colin Ryan looked at his longtime friend.

"I hate to see two more lads going down the same road I went down.''

"We're not masters in our own house," Colin answered in a low voice. "It's a troubled land, it is.''

Mike stood up and stretched. The alehouse smelled foul and his body ached and cried out for his bedroll. "I'll talk to the priest," he allowed. "It takes words I haven't got.''

2

"All things bright and beautiful, all creatures great and small, all things wise and wonderful, the Lord God made them all!" The voices of the congregation swelled and rang through the austere church.

It was not the sort of church Emerald had gone to with her mother. This church was plain, with only a single gold cross on the altar, and the altar was decorated with only a few flowers. But there was a high pulpit, and in it the vicar looked out on the assembled, leading the singing of a hymn in a loud voice that seemed to come from other than his own thin body.

Emerald could not in fact see very well. In front of her was the great bottom of a tall woman who was flanked by her thin husband and four small boys who wiggled about and made faces at Emerald whenever they twisted round in their pew.

Emerald had genuflected on entering the church, but Mrs. McArthur had roundly slapped her across the bottom and whispered, "None of that! And don't be crossing yourself, either! We don't worship graven images!"

So Emerald followed along, wondering what a graven image was. She was squeezed against Mrs. McArthur, who sat on the aisle, and Mr. McArthur, who sat on her other side. And her dress made her itch. Surely there was a dress somewhere that wouldn't make her itch. *When my freckle is gone and I am older and have some money, I shall buy a dress that doesn't itch,* Emerald promised herself.

The hymn came to a halt and everyone sat down noisily.

"Suffer the little children naught," the vicar began. "Yes, those were the words of our Lord and Savior! Words which I repeat to you today, and I repeat them in recognition of two in our flock, good Mrs. Elizabeth McArthur and her fine husband, Donald McArthur."

Heads turned around and looked at the McArthurs, who beamed and nodded at their friends and neighbors. "These two most charitable people have taken to heart the Savior's words and they suffer the little children naught, by taking into their fine Christian home a small foundling girl of dubious background."

Again heads turned, and Emerald felt eyes on her, eyes which seemed to bore straight through her. Her face went bright red and she looked at the floor, wishing to melt into it and disappear entirely.

"How kind," the fat woman in front said, smiling at Mrs. McArthur.

"Is she an urchin, Mummy?" one of the little beasts with the fat lady asked.

The fat lady did not answer; she only roughly turned the child around and mumbled, "Face the vicar!"

Perhaps, Emerald thought, no one answered any child's questions. Too bad, she decided. She would have liked to know if she was an urchin or not.

"And so we wish them good fortune in their endeavor and we hope that the little girl will bring them satisfaction." The vicar leaned over and smiled his yellow-toothed grin at the McArthurs.

"God's good works—that is the subject for today's sermon . . . God's good works."

Emerald looked down at her hands, which were folded in her lap, while the vicar droned on. Silently she began again to say her rosary and her "Our Father." I must not forget, she kept telling herself. I must not!

At last the vicar finished, and while the offering plate was passed up one row of people and down the other, the congregation sang yet another song and Emerald decided that if she liked anything, she liked the singing. The gleaming plate approached, and Mr. McArthur put in a half-crown and took back some change, though Emerald could not see how much. Emerald closed her eyes. When her mother last had taken her to church, she had paid sixpence and gotten a lovely candle.

" 'Tis a votive candle for your father," Katie O'Hearn had told her daughter. "We'll light it together and say a prayer." Alas, Emerald thought. This church was not the same at all. You paid, but you didn't get a candle to light for the person you loved. When I find a Catholic church, Mummy, I'll light a votive candle for you. Emerald made her promise silently.

There were more prayers, and then the music again began and everyone stood up and began walking out of the church. "Come along," Mr. McArthur urged, taking Emerald's hand. "It's over at last," he whispered when Mrs. McArthur was out of earshot and smiling at the vicar, who was positioned at the door of the church.

34   *Joyce Carlow*

3

It seemed to Emerald that Tuesday would never come, but
when it did, she scurried about as fast as she could, doing all
the chores so she could be free while Mrs. McArthur was at
market.

When at last Mrs. McArthur had left the house, Emerald was
out the back door like a shot and justly rewarded by Mrs.
Higgins, who met her by the loose board in the back fence.

"It's wondrous!" Emerald said as she looked through the
stereoscope. The picture that appeared was exactly like real.
Gay, happy people in strange costumes—Mrs. Higgins explained
that they were for swimming in the water—romped in the sand,
while behind them was lovely blue water with white-crested
waves. And farther down the white sand there were brightly
colored striped tents. "That's where they change their clothes,"
Mrs. Higgins said knowledgeably. "It's a place called Atlantic
City. Oh, my son says it a grand place!"

Emerald sucked on her lip and turned from the wondrous
three-dimensional picture to old Mrs. Higgins. "Are you a
Protestant?" she asked, able to contain herself no longer.

But Mrs. Higgins hardly seemed to hear her. "Well, I'm not a
Catholic, so I guess I must be a Protestant," she answered
vaguely. "Wouldn't it be nice if everyone here were rich and no
one was hungry?" Mrs. Higgins asked. "I'm lucky, you know,
so lucky because my son sends me money. There are so many
poor people here, oh, so many my heart aches for the little
children." Suddenly Mrs. Higgins' soft brown eyes filled with
tears and she hugged Emerald. "You're a sweet little girl," she
said, sniffing. "You're good to spend some time with a lonely
old lady."

Emerald looked wide-eyed at old Mrs. Higgins, and suddenly
reached up and hugged her. "Oh, I like you!" Emerald said. "I
like you so much!"

Mrs. Higgins held Emerald back a little. "So we'll have our
little secret," she promised. "You know, I think I'll teach you
to read. Would you like that?"

Emerald smiled. "Do we have time?"

"Oh, we'll make time. Yes, I'll teach you to read. It's a great
comfort, reading. I think you'll need to know how."

"Thank you," Emerald replied. And to herself she decided

that if Mrs. Higgins were a witch, then the world was upside down and witches were good people. She decided that only the Protestant world was upside down. Yes, that must be it. Protestant witches were good. Catholic witches were bad.

4

Emerald's days were spent in tedious labor. The fireplace was cleaned daily, the beds neatly made, the dishes washed, dried, and placed in the cupboards. Every few days the floors were scrubbed, and daily the chamber pots were emptied. Emerald disliked Mrs. McArthur intensely, and she came to fear Mr. McArthur as well, though his actions were unpredictable.

More often than not, he was kind and thoughtful to her. Sometimes he brought her boiled sweets, which he bought on the way home. At these times Mrs. McArthur sulked and chided that he was spoiling her. But Mr. McArthur paid her no heed. "She's only a slip of a girl," he would say. "She ought to enjoy something."

Then at other times Mr. McArthur insisted that Emerald needed discipline. These times, much to Emerald's confusion, seemed to have nothing to do with her behavior or her performance. When Mr. McArthur decided to discipline her, he pulled down her panties and lifted her dress and spanked her on her bare bottom. It stung more than it hurt, and it was humiliating. He often spanked her after some ale on Saturday night, and always it was, as far as Emerald could tell, without cause. But one time, when she chipped one of Mrs. McArthur's teacups, Mrs. McArthur asked that she be punished and Mr. McArthur merely laughed. He said that Mrs. McArthur was too harsh. On that occasion Mrs. McArthur had left the parlor in a huff and remained in her room for the better part of two days.

In the meantime, as the days, weeks, and months passed, Emerald began to learn to read words. Mrs. Higgins spent no more than half an hour with her once a week, but Emerald learned her alphabet quickly, and soon she learned sounds and began, as Mrs. Higgins had planned, to sound out words. She didn't know what the words meant, but she could sound them out.

"Don't they ever talk to you?" Mrs. Higgins asked.

Emerald shook her head.

"And they don't let you out of the house?"

"Only to go to church."

"You'll never learn about the world," Mrs. Higgins concluded sadly. She was a strange introverted woman, nearly eighty years old, Emerald learned. In her more lucid moments she knew that Emerald was being treated badly and being kept a virtual prisoner in the McArthurs' house, but she felt there was nothing she could do except be kind and teach her to read.

For her part, Emerald found Mrs. Higgins affectionate. But the old lady's mind wandered, and Emerald strained to understand disconnected sentences and half-thoughts as Mrs. Higgins unwound, spinning out anecdotes, experiences, and ideas that all related to other times and places. Still, the sound of Mrs. Higgins' calm slow voice was a source of pleasure in itself, and Emerald reacted even to Mrs. Higgins' personal aroma, which came from dried rose petals that she sprinkled in her drawers and closets. It was an aroma Emerald learned to recognize, one that gave her comfort.

"I hope knowing how to read will help you," Mrs. Higgins commented one day. Emerald, not truly understanding, but trying to, replied, "It will." Then she added, "I love you," and cuddled up, resting her head for an instant on Mrs. Higgins' shoulder.

Mrs. Higgins, as she often did, wept softly into a white hankie. "You're a nice little girl," she sobbed. "A good little girl."

Almost two years passed and Emerald knew that she was now either seven or eight, depending on when her birthday actually was. Her new front teeth had come in with no difficulty, but her freckle was still prominent in spite of the fact that it was winter and she had not been out in the sun for many weeks.

Most days it rained or drizzled cold icy drops that froze the minute they hit the ground. One day it snowed, and though it melted within two hours, Emerald was entranced with the heavy wet white snow that clung to the branches of all the trees and even coated the sagging clothesline in the backyard.

"Oh, it looks so clean! It's made everything white, snow white, and soft and fluffy!" Emerald enthused as she looked out the louvered kitchen window into the backyard.

Mrs. McArthur grunted. "Slush! Soon it'll be all gray and dirty. And it's not so pretty when you have to walk to market in it! Especially when the gout's got you and the dampness makes you ache all over!"

"Sorry, Auntie Bess," Emerald said, trying not to look at

Mrs. McArthur's great swollen legs and her feet, which appeared to be stuffed into her sensible black shoes. A wave of sympathy for Mrs. McArthur passed over her and she guessed that although Mrs. McArthur was ill-tempered and mean, she too suffered. Her sin, Emerald thought, was that she passed her suffering on to other people. She wants everyone to be as miserable as she is, Emerald concluded. But even she deserves a prayer.

"Will you be all right, Auntie Bess?"

Mrs. McArthur had already put on her coat, and now she was stuffing her electrified hair into a black crocheted hat. "I may take a carriage home," she replied. "But I'll be all right as long as you do all your chores."

"Yes, Auntie Bess." Emerald looked at the floor. In a moment Mrs. McArthur would be gone; in a moment she would be free to run to Mrs. Higgins and have her hour of freedom.

Mrs. McArthur ambled to the front door, opened it, and looked out. She made a disagreeable sound inside her throat, and then, closing the door behind her, stepped out into the snow.

Emerald watched from the window as Mrs. McArthur passed through the little front gate and onto the road. Her shoes left footprints in the snow as she headed off down the street and rounded the corner on her way to the butcher's shop, which was, Emerald knew, always her first stop. "First I go to the butcher's, then to the baker's, then to the greengrocer's. Then I stop at Otis and Blackwell and have a spot of tea."

As soon as Mrs. McArthur's black-outfitted bulk had disappeared from view around the corner onto another street, Emerald pulled her sweater about her and ran into the backyard, wincing as the cold snow got into her oxfords. She went to the loose board and lifted it sideways, slipping through easily. Then she ran up Mrs. Higgins' back steps and knocked on the door. Emerald waited, but no one answered. She knocked again, but still no one came.

"I'm a little hard of hearing," Mrs. Higgins had once told her. "Now, if I don't come to the door, you come right in and don't be shy."

It had happened only once before, when Mrs. Higgins had fallen asleep, forgetting that it was market day. Emerald waited for another minute, and then she tried the handle of the door. It opened easily, and Emerald ventured into the house.

"Mrs. Higgins!" she called softly as she passed through the kitchen and down the hall into the parlor. "It's Emerald. Are you there?"

Only silence greeted Emerald, and she proceeded on into the parlor.

There, on the settee, sat Mrs. Higgins; in front of her was a cup of tea on the table. She was leaning back against the tapestried material, her head resting on a lace doily that was pinned on the back of the settee. Her face looked like the fine bone china of her teacup, pale and fragile. Her small bony hands were folded in her lap.

"Mrs. Higgins," Emerald whispered. "Mrs. Higgins."

But Mrs. Higgins didn't answer. Emerald leaned forward and gently touched the old lady's cheek. But she withdrew her hand when she felt the cold, rigid flesh. She jumped backward and let out a little cry.

It had been three years ago and Emerald was only five, but she remembered the bare room as if it were yesterday. Her mother was sitting up in bed, and she had called Emerald to her. Emerald had come and snuggled into her arms and fallen asleep. And when she woke, she found her mother cold and stiff, just as Mrs. Higgins was now.

Emerald shuddered, and tears flooded her green eyes. "Oh, Mrs. Higgins," she sobbed. Then, half in fear of the dead body and half in grief, Emerald turned and ran from the house. Mrs. Higgins was dead, but she wasn't supposed to be there! How could she tell . . . and whom could she tell?

Emerald slipped through the fence and put the board in place. She hurried back into the McArthurs' house and for a moment stood by the kitchen window in horror. Her footprints to the fence were clearly visible. Emerald shut her eyes and began praying.

An hour passed, and Emerald, still overcome with fear, apprehension, and puzzlement as to what should be done, immersed herself in the chores.

Perhaps she could say the footprints were Mrs. Higgins'? Perhaps she could tell Mrs. McArthur that Mrs. Higgins had come by to ask Mrs. McArthur to send for the doctor. Emerald considered various possibilities, including the fact that Mrs. McArthur might well take right to her bed and not even notice the footprints. But alas, that still left the problem of letting people know that Mrs. Higgins was dead. Even Emerald knew that Mrs. Higgins had to be buried properly. She knew because she remembered that she had been alone with her mother's body for nearly three days, and when they came and took her to the foundling home, she had heard them talking about the body rotting and how, if bodies weren't properly buried, they rotted.

Emerald finished the fireplace and returned to the kitchen. "It's a miracle!" she said aloud to no one as she looked out the window. The snow had vanished, and now it rained hard, obliterating all evidence of Emerald's telltale footprints leading to Mrs. Higgins' house. Silently Emerald said two "Hail Marys" and an "Our Father."

Mrs. McArthur returned in a carriage, spluttering up to the front of the house and paying the cabbie without so much as sixpence for the extra effort of helping her in and out of the vehicle.

"Emerald!" Mrs. McArthur bellowed. "Come out and help me with these bundles."

Emerald ran out the front door to take most of the bags Mrs. McArthur carried. "What's wrong with your eyes?" she asked almost immediately. "They're all red and swollen."

Emerald sucked in her lip; she wanted to cry more. She wanted to cry and not stop. Mrs. Higgins was gone! She was gone, and so was the most important person in Emerald's life. She had waited and lived for her hour a week, she had looked forward to Mrs. Higgins teaching her, and she yearned for someone who listened, who tried to answer all her questions, who liked her.

"I got some soot from the fireplace in my eyes," Emerald lied. "It made me cry."

"You ought to be more careful. I hope you didn't get any soot anywhere else! You didn't, did you?"

Emerald shook her head. "No, Auntie Bess."

"Good," Mrs. McArthur finally said as she opened the door and staggered inside the house. They stood in the hallway and Emerald set down the bags of groceries. She took off her own wet shoes and then had to bend over to unlace Mrs. McArthur's shoes.

"I just can't bend over when the gout's got me," Mrs. McArthur mumbled. "Well, don't just stand there. Bring the groceries into the kitchen. We usually put them away, you know."

Emerald hoisted up the bags and then followed Mrs. McArthur.

"Over there on the table," she ordered. "I got a fine goose today, a good one so there'll be plenty of goose drippings. Mr. McArthur loves to spread goose drippings on bread. He'll be pleased, I'll tell you." Mrs. McArthur paused. "What's the matter, cat got your tongue?"

Emerald frowned. Sometimes Mrs. McArthur said the strangest things. There was no cat. "No, Auntie Bess," she answered honestly, "my tongue is in my mouth."

"Well, of course it is, you ninny. I meant you aren't talking as much as usual."

Emerald frowned. Most of the time when she talked, Mrs. McArthur either ignored her or told her to hush. Now that she was quiet, Mrs. McArthur wanted to know why she wasn't talking. Grown-ups, Protestant grown-ups anyway, with the exception of Mrs. Higgins, were very difficult to please.

"Well, is there something wrong? Have you done something you're afraid to tell me about?" Mrs. McArthur had her hands on her fat hips and she glared at Emerald.

"No, Auntie Bess." Emerald met her glare without blinking, and Mrs. McArthur retreated to the grocery bags, which she began to unpack with a flourish.

I shall never get through this day, Emerald thought. Then she remembered the day they had taken her to the foundling home. I never thought I would get through that day, either. But I did.

That night, Emerald spent an extra long time at her own little altar. She prayed for Mrs. Higgins and for her mother and father. She prayed for a way to let people know what had happened to Mrs. Higgins. "Oh, dear God, help me," Emerald prayed. "Virgin Mother, help me to think of something."

Emerald crawled back from her tiny altar to her bedroll. She cuddled up inside the blankets and extinguished the lamp. There in the darkness an idea came to her. She remembered the great animal held prisoner in the wall, or more precisely, what she had once several years ago thought was an animal inside the wall.

The next morning, Emerald scrambled from her bedroll and quickly dressed. The attic was cold and her skin bristled with tiny little bumps that caused the red-gold hair on her arms to stand straight up.

She pulled on her woolen work dress and added her big sweater. Then Emerald climbed down the ladder to the second floor of the house, where it was much warmer, even though a certain perpetual dampness remained.

She hurried about adding coal to the potbellied stove in the kitchen and to the fireplace in the living room. She put on the water for the McArthurs' morning tea and she warmed the bread and put the butter and jam on the table.

Mr. McArthur appeared first. He was dressed for work.

Emerald silently poured his tea and set the bread and jam before him. She smiled shyly.

"Mrs. McArthur will probably stay in bed today. Her gout's

acting up in the cold. You'll take her up some tea and bread and jam.''

"Yes, sir."

"But she's not awake yet, or she'd be bellowing through the house for you. Sounds like a bull elephant, she does. Have some tea, Emerald. And some bread and jam too.''

"I'm not allowed jam," Emerald said, pouring herself a cup of tea and taking some bread.

"Oh, have some. I'll not tell."

Mr. McArthur seemed in an extraordinarily good mood, and Emerald took the proffered jam, spreading it gleefully on her bread. It was a rare treat. She ate it with relish and then sipped her tea, waiting for what she hoped would be just the right moment.

"Mr. McArthur, sir." Mr. McArthur looked up. Emerald gulped. "Thank you for the jam," she said, really wanting to say something else.

"Quite all right." This time he didn't look up, but instead brushed crumbs from his shirt.

"Mr. McArthur, sir?" Emerald said again.

"Yes, Emma." He sounded a trifle gruffer this time.

"Sir, it's the flush toilet next door. It hasn't made a noise for several days now."

Mr. McArthur glanced toward the hall and the wall his house shared with Mrs. Higgins' house. "We should be grateful for small favors," he said cheerfully. "Damn thing makes more noise than a ship being launched down at the yards. Woosh! Woosh! All the time! Damn, that woman craps a lot!"

He seemed angry, and Emerald didn't know what to say. "But it's quiet now. It has been, ever so long. Do you suppose something has happened to the woman who lives there?"

Mr. McArthur frowned. "Maybe she's taken to her bed and is using the chamber pot. Maybe it's broken. Whatever, it's none of my affair."

Emerald nodded and felt horribly defeated. She suppressed the desire to shriek: "But Mrs. Higgins is dead on her settee and her body is rotting beyond the wall and her soul still hasn't been set free." Emerald firmly believed that a person's soul could not be set free till the priest made the sign of the cross on his forehead and he was buried. Her mother's soul probably hadn't been set free either, and Emerald only hoped that when she was older, when her freckle was gone, she could go to the church and light a votive candle for her mother. That would set her soul free, Emerald had decided.

Mr. McArthur was in the hall now, putting on his coat and his hat. Umbrella in hand, he opened the front door. "Take good care of Mrs. McArthur," he instructed, turning to Emerald.

"What if she's dead?" Emerald blurted out.

"Mrs. McArthur?" He looked aghast. "Whatever do you mean?"

Emerald shook her head. "No, no. Not Auntie Bess, the woman with the flush toilet. Suppose she's dead, suppose she's rotting, suppose nobody knows?"

Mr. McArthur looked at her quizzically. "I suppose she might be. A recluse, the old girl is, and getting on, too, I suppose. Well, I'll stop at the constable's and tell him to have a look-see. Will that satisfy you?"

Emerald nodded her head in blessed relief. She had gone further than she intended, but at last she had succeeded in getting him to listen and, more important, to do something.

Hardly had Mr. McArthur left when Mrs. McArthur called for Emerald from upstairs. "I'm all stiffened up. Oh, you don't know how painful it is! Bring me some bread and jam and some tea. Now, listen, and listen carefully. In the cupboard near the sink there's a vial of white powder. You take a teaspoon and mix it with some lukewarm water and bring it with the tea and bread and jam, understand?"

Emerald bowed. "Yes, Auntie Bess."

She scurried down the stairs and fixed the powder for Mrs. McArthur, putting it on the tray with breakfast and hurrying back upstairs.

"Now, you'll do all your chores as usual, even if I am in bed and not there to supervise you. Now, don't be a laggard, and see to it that you do everything just like it was an ordinary day."

Emerald bowed and left Mrs. McArthur. She hurried about the house doing her chores. And it was not till near noon that the sound of the bells on the hospital cart clanged loudly as it came down the street. The horses came to an abrupt halt in front of Mrs. Higgins' house. Emerald scurried to the window and drew back the lace curtain, staring into the street, which was rapidly filling with neighbors, who poured out of their houses, chattering with curiosity.

"Emma! Come here this instant!"

Breathlessly Emerald scampered up the stairs. "Yes, Auntie Bess?"

"What's all the commotion in the street, what's going on? Here, come here and help me up. Do you hear, help me out of this infernal bed!"

Emerald came round the side of the bed and held out her arms.

Mrs. McArthur half-leaned on her, half-leaned on the chair near the bed. Emerald thought she would stagger under the woman's weight.

"Ah, there," Mrs. McArthur murmured as soon as she was upright. She stretched her giant body awkwardly and struggled into her huge robe and velvet slippers. "I always miss all the excitement," she complained.

Emerald followed in her wake as Mrs. McArthur went down the stairs, gripping the banister and letting out an occasional groan. Emerald recalled Mr. McArthur's comment and wondered if she did sound like a bull elephant.

Mrs. McArthur didn't bother going to the window; she flung open the door and went straight out into the street to join the rest of her neighbors. Emerald followed.

"What's going on?" Mrs. McArthur demanded of Mrs. McCleod, who lived across the street and attended the same church as the McArthurs.

"It's old Mrs. Higgins, dead for near four days now! Found over her teacup on the settee. They say the stench in the house is something terrible! But then, you should know all about it. It's your husband who reported to the constable that you hadn't heard the toilet flush for near a week! Poor old soul."

"Poor old *rich* soul," Mrs. McArthur grumbled. She was loath to admit she didn't know that Donald had gone to the constable. "Good thing my husband cares so much for his neighbors," Mrs. McArthur said, pulling herself up and temporarily forgetting her gout. "Else the old loon might have been there forever rotting away."

"She was a good woman," Emerald whispered.

Mrs. McArthur looked down at Emerald, whose large eyes were filled with tears. "How do you know? You didn't even know the old loon. Look at you! Burbling and weeping over some old crazy you never even met; some old silly who never came out of her house! She hid all her money, she did. She must have been rich to have a flush toilet, though I can tell you I'm glad it's quiet for a while!" Mrs. McArthur paused as they brought out the stretcher with the body, covered from head to toe in a white sheet. Then she glanced down at Emerald, who was trying to hold back her tears.

"Stupid goose," Mrs. McArthur mumbled. "Go back in the house and do some work. The excitement is all over!"

1

Spring 1905

"You'll simply have to stay off your feet," the doctor pronounced solemnly. Dr. McCue was in his mid-sixties, a spare man with a long sad face and intense gray eyes.

Mrs. McArthur stared at her bare legs stretched out on the bed before her while her back was propped up against a pile of pillows. Her legs were swollen nearly three times their normal size and she could no longer stuff her feet into her shoes or stand without aid. But even if she were supported on both sides, she trembled with pain and groaned when forced upright. Her feet, she noted, were dead white and puffy, while on each leg, large blue veins stood up like a network of rail lines, each swollen and, on careful observation, pulsating.

"The swelling will go down?" Mrs. McArthur's voice was smaller than usual and her question lacked the customary tone of arrogance that resulted in most of her utterances sounding like imperious orders given from on high.

The doctor's face was serious and his eyes flitted about as he searched for the clinically right words with which to disguise his unpleasant diagnosis. "With the proper rest, food, and care, it may be reduced somewhat. Of course, there will be a restricted diet and certain exercises." He paused. "I think you should consider allowing me to order a wheelchair. You may be able to walk, but best you be getting used to it."

"A wheelchair?" Mrs. McArthur repeated the words as though Dr. McCue were referring to something she had never heard of before. "I shall never walk again," she said at length in a voice that seemed to slip away, even as she herself slipped down in the bed.

"You should perhaps consider moving your bedroom downstairs. Then your husband can have ramps built over the front steps—at least you'll be able to get around a bit."

"An invalid," Mrs. McArthur murmured.

"Now, now," Dr. McCue was saying.

Mrs. McArthur plunged her feet beneath the rolled down covers at the end of the bed. "Emma!" she called out.

Emerald appeared and bent slightly, curtsying to the doctor.

"Pull up these covers!"

Emerald nodded and pulled them up all the way to Mrs. McArthur's chin.

"Shall I order the chair?" the doctor asked.

Mrs. McArthur nodded dumbly. Then, turning her head toward the wall, "Leave me," she ordered. "Tell Donald what's to be done."

The doctor turned to leave the room, and Emerald waited. "Is there anything else?" she asked.

"Just sit down," Mrs. McArthur requested.

Emerald sat down on the edge of the chair in Mrs. McArthur's bedroom. It was a deep overstuffed chair, and Emerald was aware that her longish legs were dangling. Somehow it seemed her arms and legs were too long for her body these days; she felt clumsy and uncoordinated.

"How old are you?" Mrs. McArthur asked unexpectedly.

"Ten, Auntie Bess," Emerald replied.

Mrs. McArthur only muttered something unintelligible.

A silence that seemed to last for nearly half an hour fell between them, and Emerald wondered why she was supposed to sit in the chair. Outside, the sun was setting and long shadows fell in Mrs. McArthur's bedroom.

"When I was ten years old I had long dark curly hair and I was straight and thin. They said I was a pretty girl."

Mrs. McArthur's voice sounded truly strange to Emerald. It was small and far away. And when she paused, Emerald was not certain if she was to respond or not.

"My father was in his cups most of the time," Mrs. McArthur explained.

"Cups?" Emerald repeated, not understanding.

"A drunkard," Mrs. McArthur murmured. Her plump swollen fingers rubbed the quilt that covered her. "Irishmen drink too much. They take their ale like water till it addles their brains. When my father died, he left my mother and me an inkwell and a new quill pen. He didn't leave so much as a farthing, and we thought we'd have to go straight off to the poorhouse."

The room was in almost total darkness, but Emerald listened fascinated. Mrs. McArthur had never talked to her before. Now she sounded like a storyteller talking about someone else, and her voice continued to sound far away and defeated, like a wind-up clock running down.

"Then my uncle began coming to the house. He may have been my father's brother, but he was as unlike him as night is unlike day. He was tall and straight and very good-looking. He had eyes the color of the sea, he did. He used to bounce me on his knee and tell me tales.''

Mrs. McArthur shook her head back and forth sadly. "There was a sin," she whispered. "Oh, a terrible, terrible sin. My uncle had a wife, but she was in poor health. He took up with my mother, he did.'' Mrs. McArthur's fingers gripped the material of the quilt and squeezed it. "Oh, there were giggles when my uncle touched my mother, and then they locked themselves away behind the bedroom door. But you could hear them. I could hear them all through the night, like two animals at each other. He couldn't keep his hands off her, he couldn't. At supper he would feel her legs under the table, and in the evenings they would sit so close you couldn't slip a piece of paper between them. They did things, things no woman in mourning for her husband and no man married to a sick wife ought to do.''

Mrs. McArthur sucked on her lower lip. "When his wife died, he moved in with us. Then, when he died, he left all his belongings to Mama, who eventually left it to me. That's what I bought this house with—sinful money.''

Emerald stared into the darkness. In all truth she could not quite envisage or understand all of what Mrs. McArthur was saying.

"Donald McArthur may be better than some, but he's no better than most,'' Mrs. McArthur proclaimed. "You're old enough to know, Emma, to be told . . . men are unspeakable creatures.'' Her voice had suddenly grown low and hateful; it was a tone Emerald recognized more readily. "No matter, they all only want one thing, Emma. They want a woman's body. They want to touch it, to press themselves into it . . . it's all they care about besides their ale. They're filthy creatures, lustful and sinful! You'll have to beware, Emma.''

Mrs. McArthur struggled to sit more upright and to lean toward where Emerald was sitting. "Don't let Mr. McArthur spank you anymore. I'll tell him, but if he tries again, you tell me. Do you hear, you tell me.''

"Yes, Auntie Bess.'' Emerald tried to see Mrs. McArthur's face and grappled with the meaning of her warning. She didn't really know any men save Mr. McArthur and the vicar. The former only spanked her now and again, but was reasonable the rest of the time, while the latter's only sin was unbearably foul breath.

Mrs. McArthur seemed to be breathing heavily. "Wheelchair or no wheelchair, I shall probably never get up again. Emma, you'll have to take care of the house and bring me meals—maybe you can turn me over now and again and rub my legs. You'll have to be my eyes, Emma, you'll have to watch Mr. McArthur so he won't become a sinner, so he won't be like, like . . ." Her words trailed off. Then, more than fifteen minutes later, she began again, this time with a new subject.

"I tried to bring my sons up decent boys. They both married in the church—one married a blond woman who will, mark my words, spend every farthing on clothes. The other married a sullen girl. Well, I tell you, no sooner had they married than they were up and gone off to Rhodesia! They might as well have gone to the moon for all the good they'll be to me now that I'm sick. They don't even write, you know, it's as if they had no parents!"

Suddenly Mrs. McArthur sounded angry and hurt. She sniffed and again fell silent.

Emerald felt the gnawing pain of hunger in her stomach. It was well past suppertime, but Mr. McArthur had not called her downstairs yet. "May I get you something, Auntie Bess? Some tea or sandwiches?"

"Tea," Mrs. McArthur said with a sigh. "And see if the doctor left the special diet."

Emerald moved through the dark room and out into the dimly lit hall. Downstairs, Mr. McArthur sat in his great chair, his traditional ale mug in hand, his eyes on the dying embers in the fireplace. He started and craned his neck around when he heard Emerald coming down the stairs.

"You've been a long while," he observed.

"Auntie Bess isn't well. She wanted to talk. She wants some tea. Do you want some too, sir?"

"Nope," Mr. McArthur replied. "But if you're fixing some sandwiches, I'll have myself one or two of those."

"Yes, sir." Emerald left him, thinking he too was more solemn than usual. She went into the warmly lit kitchen and put on the teakettle. There was no telling what all this meant. Perhaps Mrs. McArthur never would get out of bed again, as she so glumly prophesied.

Emerald poured the tea and made a tray full of sandwiches. She took Mr. McArthur a plateful and quickly ate two herself. Then Emerald took Mrs. McArthur's tea upstairs.

When she returned, Emerald went to the kitchen to clean up. She finished what few dishes there were and tidied up. Then, preparing to go to bed, she stopped in the parlor.

"Mrs. McArthur wants to know if the doctor left the special diet, sir."

Mr. McArthur did not look up, but only shook his head. "He'll bring it tomorrow, with the medications and powders."

Emerald stood for a moment. Mrs. McArthur's words haunted her, though she did not completely understand the woman's mental wanderings. Were men evil? Or were only Protestant men evil—men like Mrs. McArthur's uncle and Mr. McArthur. And what were the unspeakable acts these men committed with women?

Emerald burned with curiosity—not just curiosity about men and women, but curiosity about everything that lay beyond her limited world. She read all the newspapers, but the words didn't make too much sense because they had no context in her sheltered existence. But every day more and more questions entered her head. She read about England, but where or what was England? She clung to the meager knowledge she did possess. This is Ireland, I am a Catholic, and the McArthurs are Protestant. Still, it all meant little, save for Emerald's conviction that Catholics were clearly different from Protestants, except for Mrs. Higgins. Catholics must be good people like fairies, Emerald decided. One day, she vowed, I'll run away to them.

Mr. McArthur was silent and seemed depressed. Mrs. McArthur was ill and Emerald sensed the time might be coming when running away would be possible. But how would she find the Catholics? Would she steal out in the middle of some dark night and walk the streets asking strangers: "Where are the Catholics?" No, Emerald concluded, the world, her world, had far too many Protestants, who might hold her prisoner or harm her. And how could one tell Protestants and Catholics apart? Prompted by the day's events and her own muddled thoughts, Emerald stepped closer to Mr. McArthur and dared to ask a rare question. "May I ask you a question, sir?" she asked politely, tossing her red-gold curls back.

Mr. McArthur grunted.

"Are there many Catholics here?" Emerald questioned timidly.

Again Mr. McArthur grunted. "Too many," he replied. "Here in Belfast there are more of us than there are damned croppies! They've tried to push us off this land, but we know how to hold on."

"Where do the croppies live?" Emerald asked, trying not to sound too curious.

"On the other side of Falls Road, wallowing in their filth," he replied.

Emerald only murmured a thank-you. She fled to her attic refuge, cherishing her new bit of information. "This is Belfast and the Catholics live on the other side of Falls Road! Falls Road! Falls Road!" Emerald repeated over and over. "I must not forget, I must not!"

2

The three men had already consumed two mugs of ale each and were growing loud, although they retained a friendly camaraderie. Emerald placed the tray of bread, meats, and cheeses down on the table; then she returned with two more jugs of ale.

These evenings were a development that had begun some six months after Mrs. McArthur had taken to her bed, and had continued for four years. Emerald found them intensely interesting.

Sometimes they occurred on Friday nights, but more often they occurred on Saturday nights. Mr. McArthur would invite Dr. McCue, Mr. Heardsly, the butcher, and sometimes Mr. Grant, who also worked at the Commercial Bank. But on this Saturday night Mr. Grant was not present; instead, his chair was filled by Mr. Arthur McArthur, Mr. McArthur's younger brother and an infrequent visitor to the McArthur household.

The four men gathered sometime after Mrs. McArthur had taken her powders and thus dropped off into a long drugged sleep. They played cards, they drank, and they talked politics. It was the latter that Emerald found so interesting, even though she knew that all four of them were staunch Protestants.

"In 1900 Queen Victoria, bless her soul"—Dr. McCue turned to the portrait of the prune-faced old queen which hung over the mantel and nodded his head in a half-bow of respect—"visited Dublin town herself, and there wasn't a voice of protest! Not one!" Dr. McCue took a gulp of ale and set his mug down, shaking his head. "In their hearts they know they can't begin to run their own country. My God, one only has to look at their history! 'Twas old Henry VIII who looked at Ireland and proclaimed it to be in such a state of advanced anarchy that all its land would have to be taken back by the crown and then regranted."

"The old Earl of Kildare from the venerable house of Fitzgerald was running amok," Mr. Heardsly put in.

"And 'twas his daughter Lizzie who made it a reality," Arthur McArthur added.

Emerald had loitered in the corner long enough. Mr. McArthur looked up and waved her off. She scampered back to the kitchen, where she could listen to the loud conversation and try to puzzle out its meaning.

"There were six rebellions during the reign of Elizabeth." Mr. Heardsly laughed. "They can rebel and cause troubles, but they can't govern themselves. I'll not support home rule for Ireland, I'll never support it. The minute they have it, they'll turn on us, turn us out, even though we're the only ones who can govern."

"You can't give an animal the right to govern," Arthur McArthur agreed. "Has everyone forgotten the banner we carry on our proud Orange Day Parade! The banner that commemorates what happened on the Portadown bridge on the cold, bitter November day in the year of our Lord 1641. One hundred good Protestant men, women, and even little children were thrown from the bridge into the icy waters below. And there, if they could swim, those dirty croppies in boats hit them over the head with oars or shot them right in the cold water as they struggled!"

"Aye," Dr. McCue said, his intense gray eyes looking sadly into his ale. "And they say that at midnight a woman who's been stripped naked to the waist rises out of the waters and calls out, 'Revenge! Revenge!' "

Emerald stood near the kitchen door. She fought the desire to run into the parlor and scream, "The Catholics wouldn't do such a thing!" But she stood stock still, frozen to the spot.

"There were never such atrocities as there were in the 1641 rebellion," Mr. Heardsly summed up. "And here in Ulster, here the blood of our people once flowed."

"Thirteen thousand were killed, they say." Mr. McArthur had not spoken for a long time. He had been drinking steadily while the others spoke; now he sounded weary and maudlin.

" 'Twas more than twelve thousand," Mr. Heardsly said with conviction. "Some say it was fifteen thousand! They've been known to eat Protestant children, you know."

"It'll all happen again if they're given home rule! Have you all forgotten that the rebellion in 1641 took place when there were more Protestants than Catholics in Ulster? And what would happen now, they'd stream out of the other counties, they'd kill us in our beds, they would." Mr. Arthur McArthur laid down his cards.

"No doubt, no doubt. Well, we have no choice but to make a stand this Orange Day. We have to let Westminster know that we'll not tolerate home rule." Dr. McCue also laid down his cards.

"Some Protestants say that an Irishman is an Irishman and that we should stand together against the British." Mr. McArthur smiled, and laying down his cards, picked up the few shillings in the center of the table.

"But the minute we didn't have the protection of the crown, they'd turn on us," Mr. Heardsly announced with conviction. "Mr. Yeats is a sentimental fool, and naive as well. I'll not sacrifice my home, my family, and my livelihood for his brand of nationalism."

Around the table there was a mumbled agreement. Emerald left her position near the kitchen door, sensing that the discussion was over for the time being and that now the four men would devote themselves mostly to drinking and to playing cards.

"If I only understood," Emerald said quietly to herself. Was 1641 a long time ago? Was Henry VIII the king before Queen Victoria? No, Emerald remembered one of the men saying something about Henry VIII's daughter Lizzie. So it must have been that it was Henry VIII, Queen Lizzie, and then Queen Victoria. They were all kings and queens of England and all Protestant, Emerald assumed. She shook her head and thought for a moment about dear Mrs. Higgins, long gone but still remembered. Mrs. Higgins did not want revenge; Mrs. Higgins was a good person. I must try to find out more, Emerald vowed to herself.

Abstractedly she reached up to her chest and winced. The bumps on her chest, which seemed to be getting larger, hurt a little. It seemed as if the skin were stretched out over them too tight. But I feel all right, she conceded. I must have growing pains. That, in any case, is what Mrs. McArthur always told her whenever she complained of a hurt here or there. "It's just growing pains!"

3

It was a fine May morning, warm and clear. Emerald had opened the upstairs window, and she cleaned Mrs. McArthur's room with a vigor and enthusiasm even she would have admitted was unusual.

Mrs. McArthur, now a great inanimate swollen lump of a woman, was propped up against her pillows, her frazzled hair spread out against the pillow.

"It's time you had a proper uniform," Mrs. McArthur announced. "Time for you either to cut your hair or tuck it up under a good white dust cap. I'll have to speak to Mr. McArthur about it tonight. You ought to be dressed appropriately. How old are you now?" Mrs. McArthur paused, then answered her own question. "Near fourteen, it must be."

Emerald frowned. "What year of our Lord is it?"

"Nineteen-oh-nine, you silly goose. My heavens, how can anyone not know what year it is? And it is May, May 1909. There are twelve months in every year. Don't you even know your months?"

Emerald looked down at the floor. No one had taught her; how was she to know? She shook her head. "How long ago was 1641?"

Mrs. McArthur grumbled, "Two hundred and sixty-eight years, and it was a shameful violent time! What makes you ask such questions?"

"I just heard someone mention it," Emerald replied. She dared not ask how many weeks were in a month. She understood weeks, since Mr. McArthur, at Mrs. McArthur's insistence, took her to church once a week.

"There!" Mrs. McArthur startled Emerald out of her thoughts. "There's the calendar sent round by the baker's shop. You take it off the wall and study it; maybe you can learn the names of the months."

Emerald eagerly took the calendar. "Yes, Auntie Bess," she said. "Thank you."

"You're a good girl," Mrs. McArthur allowed. "Better than I thought you'd turn out, all things considered. A bit dense, but decent."

"Yes, Auntie Bess," Emerald replied.

4

It was on the morning of July 5, 1909, that Emerald first discovered she was dying, or thought she was dying.

She awoke in her bedroll and found light pink stains where she had slept. How could it be? she asked herself, looking for some small injury.

Emerald turned her right index finger. She had cut it peeling potatoes a week ago, but it had long since healed, and in any case, she always slept with her hand outside the covers.

Emerald shivered and momentarily discarded the mystery. She dressed in her new uniform, which consisted of a plain gray wool dress, a crisp stiff white apron, and a small white dust cap which she pinned her hair up under, leaving only a few reddish-blond curls to caress her forehead.

As she did every morning, Emerald went straight out to the privy after dressing, and it was then that she discovered yet more blood. It was coming from between her legs! From somewhere inside.

Emerald paled and ran back into the house. Mrs. McArthur was not yet awake and Mr. McArthur was still upstairs dressing. Emerald could feel the liquid between her legs now; although the flow was slow, it was quite obvious that it continued. *I can't tell Mr. McArthur,* she decided.

Emerald hurried about and then finally found some old cloth. She carefully folded it and put it between her legs, holding it in place with her undergarments. The bleeding continued, and a vague childhood memory of her mother returned with frightening reality.

It was in a tiny room in an old building off Antrim Road. It might once have been a stately house with fine large rooms and servants who padded about seeing to everything. But now it was faded and dilapidated, a once-grand house that had been divided into small unheated rooms. In Emerald's memory it was like a great chest of drawers or a cupboard filled with a human collection. She could recall the long dark corridor of closed doors, and behind each one was a human being or beings, all neatly stacked away in the same way Emerald stacked dishes in Mrs. McArthur's cupboard . . . all alone, alone once the door was closed and the candle extinguished.

The room Emerald had shared with her mother was dark and damp. Darker than the attic at the McArthurs'; damper than the root cellar in midwinter, and cold, a kind of penetrating cold that Emerald knew she would never truly forget.

There had been no food. Emerald always remembered that, and even though Mrs. McArthur and sometimes her husband were strict with the food, they did not starve her, nor could Emerald ever say that since she had come to them she had ever been really hungry. But like the dampness, Emerald could remember the sensations of gnawing hunger she had known in her infancy. Daily she had watched as her beautiful mother had grown smaller and smaller. Till at last she had seemed no bigger than the fairy princess who lived beneath the great green leaf. But most vividly Emerald remembered the blood. Her mother had coughed it up, sometimes in small quantities, later more and more, as if her body were turning itself inside out before Emerald's eyes.

Finally Emerald's mother had closed her eyes and gradually grown cold and stiff. Emerald, frightened and bewildered, had sat by the bedside till at last fear, hunger, and thirst had made her scream and scream till someone came. She had only the slightest of memories about the hours and days immediately after that.

She had been taken to the foundling home and fed a watery soup. She had been dressed in clothes that were too big for her, and she had slept in a small iron bed in a room full of other sleeping children in iron beds. But those memories faded, and now, above all, Emerald remembered the vicar bringing her to the McArthurs' house, the house where she had now lived for nine long years.

Emerald examined the blood-soaked cloth between her legs as soon as Mr. McArthur ambled off to work. It was indeed bright red. Emerald shook a little. She harbored a fear of blood, remembering all too vividly her mother's coughing. Could one die from the bleeding between one's legs too?

Emerald struggled up the stairs, carrying Mrs. McArthur's breakfast. It was the usual tray and held a small pot of tea and a cup, some sliced lemon, two pieces of buttered toast, and one poached egg. She set it down, but her hands were shaking so much that every dish on the tray rattled.

"What's the matter with you?" Mrs. McArthur demanded. "I'm the one who's ill and confined to my bed."

Tears flooded Emerald's large green eyes. "I'm bleeding," she blurted out. "I'm going to die!"

Mrs. McArthur cocked a dark eyebrow and looked somewhat annoyed. "Where?" she snapped. "I don't see any bleeding." She shook her head. "Have you cut yourself again?"

Emerald bit her lower lip and pointed downward.

"Well, say something, girl!" Mrs. McArthur glared. "Don't just stand there pointing and crying like a mute goose."

"Between my legs," Emerald whispered. "I'm going to die. It's coming from inside me."

"Pshaw!" Mrs. McArthur responded with disdain. "It's only your first blood. You'll do it every single month till you're an old woman."

Emerald knew she looked puzzled. Was this something that happened to everyone? Why hadn't someone told her?

"I'm not going to die?" Emerald questioned, noting for the first time all day that she really didn't feel ill, save for the swellings on her chest, which were a bit sore.

"Of course you're not going to die. Where do you come by such stupidity?"

Emerald did not answer. Was she truly stupid? How could one know things unless one was told?

"I suppose you've made messy on your clothes, you silly girl." Mrs. McArthur paused, shaking her head in what seemed mild disgust. "Over there in the wardrobe you'll find some cloth-covered pads filled with cotton material. Take four and study how we make them."

Emerald went to the wardrobe, to where Mrs. McArthur pointed. She looked and found the peculiar-looking pads. She silently examined them.

"See they have a cover," Mrs. McArthur pointed out. "You'll need to make a dozen or so, and when they're filled up, you'll wash them first in cold water, then boil them to make them good and clean. Then dry them and save them for the next time. Is that too much for you to remember?"

Emerald again shook her head. She was still trying to make sense of it all. She would do it every month? "How long does it last?" Emerald stuttered.

"Four or five days," Mrs. McArthur informed her. "Don't you know anything? All women do it, it's the Lord's curse on us, it is. For Eve's sin! Don't you remember the Bible?"

Emerald nodded dumbly and tried to remember Eve. Yes, Eve was Adam's wife. She had spoken with the snake, and the snake had made Adam and Eve yearn for each other. Emerald wasn't at all sure what the yearning was, or what that had to do with sin.

"It's all Eve's fault!" Mrs. McArthur repeated. Emerald decided that Eve, whose fault it was that she was bleeding, must be a Protestant.

"You're such a stupid goose," Mrs. McArthur said. "Come, sit down here on the side of the bed. You know I'm a weak woman."

Emerald sat down gently. Harsh as she was, it was impossible to truly hate Mrs. McArthur. She was far too pitiful a sight, and as few knew, she was also lonely and miserable, a frightened woman who bellowed at the world and all its inhabitants more out of fear than hatred.

"I've made my bed and now I'm lying in it," Mrs. McArthur breathed in a low voice. "Soon I'll go to my reward, and none will truly mourn me. Not my worthless sons, who ran off and never even write, and not Mr. McArthur either. He might miss his ale, but he won't miss me who's given him a roof over his head all these years!" Mrs. McArthur's eyes were suddenly watery, great pale pools of blue water intersected with bloody red lines and surrounded by the puffy mountains of her face. "Will you mourn for me?"

"Of course, Auntie Bess." Emerald reached out and patted the plump hand.

There were times when Emerald disliked Mrs. McArthur, just as there were times when she yearned to talk to the brittle old woman. When she had first come to the house and Mrs. McArthur was out and about, Emerald had disliked her a great deal. But now there was not much to dislike. Mrs. McArthur, who had made a prisoner of Emerald, was no less a prisoner herself. And unlike Emerald's, Mrs. McArthur's body rebelled and gave her great pain. It was as if some invisible person were blowing Mrs. McArthur bigger and bigger, so that soon she would explode. If Mrs. McArthur died, there would be one fewer person in Emerald's life, and there were few in any case.

Beyond the house, Emerald knew nothing but the church, and she was never allowed to speak with anyone save the vicar. She did not know the streets of Belfast because she was not allowed out; she did not have friends and she knew only the McArthurs and the men who came to play cards and drink.

I am stupid, Emerald conceded. I don't know where the butcher's is, where the greengrocer has his shop, or even where Dr. McCue has his clinic. And I don't know where Falls Road is either, Emerald thought.

"I would mourn a great deal for you," she promised.

Mrs. McArthur screwed up her face and almost smiled. "You'll have to take care now," she said to Emerald. "More care than you can possibly imagine, because you are a bit dim, and the dim have to be even more careful."

"Careful?" Emerald questioned.

"Men are pure evil," Mrs. McArthur confided. "When you've had your first blood, you're ready for them and they're ready for you. You must never let one touch you, you understand. You must not."

"Touch me? I don't understand."

"Of course you don't, that's why I'm telling you. You must not let them touch you there"—Mrs. McArthur pointed to Emerald's legs—"where you're bleeding from. You mustn't let them touch you there, or first thing you know, you'll have a baby. And I know your kind. You get pregnant every time someone looks at you there, you do."

"Without my clothes on?" Emerald questioned. "I can't get pregnant if they look and I have my clothes on, can I?"

Mrs. McArthur shook her head. "No," she begrudgingly allowed. "But to remain a good girl, you'll never take your clothes off in front of any man, do you understand?"

"Yes, Auntie Bess."

"Good. Because you have to remember that men are evil. All they want is to touch and to have you. Filth! That's all they think about, filth!"

"But why do I bleed?" Emerald pressed.

"Because it's a curse. I already told you that. The only thing that's more of a curse is to get pregnant, and then you stop bleeding till you have the baby. But you start again. A curse is a curse!" Mrs. McArthur was breathing heavily; her chest heaved and she coughed for a few minutes. "Now, go downstairs and put one of the pads on. Go on, see to yourself before you bleed on your clothes."

Emerald got up, and clutching the pads, went downstairs.

"I'll have Mr. McArthur buy you some more materials to make more pads," Mrs. McArthur called out. "And when you've finished, come back and bring me some tea!"

"Yes, Auntie Bess," Emerald called back.

She ran through the yard and out to the privy. She glanced at the little garden she had planted. The sprouts were all strong and tall and the bright red, rosy tomatoes were ripening right on the vine. It's wonderful to be alive, Emerald thought. Wonderful not to be dying.

5

Mr. McArthur met Mrs. Letitia Witter while marketing. At first he had hated market day with a passion. "Why can't Emerald go?" he had argued. "She's certainly old enough."

"Too old," Mrs. McArthur had replied firmly. "First off, she might cheat on the money, and how would you ever find out? Second, you can't trust an Irish Catholic girl. She'll find some young man, and then there won't be any money or any Emma. I can't have her running off, you know. I need her now that I'm bedridden. And third, she isn't very bright. She'd never get it all straight. There's just no other way—you will have to do the marketing."

Mr. McArthur had acknowledged only the possibility that Emerald might run away. The rest of it was hogwash. If Emerald appeared naive and stupid, it was only because she had been kept in the house and never received any instruction. She was, as far as Mr. McArthur was concerned, quite a bright girl. If something was explained once, she quite understood it.

Nevertheless, he had given in and agreed to do the marketing; he had hated the task until he met Letitia—Lettice to all her friends.

Letitia Witter was a petite woman with eyes like bright shoe buttons and mounds of soft wavy brown hair that, while pinned up on her head, managed to fight discipline. The result was ringlets of escaping hair that caressed her shoulders, curled about her ears, and fell across her brow.

They had met casually and naturally by the turnips at the greengrocer's.

"Oh, you're the assistant manager at the Commercial Bank." Letitia had beamed even as her small face flushed just a bit.

Mr. McArthur had been quite taken aback that such an attractive woman had noticed him, while he himself had no memory whatsoever of her. "You have me at a disadvantage," he returned. "But I am Donald McArthur, assistant manager at the Commercial Bank. I'm terribly embarrassed, I just can't quite recall . . ." He paused and hopefully waited.

"Oh, you have no reason to remember. I opened an account only a few days ago, but you did not serve me, you were simply pointed out. And I was told, if I had any difficulty, any difficulty at all, I must see Mr. McArthur, the assistant manager."

That was how it began. Gradually, over some period of time, Mr. McArthur had learned that Mrs. Letitia Witter was a widow, that she lived off Clifftonville Road, and that she had no children.

Each time she came into the bank, Mr. McArthur had taken great care to greet her personally and to see to her needs. She, in turn, was always glad to see him, treating him like a long-lost friend.

"I know so few people in Belfast," Mrs. Witter confessed. "I should be pleased if you and your wife could come to tea one day."

Mr. McArthur looked away, trying to look distressed, giving his round face and eyes a bearing of illusory sadness. "My wife is a hopeless invalid," he confessed. "Being taken from me slowly."

"Oh, how dreadful, how perfectly dreadful!" Lettice had gushed, her fingers gripping his arm for emphasis. Then she leaned forward almost conspiratorially. "Do you think people would talk if you came alone for tea?"

Mr. McArthur took a deep breath, and now he expelled it with both relief and anticipation. "I should be delighted," he answered, speaking as softly as he ever had. "I'm certain no one would talk."

In point of fact, he wasn't certain at all, nor was he certain that he cared. Lettice was in her mid-forties, she was gay and charming, she seemed to like him. Mr. McArthur threw all caution to the wind.

It had been a full six months since he had first met Lettice at the greengrocer's, and now the culmination of his every day-dream was about to come true.

He mounted the steps to her house and knocked lightly on the door.

Lettice answered. She wore a modest light brown dress, a gold brooch, and her hair hung loose. "I see you had no difficulty finding me," she purred as she beckoned him into the parlor.

Mr. McArthur looked around. The house was neat, and like Lettice herself, it was tiny and well-groomed. She smiled and led him to a chair. "I shall get the tea," she announced crisply.

Mr. McArthur sat back uneasily. Simply being alone with her had excited him; it was the right time and moment; it seemed the fruition of his desire was at hand.

Lettice returned and set down the tray. She silently poured and handed Mr. McArthur his teacup with a devastating smile. "I thank you for coming," she said softly. "It's very lonely for me."

"And for me," Mr. McArthur added. "My wife has not gotten out of bed for some years. She is bloated with gout, and now the doctor fears there is a tumor as well."

"Oh, poor Mr. McArthur." Lettice's eyes blinked back mist and she reached out and patted his hand with hers. It was an unbloated, delicate hand, a hand with neat pink nails and soft white skin.

"I have admired you ever since we met," Mr. McArthur blurted. He was certain that his face was all red, and he cursed himself for having such a round fat belly. Could a woman like Lettice Witter really be interested in him?

"You are too kind," Lettice replied, blushing again.

"I suppose I am being too bold. I have no right. I am married . . . God help me." Mr. McArthur let his voice drop dramatically.

"It means a great deal to me," Lettice replied, looking away. "To have a man admire me, frankly, it . . . is something I have needed," she confessed.

"I can't imagine that every man does not admire you," Mr. McArthur quickly said.

"My husband didn't." Lettice gripped the edge of the settee. She cleared her throat. "We grow too personal," she quickly added. "We should change the subject."

Mr. McArthur tried not to look at her. Between his own legs he felt himself swelling as he had not for over ten long years. In his mind he clearly visualized her bush of brown curly hair, her round fine little rump, and her tight little breasts. Realizing that he was a large man, he thought that he would have to be careful with her; she was delicate, small and quite unlike any woman he had ever known.

He pulled his legs together and sat stiffly, praying that his inordinate hardness would go away, praying that Lettice would not notice his great bulge.

Lettice sipped her tea and reached for a sandwich. "It takes time to get to know one another." She smiled. "We must not get too personal too quickly. Dear Mr. McArthur, we are two people who were born to proper manners, and we appear to be in improper circumstances. I think we must consider our course of action carefully."

Mr. McArthur felt his heart beating faster and faster. Was there hope that Lettice would accept him? That he might yet live to possess so delicate a creature? "I quite agree," he replied, trying to disguise his desperate frustration.

"I shall get some more lemon." Lettice got up and walked across the room, disappearing again into the kitchen. Mr. McArthur stood up. If one asked him later why he stood up, he could not have answered. He simply stood up, the bulge in his gray trousers all too evident and emphasized by the stain resulting from his anxious secretions. As he stood, he felt as if all the blood in his body had suddenly rushed into his skull, then as if it just as suddenly drained down to his toes. He was vaguely aware of his arm aching.

"What is the matter?"

Donald McArthur heard the voice of Lettice through the fog of rushing emotions and pain. Then the room went cloudy, gray, and his chest filled with unbearable aches and he staggered forward. And then, before the eyes of Lettice Witter, he crumpled up and fell to the carpeted floor.

4

July 1909

Mr. McArthur missed the annual Orange Day Parade on the twelfth of July. He spent that day and fourteen others in the Royal Victoria Hospital, where Dr. McCue spent endless hours telling him how fortunate he was to be alive.

"I won't ask what you were doing in that woman's house." Dr. McCue smirked, and it was perfectly obvious that he wanted to know and that he had already made his own deductions.

"I went to discuss bank business," Mr. McArthur blustered. But he knew it was no use. No number of logical excuses were going to change the fact that Donald McArthur, assistant manager of the Commercial Bank, a married man, had suffered a mild heart attack while having tea with an attractive widow. Mr. McArthur considered it fortunate indeed that his wife was bedridden and that she had no friends to tell her his unfortunate tale.

Nonetheless, when Mr. McArthur returned home from the hospital, he gave up his evening of poker playing and drinking. There was no way around it. Dr. McCue would laugh and make comments. His own brother, Arthur, Mr. Heardsly, and even the staid Mr. Grant would all make jokes laden with innuendo. And though they might do it in jolly good humor, there was always the terrible possibility of Mrs. McArthur hearing. It was a possibility Mr. McArthur could simply not chance. Mrs. McArthur would have him turned out of the house, and the ensuing scandal would ruin him at the Commercial Bank. Heaven only knew that the circumstances surrounding his heart attack had been quite bad enough. In fact, had Mrs. Letitia Witter not moved away a month afterward, it might have gone on to cause further embarrassment.

During the months following his attack, Mr. McArthur grew sullen. His friends no longer came and he no longer enjoyed market day, though begrudgingly he continued to do the shopping. As summer faded into dull winter, Mr. McArthur became a man inside himself, a man who felt angered because he had been punished for that which he had not enjoyed. What's more, he continued to drink, though now he drank alone and seemingly grew angrier as he did so.

It was a foggy, rainy January night in 1910 and Mrs. McArthur was fast asleep, snoring loudly with her large mouth agape and her swollen body curled up like a gigantic baby.

Downstairs, Mr. McArthur sat in the cheerless parlor and stared at the worn settee across the room. It seemed the house and its contents, human and otherwise, were decaying before his eyes. He was as maudlin as he had ever been, and he had consumed at least four pints.

Emerald came in and out of the room several times. She was tidying up, preparing to go to bed in the attic. She felt Mr. McArthur's eyes following her, but he often stared at her, and then if she spoke, seemed startled that she was there.

After a time, he summoned her. "Come here, lass!"

Emerald came; she stood shyly in front of the worn over-stuffed chair and tried to assess his mood. He was commanding, to be sure, but he didn't sound angry or upset.

"Take off your cap," Mr. McArthur muttered. Obediently Emerald removed her white dust cap, and her long red-gold hair tumbled down, falling over her shoulders.

Mr. McArthur stared at her as if he had never seen her before. Then he lunged toward her, pulling her onto his lap.

"Closer!" he demanded, breathing his beery breath into her face.

Overcome with sudden fear, Emerald struggled, trying to escape his hairy arms, but Mr. McArthur tore the back of her dress and forced it down to her waist.

He grasped her arm with such strength that Emerald thought his fingers would go right through her skin. "Don't you make a sound, lass. Not a sound!" He hissed the words into her ear.

"What are you doing?" Emerald could feel herself begin to shake. The color had drained from her face; all of Mrs. McArthur's terrible warnings came back. For a split second she thought he might be going to spank her, something he had not done for many years.

But Mr. McArthur made no move to lift her skirts. Rather, he pulled her dress down, and Emerald knew this was wrong and dreadful. He was rough and mean; he repulsed her, so she struggled even harder. But her grappling did not stop him. He undid her camisole as well and tore it from her, revealing pink and white flesh.

Emerald turned to him aghast. His face was contorted as if he were some wild creature, and spittle drooled from the corner of his mouth as he reached for her firm hard breast, covering it with his hand and letting out a kind of sick agonized groan.

In spite of his warning, Emerald opened her mouth to scream, but Mr. McArthur's hand clamped over it. "If you scream, if you wake Mrs. McArthur, I'll put a gag in your mouth and beat the skin right off your body."

Shaking, Emerald tried to cover herself with her hands, but Mr. McArthur yanked her hands away and covered her small breasts with his hands.

His eyes were glazed over. "A bit small," he muttered. "But nice, probably even nicer than Lettice's . . . certainly you're younger, God, so much younger." He rolled his eyes heavenward. "I was punished for what I didn't do, Lord!" He burped. " 'Twas you who sent her here. I'm tempted! Sorely tempted!"

Tears were running down Emerald's face, but she was surprised to see that Mr. McArthur was crying too. "What are you doing? Please stop!" Emerald begged, her face a mask of fear.

"Just touching," Mr. McArthur replied. "Oh, God, just touching," he slurred.

Then, without warning, he pushed Emerald's torn dress down over her round white hips and roughly seized the golden fleece over her small mound.

She shivered in his arms. "I'll get pregnant," Emerald sobbed. He was looking at her, looking in that secret place, the place Mrs. McArthur had warned her about so many times since she began bleeding some time ago.

His hands seemed everywhere as Emerald wriggled and fought, trying to break away; but still fearing his threat to beat her skin off, she remained silent. His large hand slipped between her legs, and Emerald let out a whimper.

"Close your mouth! Close it or I'll really hurt you!"

He removed his hand and fumbled with his pants, withdrawing a long fat sword of flesh which made Emerald shudder in sheer horror.

"Take it! Take it in your hands, or I'll stab you with it!" His face was contorted, and Emerald thought she had never seen him look so mean.

"Take it!" he repeated.

Shaking, Emerald took the dreadful, hairy, foul-smelling object into her small hands.

"Rub it!" he ordered. Emerald did as he said, but Mr. McArthur was unsatisfied. "This way," he instructed, taking it himself. He moved its loose chicken skin up and down. "Do it this way!"

Emerald, still shaking, did as he told her, fearing that if she did not, he would surely stab her with it. And what difference could anything make now? Certainly she was pregnant already.

As Emerald moved it up and down, Mr. McArthur covered her bare breasts with his hands and toyed with her nipples, which grew hard, as they often did on cold nights or when she was deeply afraid.

Suddenly Mr. McArthur began to groan, and he went rigid, causing Emerald to think he might have died. A dreadful fluid like half-cooked egg white spurted out of the object, and Emerald withdrew her hands, feeling nauseous and afraid she might vomit.

Lost for a moment in his climax and still mumbling about temptation and punishment, Mr. McArthur released Emerald, and she scrambled away across the floor, pulling her dress up and covering herself as quickly as possible.

Mr. McArthur was breathing hard as he tucked the limp object into his pants. Emerald cowered in the corner, fearing he would lunge across the room at her.

"Next time," he threatened, looking at her with red-rimmed eyes, "next time, I'll stick it between your legs."

Emerald took in his words, and fear shot through her whole body. He had made her pregnant by looking at her and touching her. Now he was going to stab her with that thing where she bled anyway. She shivered, and with luminous fear-filled eyes she mentally measured the distance between where she crouched and the front door.

As Emerald knew, Mr. McArthur could not run fast. She did up the final button on her torn dress, but she did not replace the dust cap which lay on the floor far too close to Mr. McArthur's foot. Emerald quivered at her own plan. It was pitch dark outside, and her clothing was torn. It was raining and she wore only slippers. But she could not risk going up to the attic to get her shoes. The thought of the black night terrified her, but it did not frighten her as much as the thought of Mr. McArthur touching her again or stabbing her with his flesh-covered bone. There could be nothing worse than the feel of his hands on her skin; he was evil and mentally diseased. She decided on the spot. It would be better to be lost in the black night, to be torn by wild dogs, to be kidnapped by unknown strangers. . . . Death, Emerald decided, would be deliverance. And there was a chance that outside, somewhere near the place called Falls Road, were her people. I must find them, Emerald thought. If I live, if I survive, maybe they can help me.

Emerald took a step, and Mr. McArthur made no move. She took another and reached the long hallway. He still did not move, even though his pink-rimmed eyes followed her. Emerald eased away; his back was now to her as she rounded the corner. He must have thought she was going to the attic. But instead of going up the staircase, Emerald stepped to the front door and leaned down on the heavy latch. She flung open the door and ran out into the pouring cold rain.

She ran down the winding cobbled road as fast as her legs would carry her. She did not turn or pause; she whipped around the corner and kept going forward blindly, her eyes flooded with tears and rain. Falls Road! Falls Road! What direction might it be in? How far was it? That single question filled Emerald's mind, even as the sound of Mr. McArthur running after her filled her ears.

"Come back here! Come back here, you little croppie bitch!" Mr. McArthur waved his fat, pudgy fist in the air and shouted obscenities into the darkness. Before him he saw Mrs. McArthur's lumpish, unattractive body; then the image of Lettice floated across his mind and chased Mrs. McArthur away. He had wanted Lettice, but he had been punished even for the thought, struck down by a heart attack for simply feeling desire. His eyes too were filled with tears, bitter tears. "Ah! A man has his needs!" Mr. McArthur came to an abrupt halt. He squinted as large drops of cold rain ran through his thin hair, down his forehead, and over his nose. Emerald's form was disappearing in the distance. "She'll tell someone!" He wailed. "I'll be ruined! I am ruined!" Sobriety was returning, and Mr. McArthur shook suddenly as he remembered touching Emerald, threatening her, holding her intimately. He was torn by further desire, by a wavering guilt, by years of frustration, and by the fear that he was undone. As though once again a helpless child, Mr. McArthur stopped and cried in the darkness, only half-aware of his aching left arm and his throbbing chest now so filled with pain. He gasped once and cried out. He grasped hold of a fence post to steady himself. The night was filled with Mrs. McArthur's shrieks of agony, of her youthful protests against the sins of the flesh, of Emerald shaking with fright. Mr. McArthur panted and seized the other side of the fence post with his other hand; then, embracing it like a desirable woman, he slumped to his knees, alternately sobbing and fighting for air. "I'm undone," he wailed. "I'm a sinner found out!" Tears suddenly mingled with beery vomit and Mr. McArthur's arms let go of the fence post as he sprawled out on the ground, clutching his chest, twitching like a half-dead insect. The last involuntary spasm was in his left leg.

It lifted itself a few inches off the cobbled pavement, then dropped with a finality that marked the end of Mr. McArthur's life.

Emerald in her terror ran past the church she and Mr. McArthur had attended every Sunday. Falls Road, she decided, must be far from the Protestant church. She ran down endless dark, wet streets of row houses, houses that all looked alike, streets that seemed all the same. Emerald didn't look back, she only ran.

She ran up Lisburn to Dublin Road and past Ulster Hall, which she had never seen before. Still running, Emerald crossed a deserted Donegal Square. There she paused for a moment beneath a dripping tree. To her relief, the streets were empty, and if Mr. McArthur was still following her, he was not in sight. Emerald looked out as far as she could see. Beyond the cluster of roofs, she could make out the rolling hills against the night sky. The home of the fairies, Emerald thought as she turned wearily, only to jump and let out a startled cry.

There before her, looming like a great giant, was the queen of England herself! For a long moment Emerald stood frozen, but the queen did not move. Emerald, her eyes wide, stepped toward the queen and hesitantly reached out to discover cold metal; the queen was not real! Emerald blinked and looked up at the frightening image of Victoria, whose imposing soot-encrusted eminence compelled Emerald to back away just as a thousand church bells pealed forth.

"It's midnight!" Emerald muttered, knowing full well it was the hour when evil emerged into the world. She turned quickly and again began running.

Emerald breathed hard. Her slippers were muddy and soaked through. Her wet clothing clung to her slender body and her red-gold hair hung in damp strands; a raindrop ran down her nose. She licked it into her mouth and paused for an instant to stare back into the still blackness of the night. No one was following; there were only a few buildings and houses where warm gaslights still burned. Emerald shivered and began walking rapidly.

After a time, she approached a large building. Emerald stopped short and sounded out the words over the entrance. They proclaimed "Grand Hotel." She did not know the meaning of the words. Outside the hotel, lights still burned and there were, in the distance, a few people about. Emerald paused and decided to circumvent the large building and the people going down a dark side street. She walked along quickly, keeping to the shadows.

When she was past the large building with all the men in their strange and fearful uniforms, she crossed back again and began walking along Davis Road. In a short while she came to an intersection, and on the sign that marked it were the blessed words "Falls Road."

"On the other side of Falls Road," Mr. McArthur had told her so long ago. Emerald ran along, passing the same buildings over and over. Everything seemed to go in circles; she returned to the same spot twice.

Exhausted and excited all at once, Emerald leaned against the side of an old brick building. There were no lights now, and she felt tired. Her dress was drenched and she wrapped her arms around herself to keep from shivering as she walked more slowly in her weariness. She turned yet another corner and looked down the street at the houses filled with sleeping people. Which side of Falls Road was the "other" side? Were the houses filled with sleeping Catholics or Protestants? Were the Catholics still here? After all, her conversation had been a long time ago. Emerald sucked on her lower lip; tears were still running down her face, though they were quickly washed away by rain.

A tale her mother had once told her entered her head. It was about a child in the magical bewitched forest. The child was taken captive by an evil witch, and when the little one escaped, she ran through the forest for hours, pursued by strange beasts and plants which reached out and grasped like the arms of people. But all the while, the child was watched by the evil witch, who enjoyed seeing the child so frightened and so bewildered and who knew that, driven by fear, the child was going in circles which would end up once again at the witch's door.

Emerald feared that in her confusion she too would end up at the witch's door, and that Mr. McArthur lurked just around each unknown corner. Belfast was, after all, his forest.

If he finds me, Emerald thought, he'll beat me and beat me. He'll stab me and touch me more. Tears welled up anew, and she pushed herself to go on, feeling tired, cold, and weak. She turned yet another corner. "I'm still on the other side of Falls Road," she said aloud, more to reassure herself than out of real conviction.

Down at the end of the street there was another large building. Emerald's eyes traveled its height upward, and she saw that on the top of the spire there was a cross. But the church the McArthurs took her to also had a cross.

Emerald approached the building warily. Outside, it was surrounded by a high but delicate wrought-iron fence, and beyond

that, there was a marker. Emerald read the marker, sounding out
each word till she came to the word "Catholic."

"I'm home!" Emerald said as she leaned for a moment against
the gate. Beyond was her sanctuary; beyond were her people.

Emerald pushed open the iron gate and ran forward and up
the stone steps. She flung herself against the great wooden
doors, pounding on them wildly. "Let me in! Let me in!"
Emerald screamed as she had never screamed in her life before.
She screamed at the top of her young lungs, "Let me in, I'm a
Catholic!"

2

Emerald opened her eyes and found herself in a large high-
ceilinged room, the walls of which were painted a bilious green.
It was the ceiling she saw first, a ceiling supported by tall
columns. As Emerald fully regained consciousness, she became
aware of the room's odors, which reminded her of vinegar and
somehow of Mrs. McArthur's medicine chest.

She found herself lying on an iron cot, one of many such cots
that lined the walls of the room, standing on guard, row on row,
like sentinels. It's like the foundling home, Emerald thought in a
sudden panic. Her wet clothing had been removed, and in its
place she wore a stiff white gown. Moreover, the sides of her cot
were pulled up, and she felt like a baby in a giant crib. She was
covered from her toes right up to her neck with a heavy woolen
gray blanket, and it was tucked in to the sides of the bed so
tightly that she could hardly move. A chill of fear passed through
her.

Emerald's arms were outside the covering and had been folded
across her chest as if she were a corpse. She fumbled with her
fingers and in reality felt the magic beads of her childhood!

Emerald, her heart pounding, lifted them up and dangled them
above her face so she could examine them. They were plainer
than her mother's beads, but clearly they were for the same
purpose. They were black, and at their end, a plain black
ebony crucifix hung. Emerald fingered the rosary with wonder.
She did not move her lips, but in her mind she repeated the
words she so well remembered.

Emerald lay contentedly for a short time, fingering the beads
and saying her "Hail Marys" silently. Then gradually her ordeal
with Mr. McArthur flowed back into her mind and she recalled

with horror her nightmare of running through the streets of Belfast. Emerald was at once in the past and in the present; she found her lost voice and cried out, "I'm Catholic!"

Almost immediately, Emerald was confronted with the specter of a white angel; or perhaps, she thought, it was instead the fairy princess herself, come to rescue her.

The white angel lifted a wrinkled hand and felt Emerald's forehead; then she smiled without revealing her teeth. "We are all Catholics here," she informed Emerald in a patient, quiet voice. "But you must not scream; there are many sick people here."

'Are you Catholic?" Emerald whispered in wonderment.

Again the angel smiled. "I'm Sister Celeste of the Order of Saint Joseph's."

Emerald blinked. Did she really have a sister as well as her two brothers, Padraic and Seamus? "I didn't know I had a sister," Emerald replied. "Are you really my sister?"

The nun smiled and this time did show her teeth. "I am pleased that you have lowered your voice. I am not your sister, but a sister of the faith, a nun. I am God's bride. But a good Catholic girl found saying her rosary must know all about nuns."

"I don't," Emerald admitted quite honestly, "but I am Catholic," she repeated with conviction, lest there be any mistake.

The nun looked at her strangely but did not comment. She had dealt with mental patients, people who were temporarily lost, people young and old who were alone and afraid. "What is your name?" Sister Celeste inquired.

"Emerald O'Hearn, Emma to some. But my mother always called me Emerald—for my eyes and for the Emerald Isle."

"And where is your mother?" Sister Celeste pressed gently.

"Gone to heaven," Emerald whispered. "But I've not yet lit a votive candle for her, and I don't know if the priest has said the words over her."

Sister Celeste frowned and wondered why the young girl did not seem more upset. Surely one who had recently lost her mother should be upset. But perhaps that was a clue to Emerald's condition; perhaps she was in some kind of mental shock.

"And how old are you, Emerald?" the nun asked, testing Emerald's sense of reality.

"I don't know." Emerald could not be sure whether she was fourteen or fifteen. And she decided it would not be right not to tell the absolute truth to God's bride.

"Well, then, where do you live?"

Again Emerald shook her head, not daring to say, though in

fact she really couldn't have anyway. She had never left the McArthurs' house except to go around the corner to church. She had not even known the name of the city till Mrs. Higgins had told her.

"Can you describe where you live?" the nun asked patiently.

"In Belfast," Emerald answered.

Sister Celeste's facial expression did not change. Nor did she ask another question as Emerald thought she might. Instead, she patted Emerald on the head gently. "You're safe here," Sister Celeste affirmed, sensing that Emerald was not only confused but also frightened. "You were out for a long time in the cold rain and you were completely drenched and unconscious when you were brought here. Sleep a little more, Emerald O'Hearn, and when you wake up, we'll talk some more." Sister Celeste looked up to acknowledge two other bustling nuns who were delivering lunch trays to those able to eat. "Are you hungry, Emerald?"

"Oh, yes," Emerald quickly answered. Up until now she had not thought about food, but somehow the smell of hot tea and biscuits and broth brought on a feeling of almost desperate hunger. How long had she been here? How long had she been sleeping and unconscious?

Sister Celeste was propping up the pillows, and Emerald pushed herself up in the iron bed so that she could sit up. Another nun put a tray in front of her. It fastened to the edge of the iron bed. On it were tea, biscuits, broth with chicken, and some clear juice.

"You eat, then rest some more," Sister Celeste instructed. "I'll come back later."

Sister Celeste walked from the hospital corridor into the priest's outer office. She tapped on the door lightly.

The door opened. "Come in, come in." Father Doyle motioned.

Sister Celeste sat down in the chair opposite Father Doyle's massive oak desk, behind which he retreated instantly. She looked across at the priest, a troubled expression clouding her face.

"I've come about the girl found on the steps of the church yesterday morning. She's a puzzle, that one." Sister Celeste let out a deep sigh. "*Another* puzzle." And in truth, her life was full of puzzles. Men so full of alcohol they didn't know who they were, women who had been beaten senseless, lost children— the refuse of Belfast found its way to Sister Celeste, or so it seemed.

Father Doyle was silent, but he motioned her to continue.

"A strange girl," Sister Celeste observed. "Physically she's fine, or so it appears. As healthy as can be. It takes physical strength to suffer from exposure for so many hours and come through it so quickly without even so much as a fever." The nun shook her head. "But mentally, I don't know, I just don't know. She keeps insisting she's Catholic, and there's no doubt she knows her rosary and the 'Our Father.' But saints preserve us, she didn't know what a nun was."

Father Doyle frowned and looked at the wood grains in his oak desk.

"She's quick to answer questions, and more clear-eyed than most. She answers almost too quickly to have lost her memory, and if she weren't so bright-eyed, I'd say she was demented."

Father Doyle nodded. "Go on," he suggested.

"She must be fourteen or fifteen, but she says she doesn't know how old she is. She doesn't know where she lives either, save for the fact that she lives in Belfast. And she says her mother is dead, but she isn't sure, and I'm quoting, 'if the priest said the words over her.' She also said she had not yet lit a votive candle for her mother." Sister Celeste shook her head again and ran her hand across her brow. "She seems a sweet young girl, but not at all upset really that her mother's dead. Oh, I don't understand at all. What I do know is that she is well and that I need the bed for a body that's ill."

"Bright-eyed or not, she could be demented," Father Doyle allowed. "But considering the exposure—as I recall, she was found dressed in rags and wore no shoes—she could be suffering from some form of shock. Could be she's a runaway who's frightened and can't go home." Father Doyle scratched his chin. "What else did she say, exactly?"

"I told her I was Sister Celeste and she asked if I was her sister."

Father Doyle half-smiled and winked. "I think I had better speak with her myself. Is she rested enough to come in and have a talk this afternoon?"

Sister Celeste nodded. "I'll have her dressed and sent after lunch." She stood up and shook out her habit, then turned and went through the outer office to the ward.

After lunch, Sister Celeste once again approached Emerald's bed. She noted that Emerald was sitting up now, fingering her beads and saying her rosary. "I'm back," Sister Celeste said cheerfully. "Do you feel like getting up and dressing?"

"My clothes are all wet," Emerald answered, remembering the long night. "And I have no shoes."

"I'll get some things for you, though they may not fit you so well."

Emerald watched curiously as the bustling nun disappeared, returning a short time later with a pile of odd clothes.

"I think these will fit," Sister Celeste told her.

Sister Celeste untucked the blanket and turned back the covers. Emerald swung her long legs over the side of the cot and dropped to the cold stone floor. The beds on either side of the cot she had been in were occupied, and to Emerald it seemed as if a thousand strange eyes stared at her. She wondered vaguely how many people there were in Belfast. These were different people from the ones she saw in church. There was no familiar face, not one. That meant that there were all these people plus the ones at church, plus the ones in front of the Grand Hotel. And all the houses she passed must have been full of people as well. There were, Emerald concluded, a lot of people in Belfast. More than three hundred at least!

Emerald's next thought was more curious yet, and it was one that she vocalized. "Do all Catholics stay in bed?" Emerald asked the startled nun.

"Certainly not!" Sister Celeste replied. "This is a hospital, these people are ill."

Emerald looked around, and it occurred to her that the Protestants might have poisoned all the Catholics. "Are all the Catholics ill?" she asked with a look of such deep concern that Sister Celeste felt prone to feel her forehead to see if, in fact, she did have a fever.

"Not at all," Sister Celeste answered. Shaking her head, she quickly pulled on some long cords. Then she moved three metal objects with curtains attached to them all around Emerald's bed, blocking off Emerald's cot from all the others. "Now you can dress in privacy," the nun told her.

Emerald looked around in wonder. "Oh, it's a movable room," she said with such delight that it forced a true smile to Sister Celeste's face. "A lovely white room all my own," Emerald said sweetly.

"Don't forget I'm waiting," Sister Celeste called out.

"I'll dress quickly," Emerald replied. She found in the pile of clothes a white blouse, a navy skirt, and a navy vest. There were long heavy woolen stockings as well as new stiff black oxfords that were, like every pair of shoes she had ever had, a trifle too big. Emerald paused to inspect herself in the polished tin mirror next to her bed. She peered closer at her face and beamed. "My freckle is gone," she whispered proudly.

"I'm dressed," Emerald called out.

As quickly as the nun had moved the white screens into place, she removed them. She looked Emerald up and down. Every article of clothing was on properly and she had tied her shoes with neat bows. Most demented youngsters, Sister Celeste recalled, had great difficulty dressing themselves. Demented, this Emerald O'Hearn might be; to Sister Celeste's relief, she appeared to be capable of dressing and no doubt of working. And why do I care? Sister Celeste asked herself. The demented are granted a certain bliss by God, and I do see a lot of them. It occurred to her that in so short a time she had, however, formed a quite different feeling for this young girl. She didn't want this bright-eyed, red-haired little beauty to be demented. There was something about this girl, something Sister Celeste sensed but could not yet verbalize. Emerald's questions and outlook had a kind of naive intelligence; it was as if she had just disembarked from some distant planet.

"Follow me," Sister Celeste said briskly, leading Emerald out of the ward, through the outer office, and into the priest's inner office.

"This is Emma O'Hearn. She tells me her mother called her Emerald. Emerald, this is Father Doyle."

Father Doyle was middle-aged, perhaps forty or forty-three. His face was long and thin, but his eyes were a twinkling blue and his complexion was rosy. He was dressed in a long black cassock and he wore a tight white collar.

Emerald stared at him. "You are not my father," she said, standing back, her large curious green eyes wandering the length of his cassock. Emerald had never seen a man in a dress before—if he *was* a man, and he did appear to be one from the neck up.

"Sit down," Father Doyle invited, motioning her to the same stiff-backed chair that Sister Celeste had been sitting in only a short time ago. "I think it might be best if Emerald and I talked alone," Father Doyle suggested.

Emerald shot an uneasy glance at the nun and then she looked back into Father's Doyle's face. "Are you Catholic?" she asked, not wanting to be left alone with any man who wasn't.

"I am," Father Doyle answered, unable to disguise the amused look on his face. "I'm a priest. That's why they call me 'father.' "

Emerald looked at the floor. "I forgot," she confessed. "I forgot that priests are called 'father.' "

"Sit down, Emerald."

Uneasily Emerald sat down, perching on the edge of the chair like a bird on the edge of a garden fence.

Sister Celeste closed the door behind her, and Father Doyle sat down behind his own desk, folded his arms, and looked across the expanse of golden wood at Emerald.

"I want you to start with the very first thing you remember about your life, Emerald. I want you to tell me everything."

Emerald bit her lower lip and let out her breath. "My brothers went away," she said slowly. "Padraic and Seamus were sent out to work . . ." She paused and frowned. "No, that's not right. My father went away first. Then when he didn't come back, my mother cried a lot, and there wasn't enough food. Then Padraic and Seamus went out to work."

Emerald looked up at Father Doyle. "I don't remember too much. I remember the dark room and Mama coughing. Then Mama went to heaven and I cried all night. I prayed for the angels to send her back. I did, I really did." Tears had suddenly flooded Emerald's large eyes.

Father Doyle listened intently, fascinated by the childish expression of her story. For a girl her age, she seemed terribly young. Perhaps Sister Celeste was correct, perhaps she had mentally reduced capacities. But still her eyes seemed to shine, and there was an open honesty that interested him and made him curious.

"Then they came for me," Emerald continued. "They came and took me to the home. A place rather like this," Emerald concluded. "But full of Protestants."

"Why did they take you there?" Father Doyle asked, tilting his head slightly.

"Mama was Catholic and she taught me I was Catholic too. But they said Papa was a Protestant, so they said I belonged with them. But then they called me a croppy." Emerald lifted her hand and wiped her cheek. "Then the vicar took me to the McArthurs' . . ." Suddenly fear flickered in Emerald's eyes. "Oh, don't send me back there . . . oh, please. Mr. McArthur said he'd stab me and beat the skin off me!" She was shaking now, and the tears were running down her face.

"It's all right, it's all right." Father Doyle stood up and reached across the table. He gently patted her arm. "It's all right, we won't send you back, it's all right."

Gradually Emerald's tears and shaking subsided.

"Now, go on," he urged. "Tell me more, tell me how long you were with the McArthurs."

Emerald scowled. "I came, or they said I came, in 1900.

They thought I was five then, but no one was certain. It's 1910 now, and I've been with them since 1900.''

Father Doyle put his hand over his eyes. The reality of Emerald O'Hearn was becoming agonizingly clear. "And what did you do there?" he queried.

"I cleaned," Emerald replied. "And after Mrs. McArthur got sick, I took care of her too."

"And you were never taught?"

"Not since Mrs. Higgins died."

"And who was Mrs. Higgins?"

Emerald quickly told Father Doyle about Mrs. Higgins. "She taught me to read, but I can't understand everything I can sound out."

"And since you had to hide the fact that you visited Mrs. Higgins, did they not allow you out of the house?"

"Oh, no," Emerald answered. "Only to go around the corner to church, and only with them."

"And you never played with other children? You never talked with them?"

"Played?" The way she said the word answered the question for Father Doyle.

"You knew nothing beyond the street where you lived? But how do you know your rosary?"

"I remember it. I said it every single day. Even though they took my beads away."

Far from being retarded, the young girl in front of him was bright as a button. She had been a virtual prisoner for ten years, she had been denied all knowledge of the outside world, and what she knew of her Catholicism was based on her early-childhood memories and mixed with folk tales. No, Emerald O'Hearn was not incapacitated, she was a small wonder! A virtual inspiration! She had kept her memory alive repeating what she did know, and she had survived to find her way back to safety.

"You never received Catholic instruction?" he asked, seeking to confirm the opinion he had already formed.

Emerald shook her head. "The McArthurs didn't know any Catholics. They didn't like Catholics."

"Now tell me how you came to run away from the McArthurs. You did run away, didn't you?"

Emerald nodded in agreement.

She told the story as well as she could and noticed that Father Doyle went pale, then bright red. But at the same time, she noted that he was angry, though she was quite certain he was not angry with her.

For his part, Father Doyle was shocked that Emerald had nearly been raped, and certainly she had been subjected to untold indignities. But she was a total innocent who knew instinctively that she had to escape the evil she was subjected to. Poor child! She was like a character from a folk tale! No, Father Doyle thought, she was more like Ireland itself. Through long years she had been subjected to deprivation both mental and physical; like all Irish Catholics, she had been denied an education and everything had been done to make her forget. And Emerald O'Hearn was like Ireland in another way, perhaps a more important way. Her spirit and her religion were intact; the violent act of suppression committed against her had failed.

Tears filled Father Doyle's eyes. "I'm proud of you, Emerald O'Hearn," he said softly. "And we'll see to it that it's all made up to you."

Emerald didn't say anything. She didn't quite understand, but she sensed the fact that Father Doyle intended to help her.

Father Doyle ignored his own tears and picked up a pencil, abstractedly putting one end in his mouth. Then he withdrew a long piece of paper from his desk. He wrote down her name, her brothers' names, and the year 1900.

"So your mother died in 1900. Do you know when your father died, or how?"

Emerald's face clouded over as she searched her memory for details. "Far away," she answered. "In a place with elephants . . . that's what my mother said, it was . . . a jungle, that's it, a place with big animals."

"South Africa," Father Doyle surmised. Emerald broke into a wide grin. "That's it! Mr. McArthur said he died fighting against the Empire! That he was a traitor."

"That's a matter of opinion," Father Doyle said, not bothering to hide his disdain. He leaned back in his chair. "I'll have to check some records," he mused. "I may . . . Now, I'm not making any promises, but I may be able to locate one or both of your brothers."

Emerald's smile was broad and wide. Then, as she thought of it, the smile faded from her face. "If you can't, would I have to go back?"

Father Doyle was up out of his chair in a shot and standing by her side. He patted her gently on the back. "Poor innocent lamb, we would never send you back, never."

Emerald looked up into the folds of his cassock. She shivered slightly and thought to herself that her long nightmare was over.

"You'll have to stay in the convent for the time being," Father Doyle told her. "You'll have to study, for there are many, many things you don't understand. But we will make inquiries, we will try to find your family."

1

July 1911

"You can tell an Irishman from an Englishman by the calluses on his hands." Padraic O'Hearn studied the hardened skin on his palms as he turned his hands over slowly. "A lifetime of work before you're twenty-five, and the tale is told in a man's hands."

"It's not the actual work I resent," Thomas Hughes commented. "It's the work they don't do. They're paper princes, they are. An Irishman grows poor shoveling English shit; an Englishman grows rich shoveling paper. And they call them civil servants! They're not civil and they're nobody's servants."

Padraic slumped into the straight-backed chair, and reaching across the table for the tin pitcher, poured himself another pint of porter. He surveyed the room for the hundredth time. He wondered, as he often did, what color the walls had once been. A cheerful yellow perhaps? Maybe a subdued white . . . but no more. Now they were a hue no artist would put on his palette; a kind of gray-mustard color with off-white streaks where a century of paint and paper had worn off and the plaster beneath erupted as if the building were being deeply ill in the bowels of its ancient construction.

Padraic's eyes moved to the windows, where snow-white lace curtains, incongruously delicate veils, shielded the drab room from the even drabber view.

Padraic sipped his warm porter. If the lace curtains that hung over the window kept the people outside from seeing in, they did not keep the odors of the street from drifting into the room. They were smells familiar to the inhabitants of the area, but no doubt revolting to the visitor: a mixture of garbage, the sweat of too many bodies living too close together, freshly baked bread and biscuits, the mouth-watering contents of a hundred iron cooking pots, and the refuse of a partially open sewer. The multiple odors mingled and blended, and the result was a peculiarity that might simply be described as "the smell of the impoverished."

Nor did the curtains keep out sound. There was often the crying of babies, and from the cobbled street the collective voices of children rose easily to the level of the window, so that Padraic O'Hearn was often treated to the songs of the street and the games of the youngsters. And late at night, when men grown old before their time returned home with a belly full of ale, their round frustrated wives raised a ballyholly—a fine tongue-lashing, a torrent of fearful angry abuse that somehow echoed love and the certain knowledge that all too many men who were out late drinking were vulnerable to the violent hatreds that held Belfast in its historic vise.

The room was not unique in any way from a hundred or even a thousand others. It was located on the fourth floor of a decaying building near the shipyards and the scrap heaps. Here Padraic O'Hearn, Thomas Hughes, Terry McKenna, and Wee Willie O'Brien bunked together, their bedrolls spread out untidily next to the wall of their choosing.

A plain wooden table with four straight-backed chairs stood in the center of the room, and against one wall a torn settee that had either been rescued from the trash heap of the wealthy or had been a part of the room for a century offered some comfort. Along the wall that was nearest the exit into the bleak hallway, there was a yellowed basin over which hung a tin mirror, and near it were a small gas burner and a screened pantry box.

The lace curtains, which fluttered in the breeze, were a gift from Thomas' mother, and the plain ebony crucifix that hung on the side wall belonged to Terry McKenna. Near Padraic's bedroll there was a small table, and on it, three yellowed tintypes. One depicted his father posing with a gun, and in the background, lavish vegetation revealed a tropical locale. The second showed a beautiful young woman and the same handsome face of his father. It was his parents' wedding photo. The third portrayed a wide-eyed baby in a long flowing christening gown. It was his sister, Emerald.

Apart from these individual signs of home, the room was the barren digs of four men who ranged in age from twenty-seven to forty. They were men without women, because few could afford a wife before the age of forty. Their living conditions, their struggle to earn sufficient money, and their twelve-hour workdays were duplicated in Ireland thousands of times over.

Padraic, Tom, Terry, and Wee Willie might have chosen to live in the barracks offered by the companies they worked for, rather than in this room. But here, at least, they were surrounded by families and the sounds of children. Here there were neighbors and the possibility of an occasional gathering. Living here made life seem more normal to the four men who were, either by circumstances or financial need, separated from their families.

Padraic was an orphan whose only brother had moved to

Dublin. Thomas Hughes had recently lost his mother, and his
father had died some years before. He was an only child, and
like Padraic, all other relatives were lost to him. Terry McKenna
came from a large family in County Galway and had left home to
relieve the economic situation as well as to find work. Wee
Willie O'Brien had a sister who was a nun and a brother who
still worked in the peat bogs. But like Thomas Hughes and
Padraic O'Hearn, his parents too were dead.

"The Kaffirs in Joburg live this way," Terry McKenna had
once commented. "They're dragged from their homes and live
out solitary lives waiting on their masters." Terry McKenna
knew because he had once been in Johannesburg. He hadn't
understood the Kaffirs because when they dared to speak, they
spoke a foreign language. But though he could not understand
their words, and though their black skin troubled him, Terry
McKenna recognized the sweat on their backs and the calluses
on their hands. It was in South Africa that Terry McKenna had
first heard and come to understand the word "colonialism." It was
in that land that was so vast, so beautiful, and so rich that he had
first discovered the English penchant for building open sewers
and for governing men with paper.

"The Irish are no better than Kaffirs," Terry McKenna
mumbled.

Padraic was the youngest of the four roommates. He was tall,
with an angular face and the piercing eyes of a dreamer, a poet
caught and held fast by grim reality. He was twenty-seven and
was resigned to the life of a bachelor.

Padraic had a special fondness for Terry McKenna because
Terry had fought in South Africa with the Boers and against the
Empire. Padraic's own Protestant father had done that because
he was an Irish nationalist who, like the poet Yeats, believed in
the destiny of Ireland as an independent nation.

But Padraic's father had died from an English bullet and was
buried in a land made real only by Terry McKenna's vivid
descriptions.

"We never had much in common with the Boers," Terry
McKenna explained once. "But you see, our going was the
manifestation of an old saying—'Let England's difficulties be
Ireland's opportunities!' That's the motto of the nationalists, be
they Catholic or Protestant. Wolfe Tone said it back in 1798,
and it's as true today as it was then."

It's difficult for an outsider to understand, Padraic thought.
The Protestants and Catholics shared a hatred for one another

generally, but there were groups of them who shared being Irish and who hated the British more than each other.

Apart from a few firm political pronouncements, vague memories of his face and smile, and the faded tintype photograph, Padraic remembered little of his father save his departure. Shortly thereafter, the family's poverty forced Padraic and his older brother, Seamus, to hire out to work in the peat bogs. Padraic was thirteen then and Seamus fifteen. Both boys had worked in the textile mills before they left home, beginning their working lives at nine and eleven. But jobs for young sweepers didn't last long, and the peat bogs were the only alternative.

Seamus and Padraic had lived in a community of men, and one, Mike Flannery, had befriended them. He had even tried to help them find their mother and Emerald when the letters ceased to come.

It was Mike Flannery who learned of Padraic's father's death, and it was Mike Flannery who spent so much time trying to find where Mrs. O'Hearn had moved. Finally he traced Katie O'Hearn and her small daughter to a tenement. He learned from belligerent neighbors that Katie O'Hearn had died and that little Emerald had disappeared.

Mike Flannery was like a father to Padraic and Seamus, and when he died, since he had no family of his own, he left what little he had in the world to Seamus and Padraic. Seamus used his share to go to Dublin in order to make a new start. Padraic saved most of his share. He used some to leave the peat bogs and find work in Belfast; the rest he stored away, dreaming of an eventual trip to America.

Both Padraic and Seamus had searched for Emerald, but there were no records, no way to trace her. Padraic had obtained work in the rope factory, and Seamus wrote from Dublin that he had work in a linen mill.

Thomas Hughes joined Padraic at the table. "It's a grubby life," he commented, staring into the tin of porter. "A grubby life."

"A man with work in the shipyards ought not to complain." Padraic smiled. Jobs in the shipyards were hard for Catholics to find; Hughes was fortunate. He worked for Harland and Wolff, and the firm was building the *Titanic*, which they hoped to launch in one year's time.

Thomas Hughes grimaced. It was Orange Day. "There'll be no pay this day. It's an enforced holiday—Orange Day is no holiday of mine."

"Pay or no pay, be glad you don't have to work today," Padraic said knowingly. There were things that didn't need saying. Orange Day was a day a Catholic ought to be grateful to keep to his house. If one had to go out, one was certain to encounter hooliganism. A wise man was glad to keep to the Catholic communities unless he was one who sought to return the violence of the Orangemen, who traditionally used this day to repay old grudges. It was a day when demonstrations often collided, when a man's head could be flattened with a truncheon, a day when ruffians might be around any peaceful corner.

Outside in the hallway, Mrs. Malone could be heard pursuing one of her children. It was a familiar sound, and in his mind's eye Padraic could see her. She would be carrying the baby in one arm and dragging little Paddy with the other as she ran after her always wandering four-year-old, Jimmy Joe, whose adventurous spirit led him out of the tenement house and into the street on warm July days such as this.

"Come back here, you little devil," Mrs. Malone shouted, "or you'll end up flattened out like a pancake by one of King Billy's henchmen!"

Padraic flung open the door that led to the hall and captured little Jimmy Joe Malone as he ran pell-mell down the long corridor. Mrs. Malone, just as Padraic had imagined her, was advancing from the far end of the hall.

Jimmy Malone wiggled and let out a disgruntled cry.

"And where might you be going?" Padraic asked good-naturedly.

"Running amok, as usual!" Maureen Malone replied breathlessly. "I'll skin you alive, child! This is a day you'll stay inside, otherwise you'll end up being hurt, beaten up by King Billy's henchmen!"

Maureen Malone waved her long finger in Jimmy Joe's face, and his big blue eyes filled with huge tears.

"Hard to keep them penned up on a summer's day," Mrs. Malone observed saucily. She let go of little Paddy's hand and wiped her hand on her skirt. She shook her head and looked at the squirming child in Padraic's arms. "You can't tell," she went on. "You can't tell when there might be trouble in the streets. I've seen it come sudden." She shuddered slightly. "I remember one Orange Day when the children were out playing . . . some rowdy proddy boys come whipping around the corner wielding bricks and bats, and two little ones were . . . were . . ." Her voice choked. "Hurt," she concluded. Padraic knew that "hurt" was an understatement of a bad memory.

Padraic shook his head knowingly. "I'll carry him to your flat for you," he volunteered. "Your arms are full."

"Trouble," Maureen Malone repeated. "We have children of the troubles . . . growing up with hate and fear, nothing but troubles."

Maureen Malone shifted her grip on the baby, whose diapers were soaked with urine. She took little Paddy's hand, and Padraic followed in her wake, carrying little Jimmy Joe, whose full name was James Joseph Malone. "James Joseph" for two saints, but little blue-eyed Jimmy Joe was no saint. He was a blooming little terror and one of his mother's six worries. She worried how to feed and clothe all of them, how to keep them from taking to the streets like the other urchins, how to raise them loving and good in a world that seemed to offer neither love nor goodness in any quantity.

And how old was Maureen Malone, whose plump figure was disguised in a wretched housedress that had seen better days before she acquired it? She was a young woman, only twenty-six. But her face was etched with the mark of the troubles—worry lines on her forehead, small creases about the mouth, circles under blue eyes. She might have been forty. And Maureen Malone's husband, Kevin, was forty-five and might have been sixty. He too worked in the linen mills, and though he earned enough to feed three, they were eight.

Padraic looked at the damp curls that clung to Maureen Malone's forehead, and because of the weariness in her face, he felt a surge of hatred for the circumstances that kept a hardworking man like Kevin Malone from earning enough to feed and clothe his family adequately. The Protestants of Ulster prevented Catholics from getting good jobs, though Padraic knew full well that there were poor proddies too. In all, he blamed the English, who stole the land, ran the factories, and had, albeit long ago, planted the Protestant settlers in Ireland and divided a once-proud, strong land.

Maureen Malone walked through the open door of her apartment and deposited her youngest child in a cradle on the far side of the main room. She pushed little Paddy into a chair and returned to rescue Jimmy Joe from Padraic's arms.

"I'll be thanking you for your kind assistance," she said briskly. Maureen Malone was a proper woman. Her husband wasn't at home; she would not invite a single man in for a spot of tea.

Padraic turned with a wave of his hand and walked down the hallway. At the far end, he saw a priest.

"May I help you, Father?" Padraic called out cheerfully.

"Only if you know where one Padraic O'Hearn lives," the priest answered.

"You're looking at him, Father. What brings you out on a day such as this?"

"Are you Padraic O'Hearn?" the priest asked in order to confirm Padraic's first answer.

"I am."

The priest let out a sigh and wiped his brow. "Then I can hope my search is over. May we talk?"

Padraic ushered the priest into his rooms and Thomas Hughes, slightly blurry-eyed from the warm porter, scrambled to his feet, stuttering, "An unexpected guest." He quickly wiped the table with his hand and moved the pitcher of porter to the sideboard. "Only a little drink on a hot day, Father."

Father Doyle seemed scarcely interested. In any case, he had seen it all before—too many times, as a matter of fact. And what were men to do, anyway?

"Please sit down, Father," Padraic invited. A visit from a priest was rare indeed. And this was not one of the priests from the church Padraic attended. This priest was a total stranger.

"Allow me to introduce myself. I'm Father Doyle, from Saint Joseph's Hospital."

Padraic frowned and his heart pounded. Terry McKenna and Wee Willie O'Brien were not home. Had they gotten into some trouble? Had they been attacked? Hurt?

Thomas Hughes tensed as well, and though Padraic did not look at him, he felt his tension. Terry and Willie could be rabble-rousers, and unlike Thomas and Padraic, they did not avoid the taverns on Orange Day.

"Have you come about Terry McKenna or Willie O'Brien?" Padraic asked.

Father Doyle shook his head. "No, I've come to speak to Padraic O'Hearn on a personal matter, and not a soul is hurt."

Both men relaxed. Father Doyle's eyes settled on the sideboard. "You wouldn't have a bit of porter left, would you?"

"Why, of course, Father." Padraic went to the sideboard and began to clean off a dirty glass with the edge of his shirt. Satisfied that he would not be insulting the good father, he poured some porter into the glass and handed it to Father Doyle.

"What can I do for you, Father?" Padraic asked as he sat down.

"A lot, if you are the right Padraic O'Hearn. Nothing, if you aren't, I fear. I've been looking for over a year, and I've searched out more Paddy O'Hearns in Belfast than I ever dreamed existed." He didn't mention that he had given up one or two times, nor the fact that he hadn't devoted himself full time to his quest. Nonetheless, he had promised Emerald he would look, and look he had.

"And how will you know if I'm the right one?" Padraic asked.

"We could begin with a few questions about your family," Father Doyle suggested.

Padraic poured himself another glass of the porter. "What I remember," he said hesitantly. "I was sent to work in the peat bogs when I was quite young. My family was lost to me."

"Tell me what you can," Father Doyle urged.

"My father died in 1899, fighting in South Africa. A year later, I was told, my mother died." Padraic lowered his head and crossed himself. "My brother, Seamus, is in Dublin town, and I have a sister, Emerald. That's her picture as a baby, at her christening." Padraic paused. "But she disappeared after my mother's death. . . . You see, we weren't there. Our friend Mike Flannery, bless his soul, found out about our mother, and he tried to find our sister, but no one knew . . . We came back years later."

Father Doyle's eyes flickered with warmth. "It's Emerald I've come about," he admitted. "But I had to make certain you were the right Padraic O'Hearn."

Padraic's eyes brightened and misted over. "Sweet Jesus, Emerald! You know where Emerald is?" He felt like leaping right across the table. He turned to Thomas Hughes. "He's found Emerald! Sweet Jesus! She's alive!"

"She found me," Father Doyle retorted cheerfully. "Nearly a year ago, it was. She's been living with the sisters. She'd been given over to a Protestant family who abused her badly, but she remembered her mother and her faith. God be praised, she ran away when she was a slip of a girl, fifteen, and she ran straight to the nearest Catholic church."

"A Proddie family? Abused?" Padraic's face paled. Thoughts of his baby sister being abused filled him with guilt. "We should have searched harder. Seamus and I should have turned Belfast upside down looking for her!" He lifted his hand to his forehead.

"You were mere boys then," Father Doyle pointed out. "Boys without resources to care for her even if you had found her. Don't be blaming yourselves now."

"Is she all right?" Padraic asked with hesitation.

"Oh, she's fine. A fine, beautiful, healthy young woman, as

bright and as smart as can be. She has worked hard all her young
life, and although she missed her rightful childhood, she isn't
hurt in any way save some blank spaces, so to speak. But the
sisters have helped, and she's blossomed like a flower. But I
don't think she wants to stay in the convent. Her strongest desire
has always been to find you and her brother Seamus.''

Padraic let out his breath and thought about his limited resources.
A fine family young Emerald had found. One dirt-poor brother
with little or nothing to offer.

"I have little, as you can see," Padraic admitted, as if it were
necessary to vocalize his poverty. "Seamus lives in Dublin," he
reiterated.

"You have what Emerald needs," Father Doyle said with
conviction. "You're her family, the key to her past, you are
blood relatives."

"But of course I want her!" Padraic said quickly. He looked
around. "But we're four men," he said, shaking his head. "In
poor digs. But I do have a little set aside. Perhaps I could board
her with married friends in exchange for a bit of money, and
maybe she could help with the children."

"It doesn't have to be right away," Father Doyle replied. "Of
course a young woman cannot live with four men. Come to the
convent and visit her. Then we'll see what arrangements can be
made."

Padraic shook his head. His mind focused on Mrs. Malone.
She could certainly use some help, and perhaps for a small sum
she could take Emerald in. If not Mrs. Malone, then perhaps one
of the other neighbors.

"I'll come right away," Padraic promised. "It's been too
many years already."

2

August 5, 1911

Emerald sat on the edge of the chair and leaned on the table as
she looked into Padraic's eyes. The reception room in the convent was too solemn a setting for the emotions that were pent up
in both of them. It was Padraic's third visit in two weeks, but
this was a special visit indeed.

"Go on, open it." Padraic pushed the small package across
the table and winked.

Emerald smiled and her green eyes danced with anticipation.
"You know, this is the first birthday I've ever had in my whole

life! I didn't know when my birthday was before . . . I wasn't even sure how old I was."

"It's August 5, 1911, and you, my darling sister, are sixteen years old today."

Emerald fumbled with the string of the package and unfolded a tissue-wrapped tintype photograph. She studied the picture and her eyes filled with tears as the woman's face became an animated reality in her long-held memory. "Mother," she whispered, tears running down her cheek. "And father."

"On their wedding day," Padraic said. "It's a poor man's gift, but I want you to have it."

"Oh, Padraic, you couldn't have given me anything better . . ." Emerald's voice trailed off; it was clear to Padraic that she was too filled with emotion to speak.

"One day, my girl, and I'll be giving you away in marriage . . ." his face was red, and he looked down.

Emerald smiled and reached across the table and squeezed Padraic's hand softly.

"It should have been more, something to make up for all the birthdays I wasn't there. . . ."

"I can't stay here forever," Emerald announced after a moment's silence. "Especially now that I know you and Seamus are alive and that I have a family."

"There's not much money," Padraic admitted.

"Surely I can work, Padraic . . . I've been working all my life."

Padraic looked at the table, sensing the earnestness in her voice and knowing that she was correct. But it wasn't what he wanted for Emerald. He wanted a better life for her, a life removed from his own. Unhappily, a better life was not his to give.

"Mrs. Malone is willing to have you come and stay with her. You can help with the children—God knows she needs help— and you'll be able to sleep in the room with them. I have a little money, Emerald, enough to provide for your room and board until something better comes up."

Emerald's smile lit up her whole face and her eyes danced merrily. "Helping with the children . . . Oh, Padraic, it's wonderful! It's not only the first birthday I ever had, but I'm sure it will be the best!"

Emerald pulled her chair away from the table and stood up and stretched. Padraic smiled to himself. His sister was a rare beauty, but she was totally unconscious of her appearance and seemingly ignorant of how truly lovely she was.

"What's the matter? You look so worried," Emerald teased.

"Just thinking I'd have to keep my eye on you, or first thing I know, you'll be up and getting married."

Emerald laughed, and it seemed to Padraic as if she filled the room with music. "Oh, I'll not be marrying so young," she told him. "I want to study with the sisters and become a nurse. I want to work in the hospital."

Padraic smiled broadly. "That's good, but what prevents you from starting now?"

"Myself." Emerald smiled back. "Father Doyle and Sister Celeste say I have the ability and that I can begin training anytime. But, Padraic . . . oh, Padraic, I've seen so little of the world! I want to live among people for a while, learn to talk properly and to feel at ease. Padraic, all my learning is from books." Emerald sighed, and having moved around the table, touched his shoulder lightly. "I know it's hard to understand."

Padraic reached up to his shoulder and patted her hand. "I've been illiterate all my life. It is hard indeed to imagine someone's learning coming from books, when all mine has come from living."

It's not surprising she's chosen to wait a bit, Padraic thought. She could certainly read, and the sisters at the convent had taught her the meanings of all the words she could sound out. She knew many things that Padraic did not know, but in other ways Emerald was naive and childlike. Her clear lovely eyes still held the wonder of discovery, and her delight in the world could only have come to one so long deprived.

"If you're unhappy with the Malones and with our life—and it's not the best of all lives—you can come back and take up your nursing."

"Yes," Emerald answered. "But I hope not right away. In a year, perhaps." Her eyes were luminous. "Oh, Padraic, how much can I learn in a year's time? How different will I be?"

Padraic stood up and hugged her. "I hope you will never lose your enchantment with life," he told her. Then he whispered, "Happy birthday, Emerald. Happy sixteenth year."

3

May 1912

"He's fast asleep, you know." Maureen Malone wiped her hands on her white apron.

On the worn settee in the Malones' living room, little Jimmy Joe Malone sat curled in Emerald's lap. The little horror was a beast no more, Emerald thought. His bright little blue eyes were closed fast, and he was nestled up against Emerald, fast asleep.

Emerald eased his small tousled head off her shoulder. "I'll take him to bed," she whispered, picking him up with some effort and carrying him into the children's room, where she also slept. There were seven beds—three on one side of the room and four on the other—all stacked up, one atop the other. On each of the other beds, save Emerald's, one of the six Malone children was sprawled out peacefully, covers askew and small toes visible. Carefully Emerald set little Jimmy Joe in his bed; then she pulled his blanket over him. She kissed the tips of her fingers and lightly touched his cheek. His huge eyes opened and his dark lashes fluttered for an instant. He made a muffled good-night sound, and again his eyes closed.

"Good night, my darling," Emerald whispered. She covered all the rest of the Malone brood and again whispered, "Good night, my darlings."

Emerald closed the door behind her and went to rejoin Maureen Malone.

"You can't imagine what a difference you've made." Maureen was full of praise. "That child's not the same since you came. He'll do anything for you. You've cast a spell over him, you have. It's a miracle."

"He's adorable," Emerald said, sitting down and taking up her sewing.

"An adorable hellion." Maureen beamed. "I used to think he spent his nights dreaming of ways to plague me."

Emerald laughed. It was quite true that Jimmy Joe delighted in running away, that he drew on walls, and that he chased Mrs. Finney's cat. But he was only a typical little boy, active, curious, and fun-loving.

"I'm teaching him to read," Emerald confessed. "He's such a bright youngster."

Again Maureen murmured her thanks. "Learning is the way out of here," she observed. "Those that have learning don't stay, they don't have to." Maureen looked up, and her blue eyes met Emerald's clear green ones. "Sometimes I think I would sell my soul to the devil if just one of my children could make something of themself, could get out of Belfast and out of Ireland. In America an Irishman can accomplish something, in America an Irishman isn't dirt under the feet of everyone who comes along."

"I'll do my best to see to it that he reads, and reads well," Emerald promised. "In fact, I'll see to it they all do."

Maureen nodded and did not say that she believed it a waste to teach girls. After all, where had learning gotten Emerald? A woman who read was, after all, still a woman, and women's work was to serve their men and to bear children. In her heart, Maureen had a fear that a literate girl would be discontented with her lot. And silently, Maureen vowed to speak to Emerald later about teaching the girls to read too—or, more precisely, not teaching them to read.

At ten o'clock Emerald folded up her sewing and said good night to Maureen. She went to her bed in the crowded little room and undressed silently, putting on her long nightie. She crawled into bed and pulled the covers up, listening to the sound of the children breathing around her, making their strange night noises. In truth, she loved it, feeling like a puppy in its lair, surrounded by warm sleeping bodies. No more the lonely darkness of the pitch-black attic, no longer the solemn quiet of her room in the nunnery. Emerald drifted off to sleep with a faint smile on her face, feeling as if she finally belonged to someone, that she finally knew the meaning of human affection and family love.

"Mama!" The weak cry brought her to sudden consciousness, and Emerald sat up quickly, so quickly that she bumped her head on the bed above, forgetting that it was there.

"Mama!" Emerald shook her head and rolled from the bed, reaching up to Jimmy Joe, who had tossed off his blankets and moved restlessly.

Emerald reached up and touched him. His forehead was hot and his little body shivered.

The door opened. "What is it?" Maureen peered into the room.

"He's burning up with fever," Emerald answered.

Maureen let out a little groan. "He seemed all right earlier."

"Fevers come up quickly in little ones," Emerald replied. She had been reading some nursing books, preparing herself for the examinations she hoped to take soon so that she could enter St. Joseph's for nurse's training in a year's time. "Best we should bathe him with cool cloths, and if his fever doesn't go down, we'd best take him to the hospital."

Maureen scurried to the kitchen for cloths while Emerald remained by the bed. "Is your throat sore?" she prodded.

Jimmy Joe shook his head.

"Do you hurt anywhere?"

"I'm sick all over," he complained. Then, with little warning, his hand flew to his mouth and he vomited. Emerald stepped back. "I'm sorry," he sobbed incoherently. "Mama will be angry, I got the bed all dirty."

Emerald picked him up. "I'll clean it up," she promised, hugging him. "But you'd better sleep in the other room tonight." Holding him to her, Emerald carried him into the front room, where she and Maureen made a bed for him and covered him with cool cloths.

"Oh, dear," Maureen exclaimed as she and Emerald gently rolled the youngster over. "Look at that!"

Emerald looked at the bright red bump, which might have been a large pimple but didn't look quite like one.

"It's the first pox!" Maureen said, half-relieved, half-annoyed at the thought. "I've not had six children not to know it when I see it."

Emerald looked at the swelling. "Chicken pox?"

"Yes, and a messy illness it is. But it's better they get it. First you get the one pox, then the fever. In a few hours he'll have a rash all over, then it'll itch and itch, and finally the scabs will fall off and he'll be better. Some say that if you get the chicken pox you can't get smallpox."

"That's not true," Emerald said. "I've read that many who get chicken pox also get smallpox. Only a vaccination of cowpox prevents smallpox."

Maureen nodded and was afraid she looked annoyed. She liked Emerald, but she found having a literate person about disconcerting at times. Emerald didn't mean to do it, but she constantly referred to reading this or that, not realizing that with every book and every bit of new knowledge, she was building a wall that would separate her from other Irishwomen. Again Maureen vowed to speak to Emerald, but again she put it off.

"You've had it, of course?" Maureen asked.

Emerald looked at her curiously. "No," she answered, "I've not had it."

"Oh, my." Maureen's hand flew to her mouth as she vaguely remembered Emerald's background. Of course, as an isolated child, Emerald had had none of the childhood diseases that invaded Maureen Malone's household.

"Can I get it?" Emerald asked.

Maureen laughed—it was a somewhat triumphant laugh. For all her book learning, she didn't know about measles, chicken pox, or whooping cough. "Of course you can," Maureen replied. "And it's much worse in an adult."

"Oh," Emerald answered. She looked down at little Jimmy Joe; he had fallen asleep on the bedroll they had made for him after bathing him in cool cloths. His fever was a bit lower. Emerald, who had been sitting on her knees, sat back, extending her legs sideways. "I didn't know adults could get it."

"There's a lot you can't learn in books," Maureen said, unable to keep her real meaning out of the tone of her voice.

"You've had so many experiences I haven't," Emerald said softly. "I try to make up for my lack of living by reading."

Maureen sucked her lower lip and looked at Emerald. Suddenly she felt sheepish, admitting to herself for the first time that she was jealous of Emerald, who could read, and in some ways jealous of Emerald herself, of her calm, of her ability to deal with the children, of her good humor, even of her stunning good looks.

"I can't read a word," Maureen admitted. "Not even the directions on the medicine bottles." She moved her eyes away and looked at the floor. "It seems there's no use for women to read. When a woman reads, she puts herself in a man's world, and I fear . . . I fear dissatisfaction for my daughters, maybe even for myself."

Emerald reached out and touched Maureen. "And should you be satisfied? Should any of us be satisfied?"

"I'm afraid to know how others live," Maureen blurted out tearfully, surprised by her own words.

"To want is not a sin," Emerald said. "To want for children isn't wrong—it's not wrong to want for yourself. Learning might help you understand what ought to be yours, but it doesn't mean you have to be discontented."

"I love you, like you were a sister," Maureen said. "But there's a wall between us now. It's a wall created by your learning and my ignorance, by your ambition and my fear."

"Is it wrong for me to want to be a nurse?"

Maureen shook her head. "It's an honorable profession for a woman. But not all nurses can read. Reading is something special, it's something that makes you different."

"I'm as much an Irishwoman as you," Emerald answered.

But Maureen shook her head. "No," she answered softly. "You're on your way out of this oppression. I know it in my heart and I'm glad for you, Emerald O'Hearn, but know that you're different. You don't have to depend on stories and hand-me-down tales, you don't have to depend on hearing what men tell you and trying to understand what they think. You don't even have to marry and have so many children . . . though I love my children.''

"But I think I want children, I want to marry," Emerald protested.

"You want to," Maureen insisted, "but you don't have to."

6

1

July 1912

Padraic studied the poster with some disgust. It featured Sir Edward Carson flanked by Colonel Wallace and Captain Craig, who was a Member of Parliament. Beneath their stony countenances were the words "WE WON'T HAVE HOME RULE!" Above the picture was the British crown, and from it fell a banner. On the bottom was a picture of King Willy on his horse, sword pointed outward. And the motto? "OUR CIVIL AND RELIGIOUS LIBERTIES WE WILL MAINTAIN." *Our*, thought Padraic. "Our" was the key word, the underlined word. Not one of the proddie leaders, and doubtless few of the proddies in general, were concerned with the civil liberties and rights of the Catholics. No, the Protestants built a wall around Ulster and held it as if at siege. "NO HOME RULE!" the poster proclaimed. And an arm holding an eagle stretched across a British flag. Yes, that was how Carson and his cohorts intended to prevent home rule; they intended to prevent it with a gun.

Padraic made his way along the street. He looked down and walked rapidly. He was anxious to get back home, anxious to get off the streets, which he sensed might turn into a river of blood. Protestant Ulstermen outnumbered Catholics, they were up in arms over the proposed Home Rule Bill, and they would try to create a situation that would threaten Britain with civil war. It was a tried-and-true tactic. Demonstrations, violence, retaliation, clamp-down. Then long political negotiations, and the cycle would begin again. It was a circle, a never-ending trip on a merry-go-round.

Padraic passed a huge old woman, clearly on her way to the parade. She was draped in the red, white, and blue of the Union Jack—out of which she had fashioned a dress that clung unpleasantly to her bulges. She even wore a knit red-white-and-blue cap in spite of the warm July sun.

And there was music in the distance. The pipes sounded and the drums rolled as line after line of men in bowler hats strutted down the streets of Belfast, proclaiming their right to rule and their right to civil liberties, though they marched on Ireland's soil and they spoke a foreign language.

Padraic hurried across Falls Road and down a side street. He moved near the buildings, and finally he rounded a corner and felt safer in the realization that he was at least in the right neighborhood. In another ten minutes he reached home.

Padraic closed the door of the flat behind him and sat down at the table. He was about to get up and pour himself a drink when there was a knock on the door.

When Padraic opened it, he was confronted with an anxious Maureen Malone.

"It's the baby," she announced. "She's had a fever all night and she's wheezing badly. Emerald's with the other children, but she thought I ought to take the baby to the hospital, and I think she's right."

Maureen looked at him pleadingly. "Kevin is working an extra shift at the tavern to make some extra money—there's no one here I can ask except you. I can't go out alone today with the baby, it's too dangerous . . . could you walk with us to the hospital?"

Padraic nodded. He didn't want to go out again, but the hospital wasn't that far, and there were no Protestant neighborhoods to pass through. One mixed neighborhood, to be sure, but it was all right if one walked right along and didn't pause.

"Of course," Padraic answered. "Of course I'll go."

They walked briskly to the hospital, taking the side streets. Maureen Malone chattered incoherently and didn't stop talking or break her pace even when the sound of gunfire shattered the morning air.

"Firecrackers," Padraic mumbled, wanting to make Maureen less frightened. But she was not afraid. She seemed to be in some sort of a trance, distracted by the baby's illness too much to allow thoughts of the parading proddies to deter her.

"To hell with them." She grimaced as she plodded on across a trash-strewn street, holding the baby close. "Have to think twice just to go to the hospital! It's not right, it's just not right!"

2

"Emerald!" Little Paddy's voice summoned Emerald from the children's room, where she had been picking up and making beds.

She hurried into the center room and immediately saw that the front door was open. "Jimmy?" Emerald bit her lip. Jimmy Joe had wanted to go with his mother and Padraic to the hospital; now the door was open and it seemed clear that little Jimmy Joe had decided to follow on his own.

Emerald stepped into the corridor and saw Annie Murphy opening the door to her flat at the opposite end of the corridor. She ran to her. "Annie, little Jimmy's gone off and Maureen's at the hospital. Can you . . . ?"

"I'll watch them," she answered. "No explanations, off with you. That little horror travels, he does."

Emerald ran down the stairs and out into the warm July sun. She paused momentarily—which way would he have gone? He certainly didn't know in which direction the hospital was.

Then, in the distance, Emerald heard the sound of the pipes and drums. "Music—oh, dear God!" Instinctively she whirled about and followed the sound of the music, certain that little Jimmy Joe had done the same.

Breathless, Emerald paused when she saw a sweep going about his business. "Have you seen a little boy pass this way—dark hair and blue eyes, wearing a little green shirt?"

The sweep looked up at her and then spit on the sidewalk through his yellowed teeth. "That way." He motioned with his broom and watched, shaking his head, as Emerald ran down the street.

"Jimmy Joe!" she called out. Her heart pounded as she rounded the next corner. There, half a block up the street, five older boys stood menacingly above little Jimmy Joe Malone. One, Emerald saw, carried a bat, another had a chain of some sort, and all were dressed in the orange colors that clearly identified them, while Jimmy Joe, wearing his green shirt and his St. Christopher's medal around his little neck, was just as clearly identifiable.

"Jimmy Joe!" Emerald called out, hoping that the youngster would break away and run toward her. And he did turn around.

Run, Emerald thought. No one is holding you, run to me! But she dared not call out . . . she dared not make the rowdies angry when Jimmy Joe was so close to them.

Jimmy Joe took one step toward her, and Emerald saw that he was yanked rudely back into the middle of the circle the boys had now formed. Emerald walked toward them, fighting to look calm.

"Throwing stones ain't nice," one of the boys said. He towered over Jimmy Joe, who looked up, undaunted.

"Little croppie bugger!" another sneered.

"Hey, you was reciting a rhyme, weren't you. Now, say it again—come on." The boy reached out and shook Jimmy Joe roughly by the collar of his shirt. "Sing it again!" The boy delivered a swift kick, and Jimmy Joe doubled, screaming in pain.

"Leave him alone! He's only six years old!" Emerald ran toward them, but stopped when one poised his bat above Jimmy Joe's head.

"I do believe it's the croppie's bitch mother! Well, you're just in time to hear him sing a little ditty for us. Sang it before, he did. And threw some stones, too. Sing it again!" The boy lifted his leg but did not kick.

Jimmy Joe looked at them. Tears were running down his face and he was shaking.

" 'Up the long ladder . . .' " he began. His voice was low and frightened. " 'Down the short rope, to hell with King Willy, and God Save the Pope. If that won't do, then slice him in two, and send him to hell in his red, white, and blue.' "

The last few words were barely audible. The older boy kicked, and Jimmy Joe fell to the ground.

"Stop it! It's a silly rhyme, he's a baby!" She threw herself into the fray and felt the pain as one of the boys hit her in the face with his fist. Another hit Jimmy Joe with his bat, and the youngster fell—this time facedown in silence.

Emerald screamed and fell on top of the child in order to protect him from another vicious blow. Blood trickled from her nose, and one of the boys viciously kicked her in the stomach. Emerald was fighting pain and blackness and somewhere in the distance she heard the sound of trampling feet and running—she heard sounds of swearing and shouts. Then she felt a strong arm around her waist, lifting her up.

Her head and stomach ached with pain; more blood ran from a small cut near her mouth, and scratches on her arms bled freely.

"Jimmy . . ." Emerald whispered. "Help him, dear God, help him." Emerald blinked. She couldn't quite focus her eyes, but she clearly saw that it was Thomas Hughes who had lifted her into his arms. In her fear and pain, she clung to him. Then she passed out.

"It's my fault," Emerald said, turning her face to the wall. "It's my fault for not finding him sooner, my fault for letting him run away."

Thomas Hughes sat on a chair near her hospital bed. "It's not your fault . . . and, my girl, they'd have gladly killed you too."

She shook her head. A week had passed and the doctors said she could go home—but what home? Could she face Maureen Malone?

"Even Maureen doesn't blame you," Thomas said, as if he were reading her mind. "She wants you to come back, she wants to share her grief with you. . . . Emerald, it is not your fault. It's the fault of Ulster. This place is a boiling witch's brew—a caldron of steaming hate."

Emerald turned to him and frowned. "My mother used to tell me a story like that. . . ." She looked into his eyes. He had soft kind eyes and his hair was thick and dark, tinged ever so slightly with gray. He was extraordinarily handsome—Emerald had always thought so—but now she realized how sensitive he was as well.

"When children grow up hating one another, it can't end. They adopt their parents' prejudices, they know all the mean nasty little songs and ditties, and though it begins with a pinprick, it turns into a river of Irish blood."

"He was singing a ditty and he'd thrown rocks, but . . ."

"Of course that's no excuse to have . . . have . . ." Thomas Hughes couldn't say the word "killed" either; it was all too close, too terrible.

Emerald leaned back against her pillow. "I used to regret missing my childhood, but now I wonder what I missed."

"You didn't hate the McArthurs?"

"No," Emerald answered truthfully. "I didn't like them, but that's not the same as hate. And I loved Mrs. Higgins . . . there are good Protestants, Tom, I know there are."

He nodded. "There are some who haven't grown up with hate." He stood up. "My shift at the shipyards starts soon. I have to go, but Padraic said he'd be coming by this evening."

Emerald looked at him as he towered above her. She'd known him for over a year, yet this was the first time she'd ever noticed him—really noticed him.

He cleared his throat. "You'll be coming home soon?"

"Perhaps tomorrow," Emerald replied.

He looked around, shifting his weight from one foot to the other; he looked a little embarrassed. "Your birthday's in August, isn't it?"

"Yes, I'll be seventeen," she answered.

"I'm much older than you."

It was an unfinished sentence, Emerald thought. As if he wanted to say more but didn't know how.

"I enjoy talking to you," she replied. "I really do."

He smiled almost shyly. "I'd like to ask your brother for permission to take you out now and again . . . if you would agree."

"Of course I'll agree." She smiled up at him in spite of herself.

Thomas Hughes thrust his hands in his pockets and hurried out of the hospital. Little Jimmy Joe's death had cast a pall over the entire tenement block, and though the pall and the mourning continued, he himself suddenly felt younger, happier, and more full of hope than he had ever felt before. Emerald O'Hearn was beautiful, kind, loving, and intelligent. Young though she was, she seemed older, more mature, and was certainly the most interesting woman he had ever met. He had money in the bank, for unlike his three roommates, he had a fine job and had managed to save. "I can afford a wife," he said out loud. Then, aware that he felt like flying, he began to whistle an old Irish tune.

"Are you certain you feel strong enough to come home?" Padraic looked at Emerald in concern.

"Quite sure," she said as they stood in the hospital foyer. "The doctors say I'm fine, and I've had long talks with Father Doyle . . . he talked to Maureen too."

Padraic picked up her bundle of books. She had requested them while she was in the hospital, and Thomas Hughes had been kind enough to bring them over.

"It was nice of Thomas to come and visit with me," Emerald said as they walked along out of the hospital.

"I'll get us a cab," Padraic suggested.

"You'll do no such thing, Padraic O'Hearn. It costs too much. I'm absolutely fine, it's warm, it's a short walk, and I need the exercise."

"You're just leaving hospital," Padraic protested.

"I ought to have left three days ago," Emerald reiterated. "Please, Padraic, walking will make me feel better. . . . He's a very nice man," she said after a moment.

"Who?"

"Why, Tom Hughes of course. He came to visit me, he's a nice man. Very good-looking."

Padraic turned to her and shrugged. "I never noticed."

"Tell me about him."

"Well, he's got no family now. His mother died a while back and he works in the shipyards, and I think he can read a little.

He's got a better job than the rest of us. He's a quiet sort. I like him.''

"So do I." Emerald smirked.

Padraic turned to her, suddenly looking quite solemn. "What does that mean?"

"He's going to ask your permission to take me out."

"To court you? You're much too young! He's too old!''

"And the sun is too warm." Emerald laughed. "I want him to take me out—if that's courting.'' She stopped walking and looked at Padraic. "I've already made up my mind."

"To do what?"

"To let him take me out."

"And I don't have a thing to say."

"Say yes."

Padraic studied her expression. She was every inch an O'Hearn, stubborn to the core. "Yes," Padraic agreed. "But he better mind his manners if he's going to be seeing my sister."

"I'm sure he will," Emerald answered, though if she imagined Thomas Hughes kissing her, it sent a chill down her spine and she honestly hoped he wouldn't mind his manners too well.

3

September 1912

Thomas Hughes sat on the sand. His pants legs were rolled up, as were his shirt sleeves, and he had taken off his shoes and socks. A great Irish knit sweater lay beside him and next to it was the empty picnic basket.

A few feet away, Emerald too sat on the sand. Her hair hung loose and fell in ringlets because of the humidity from the sea. Her facial expression was one of intensity, as she packed the sand into place, enchanted with her creation. She revealed a childlike joy in her activity.

"That's a wonderful sand castle," he said in admiration.

Emerald looked up. "A sand castle? Is that what it's called?"

Thomas Hughes smiled; he often forgot her past. "Yes, a sand castle. The children build them in the sand."

"It's great fun to play in the sand," Emerald said, looking up. "I love the way it feels when it oozes between your toes, and as for my masterpiece, I think when the tide comes in it will be washed away."

"It's the fate of most sand castles," Tom Hughes replied.

"But they live on for a long while in the imagination, and as long as your memory keeps them, they're not really gone."

Emerald smiled at him and crawled over to him. He put his arm around her, and she nestled against his shoulder. "I love the sea, and the Irish Sea is something special."

"I love going places with you," he answered. "The sun always shines—are you an intimate of the little people? You know, it's September and the weather is not usually seashore weather in September. I think you've had one of your magical intimates conjure up a good day. I can't believe the sun's so warm on my back."

"I don't know any little people who live at the seashore," Emerald answered. "All the ones I know are the elves and fairies of the woods."

He touched her arm and then brushed her hair with his lips, afraid to do more. "I love you, Emerald O'Hearn."

She cuddled closer. "I think I love you too," she answered.

"I'm twice your age—sometimes I watch you, you have the wonder of a child. You make me feel even older."

Emerald looked at him reproachfully. "You're a young man of thirty-five, and I'm certain you'll live to be at least a hundred."

He patted her hair. "It will still be a long courtship. I want you to be sure, I want you to be absolutely certain."

Emerald nodded. "And you don't mind that I'm going into nursing? You don't mind if I have a vocation?"

He smiled at her tenderly. "I can't imagine minding anything you do. But it's right—you'll be out of training in two years' time and then, God willing and if you still want to, we'll be married."

Emerald covered his hand with hers. "I'll still want to," she vowed.

4

August 1913

"I feel a bit silly," Emerald announced. She was wearing her bright white uniform with the big red cross on the top of its stiffly starched apron.

"You don't look a bit silly, but you will have to move just a little to the left," Thomas Hughes suggested. He had posed her under a great spreading blackthorn tree and now turned to the nervous photographer, whose awkward Graflex camera was perched on the tripod. "Now," he instructed.

The man mumbled, and with a flourish, clicked the button. "Eight shillings," he said, holding out his hand. "And you can pick the pictures up next week at my studio."

Tom Hughes paid the man and went back to where Emerald was standing.

"Eight shillings! Tom, that's a lot!"

"Not for your picture, not in your uniform—it's your birthday anyway." He leaned down and kissed the tip of her nose. "Happy birthday, my darling."

Emerald looked into his eyes—he was so kind; she was overwhelmed with his kindness and his caring. He treated her like a china doll; he was protective and at the same time passionate when he kissed her, and his kisses always made her yearn for him.

Sometimes they walked for hours in Alexandria Park and sometimes they sat under the trees and read poetry to one another. Thomas, Emerald discovered, did read, and under her tutelege, he improved and learned to write as well. Often he read poetry to her, and his voice was so deep, so filled with emotion, so strong that the words came alive for her and she was able to build word pictures in her head as she listened to his strong Irish brogue.

Her thoughts returned to the present and she shook her head. "Birthday or no, it's a lot to spend. Eight shillings!"

He laughed at her. "Thrifty, are you? I'll be thinking you've been brought up Scots instead of Irish." He imitated a Scots accent, and Emerald giggled. "You sound like one of Mr. McArthur's friends!"

He slipped his arm around her waist. "But I'm not. Emerald, have you thought about America?"

She nodded. It was a subject they often discussed. But each time, he brought it up anew, and Emerald knew he was testing her. "I've thought about it a lot. I've wondered what a land so vast is like. I've wondered how it is where everyone is equal."

"And would you consider leaving Ireland one day?"

Emerald let out her breath. "If that's what you want," she simply replied.

"I wouldn't want to go unless you really wanted to. I want you to be happy—that's my only concern." Emerald felt his arm around her and thought how very lucky she was. Many men would assume that such a decision was theirs and theirs alone, but not Tom Hughes.

She paused by the small pond in the park. A stately swan glided on the placid waters. "I'll go where you want me to, I'll be happy as long as I'm with you." She looked up into his face and he bent down, his own eyes misty, and kissed her.

Emerald responded to his lips on hers and moved in his arms as he gently rubbed her back while holding her close. His very nearness filled her with that vague feeling of longing she had so much difficulty describing. She pressed herself to him, feeling the imprint of his jacket buttons, he held her so close. And she felt his breath quicken and become deeper. Reluctantly he let his arms drop and he stepped back. "God, I love you," he said quietly.

"Why don't we get married?" Emerald asked. "I'm eighteen —oh, Tom, I know my own mind."

He shook his head. "Not yet—next year. Next August."

She smiled faintly. "Is that a promise?"

"It is."

5

August 1914

When Seamus hugged Emerald, it was a great bear hug. "That was breathtaking," she laughed.

Seamus O'Hearn was shorter and heavier than Padraic. From the very first day they were reunited, Seamus always reminded Emerald of an elf. Padraic had dark brooding eyes; Seamus had laughing merry eyes. Padraic looked the dreamer, but Seamus looked as if he ought to be dancing a jig, waving his shillelagh in the air.

Seamus came up to Belfast two weeks after Padraic and Emerald were reunited. They had spent a wonderful weekend together. Emerald thought that she would never forget the sense of sadness she had the first time she had met Seamus. It was caused by the single realization that she might have passed him on the street a thousand times and not known he was her brother. "This is your brother," Padraic had to say when Seamus emerged out of the crowd at the train station. But that was no more. Three years had passed since the O'Hearns had been reunited, and though he came no more than every few months, Seamus' face was known to her.

Seamus' eyes devoured Emerald with fondness. "Married," he said, hugging her again. "I can't believe you're getting married. Do you think Tom Hughes is good enough for her, Padraic?"

Emerald stepped between them and linked arms with both of

them. "Good enough in your eyes, or in mine? I'll have no talk like this—I've chosen Tom Hughes, and it's Tom Hughes I'll marry."

"You had better, my girl. I've already rented the Hibernian Hall and hired a fiddler or two." Seamus laughed and passersby in the station turned to look at him. His voice was always loud and always jolly.

"You ought to have gone on the stage," Padraic joked. "When you whisper, they can hear you in County Cork."

"We little people can't have wee voices too," Seamus joked back. "I haven't seen you in your nurse's uniform, Emerald. Do you look all starched and stiff?"

"I look like the other nurses." She smiled.

"But much lovelier, I'll wager."

Emerald ignored Seamus' compliment. He made them all the time, and she excused them as a brother's prejudice. Still, she was proud of her uniform and having finished her two years of training; she was equally proud to think that she could actually earn her own living.

"Are you excited?" Seamus beamed.

"Of course! So excited I can think of nothing else and I can't sit still."

"Then we'll have lots of dancing at the wedding! We'll whirl you around till you're so tired you'll drop into your Thomas' arms."

"Seamus, I love to dance, and everyone is looking forward to the party, but you ought not to have spent so much money."

"It's my money, you're my sister, and besides, I've just had a promotion. You let me worry about my money."

Emerald glanced at Padraic, who merely shrugged. Both had tried to dissuade him from spending so much, but it was to no avail.

Seamus O'Hearn was an outgoing, generous man who refused to take their arguments seriously. "I'll spend it on Emerald, or I'll spend it on John Jameson whiskey, or I'll lose it."

"You've saved it, and you should use it when you get married."

But Seamus had only shaken his head. "I won't be marrying," he answered, looking away. He said something Emerald couldn't forget; something out of character. "I'm a man with little past and less future," he told her. She had argued with him at the time, but he had put her off, refusing to explain his comment. "Irish black humor," he told her. "Don't take me seriously."

Briefly she thought of that comment now as they headed out of the crowded Central Station. But Seamus was laughing with Padraic, and the thought fled her mind.

7

1

August 15, 1914

"Seamus! You've done us all proud! It's a day we'll all remember! It's as fine a wedding as our friends have ever enjoyed!" Padraic embraced his older brother, and the two of them moved closer to the wall in order to avoid the dancing, which had just begun. The Hibernian Hall was filled to capacity in celebration of the wedding of Emerald O'Hearn and Thomas Hughes. The stomping of feet and the music of the fiddles caused the floor to vibrate.

"She's a beautiful woman," Seamus said with pride as his eyes followed his sister, who was happily dancing with Thomas.

"Her eyes are glistening like the dew-covered shamrocks," Padraic boasted proudly.

"After what she's been through, she deserves some happiness." Seamus' face was red from drinking Bushmill's, but he was not drunk. His eyes twinkled and his round cheeks were shiny with perspiration. His hair was just beginning to thin out on top, and there was a small round bald spot right in the middle of his skull. But if the hair on his head was soft, fine, and thinning, Seamus O'Hearn's beard was full, bristly, and reddish in color. He was a trifle bowlegged, like a rider without a horse, and lately he had developed a slight paunch. "Broad-shouldered and short in the legs, like all good Irishmen," his father would have joked. In all, Padraic thought, Seamus looked like an impish monk without a habit. But in spite of his looks, Seamus was consumed with politics, not an unusual obsession for an Irishman.

"No one will be able to stand up to the hatred and violence that Carson and his so-called volunteers will be creating." Seamus shook his head. "It'll be worse than ever before! And, Heavenly Father, how much more can people take!" Seamus' voice rose slightly as he nodded off toward Maureen Malone. "It's true I don't know her well, but how much can she and those like her take? I've heard the tale, not lived through it, mind you, but her son's tragic death is a story that's been repeated in Ulster far too often. Far, far too often." Seamus' eyes narrowed, his voice had an edge to it, and Padraic, almost for the first time, actually sensed the hatred that lay buried beneath Seamus' cheerful exterior.

"It's not a good situation," Padraic agreed. He hesitated to go too far with Seamús in political discussions because although they were close and had shared a troubled childhood, Seamus had changed since moving to Dublin. His new environment had affected him profoundly, and now, Padraic thought, Seamus not only "feels," but knows why he "feels."

To *feel* was the best way Padraic could define Irishmen. Once he had heard a priest call it "primordial instinct" and explain how a female cat, without benefit of instruction, knew how to twist and knot the umbilical cord of her newly born kittens; an Irishman, the priest explained, is born *feeling,* knowing without being taught what oppression passed before.

Padraic was illiterate; though Emerald had taught him something about reading, he still could not write. He was not proud of his illiteracy as some of his friends were. Some wore it as a badge of distinction, a tangible symbol of their hatred for the British, who had banned education for Catholics for so many centuries. Nor was Padraic like an Irish Catholic intellectual who rose above poverty and prejudice, only to find himself separated from his people by education.

Padraic O'Hearn considered himself a simple man, and though he could not read well himself, he was proud that Emerald could. He was equally proud that his brother, Seamus, since moving to Dublin, had also mastered the mysteries of written language.

It was Seamus' knowledge that made him rare to Padraic. Seamus not only felt in that primordial way, but he knew why he felt. Seamus could do more than talk about oppression, he seemed to understand how it had come about and what should be done about it; he seemed to know a hundred and one things that had never occurred to Padraic.

Seamus' metamorphosis had come about in Dublin, and the person most responsible, or at least the person Seamus gave most credit to, was Lady Constance Georgina Gore Booth, who, having married a Polish count, was now known as the Countess Markievicz. When Seamus described her, Padraic could hardly imagine such a woman.

The Countess Markievicz, according to Seamus, had formed a Boy Scout troop, the Fianna Nae Eireann. A staunch Irish Nationalist, the countess deemed the British Scout movement unsuitable for Irish lads. In the Fianna Nae Eireann, the young men who joined learned Gaelic, they had lessons in language and history, and they kept physically fit learning commando tactics. Seamus had become actively involved in the training program

with his close friend Sean Heuston. And Seamus both took and
gave orders in Gaelic. That was the strangest thing to Padraic;
they were brothers, but Seamus could speak the language of
Ireland and Padraic couldn't understand a word.

"Aren't you going to dance?" Maureen Malone called out as
she passed the spot near where Padraic and Seamus stood.

Seamus waved at her. "I'll want a dance with you soon
enough!" he called back. Then he turned back to Padraic.
"Carson and his followers will run amok!" he said, shaking his
head with disgust. "They'll kill us in our beds."

"Will it be that bad?" Padraic asked.

"In Ulster, they'll not allow home rule. I tell you, only a man
with a gun who knows how to use it will survive. It's all they
understand."

Padraic thought of one of his fellow workers who always
argued that there were two sides to every question. But there
were more than two sides to the question of Ireland just in this
hall, and outside there were yet more opinions. There were the
British and their transplanted Protestant supporters; there were
Irish Nationalists, who were both Protestant and Catholic; there
were just plain Protestants and Catholics. And, Padraic thought,
a man, any man, even Seamus, formed his loyalties in terms of
first priorities. Home rule for Ireland was the first priority for
Nationalists of both religions, but for many Catholics, independence was the next logical step and then the restoration of a
Catholic state.

And finally there existed the Ulster Nationalists, who wanted
no change, but were willing to accept limited home rule within
the British Empire with the right to bear and use arms against
anyone who might stand in their way. And today, at this moment,
the Ulster Nationalists were a real danger because they had
modern weapons, were well trained, and now seemed to have the
tacit support of London.

"It was three hundred years ago," Seamus said somberly,
"that Cromwell began to transplant Scots into Ulster, and since
that time all laws and pronouncements emanating from London
have been for their benefit."

"They've promised us home rule," Padraic said.

Seamus laughed. "They'll cancel it! And what would happen
if they granted it? The Ulster Volunteers would fight to the
death!" He shook his head in disgust. "The British do have one
talent. They're able to resort to high-flung rhetoric in Westminster,
rhetoric so clever that it lulls the inhabitants into believing they
actually live in a democracy, or, as sometimes happens, they

simply go to sleep. The English parliamentarian is a master of mass hypnosis. We're a conquered people, we'll only be free when we fight. Rebellion, full-fledged rebellion—that's what the British understand.''

"Oh, Seamus, our resources are not great enough. The English believe their democracy is the greatest in the world—they defend it with more guns than we can steal.''

"Surely they do. And on Sundays the poor miners and working-class blokes stroll through the grounds of Hampton Court, and they tell each other how nice it is that they are allowed to do so. Nice? Allowed? Who keeps the grounds?''

"Are you suggesting that the English working-class proddies would support us if we rebelled?''

Seamus shook his head and roared with sardonic laughter. "No! Would that they would! Of course they might if they had the sense God gave to pigs. But we know they do not.''

"Not politics again!'' Emerald's eyes glowed as she searched her brothers' faces. Seamus and Padraic could not resist. When they were together, it was always politics.

Thomas' arm encircled her slender waist; he held her close, pressing his fingers against the white lace of her dress.

Seamus smiled indulgently at Emerald, then unabashedly turned to Tom Hughes, his new brother-in-law. "And what do you think?''

Thomas shifted from one foot to the other. He was distracted because of the wedding, because of his bride, and most of all because all day he had kept a secret and now he was unsure of how best to reveal it. "About what?'' he answered.

"About Carson. About home rule. About Ulster, man, about rebellion and the future of Ireland.''

Thomas Hughes laughed. "A mouthful of questions. . . . I think we'll have home rule eventually . . . I think if we're rational we'll eventually gain our freedom. But I also think there are great threats in the world today—far greater than Mr. Carson.''

"And what does that mean?'' Seamus scowled.

Thomas squeezed Emerald. He had wanted to tell her all day. "It means I think the kaiser is more of a threat than Carson. I feel it so strongly that I've joined the British Army.''

Emerald drew away from him and looked into his face. She was flooded with a troubled feeling, and her own bewilderment was augmented by the sudden tension she felt in her brothers' instant reaction to her husband's words.

"Joined the Army! Joined the British Army!'' Seamus half-shouted, half-spit the words. "Have you gone daft, man? Now is the time to fight against England, just as Paddy O'Neill did in ninety-nine!''

"This is not our war," Padraic said, shaking his head.

"If able-bodied Catholics join the British Army, who's going to stand up against the proddies the next time they decide the folks on Falls Road need a lesson?'' The question came from Kevin Malone, who had stopped dancing to join the argument. "You of all people, Thomas Hughes! You just married a victim of the proddies! You who saw with your own eyes what they did to my little son . . . how could you join the British Army?'' Kevin Malone's voice was near to breaking; mist filled his eyes even as his emotion-packed words poured forth.

A small group gathered. "Do you remember when they torched the homes on Flax Street last year?'' Kevin Malone spit on the wooden floor.

"Fight for the Empire!'' Seamus sneered. "What have they ever done for us? They rejoiced during the famine when near a million Irish died. They wept when we survived on foreign soil in America! They kept our children barefoot, hungry, and ignorant, not by necessity, but by law! Now they're arming the proddies to kill more of us! Dammit, man! I respect your bravery, but it's misguided bravery.''

"Seamus O'Hearn, you're my brother and I love you. But Tom has made a decision. At least he'll be fighting in a war where Irishmen are not killing Irishmen.''

"Praise the saints," Maureen Malone added, crossing herself. "First someone kills my son, then one of ours kills a son of theirs. Kill and kill and kill! If that's the way Thomas Hughes feels—if he wants to fight tyrants, then he has a right! He has a right to stop this hating!''

"Shame on you, who lost a son to a proddie truncheon!'' Kevin Malone said, shaking his finger at his wife. But Maureen did not retreat before his words.

"I've already enlisted," Thomas said defensively. "I look on this as an opportunity.''

"To have some proddie bastard Brit push you in front of a German gun! An opportunity to get your guts blown out for king and country! What an opportunity,'' Seamus hissed.

Emerald drew herself up and stepped between her brothers and Tom Hughes. "If this is what Thomas wants, I'll stand by him. He's my husband and he's as good an Irishman as any man in this room!''

For a moment there was silence. "This family is not to be divided again," Padraic finally said. "No more.''

Seamus grumbled slightly under his breath and picked up his glass of whiskey, draining it. Emerald put her arm around him and kissed him. "You listen, you're going to dance with me now. I'll not have you ruin my wedding, Seamus O'Hearn."

Seamus set his glass down. "You're right," he agreed. "No more tonight."

They danced an Irish jig, the beer and whiskey flowed, and the music filled the Hibernian Hall till near dawn, when finally the drunken, merry celebrants staggered forth into the dawn.

Thomas Hughes held Emerald tight and looked into her face. "We'll miss our train," he reminded her.

Emerald leaned against his broad chest. "I'll sleep all the way to Galway."

"It's not the grandest hotel," Thomas Hughes said as he opened the door to their room in the tiny inn.

Emerald went to the window and looked out. They had taken the morning train; now the afternoon sun was setting and Galway Bay shimmered in the distance. "It's beautiful here, so peaceful, so tranquil."

"I came here once when I was a boy, and I always remembered it." He set down their suitcase and then sat down on the side of the bed. It was a small quaint room with a slanted ceiling that bowed to the front window, which overlooked the bay. It had a dresser and a huge bed; it had a small table and on it a washbasin.

"I'm sorry we can't stay more than a few days," he said, looking at the blue carpet that failed to entirely cover the uneven floorboards.

Emerald turned from the window. "We'll make the most of our quiet time together."

Thomas yawned and lay down.

"I'll go undress," Emerald said. She opened the suitcase and took out her things. "I'll be back in a few moments," she promised.

She slipped behind the door and into the small alcove that served as both dressing room and closet. She shivered slightly. When she came back, Thomas would be waiting naked in bed for her. The memory of his last passionate kiss lingered on her lips, but in the deep recesses of her memory she still recalled Mr. McArthur's assault and his threats. She could still picture his bonelike appendage. . . . Emerald slipped into her nightdress. She loved Thomas with all her heart; she trusted him with her life. But the distant fear lingered, a fear that she herself might freeze and run away, a fear that she could not make him happy.

Once she had tried to discuss her fear with Maureen Malone, but Maureen could not quite seem to understand. "Better to fear the results," she had said. "Birthing a baby isn't easy."

But the thought of being with child did not trouble Emerald. She wanted Tom's children; she wanted to bear him fine strong sons and beautiful daughters. If there was pain, it was wanted pain because she loved Tom. It was not birthing, but the act of intimacy itself that she was wary of, and even where that was concerned, she found herself of two minds. She wanted him terribly; she feared the unknown.

Emerald took one last look at the doorknob. It turned with a slight creak and she opened the door, slipping back into the room.

Tom had drawn the curtains and lit a lamp. He looked at his bride with moist eyes; he looked almost as if he were going to cry. They were soft wonderful eyes, Emerald thought. Like a lost puppy's—great watery pools of love and longing that drew her to him.

"You're the vision of an angel," he said with undisguised admiration. He held out his arms to her and Emerald walked across the room. She sat down on the side of the bed, and Thomas drew her into his arms, kissing her on the mouth, moving his lips against hers as he always did.

"Lie down next to me," he whispered.

Emerald lay down beside him, her long lace nightdress around her.

Thomas ran his hand underneath her neck and lifted her thick red hair, spreading it out on the white pillow. "You're an angel with a glowing halo," he told her, lowering his face and kissing her neck and ears again and again.

He was covered only by the white sheet, and Emerald knew that beneath the sheet that separated their two bodies, he was undressed. She could feel his bone hardening, and it sent a shiver of apprehension through her. She pressed herself to him, feeling both safe and threatened by the strength of his embrace.

"I know you're afraid," he whispered. "You don't have to be. I'll be gentle, tender, and loving. Lie still, my love, lie still and let me show you poetry in the making." Thomas' deep voice and Gaelic lilt lulled Emerald, and she nodded her head in silent acquiescence.

Thomas slid down in the bed, and the sheet that covered him

fell away, revealing his broad hairy chest and his large muscular shoulders and arms. Emerald suddenly felt like the tiny fairy princess who lived beneath the leaves in the great forest. She felt that Thomas, like a great friendly giant, could pick her up and cup her in his large hands and that he could bend her to his will. A chill passed through her, though she avoided looking at his nakedness fully.

"Would you be more comfortable in darkness?" he asked. Emerald didn't answer, but Thomas sensed her wishes and in one swift motion he straightened up, leaned over, and turned out the lamp on the bedside table. "Later I want to make love to you in the light," he said softly, "but for now I will love you blindly."

He again moved down in the bed, and Emerald lay still as he kissed her toes and her ankles, moving his lips and his tongue up her long white legs to her knees. She hardly noticed that he lifted the lace gown and kissed her thighs, settling at last on her mound and nestling his lips into the light red-blond curls that covered it.

Emerald felt paralyzed with pleasure, unable to move. His intimate caresses caused her to go cold, then warm as her sleeping passion was aroused. She felt damp between her legs and her whole body flushed as if she had a fever. When he ceased the caress, she made a small sound and moved herself against him, wanting him to begin again, though he did not. Instead, he moved upward, kissing her flat stomach and tickling her navel till she laughed and wiggled beneath him. Then his hand returned to her center of pleasure and with quick gentle movements he silenced her giggling and brought her to a panting urgency.

"It's the center of pleasure," he whispered. "A pleasure we can both share soon." But again he moved his hand away. He undid the ribbons of her nightdress and carefully and slowly uncovered her. "I can't see in the darkness," he breathed in her ear, "but I know they are lovelier than all the rosebuds in Ireland." His tongue caressed her nipples, moving around them, flicking them gently. Now and again his hand returned to her mound and moved across it with a teasing motion that caused Emerald to lift her hips—reaching for what, she was unsure. He suckled the tip of her left breast as if he were a small child and Emerald groaned with pleasure, and again he moved his hand across her. She was lost in his arms and she ached inside as her desire grew to a pitch she could not explain and in truth did not understand. It was as if all else was lost and nothing save the sensations she felt were real.

"It might hurt a little at first," he warned her. "You tell me."

Emerald hardly heard a word. She had abandoned herself entirely to the sensations she was experiencing. Her nipples were hard and she imagined them to be small light pink stones. She longed, but could not describe her longing. It was not hunger, but it was a kind of hunger.

Again his fingers moved, and she responded to his touch. When he lifted his hand away, she moved. "Please, don't stop," she begged. But he did stop; he stopped to move her legs apart, then returned to her. Emerald could feel his long appendage, but it no longer frightened her. She wanted it, understanding now that he would enter her and they would become one. She lifted herself to him and kissed his face as she wrapped her arms around him.

"My beautiful little virgin," he murmured as he gently prodded her. "Tell me if I hurt you. I would not hurt you for anything in the world."

Emerald lifted her hips and she felt a slight pain, but the dampness between her legs eased his entry and his lips again touched her nipples, and she clung to him. He began a steady rhythm, moving in and out of her, and the stem of his appendage rubbed against her mound just as his hand had. Emerald yielded herself completely to the feelings of her body. At first she experienced blackness; a void. Then there were raging colors, all the colors of a distant rainbow. It was as if she were a small child who had climbed atop the rainbow and who had begun, quite out of control, to slide down one side. Emerald fell, allowing herself to tumble. . . . She felt a throbbing relief that racked her entire body. She pressed herself against Thomas and shook violently in the pleasure of pure release.

At the same time, she felt him vibrate against her and into her. He let out a kind of muffled cry and they held each other tightly. Emerald thought they would melt into each other; surely they had become one person.

"I shall remember this night as long as I live," Emerald said after a long while.

"I too," Thomas replied. "Your love will sustain me, Emerald. I'm a rare Irishman; I have something to come back to. I have someone very important."

Emerald leaned against him. "I don't want to talk about your leaving. I don't even want to think about it."

He kissed her cheek. "When I come home, I'll have enough money for us to go to America. It's my dream, Emerald."

2

September 1914

There were five gentlemen in all. Each of them was impeccably dressed in dark morning coat, tall formal hat, white spats, cane, and the perennial umbrella. Pin-stripped trousers shimmered under the light from the crystal chandeliers that lit the long high-ceilinged corridor. On either side of the large double doors, two red velvet settees stood like old well-dressed ladies on spindle legs. To one side, two tin-helmeted guards stood at ease, each with a stony expressionless face that might have matched any figure in the waxworks. Indeed, the guards looked more like wax figures than living men.

The five unofficial delegates who waited to be granted an audience beyond the double doors might have been British if one judged men by their appearance and language. But they were not British. The British sent no delegations to Hamburg in the Indian summer of 1914, because the British had declared war on Germany, August 4, over a month ago.

The men who waited outside the double doors were Irish and their spokesman was Sir Roger Casement, OBE, K.G.

"If they wanted to see us, why are we kept waiting?" one of the men asked Sir Roger. His voice was full of irritation and he looked weary.

Sir Roger gave the man a withering look. "The Germans are a peculiar people." He mouthed the comment without actually speaking the words.

There was movement behind the double doors and they were dramatically flung open. The guards stiffened and shifted their rifles formally.

The gentleman who opened the door was dressed in black morning coat with proper tails and a white ruffled shirt transected by a bright red sash. In the middle of the sash, across his narrow chest, he wore a large medal: the Order of Hohenzollern. He had long, well-manicured, but yellowed nails. He spoke with a perfect British accent and might easily have passed for an Oxford don. "General von Seeckt will see you now," he announced in almost a whisper.

Sir Roger strode past him, paying him no mind. The others followed more shyly in his wake, their eyes taking in the ornate room. The walls were framed with heavy wooden beams carved with endless curlicues that gave the room the appearance of being an overfrosted gingerbread house. The rich floor coverings which clung to the inlaid oak floors were Persian—deep and rich, they bore designs of some martyred Armenian who probably died producing them in a Turkish carpet factory. The furniture was all antique, the majority being Louis XIV.

Across the room, behind the great expanse of highly polished wood, General von Seeckt sat stiffly. In his left eye he wore a monocle, and holding it in place caused a permanent and premature wrinkle in his forty-eight-year-old brow. Von Seeckt was not a large man, but his desk was cleverly placed on a raised dais and thus his guests felt small, since they were forced to look up at him.

General von Seeckt stood, clicked his heels, and bowed formally from the waist. "It is kind of you to come. We are always pleased to entertain our Irish guests." The general bowed again, and the light from the crystal chandelier shone on his balding head.

Sir Roger, who was somewhat effeminate most of the time, moved as if he were wearing a flowing cloak. And had he been wearing one, he doubtless would have flicked it over his shoulder. Instead, he simply flicked his shoulder. "We have come on urgent business," he pressed. His face was knit with concern, and he fairly glowed with his sense of true purpose.

A vague image of Lord Byron flashed across Sir Roger's mind; it was a rare moment and he relished the thought of himself as Ireland's savior.

The reality, thought one of his silent cohorts, was quite different. To him Sir Roger projected the image of Don Quixote. Lance aimed, he tilted forever at a British windmill. Unhappily, there was no one among his intimates who had the insight of Sancho Panza, though they were all equally long-suffering.

Sir Roger dared not step onto the dais unless invited. But he did lean over it. "We can be of mutual service to one another," he stressed, sounding more than a little conspiratorial. "We know where all the British bases are, we can get our people inside the bases. We could help you in your efforts."

General von Seeckt cleared his throat. His eyes fell on stacks of paper that were neatly piled on his desk. At the end of this day, like all the days, his secretary would sort through and rearrange the piles. General von Seeckt did not like his temporary role of bureaucrat; he was chief of staff of the Eleventh Army, the boy wonder of the German general staff. He preferred combat against the enemy to dealing with overwrought would-be allies.

"And in return?" the general questioned. It was nearly time for tea, and the general fully intended to dispose of these people well before his tea and afternoon cognac arrived.

"We want arms to fight the British!" Sir Roger intoned grandly. "Vast sums of money are now being raised in the United States to enable us to buy the best you have to sell. At the same time, we can develop a coordinated attack on the British bases. I tell you, not since Wolfe Tone in 1798 has such an opportunity presented itself! A German naval blockade, the Irish soldiers together against a common foe. Think of it!"

Think of it indeed, General von Seeckt contemplated. Given the record of the Irish, they would probably blow themselves to kingdom come and take half the German Army and Navy with them. They were inept, and doubtless that had something to do with their brooding Celtic emotionalism. General von Seeckt did not approve of emotional men. Armies were not built on tears, but with men who could act like efficient robots. It all took training, and above all, discipline; a discipline of both body and spirit. The Irish had neither, though if wars were won with poetry, storytelling, and song, the Irish might have ruled the world.

The general stood up and looked at the delegation. He did not look directly into Sir Roger's eyes, but rather focused on the intricate patterns and designs of the Armenian carpetmaker. For a moment he wished the Irish were Turks, and he wondered if they had been Muslim instead of Catholic if they would be fighters. On reflection, he decided that the Turks were not all that much better. It was more that in the Balkans they had a frightening reputation and people simply surrendered before them. No, it could not be Catholicism. After all, many Germans were Catholic too, and it didn't make them bad soldiers.

He sighed. It was truly difficult for the Germans to find suitable allies. "We shall have to take this matter under our most considered thought," General von Seeckt hedged. "Not for a moment do we doubt your sincerity . . . or your ability." The latter part of his statement almost caught in his throat. "But we have vast commitments and we must consider opening any new front carefully. There's a question of supply lines, of stretching our resources too far, of communications, of bringing in other powers. . . . So many questions. I fear this matter must be meticulously considered and analyzed. Let me assure you we will let you know at the earliest opportunity what our decision is."

Sir Roger's face muscles twitched and his cheekbones seemed to settle into a stony position. He raised one bushy eyebrow. "We cannot wait long," he said arrogantly. "We are prepared to fight!"

The intended insult of the last comment did not elude General von Seeckt, but he could hear the cart which carried his tea and cognac being wheeled down the corridor and he knew its pleasantries were waiting, so he allowed Sir Roger's comment to pass without retort. "We will let you know," he reiterated.

Sir Roger turned to his waiting silent friends. He shrugged and they followed him to the double doors that opened as if on signal. "Good day," the gentleman in black who sounded so British said. "Another time."

"And do enjoy your visit to Berlin," General von Seeckt called after them. "You are, after all, our guests."

The group walked down the long hallway in silence. Sir Roger led them in long purposeful strides.

"I suggest we plan our own rebellion," one of them commented.

"If the Germans won't help us, Irish Americans will!" another added.

Sir Roger smiled at the last thought. True, there were plenty of Irish in New York, Boston, and Philadelphia who could be counted on for cash. And money could buy arms elsewhere.

3

October 1914

"One night?" Emerald looked at Thomas sadly. "It's not long enough, it's not!"

He kissed her cheek. "I'm lucky enough to get that."

"But you've been gone six weeks in training. . . . Have they no mercy?"

He shook his head. "It's the Germans who have no mercy."

"How long will you be gone?" Her eyes searched his face.

"If I knew that, I'd be a fortune-teller." He looked around the small room that Emerald had rented. "Are you happy here?"

"It's small and it's cozy. I don't mind it. Padraic's flat is not far."

"And the hospital? How is it?"

"Oh, Thomas . . ." Emerald flung herself into his arms. "We've got twenty-four hours, don't ask me things I write you every day in letters. Kiss me, hold me, make love to me, and pretend you'll never leave, even though I know you will." She was starting to cry, and she wondered if she should tell him the only important news she had—the one thing she hadn't written. But his lips were on her neck and he swept her into his arms and carried her to the bed.

He undressed her slowly, lingering over each button, kissing her, caressing her. She in turn moved soft hands over him and felt him warm to her touch, growing larger and ready for lovemaking.

"I adore you," he said as he gently kissed her knees. "I missed you more each day I was gone, I dreamed of you every night."

"And I of you," Emerald answered, yielding to his touch, shivering as he aroused her.

He entered her and they were welded together in mutual passion, climbing the heights, falling together. Then they lay in one another's arms till at last Emerald knew they had to talk.

"Padraic's going to America," she finally said. It wasn't her big news, but it was a prelude to it.

Thomas propped himself up and looked across at her. "Soon?"

"In a month's time. I'll miss him, but you said we would go too when you come home, so, God willing, I won't have to miss him for long."

"That means you'll be alone in Belfast. I don't like that."

Emerald sighed. "Nor do I. Especially now."

Thomas looked at her; it was true that there were difficulties, but there were no more than usual. "I don't understand."

Emerald let out her breath. "Well, I'm not certain . . . it's too soon to be certain. But, Tom, I think I'm pregnant. I've missed one month. . . . I just can't be sure yet."

His face lit up with such joy that Emerald immediately felt she had done the right thing. "A baby? We're going to have a baby?"

He drew her to him and devoured her with kisses while Emerald turned in his arms, laughing herself. "Oh, I hope it's true," she said, pressing herself to him.

He held her close. "If it is, you can't stay here alone."

Emerald nodded against him. "I'd like to go to Dublin so I could at least be near Seamus."

Thomas Hughes agreed. "It's a fine idea. I'd feel better about leaving."

"Leaving . . . Oh, God, don't even say it." She rolled over and kissed his lips and his brow. The tiny dark rented room seemed to close in on them, and Emerald closed her eyes, abandoning herself to everything but the feel of her husband, the sound of his breathing, his nearness. "I love you," she said, pressing to him. "I love you."

Book II

8

1

March 1916

Day after tedious day for the last three months, Sir Roger Casement had been a frequent if not eager visitor to various government ministries in Berlin. Each, in turn, had passed him on to another ministry, department, or subdepartment for the necessary approval to purchase and ship arms to Ireland.

In spite of the frustrations of the German bureaucracy, this trip to Berlin was at least less embarrassing than his last effort. Then he had agreed to reorganize Irish prisoners of war into a battalion to fight against the British. Alas, none of the captured Irish would agree. And what could he have said to the impatient Germans? "You didn't capture the *right* kind of Irishmen."

No, he reflected, there was no way to make the Germans truly understand the Irish or the Irish situation. Certainly, even he was annoyed at the Irish penchant for forming three political opinions when only two people were present, but if he was annoyed at this phenomenon, the Germans were incredulous. They had no such variance of opinion; in fact they allowed no such variance of opinion. But deep down, Sir Roger took a certain perverse pride in the fact that the Irish couldn't agree; their internal squabbles gave them a certain charm.

I will put past failures out of my mind, Sir Roger vowed. After all, the Germans have finally agreed to return me to Ireland, along with the arms I have procured.

Of course, it was humiliating to have haggled over every round of ammunition and every gun. Herr Stock, the gentleman from Mellor und Sohne, was quite willing to sell three ships full of armaments, knowing full well that Sir Roger had been given only one ship in which to transport them.

"Ach, Herr Casement," Stock growled with superiority, "I did not realize that your means of transportation was so limited. I fear that if you only seek this small quantity, the price will be, well, higher." Herr Stock fingered his mustache. "Yes, higher."

"Naturally," Sir Roger replied. Herr Stock was greasy and irritated him.

The Germans, it turned out, did not barter with the charm of the Arabs or the humor of the Spanish. They bartered with an all-consuming sense of purpose and a positive busybodiness that constantly hinted at insult.

The Germans did not, as one might expect, simply sell bullets. Rather, they discussed how many bullets would be necessary per weapon given the "below-average marksmanship" of the Irish. "Below-average marksmanship" was a description that applied to everyone who was not German-trained, with the exception of those from the Southwestern United States. The Germans were in awe of Western legend, and Sir Roger decided that was because American Westerners were as crass as the Germans themselves.

But it was not only the issue of the marksmanship that was tiring. It was the slavishness of the Germans to mathematics. Naturally they worked out a ratio of guns to ammunition. You might purchase X number of guns, and if the guns were to be used by soldiers who were German-trained, then you required X number of bullets. But if they were to be used by others, you needed fewer guns and ten times the number of bullets. Further, there was no need for more than X number of guns when you had only one ship, because you could not carry sufficient bullets. Behind this merry-go-round logic was the German insult; mathematical ratio or no, it all proclaimed German superiority.

Thus the meetings had been long and tiring and Sir Roger had more than once bitten his tongue to keep from screaming, "If I pay for them, it's none of your fucking business how or by whom they're used!" And he might have added, "The good Irish Americans who donated this money don't care as much as you do!"

But Sir Roger had said none of these things. Instead, he sat across the table while prices and quantities were bandied about, and until final agreement was reached. He shook hands politely and left, but the whole experience made him feel dirty and common. "God! How I hate tradespeople!" he mumbled to himself as he hurried down the street. Five hours of bargaining with a merchant might be all right for some people, but it did not suit his image of himself. The odor of Herr Stock's foul-smelling cigars seemed to have permeated his clothing, relentlessly attacking him till his olfactory senses were numbed. Sir Roger shook his head in disgust. In the act of being a true Irish patriot, one had to lower oneself to incredible depths. Auch! Indeed.

Sir Roger walked aimlessly along the waterfront, down the winding streets of the old port city. It was like other port cities: Panama, Port Said, Naples, Marseilles . . . Their inhabitants might have been from Dante's inner circle. Any pleasure, any

depravity, was available for cash. The abundance of female flesh
offering favors for a few marks was utterly repulsive. He saw an
overweight fräulein who stood in the doorway of her establishment on the Reeperbahn, one large mammary gland being openly
displayed while her tongue shamelessly circumvented a banana.
Sir Roger felt the bile in his stomach rise and he quickened his
pace and hurried onward into the night.

He came to an intersection, turned the corner, and stopped in
front of an old stone building displaying a sign which read
"BADANSTALT."

Exactly what I need, he thought. He turned the great brass
doorknob and entered the ancient building. It was one of those
structures that had known a grander time, or perhaps it was only
the war that cast a pall on taking mineral baths. He looked
around and smiled to himself. The foyer was huge, with great
high ceilings, a stark marble floor, and stone walls that were
bare. He could not help but notice the marked increase in
humidity; somewhere there was a faint odor of chemicals and
sweat which mixed with the various colognes employed after the
bath.

Sir Roger approached a desk which might have been in any
hotel. He agreed to the price of five marks for a steambath and
massage; he rejoiced that this had to be the only place in
Germany where there was no price gouging.

"Your key. It's that way." The clerk pointed off down a
corridor and indicated the number on the key, which would
match the number of the cubicle assigned him.

Sir Roger paid the bill and proceeded along the faintly lit
corridor. Somehow he found his room and stripped down, wrap-
ping himself in a towel. He went gingerly to the steambath,
noting that the doors to the other cubicles were open, displaying
a motley assortment of German manhood. Looking at the various
"boys," Sir Roger felt that he was in a day-old bake shop. They
all seemed stale and tasteless; some looked old and withered
before their time, others had a garish appearance even without
their clothes. He sighed and thought: All I shall leave here with
is a clean body. But the steambath proved to be equally
disappointing. It was as if the horrid "boys" he saw in their
cubicles had all been cloned.

When he finally found a bench to sit on, he began taking deep
breaths and at last succeeded in obtaining a level of bodily
relaxation he had not felt in months. He closed his eyes and
inhaled and exhaled slowly; he felt the perspiration forming on
his forehead and trickling down his chest. Relax, relax, he

repeated to himself over and over. But there was no relaxation. Suddenly it was as if everyone in the room were an octopus; hands began groping and fondling his slim athletic body. But the hands were callused and coarse; their touch was totally offensive, and even with his eyes closed he could not help but think that he had been more tenderly caressed in a crowded lift.

It was no use. He felt his anger, but nothing else, rise. He stood up, shaking the hands off him, and stormed from the steambath into the massage room. At least the hands of the masseur would be professional, and the tension in his muscles was tight beyond endurance.

The room was empty when he entered, and steeling himself for another disappointment, he quickly lay down on the table. He did not even offer a glance toward the young masseur when he entered the room and walked over to the table.

Without saying a word, the masseur gently removed the towel covering Sir Roger's buttocks and with a delicately applied grace and skill began covering Sir Roger's body with oil. Pomegranates, he thought. The room was filled with the sublime fragrance of that unique tropical fruit.

Through the masseur's magic fingers, Sir Roger felt his life being restored. Without looking up from the table, he asked the masseur his name.

"Adel, sir," the velvet voice replied.

"You're Egyptian, yes?"

"No, sir. Tunisian." Adel continued the gentle circular motions across Sir Roger's flesh.

"Have you been here long?"

"Here?"

"I mean in Hamburg," Sir Roger answered, trying to be both rebel and consummate English lord of the realm.

"Nearly three years," Adel replied.

Lines from Byron began running through Sir Roger's mind. "You're quite good at your work," Sir Roger finally said, aware that his senses were all alert and his yearning was growing by the second.

"Thank you, sir."

"You're not a talkative fellow, are you?"

"I allow my fingers to express my feelings. They communicate better than words."

Sir Roger sighed deeply. "I've been very lonely since I've been in Hamburg. I crave quality, and this city . . . this country, is rather crude. You're the first genteel experience I've had here."

"Thank you, sir. But it's only my job."

"Is that all it is to you? Don't you derive any pleasure from your work? I've missed pleasure since I've been in Germany. I can pay you handsomely for what happiness you can offer."

"You insult me, sir." Adel had a hurt tone in his voice.

"But I thought . . ."

"Sir," Adel said, leaning a bit closer, "pleasure is to give and receive, not to be bought and sold like a pair of fashionable shoes. The truest pleasures are those freely given and freely received."

"I'm sorry," Sir Roger stuttered.

"You're becoming tense . . . allow me to relieve you. Please turn over."

Lying on his back, Sir Roger looked into Adel's face; surely he was no more than twenty-five. Adel was perfectly tanned; his face was a kind of desert sculpture, his hands were soft . . . Sir Roger was about to speak, but Adel put his finger to his mouth in the universal sign of silence.

As Sir Roger closed his mouth, the young masseur bent over. Sir Roger pressed his eyes closed; he imagined himself having penetrated a Grecian cave, while a thousand delicate-tongued nymphs inside caressed him. Sir Roger grew larger, yet the young masseur received all that was given.

The man must come from a family of sword swallowers, Sir Roger thought, as Adel was now gently sucking on his testicles. It was as if Adel had ten tongues, all working in unison with his fingers. Sir Roger tensed, fighting to control the inevitable explosion. Then, unable to restrain himself any longer, he burst forth in a torrent.

To Sir Roger's surprise, the young man continued, and much to Sir Roger's joy, the second orgasm was achieved in due course of time. It was a long delicious night, with each man loving and touching the other. There was no thought of rest or sleep, and each gave the other pleasure many times.

Dawn finally peered through the skylight overhead and Sir Roger knew it was time to leave for Bremerhaven and his rendezvous with the unknown submarine captain.

Sir Roger dressed silently. Leaving an encounter like this one was always difficult. What did one say? "Thank you"? It sounded too formal, too insincere. And promises of future meetings were so seldom kept.

"Adel," Sir Roger asked, putting his hand on the young man's shoulder, "does your name have a meaning?"

" 'Eagle,' sir," Adel replied.

"I must leave now, my Eagle."

As quietly as he had entered the room, Adel left. Sir Roger drew a deep satisfied breath and finished dressing. He paused at the front desk, and taking out a hundred-mark note, handed it to the clerk. "Give this to Adel," he said, putting on his hat with a flourish.

2

April 16, 1916

It's a truly lovely day, Emerald thought as she looked around, taking in the beauty of the countryside. An unusual day for mid-April. The sky was absolutely clear and a deep blue. The rolling hills were carpeted in dark green, and atop a distant knoll, a flock of sheep grazed under the afternoon sun, looking like a pastoral painting.

Early that morning, Seamus had packed Emerald and little Tom off to the country, insisting that a day away from Dublin would be good for the baby and for Emerald.

"We'll take the train to Glendalough and spend the day outside. We'll have a picnic and little Tom can crawl around to his heart's content. And you, my girl, you need a rest from the routine of your daily life and some good clean, fresh country air."

Ah, Seamus, Emerald reflected, you're always trying to make me forget the death of Thomas Hughes, you're always trying to heal me and make me whole again. But what would I do without you? You've been a tower of strength, and a near-father to little Tom.

Emerald looked back on the last year with deep sadness. Her beloved husband had died almost a year ago; then, only a month later, little Tom had been born. Emerald let out her breath and held back the tears that were always ready to come.

She forced the thought of Thomas Hughes's death out of her mind and looked at Tom and his Uncle Seamus. Under the large spreading tree, Seamus had laid down a blanket and a large tablecloth. They had eaten their lunch and drunk some Guinness, and Tom had crawled around uninhibited till he was absolutely exhausted, as drowsy from exercise as Seamus was from his drink.

Then Seamus had taken out his autoharp and played some old songs, singing to Tom in his deep voice; the sweet sound echoed through the pleasant little valley. For a time, Emerald closed her eyes to listen as Seamus sang "The Fairies Dancing on The Green." Tom Hughes, Jr., at eleven months of age, was too young to understand the song stories, but he adored the autoharp and delighted in plucking its strings when given the opportunity by his indulgent uncle.

After a time, Seamus fell silent, and when Emerald opened her own eyes, she saw that Seamus was fast asleep under the tree and that little Tom was also napping, his head in his uncle's lap.

Emerald pulled her shawl about her and stood up. In the distance, a winding row of trees proclaimed a sinuous little stream, and Emerald began to walk toward it, feeling the need to move about.

The ground was firm and not soggy as it often was. She descended a slope and continued off toward the stream. Then, as she approached the water, she stopped short, frozen with a cold chill.

Because the day was warm and the water still cool, a white ghostly mist rose off it, curling around the great tree trunks near the riverlet, caressing the thick damp moss on the nearby rocks.

"Thomas . . ." Emerald whispered her husband's name and stared at the ghostly white vapor. She imagined she saw him in the vapor's midst, holding his arms out to her, even though his face was twisted in pain as his lungs turned themselves inside out.

"No, no, no . . ." Emerald murmured. Then, unable to hold back the tears, she wept as she envisaged the words on the cross in Flanders:

Thomas Andrew Hughes, born 1877 near Donegal; died April 22, 1915, in Ypres, France, while serving his eighth month with His Majesty's Forces. Age 38, he is survived by his loving wife, Emma Hughes, and his infant son, Thomas Hughes, Jr.

Someday I'll visit your grave, Emerald vowed. She blinked back more tears. I will never be able to look at mist again without thinking of chlorine gas, without imagining your face and your suffering. "Blessed are the dead," one doctor told her. "It's painful, but it's over. Those who survive die slowly and in agony."

"I should be grateful you didn't suffer too long," Emerald said aloud to the rising mist. She shook her head as if to dispel her thoughts. For nearly a year the specter of Thomas Hughes had haunted her, and in her nightmares she always saw him in the cloud of transparent poison, gasping, fighting for air, and calling out to her. The Germans called it a new weapon, but it was a ghastly weapon, a torture.

"It burns," one man told her. "It burns your lungs till you vomit them out your mouth."

Emerald leaned against a tree trunk and abstractedly ran her hand over the soft moss. "Dear God, let me be at peace. This is such a happy day; I'd almost forgotten. Lord, let me be strong and healthy for my baby boy; let me be grateful I have a position at the hospital, and thank you for Seamus, who has helped me so much. No woman could have a better brother. . . ."

Emerald finished her prayer and crossed herself. Then she turned and hurried back to Seamus and Tom, running from her most persistent and haunting memories.

3

April 16, 1916

"Dive!" Captain Lothar von Hofmann commanded. This was potentially a perilous voyage for von Hofmann and the crew of U-boat 36, and, as far as Lothar was concerned, one with little tangible reward that he could discern.

Wearily he reminded himself that life was not always what one wanted. Ever since he had been awarded the Eisen Kreuz for his involvement in sinking the *Lusitania*, his duties had become more ceremonial than useful.

Germany needs live heroes, Lothar was told. He glanced over at Sir Roger Casement, the source of his irritation, and made a slight face. It seemed the Irish preferred dead martyrs. Certainly, given the plan, Sir Roger's chances of survival seemed limited.

Live hero . . . dead martyr. Lothar desired neither; he only wanted to return to active duty. And even if he couldn't understand this assignment, at least it was better than raising funds for the German war effort.

Six months on the beer-and-schnitzel circuit was too much. He had been sent out to give patriotic speeches, and he found such activity humiliating, boring, and fattening. Lothar glanced up and caught sight of his image in the metal bulkhead. Of course it was a distorted view, but there was no doubt he had gained twenty pounds in the past six months. Shit! He felt and looked like the rotund burgermeister of Munich.

If he could have just given speeches, it might not have been so bad, but he was forced to do other things as well, silly things.

He was given a bag of fifty models of his U-boat to take with him on the speaking circuit. But they were in pieces and came with a hammer and nails—each one a tiny prefabricated balsa-wood replica. After his speech, Lothar was expected to assemble the model, and each nail used in the assembly represented one mark donated to the cause. At schools Lothar usually raised two hundred marks, but at the Seimens factory in Wannsee he had taken in over ten thousand marks. Happily, he had not had to drive in ten thousand nails.

But no matter, raising funds did not give him a feeling of fulfillment. What did give him pride and fulfillment was to command one of the Deutschland-class U-boats. Each one was ninety-five meters in length, each had two long storage compartments, and, submerged, the Deutschland submarines could carry either seven hundred tons of armaments or seven hundred tons of supply cargo.

But was U-36 carrying armaments or a valuable cargo? No, Lothar thought bitterly. This submarine carried Sir Roger Casement and two of his compatriots. This submarine was meant only to rendezvous with the *Aud,* which was carrying armaments for Sir Roger.

Moreover, the rendezvous was to take place off the coast of Ireland, which made this a dangerous mission indeed. After all, he had sunk the *Lusitania* off Ireland, and Lothar knew full well that every sailor in the British Navy was gunning for him. The *Lusitania* was a civilian passenger liner and carried nineteen hundred civilians, of whom only seven hundred survived. It's small comfort that this isn't the same U-boat, Lothar thought.

The submarine completed its dive, and Lothar sat down. He was following orders; he was headed for Ireland. His sole cargo was a strange, effeminate, overdramatic English lord and his two sullen companions, who had come aboard late, having traveled from Berlin instead of Hamburg.

Rendezvous with a large ship carrying arms right under the noses of the British? Support the Irish in some sort of uprising? Lothar stared at Sir Roger. Was this man a rebel? The leader of a putsch? He shook his head to himself. Someone in the German high command was slipping.

4

April 17, 1916

Spring was Franz von Papen's favorite time of year. Unlike
the climate in Pomerania, where he had an estate, spring arrived
on time in New York. He walked down the street toward his
office on Wall Street; he relished the warm sunshine.

Surely my worst time in America is over now and relations
between Germany and the United States will improve. After the
sinking of the *Lusitania* eleven months ago, it seemed that the
mighty industrial machine of America would go to war with
Germany too. Von Papen pondered the six months he had spent
using every resource available to stem the tide of anti-German
sentiment in America, and in this regard the Irish and their
growing political influence were most useful.

It seemed that almost every factory, mill, and harbor was
worked by the Irish, and the large cities of America—New York,
Boston, Philadelphia, and Chicago—had populations that were
predominantly either Irish or German in heritage. Von Papen
decided it would be difficult to get German-Americans or Irish-
Americans to fight. The Germans would not fight against the
country of their origin and the Irish would not fight with the
British. Still, after the *Lusitania*, von Papen admitted he had
been through a tough diplomatic battle.

He had planted stories in the newspapers, and he had actually
had to purchase several leading Irish and German papers. Sometimes he made outright bribes to columnists. But he was able to
congratulate himself; he had been careful and discreet, mindful
that one slip and anti-German sentiment would double overnight.

Fortunately, his battle was less bloody than those fought by
his friends and comrades on the western front and in Russia.
That was, of course, a frustration. He never really knew how the
battles were developing. True, there were the usual cables to the
embassy, but how much could be believed? The enemy casualty
figures were obviously exaggerated. If they were not, France
would have no population at all and Britain would be a desert
island. Even the *Frankfurter Zeitung*, despite heavy censorship,
would present a truer story than the reports to the embassy did.

As von Papen approached Wall Street, he decided to enter
Trinity Church and give thanks to God for the lovely spring day.
In spite of his reverence, von Papen could never resist musing
over the peculiarity of the church's location. Unlike Germany

and most other civilized countries, in which churches would be situated in the center of town, America had churches overlooking Mammon—the financial district. He shrugged and smiled. Render unto God the things that are God's and unto Caesar the things that are Caesar's—it certainly seemed easier when the two were next door to one another.

When von Papen entered the anteroom of his office, he found two men waiting. They were John Corbett and James Sullivan, both members of the Fenian movement in the United States. Von Papen had met with the two over a week ago, and assumed all their mutual business was settled. What, he asked himself, did they want now?

Both men rose when he entered the room. Von Papen was not unaware of his aristocratic bearing and the respect it usually brought. He waved them aside and went into his office.

The Irish, von Papen decided, were disorganized at the best of times. He had no intention of allowing these two unannounced visitors to throw his morning regimen off schedule. Thus he vowed to review the morning dispatches. When he had finished, he invited the two Fenians in.

"You look distressed," von Papen commented as he motioned them to chairs. Both men sat down, and von Papen felt a strange foreboding as he studied their expressions. They sat on the edges of their chairs, their faces clouded with concern. It occurred to him that perhaps he should not have kept them waiting so long.

"The arms shipment must be delayed," Corbett blurted out. He was a short stocky man, direct and not given to social graces.

"Really?" von Papen replied. He placed his monocle in his left eyes, aware it served to maintain a physical and emotional distance from those who sat on the other side of his desk. "And how do you propose that we accomplish this . . . uh, feat?"

The two Fenians looked at one another blankly. "Send a wireless message, I guess," Corbett answered.

"You realize, of course, that there is a war on and that the war has severely altered the ease with which such a message might be sent." Why am I having this conversation with these two dolts? he asked himself silently.

He decided to make short shrift of this meeting so he could finish his duties and go out and enjoy the sunshine. "It's virtually impossible." He took out one of the folders from his desk drawer and passed it to Corbett. "Here, look at this and tell me how it can be done."

The contents of the folder were written in German, a language the two Fenians didn't understand. Of course, they probably didn't read English either. Mentally von Papen congratulated the British for choosing illiteracy as a form of oppression.

The folder contained only information on the establishment of weather stations in the Atlantic, but it still took some moments for the Irish to confess their ignorance. At that moment, von Papen spoke. "As you can see, the plans are in motion. Now, had you come yesterday, I might have been able to help. The *Aud* is carrying arms, and it left Bremerhaven two days ago. The *Aud* and the U-boat which is carrying Herr Casement are under strict orders to maintain radio silence. They are to rendezvous, and Herr Casement is to go aboard the *Aud*. Failing a rendezvous, the U-boat captain has orders to put Herr Casement ashore. But with radio silence, I cannot order a delay."

The two Fenians looked even more distressed than before.

"Why is there a change in your plans?" von Papen asked, trying to sound a little less arrogant and a little more concerned.

"It's informers," Corbett confessed.

"And liaison," Sullivan added.

"I don't understand," von Papen hedged.

"The ship with the arms will arrive at Tralee at least two days before the rising is scheduled. The British are bound to find out. You can't hide a German ship for two days."

Von Papen was indignant. "But it is arriving on the day you requested."

"We've been informed that the rising is scheduled for Easter Sunday, April 23. That means the fine cargo of German guns will be sitting on some dock for two, three days—that's assuming they get ashore in the first place. With all due respect, sir, that means they will likely fall into the hands of the British. The freedom of Ireland will be set back another generation."

"If we could delay the shipment till the twenty second or even the morning of the twenty third . . . at least that way, if anything should go wrong, the British won't be given advance warning of the rising," Corbett implored.

Von Papen nodded. Confusion reigned supreme, and he cursed himself for getting involved with this tawdry little plot in the first place. "Yes, yes, I'll do my best," he promised. "But please, you should leave now."

Von Papen watched as the two left. Perhaps he ought to request German troops be landed in Ireland. He toyed with the idea. Then he thought: Perhaps just a recommendation.

5

April 21, 1916

Good Friday Evening

Tomorrow would make it one year exactly since Thomas Hughes had been killed. For Emerald, the year was an eternity of loneliness, of endless days filled with memories which were all too few.

There were days when Emerald took sheer pleasure in living, when she felt contented in her work and happy to come home and play with Tom. But then, as soon as she managed to forget, her sadness flooded over her and she returned to the melancholy of her mourning.

Enough of the past, Emerald commanded herself. Today is Good Friday. She lifted her green eyes to the cross and steadied herself on the pew in front of her. The church was nearly full, the priest was just finishing the service. It's the nearness of the anniversary of Thomas' death; it's the sight of incense; it's the accumulation of events—that's why I'm so maudlin. Think of Tom, think of Easter, think of joy, hope for tomorrow.

Emerald left church with the others and walked rapidly home. She stopped at Mrs. O'Shea's ground-floor flat and picked up little Tom. Mrs. O'Shea played the role of substitute grandmother so well that sometimes it seemed as if she were the real thing.

Tom was already asleep, so she took him to their room and put him in his bed. She returned to the center room and lit the lamp.

It was hardly a sumptuous flat, but it was homey. More important, she could afford it on her nurse's salary. Not that Seamus didn't help. He brought her many gifts, and Padraic sent clothes from America for her and little Tom.

The main room of her flat was furnished with a worn settee, a table, four chairs, and a wooden pantry. Perishables were purchased every day, but many other items were kept in the screened pantry, which was not vulnerable to insects. Emerald counted herself lucky that unlike a good many other flats in Dublin, this one did not seem to have rats or mice. The former were a danger to a small child, the latter an annoyance she could well do without.

The second room of the flat was a small bedroom and held Emerald's iron bed and little Tom's small bed. Seamus had made Tom's bed himself, carving on it gay shamrocks and little flowers he had painted red.

Down the corridor there was a communal bathroom shared by fourteen tenants. It had tubs and toilets, but every flat had its own sink and chamber pot.

Emerald went to the tiny stove and lit it. I'll have some tea, she thought. She prepared the tea. With Tom asleep, it was deadly silent, and his toys, which were piled neatly in a basket in the corner, looked dead and abandoned.

"Oh, I hate the silence!" Emerald said aloud. She sipped some tea.

"Emerald! Are you home!" It was Seamus, and his query was followed by a loud knock.

"Your shouting and knocking would wake the dead," she called back, opening the door.

Seamus looked sheepish. "Did I wake the baby?"

Emerald cocked her head and listened. "No," she answered, smiling. "I'm glad you've come," she said honestly.

"I have news," he said, plunking himself down at the table. His eyes twinkled, and once again Emerald saw the mischievous elf.

"Might I trouble you for a small glass of Mr. Jameson?"

Emerald went to the cupboard. Her small collection of dishes was arranged on the left side, while on the right there were condiments and a half-full bottle of John Jameson which she kept on hand for her brother and his friends, should they drop in. She poured the whiskey into a glass and handed it to him.

"You're all dressed in your uniform," she commented. Seamus was an Irish Volunteer.

Emerald smiled to herself. It didn't seem to matter if one were an Ulster Volunteer and supported the British like Mr. McArthur's friends, or if one were an Irish Volunteer and a nationalist like Seamus. They both shared a love of John Jameson, their Irish whiskey.

"We're going to have a march on Sunday! Now I want you to wear your Volunteer uniform too. I want you to wear it proudly."

Emerald shook her head. "It's hardly a uniform. I wear it to the hospital every day."

"Well, put a Volunteer's green sash on it! Drape it across your heart."

Emerald laughed. "I knew there was to be a march, but I didn't know it was to be a parade." She glanced at the bottle she was still holding. She leaned over the table and refilled Seamus' glass. Then she poured a small drink for herself.

"I see you're acquiring a fondness for whiskey," Seamus joked.

"Be gone with you," Emerald retorted. Then, more seriously, she looked at him and covered his hand with hers. "I'm glad you came. It's not a good weekend for me. It's the anniversary of Tom's death. . . . Today I lit a votive candle for our parents, for Tom, for Mrs. Higgins . . . Oh, Seamus, I keep losing the people I love."

Seamus blushed. "And you miss Padraic, too."

Emerald nodded.

"But we've waited a long time for Sunday's march, Emerald. Here, join me in a toast. Don't think about Tom just now." Seamus raised his glass. "To ourselves alone and a free Ireland!"

"If only the English prime minister, Mr. Asquith, and Mr. Carson could join us in a glass of whiskey. Mr. Jameson always lets us see each other more clearly. I know all of Ireland's problems could be solved with a little friendly understanding."

The prime minister of England might be willing, Seamus thought, but not Sir Edward Carson, M.P. and organizer of the Ulster Volunteers. No, Mr. Carson was the most charismatic leader to oppose home rule and Irish nationalism. There would be no drinking with him. Seamus burst out laughing at the thought. "Ah, Emerald. Mr. Jameson can do a lot, but drinking Irish whiskey with those bastards would not solve Ireland's problems. If only it were true! But I know you're not that naive! I know you know that action, not words, will bring our solution."

"And is marching action?" Emerald asked. "Will we accomplish more than a lovely walk down O'Connell Street on Sunday? Of course, we're assuming it doesn't rain." Emerald shook her head, and a curl fell on her forehead. "I think I'll take my letter to Padraic and mail it, just to make certain the march has some positive meaning."

"That's a fine idea. Yes, mail a letter, the post office is always open to legitimate business."

"Are you being serious, Seamus?"

"I'm serious. This march means a lot. It's you who are not taking it seriously enough."

"March, march, march to our graves, Seamus. Lord knows there's no trouble getting enough Irishmen for a march—all we ever do is march and talk to each other. We've marched against one thing and another since Brian Boru first raised the call to unite the kingdoms of Ireland over nine hundred years ago. Well, he succeeded in defeating the other chieftains, but their defeat left us vulnerable. And we're still marching, and we haven't got our freedom either. Tell me, Seamus, why can't the Irish and the British just sit down and talk?"

"In whose language?" Seamus returned sarcastically. "Emerald, I know you care, I know you have book learning. Emerald, I want you to feel!"

"I do feel," Emerald answered quietly. She studied her brother. Politics was his life, his reason for existence. And she found politics fascinating too, but in a different way. Seamus' brand of politics was militant, and militancy could easily turn into violence; her brand of politics involved negotiation, give and take.

"Will you come, then, will you march on Sunday? Perhaps after we've celebrated the Feast of the Resurrection, we'll find a way to talk to Mr. Asquith."

"Oh, I'll come," she replied.

Seamus lifted his glass and drained it. "One thing, could you bring your medical kit?"

"Of course," she replied, and thought to herself that doubtless Seamus had volunteered her. There was always the possibility of someone fainting or falling. And some of the old people had heart conditions. One never knew what a demonstration might produce in the way of minor injuries.

Seamus stood up and stretched. "Do you think I look like Brian Boru?"

"You look like all Irishmen, Seamus O'Hearn. You look cheerful and serious, loving and brooding, harmless and wild with anger; you're the face of Irish contradiction. Ah, Seamus, we sing on our way marching to the gallows."

"One day, Emerald O'Hearn Hughes, I'll be dancing a dance of freedom with you! An Irish independence jig! Maybe sometime after Sunday!"

"It's not easy to be optimistic after seven hundred years of British rule, Seamus."

"Try," he said, winking at her.

9

1

Saturday, April 22, 1916

Early Morning at Tralee Barracks

"You look a mite familiar, mate." His interrogator was oval-faced and rosy-cheeked, a mountain of a man who was as round as he was tall. He leaned over Sir Roger Casement and Sir Roger detected the distinct odor of garlic on the man's breath. He immediately thought of Germany and unconsciously winced.

The man drew back. "What's the matter?" he asked harshly, sensing Sir Roger's disdain of his person.

"You are ruining my good humor," Sir Roger replied. And it was so, Sir Roger thought. Only yesterday he had been in the best humor he had been in for a whole year—with the possible exception of the night he had spent in the exquisite company of Adel. But that brief interlude now seemed like a dream.

He had entered Tralee Bay on Good Friday morning aboard the U-boat which had orders to rendezvous with the *Aud*. But the rendezvous did not take place, so, following orders, the U-boat went on to Ballyheigue Bay, and there, in the early-morning hours, Sir Roger and his two companions had been put ashore on Banna Strand along the somber Kerry coast.

Sir Roger had felt instant ecstasy at being home in Ireland. He sent one of his companions on to Tralee for help, and the other carried a dispatch to Dublin. Alone, Sir Roger sat down near an old fort where he could watch both land and sea, and set about writing a poem to commemorate his homecoming. "The sandhills were full of skylarks, rising in the dawn . . ." He went on to write about the primroses, the violets, and the songs of the birds.

It was later that day that police had come from Ardfort Barracks and found him. They arrested him, and Sir Roger had bluffed, "My name is Richard Morten and I live in Denham, Buckinghamshire."

But they had not believed him, because he had no papers and no passport. And doubtless, he reflected, they noticed the wet sand caked on his trousers. Nonetheless, they had not questioned him extensively. Instead, they moved him to Tralee Barracks for the night. But now he faced an interrogator.

"You do look familiar," the man repeated.

"I'm quite certain we've never met," Sir Roger said coldly. And implicit in his tone was all the charming snobbery of his class. It was a snobbery which he admitted; indeed, he cultivated it. It was useful, and now he employed it, noting with pleasure the discomfort it caused the oaf who kept questioning him.

"We could have met," the dim-witted sergeant insisted.

"Not likely," Sir Roger retorted, looking at his nails. They were grubby, badly in need of a manicure.

The man was studying Sir Roger's face closely, and again the odor of garlic attacked Sir Roger's olfactory senses.

"You cut yourself," his interrogator said triumphantly, as if he were Sherlock Holmes and had just made a major deduction.

"How clumsy of me," Sir Roger replied dryly.

The man reached out and stroked Sir Roger's cheek, and Sir Roger jumped. "I'll have none of that!" he intoned angrily.

The man jumped backward, and a distinctly hurt look filled his eyes. "Just business," he muttered. "I ain't no fairy."

Sir Roger swallowed a smirk. "I should think not," he said with indignation.

"Your cheeks and chin are whiter than the rest of your face." The man's dull eyes seemed to light up slightly, and Sir Roger felt a chill run down his spine. The dim-witted dolt had tumbled to it.

"You had a beard! That's it! You've recently shaved off a ruddy beard."

Sir Roger fought to keep his expression bland, but the man literally ran from the room and returned a few seconds later holding a picture in his hands.

"Ain't no doubt about it!" he uttered with a note of true triumph. "You're Sir Roger Casement!"

"And you are a nit-witted, fat-bellied bore," Sir Roger returned.

"Don't matter, governor. I'm sending you on to Dublin. Right now! Ah, a ruddy, fluffy lordship of a spy you are. I always said the upper classes had too much as was good for 'um. Dissipation, aye, that's what it is."

Sir Roger blinked and fought the desire to put him in his place. No, he decided, that might make things worse. Besides, he was being sent to Dublin, and with any luck at all, he would be liberated during the rising on Sunday. He sighed internally. If worse came to worst, he could always go to America until Ireland was free.

2

Saturday, April 22, 1916

Early Morning, Dublin Barracks

"Captain Bowen-Colthurst, reporting as ordered, sir!" Bowen-Colthurst was a descendant of the settlers brought to Ireland by Cromwell. He was a Protestant, a man of background, a loyal supporter of the British crown. And on this chilly early morning in April, he was also all spit and polish.

Colonel Henry Falconer looked up and winced. "I'm not deaf," he mumbled. At that moment, Bowen-Colthurst felt intense apprehension. He wanted to bolt from the room and reenter more quietly. He was well aware of his own shrill voice.

Colonel Henry Falconer was in his early sixties. He had been wounded in the leg while serving in the Transvaal, and as a result, he moved slowly. Obviously he thought slowly too, Bowen-Colthurst observed. The proof of that assumption lay in the fact that all of Falconer's fellow officers, men who had been at Sandhurst with him, were now in senior positions, and some were even generals.

Bowel-Colthurst cleared his throat and apologized for his voice.

"It's all right, quite all right," Falconer replied. "Actually, I'm glad you're enthusiastic. This isn't an easy post, you know. It's tiresome playing nursemaid to a pack of whining Irishmen, not to mention the convalescing soldiers who make up this regiment."

"I know, sir."

Colonel Falconer shuffled the papers on his desk. He knew what was there, but he enjoyed the effect. "These are . . . ah, somewhat ominous reports here. They will not do," he mumbled, somewhat more loudly.

"Pardon, sir?" Bowen-Colthurst could hardly make out Falconer's mumbling. He leaned closer.

Falconer looked up. "Sorry, old chap. I was merely thinking aloud. A trick I learned from Kitchener at Khartoum. It serves to clear the mind of useless information. Lord Kitchener always talks under his breath. British mumbling is what made the Empire great, what?"

Bowen-Colthurst nodded. Falconer was more than a doddering old fool; he was an idiot too, he decided. "Yes, sir!"

Falconer cleared his throat. "Another of Kitchener's tricks, Captain—"

"Yes, sir."

"Please don't interrupt me till I've finished speaking." Falconer had suddenly developed a fatherly tone, and Bowen-Colthurst knew it to be yet another of Kitchener's affectations—something he did while speaking to junior officers.

"Sorry, sir."

"Yes, very well . . . as I was saying, there seems to be some sort of trouble brewing here in Dublin right now, Captain. Our intelligence branch has gathered these reports on the activities of known terrorist organizations. By the way, do pass on my compliments to Captain Spear for his fine work in assembling these data."

"Yes, sir." Captain Bowen-Colthurst felt like retching. He disliked Captain Spear. No, he hated him.

"There's a serious shortcoming in this report, however . . ." Colonel Falconer paused for effect. "There's no conclusion to be derived from it. We seem to know something is about to happen, but we don't know when, what, or where."

Captain Bowen-Colthurst tried to keep his voice even; he held his facial expression, trying to make himself look bland and efficient. There mustn't be a hint of personal triumph in my voice, he thought. I must be calm, I must appear concerned. "Yes, sir." A little more rope, he decided, hoping that he had not lost this golden opportunity.

"I don't like it one bit," Falconer intoned solemnly. "Remember the faulty intelligence information concerning the enemy's strength at Balaklava? That caused a real setback for the Empire, I'll tell you. We cannot have a repetition of that nature." Colonel Falconer's lips quivered and he leaned back, recalling Balaklava. " 'Theirs not to make reply, Theirs not to reason why, Theirs but to do and die. Into the valley of death rode the six hundred!' " He paused and wiped his eyes. " 'Cannon to right of them, Cannon to left of them, Cannon in front of them, Volleyed and thundered; Stormed at with shot and shell, While horse and hero fell, They that had fought so well, Came thro' the jaws of hell, All that was left of them, Left of six hundred. When will their glory fade? O the wild charge they made! All the world wondered. Honour the charge they made! Honour the Light Brigade.' " Colonel Falconer's voice dropped and he sniffed. "God, I love Tennyson. What a tribute to Balaklava!"

Bowen-Colthurst resisted the terrible temptation to add that it was a tribute made possible only by bad intelligence reports.

"Do you have any thoughts, Bowen-Colthurst?"

"May I speak freely, sir?"

"By all means," Falconer answered.

"It appears to me, sir, that Captain Spear has made a rather nasty mess of things. As you know, he lost track of some of the so-called Irish Republican Brotherhood's ringleaders more than fourteen days ago. And only recently, two of Spear's informers were fished out of the River Liffey with their throats slit. Rather gruesome, I must confess." Bowen-Colthurst mouthed the words. In point of fact, he didn't consider the throat slittings a bit gruesome. In fact, he looked forward to slitting some throats himself, all under the Defense of the Realm Act which suspended civil rights.

"Bloody kaffirs all of them," Colonel Falconer stormed with disgust. He referred to all groups other than white Anglo-Saxon Protestant English as kaffirs. "Can you draw any conclusions?"

"Indeed. These Irish thugs have been talking endlessly about the march tomorrow. With the disappearance of their leaders and the brutal execution of our informants, I believe it would be prudent to assume that more than a mere protest march is being planned. I believe we are facing a bloody insurrection against His Majesty's government in Ireland."

"How can you be certain of this?" Falconer asked.

"A process of elimination, sir. I see no other possible explanation, sir. We generally know every move they make, before they make it. That we know nothing suggests to me that something big will happen. Their security wouldn't be this tight if all they were truly planning was a march. It's more, sir. Much, much more."

"I do catch your logic, quite clearly, actually. What do you suggest?" Falconer asked.

Captain Bowen-Colthurst moved over to a map of Dublin. "With your permission, sir."

"Certainly, certainly."

"Here, here, and here." Captain Bowen-Colthurst indicated the bridges, using a pointer. "I propose a detachment of regulars posted and fully armed. Furthermore, I have taken the liberty of speaking to my counterpart in the Royal Navy, strictly off the record, sir. But there will be increased guards at the port facilities. All roads leading in and out of the city will be closely watched, and all suspicious persons detained for questioning."

Colonel Falconer leaned back with a satisfied expression on

his face, and it was at that moment that Captain Bowen-Colthurst knew he would play an important role in command.

"It sounds convincing, Captain."

"Sir, not a pip will squeak in Dublin tomorrow without our permission. We shall have the element of surprise, and we will nip any insurrection rose in the bud. Tomorrow shall be a victory for the Empire, and the Irish will have been given yet another lesson. God knows, one day they might finally learn to respect and submit to the British crown!"

"Very good, Captain. Those are your orders, England expects you to do your duty, and so you shall!"

Bowen-Colthurst saluted and turned on his heel. We can't have a defeat, he thought. Tennyson is dead.

3

Saturday, April 22, 1916

Noon, Dublin

James Connolly—Jim to his friends—was the first to arrive at Clancey's pub. A commander in the Citizen's Army and a prominent labor leader, he was in his late forties, a short, chubby, good-natured leprechaun in outward appearance. Jim Connolly was already a hero as a result of his valiant role during the Dublin transport workers' strike in 1913. He was also a cautious man, because with his reputation and a known face, he couldn't be too careful. Especially now.

Clancey's, he concluded, was a reasonably safe pub, and since it was lunchtime, the five men he expected to join him would filter in at five-minute intervals, likely unnoticed owing to the usual crowd of hungry, thirsty noon-hour customers.

James Connolly leaned over and ordered a pint of Guinness; then he slowly made his way down the stairs to the basement meeting room.

By one P.M. they were all assembled: Padraic Pearse, a fine leader, organizer, and poet; Padraic's younger brother, William Pearse, who was a quiet sensitive young man assisting Padraic in all his endeavors; Michael Mallin, another organizer; Sean Heuston, a tall red-haired youth with sky-blue eyes. Sean was a charter member of the Fianna Nae Eireann, the Boy Scouts organized by the Countess Markievicz; and John MacBride, a man in his late thirties. He had fought against the British in South Africa.

Michael Mallin shook his head and gulped down some Guinness. "What in God's sweet name are we doing here in the heart of Dublin less than twenty-four hours before the rising?"

"What indeed," Jim Connolly muttered.

Heuston and MacBride joined in.

"Imagine what someone would get for turning the lot of us in," MacBride joked.

"Just being together offers proof of conspiracy," Sean added.

Padraic Pearse, who had called them together, tapped his hand on the table as if to silence their collective objections. "I've called you here to announce that we must delay the rising."

His words hung for a minute in the sudden silence they created. It was as if each of the five others had been struck dumb.

Sunday had been planned as no other rising had been planned. And the time was right. It was right internally as well as internationally. Britain was bound, gagged, and tied up in a war with Germany; Irish-Americans would see to it that maximum pressure was put on the U.S. government to pressure the British.

"No, the rising must take place!" Mallin said firmly. "People can't be held back once a pitch has been reached."

Pearse stood up and set his mug down on the table with a bang. "It's only to be delayed by twenty-four hours, there's no need to fear!"

There was an audible collective sigh of relief.

"There's been a delay in the arms shipment to our men in the west. As you all well know, they'll not come unarmed."

"To hell with them!" Connolly exploded. "Delays are dangerous. There's too many people to be told and too many who could find out because of the telling. We don't need the westerners!"

Heuston, the young good-looking firebrand of Fianna Nae Eireann, reached out for Connolly's arm. "He's right, the schedule ought to be maintained. The orders have been given. We can't recall or notify some of our people."

"From the roads of Kilkenny to the plains of South Africa," John MacBride intoned dramatically. "I've been fighting against the British since I was twenty. Now, when I was in Africa, I observed these ants, giant ants they were, large and black. But like the Irish, they had no homes save the temporary clay coverings out on the grass. And like the Irish, they were always on the march. But when they marched, they flattened everything in sight, so great were their numbers. Tales had it that they could devour a tethered horse in seconds, leaving only the skeleton tied

to the trough. I once heard tell they walked, only walked across
a drunk man's legs, and they left scars near three inches deep.
So I asked, how was it I saw so few in the grass, but when they
marched, I saw millions? And I was told that they send out an
electrical impulse caused by their excitement and their energy
and that all the ants for one hundred miles pick up that impulse
and join the march.'' John MacBride paused and relished the
silence he always created when he spoke. He had made his
analogy, and now he waited for the point to sink in.

John MacBride looked about; then he continued. "I don't care
if the boys from County Clare and Limerick will miss our little
party. It was never the intention for them to be here in the first
place. On Sunday we liberate Dublin, and on Monday we are
joined by our loyal brothers and sisters from throughout the land.
Wasn't that the plan, Padraic Pearse? Weren't we to send out the
electrical waves, the energy to excite all Ireland?''

Padraic nodded. "It's true. But we ought to be reasonable.
We still do not have enough men to occupy key positions, let
alone hold Dublin. We need those men and we need those arms.
I say a delay of one day will not hurt us.''

"Why not wait another week?'' Connolly mocked. "Perhaps
by then all of Ireland will be armed and ready to march. If
they're not, well, we can wait another week, and then another
and another. God, man, seven hundred years of waiting! And
some waited for blessed, promised home rule, but the British put
it on the shelf again till their war is over!''

"Be still, James Connolly!'' shouted Michael Mallin. "When
the Brotherhood brought you into our plan, we had to lock you
away in Kilkenny for close to a week before you accepted the
discipline and orders of the Brotherhood! As for home rule and
waiting for it, it had nothing to do with any of us. Not one of us
would accept home rule! We want our freedom, man! Absolute
and unconditional!''

"And that's what I want too!'' Connolly retorted defensively.

"Then give us one little day, Jim.'' Padraic looked at him
steadily. "Give me one day. I'll give you a free Ireland!''

Connolly drained his mug. "I'll give you one day. I've been
scratching at the thought of Mr. MacBride's ants, I have.''

There was laughter, and Jim Connolly leaned back in his
chair. "If we lose, we win . . . and if we win, we win,'' he
mused.

"What does that mean?'' Pearse queried.

"Ask me on Tuesday next week,'' Connolly answered.

4

Saturday, April 22, 1916

2 P.M., Dublin

Emerald walked toward St. Stephen's Green, one of Dublin's largest parks.

"It's a fine outing for both of us," she said to little Tom as he peered up at her from his carriage. "And soon you'll be running around the green and I'll be chasing you." She chucked him under the chin and he giggled, displaying two teeth.

"I look forward to your walking, Tom. But not to chasing you all over. Now, you'll have to be good today," she continued. "One of the boys will watch you, but I have to help the countess. See, my kit is right there, tucked down at the bottom of your carriage. I'll need that, because I'm going to be giving lessons today."

Emerald adjusted her bonnet and tilted the pram so it would go over the curb. She was fortunate to have the pram. The countess had obtained it from a friend, but it was in fine condition.

Saturday was training day for the Fianna Nae Eireann, and Emerald enjoyed watching them as well as teaching them first aid. They were young and full of life, joking and yet polite. In a way, however, the boys seemed older than Emerald knew them to be. Perhaps, she reasoned, it was their good manners, or the fact that they spoke and read Gaelic, a language she was trying to learn.

"First aid is something everyone should know," the countess told the boys. "You will listen carefully and you will treat Mrs. Hughes with great respect. She will be your teacher. What she teaches you could save your life."

Emerald thought the countess overstated it a bit, but on the other hand, she felt the more skills the lads had, the better, and she admired the countess' dedication to learning.

Added to that was a more personal factor. The countess had done a great deal for Seamus and for her as well. Seamus had learned to read and write working with the lads of Fianna Nae Eireann, and he learned history too. Now, thanks to those skills, he had a job and a future.

And from the day Seamus introduced Emerald to the countess, the countess had been kind in the extreme. She helped Emerald

get a job at the hospital and she passed on clothing for little
Tom. "It's nothing," she would always say. "I have so many
wealthy friends and they're so wasteful! Imagine buying a baby
lace clothing, they grow so fast! Well, here, you take it. Better
to have it worn twice."

Emerald regarded the countess as a strange mixture: practical
and a dreamer; feminine and military; disciplined, yet deeply
emotional.

Emerald approached St. Stephen's Green and in the distance
saw the Countess Markievicz. She was dressed in her semimilitary
garb, and as usual, it looked several sizes too large. Even though
the clothing gave her an ungainly appearance, the countess still
managed to assume the attitude of the Polish court, where she
had spent her honeymoon.

Emerald watched her for a moment and thought that her
slender, angular body might have been clothed in the finest silks
from the Orient instead of field-gray army issue.

"Settle down, settle down!" the countess blew her whistle,
and the hum of conversation became instant silence as the group
of boys sat on the grass.

"They're all excited about tomorrow's march. Everyone in
Dublin is preparing," the countess said by way of explanation.
Then, looking at them again, she added, "And they're here in
their work clothes so they won't get their uniforms dirty before
the march."

"I thought they looked a scruffy lot," Emerald joked.

"It's better for them to look smart tomorrow."

She's not a woman of great humor, Emerald thought. The
countess was, however, endowed with other qualities. She was
selfless and dedicated, and like Seamus, she was deeply involved
in politics and in freedom for Ireland. Indeed, that was how the
Fianna Nae Eireann had come about in the first place.

The countess studied Baden-Powell's Boy Scout organization
and decided to train the future leaders of a new free Ireland in a
similar way. Privately, to other nationalists, she confided her
political view that "Our struggle will never be settled in
Westminster, but rather on the streets and in the countryside.
Our young men must be trained for combat; they must have
healthy bodies and educated minds."

With the posture of a ballerina and the force of a sergeant
major, the countess blew her whistle a second time.

"We have a busy schedule today," she announced, "and the
sooner we start, the sooner we'll be finished."

The countess made a long speech in Gaelic. It seemed to

concern marching tomorrow; she said something about Sean Heuston and something about being on time.

At that moment the countess stopped speaking Gaelic and turned to Emerald, speaking in English. "Tourniquets?"

Emerald nodded.

The countess turned back to her young men. She knew how to get them to pay attention. "You remember back two years ago when the British attacked us in Phoenix Park? Do you remember or have you heard of little Michael McSorley? He was badly injured, poor lad. And though he was dragged from the spot, his wound was not properly tended. Sure enough, gangrene set in and little Michael lost his leg. Now, if the people tending him had known first aid, that little boy would have two legs today. Now, it's bad enough for the British to harm us," the countess concluded, "but it's twice as bad when we harm ourselves as the result of neglect and lack of knowledge. So now you listen to Mrs. Hughes."

Emerald leaned over to the countess. "Could you please not translate into Gaelic while I'm demonstrating? I get nervous enough when I'm speaking. I am improving with my Gaelic, though." She always felt she had to apologize about her lack of proficiency in the language.

The countess merely nodded her agreement. "Excuse me," she said abstractedly.

Emerald watched as she walked off toward two men who were some distance off, under the shade of the trees. One of them looked like Willie Pearse, Emerald noticed as she turned back to her pupils.

Taking her lead from the countess' example, Emerald began her course. "Now, if it's at all possible, you should wash your own hands well before you begin treating a wound. If you can't, try to use some disinfectant, like rubbing alcohol, or just plain alcohol." She paused at the twitter that ran through her audience. "I know some of you carry whiskey," she said, arching her eyebrow. "Well, it's good for more than warming your gut. You can use it on wounds and you can use it on your own hands. But when it's possible, use soap and water. Be sure to wash around the abrasion or laceration and remove all visible dirt particles. Now, most wounds will stop bleeding by themselves, unless a large blood vessel has been severed. If that happens, you have to apply a tourniquet above the wound. We'll come back to that in a moment. First let's talk about bandaging the laceration or abrasion."

"What about gunshot wounds?" one of the lads piped up.

Emerald frowned. She almost never referred to gunshot wounds specifically, but every week someone asked about them. It was a constant reminder of the day-to-day violence, the ever-present possibility of harm coming to one of their number, and Emerald realized that she hated being reminded of that reality. Unconsciously she glanced over at Tom in his carriage. He was asleep, peaceful and watched over. But he was going to grow up like these boys, victims of Ireland's troubles. They grow up too fast, Emerald thought. One day they're playing soldier; the next, like Thomas Hughes, they're dead. And how would they die? They would die fighting British tyranny in Ireland, or defending Britain from another tyranny. Who was right? The answer was everyone and no one, Emerald concluded. Seamus and the countess were right about some elements of the situation, but they were wrong about others. And Tom Hughes had been right and wrong too.

"What about gunshot wounds?" the boy persisted.

"It's better to leave the bullet in till a proper doctor comes. Yours is first aid, and it means just that, the *first* aid a victim gets. Now, take a knife wound. Sometimes if you pull the knife out, you can't stop the bleeding. It's the knife that is preventing the bleeding, and when you pull it, it's like taking the cork out of a bottle. But with both a knife and a gunshot, you have to clean around the wound. In the case of a bullet, it can be taken out later if there's no internal damage and if the patient doesn't have an infection. Now, let's demonstrate . . ."

Emerald pointed to one of the boys, and he came forward. Emerald drew a large X on his leg with a piece of chalk. "This is your wound," she explained. "Now, let's say it's a gunshot and the skin has been torn and these little vessels under the skin are broken. What are you going to do first?"

One of the boys, Sean, came over and knelt down. He began to speak, and Emerald glanced up. The countess had returned and stood behind her; she looked distressed.

Sean finished his explanation. "That's good," Emerald praised. "Now, if the bleeding doesn't stop, it's because a large blood vessel has been severed. In that case, we apply a tourniquet above the wound." Emerald took out a piece of triangular white cloth. "You carry this shape cloth in your first-aid kit, and it's normally used for slings. Now, if you don't have one, you can use a scarf, or any piece of material this long. Now, let me demonstrate. Rory, would you come here, please?"

Rory came immediately, and Emerald slowly wound the cloth.

"Now, you insert a stick here—you can use any piece of wood—even a shillelagh will do. If you have a watch and chalk, you will mark the time on the tourniquet. Now, this is important, really important. The tourniquet must be released every fifteen minutes and not one second later, although sooner is all right. If it's not released every fifteen minutes, the tissues that are fed by the flowing blood will die and you might lose your arm or leg. Now, if you don't have a watch, you have to count the seconds. There are 720 seconds in twelve minutes, so count to 720 and you will have a margin for error."

Emerald took a breath. "So the most important things to do are keep the wound clean and stop the bleeding. I think most of you know that maggots can be used to clean infections out of wounds. And you all know there's not a garbage heap in Dublin without maggots."

"They're fly eggs!" one of the boys complained.

Emerald smiled. "Larvae," she corrected. "And as sterile as flies are full of germs.

"Now, the third point is to be certain to release the tourniquet. Any questions?"

A boy in the back stood up and fired off a question in Gaelic.

"He wants to know if it makes any difference which way you wind the tourniquet," the countess translated.

Emerald shook her head. "No difference at all."

The countess stepped front and center once again. For good measure, she blew her whistle again. "There's been a change of plans," she revealed. "We are not going to march tomorrow."

A groan went up instantly from the assembled group. The disappointment appeared universal, as if they thought tomorrow's march would be different from all the other marches. Emerald was puzzled; she was also aware of a vague suspicion.

"Hush!" the countess ordered. "You call yourselves future soldiers of Ireland and you whine like wee little babies who cannot go outside and play." Her words of shame worked instant wonders. The boys were silent; they stood at attention.

"We are not marching tomorrow, but we will march on Easter Monday."

There were no groans now. But there was still some disappointment evident Youth, thought Emerald, cannot be delayed for even one day.

Dismissed with an anticlimactic shrill of the whistle, the boys romped off across the green. Some would be off for a little afternoon football, others would be heading home to do chores for their parents, still others would return to the streets where they lived when they were not working in the mills.

"You did well today," the countess said, turning toward Emerald.

"I'll be glad when I master Gaelic," Emerald confessed.

"Keep at it. It'll mean more to you if you keep reminding yourself that it was once a forbidden tongue. Nothing is more important than the preservation of culture, our way of life and our language."

"And religion?" Emerald asked.

"You know I'm not Catholic," the countess confessed. "Though I am thinking of converting. Yes, our religion is important, that's why I'm considering conversion. Out there, Emerald, out in the rolling hills among the ruins of ancient Irish castles and Viking strongholds, out there hidden away are a thousand rock altars where mass was secretly said beneath the blue sky and God's own cathedral. That which is threatened grows strong, Emerald. The Irish have grown strong. We have freedom of religion, we're being educated, we're becoming a disciplined people, and when we return to the Gaelic, we'll be returned to our history. Study it, Emerald, it's the mother tongue of all Ireland, the key to our glorious past. We're Irish Nationalists, Emerald. We relish our Celtic revival."

In spite of her reservations, reservations caused largely by a true revulsion to violence, Emerald felt the strength of the countess' convictions. Small wonder the woman could bring rowdy little boys to utter silence and thrill them with inspirational words and patriotic poems. She was truly a charismatic woman who felt that women, especially Irish women, were equal to any task.

"You've done a great deal," Emerald said, knowing that it was an understatement. Once the toast of Dublin society, the wife of a Polish count, the countess could have had a very different kind of life from the one she voluntarily led.

The countess looked at Emerald thoughtfully, and raising one eyebrow, she smiled sardonically. "It's my nature," she said in a near-whisper. "We're different, Emerald. You're a natural healer, a peacemaker. I'm a rebel. And I'll never complete my rebellion—it's only that I have chosen to order my causes. If I weren't Irish, I would be rebelling against the power of men over women. If I were English, I imagine I would be standing side by side with Pankhurst, demanding the vote for women. But I can't do that first because I'm Irish. We Irish women can't demand our rights till our men have theirs . . . we're all oppressed.

And after men and women, there's children. Tell me, Emerald Hughes, why should a little child labor in a factory, why should a little one work his young life away, till he's finally struck down by tuberculosis? No, I expect I'm in no danger of running out of injustices to rebel against.''

"Does injustice have to be fought with violence? I would fight those same injustices," Emerald replied.

The countess tilted her head and studied Emerald. "We're both fighters," she gave in. "And let me say I have a feeling about you. I've had it since the day Seamus brought you to me. You're not the rebel I am, not in the active sense. But one day, Emerald Hughes, you're going to have power, you're going to have the opportunity to redress injustices. I feel it."

Emerald laughed and took the countess' arm. "First a rebel, now a soothsayer," she teased.

3

Saturday, April 22, 1916

6 P.M.

James Connolly sat in the untidy flat, relaxed in an easy chair, with his large feet up on a nearby table. He held a glass of whiskey in his hand; his bulk filled the chair.

Connolly was a melancholy man, a fanatic, but also a romantic with a sense of history, or more precisely, the poetry of history: that ebb and flow of conflict, resolution, and progress. He hardly expected the rising to achieve anything but a new and poignant set of martyrs, and these martyrs, he believed, would cause both British guilt and Irish anger. Thus, if the rising was a failure and they were all killed, it would be a success. And if by some fluke of history or fate it was a success, well, then it was a success.

Connolly drained his glass and looked around. This wasn't his flat, and for that reason he always had to think where things were. Yes, that was right. The bottles were kept in the sideboard. He pulled himself out of the chair and ambled over to the sideboard. He fished for the bottle, then poured himself another drink.

James Connolly had moved into the flat of an acquaintance for the few days before the rising in case the British got wind of it and of his involvement. He sent his casual acquaintance off to the west country and congratulated himself that only two of the council members even knew where he was. The trouble with the Irish, even he was willing to admit, was that they all talked too much and too loud.

He took a sip of whiskey and turned back toward the chair. He stopped short at the slight tap on the door. He set down the glass and walked to the door on tiptoes. "Who is it?" he asked in a voice pitched higher than his own.

"Sean, Sean Heuston."

Connolly shrugged and made a face to himself. But he opened the door a crack. "Are you alone?" He looked furtively up and down the hall.

Sean grumbled his reply and Connolly opened the door, allowing Sean to slip in.

"You look exhausted," Connolly observed.

Sean nodded. "I've been over half of Dublin. I was at Clancey's this afternoon and I learned something astounding, really astounding, tragic, terrible—we can't go through with the rising, and so I've spread the word."

Connolly's eyes grew wide and round. "You did what?" he bellowed loud enough so that the occupants of the entire four-story flat might have started upright.

"Sir, we absolutely can't go through with the rising."

"Sit down!" Connolly shoved Sean into a chair, and heading for the sideboard, grasped the entire bottle. Shit, he thought, what was this young idiot talking about? He gulped down some more whiskey. "Explain." He spit out the word, so angry he was unable to say anything else.

"Sir, I've learned that the arms shipment was captured—fortunately, before the British could take possession, the Germans blew it up. So there won't be any arms, I mean not even on Monday. They're all at the bottom of Tralee Bay. That means the westerners won't come, because they won't come unarmed. And that's not the worst of it, sir. The worst is that Sir Roger Casement has been captured."

"And this is why you have taken it upon yourself to call off the rising?" He could hardly control himself.

"Yes, sir."

"Well, my fine young man," Connolly said mockingly, "you'd better just move your bloody arse and unspread the word. The council met and there's nothing you've said that makes the least bit of difference."

"But, sir," Heuston stuttered, struggling to sound respectful even though he was totally confused, "I thought we were depending on the boys from the west."

"What the hell were you doing earlier this afternoon?" Connolly could feel the heat in his face, and he hoped he didn't have a stroke. "First, we are going to inspire the ants to march, as Mr. MacBride put it. Then we are going to create martyrs, who will create the force that will free Ireland. I almost hope I survive this rising," Connolly mumbled. "But in case I don't, I intend to pass on my last wishes! For should you fall in battle, Sean Heuston, I would want to see the proper number of years devoted to your memorial."

"Thank you very much, sir."

Connolly pinched his lips together. Heuston was a moron; he was made for martyrdom. He was brave, beautiful, and the stuff of legends. He was also stupid. "I know, we'll change the name of Kingsbridge Station and name it after you. That will be a fitting memorial!"

"Why's that, sir?" Heuston looked genuinely pleased.

"Simple. You remind me of a train station. A most imposing facade, tall and strong. And like a train station, everything goes in one end and out the other," Connolly said, rather proud of his convoluted insult.

"Mr. Connolly, sir, well—"

"Mr. Heuston," Connolly interjected, "I will be simple and direct in the fond hope that all I say will be understood: we rise on Monday, period. There is *no*, and I repeat *no*, change of plans. Do you understand?"

Sean Heuston looked at the floorboards and shuffled his feet. "Yes, sir," he replied meekly.

"Good, and God help you if you can't undo all the damage you have done. Go!"

"Sir?"

"Yes," Connolly replied. He felt strained beyond all endurance.

"If you're angry with me, will you still name the train station after me?"

"Shit!" Connolly swore. "Get going! Get out of here!"

6

Saturday, April 22, 1916

7 P.M.

Emerald had left Tom with Mrs. O'Shea so that she could do her afternoon shopping. And what a shopping! The greengrocer's had been nearly out of everything, and the line at the butcher's shop ran right straight out the door and down the street. Then, at the dry-goods store Emerald had stood in line for another half-hour. Of course it was a holiday weekend and the stores would not be open again until Tuesday. And of course Easter Sunday was the feast that followed the forty days of Lent, so all the stores stocked special foods and all the women in Dublin were stocking up. But to Emerald it seemed as if the shops were more crowded than usual, even for a holiday. I did leave St. Stephen's Green late, she reminded herself, and I did bring Tom home to Mrs. O'Shea, which means I started late with the shopping. I always leave everything till the last minute, she admitted to herself. But in the end, she had gotten all the groceries and three bottles of whiskey for company. Surely Seamus and his friends would come by after the march on Monday. It was best to be prepared.

"I'm sorry I'm late," Emerald apologized to Mrs. O'Shea. "The stores were packed! I never dreamed they would be so crowded."

"You'd think people were preparing for a siege," Mrs. O'Shea commented, "instead of Easter and the rising of our Lord."

Emerald smiled and took Tom into her arms. "I'd better be getting upstairs and putting this all away."

Mrs. O'Shea held out her arms to Emerald, who was already overburdened with bundles. "Come on, let me carry something upstairs for you."

"Thank you," Emerald murmured. She didn't know what she would do without Mrs. O'Shea, who always seemed to be there when needed and who cared for Tom with kindness and affection. But then, Maggie O'Shea had brought Tom into the world, and as midwife and adoptive grandmother she had loved him from the beginning.

They reached Emerald's flat and deposited the bundles. Emerald put Tom in the playpen Seamus had made for him. "Would you like some tea?" she invited.

"Heavens no, not now. I have to be getting back to my dinner, the boys will be home soon." Mrs. O'Shea had six children, and four of her grown boys still lived with her. She turned and bustled down the corridor. "I'll see you in the morning," she called out as she left.

Emerald finished unpacking the groceries and putting them away. Then she sat down at the table and looked over at her son in his playpen.

Little Tom had Thomas Hughes's large soft eyes and ivory complexion. And although his hair was still fine and soft, it was the same color as Thomas Hughes's hair.

"You're going to look like your daddy," Emerald said sadly.

She sat for a time and watched as Tom became engrossed in his wooden blocks, but in spite of his giggles and baby sounds, the room was silent and the silence seemed to close in on Emerald.

"We're alone," she said to him. "I've been avoiding this moment all day long, but you won't tell anyone that I'm not very brave, will you?" The baby looked up innocently and smiled.

Emerald covered her eyes with her hand. Running . . . running, all day I've been running from the fact that today is the anniversary of your father's death.

Emerald got up and walked across the room to the dresser. She took out a box. It had been opened before, but it still had its original paper wrapped around it. It was addressed to Mrs. Emma Hughes and the return address was the War Office. Emerald carefully removed the paper and lifted the lid of the box. On top was a letter, a short formal letter that simply explained that the items enclosed were her husband's personal belongings, which were being returned to her. It included a medal and a line of thanks.

Emerald had opened the box when it first came a year ago. Since then it had sat in the drawer, untouched, a sacred object that conjured up far too many emotions for Emerald to risk feeling.

"Thanks for your life," she said bitterly as she looked at the letter. What "thanks" could there be for a man's life? She took Thomas Hughes's wool scarf out of the box and held it to her lips, kissing it tenderly.

A letter, a medal, a scarf, an identification tag, a picture of Emerald in her nurse's uniform, a rosary, and a plain prayer book inside which was pressed a lock of her own hair.

"The possessions of an Irishman," Emerald said aloud. Tears were running down her face and she bit her lip and closed her eyes. Stop being maudlin, she tried to tell herself. You might yet get married again and find some happiness. But it didn't matter how many times she told herself about a possible future; the thought meant nothing. One had to love to marry, and I still love Thomas Hughes, she admitted. I still love him passionately, so passionately that I can't yet give him up.

10

1
___

April 23, 1916

Dawn, Easter Sunday

Captain Bowen-Colthurst surmised that Colonel Falconer was still fast asleep, dressed in his nightshirt, with his foot warmer gone quite cold. "Let sleeping idiots lie," Bowen-Colthurst muttered as he peered into the utter darkness. Today is going to be my day of utter and complete triumph.

Bowen-Colthurst shivered slightly. It was always chilliest in the hour before dawn, and April was a damp month in any case. Of course, Dublin Castle, the seat of the British government in Dublin was always damp.

He sipped his cup of tea as he looked forward with relish to the day's events. In a minute he would go out and speak to his men. If his intelligence reports were correct, this would be a day of attempted treachery. And the fact seemed clear enough. The German arms shipment, the arrest of Sir Roger Casement, the disappearance of the known leaders . . . Bowen-Colthurst smiled on one count. Sir Roger Casement was to be sent to Dublin, but a change of orders sent him directly to London. That, Bowen-Colthurst decided, would prevent any organized attempt to rescue him. Bowen-Colthurst shook his head. Personally, he'd have slit Sir Roger's throat if it had been up to him. The man was a queer and a lunatic, he was a traitor of the first order, and he deserved to die in the slowest, most painful way possible. Little beads of sweat broke out on Bowen-Colthurst's forehead and a chill ran down his spine. He shook his head. Casement was gone; his main concern was today.

It's a real pity the colonel wouldn't push for a proclamation of martial law, he thought. Then I could arrest every man-jack one of those damn troublemaking croppie rebels.

On reflection, however, this did seem a more prudent course of action. Nip an insurrection in the bud. Almost all of the men serving under him had relatives fighting the Germans. They certainly wouldn't look kindly on this Irish stab in the back. My God, the Irish actually wanted to make the Germans their allies. Yes, a lot of Irish blood will be spilled today, he decided. The thought excited him.

Captain Bowen-Colthurst got up from the table and proceded outside. "Men!" he called as row on row of his men snapped to attention. "You have a great and noble duty to perform today. The Empire is being threatened, and we are the first line of defense!" Captain Bowen-Colthurst strained to hear himself as he spoke. Sometimes the men snickered because his voice was so shrill. People were always making fun of him. He paused; then, gripping his coat jacket, he continued.

"We shall not let, we must not let England down! Even as our brave brothers are fighting in France, victims of brutal chemical warfare used by the Germans, we must let them know their rear is safe!"

There was a slight twitter at the captain's turn of phrase, and he himself did not miss it. "Plotting with the Germans is treason!" He boomed out those words and brought an end to the twittering. In fact, those words brought absolute silence. "Our boys in France will know that the crown is secure in Ireland because you are here. Good luck, men! God's speed!"

Bowen-Colthurst checked his watch. By seven-thirty A.M. every bridge over the Liffey River would be guarded by a detachment of regulars. There would be one detachment at each end of each bridge. In the heart of Dublin every government building and the telephone company would also be placed under heavy guard. An alert had been issued to all British forces in Ireland, and patrols along the highway would be doubled. The captain smiled with enormous self-satisfaction.

After today I will have apprehended an insurrection, and no one, no one, will laugh at me.

2

April 23, 1916

9 A.M., *Easter Sunday*

Emerald left her flat with Tom and pushed the pram down Bride Street. They were strolling toward Christ Church Cathedral, which overlooked the Liffey River. It was nine in the morning, but already the streets were filled with people. High mass at eleven would be terribly crowded, so many of the faithful took mass at seven, eight, nine, or ten.

On a normal Sunday, the walk from her flat to her local church took no more than ten minutes. Today it took her ten minutes just to reach the corner. It seemed that everyone wanted a glimpse of Tom. For his part, Tom accepted the affection and smiled, gurgled, and waved at all the passersby who stopped to chuck him under the chin.

"What a fine young lad! So big for his age. How old is he?" Mrs. O'Rourke cooed.

"Eleven months, his birthday's in May," Emerald explained patiently.

"Oh, and I thought he was over a year!" Mrs. O'Rourke bent over and patted Tom on the cheek.

"He's the living image of you." Mrs. Finnigan smiled.

"Thank you, but truly he looks like his father," Emerald answered.

"A strong broth of a boy, a proud son of Ireland!" intoned Cory Mulligan.

"And aren't you coming to St. Patrick's for Easter mass?" Father Marron asked. He stood at the base of the steps that led up to the church. He had just finished nine-o'clock mass.

"I hope you'll forgive me, Father. But I promised my brother Seamus that young Tom and I would be joining him today at Christ Church. Seamus does love his nephew."

"We all do." Father Marron beamed. "Though some of us hope he will outgrow his bad sense of timing."

Emerald blushed and laughed at Father Marron's comment. Bad sense of timing indeed! During his christening—and a beautiful christening it was—little Tom, all dressed in his long white christening dress, had soaked Father Marron near through, and Seamus, poor Seamus, could hardly control himself and keep from laughing.

Two elderly women smiled at Tom and then began talking to Father Marron. Grateful for the opportunity, Emerald broke away from her friends and neighbors in front of St. Patrick's and continued walking down Bride Street. She quickened her pace, though it seemed that Tom preferred the leisurely stroll, as it gave him the opportunity to be on display for much longer. "You're going to develop a swelled head," Emerald teased. "Of course, you are the most beautiful baby in all Dublin."

Emerald looked up. "Here comes your uncle now." One could always tell when it was Seamus O'Hearn in the distance. He had a strident, purposeful, and bowlegged walk.

"You're a fit sight for the Easter Parade," Seamus said, winking. And there was no doubt Emerald looked stunning. She was wearing a jaunty straw hat with a yellow flower on the top, a russet suit with a white collar, and high-topped shoes. Part of her hair was in a roll; the rest fell to her shoulders, beneath the brim of her hat. Her skin was flawless, and in spite of her tears of the night before, her eyes were clear. Everything about her looked young, but Emerald Hughes had a maturity that was unusual in a twenty-year-old.

Seamus took her arm. "Hurry along, let's get into the church quickly. It looks as if there might be some trouble brewing." He leaned over and whispered in her ear, "The bastard Brits are all over the place, in force!"

"We're only going to church," Emerald said indignantly. "Is it again a crime to be Catholic in Ireland?"

Seamus shook his head. "No crime in being Catholic, only in trying to overthrow the British. Every single bridge over the Liffey is guarded and all citizens are being stopped and searched."

Emerald laughed. "All they'll find on me is a change of diapers and my rosary." Emerald paused and turned to Seamus. "Does this have anything to do with the march that was supposed to happen?"

Seamus unfolded the newspaper he was carrying and gave it to her. "What do you make of this?"

It was the *Sunday Independent* and Seamus had marked off several stories. One was the headline which read: "NO PARADES. IRISH VOLUNTEER MARCHES CANCELED. A SUDDEN ORDER."

Seamus ran his hand down the page. The next story read: "ARMS SEIZED."

And below that was a series of stories: "COLLAPSIBLE BOAT ON KERRY COAST"; "MAN OF UNKNOWN NATIONALITY PICKED UP"; "TRAGIC MOTORING AFFAIR IN KERRY. A WRONG TURNING."

Emerald read the unilluminating items and turned to her brother. "Do the British think all these things are related?"

"They might. Over in Europe the damn British say they're fighting for our freedom. Here in Ireland, where we only want to express our freedom, they post armed guards at every crossing."

Emerald frowned at Seamus. He seemed positively distraught. And she thought: I have my suspicions too. Yesterday's events at St. Stephen's Green came back to her and she tried to piece together both events and the strange stories in the paper.

"Is the march supposed to go on tomorrow?" she queried.

This time it was Seamus who shrugged. "It says Eion MacNeill canceled all marches."

Emerald knew that Eion MacNeill was head of the Irish Volunteers, but her mind wandered back to the countess.

"Seamus, let's go to church and celebrate this day. Easter,

Seamus, is always a new beginning. But when we get home, we're going to discuss this.''

Seamus smiled. Emerald had a way about her. New beginning or no, she sounded as if she meant to find out what was going on. And for his part, he was prepared to tell her. At least he was prepared to tell her as much as he knew, which at this point was not a great deal.

3

April 23, 1916

Late Afternoon, Easter Sunday

They had eaten baked ham, roast potatoes, and greens. Then Emerald served a homemade cake and they both laughed as Tom smeared his face with chocolate frosting.

Emerald washed him off and lifted him off his little seat. "Now I'll let you be free, if you're good," she said cheerfully. "He gets so discontented in the playpen," Emerald told Seamus. "He can stand up, but he can't sit down yet."

Seamus laughed and Tom crawled away into the bedroom.

"It's all right. There's nothing he can do there, and he'll be back as soon as he discovers he's alone."

Seamus had cleared the table and gotten out a bottle of whiskey. "Will you join me?"

"Of course. And I think this a good time for our little talk. Seamus O'Hearn, what's going on? You've been keeping secrets from me."

"That's not easy."

"Out with it." Emerald looked at him with her eyebrow arched, but she smiled good-naturedly.

Seamus sighed. "Well, the march we'd planned for today was to have been a bit more; a sort of rising, or the beginning of one. We had planned to occupy the post office."

"And you weren't going to tell me!"

"I was, but I thought you might not come, and I was afraid we'd be short of nurses. But I was going to tell you."

"When? After we'd all been shot?"

"No, no. I didn't want you to take part. I know your mind and heart. I only wanted you there to nurse, and I was going to send you home when anything happened."

"Then I was right. I knew something was going on. I sensed

it yesterday with the boys and then again when I was shopping. Honestly, Seamus, you should have told me.''

He took another gulp of whiskey. ''I'm sorry.''

''And now?'' Emerald asked.

''Damned if I know,'' Seamus said honestly. ''First I hear we're rising, then I hear we're just marching. Then I hear we're not marching or rising. Then I hear we're marching but not rising.''

''And do you think it's safe to assume that tomorrow is a mere march?'' Emerald asked.

''Judging from the papers, yes. But no, I don't know for sure.''

Emerald poured herself a drink. ''I'll come to the march if there is one. I'll help with first aid if I'm needed. But, Seamus, I will not be involved in violence.''

''I respect your conviction, Emerald.''

She took a sip. ''I'll ask Mrs. O'Shea to stay with Tom. Just in case.''

''Good!'' Seamus laughed. ''That woman could stand off the whole British Army! I remember when little Tom was born. She shooed me out!''

Emerald leaned back in her chair. Tom's birth had been bittersweet—it had come only a month after Thomas' death, and the thoughts of the child she carried were all that had sustained her.

''Oh, little Tom!'' Emerald jumped up and ran in the bedroom. Silence was never a good sign. But the next thing that Seamus heard was Emerald's peals of laughter.

He came running.

There in the middle of the bedroom floor sat a delighted baby. He had opened Emerald's medical kit and played with her stethoscope; it lay on the rug in one corner. But his current delight was a large roll of gauze, which, like some curious kitten, he had unraveled and bandaged himself in from head to toe.

''Don't you look like a fine Egyptian king!'' Seamus said as he joined Emerald in laughter.

''And for you, Seamus O'Hearn, for laughing, you can just help me rewind all of that!''

Emerald leaned over and removed the tangled web from Tom. ''Here, you go to your Uncle Seamus, he'll tell you what happens to bad little boys.''

''Will I!'' Seamus took a giggling baby into his arms and

carried him to the armchair in the living room. "Bad babies are kidnapped by giants!"

"You'll frighten him." Emerald followed behind.

Seamus held Tom above his head. "He doesn't look frightened. Here, here, come sit down in the big chair and Uncle Seamus will sing you a song." Seamus sat down and began to sing one of his favorite Irish ballads, "The Rising of the Moon":

Oh, tell me, Sean O'Farrell,
Tell me why you worry so,
Hush, my little bushel, hush and listen.

His cheeks were red with glow. Seamus began to hum, and then took up the song again:

For the pikes must be together,
At the rising of the moon.

"He's asleep," Emerald said, pressing her finger to her lips. Tom's tousled hair lay against Seamus' shoulder.

Seamus carried Tom to his bed and covered him. Then he returned to his whiskey. "Did you go to the Margamore on Saturday?" he asked.

Emerald nodded. Seamus referred to the great market held before Easter and Christmas. It was a Derry word and custom, but there were always markets before Christmas and Easter, and *margadh* was the Gaelic for "market."

"I did, and to the greengrocer's, the butcher's, and about everywhere else in Dublin."

Seamus poured his sister a drink and handed it to her. "It's good you kept busy," he said with vague reference to the anniversary of Tom Hughes's death. But then he turned to her. "Were you all right? I didn't know if I should come or stay away."

"I was all right, Seamus. Yesterday wasn't as bad as I thought it might be, nor as good as I'd hoped. But, Seamus, this is Easter, and you know I do believe in new beginnings."

Seamus lifted his glass. "Then to all your tomorrows, my darling." He leaned over and kissed her cheek. Then he drained his glass. "I think, with your permission, I'll leave. I'd like to get to the bottom of these rumors."

"I don't mind," Emerald agreed.

"Shall I meet you tomorrow in front of Liberty Hall?"

Emerald smiled. "You mean in case there's a march?"

Seamus nodded. "You never know."

"I'll come, but we'll probably be alone."

Seamus kissed her cheek. "Till tomorrow," he said as he waved good night.

4

April 23, 1916

8 P.M., *Easter Sunday*

Colonel Falconer studied the dispatches which covered his cluttered desk. "Balls!" he muttered. This would mean yet another black mark on his undistinguished record. Not only am I never in the right place at the right time, but even when I think I'm prepared, nothing happens, he thought. Merciful heavens, the ministry wasn't going to like any of this. Every time there was a mobilization, it cost money, and all the money was needed for the real war in Europe. The ministry would not take well to the cost of an unnecessary mobilization.

At two o'clock Falconer had taken matters into his own hands and canceled the alert, ordering all nonessential personnel to return to barracks. Nothing—in fact less than nothing—had happened. A more peaceful Easter Sunday would be difficult to imagine. Were I in good humor, I might laugh about this. On any ordinary day in Dublin, a search of so many people would at least have yielded some firearms and a pile of knives and home-made weapons. But not this Easter Sunday. The most that had been recovered was an unseemly number of bottle openers.

"What in God's name is the meaning of this fiasco, Captain?" Colonel Falconer was shouting; he enjoyed the sound of his voice when he was angry. "Where was the rebel uprising that caused the entire British Army in Ireland to be put on alert?" His eyes blazed as he first thought of Kitchener, then Tennyson.

"Sir," Captain Bowen-Colthurst was stuttering.

"What would Lord Kitchener think of this mess?" the colonel interrupted. "Weren't you taught to check, check, and double check? Well, Captain, how do you propose to extricate us from this sorry mess?"

"Begging your pardon," Bowen-Colthurst blurted out, "but the evidence indicated that there would be an uprising today!"

"Your voice is shrill, Captain. Evidence, what evidence? A scuttled German freighter? A captured maniac? The tales of a few washerwomen? These things do not constitute evidence, Captain.''

"If I might, sir . . ." Captain Bowen-Colthurst looked terribly agitated to Colonel Falconer, more agitated than he ought to be, even during a dressing-down. In fact, to use his friend Admiral Harrington's favorite phrase, Captain Bowen-Colthurst looked a bit green around the gills. In fact, the man was actually trembling. It all made Falconer feel more powerful than usual.

"We did manage to put a lid on them today, and if I could continue this operation for a while longer, we could crush them . . ." Bowen-Colthurst finished, but his words trailed off.

"My dear young Captain . . ." Falconer reminded himself to sound fatherly. "If the lid was any tighter, the entire city of Dublin, if not the entire country, would explode in our very faces." He sighed deeply. "I was personally derelict in my duty by allowing you to have your head, and then by following your advice."

"Sir, something went wrong. The information I had was accurate. There was going to be an uprising, but something went wrong."

Falconer straightened up in front of his chair. It was eight o'clock, and he yearned for a brandy and some relaxation. "I'll tell you what went wrong. You went wrong."

"Colonel, all I ask is one more day. I am certain something is going to happen."

Falconer was shaking his head. "No, no. I'm afraid not, Captain. My phones have been ringing all day. London wants to know what the hell is happening. The authorities here want to know what's happening, and let me tell you, loyal Irish citizens are furious at being stopped and searched on virtually every street corner." Falconer paused. "The only bright mark on this dismal day is that we've demonstrated what we could do if there was trouble, but, by God, man, I'm not going to be the cause of that trouble."

"But, sir—"

"Captain, you are immediately ordered to have all your men stand down and return to their barracks."

"Begging your pardon, sir—"

"Captain, am I speaking Swahili? Perhaps you believe I'm talking to you in Urdu, or have you forgotten the king's English? Stand down, Captain! That's an order!"

Colonel Henry Falconer clenched his hands and stared at the departing figure of the captain. "Christ, let me be right! Just once!" he mumbled.

5

April 23, 1916

10 P.M. *Easter Sunday*

If anyone in all Dublin knew what was happening, it would be Eamon de Valera, and so it was de Valera that Seamus went in search of. De Valera seemed to possess a somber strength and had a quiet negotiating skill that calmed ruffled feathers. He moved from one group of nationalists to another; he brought them together; he helped the disparate to unite.

Seamus regarded de Valera as intense and determined; he commanded men, they obeyed. Born of a Spanish father and an Irish mother in New York City, de Valera was the type of man who could have risen easily in the ranks of the Jesuits. Seamus thought that, unlike many leaders, de Valera had an intelligence that matched his emotions.

"I've been there four times already!" Seamus smiled at his own exaggeration. Actually, he had been to the Shelbourne three times, as well as to the other pubs frequented by the nationalists. In the other three pubs, however, he had encountered people who had just come from the Shelbourne. "If I appear at the Shelbourne one more time, they'll be charging me rent."

"I'm sure the commander will be there now," Kevin Moriarty said, lifting his pint to his lips and gulping down the liquor.

"How can you be so cocksure, Kevin?"

"Well, it's a long story, if you have the time, which I can tell by your agitation you don't. But to make it short: Flannagan saw Brody, who's spoken to Hanrahan, after seeing McTavish, who saw Heuston and MacBride walking out of the Shelbourne. Both men claimed to be early for a meeting with de Valera."

"What a lot of cugger-miggering," Seamus said with irritation.

"You could at least say thank you for all the help I've been." Kevin Moriarty was in his cups as he drained his glass and called for more. He slurred his words and slapped Seamus on the back.

"You're fit for a rising," Seamus uttered. "And I'm sure you'll have no need to do anything but breathe on the bloody British and they'll pass out right in front of you."

Seamus shoved his pint over to Kevin. "Here, finish mine, I've business to attend to."

He left the pub and took a shortcut across St. Stephen's

Green, virtually colliding with his unit commander, Eamon de Valera.

"Seamus O'Hearn, you look exhausted. Come over to the Shelbourne with me and we'll sit and have a pint." De Valera took Seamus' arm.

"You seem calm, even cheerful I might say," Seamus observed. "All Dublin's in chaos, and you look so placid it's unnerving. We must speak immediately."

"And what requires immediacy? What will happen will happen," de Valera philosophized.

"That's just it," Seamus said, allowing his exasperation to become fully evident. "What is going to happen? I've heard more instructions, plans, and counterplans than there are saints in Mother Church."

They entered the public room of the Shelbourne. It was only an hour before the eleven-P.M. closing, and fortunately, the room was crowded and noisy. After ordering their Guinness, de Valera turned to Seamus. "We can talk. I doubt anyone can hear us over this din. Now, tell me, Seamus, what are your orders for tomorrow?"

Seamus smiled. "I'm to wait for further instructions."

"Who told you that?" de Valera asked. His voice took on a slight edge.

"Joe Kennedy, sir. Said he was acting on the instructions of Eoin MacNeill. Then too, I heard it was all being called off from Sean Heuston."

"Damn!" de Valera interrupted. His voice sounded full of bitter resignation and frustration. But he turned to Seamus calmly. "Tell me, from whom do you take your orders?"

"You, sir."

"Very well, then, we rise tomorrow." De Valera was speaking in a whisper.

"Should I inform others?" Seamus asked.

De Valera shook his head. "I seriously doubt it would do any good. At best, we would be confusing the brothers and sisters even more. You'd be just one more voice roaming the streets of Dublin, telling people to come out or stay in."

Seamus didn't answer, but he agreed silently.

"There's nothing we can do but have a few more pints. Get a good night's rest, and march with all the boys tomorrow." De Valera raised his Guinness. "To a good night's rest," he toasted.

Seamus drank his Guinness and shifted on his stool. The Shebourne had a curious quality, he thought. Usually there was a group of men in the corner singing, but not tonight. Tonight, many men seemed to be drinking mournfully, as if more than a few of them thought they were spending their last night in the Shelbourne. It was close to midnight when the room emptied, with Seamus O'Hearn and de Valera being among the last to leave.

The steeple of Christ Church Cathedral could be seen as they walked out of the Shelbourne. "Come, Seamus, let's take a short walk and enjoy whatever calmness and tranquillity may be left in this city. God knows that after tomorrow, Dublin and Ireland will never be the same again."

Seamus and de Valera walked toward the river. As the bells of the churches of Dublin pealed out the hour of midnight, de Valera looked into the night sky. The moon was gloriously full; not a cloud was in the sky. "If only I believed in omens," de Valera sadly intoned.

"A ring around the moon," Seamus mumbled.

De Valera kicked a lose pebble off the path. "One of the disadvantages of being brought up in New York City is that I never learned all the old Irish songs. My father was Spanish, you know. Now I can sing of bullfighters, but I can't sing of rebels."

"There's a song about the full moon," Seamus mused. "It's called 'The Rising of the Moon.' "

"Sing me a bit," de Valera requested.

The two of them strolled along the quay, and Seamus thought they must look a strange pair. One man singing in a deep baritone voice, and the tall lanky man humming. Then, when Seamus got to the chorus for the second time, de Valera joined in and together they bellowed their song into the night:

> At the rising of the moon,
> At the rising of the moon,
> Around me boys in freedom,
> 'Tis the rising of the moon!

11

1

April 24, 1916

Easter Monday Morning

Emerald walked through the sparse crowd in front of Liberty Hall. She searched for Seamus, wondering if, after all, even the march had been canceled. As she moved among those present— and they were few in number—she did note a disgruntled, disorganized atmosphere.

"May as well march and get it over with!" one woman mumbled to another as Emerald passed them. She stopped for a moment and checked behind her; then, turning, Emerald saw Seamus. He was surrounded by a small group of men and seemed to be dividing them up, sending them off in different directions.

"We need more men and we need more weapons," Emerald heard Seamus saying as she approached. She stopped short as he held out his hand acknowledging her. "Can you wait over there, Emerald? I've a few details to straighten out."

Emerald turned and went over to the lamppost a few feet away. Men and arms—that meant there was intended violence; there had been yet another change of plans.

"There," Seamus said with a sigh.

Emerald looked at Seamus; his sigh was too deep and his brow too furrowed. "What's happening?" Emerald said quietly. "What's going on?"

"It's on, but we were expecting more people." He expelled his breath. "I don't know, honest to God, I'm really not sure."

Emerald could feel her hands grow cold and clammy; a shiver of apprehension ran through her. There were children here, and many people who just thought they were coming out for a demonstration. But there were also others, and Emerald recognized them as they filtered into the square. They were members of organized Irish nationalist groups, and they were armed.

"Seamus, I wish you would come home with me. I have the feeling of impending tragedy. Seamus, we're not ready for an uprising." Her eyes pleaded with his, and though Emerald knew her brother would reject her plea, it was one she had to make.

Seamus met her gaze, and Emerald could not help but notice

that the merriment had gone out of his eyes. He looked tired, but he also looked serious. "I'm a part of this, I'm deeply involved. I can't leave, Emerald. This is something I have to do. I have to fight for what I believe in."

"Seamus . . ."

"Rebellion is the call of the day, Emerald. We're going to give King Georgie a good kick in the arse that he'll not soon forget. And it will be a kick hard felt because it comes from the Irish."

Emerald closed her eyes, allowing Seamus' words to sink in, to form, to have meaning. She was filled with sadness and melancholy, a longing for little Tom that was simultaneously coupled with a sense of relief that he wasn't here.

Seamus put his hand on her arm. "I'm not asking you to take part. I told you that last night. But there are going to be casualties, Emerald. We've two doctors and only one other nurse. There are young boys here, Emma, there are men with families. Don't you believe in a free Ireland enough to tend its martyrs?"

Emerald steadied herself, leaning against the lamppost. She felt as if little Tom were pulling one arm, and Seamus the other.

"You're certainly free to go if you want. Lord knows, there's so few of us, it won't matter much anyway."

"I'll stay," Emerald whispered. "I won't pick up a gun, but I'll stay to do what I've been trained to do. Save lives, Seamus, not take them, save them."

Seamus blinked back his own tears. He leaned over and kissed Emerald's cheek. "You're the dearest sister a man could have," he said, squeezing her arm.

Emerald nodded. "Tell me everything," she requested.

"We're dividing ourselves into six groups. The First Battalion will take and hold Boland's Mill; the Fourth Battalion will hold the South Dublin Union; the Citizens' Army will take and hold the General Post Office. As you can see, there are plans. . . ."

"And where will you be going, Seamus?" Emerald asked the question with resignation.

"Originally I was attached to the Third Battalion under Eamon de Valera, but plans have been changed . . . again. I'm to be attatched to headquarters for the duration, that is, to the post office."

"Then that's where I should be too," Emerald said.

A sudden hush fell over the milling crowd, and Emerald and Seamus both turned toward Liberty Hall. James Connolly was standing on the steps and he was dressed smartly in a uniform that appeared to have been designed especially for this occasion.

"He must think we're a motley crew," Emerald whispered to Seamus. The small band of the Citizens' Army had moved to the forefront, but only a handful were wearing their traditional uniforms of dark green. Even the detachment of Irish Volunteers was dressed oddly, and only a few had on their uniforms of heather green. The rest of the men looked as if they were going out hunting. As for the arms, some men carried German Mausers, others had hunting rifles and shotguns, and some even carried axes and pikes.

It took a few seconds for everyone in the crowd, which was still assembling, to recognize James Connolly. But when they did, a cheer went up.

Connolly raised his hand and doubled his fist. In a dramatic gesture he beckoned the crowd to follow him, and another cheer burst forth as he strode down the steps and marched down Abbey Street with the crowd in his wake.

"We're going to be slaughtered," Emerald heard one man mutter. She pressed her lips together and walked on, her arm through Seamus' arm.

Ahead of them loomed the General Post Office, a magnificent building with six graceful Ionic columns and three statues atop the portico. Emerald sighed. It was the most beautiful building in all Ireland, but this was not a day to look at landmarks.

"Charge!" Connolly's voice boomed out.

In the ensuing crush, Emerald had to let go of Seamus' arm as the people behind them began to run, walk, and stomp toward the GPO.

"It's ours!" one man screamed as the doors were flung open. "To a free Ireland! To independence!"

Emerald passed through the doors and stopped to take in the solemn grandeur of the building. People were dashing around her; the usual bureaucratic orderliness was gone, lost underneath the echo of trampling feet in the high-ceilinged foyer. No one today would stand in long queues.

Emerald was so distracted, her mind traveled back to last week when she had waited in line for nearly an hour to retrieve a package sent by Padraic to little Tom. The man behind the counter had been surly, as if he were bothered by having to do his job. But Emerald had waited patiently for her turn to come, and in spite of the man's bad manners had finally gotten her parcel. Yet it lingered in her mind that he had deliberately taken a long while to find it, and would have gladly misplaced it, had he thought it contained anything of real value. Why am I thinking about this now? Emerald suddenly asked herself. It was as if her mind was forced to think about everything besides what was going on.

"Mrs. Hughes . . ." James Connolly had come up to her. "The doctors and nurses are setting up a surgery in the basement. I'd like you to set up a first-aid station and to be in charge of it. I'd like you to investigate, find out where the first-aid supplies are kept."

Emerald agreed and moved away. She walked behind the counter and saw the same rude clerk who had waited on her last week. He was tied up, as were the others who had been on duty. She looked directly at him. If she remembered him, he clearly did not remember her.

Emerald smiled as she walked behind the counter. It was a rather nice feeling. "Today I own the post office," she said with good humor. And she thought: There'll be no more rudeness and ill-mannered behavior. It was a passing silly thought, and again Emerald checked herself. I'm nervous, she conceded, and filled with undirected energy.

The clerk looked up at her defiantly in spite of his position. Emerald ignored him and continued to go through the drawers and cupboards that lined one wall. Finally Emerald went over to the clerk. "Pardon me, but could you tell me where you keep the first-aid supplies?"

The man looked at her with pure hatred and contempt. He actually spit, "To hell with you, you bloody croppie cunt!" The veins on his forehead were extended as he spit out the words; in fact, he looked as if his head might explode.

His mouth was open as if he were about to say more, but he didn't have the opportunity. No sooner had he finished his disgusting curse than Paddy O'Rourke came from out of nowhere and punched him in the face so hard that Emerald actually heard the man's nose break.

"You'll not speak to a lady like that! You bloody son of a bitch! Now, answer the lady, and be quick about it, or I'll gladly crack your empty skull like a ripe melon!"

Emerald backed herself against the counter. The tone of Paddy's voice took her aback. It was the voice of a man who was beyond hatred, who reached across the recesses of seven hundred years of oppression and came up inhuman. Paddy was willing to kill without thought; he struck out at the ghosts of the Irish past. And I am his excuse! Emerald cringed and shook her head, unable to speak though words formed, waiting to be uttered.

But the clerk didn't hesitate. His eyes rolled in pain, and they fastened on the butt of Paddy's rifle, which was poised above his head. "Upstairs, second room on the left . . . those stairs . . ."

The blood was pouring down his face. Emerald bent over, opening her own first-aid kit. It had pitifully little in it, she thought.

"Don't waste supplies on the likes of him," Paddy O'Rourke muttered.

Emerald looked up, vaguely aware that the cuffs of her sleeves bore bloodstains from having reached out to the clerk on the floor. "Please . . ." was all she could say to Paddy O'Rourke, whose face was still tight with anger. But Paddy shook his head and turned on his heel, stomping off to join the others. It was a small wordless drama, but it shook Emerald to her core.

"I'm here to treat those who are injured," she said, turning back to the clerk. But they were words she need not have spoken. The man had passed into blessed unconsciousness and the blood that had poured from his nose so freely now congealed into a drying scab on his face. He's stopped bleeding, Emerald thought. Still she rolled him on his side so that if he began again, he would not choke. Then, already weary, she got up and went to the second floor.

The room the clerk sent her to was the office of the assistant superintendent. It was a large room, larger than Emerald's entire flat. On the wall directly behind the desk was a faded portrait of Queen Victoria done at the time of her Diamond Jubilee. It reminded Emerald of the portrait over the McArthurs' mantel.

"It's more like a crypt than an office," Emerald said aloud. She walked around the room, afraid to misplace anything and at the same time chastising herself for her foolishness. Finally she found a quantity of medical supplies in the closet. Briefly she wondered if other public buildings had the same number of supplies—in case of an insurrection or a civil war, she reasoned.

"Emerald Hughes?" The round-faced man at the door was an acquaintance of Seamus', but Emerald didn't know his name. She looked up expectantly.

"Padraic Pearse is about to read our proclamation of independence. You'd best come, or you'll miss it."

"Can you take a few of these boxes?" Emerald lifted one and straightened up, shaking out her skirt. The man picked up three more and followed behind her.

It was 12:45 when Emerald joined a handful of rebels at the entrance to the General Post Office. Padraic Pearse and James Connolly were standing together, directly between the center columns of the building. A small crowd had gathered outside, and one could tell from the expressions on their faces that they had come more out of curiosity than out of sympathy with the cause. But Pearse did not seem dismayed.

"He's speaking to all of Ireland," Seamus said as he came up and stood near Emerald.

> Irishmen and Irishwomen: in the name of God and of the dead generations from which she receives her old traditions of nationhood, Ireland, through us, summons her children to the flag and strikes for her freedom.

Emerald listened and could not help being moved by Pearse's voice and words. Her objection was to violence, not to Irish nationalism. And no one could deny that Pearse was inspirational. He went on to discuss the Irish Republican Brotherhood, the Irish Volunteers, and the Irish Citizens' Army. He spoke of seizing this moment because Ireland was supported by Irish-Americans and because the British were distracted by the war in Europe.

Pearse's words caused an electricity in the crowd, and in spite of her many reservations about what was happening, Emerald felt a part of history in the making; she felt like an honored observer hovering on the edge of the crowd.

> We declare the right of the people of Ireland to the ownership of Ireland, and to the unfettered control of Irish destinies, to be sovereign and indefeasible. The long usurpation of that right by a foreign people and the government has not extinguished the right, nor can it ever be extinguished except by the destruction of the Irish people. In every generation the Irish people have asserted their right to national freedom and sovereignty; six times during the past three hundred years they have asserted it in arms. Standing on that fundamental right and again asserting it in arms in the face of the world, we hereby proclaim the Irish Republic as a Sovereign Independent State, and we pledge our lives and the lives of our comrades-in-arms to the cause of its freedom, of its welfare, and of its exaltation among the nations.

Emerald wiped a tear from her cheek. She certainly wasn't the only one in the crowd moved to tears by Padraic Pearse's proclamation. His words had conjured up powerful images of injustice and of the famine; of ignorance and of prejudice; of sickness and of death. It was evident to Emerald that if one could not relate to the enormity of the whole of Irish history, there wasn't an Irishman alive who didn't carry the details of specific events in his mind, and there, like a cancerous growth, the collective memory of a people settled on the subconscious of the individual, bursting forth now and again in acts of terror-filled frustration. For women, the image of a single child lost, alone and hungry, loomed large in the imagination. A burned house, a slaughtered family, and a lone survivor; a helpless survivor. Perhaps others carried images like the one Emerald carried—the memory of a young child whose skull was crushed to commemorate the victory of King William.

And for the men of Ireland there was impotence in the face of having their houses burned, their lands pillaged, their women taken, and their children killed. And so the Brennans, the Wolfe Tones, and the Emmetts of Irish history loomed larger than life and stepped into the shoes of the heroes of Irish folk tales, becoming the subject of new folk tales.

The men who called out for freedom, even as Padraic Pearse did now, the men who led brief battles against the oppressor, these men grew into giants, and around them a hundred stories were woven from the threads of Irish desire. And there is no one, not even me, Emerald thought, who does not believe the desires are just.

Pearse continued his proclamation. He declared the provisional government and concluded with a final call to arms.

> In this supreme hour the Irish nation must, by its valour and discipline and by the readiness of its children to sacrifice themselves for the common good, prove itself worthy of the august destiny to which it is called.

Cheers went up from Pearse's supporters in the crowd outside the post office. And on the streets, broadsheets printed the day before were being distributed.

Emerald stood like one of the statues on top of the GPO. Her mind was still filled with conflicting thoughts that danced to a fugue, one chasing the other away. She felt mildly ill, and giddy all at the same time.

"We need to know what's happening in the rest of the city," Connolly mumbled to Seamus. "Apparently we've failed to capture the telephone exchange. That means communications are in the hands of the British. Damn!'' His eyes searched the crowds. "I wanted more people . . .''

Emerald glanced at her brother as he stood at Connolly's side. She could hear them clearly and she knew the distress she felt was evident in her facial expression.

"You're the liaison with de Valera,'' Connolly was saying. "It's time we liaised. Here's a list of the objectives to be taken. We must know which of the objectives has been gained. Get out of your uniform and try to be back within two hours. We'll be expecting you.''

"Seamus . . .'' Emerald held out her hand.

"Orders.'' His jaw was set. His eyes still glowed with the fire caused by Padraic Pearse's speech.

"Be careful, Seamus. God be with you.''

He nodded. Emerald wasn't sure he had even heard her.

Two hours passed like two days for Emerald. But when Seamus returned, though he went immediately to Connolly, she saw him and they had time to exchange looks. Each clearly understood the other's anxiety.

"Report,'' Connolly ordered. "How are our gallant comrades holding out against the British?''

Seamus looked into James Connolly's face. The man was an enigma to him. He was involved, deeply involved. He was a fine organizer, a man whom other men willingly followed. But he didn't have the look of fiery passion the others had; he seemed cool and calm, as if he had already read tomorrow's paper and knew the outcome of every endeavor.

"With the exception of Dublin Castle,'' Seamus began, "all positions have been secured. We have effective control of the Four Courts, Jacob's Factory, Boland's Mill, the College of Surgeons, and the South Dublin Union.''

"Casualties?''

"Captain Sean Connolly was gunned down in the attempt to seize the castle. But his group did manage to kill a policeman before withdrawing. Otherwise, the only other casualties are several other police killed by Commander Mallin's men near the College of Surgeons.''

Seamus paused. "There doesn't seem to be any response yet from the British. In most parts of the city, police and soldiers are still walking about as if nothing were happening.''

The door opened and Pearse came in. Connolly repeated Seamus' report and brought Pearse up-to-date.

"Are there any discipline problems?" Pearse asked.

"None whatsoever," Seamus reported. Everyone had been ordered not to drink, and even he was surprised the order was being observed.

"Let's get to the business of setting up our defenses," Connolly suggested. Seamus looked at the man and sensed Connolly had a few good ideas up his sleeve.

2

April 24, 1916

Dublin Castle, 2 P.M.

Dublin Castle hummed with activity, tension, and pure confusion. The rising, which many felt was imminent but which most believed had been averted through diligence, was in full blossom. As for the numbers of rebels involved, their actions to date, and their aims, all of these were currently unknown.

Sir Matthew Nathan, the undersecretary of Irish affairs, was in his late fifties, a man with a distinguished record. Yesterday he had felt healthy and fit, but today he felt ill and looked haggard.

Sir Matthew Nathan had always considered himself the model civil servant—moderate in all actions, humane, and deeply concerned with Ireland, which was his domain. Through one political battle after another, Sir Matthew had championed the Irish cause and supported home rule. Unhappily, those whom he sponsored, those whom he championed, were at this moment in full-fledged insurrection. Their action, he realized, would spell the end of his career.

They say a man's life flashes before him in the moment before his death. And though Sir Matthew Nathan was not dying, his life nevertheless appeared before him as his dreams of reconciliation died with the morning's dispatches.

It was two P.M. and Sir Matthew had composed himself through force of sheer will. He came into the operations room and took his seat. Major Price, his chief of intelligence, was present, as were all the commanders and deputy commanders of military posts which were scattered throughout and around the outskirts of Dublin. The shades on the windows were drawn tight, and outside, the sound of gunfire seemed all too close.

"Order," Nathan said, clearing his throat. "Price, let's have your report first."

"At present, a handful of men are occupying various buildings around the city: the Four Courts, the South Dublin Union, Jacob's Factory, Boland's Mill, directly adjacent to our barracks at Beggar's Bush, the College of Surgeons, and, as we all know, the General Post Office. We estimate the total number of traitors to be no more than a thousand, although we can't be absolutely certain."

Price stopped and eyed the pitcher of water on the desk. "May I?"

Nathan nodded, and Price took a moment to pour himself a glass of water. He gulped it down and returned to his report.

"Reports from the rest of the country indicate that the rebellion is restricted to Dublin. All communications are functioning and there have been no reported acts of sabotage along the railroad or at the port facilities. I've already taken the liberty of requisitioning train cars, and have dispatched them to peaceful parts of the country in order to obtain additional troops. The first contingents should be here by five o'clock."

Abruptly an aide to Intelligence Officer Price entered the room. He handed Price a slip of paper, then turned and left on the run.

"Oh, my God." Price breathed the words and set the note down. He trembled slightly and his face had gone dead white.

"What is it?" Nathan pressed.

"It seems we have problems in our own communications. Four of our Lancers are dead in front of the post office, and eight are wounded. The surviving members of the platoon have indicated they didn't know there was any trouble in the city. They were merely taking a walk down Sackville Street."

"You mean our own units haven't been put on alert?" Nathan shook his head in disbelief.

"I presume not all of them," Price fumbled. "That's why I said we had a serious communications problem."

Colonel Falconer was opening and closing his mouth like a fish. Nathan glanced at him, acknowledging him without making reference to the premature and bungled alert of the previous day.

Falconer finally found his voice. "Mr. Secretary, I can have a troop of cavalry storm their position within the hour. We'll force those bloody kaffirs out and put an end to this nonsense once and for all."

The man was clearly past it, Nathan decided. But there was no doubt he was trying to redeem himself.

Nathan nodded and asked the other commanders. They mumbled about for fifteen minutes and finally agreed to Falconer's plan, reasoning no doubt that the rebels might kill unarmed constables but would react differently to a full-scale charge of his majesty's cavalry.

"It will show a positive resolve on the part of the government," Nathan intoned.

"And buy more time till troops arrive," Price added under his breath.

Nathan shot Price a dirty look even though he too was uncomfortable with the situation. The honest truth was, at this moment there weren't more than twenty-five hundred troops available, and most of them were old or had been wounded in France. It was not an army to quell a rebellion.

3

April 24, 1916

3 P.M., Easter Monday

The number of rebels in the General Post Office had grown to two hundred men and women. Mailbags were brought to the main floor and everything movable was put in them. Nails, letters, coal, and rubbish were stuffed in them. Windows were broken and the bags put in front of the empty panes.

Meanwhile a small group of rebels sent out by Connolly made a lightning raid on the waxworks on Henry Street and absconded with a group of effigies. The occupants of the post office took great delight in positioning Queen Victoria, King George, and Lord Kitchener in the windows to serve as noble targets for the British.

"The cavalry's coming!" one of the rebels called out. "They're in full battle dress, they're marching down O'Connell Street, they are!"

Armed men rushed to the windows, guns at the ready, and Emerald hovered close to the wall, crouching down and feeling out of place and lost among the shouts and the catcalls.

"I guess they're believing that the sight of them in their pretty uniforms will scare us away!" someone said.

"Come and get us!" another called out.

"Slimy bastards!"

Connolly went to the windows and peered over Lord Kitchener's shoulder. "There's only about twenty of them. . . . Hold your fire until they're clearly in range. When the last horse passes Moore Street, aim carefully and fire. But no more than two rounds each."

Connolly climbed down. "No need to engage in a full-blown battle," he told Paddy O'Rourke, who stood nearby. "Unless more men, arms, and ammunition come, we can hold out more than a few days anyway. Best to conserve what we have."

The last horse crossed Moore Street. A split second passed and there was an ear-splitting sound of gunfire followed by an eerie silence. "Eleven . . . no, twelve!" someone shouted.

"That's right, looks like four dead and twelve being carted off wounded. There they go, all scurrying back across the bridge to Dublin Castle!"

A boisterous cheer went up and echoed through the General Post Office.

"A great battle," one woman called out.

"In no time the British will be seeking terms!"

"O'Rourke!" Connolly called out. "Get out there and gather whatever arms and ammunition you can find from the fallen soldiers."

"Surely we can win with what we have," O'Rourke protested.

Connolly bit his lip, and Emerald, who was only a few feet away, could see that he was restraining himself.

"O'Rourke, I don't have time to develop the true extent of my thoughts, but I'll do it for you once, just this once. I'm ordering you to strip those fallen soldiers because we need every bullet and gun we can get. While I am prepared to fight, and I might add die, I would like to prolong the experience of living as long as I can. Now, move! And in the future, move whenever you're told!"

Connolly sneered at O'Rourke. "Our success will not be measured by the traditional military victory. King George won't be riding down O'Connell street with a white flag in his hand, begging us to take Ireland off his hands. We have one task, and that's to survive as long as possible. People need to have time to get fond of martyrs."

Emerald took in Connolly's words and allowed herself to sink down the side of the wall against which she was leaning. Her legs begged her to sit down in any case, and the cool stone felt good. "Tom," she said to herself, facing for the first time the

true meaning of her involvement and the real possibility that she
might be killed. Then Tom would be like me, a motherless child
in a hostile world. But of course Mrs. O'Shea would look after
him, and Padraic would send for him.

"I love you, my darling," she whispered to herself, thinking
of her baby. Then she crossed herself. "I'm in your hands,
God," she whispered under her breath. And for the first time in
a long while Emerald found herself repeating the "Hail Mary"
without her beads in hand.

4

April 24, 1916

9 P.M., *Easter Monday*

In spite of the fact that the streets outside were reasonably well
patrolled by the British, reports continued to filter into the
General Post Office.

Connolly called a meeting of the military council. It was, he
reasoned, the last meeting any of them would have time for.

He moved into the post office superintendent's office, and
there held court like a general well behind the lines instead of a
rebel in the midst of battle.

There was no denying, Connolly thought as he looked at those
attending the meeting, that their mood was excited and jubilant.
They had met British steel twice and dealt the enemy a resounding defeat. The younger men really believed that it was only a
matter of time until final victory was achieved.

Connolly brought his hand flat down on the table. "Before
you adjourn to dance a jig, perhaps you ought to know what the
situation is at the moment."

He paused and waited for the total silence he knew his words
would bring. "It's true that our immediate goals—with the
exception of Dublin Castle—have been realized. It is also true,
my friends, that we have inflicted a number of casualties on the
British, with minuscule cost to ourselves."

"And there'll be more British blood adorning the streets of
Dublin before we're finished." Paddy Lynch was clearly pleased.

Connolly leaned forward. "We've gained the initiative because we surprised them. And that's probably the end of it."

Paddy Lynch made a disagreeable sound through his teeth. He
started out recounting the afternoon's events as if Connolly

hadn't been there. "And they won't dare attack again. Besides, the people of Dublin will be rushing to join us tomorrow."

"You're a fool, Paddy Lynch." Connolly's tone was more sad than angry. "Do you know what your glorious people of Dublin are doing right now?"

Connolly didn't give Lynch the opportunity to speak. "Just go and look across the street at Clery's. There are the people of Dublin in a great show of patriotic fervor—they're breaking into the store and carrying off everything that's not nailed down. Why, I do believe if you listen you can hear them crying out 'Long live the Irish republic!' as they fill up their shopping bags."

Connolly got up and walked over to Lynch. No one said a word; no one dared breathe too loudly. Connolly pulled Lynch to the window. "Look for yourself, you poor dumb idealistic bastard. There are our glorious supporters, acting like the bloody selfish rabble they are."

Connolly stood for a moment, and Lynch, truly shocked, hurried back to his chair as if it were a refuge from the reality of the world. "I'll continue my report now," Connolly said, satisfied that he had done his bit to kill unreality. "According to the messenger who just arrived from the Fourth Battalion, British troops are beginning to arrive at Kingsbridge Station. Not many, mind you, but it's the beginning.

"There's a report from Boland's Mill that indicates that soldiers have been pouring into the Beggar's Bush Barracks since early afternoon. There's been some shooting, but it's only sporadic. Reports from the Second Battalion suggest that Portobello has been emptied of its troops and they have gone to reinforce Dublin Castle. Fortunately, I might add, not too many made it. Not as many as tried, in any case."

"And what now?" Padraic Pearse asked. "We were depending on the people of Dublin to support us, and that seems like a lost dream." He glanced toward the window and the looters across the street. "And the boys from the west aren't here. Are there reports from the countryside?"

Connolly shook his head. "And there's nothing from our gallant allies, either." Connolly spoke his last words sarcastically. "Whatever possessed you to write that phrase into your speech, Padraic? 'Gallant allies,' my sweet Irish arse! The Germans sent a tub to the West Coast, loaded with outdated weapons, and sailed around Tralee Bay for two days. By God, I don't know why they didn't bring one of those um-pa-pa bands to serenade the British while they were waiting around to be captured."

"So what do we do?"

"Our only hope for victory is a glorious defeat. You know, the years I spent in America were not a total waste. It's a glorious and mighty land, which I chanced to travel from coast to coast."

As Connolly began to speak, the others settled down to listen. Agree with the man or not, there were few among them, or even in Ireland for that matter, who could tell a story as well as Jim Connolly. With the magic of his words and the texture of his voice he could weave the most delightful tales of valor and heroism, even if the objective reality was misery and squalor.

"One day my travels," the consummate storyteller recounted, "took me through the American state of Texas. As you know, I was organizing the railroad workers into a union. Mind you, I always suspected that the savages of the West in their feathers and loincloths would have given me a better hearing than those railroad bosses." He laughed and shook his head. "But I digress.

"I chanced one day to be in the colorful little town called San Antonio. An old Spanish town, as the name would indicate, named after good Saint Anthony. Right smack in the town center is as charming an old mission as one could hope to see, a place right out of a storybook, it was. Well, it seems that in 1836, some eighty years ago, the mission became a fortress for battling Texans against the tyranny of Mexico, which at that time owned that part of Texas. Over one hundred eighty men fought off thousands of Mexican soldiers for weeks. In the end, they all died. And when the Mexicans stormed the mission, they executed those whom they had failed to kill.

"A short time later, a mighty army of Texans was raised from the charred bones of that ignominious defeat. It wasn't an army of trained, disciplined soldiers, but an army of farmers, merchants, and townspeople. The very kind of army you want to rise up and support you. Well, they met the Mexican Army in battle, and although outnumbered, brought about its defeat. The battle cry of the Texans was 'Remember the Alamo!' "

Connolly paused. "What idiot among you ever thought we could win against the British . . . we can't. But we can cause the people of Ireland to rise in mass shouting, 'Remember the GPO!' In that hope, gentlemen, lies our victory. But time is what we must have. We must hold out until the people of Ireland have something to remember!"

When Jim Connolly finished, there was utter silence in the room. After a few minutes Padraic Pearse got up and went over to Connolly. Silently he shook his hand.

5

April 24, 1916

10 P.M., *Easter Monday*

Emerald had taken four boxes of first-aid supplies downstairs.
The remainder she left upstairs in the assistant superintendent's
office. She had just finished taking an inventory of those in the
office when Seamus came into the room.

"I'm glad you're alone," he said, sitting down.

Emerald wiped her hands on her skirt. "I don't think I'll be
able to sleep. It's the first night I've been away from the baby."
It's an understatement, Emerald thought. But it seemed impossible to describe the feeling she had to Seamus. It's a feeling only
women have, she decided. During those weeks after birth, a
mother becomes one with her infant's needs, and as the baby
grows, the bond grows. And it's stronger with Tom and me
because we're alone, Emerald acknowledged. This is the time of
day I'm with him, but our routine has been interrupted and I
ache for him, and it's a lonely, empty feeling.

Seamus stared at the floor. "It's my fault you're here, my
fault you and Tom are separated."

"I could have gone home," Emerald replied. "And I suppose
I would have if I'd understood the implications this morning.
Somehow I wasn't thinking about the nights . . . or the weeks."
Emerald choked back tears. "Maybe getting killed and leaving
Tom an orphan." She didn't add, "like us."

Emerald closed her eyes and felt Seamus' arms around her.
Gratefully she leaned on his shoulder. Seamus began telling her
what was going on outside the post office, and Emerald listened
while silent tears ran down her cheeks.

"It'll be all right," Seamus kept saying. "Little Tom is safe,
and when the time comes, you'll go out of here under a white
flag of truce. I'll see to that. You're a nurse. Even the British
respect that."

Emerald nodded as if she and Seamus were making a solemn
agreement. "Do you think they might just talk? Negotiate?" It
helps to ask questions, Emerald thought; it helps to know what's
happening. It's good to try to make some sort of plan. After all,
they must have better use for their soldiers than shooting up the
streets of Dublin.

"With the mighty British Empire in jeopardy all over the world, they don't have much time to talk." Seamus patted her long red hair. It was still tied behind her head, but some of it had fallen loose and hung in long thick strands. "Don't cry. Bloody bastards they may be, but they don't go around shooting women with white flags. You'll get home to little Tom, you will, I promise."

Emerald drew back. "It's the ghost of Thomas Hughes I fear," she finally said.

"I don't understand," Seamus said, shaking his head.

"Seamus, if he were alive, God willing, Thomas Hughes would come walking right down O'Connell Street dressed in his Tommie khaki—his British uniform—and you'd have to kill him, or he'd have to kill you. Thomas Hughes, my husband, little Tom's father, died wearing the uniform of the British."

Seamus paused and bit his lip. Emerald could see the confusion on his face. "Emerald, there's nothing to worry about. Thomas Hughes is dead, buried in France."

"But, Seamus, what if they start bringing back men like Thomas, Irishmen?" Suddenly the whole question loomed large in Emerald's mind, and the contradictions of Ireland came into a new, sharper focus.

"It's not likely," Seamus was saying. "I've followed the battles. For over two months now, each side has been throwing in its men at . . . at . . . ah, Verdun. From what I gather, hundreds and thousands are fighting at Verdun. I doubt with that much at stake, Britain is going to send back its crack troops."

Emerald looked at her brother seriously. He answered the question reasonably, without understanding the symbolic nature of her question. I don't care about the reality of British strategy, Emerald thought. I want to understand if you could kill Thomas Hughes. But she did not rephrase her question. She let Seamus' answer stand unchallenged.

Emerald left her brother's arms and sat down on the floor next to the boxes she had just emptied of their supplies.

"I'm always frightened that Tom will die like his father and grandfather. One buried in France, one in Africa. . . . Why, Seamus? When will the killing stop? Is the value we place on our lives so little? Surely there are answers that don't involve bullets? Surely people don't have to go around killing to make themselves heard." But you can't understand, can you, Seamus? She asked that question silently.

"Talk? You can't talk to an enemy that's oppressed you for seven hundred years."

"Then, Seamus, we're trapped, trapped by our history. And my son will die with a British bullet, but should he live long enough, he'll produce another generation and they'll die by British bullets. But, Seamus, it will be our history pulling the trigger, we'll be generations and generations of O'Hearns murdered because of our commitment to history. Seamus, I hate history, I hate our inability to change it!"

Seamus went over to her and kissed her cheeks. "I don't always understand you," he admitted. "But I can't stand to see you cry." He paused, then looking up, peered into her hypnotic eyes. "I wish you'd known our father," he said. "He was a fine jolly man. When I was young, just a pup like little Tom, and I'd be crying, he'd take me in his arms, just like this, and he'd sing to me. His favorite old song was 'A Jug of Punch.'

" 'Too, ra, loo, ra loo, ra, too ra loo, ra lie, too, ra loo, la loo, la . . .' " and Seamus went on singing. Emerald closed her eyes and leaned against him. He doesn't understand, and we'll never agree, she thought. But his arms are warm and his voice is soft and there are times when one ought to give in to weariness and loneliness, there are times when one ought to allow comfort without questions and love without conditions.

"And what's going on in here!" Connolly flung open the door. "Have you two been drinking?"

Emerald turned her tearstained face toward him, less in anger than in surprise. "How dare you presume that! We're not breaking your regulations! Is it against your almighty regulations that two people comfort one another? You may not have much to recall, but Seamus and I remember better days." He looks like a cold man, she thought to herself. "I'd like you to apologize," Emerald said.

Connolly paused. He looked a little taken aback. "And I do," he muttered, then added, "We're all a little on edge."

"The question, Mr. Connolly, is on the edge of what?" She looked at him unblinkingly and for the first time in several hours felt some strength flowing back into her body.

Connolly did not answer her. "You're scheduled for the four-A.M. watch," he told Seamus. "Best you get some sleep."

12

1

April 25, 1916

Dawn, Tuesday

Captain Bowen-Colthurst looked into his regulation army tea-cup for a full two minutes before gaining the courage to lift it to his lips. It was all a matter of resolve . . . of willpower. He had to force his mind to control his body, and as much as he wanted the hot tea, he would not pick it up till his hand stopped trembling.

If at this moment Bowen-Colthurst had been asked to draw a picture of himself, he would have drawn a detailed anatomical figure; its tendons stretched as if on a medieval torture rack, nerves raw and red, quivering at the slightest disturbance, muscles tense and aching from the forced restraint of his mind and imagination. He was a glass in that instant before the high note of the soprano shatters it; he was the bullet just before it bursts exploding inside its victim; he was a cat in midair between ledge and prey.

Images of his past ran through his mind. He visualized the family estate in Cork. For more than two hundred years the Bowen-Colthursts had been fervently loyal to the British crown. And wasn't he Irish? Wasn't two hundred years enough? Now once again the illiterate rabble was threatening the civilizing influence of families like his; in days they could destroy what two hundred years' work had built. He sipped his tea, set it down, and squeezed some more lemon into it. It shamed him personally that it was always the Irish that caused trouble. After all, everyone knew he was Irish, all of his superior officers knew. That's why they look at me all the time, he decided. A flood of past comments came to mind, little indignities he always tried to forget.

Once he had gone into Barclays in London with a letter of credit and the clerk had sneered at him and treated him like a forger.

"You're Irish," the little man with spectacles announced. "I'll have to see about this letter . . ."

But of course when the clerk consulted the more learned manager, and the manager saw the name Bowen-Colthurst, there were no more questions. Still, the memory of the slight and its implications weighed heavily on Bowen-Colthurst.

Deep in his soul Bowen-Colthurst ached with anger because the Irish said he wasn't Irish and the English treated him as if he were. And he hated, truly hated the Irish Catholic rabble-rousers with their illiterate slogans. It was they who made pride in being Irish impossible.

"They'll die," he muttered to himself, fingering the knife that came with his bread and jelly. "I'd kill every fucking one of them barehanded, and, by God, I'd do it slowly so I could watch them die." He shivered at his whispered articulation of what was becoming a frequent daydream. And when they're all dead, he thought, then I can be proud to be Irish.

2

April 25, 1916

8 A.M., *Tuesday*

Emerald had slept alone in the assistant superintendent's office with the first-aid supplies spread out around her. She thought for a long while that she would not be able to sleep, but sometime after midnight she took one of the government-regulation wool blankets and wrapped it around herself, curling up in the corner. Outside, the random sound of gunfire slowly died out, and in the silence, Emerald drifted off into blessed sleep.

When she opened her eyes Tuesday morning, it was to respond sleepily to a loud knock on the door. She shook her head, trying to clear it and put things in order. She had been dreaming about getting up and feeding Tom, and in her dream, she had done so. She was therefore doubly stunned and confused to be awakened and find out she had only been dreaming.

"Come in," Emerald called out. As if this were her private suite in a hotel. What a silly thought, she acknowledged.

"Found him outside. Poor bloke's one of ours. Doctor's busy. Anyway, he doesn't really need a doctor." Connolly dragged the man inside. "See what you can do, and when you're finished, move your station downstairs."

Emerald, bewildered, crawled over to the litter and looked into the handsome face of a man who was perhaps thirty-five. His eyes were closed, his lips pressed together in pain. Instinctively Emerald put her hand on his forehead, and responding to her touch, he opened his eyes. They were the color of Tom Hughes's eyes and they looked into hers pleadingly.

Emerald gently pulled back the cover and saw the dried blood. The wound only trickled now, but he had lost a great deal earlier. Emerald tried to smile at him. "I'm going to cut away some of your clothing," she told him in a near-whisper. She reached in her pocket for her scissors. "It won't hurt." He groaned slightly, but Emerald persisted. She applied some cool water and cleaned the wound. "You've been outside for a long while?" It was half a question, half a statement. He was terribly pale and his lips quivered slightly.

Emerald bit her own lip and fought to keep a bland expression on her face as she explored the wound. Clearly it had entered a critical area and in all likelihood penetrated a vital organ.

His mouth moved. "You're a beautiful angel," he said softly. "The most beautiful woman I've ever seen."

Emerald blushed, then cringed because a trickle of blood was running from his mouth. He must have been hit by some kind of bullet that exploded inside. She knew her eyes must not reveal her stricken look. That's why Connolly brought him here instead of to the doctor. He was dying.

"What's your name?" she stammered. Perhaps he had friends or relatives in the building.

"Thomas . . ."

Emerald froze. "Thomas . . ." She repeated the name in a faraway voice; her eyes studied him and filled with tears she couldn't hold back.

"Thomas Reilly," he finished with difficulty.

Emerald put her hands on his cheeks. "Thomas . . . I used to have a Thomas . . ."

He managed to lift his hand and touch hers. "I don't have anyone." His words were labored, but his eyes seemed to devour her with the same loving lust that Thomas Hughes's eyes had devoured her with on their wedding night. "Tell me your name."

"Emerald."

They were silent for a time, and Thomas' hand still covered hers.

"Stay with me till I go," he finally breathed. Emerald nodded. His face had become the face of Thomas Hughes; his touch on her hand was Thomas Hughes's touch.

"Let me love you for a few minutes," he asked, and Emerald in a trance nodded.

"I wasn't in France," she heard herself saying. "I should

have been with you then, I should have been holding you in my arms, we ought to have been together.'' Her tears were flowing freely and she felt the dying man by her side stroking her hand, trying to comfort her.

"I want to come with you," she sobbed incoherently.

"No, you have to stay here," he replied. "You can't come, you have to stay here where I can see you and remember you."

"It's unfair," Emerald sobbed. "I love you so much, I love you too much!" His hand tightened on hers.

"Lean down, Emerald my love, give me a kiss . . . no, give me two. One for your Tom, one for me."

Emerald fought back her desire to throw herself across his body and curse the God of war who had taken Thomas Hughes from her. Instead, she leaned over and kissed the dying man twice. She tasted his blood on her lips and felt his hand as it touched her breast softly with a boyish wonder and a man's desire. She lifted her head after a long while. His eyes were filled with tears too.

"I'll take that kiss to heaven for your Tom," he gasped.

Emerald bent over him again, and this time she kissed him passionately, moving her lips on his. "Don't die," she begged. "Oh, please don't die."

But his hand pressing hers grew weaker, and even as she moved her lips on his, Emerald felt the life ebb out of him. There was a final spasmodic gurgle, then the terrible silence of death.

Long moments passed, perhaps a half-hour. Emerald sat by his side, her hand covering his brow. She reached up and closed his open eyes. "Dear God," she said, coming out of her trance. Was it because she had been so soundly asleep? Because his eyes were like Thomas' eyes? Because his name was Thomas? No, Emerald concluded. The merciful God had given her the opportunity to be with Tom when he died.

"You must stay here," he had said. "You cannot come."

Emerald pulled the blanket over his sensitive face. She stood up and went to the door, summoning someone to take the body away and help her to take her things downstairs to set up her station.

3

April 25, 1916

7 P.M., *Tuesday*

"You look a bit done in."

Emerald looked up from her bowl of soup into the eyes of an exceptionally handsome man. He was tall and dark, with deep brooding eyes and a perfect smile. He looked as if he'd just stepped in off the street; he wasn't grubby like the rest of the inhabitants of the post office, and he had a calm, detached appearance.

Seamus finished gulping his soup. "Meet Michael Collins," he said offhandedly. "Michael, this is my sister, Emerald Hughes."

Seamus turned to Emerald and winked. "Better watch him, he's got quite a reputation, lulls his women with poetry, he does."

"Emerald . . . I like your name . . . it conjures up the green hills, the mountain streams, the smell of spring."

His voice was deep and resonant. But there was something about Michael Collins that was hard to take seriously.

"Now, now," she answered. "The only smells we have today are gunpowder."

"There's always time for a beautiful thought. You know, as much as I like your name—which speaks of Ireland—I think I'd rather call you 'Lady Ireland.' "

"That seems a bit presumptuous," Emerald returned.

"Is Lady Ireland married, Seamus?"

"She's a widow," Seamus answered.

"Stop talking about me as if I weren't here," Emerald interrupted indignantly.

Michael Collins laughed wickedly. And it occurred to Emerald that it was the first laugh she had heard in thirty-six hours. She thought he was laughing at her, but at the moment she didn't care. Who was Michael Collins anyway?

"It's been eerie calm all day," Seamus commented.

"The British are waiting for us to make the first move. We're waiting for them to make the first move."

Seamus took a gulp of soup. "What do you know from outside here?"

Michael Collins shrugged. "The British have secured the countryside, and I'd say that Dublin was secure too. There are now sharpshooters on the roofs of most of the tall buildings about. It's damn hard to move around. We're, shall I say, pinned down."

Seamus nodded. "Their accuracy is awesome. We've already lost three today who were messengers."

"Don't go out again, Seamus." Emerald had finished her soup and she looked into her brother's eyes. "Please."

Seamus blushed. "I'll see when the time comes," he replied, getting up. "I need some more soup," he said, walking off.

Michael Collins shook his head. "See what you did, Lady Ireland? You embarrassed the man, you asked him to commit himself to staying with you in front of another man. He can't do that, you know."

Emerald scowled at Michael Collins, who somehow irritated her. "He'll stay if I ask him to," she said confidently.

Collins shook his head. "No, he won't, Lady Ireland. He'll do what a man has to do."

"And must all men go out and get killed?"

He smiled. "It's a habit we have. Now, Seamus O'Hearn is a brave man, he's going to do what brave men do. And he won't be dissuaded by his sister."

Emerald pressed her lips together and didn't answer. She was afraid he was right, and that irritated her even further.

"Now, if you, as beautiful as you are, asked me to stay, I just might."

Emerald stood up and brushed off her skirt. "You're full of it," she said, turning in a mild huff. And she heard him laugh, though not loudly.

4

April 26, 1916

10 A.M.; Wednesday

Colonel Albert Jenkins settled in behind his desk, though in fact he had no intention of spending a great deal of time behind it. His suitcase was still in the corner of the office, and as yet he had no idea where he was going to be accommodated. He had arrived at one o'clock from Belfast.

His briefcase was full of documents which included information on the political situation in London, a detailed report on conditions in Dublin, a report on the rest of Ireland, and last, but not least, a horrifying report from one Major Vane, who detailed the actions of one Captain Bowen-Colthurst and recommended the captain's detention, if not arrest.

It all involved one Francis Sheehy-Skeffington, a small, wiry, elfin man with reddish-brown hair and a beard to match. In his time, according to the information in the folder, Francis Sheehy-Skeffington had been a feminist, a vegetarian, a teetotaler, a pacifist, a socialist, and an Irish nationalist. Though it had to be admitted that he gave more time to the antitobacco and antivivi-sectionest leagues than to the Irish nationalists.

From all that Jenkins had read, the man could only be regarded as a good-natured, completely harmless crank. Indeed, a somewhat humorous crank who happened to be married to Hanna Sheehy, the daughter of a nationalist M.P.

It was true enough that Francis Sheehy-Skeffington had been in jail. He had also been released, however, under the Cat and Mouse Act, as it was known; he could be rearrested at any time. Until Tuesday evening, no one bothered.

Apparently Francis Sheehy-Skeffington had gone to an anti-looting conference on Tuesday evening and was arrested and taken to Portobello Barracks by Captain Bowen-Colthurst.

According to the information given Jenkins, Sheehy-Skeffington had been asked if he were in sympathy with the rebels. Sheehy-Skeffington had replied that he was, but not with their militarism. No more contradictory answer could be given, Jenkins thought. In any case, what cause was poor Sheehy-Skeffington not in favor of?

But of course it didn't end there. According to informed sources—Bowen-Colthurst appeared to have frightened some of his own men rather badly—he had taken Sheehy-Skeffington as a hostage on tour with him to Rathmines. There Bowen-Colthurst killed a small boy outside a church and later seized two magazine editors: Mr. Dickson of the *Eye-Opener* and Mr. McIntyre of *The Searchlight.* Both editors were loyalist Redmonite writers. At dawn this morning, all three of them were shot by Bowen-Colthurst without trial.

Jenkins was furious when he read the report and, strangely, he read it first. It had been given to him by Major Francis Vane on his arrival, and Jenkins liked Vane. It was as important for him to know this sort of thing as what was going on in London and what was happening in Dublin among the rebels. "But this I will handle first," he said aloud. "These aren't the actions of a soldier doing his duty; these are the actions of a lunatic and a murderer." Jenkins picked up the phone and gave the orders. "Have Captain Bowen-Colthurst confined to barracks until further notification."

Jenkins got up and walked to a map of Dublin. He had been sent here to work under General Maxwell—when and if Maxwell arrived. He had been sent because the Prime Minister wanted this over; he wanted it over quickly and with the least loss of life possible. Jenkins was the top artillery officer available.

Colonel Albert Jenkins was a graduate of Sandhurst, a tall handsome man of thirty-three who was cultured, well-educated, and lonely. On his father's side of the family, everyone for four generations back had served the crown. His father had been a general, his grandfather had been a general, and certainly he was on his way to becoming a general.

His mother's side of the family were hardworking people who, while rich, were what many called nouveau riche. His mother's father had come up through industry and eventually came to own his own profitable factory. It was from his mother that he had inherited his rambling estate in Wales, a refuge from war and the military, a place where Colonel Albert Jenkins became, simply, Albert Jenkins.

He stood up and stretched. He was tall, had a full head of straight black hair, a fine complexion, and stood straight and tall in spite of the recent wound he had received in France. War in France, riots in Belfast, now insurrection in Dublin.

Colonel Jenkins checked the figures on troop arrivals. There was no doubt he had enough now. He called his staff to assemble at noon.

War on the western front had taught Jenkins at great deal. He believed in artillery. As far as he was concerned, frontal assaults by large bodies of troops were outmoded and their death knell had sounded at Sebastopol. Kipling and Tennyson might immortalize the suicidal assaults, but it was Albert Jenkins who had to inform the parents and sign the letters telling them how their brave young sons died for king and country. Death was to be expected in combat, but Albert Jenkins was not one to foolishly sacrifice one single man to achieve his end.

"I want a ring of artillery fire around the post office," he ordered. He hoped the building would not have to be totally obliterated, but that would be the choice of the people inside. Whenever they decided they had had enough, they could march out under a white flag of truce with their hands in the air. Then and only then would the guns cease.

"I want the *Helga* to be armed immediately with twelve-pounders and placed in position on the River Liffey." He leaned back and lit his pipe. "Next I want all guns turned on Liberty Hall. I want it flattened."

"But there's not a soul in the building," one of his junior staff members argued.

"Exactly," Jenkins replied. "Those rebel bastards are positioned across the street. I should like to give them a demonstration of the power I have at my disposal, and I should like to illustrate, without killing anyone, that I intend to use it."

"But, sir. That's the wanton destruction of public property. How can we possibly justify the gutting of this city?"

"We'll be reviled by the loyal Irish citizens of Dublin and by the War Office," another officer complained.

"Balls!" Jenkins barked. "I would rather be remembered for destroying cities than murdering the men under my command. Those bastards are in an almost impregnable position. You know what happened on Monday when the cavalry attacked them. The cavalry were like sitting ducks in a shooting gallery. I refuse to have a similar incident occur. Furthermore, look at those under your command. When, if ever, did they fire a shot in anger?"

The staff sat in silence. The new colonel was correct. Although they now had over twenty-five thousand men at their disposal, they were, in the main, untested. Many of them were fresh off ships from England and did not even know where they were. They had thought they were on their way to France and had woken to find themselves in Dublin.

"Look at it this way," Jenkins said. "Chances are, your men would destroy Liberty Hall anyway. At least we can give them some field training in artillery. Once we get this show moving, even under the best of circumstances, each shot will be as if we're threading a needle. Let your men have some practice, and at the same time, we can show those rebels we are quite clear in our intentions."

Jenkins concluded his staff meeting and went about his business. But within the hour, he had news that doubled his resolve.

Owing to a mistake in orders, the men of the Sherwood Foresters were ordered to march to the Royal Hospital by way of the Mount Street Bridge. They had just arrived from England, they had not realized that the bridge and its approaches were held by the rebels.

The slaughter occurred at twelve-thirty according to the dispatch Jenkins was handed. The men of the Sherwood Foresters marched along Northumberland Road toward the bridge and right into a rebel trap. Their guns were on their shoulders and they were still tired after the long trip from England. Apparently the fighting was still going on, but the reports indicated heavy casualties. Jenkins ordered his artillery into the fray; then he turned his attention back to his work, still fuming in anger.

5

April 26, 1916

3 P.M., Wednesday

The British fired furiously at a lone figure that darted down O'Connell Street toward the General Post Office. The men inside, alerted by the firing, saw him running in a zigzag pattern.

"It's Sean Flynn, from the Fourth Battalion!" Someone shouted out a cry of welcome, but the cry was quickly stifled when Sean Flynn fell to the ground a hundred yards from the front door.

"He's been hit in the leg!"

Michael Collins didn't wait. He opened the door and ran outside. He grabbed the man in a fireman's grip and brought him in to safety. There was a cheer and a round of applause.

Emerald had been watching, and she followed Collins into the mail room, which had been converted into an infirmary. Michael Collins gently placed the man on an empty bed and stepped aside so Emerald could see to his wound.

"Connolly. I must speak to James Connolly!"

"There's time enough for that," Emerald replied, feeling relieved. It was only a flesh wound. "Let me see what I can do for you first."

"I beg your pardon, ma'am. But I've been ordered by Commander Ceannt of the Fourth Battalion to report immediately to Mr. Connolly. I've never been shot before, and I don't know how long I might be alive. I must speak with Mr. Connolly."

In spite of herself, Emerald laughed lightly. It was a musical kind of laugh. "Begone with you, it's only a flesh wound, as the bullet passed clean through. You'll be living about sixty more years, if you stay out of the way of the British bullets."

The intense young man smiled back at her. Sixteen, Emerald thought. He couldn't have been more than sixteen.

"Thank you," he said gratefully, "but I still have to speak with Mr. Connolly."

"Oh, don't thank me, thank the British soldier with the bad aim. Or better yet, thank God, who was watching over you." She turned to Michael Collins. "Or you could thank Mr. Collins, who came out after you."

"I thought you didn't like me, Lady Ireland."

Emerald smiled at him. "He's a boy, you saved his life. I like you for that."

"Mr. Connolly," Sean Flynn protested.

"Best you get Mr. Connolly," Emerald suggested.

James Connolly came on the run, and Sean Flynn spoke slowly; it was obvious he had memorized his entire report.

"Commander Ceannt sends his cordial regards, but regrets he cannot be here in person. Since last night the British have been attacking our positions from all sides. The Mendicity Institute was the first to fall in the early hours before dawn. Sean Heuston was captured. By eight o'clock this morning, the artillery that fell on the South Dublin Union sounded like the gates of hell opening up. We're out of ammunition, half our force is dead or dying. Commander Ceannt felt he had no choice but to surrender."

Connolly listened carefully and then thanked the young man for his report. "They'll not be able to use artillery on us," he said. "They'd never destroy the heart of the city."

Michael Collins shrugged his shoulders. "I wouldn't count on it."

"Assemble the men," Connolly said. "We should pass on this young man's report."

An hour and a half passed, and then the shelling began.

"Why are they firing on Liberty Hall?" Sean Flynn asked. "There's not a soul inside it."

"They're hitting the wrong building," Padraic Pearse agreed.

Those standing about clapped and cheered as each shell pounded into the empty structure across the street. There was laughter, hoots and jeering, but the laughter held no humor, and even though several people went to the windows to shout about the British aim, the shelling brought an uneasy feeling to most in the General Post Office.

Emerald's first-aid station had been moved into the mail
room while the other doctors and nurses set up an operating room
in the basement. Sean Flynn's leg had been seen to and he was
up and about, though limping somewhat. Emerald remained in
the mail room, though at the moment her station was quiet.

"No wounded?" Michael Collins asked as he entered bearing a
cup of hot tea.

Emerald shook her head. "I only get those with minor wounds,
or those who are dying. The rest go downstairs."

Michael Collins held out the tea. "Here," he offered. "Drink
it while you can. From the shelling across the street, I'd say
things will get worse, not better."

Emerald took the teacup and thanked him. The hot brew tasted
good and she sipped it slowly, wanting to make it last. "It's the
noise," she admitted. "It's unnerving."

Michael Collins laughed. "Unnerving and deadly, Lady Ireland.
Very deadly."

"Their aim isn't bad, is it? They meant to hit Liberty Hall,
didn't they?"

Michael Collins nodded. "I daresay it's a warning."

Emerald finished the tea.

"Better get some rest now," Michael Collins advised.
"Tomorrow may be a long day indeed."

6

April 26, 1916

6 P.M., *Wednesday*

"O'Connell Street is completely sealed off at both ends by
artillery and machine-gun emplacements which effectively prevent us from all outside activity. All tall buildings in our immediate vicinity are firmly in British hands. They're shooting at
anything that moves. Unless, of course, there's a white flag of
surrender."

Connolly finished reading his report, and it was punctuated
with yet another shell.

"I never believed they'd do this," Paddy Flynn mumbled.
"We're dying without honor, without a chance to fight man-to-
man. I hate the sons of bitches for that!" His eyes were blood-
shot and narrowed, his fists were clenched.

"They're safe behind their howitzers. We can't do a damn thing with rifles," Seamus O'Hearn added.

Connolly stood up. "Michael, can you round up a group of thirty volunteers? I'd like to try to seize and hold the offices of the *Irish Independent* across the street. I believe it would give us a chance to break out of this."

"I'll go!" Paddy volunteered. "I'm going to die in one of three ways in any case. By a British bullet now, by a British bullet later, or on the end of a hangman's noose. A British bullet now is fast, at least."

"Fast and painless," Seamus said wryly. "The last person who went out that door was pumped full of thirty bullets in as many seconds."

"I'll be in charge of the assault and providing the cover," Connolly announced. "You, Seamus, will take the offices of the newspaper with your men, and as soon as you've secured it, commence firing on the British position at the Four Courts."

Seamus nodded.

"Men," Connolly was saying, "it's up to you to determine how we shall die. If you can take and hold the *Independent*, a few of us can die honorably, the rest will probably become prisoners. Should you fail, then I fear we shall all die like dogs."

"Are you really going to leave us?" Paddy Flynn asked.

Connolly nodded. "I'm not all talk." He smiled.

Seamus shouldered his rifle, and as the men headed toward the door of the post office, he caught sight of Francis Grady. He caught Grady's arm. "If I don't come back, tell my sister I love her, and I'm sorry. It's just something I have to do."

"That's all?" Grady asked.

Seamus shrugged. "What else could there be? I'm not a man with a large legacy."

Seamus turned toward the door. In Belfast, he thought, Padraic and I used to play tag. I never got caught. . . . It's fifty yards, only fifty yards. . . . Small beads of perspiration formed on his forehead and across his upper lip, resting on his beard like dew drops in the morning grass.

Then Connolly shouted the order and Seamus ran with the others. He felt nothing but the pavement beneath his feet, which hardly seemed to touch the ground.

A torrent of bullets shattered the silence. They came from both ends of O'Connell Street and from the rooftops of the surrounding buildings. Thirty men began the dash, six returned, dragging the bodies of those who fell next to them.

James Connolly and Seamus were both dragged inside. Connolly was hit in the leg; Seamus had a bullet wound in his shoulder, a hole no larger than the tip of a pencil. He lay on the floor, his eyes open.

"Seamus!" Emerald had come running. She knelt down. It was such a small hole, and only in the shoulder. She moved him slightly and turned him. There, on his back, was a hole the size of a fist. Every ounce of blood his heart was pumping gushed onto the grimy floor.

"An exploding bullet," someone said. The voice seemed to come from elsewhere.

"Seamus . . ." Emerald lifted his lifeless form into her arms and wept as she rocked back and forth. His blood soaked her uniform and she could feel his blood in a puddle around her bare knees. She sat, unaware of anyone, uncomprehending.

One of the nursing assistants came and tried to wrench Seamus from her arms, but like an animal with its young, Emerald shook the woman away ferociously. "Leave us alone!" she screamed out, and her scream seemed to echo through the room. The huddle of people shrank back and away from her. She heard their murmurs, but not their words.

The sun set, and darkness settled over the post office. Emerald struggled to her feet and laboriously dragged Seamus with her, across the floor to the dead-letter office, where the bodies were now laid out, row on row.

"Come, Emerald." She turned to see Michael Collins, who towered over her.

"He's dead. Seamus is dead."

"We must see to the living," Collins said softly.

"He's my brother," Emerald wailed.

"And mine," Michael Collins replied. "But he's dead, he's at peace, and unless we tend the wounded, they'll be joining him in whatever heaven he now resides."

"We were separated for too long," Emerald whispered. "I can't leave him now . . . I can't."

"Emerald, we have over fifty wounded. Come . . ."

"Seamus . . ." Tears flowed from her eyes. "He's my brother!" She grasped Michael Collins' shirt, and her whole body shook.

Collins bent over and picked her up into his arms, lifting her against him. "There's no time for love, Emerald, and there's less time for mourning. Mother Ireland and you can mourn your sons at a more tranquil time. Tend the wounded."

He carried her out of the dead-letter office and toward the infirmary. He stopped at a basin of water, and using her own apron, washed her face clean of Seamus' blood. Then he bent down and kissed her brow. "You're not a pretty sight, Lady Ireland. You're bloodied and frightened, but you're brave and beautiful too. And, my girl, you'll be free. That I promise you."

Emerald watched as he disappeared into the darkness. "God give me strength," she prayed.

13

April 27, 1916

10 A.M., *Thursday*

Augustine Birrell was chief secretary for Irish affairs, a faithful member of the Liberal party, and a friend of the prime minister, Herbert Asquith.

He had a reputation for implementing not only the letter of the law in Ireland but also the spirit of the law. Birrell's chief aim was home rule—peace and justice for Ireland—and he believed that only a steady, caring hand could bring the Irish around to his own belief that independence was to be earned, a matter of evolution rather than revolution.

On Easter Monday evening he began receiving the first reports about the insurrection, and he was shattered by the news. Tuesday in Parliament was a nightmare. There were no newspapers in London over the Easter weekend, thus parliamentarians received all the weekend news on Tuesday morning. Anyone, including Augustine Birrell, would have to admit that, taken together, the stories seemed ominous indeed. First, the capture and subsequent sinking of the *Aud*; second, the arrest of Sir Roger Casement; next, German air raids along the coast; now, last, the insurrection in Dublin.

Birrell believed most of the events to be unrelated, but the same could not be said for Parliament. There the opposition raged about treachery; John Redmond's Irish M.P.'s groveled and apologized for the actions of the rebels, and even Asquith went into a fury, demanding that the rebellion be quashed as quickly as possible and that "the Irish be taught a lesson."

Thus a sad and confused Augustine Birrell was dispatched to Dublin posthaste to watch over the burning embers of his enlightened Irish policy.

He arrived in Dublin Thursday at dawn, aboard HMS *Dove*. He went directly to the Vice Regal Lodge, and from its windows he gazed down on Dublin in tears. The city was aflame.

Now it was ten A.M. and the day already seemed a hundred hours long. He was in the office of Colonel Jenkins.

Colonel Jenkins handed him a sheaf of papers. It was an account of the men of the Sherwood Foresters. Their battle with the rebels had lasted all day, and the results were horrendous. Of the four hundred men who had stumbled into the rebel trap, 230 were dead. The rebels who attacked the Sherwood Foresters were now all dead; they numbered a mere seventeen.

"I don't like statistics," Jenkins said, leaning over. "If a man is dead, he's dead. But they killed over thirteen of our men to one of theirs, and those statistics are not acceptable in any kind of warfare. Their positions, for the most part, are impregnable. We have to use artillery, we have to proceed along the road I've chosen . . . dammit, man, we'll save more lives on both sides."

Augustine Birrell nodded dumbly. In a sense, he was Jenkins' superior, but Jenkins was a difficult man to argue with because he was not only a good soldier but also a man deeply concerned with human life.

"This," Jenkins continued, "is what happens when one develops a reverence for buildings and bridges. It's a fine example of how a few men, in the right place, can wreak havoc and cause casualties all out of proportion to their own numbers."

"Weren't you using artillery, then?"

Jenkins shook his head. "Not there. We couldn't get it placed in time to save the lives of the Sherwood Foresters."

"It just saddens me terribly," Birrell admitted.

"But artillery will ultimately decide this issue. We possess it, the rebels do not."

Birrell leaned back in his chair and closed his eyes. The trip from Liverpool had been a nightmare, his mind was in total chaos. The strong winds had caused eight-foot swells and delayed the ship for more than twelve hours. And the delay in his arrival made him more anxious. *But I couldn't have stopped any of this,* he tried to tell himself.

Birrell opened his eyes. Jenkins smiled understandingly at him. "You're tired, bad trip?"

Birrell nodded. "I just don't want this to turn into a bloodbath," he confided. "Asquith seems to want that, and the British public stands behind him because they feel the Irish are traitors who would willingly ally themselves with Germany. At least that's the impression you get from reading the papers. Let me tell you, Fleet Street is having a field day."

Jenkins agreed. "Our most pressing difficulty is that we're facing a foe that's untrained and therefore unsoldierly. Any soldier with a modicum of common sense would have surrendered yesterday. Their inability to understand the futility of their position is only causing more death and destruction."

"Martyrs," Birrell mumbled. "It's a secret weapon."

2

April 27, 1916

4 P.M., *Thursday*

Emerald huddled behind a giant mail bag. Her hands covered her ears; every part of her yearned for silence. The noise was terrifying and deafening. Then there *was* silence, and Emerald looked up. She looked up to see a man near one of the windows, and almost as if she sensed the coming blast, she cried out, "Stand back!" But her cry was lost in the sound of the shell exploding and in the smoke.

The man was dragged into the mail room, and Emerald stared at him in cold horror.

"Hit by a flying piece of shrapnel," the man who dragged him said.

Emerald bit her lip. The fragment had cut him cleanly in half. It was like a surgical cut, and the heat of the flying fragment must have cauterized the nerve endings as it sliced through his body.

But an unmerciful God played a cruel trick. The man was alive and conscious; he clearly did not realize the extent of his injury. He looked at Emerald with clear eyes; he was smiling.

Emerald's nostrils filled with the smell of burning intestines, and a river of blood gushed from his lower torso.

Emerald felt the vomit rise in her throat, and she turned away and retched, feeling as if all her insides would come up.

Pale and shattered, she turned back, forcing herself to look into the face of a horrible living death.

"There, there," the wounded man muttered. "It's only a little stomach wound. Just patch me up, my dear, and I'll go back to my post."

Emerald turned away again and retched. The half man reached out to her and patted her arm. "Now, there, haven't you ever seen blood? I'm sure I've been hurt worse on Saturday night after a donnybrook at the pub."

Emerald bit her lip again, this time so hard that she tasted her own blood. The man reached into his shirt pocket for a cigarette and put it in his mouth. He groped in his pants pocket where his matches had been. "My legs and fingertips are numb from the explosion," he muttered. "Can you get me a pillow to prop up my head, and can you light my cigarette?"

Emerald found the matches and lit his cigarette. Then she propped up his head a little. He sucked on the cigarette and expelled the smoke with obvious pleasure. Then he looked down over his rounded stomach and saw that the lower half of his body was gone and that his intestines were spread out like a coiled snake on the floor. The moment of shocked silence was followed by a long bloodcurdling shriek. "God! Oh, God!" he wailed, and his anguished cry brought Michael Collins from the other room. He looked at the man and, like Emerald, turned and retched at the sight.

"Help me! Oh, God, help me!" the man continued to scream.

Collins wiped his mouth off. "Go away, Emerald," he ordered. His voice was hoarse and strained, his handsome face deathly pale. "Go away," he repeated.

Emerald didn't hesitate. She turned her back and took rapid steps toward the door; then, unable not to, she turned back to witness the scene.

Michael Collins bent over and kissed the man's forehead. "You're a brave man," he whispered. Then he took out his service revolver and held it to the man's head. Then he fired. He replaced his revolver and crossed himself, bowing his head.

Emerald let out her breath, and the man, trailing blood, was dragged across the floor and out of sight. She steadied herself against the wall, and Collins came over to her and gently drew her into his arms. He stroked her hair and held her for a long moment. "Had I time, Lady Ireland, I'd love you. But our time is running out." He released her and without another word left the room.

Emerald followed him with her eyes. His words sang in her ears like a bit of Gaelic verse, a reminder of a song sung in a different time, in a peaceful place. Michael Collins, Emerald decided, had a strange tenderness about him.

There is nothing between us, she thought. But we have shared horror, and for a moment we shared a retreat back into the world as it was before Easter Monday. Today was Thursday, three nights, two and one-half days, and it seemed like an eternity; time eclipsed; experiences intensified; a life lived in hours and minutes. . . . I shall never be the same, Emerald thought. If I survive.

Hours passed, and more and more wounded were brought to her. Nothing in her training could have prepared her for this situation. The hospital was clean and sterile; here it was more often than not an unswept floor.

And in hospitals doctors made the decisions, while here Emerald sorted out the cases, sending the serious ones to the doctors in the basement. It became a task of establishing a priority for those in pain. There wasn't enough morphine to be indiscriminate in its use, so she and the others were forced to differentiate between those in deadly pain and those in moderate pain; between those who might die and those who would die.

For Emerald, her world became the several rooms in which she now worked. At five-thirty, because of the shelling, she too was moved to the basement and set up in a small room adjacent to the main operating room. And in spite of the lights which hung from the ceiling, the basement was a world without time, without sun, without nightfall. It was a world filled with distressing rumors, with stories that caused Emerald great anxiety for the safety of little Tom, whom she alternatively wished was with her and then thanked God he wasn't.

James Connolly had set up stations on the streets around the post office, and many of the wounded came not from within the building, though there were plenty who did, but from the surrounding streets. When the guns were not firing, the British from their vantage point atop high buildings were strafing the streets, spraying them with a rain of death.

"Dublin cries out in agony!" one wounded man cried; tears streamed down his wrinkled old face. "Fires have been set and rage mercilessly in the heart of the city's center, and as people flee from the burning buildings, the British pick them off one by one with snipers. And the shells! One goes off every fifteen minutes!"

Images of Mrs. O'Shea running from a burning building with Tom in her arms haunted Emerald, and in her mind she could see them being sprayed with machine-gun fire; then she imagined them sprawled like rag dolls on the road.

"I hear the Germans are coming to our aid," a wounded man from County Cork said, waving his bloodied arm around.

His words shook Emerald out of her momentary nightmare thoughts. She turned and looked at the man in amazement. "What?" she asked.

"I was going to ask you when they're expected. Don't you know?"

"And how's the battle going at Newry?" asked another of the wounded. He was from Galway, and his shoulder was gushing blood.

"What battle?" Emerald asked. Was the country on fire?

"Must be top-secret," the man winked. "Aye, but all the boys know about it. The Jerries have their army up at Newry on the road to Belfast. It's only a matter of time till the Brits are forced to withdraw from Ireland."

Emerald looked at the man and didn't smile. She didn't want to be rescued by the Germans who had killed Thomas Hughes and who used chlorine gas. "It's not true," she replied. "The only fighting is here in Dublin."

"Isn't it the Germans who are coming?" another man interjected.

"No, it's the Yanks. They're going to force the British to surrender by refusing to fight the Jerries if we're not given our rights. It's Yankee money that bought the bullets we're fighting with."

Emerald turned abruptly and went to James Connolly, whose serious leg wound now forced him to command from a bed.

"You've got to stop these rumors," Emerald insisted without hesitation. "Before they get out of hand."

Connolly rubbed his chin. "And why would I be doing that?"

Emerald frowned. "It's not fair to the men to let them believe that help is on the way. It's false hope they're clinging to."

"And what hope should I replace it with?" he mocked her.

"The truth would be better," Emerald returned, ignoring his tone.

"And what purpose would that serve?"

"It's only fair. Those men are fighting and dying, and they actually believe they're going to be rescued either by the Germans or the Americans. It's just not fair!"

Connolly opened his mouth to speak, then closed it before a word was uttered. He seemed to be searching for the right words. Finally he spoke. "Mrs. Hughes, no doubt you are a worldly woman, even though you are young. You have experienced both pain and joy. You have a son, someone to live for. These rumors are spread by men who have very little to live for, save victory or the thought of it. You spoke of fighting and dying; it is I who have asked them to fight and to die; it is I who have the final responsibility for their deaths. Every second longer that they can hold out is one second closer to our ultimate victory, and I will use every means at our disposal to obtain that victory." His tone revealed a touch of his famous temper toward the end of his speech, but Emerald did not back off. She simply stood her ground and stared at him.

"You cannot be that deceitful to dying men. Have you told them they were meant for martyrdom rather than victory?"

"If they have hope, they will keep fighting."

"That's cruel. You're causing more deaths than need be."

"Cruel, but effective. Cruel, but honest. Whether we die fighting or with a white flag in our hands, most of us are going to die. If Ireland is to be free, then we must die as freedom fighters, we must die with guns in our hands, fighting to our last breath."

Emerald grasped the side of the desk and fought to control herself. "How very theatrical," she said coldly.

"We're close to victory," Connolly boasted.

Emerald shook her head. "I won't leave now, because I can't. But, Mr. Connolly, you're little better than the British whom you claim to despise. You're sending men to their death, not to free Ireland, but because you're guilty of the sin of pride. Mr. Connolly, it is 'God who giveth and God who taketh away.' God, Mr. Connolly, not you. Not James Connolly, who has turned the General Post Office into hell! Mr. Connolly, I believe in a free Ireland too. But we must have free minds, too, free from guilt."

"And I suppose you'll blame me for your brother's death too." Connolly was trying to sound hard and cold. But sitting in bed, his leg obviously hurting a great deal, his image failed him.

"No," Emerald said softly. "Seamus chose to go. He chose to die, though I would have stopped him if I could have. No, for that I do not blame you."

"I think I'm right," he finally said.

Emerald looked into his weary eyes. The man seemed to have aged ten years since Monday. "You're wrong," she said with determination; then she left. It was no use; they had agreed to disagree.

3

April 29, 1916

10 A.M., Saturday

James Connolly listened to the report on Friday's events. Michael O'Rahilly, known as "The O'Rahilly," had come to join the rebellion. He had taken a group of wounded out and, according to reports, all had been killed. Friday, like Thursday, was a nightmare of destruction.

The post office roof had caved in, and damage to the building was severe. And what was left of the rebels was a sorry lot of wounded, weary men and women.

"It's over," Connolly said sadly. "There's nothing I can do but surrender. If we don't surrender, they'll kill us all, even the women.

"Ah, Mrs. Hughes." Connolly signaled Emerald to his side. "I have a request of you, if you don't mind."

Emerald looked at the wounded man whom she had challenged two days before. The life was being sapped out of him. And she had heard stories, all the terrible stories of what was happening all around Dublin.

People who had nothing to do with the rising were being shot, mass arrests had been made, and there had been a senseless destruction that no one could have imagined would occur. And Seamus was dead. Emerald shuddered and again put her anxiety for Tom out of her mind.

"Ask, Mr. Connolly," she invited.

"If I had the strength, Mrs. Hughes, I would walk with the white flag in my own hand, even though I know I would be shot on sight. Regrettably, I can't even stand up. Will you perform the task, Mrs. Hughes?"

Emerald nodded. "If you think it's right."

"No, Mrs. Hughes, it's not right. But I have no choice." He had tears in his eyes and Emerald looked at him, wondering what manner of man he really was.

"And if I send a man out there, he too would be shot on sight. Now, I don't trust the British all that much, but somehow I don't believe even they would shoot a defenseless nurse. And while I don't mind dying myself, I have some responsibility to get the women and wounded out of here."

Emerald nodded, clenching her fists together and thinking how much she wanted to walk out the damnable door and run straight home, straight to Tom.

"You'll tell them I'm ordering all the men under my command to surrender."

Again Emerald nodded.

"Have you a white flag?" James Connolly asked.

Emerald looked around. There was nothing. Then she remembered her petticoat. The front was saturated with dry blood, but the back was still white. She twisted it around and lifted her skirt, tearing a large piece from it. "Here," she answered. "This will have to do."

Emerald took a long deep breath and poked the flag, which had been attached to a pole, through the door.

"Good-bye, Lady Ireland."

Emerald paused for a second when she heard Michael Collins speak. She turned to him for a second, "What will happen?"

He smiled at her and winked. "If I survive, we'll meet on another day. If I'm hung, you look for me resurrected and leading a band of rebels to a real victory. The ghosts of Ireland are going to rise up, Emerald. And you can't kill a ghost."

Emerald turned away from him and stepped out the door, half-expecting to be greeted by a rain of bullets. She walked to the street, and there, for an instant, stood still. She inhaled as the smell of blood was left behind.

It was an eerie silence that greeted her as she walked down O'Connell Street and proceeded toward the British barricade at the far end.

"That's how I likes me women, surrendering to me charms," a soldier called out.

"Over here, my pretty. And I'll thrust some British truce into you!" another called.

"Your flag's not white enough, tear off more of your dress, you filthy mick cunt!"

"No wonder they stayed in there so long—brought all their whores with them, they did."

A man whistled through his teeth. "Bet she's banged half of Ireland!"

Emerald fought back her tears, though she was not crying because of the verbal abuse, which she hardly heard. She was only vaguely aware of the filthy insults, because after five days of death and dying, five days which seemed a lifetime, the words meant nothing. Emerald lifted her head and continued walking, successfully navigating the gauntlet of swearing men. Mercifully, no one tried to touch her.

A captain met her and motioned his men to instant silence. "This way," he beckoned. "Follow me."

They got into his car and drove. Emerald closed her eyes, but continued to clutch her white flag. How long had it been since she slept? She couldn't remember.

They reached the field command post—or at least that's what Emerald assumed it was. The captain ushered her inside. "Colonel Jenkins, miss."

Colonel Albert Jenkins bowed from the waist and ushered Emerald to a canvas chair. "How may I assist you?"

"Mr. Connolly has ordered the remaining soldiers who are under his command at provisional headquarters to surrender and cease firing immediately. He has empowered me to ask you for terms of surrender."

Jenkins smiled. "No offense, madam, but do you have the power of agreement?"

"I do," Emerald answered. She looked down at her dress. It was filthy and bloodstained. Her hair was a tangled mass of snarls, her eyes were red and puffy, and she felt less than human.

"One more point. I do not know your name."

"Emerald Hughes. Mrs. Hughes."

"Is your husband inside the post office, madam?"

"No, sir, my husband is dead—he was killed at Ypres fighting with the British Army."

Jenkins looked at her, and Emerald could feel his bewilderment. "My deepest regrets," he stuttered. "Your husband died in combat fighting for the United Kingdom, while you have been aiding and abetting those who sought to injure and destroy the very uniform I'm sure he wore so proudly. Can you explain this to me?"

Emerald opened her mouth to speak; she ran her tongue around her lips, aware of her thirst and the fact that she had not had any water for some time. "I can," she answered, "but may I have a glass of water?"

Jenkins poured it for her and handed it to her. She drank it all down, savoring it as if it were whiskey.

"To explain my late husband's actions in relation to those of my own would take far more time than either of us has at this moment. Neither my husband nor I hate England. We do . . . he *did*, however, love Ireland. To love Ireland is, among other things, to hate tyranny in all its forms. In 1914 the Germans invaded France, an event similar to your invasion of Ireland in the twelfth century. Since the twelfth century you British have viewed Ireland as your private fief, destroying our language, freedom, and religion. The very same principles that compelled my late husband to go to France are identified with the principles held by the brave men and women who have held the city of Dublin for the past week."

Emerald finished and felt suddenly as if she had articulated her own beliefs for the first time. In spite of her weariness, she saw a sudden clarity to the week's events. It was as if the mist had lifted from her mind.

"My God, woman!" Jenkins was slightly flushed. "That was seven hundred years ago!"

"And, General, your soldiers and administrators are still here. Does it mean anything to you that in order to have this little talk right now, I am compelled to speak *your* language in *my* country? It was not until recently that it was possible for us to learn our own Gaelic language. It's only been in the last hundred years that mothers like myself have been able to take their infants to church freely and openly to receive holy baptism. All you have given us is foreign-born landlords, foreign-born administrators, and each time we demand the same justice as the French and the Belgians, we receive foreign-made bullets and steel."

"My dear lady, your words both interest and trouble me."

Emerald leaned over, and pointing to the water, asked if she might have more.

The colonel poured it. "The business of war and peace is our priority," he finally said.

"May I have your terms?" Emerald answered.

"Unconditional surrender," Jenkins said. "You have one hour to give me your decision."

"On behalf of James Connolly and the provisional government of the republic of Ireland, I accept your terms." Emerald could hardly hold back her own tears—the words "on behalf of the republic of Ireland" had come out proudly, and she was aware of the pride she felt uttering them.

"I'll have the terms drawn up," Jenkins informed her. "But I fear I must make an additional request for your services. In order to prevent further bloodshed, would you be so kind as to transmit the document of surrender to all the other positions held by your people? A detachment of my men will escort you on these rounds, and I personally guarantee that no abuse, verbal or otherwise, will be directed toward you."

Emerald scrutinized Colonel Jenkins. She was at war with herself, and terribly afraid she might trust too easily. But she had to know about her son.

"If I may request one favor from you," she answered cautiously. "I should like you to send two unarmed men who can be trusted to an address I will give you. I would like those men to bring a Mrs. Maggie O'Shea and my baby here, so when I am finished I may see that they are well and unharmed."

Jenkins seemed to be studying her; then he agreed. He gave her paper, and she wrote down the address.

"I shall do my best," he said, taking the paper from her. "But you realize you will be arrested."

"But not my baby or Mrs. O'Shea. They had nothing to do with this. And I want your word that they will be left alone and that no retribution will be taken against them."

Jenkins smiled slightly. "We do not arrest babies," he replied.

"And the rest of it?" Emerald was staring at him intensely.

Jenkins met her gaze. He had been stationed in Belfast and he knew about retribution. Doubtless this woman knew the kinds of atrocities that could occur. He thought of Bowen-Colthurst, and a chill ran down his spine. "You have my word. They shall be placed under my personal protection for as long as necessary."

Emerald stood up and picked up her flag. "I'm ready," she announced.

He nodded. "It'll just be a few minutes before the documents are ready."

Emerald waited outside, breathing the fresh air and wishing it were completely over. But it would not be over for a long while, she admitted. She would be arrested, she would go to jail . . . God only knew for how long!

"The documents are ready." The man who spoke was fresh and clean-looking. He was also young.

"I'm ready," Emerald told him.

The rebels at the Four Courts surrendered to the British, and next Emerald led her detachment to the main gate of the College of Surgeons.

She walked alone to the sentry at the gate. "I'm Emerald Hughes. I must speak with the Countess Markievicz. I come in place of James Connolly."

The man screwed up his face. "I don't know you," he muttered. His eyes were red and swollen. *He's had no more sleep than I have,* Emerald thought.

"Is this some new kind of British trick?"

"No, I come from the post office, and Mr. Connolly has ordered a surrender. The provisional government has ordered everyone to lay down their arms. Please, I am unarmed and the countess knows me."

The man examined her again; then reluctantly he stepped aside.

Emerald walked up to the door, and it was the countess herself who opened it. She was clad all in green, wearing breeches and a military jacket. "I take it we're surrendering," she said crisply. Her tone was one of resignation rather than actual desire. "We put on one hell of a good show!" Her eyes danced with merriment, and for a moment Emerald felt as if the countess must have fallen to earth from a distant planet.

"I'll fetch co-commander Mallin." She disappeared and in a few moments returned.

"I need a pistol," she announced, much to Emerald's surprise. "Mine was damaged during the fighting." She turned to Emerald. "I see you don't understand. Well, one must surrender something. I certainly can't surrender my feathered hat to those idiot soldiers." She smiled wickedly. "And I don't believe we're allowed to return fire when we're put in front of a firing squad."

"I don't think they'll be shooting us," Mallin interjected. "I rather imagine we shall be hanged."

"They wouldn't! We're prisoners of war. I for one demand to be executed as such. Hangings are for criminals and traitors. We are neither! We're Irish and we've been defeated in combat against a foreign enemy. Surely even the British will see the essential difference."

"Dear Georgina, it's the British, who have always considered us traitors, that you'll have to convince, not me. But if they admit this is a political struggle, then they admit their own guilt."

"They wouldn't dare hang me," the countess retorted.

"The British are waiting," Mallin reminded her.

"I must find my hat. A lady should never go anywhere without her hat." The countess walked about, disappearing for a while.

"It's her slouch hat, given to her by an Australian friend," Mallin explained.

"I have it!" the countess called out. "Oh, the feather is missing!"

Emerald leaned against the wall. She was so tired she thought she would drop, and her thoughts were now fully concentrated on seeing Tom. Everything around her, everyone, took on an air of unreality. She felt as if she were onstage finishing the last act of a long, tedious play.

"A miracle!" Mallin announced. "We've found a feather! Not as grand as the ostrich-plume original, but I think it will do."

The countess placed the feather in her hat band, and tilting her head, placed her hat on. It gave her a jaunty, fighting appearance that belied her petite stature. Michael Mallin handed her a pistol.

The three of them, followed by the remaining fighters, walked out of the building, through the gate, and over to the British detachment.

Withdrawing the pistol that Mallin had given her, the countess lifted the gun in the air, exhibiting it to the whole stunned group of soldiers. She pressed it to her lips and kissed it tenderly, then extended it to the British officer and murmured, "I'm ready."

The line of rebel prisoners wound through the streets of Dublin like a long snake. From all their previously held positions, the rebels laid down their arms and joined their comrades in surrender; an uncertain fate.

Close to one thousand men and women marched with their heads bowed, to the detention camps the British had established in anticipation of the surrender.

But it was not an inspiring march. All along the route, the besieged inhabitants of Dublin, divided at the best of times, screamed, hooted, jeered, and swore at the rebels.

"Traitors!"

"Huns!"

"Filth!" The cries were anguished and angry. A few onlookers hurled stones.

"This is the thanks we get. For near a week we've fought for the freedom and independence of Ireland. For *their* independence!" The rebel prisoner pointed at the people who lined the sidewalk.

"Ridicule and derision," another mumbled. "A thousand dead, a thousand prisoners, and we get ridicule!"

But Emerald was not forced to march. In the silence of Colonel Jenkins' command post, she embraced her son and let her tears run freely down her face.

"Oh, I was frantic," she confessed to Mrs. O'Shea, who stood white-faced and rigid.

Colonel Jenkins came in. He had waited discreetly outside. "I'm afraid you'll have to come with me now," he told Emerald.

She reluctantly handed Tom back to Mrs. O'Shea. She shook her head in misery. "I'm going to miss your birthday, darling . . . your first birthday." She choked on her tears, and the baby held out his arms to her and cried to be taken back.

Emerald braced herself against the table. "I'll be back," she said softly. "Please watch over him."

Maggie O'Shea mumbled her answer. Then she took the crying baby away.

"You have my word they'll not be harmed," Colonel Jenkins promised.

From outside, Emerald heard Tom cry, "Mama!"

She listened and wiped her tears with her hand. "That's the first time he's spoken," she said.

"A lovely child," Colonel Jenkins said awkwardly.

Emerald put down her hand and looked him in the eyes. "Not unlike other Irish children," she said, turning away.

14

1

December 14, 1916

A cold rain had turned to ice that now coated the trees on St. Stephen's Green so that they looked like crystal. Emerald thrust her hands into the pockets of her threadbare coat and inhaled deeply. Even if it was cold and damp, she savored the fresh air and delighted in the sights and smells that assaulted her.

No one, Emerald reflected, could ever appreciate freedom until he had been incarcerated. And though she had grown up in the small world of the McArthurs' house and garden, she had run free on her release and embraced the outside world with a passion that made her recent confinement even more of a nightmare; it was a temporary return to her deprived childhood.

Emerald, like the others, was arrested under the "Defense of the Realm Act," which came into force automatically when martial law was proclaimed. This act enabled the British government to suspend its own democratic laws of *habeas corpus* and trial. Anyone could be arrested and held without trial, but a court-martial—a summary trial by a military court—could be carried out and those judged treasonous could be executed.

On May 3, Padraic Pearse, Thomas MacDonagh, and Thomas Clarke were shot; on May 4, William Pearse, Joseph Plunkett, Edward Daly, and Michael O'Hanrahan were shot; on May 5, John MacBride; on May 8, Cornelius Colbert, Eamonn Ceannt, Michael Mallin, and Sean Heuston were shot; and finally, on May 12, James Connolly and Sean MacDiarmida were executed.

It was said that James Connolly had developed gangrene in his severely wounded leg and that he could not stand against the wall to face the firing squad. So, the story went, he had been tied to a chair, and there, his brain muddled by a high fever, he lifted his head so that he might die looking up at God, his maker, and facing his murderers bravely. He was, Emerald contemplated, the very essence of the martyrdom he wanted to create.

Connolly's was the last execution except for one in the countryside. In all, the executions had the effect Connolly had so desired: they turned all Dublin against the British. Those who had jeered in the streets at the defenders of the post office and the other rebel strongholds were now jeering the British, who had turned on the populace with undeserved retaliation for the rising. Thousands had been arrested and detained, over a thousand had been sent to England, and horrible stories about completely uninvolved Irish families murdered by the British spread like wildfire. Each new story kindled a spark that became a flame in the heart of Ireland, giving rise to a new ferocious nationalism and a heightened desire for freedom.

But Emerald did not know these things while she was detained. She had heard that in Britain and Ireland the public reaction to the executions and arrests was so great that they were suspended and that the Countess Markievicz and Michael Collins had their sentences commuted to life. She also learned that Mr. de Valera, whom Seamus liked so much, was given life because he had been born in the United States and the British were reluctant to irritate Irish-American sentiment at a time when America would go to war with Germany.

Emerald stopped and leaned against a tree trunk. She had been released fourteen days ago on the first of December, and she still couldn't get sufficient fresh air or see enough of the world.

But I'm more fortunate than most, she admitted. She had been tried by a group of officers who merely asked her name and what she was doing in the post office.

"Looking after the wounded," she had explained.

"And did you take up arms?" one officer asked; he didn't even look up at her.

"No," Emerald replied.

"One year in detention," was the verdict. I wanted to cry out, she remembered, but she couldn't.

Shortly after being taken to the detention center, she was removed to a military prison where there was an infirmary. She spent her days working in the wards as a nurse and her nights in a locked room alone. No one spoke with her. At least I was able to work at my profession, she thought. Other nurses were sent to hard labor, and Emerald questioned her good fortune more than once.

And Mrs. O'Shea was allowed to visit once a month and bring Tom. They were happy, joyous visits and Emerald had lived from one visiting day to the next.

Then there was a Christmas amnesty and Emerald's name was on the list of amnestied prisoners.

Emerald sat down on a damp bench and took Padraic's letter out of her purse. She reread it for the third time, trying to picture him, yearning to see him.

My dearest sister,

My heart weeps for you in prison and I pray every day that you will be released. There is talk here of a Christmas amnesty. I pray it will apply to you, who do not in any case belong in jail.

I hope that when you are free you will bundle little Tom up and come to America. Emerald, what does Ireland hold for you now? I have sent you some money in care of Mrs. O'Shea. I will send more every month, since I make a good living as a policeman—now, Emerald, don't jump to conclusions—the police in America are not like the police in Ireland. We only deal with criminals, not honest citizens who only want their freedom.

Please consider coming. Please. I can save enough money for you in a few months' time. Oh, Emerald, you would love it! The stores are full of lovely things, and there's opportunity aplenty.

We'll both weep for Seamus, but, Emerald, you must live now.

Love,
Padraic

"I've sent you a telegram," Emerald said aloud. "And a letter, just in case." Damn the war, Emerald thought. It takes months to get mail to America, and if he didn't get my cable, he still thinks I'm in detention.

Emerald got up and began walking toward home to the flat she now shared with Maggie O'Shea, whose sons had been killed in the rising. No wonder she looked so pale when she brought Tom. Such an unselfish woman . . . she didn't even tell me then.

"Bless you, Padraic, and bless you, Mrs. O'Shea," Emerald whispered. But there was hope. Next week she would return to the hospital, and she'd be earning a salary. And did they need it! What funds there were had been used. This will not be the merriest of Christmases, she admitted.

Emerald climbed the stairs to the flat, and Mrs. O'Shea flung open the door as she walked down the corridor. "Oh, I couldn't wait for you to come home! You know how I am, I'm filled with the devil's own curiosity!"

"Mama! Mama!" Tom flew into her arms.

"At eighteen months, you're a real armful, you are!" Emerald hugged and kissed him. "Ah, my darling." She nuzzled her cold face into his warm neck and he giggled and squealed in delight. She tickled and cuddled him, then sent him off running into the bedroom.

"It's here, it came right after you left. I really think the delivery boy thought he'd gotten the wrong address. He asked if you lived here three times."

Emerald studied the huge carton that sat in the middle of the table. "What on earth?" She walked over to it and examined it closely. "Is there no card?"

Mrs. O'Shea shook her head.

"Well, perhaps it's inside." Emerald tore open the top of the brown corrugated carton carefully and gasped. "Lo and behold, it's full of Christmas presents!"

Mrs. O'Shea peered inside, and her round face broke into a smile. It's the first time she's smiled in a long while, Emerald observed.

Inside the box were a number of smaller parcels, each one individually wrapped in a different color of paper. "It's a rainbow of gifts!" Mrs. O'Shea laughed.

One by one, Emerald took them out. Each one bore a label. There were three small parcels for Tom and three for herself, though one of hers was quite large. There was one for Mrs. O'Shea and on the bottom were a fine ham, two tins of jam, a large cheese, and some fruit.

"I can't believe it!" Emerald exclaimed. "It's our whole Christmas in a giant box!"

"But no card." Mrs. O'Shea sounded mystified.

Emerald frowned. "It's certainly from someone with money," she said finally. Then added, "Perhaps it's from the countess' family." In fact, the countess and her friends were the only wealthy people Emerald knew. All of her other friends and acquaintances were like her, as poor as church mice.

"Why would the countess' family send a gift without a card?" Mrs. O'Shea did not reject the contents of the box, but she looked on them suspiciously.

"Whoever it's from, we ought to accept it graciously and hope that the person will come forward to be thanked."

"Shall we open them now?" Mrs. O'Shea asked.

"No, we'll keep them for Christmas morning and we'll have the ham for our Christmas dinner. What do you think?"

"I think I've forgotten what ham tastes like," she joked back. "And, my, won't that bone make a fine soup?"

"It will indeed," Emerald answered.

2

December 17, 1916

Colonel Jenkins sipped his brandy and watched the dying embers of the fire. Christmas season was a lonely time, and this Christmas, so far from home, seemed more lonely than most.

Sophie, his wife, had died three years ago in childbirth, and though they had never been passionate lovers, they were good friends and it was Sophie's warmth and companionship he missed.

"More brandy, sir?" Jeffries came into the study so silently that the sound of his voice startled Jenkins.

"A bit," Jenkins answered, extending the large gold-trimmed brandy snifter.

Jeffries filled it. "Will that be all, sir?"

Jenkins nodded.

"I'll be retiring, then. Shall I leave the bottle?"

"Please," Jenkins responded. He waved Jeffries off. He sipped his brandy slowly. I wonder if she's received the package, and I wonder what she thinks . . . at least she'll have a good Christmas dinner. He sighed. Does behaving like Scrooge make me happy? he asked himself. That's what he felt like, and Mrs. Hughes is Bob Cratchit and her baby is Tiny Tim. God bless them every one. He drank some more brandy and chastised himself for not enclosing a card. "But she might have sent it back," he mused aloud. "At least if I don't tell her till after Christmas, she will have enjoyed the food."

He had made an agreement with himself. He had promised himself that he would wait until after Christmas and then call on her. She could accept him or reject him then, though he hoped she would accept him by allowing him to call again.

The truth of the matter was that since the day of the surrender nearly nine months ago, he had been haunted by his memory of Emerald Hughes, the extraordinarily beautiful nurse who had brought him Connolly's surrender and who at considerable danger to herself had gone to the other rebel strongholds and obtained their surrender as well. She was a strange sight that day in her tattered, bloodstained uniform with her hair a tangle and her eyes heavy with the need for sleep.

Yes, Emerald Hughes had struck a chord that day, and though he had not done so openly, he had more or less extended his protection to her by seeing to it that she was removed from the prison and sent to an infirmary and then by making certain her name appeared on the Christmas amnesty lists.

And now that she was free, Colonel Jenkins was unsure of how, exactly, to proceed. Odd, he conceded, he could plan battles and make life-and-death decisions, but he was at a loss when it came to making his admiration for a woman known. It was cowardly to send a gift without a card, he decided. Then he dismissed the thought. "I'll make up for it."

Emerald Hughes was, he sensed, a woman among women. She appeared to be physically flawless, and even from his short conversation with her—it made him smile just to remember it—he knew she was highly intelligent. And there was wit too, and just that tip of a temper that made a woman desirable; the fire of life, he called it. He admitted that it was desire he felt, though in fact he also felt a deep respect for her. She had taken the trouble to lecture him, and though she hadn't told him anything he didn't already know, she had done it with style and conviction.

But how would she react to him? In fact, would she even remember him? They had certainly experienced a fleeting encounter. He wondered if there would be too much between them, he wondered if she could understand his position militarily: that breaking the back of the rebellion was his job, just as nursing was hers. And his job had nothing to do with his analysis of the Irish situation or his feelings toward the Irish; his actions, in fact, had little to do with his own convictions. After all, nothing could be solved by war—who knew that better than a good soldier? But before there could be peace, there had to be order, and it was his job to bring about order and to maintain it.

He took another sip of his brandy and wiped his brow. The authorities had mucked up Ireland; there was no doubt about it. The repression during and after the uprising had been extreme, and it had rallied more supporters for Irish independence than any speech by an Irish nationalist could ever do.

Stories circulated all over Dublin about the cold-blooded crimes of Bowen-Colthurst and others like him. Fortunately, Bowen-Colthurst had been put away in a mental institution. But the British public was screaming about that too. Rumor had it that Bowen-Colthurst would be sent off to the far Canadian province of British Columbia for the rest of his life. It was the kind of thing the British Army did frequently. The shell-shocked, as Bowen-Colthurst was described by his doctors: the mentally ill officers who went too far in the line of duty and betrayed themselves and their rank, they were all pensioned off and sent out to British Columbia, where, it was assumed, a life of rest and sunshine would cure most of them.

Perhaps, he mused, if his superiors knew he was behaving like a puppy in springtime over an Irish rebel, one who had taken part in the recent uprising, he too would be sent to an institution or off to British Columbia. But no, no one would think him strange who saw Emerald Hughes and felt the compelling strength of her presence. No, a man who found Mrs. Hughes attractive was quite, quite sane.

3

January 4, 1917

Colonel Albert Jenkins looked at the startled expression on Mrs. Hughes's face as he stood before her, albeit in civilian dress.

"May I come in?" He stood stiffly, and in spite of his manner of dress, he still looked every inch the military man.

Emerald motioned him inside.

"Are you alone?" he asked, looking about the spotlessly neat and homey little room.

"Mrs. O'Shea is out for the evening and the baby's asleep." Emerald was glad Maggie wasn't home. Having lost her sons to British bullets, she could hardly be expected to greet a British officer with any kind of friendliness.

Colonel Jenkins shifted his weight from one foot to the other. "May I sit down?"

Emerald nodded. "To what do I owe this unusual visit?"

"Is it so unusual?" He tried to sound casual. His gray eyes studied her.

Emerald sat down too, but she felt uncomfortable; he seemed to be staring right through her. She sighed. No, that wasn't why she was uncomfortable. It was that Christmas had just passed and she had felt warmth and comfort during the holiday season. Now she was suddenly reminded of the rising and its aftermath.

"It seems unusual. I shouldn't think that a British officer would be calling on a rebel so recently released from prison."

"You weren't exactly in prison, you were working in a hospital."

"I was detained, locked up and deprived of my freedom. That, Colonal Jenkins, is being in prison."

The colonel moved in his chair uncomfortably. He didn't

answer immediately, but rather fumbled in his unfamiliar tweed jacket, withdrawing a briar pipe. "May I?"

"Yes." She watched as he stuffed it with tobacco and lit it, sending billows of sweet-smelling smoke into the room.

"I suppose you'd like some tea, too," Emerald stated.

"That would be delightful." He actually smiled.

"I was going to fix some for myself anyway." Emerald got up and walked to the small stove in the alcove that served as a kitchen.

Albert Jenkins followed her with his eyes. "This room expresses your personality," he said, looking around. It was not a large room, but the sofa was covered with soft material which was russet in color, and so was the overstuffed chair he was sitting in. On a small table was a picture of a young British soldier, and Jenkins assumed it must be a photo of her husband. In another picture, on a second table, he could clearly see her in a wedding dress . . . yes, the man with his arm around her was the same young man in soldier's dress. Behind the huddle of furniture was a table, and in the alcove were a pantry, a cupboard, a sink, and an icebox. The center of the room was covered with a round carpet, and in one corner some shelves held a collection of books; quite a lot of books, as a matter of fact. And there was another photo; it was of a man standing in a lush jungle area— South Africa, Jenkins decided.

"What do you mean the room expresses my personality? How do you know what I'm like?" Emerald set the teacups down on the table and Jenkins got up and went over to it.

"I'm a good judge of character, and you showed a lot of character in a short period of time on April 29." He smiled and sat down.

They were silent for a moment, and Emerald sipped some tea.

"Was it too terrible?" His expression was one of deep concern.

"Was what too terrible?"

"Prison," he answered, not even liking the word. "I tried to make it easier for you by having you transferred to the hospital."

Emerald set down her cup, aware that she looked surprised. "You arranged for me to be transferred?"

"I was . . . I am very grateful to you for the role you played in bringing the rebellion to an end. I admired your courage—you do have courage, Mrs. Hughes. I wanted to do something to repay you."

Emerald scowled at him. "I did what I did to prevent further bloodshed, for no other reason."

"I couldn't keep you from going to prison, I only tried to

make it more comfortable for you. And I got your name on the Christmas amnesty lists so you could come home to your child, Mrs. Hughes." His face had gone red, and again he moved uneasily. "For your husband, Mrs. Hughes. For his memory."

Emerald poured some more tea into her cup. "How kind of you," she said sarcastically. "But I was in the post office, and I saw my brother killed by British bullets. I was one of them, Colonel Jenkins, and there are thousands of people in British jails who are completely innocent of even taking part in the rebellion. Do they deserve to be in jail while I am free?"

He stared at the floor and finally admitted, "I can't extend my personal protection to everyone, Mrs. Hughes."

Emerald covered her eyes with her hand in exasperation. The man was impossible, and why couldn't he understand? "Your personal protection embarrasses me," she answered in a low, sad voice. "It places me in a position of privilege. Colonel, I'm Irish, I'm a Catholic, and I'm no less guilty than the others."

"You never took up arms," he protested.

Emerald stared at him, her green eyes large. "I bandaged the hands that held the guns," she answered. "And I have no regrets."

He leaned back. "And I gave the orders to the men who pulled the triggers, though I myself have never killed anyone. And I have no regrets either. I'd say that makes us rather alike."

"We are not alike!" Emerald quickly replied, not even trying to control her voice.

Colonel Jenkins sucked on his pipe, then sipped on his tea. Then he leaned across the table. "You're arrogant, Mrs. Hughes. You gave me a lecture on Ireland and supposed that the things you were saying were somehow new to me. They were not. I am perfectly aware of Irish grievances and I am perfectly aware of the justice of those grievances. I would see them redressed—all of them. But, Mrs. Hughes, that is the duty of negotiators and of politicians. My job is to keep order and to restore order when it has been threatened."

"And to that end you leveled half of Dublin and walked over the rights of completely innocent people, even to the point of allowing your underlings to kill little children! That is not order, Colonel, that is despotism, pure and simple."

"I did not kill children and I did not give orders to kill children. As a matter of fact, I was instrumental in the arrest and conviction of a lunatic British soldier who did commit such crimes. Mrs. Hughes, I beg you to look at the role the rebels played in the killing of innocent people. They pushed us into a position where we had to retaliate with full force. By choosing to fight where and how they fought, they literally thrust people into British bullets and then accused us of murder. Mrs. Hughes, you are seeing this whole situation from a very one-sided position!"

Emerald set her cup down. "Perhaps, but you are in my house and I don't even know why you are here, except to tell me how grateful I ought to be to you!"

"I didn't say that." He was close to stuttering.

"You intimated it."

"I came to see you. I came to see if you were well. I came to see if you received my Christmas gifts . . ." His face was quite red.

Emerald felt herself flushing too, but with anger rather than embarrassment. "Your presents!" She was completely taken aback. "I don't want your presents. . . . I . . . You can keep them!"

He leaned back and looked at her appraisingly. In point of fact, she was wearing the dress he had sent. A modest gray dress trimmed in white. Her hair was hanging loose; it was a most becoming dress. And he was just as sure that little Thomas Hughes was wearing his new little shirt and already playing with the two toys. No doubt the food was eaten as well.

"I hardly think I want them back now," he said. "They're used."

Emerald stared at his face and thought her consternation must certainly be evident. And to make matters worse, he seemed to be smirking at her now.

"I didn't know they were from you. I thought they were from the countess' family . . . or somebody."

"They were from somebody." He drained his cup and stood up. "Please keep them with my compliments. And I may say, the dress looks lovely on you."

Emerald stood up too. "Thank you," she said slowly, "for your thoughtfulness. But please, don't send me anything else."

"I shan't promise, Mrs. Hughes. But I would like to come and visit."

"You are not entirely welcome." Emerald tried to sound cold, but she could barely hide her confusion.

"I hope you will change your mind, Mrs. Hughes. I come entirely in friendship. I admire you and I find you most interesting. Frankly, I enjoy arguing with you."

"I doubt there is any shortage of people to argue with in Dublin," she retorted.

He was standing at the door and he bowed slightly from the waist. "But none of them, Mrs. Hughes, are as beautiful as you."

4

January 29, 1917

Maggie O'Shea stood over the stove and stirred a pot of stew. She was a short, round woman with wisps of gray hair that refused to be held prisoner by the bun she attempted to push them into. Her face was deeply lined, but her eyes were still bright, and in spite of the tragedy she had experienced when her two sons had been killed, she retained her wit.

On New Year's Day she had traveled to Limerick to visit her other children, who were all married and who had children of their own. She returned a renewed woman, bustling and active as ever.

"Politics!" Maggie O'Shea shook her head. "I never expect politicians to do much of anything!"

"Political pressure is better than killing," Emerald insisted. She lifted Tom into his high chair and did up the strap that held him in. He smiled impishly at her and cried out for a piece of bread. "And do you want Mama to butter it?" Emerald kissed his hair. Tom nodded vigorously. Emerald buttered the bread and handed it to him. "That should keep you busy till dinner's ready."

"Well, I don't understand this whole political idea," Maggie admitted as she put the spoon down. "Ireland has had representatives in Westminster, but they've never done a thing for us. Paid to sit on his arse, John Redmond is."

"This is different,'\ Emerald explained. "Mr. Kelly—he was the M.P. from North Roscommon—has died, and Count Plunkett, whose son was killed in the rising, is running in the by-election to fill the vacant seat. He's running as Sinn Fein's candidate."

Sinn Fein was the nationalist political party. It had first been organized by Arthur Griffith, editor of *The United Irishman*. His original organization was called Cumann na naGaedheal—the Society of Gaels—and it dated back to 1902. The philosophy espoused by the Society of Gaels came to be called Sinn Fein, which meant "we ourselves." And now, much to Emerald's

delight, Sinn Fein had become a rallying point for Irish nationalists who believed in political action.

Emerald smiled to herself and decided to try her best tactic.
"Michael Collins is working for Count Plunkett's election. He's
been working on it since the day he was released."

Maggie turned around. She adored Michael Collins and, Emerald thought, if Michael Collins told her to sprout wings and fly
to the moon, she would do it out of the pure desire to please
him.

"Is he, now? Well, if Michael Collins wants Count Plunkett
elected, I want him elected. But I still think all politicians were
meant to bore people to death. And please tell me this—how can
Plunkett run for the British Parliament when the British killed his
two sons? I don't understand."

Emerald shook her head. "No, no. If Count Plunkett is elected
to Westminster, he won't take his seat. He's a Republican and
can't go off to Westminster."

"So if he won't go, why is he running?" Maggie frowned.

"It's a form of political protest," Emerald said. It was difficult to explain the finer points of political strategy to Maggie,
and reluctantly Emerald admitted to herself that, good though
Maggie O'Shea was, she didn't have much of a mind for politics.

"If Sinn Fein can elect, and continue to elect, candidates to
Westminster who refuse to take their seats, the English can no
longer claim that Ireland is represented. As long as the Redmonites
are in Westminster, they can go on saying we have our elected
officials.

"Michael Collins and Arthur Griffith think that Count Plunkett's
election would be a strong political demonstration, especially
now that Lloyd George is prime minister. They say Lloyd George
is more susceptible to pressure, and he has released a lot of the
prisoners," Emerald concluded.

"And will Mr. Lloyd George be bringing back the dead? I for
one have no intention of forgetting what happened nine months
ago."

"Nor I," Emerald said softly. "Maggie, we've been dying for
centuries. This is worth a try."

"And Michael Collins really wants him elected?"

Emerald nodded. Maggie looked on Michael as the voice
of Ireland and always said, "He's handsome, gallant, and
brave."

"What do you want me to do?"

"Help me." Emerald smiled. "It's important to get everyone

to the polls. Michael wants you to help because of your sons. He says people will listen to you.''

Mrs. O'Shea laughed. "Not even my sons listened to me! But if that's what Michael wants, I'll do it.''

Emerald smiled. "I knew you'd help.''

5

January 30, 1917

Emerald sipped her glass of Irish whiskey. Its taste reminded her of time spent with Padraic and Seamus. But the person who shared the bottle of John Jameson with her was not a relative, but rather the persistent Colonel Albert Jenkins, who was calling on her for the fourth time.

"You ought not to be here,'' she said, looking into the amber liquid. Yet, she admitted to herself, she always invited him in, she had told him what nights Mrs. O'Shea was out and when Tom went to bed. In fact, it was he who had brought the bottle of whiskey they were now enjoying. She sighed. His visits always followed the same pattern. They talked, they argued, and he politely said good night.

"I think you enjoy my visits,'' Jenkins observed. He poured a little more from the bottle.

Emerald didn't reply, but the truth was, he was right. She detested everything he stood for—English authority in Ireland, a soldier, the man now credited with the strategy that broke the back of the rebellion—but at the same time she felt a curious liking for the man himself. He wasn't what she'd expected a British soldier to be, and she felt challenged by him. He keeps me on the defensive, Emerald reflected. And I enjoy the verbal jousting, dammit!

"You look distressed. Did I hit a raw nerve?''

"I suppose you did.''

"You mean you're going to admit you like my visits?''

He beamed, and suddenly he wasn't the prim, proper, authoritarian British colonel. He was a young man whose gray eyes had compelling charm. But lest his appeal be too compelling, Emerald turned away, breaking his visual hold on her.

"I like the gifts you bring,'' she said curtly as she indicated the whiskey. "It's a luxury I've not been able to afford lately.''

She returned her eyes to his face and watched him intently, because she had intended her comment to wound, but as the twinkle in his gray eyes faded and turned to pain, she regretted her callousness.

"I didn't mean that. I'm sorry—your gifts are generous and I didn't invite you in because you had a bottle of whiskey."

He smiled and acknowledged her discomfort. "I understand your feelings better than you think," he said quietly.

He's a sensitive man, Emerald realized. "I enjoy talking with you, perhaps I enjoy arguing with you," she finally acknowledged.

"Good. Does that mean I can continue to come?"

"Are you leaving?"

"No. I was just seeing where I stood. A good soldier does that."

Emerald laughed lightly. "You may come again."

He leaned across the table and filled her glass. "You know, I'm getting used to this drink. Though I admit to being a Scotch man. You know, once I was in America and I tried bourbon. Ah, there's a nice smooth drink."

Emerald lifted up the bottle of John Jameson. "But this means something to the Irish. It's something we share whether we're Catholic or Protestant, nationalists or unionists. If you can get two Irishmen to agree on anything, it will be on the whiskey they drink."

Jenkins laughed. Then he leaned over and the smile faded from his face. "You're different, Mrs. Hughes. When I argue with a person, I always want to know about them. . . . Tell me about yourself. Tell me why you're different—not from the Irish, different from other women."

"I don't think I'm that different. You're trying to flatter me."

He shook his head. "No, tell me about yourself."

"Well, I have a brother in America. His name is Padraic."

"And do you hear from him?"

"Oh, yes. He sends us money and presents. If he didn't, I don't know how we'd survive. I don't make much, you know, and while I was in prison . . . well, Padraic was a great help. He wants me to come to America."

"And will you?"

"I don't know . . . I haven't made up my mind."

"And what do his letters tell you about America?"

"Not too much. Padraic learned to read and write in America, going to night school. His letters are not . . . well, terribly descriptive. He talks about what's in the shops and about opportunities. He's a policeman, he is. In New York City."

Jenkins looked at her in surprise. "He was illiterate? But

you're not. I assumed you came from a learned family because you read, and it's rare for a woman to read in any case.''

Emerald shook her head. ''No, not a learned family. No,'' she said thoughtfully. ''We were separated, you see. I was brought up in someone else's home and I wasn't reunited with my brothers until I was nearly sixteen.'' Emerald's voice dropped almost to a whisper.

''Tell me about it,'' Jenkins prodded.

''It began with a fairy princess,'' she said, knowing that Colonel Jenkins would certainly see the tears in her eyes. ''No,'' she started over, ''it began when my mother died.''

Jenkins listened intently. In turns his expression registered surprise, shock, and sympathy. When she had finished, he let out his breath as if he had been holding it for the longest time. ''The bounder!'' he said with reference to Mr. McArthur. ''The filthy old bounder!''

Jenkins' look of disdain was so pronounced that it made Emerald laugh.

''Why are you laughing?'' he asked, mystified.

''I suppose because you're so outraged. Do you think your soldiers haven't done worse to the women of Ireland?''

''But they don't get away with it if I find out!''

''And I doubt you find out all that often,'' Emerald added.

''Perhaps not,'' he allowed. ''Let's not argue tonight.'' He brushed a shock of his graying hair off his forehead and leaned back in the chair, looking a thoroughly relaxed man. ''I like country living,'' he announced offhandedly. ''Dublin is not for me, it's too industrial, too big, and far too dirty. My God, if you fell in the Liffey River, you'd die. At least you'd come out covered with sh . . . ah, excrement.''

Emerald laughed.

''You have a very musical laugh, Mrs. Hughes.'' His voice was cheery and his face a trifle flushed. He took another shot of whiskey. ''I'd better make this my last drink, or I'll be in my cups. Anyway, I have a house in the country. It's lovely. There are horses, dogs, and sheep. My God, it's beautiful.'' His eyes seemed to take on a faraway look and he nodded to himself as if confirming his mental vision. ''It's a big rambling house and we have our own stream, a stream you can fish in, and in the summer you can swim in it. Acres and acres of land and woods.''

''Why did you leave?''

''Because I had to be a soldier, don't you see. My father was a general and my grandfather was a general . . . and before him . . . Ah, woman, no one in my family wasn't a general. We have our own room reserved at Sandhurst.''

"Do you want to be a general?" Emerald asked.

"Want doesn't enter into it." He laughed and slapped the table. "Ah, you Irish have too much history and are ruled by it; we British have too much tradition and are driven by it. We are the willow and the wind—one blowing, the other unbending. In my family, tradition demands that the firstborn son becomes a general. That's the long and short of it.''

Emerald glanced at the clock. Mrs. O'Shea would be home shortly. "It's nearly ten," she reminded him.

Colonel Jenkins stood up and stretched; then he strode to the door, putting some effort into maintaining his straight posture after so much to drink.

Emerald walked behind him to the door. He turned and took her hand as he bowed from the waist. He lifted it and kissed her fingertips.

"Colonel Jenkins . . ." Emerald's face flushed, and he looked up at her boyishly.

"I think we're entering a new era," he slurred. "A more peaceful one, I hope.''

Book III

15

1

February 24, 1917

Boston

Big Joe Scanlon, Sr., had left County Cork in Ireland at the age of thirteen and landed in the United States at the port of New York in 1847.

"You can't imagine," he told his son, Joe Scanlon, Jr. "You can't imagine because your belly's always full. But I remember the aching in my gut, the longing for just a cup of watery soup. It was the Great Famine, you know . . . a hunger that swept County Cork, County Clare, County Mayo, and County Donegal . . . Oh, the others suffered, but not as we did. We produced only potatoes; they were our sustenance, our only food. I'll tell you how it was. We had small farms, but we didn't own the land. No, the Irish didn't own the land—that was owned by the absentee landlords and they divided and split the land into tiny parcels in order to inflate the rents they collected. But when the potato crops failed, no one could pay their rent and there was no food either. So the landlords rented ships, old wrecks of ships, vessels that weren't even seaworthy. They say that one of those ships was built in 1763, but she sailed, she sailed with her hold full of people stacked like boxes, with no air, no proper food, no place to shit and piss, no fresh water—that's what they did, they packed us up like cargo and shipped us out of Ireland. Then in forty-seven, the year my father and I were packed out, typhus broke out. We started out three hundred and twelve people, and when we reached the detention centers we were one hundred and eighty.

"I'd been clinging to my father's breeches for nearly sixteen hours before I found out he was dead of the fever. I'll not forget that black hold in the bowels of that ship, nor the stench and the vermin. Buried at sea, my father was, and I came here as an orphan . . . but I built.

"Then they talked about sending me back, but one of the big officials said, 'Hell no! That youngster's thirteen and there's work for him. Besides, he's a big lad, a good strong boy, and he can take care of himself.' So they sent me out to a sweat shop—that's what we called 'um. Got a couple of cents an hour,

worked twelve hours a day and boarded with a family of twelve
living in two little rooms. After a couple of years, when I was
seventeen, I up and said the hell with this. So I walked to
Boston, I did, working on farms along the way.

"When I got here, I started working in construction and I
moved myself into South Roxbury. Old South Roxbury was like
it was everywhere for the Irish—immigrants stacked up like
cartons on a dock. But all Irish, every damn one.

"When I was thirty, I'd saved a sum. Then I started my own
construction firm, and damned if it didn't work out pretty good.
Made a bundle, I did. And when I was forty-nine, I could finally
afford a wife—your mother, bless her soul, little Annie Finlay.
A pretty lass, a mere twenty, she was. And you, let's see, you
were born in 1885 it was.

"After you, Annie didn't have no more children. Doctor
thought she was barren. Then the Lord up and said, 'No good
Irish woman is ever barren!' Yup, your little brother Mike was
born a month before your fifteenth birthday, in 1900, when I was
near sixty-five years old and had made enough money in construction to spit at any Bostonian Brahmin bastard that walked
down Tremont Street with his head in the air!''

Joe Scanlon, Jr., smiled as he thought of his father's oft-told
tale. Today was the anniversary of his father's death some ten
years ago, and Joe Scanlon had just visited the cemetery to lay a
wreath of flowers beneath the towering Celtic cross that marked
his father's grave.

Joseph Francis Scanlon, Jr., was known to most of his friends
as "Big Joe Scanlon"; it was what they had called his father and
he had inherited the mantle of both his father's wealth and his
father's reputation in ward politics. He was, in fact, big, a
rabbit's hair under six feet tall, with wide shoulders and strong
muscular arms. His hair was thick, light brown, and wavy. He
had brown eyes and his face was square. The angle of his jaw
gave him a look of strength and determination; but at this
moment he felt neither strong nor determined.

Joe Scanlon had reared his younger brother, and though the
two were different in temperament, they were close, so close that
Joe felt torn by conflict. Joe's wife was the former Kitty Corbett,
and he had married her ten years ago, hoping she would make a
home for his younger brother as well as for their own children—
Joe wanted lots of children.

But fate intervened. Kitty was not the woman Joe had imagined her to be and she disliked Mike, treated him coldly. Kitty

also did not have children, and Joe was unsure, given their current situation, if that was a blessing or a curse. He shook his head as he rounded the corner and turned onto Brimmer Street. His home life was an armed camp; he felt betrayed and confused. "I'm thirty-two years old," he muttered as he climbed the steps of the old brownstone, "thirty-two, childless, and trapped."

He glanced up, and there, like an old bird looking down from a telephone wire, was his neighbor, Mrs. Ernestine Clapp, staring from her window, offering her daily challenge. If nothing else in his life gave him great pleasure, Mrs. Clapp did. It was broad daylight, and the sight of him, a stubborn Irishman, in this cool, tight Brahmin neighborhood, galled his neighbors. Dear Mrs. Clapp—as wiry an old Brahmin as there was this side of the Charles River—she waited each day for his return, hoping no doubt that he would be run over by a tram or savaged in a brawl in "one-of-those-places-people-like-that-go." He always disappointed her. He waved—that was the challenge. But Mrs. Clapp did not respond. Instead, she made a disgusted face and thrust her tiny chin into the air, dropping the curtain and disappearing from view. Her answer was a snub: dare wave, and I shall snub you—challenge and response. He regarded it as a game.

Joe Scanlon could laugh at Mrs. Ernestine Clapp because he now had Scanlon Construction, half-interest in a shipbuilding firm in Gloucester, a contract to build a chain of restaurants, an electrical- and plumbing-supply house, and a newly acquired paper mill upstate. I could buy out her brownstone, he thought, or half the street for that matter. That's what his father would have done, but Joe found it more enjoyable to live next door to Mrs. Clapp, to rile her prissy Brahmin values; to make her aware of his comings and goings.

Unhappily, Kitty, his wife, could not laugh. The slobbering, stuck-up sons of bitches hurt her and caused her immense pain, pain which Joe Scanlon could neither condone nor heal. More often than not, he found himself angry because Kitty was too sensitive and allowed herself to feel hurt because she had been excluded from the Brahmin midst. Kitty Scanlon's gifts to the children's wing at the hospital were more than welcome, as were her generous donations to the art gallery and the symphony. But Kitty Scanlon was not invited to the tea parties and recitals that were both a routine and a way of life for the Boston Brahmins. Kitty Scanlon was called "nouveau riche" or "lace-curtain Irish nouveau riche." Sometimes, as Joe Scanlon well knew, she was called worse.

"We'll have our own parties and invite our own friends!" Joe insisted. But Kitty was not to be consoled. She wanted to be a part of that society that rejected her so openly and so often. Her desire to be stepped on infuriated him because he wanted her to fight their discrimination with dignity.

But in spite of his wife and his anger, Joe Scanlon had a gut understanding of the Boston Brahmins. He even acknowledged that the Irish needed them because unless they were prejudiced against, the Irish wouldn't struggle to better themselves and overcome the prejudice. The more the Boston establishment railed against the Irish immigrants, the more the Irish used their political power to gain control of the city's institutions.

Joe opened the door and stepped into the hallway, hanging his coat on the rack and pulling off his galoshes, which were caked with snow

"Kitt!" Silence greeted him and reminded Joe of his deepest regret. He had no sons to run up and hug him, no daughters to kiss him. "Kitty!" he called out again, hoping that his slight annoyance was not evident.

"Yes," her small childlike voice answered from the head of the stairs. He lifted his eyes and looked up at her, knowing instantly that again she had been wounded. Her coal-black hair hung over her shoulders; it was loose and unkempt, almost stringy. She was thin and pale, with skin that sometimes looked almost blue. Her light blue eyes were ringed with dark circles and her mouth was small and tight, as tight as her hand gripping the banister. He knew, without taking a step toward her, that she had been alone in her room drinking and that she had been crying as well.

"What's the matter?" he asked. And he knew that his voice conveyed anger. He might as well have sighed, "What is it now?"

"It's nothing," Kitty replied as she turned away from him.

"Shit!" he mumbled under his breath. If he behaved as usual, he would follow her into their room and listen to her cry while she blurted out her tale of woe, an incident that loomed larger and more important because it was seen through the clouded dark glass on the bottom of a whiskey bottle.

He would rock her in his arms and let her bury herself in his chest, clinging and complaining. Then, because her presence would press on him, he would try to make love to her and she would push him away, saying only that she was too tired. And he would persist till she lay passive and cold, spread out on the bed before him. Then, as much out of curiosity as desire, he would kiss her breasts and look at the blue veins that transected her pale skin. He would find idle physical satisfaction in their coupling, though in fact she never moved nor cried out, nor responded in any way. When he would finish throbbing into her, he would go away feeling slightly ill and wondering why he had once again taken her.

It was in those moments that Joe Scanlon acknowledged the unthinkable; he admitted that he did not love his wife and that he was forever trapped in a loveless, childless marriage.

He stood quite still and listened as she retreated back to her holy tower—their room, which had become hers. Then he decided not to follow his usual practice. Instead, he walked into the parlor and sat down in his favorite chair, opening the newspaper. He perused the stories and let the paper fall into his lap. America was edging toward war; his brother didn't like school and wanted to drop out; Kitty was moving closer to a total nervous breakdown.

Joe Scanlon closed his eyes. He felt powerless in the face of multiple threats; he had the sensation that he was being tossed and battered.

2

April 1, 1917

Dublin

"The devil take them!" Mrs. O'Shea cursed. "I've lost two sons in the rising, and now the British want to conscript the others—who have wives and families to care for—into the army to fight their bloody hell of a war!" She blushed and turned to Emerald. "No harm . . . I know Thomas Hughes joined and died in the British Army, but he went because he wanted to go, he wasn't conscripted! Seven hundred years of suppression and now they want our fine able-bodied young men to save their hides! I'll fight them, I will. I'll fight them as I never did before!"

"It's a political fight we'll have to wage," Emerald said with an air of confidence. Now that Count Plunkett had won his seat, Emerald felt the fire of success.

"The Sinn Fein National Council is going to run Joseph MacGuiness for election. And he's an IRB man, still in jail." Emerald laughed. "Oh, the British will be fit to be tied if he's elected to Westminster!"

"And how will another M.P. who doesn't take his seat prevent conscription?" Mrs. O'Shea asked.

"Sinn Fein is against a foreign parliament making laws for Ireland. Conscription is such a law. We must show the British that the people of Ireland are prepared to separate from Britain peacefully. We must demonstrate our own political power by depriving the British of puppet Irish M.P.'s who say yea, but seldom nay to the prime minister."

"Without Ulster?" Mrs. O'Shea asked, raising a suspicious eyebrow.

"Certainly not! Ireland is one nation. A part cannot be separated from the whole!"

"I should think not," Mrs. O'Shea mumbled as she finished up the dishes.

Emerald looked at the newspaper on the floor. It blared headlines about conscription, protest marches, and more protest marches. No one wanted it; the Irish would not accept it.

To an outsider, Emerald would concede, it was difficult to explain. Her husband had volunteered, and so had many other Irishmen like him. But such volunteers believed in the sanctity of smaller nations; as individuals, many Irish did not approve of the kaiser's aims.

Conscription, on the other hand, would establish a terrible precedent that almost no Irishman in or out of uniform wanted to see. It would be the final humiliation—the citizens' surrender to a foreign parliament. Irishmen who were conscripted would have to take an oath to the king; denial of that oath at a later time would be treason. And what if conscripted troops were used against the Irish themselves? It had almost happened; it might happen in the future.

Mrs. O'Shea hung up her apron and was putting on her cloak and bonnet. It was her night out, and she usually spent it at the church, where she talked to her friends and met with people her own age, telling old stories, listening to music, dancing a jig now and again.

"Are you certain you don't mind?" Mrs. O'Shea asked. She asked the same question every Wednesday night.

Emerald shook her head. Tom was fast asleep, and she was expecting Colonel Jenkins. Mrs. O'Shea knew a man came to call, but she did not know he was a British officer. That was Emerald's closely guarded secret, and Albert Jenkins always obliged her by coming in civilian dress.

"Is your young man coming?" Mrs. O'Shea queried.

"He's not my young man," Emerald replied. "He's simply a friend."

"Of course," Mrs. O'Shea agreed, but her eyes twinkled, and it was quite obvious she was teasing.

I ought to put an end to it, Emerald reflected. She had toyed with the idea before, but she hadn't done it. Every Wednesday, Colonel Jenkins appeared, and more often than not, he brought a small gift for her, or a toy for Tom, who was nearly two.

Reluctantly, Emerald admitted that she looked forward to Colonel Jenkins' visits. He was an interesting man; he made her laugh; he was well-educated and well-read, and above all, he was kind.

In a rare moment, Emerald had confessed to herself that she even found Albert Jenkins attractive. His steel-gray hair and his soft gray eyes were a strong combination, and Emerald felt a certain warmth when his eyes caressed her. At the same time, she felt more than a little guilt for encouraging him. But as if he sensed that guilt, he assured her over and over that he valued her friendship alone. Given that rationalization, Emerald allowed his continued visits.

"I won't be home till after ten," Mrs. O'Shea informed her with a wink.

In the several months Colonel Jenkins had been visiting, Mrs. O'Shea had met him only once. That, to Emerald's relief, was in a darkened corridor. Mrs. O'Shea had not recognized the gentleman in tweeds as the officer who had summoned her with little Tom that day in April when Emerald had surrendered the post office on behalf of James Connolly. Whatever Mrs. O'Shea's memory of that day when she and Tom had said good-bye to Emerald, who was being arrested, she did not realize that the officer and Albert Jenkins were one and the same person. Thanks, no doubt, to the darkness of the corridor and to Albert's Welsh accent.

Mrs. O'Shea disappeared out the door with a wave, and Emerald got up. The table had been cleared and she gathered up the newspapers, setting them aside in one neat pile. Then she went to the mirror and looked into it. She picked up the brush and ran it through her loose hair. She smoothed out her long dress.

The knock on the door was only a few moments coming. Colonel Jenkins was always prompt, so prompt that Emerald teased him that she could have set her clock by his arrival.

She opened the door and he bent and took her hand, kissing it. "Good evening," he said formally. He handed her a bouquet of flowers. "It's spring," he commented as he took off his light coat and hung it up.

"They're lovely. But you must have gotten them from the florist. It's much too early for roses."

"They'll be in bloom soon, though. Then I will bring you another bouquet picked by my own hands."

"You're so gallant," Emerald joked. She went to the sideboard and withdrew a bottle of whiskey. They always had a few drinks together; it was such a habit now, she didn't have to ask.

"Make mine a double," he requested.

"Has it been that bad a day?" Emerald smiled warmly, and Colonel Jenkins smiled back.

"It has, but it's looking up." He followed her with his eyes, and Emerald felt his gaze penetrating her, breaking down her defenses. It was as if he kept saying, "Like me for myself, just for myself. . . ."

She handed him a glass and watched as he made himself comfortable in the easy chair. "Young lad asleep?"

On a few occasions Colonel Jenkins had come when young Tom was awake. Then he had sat down on the floor and played with him, seemingly taking as much delight in Tom's building blocks as Tom himself took.

Emerald nodded as she arranged the roses in a vase. "I'm afraid so. It was such a nice day, Mrs. O'Shea took him to the park. Now he's drugged on fresh air."

Jenkins chuckled. "Took a nap myself after lunch," he confessed. "Springtime is sleepy weather, no matter how old you are."

Emerald put the vase on the table. "They do brighten up the room."

"Emerald, how long have I been calling on you?"

His question took her by surprise. She had gotten out of prison in December and he had first come after the new year—the fourth, it was.

"Three months," she responded.

His expression was serious, and Emerald felt a twinge of anticipation. She wanted to say, "Don't say anything, just let it go on as it has been. Don't spoil it now." But instead, she held her tongue.

"You have a wonderful son," Jenkins said. "And you're a wonderful woman."

"Albert . . ." She paused and bit her lip.

"Emerald, I could give you comfort and security. I could see to it that Tom went to the finest schools, you'd live in a country house, rear your son in peace, quiet, and safety. We have horses, Tom would love the horses . . ."

"Don't, Albert . . ." Emerald turned away. She had suspected for some weeks that this moment would come, and she dreaded it. And yet there was a sense of relief, too.

"Emerald, I love you, but I don't expect you to love me . . . not yet in any case. I don't expect anything from you, and I don't want you to answer me now. I want you to think about it."

Emerald faced the wall of her flat. She had just had the courage to hang the last photograph of Seamus. His face smiled at her from the frame of the picture, and at the same time she knew Albert Jenkins had gotten up out of the easy chair and was standing just behind her.

"There wouldn't be any more prejudice if you were my wife. We'd move to Wales . . ."

There was a long pause and Emerald couldn't say anything. She could only hear the sound of his voice echoing in her ears, pleading with her, and the obvious depth of his feeling for her made her feel empty inside, incapable of hurting him or rejecting him outright.

"I'm a high-church Anglican. I've thought about it. I'd be willing to convert."

Emerald turned toward him and found him looking down at her with his eyes misty. "You would?" she asked softly. There was an overwelming sense of sacrifice in his last offer. Not that their religions were so different; it was more that worlds of social station separated them. And it was Albert who had once told her that the Irish were ruled by their history and the English by their traditions. Emerald wondered if history and tradition could be reconciled. She wondered if a relationship between them were possible.

He reached out to her, and Emerald felt his warm hands on her bare arms. He pulled her toward him and bent, kissing her on the lips. Albert Jenkins' arms around her were solid and strong, warm and comforting. His broad chest brought back a whirl of memories and longing. The simple feel of his male body pressing against her caused a stirring in Emerald, and she moved her lips beneath his almost unconsciously, lost for a long moment in a memory painfully buried.

Colonel Albert Jenkins held her gently, and then, releasing her mouth, breathed in her ear, "My God, I love you, you're pure passion and I long for you."

Emerald leaned against him as she expelled her breath. By pure force of will, she pulled herself away from him. "Oh,

Albert, I'm so sorry, I . . . You don't understand . . . I'm not
sure I do.''

"I told you, I don't want your answer now."

Emerald nodded gratefully, afraid to see any hurt in his eyes,
desperately afraid of her own sympathy and her own memories.
How could she make him understand that she had just responded
because for an instant, just one instant, he was someone else and
it was another time and another place? It's not right, she told
herself. It can't be right.

"There's so much between us . . .'' She spoke the words and
knew they were inadequate. A British officer and an Irish
nationalist. A man from Sandhurst and an orphan from the slums
of Belfast, and between them, between them, seven hundred
years of history and tradition, of pride and passion, of hate and
war.

"Perhaps we can overcome it all," he said. "Please, Emerald,
think about it. Come to Wales with me, give me a chance before
you make up your mind. Then, my dearest one, I'll respect your
decision, whatever it is."

Emerald lifted her large green eyes to look at him. In a way,
she owed it to him to consider the decision outside of her present
environment. She certainly owed it to him to take him seriously.
If I don't, she conceded, I'll be as unfair as any Englishman who
ever walked the face of the earth. I'd be rejecting out of hand a
man who has done nothing to me personally but be there when I
needed someone. And of course, that's why I allowed him to
keep visiting—I needed someone.

"I'll think about it," she promised.

"And you will come to Wales with me? Will you come and
spend two or three days on the estate? It's beautiful now, it's
spring."

"When do you want me to come?"

"Easter weekend," he answered as surely as if he had already
made the plans.

"Easter weekend," Emerald promised.

3

April 1, 1917

Boston

Joe Scanlon crossed himself and stood up, stretching his large frame. He genuflected and headed up the long aisle to the foyer of the church. Kitty had refused to come to mass, but he came because his seventeen-year-old brother was acting as altar boy and Joe had promised to meet him for lunch and a pint at Dooley's.

He waited awkwardly in the foyer of the church, glanced through the assorted publications and prayer books offered for sale, then walked through the big door and stood outside on the steps. He lit a cigarette and watched as the breeze carried the smoke away.

"Joe!" Mike's voice was deep like his own, and his face was roundish and younger-looking.

Joe Scanlon turned and Mike stood next to him. They were nearly the same height, but Mike was not as muscular or as heavy. Mike tended to be more vulnerable to illness, and he pushed himself too hard, wanting to be more like his older brother. Joe hugged Mike, then slapped him on the back. "How's it going?" he asked cagily.

Mike blushed and shrugged. "All right."

"You didn't come home last night," Joe observed.

Again Mike shurgged. "I went to the Howard Theater with some of the boys to hear John McCormick sing." John McCormick was the leading Irish tenor of the day, and on Saturday nights the old Howard Theater was packed with Irishmen and women who listened in rapt pleasure as John belted out the sentimental Irish ballads of yore. Seldom, Joe Scanlon knew, was there a dry eye in the house.

"And then?"

"And then we went to see the naked lady wrestlers in Scollay Square. I drank a little too much and spent the night with Emmet Kelly."

Joe laughed. Ah, yes. The naked lady wrestlers were a sight: four hundred pounds of bouncing flesh being hurled about; hair pulling galore; screams, cheers, and beer. Lots of beer.

"Were you worried?" Mike asked, mindful of the fact that he hadn't spent many nights at home lately.

Joe shook his head. "No. I just wondered. You've been away a lot lately."

Joe Scanlon paused. Mike wasn't going to say that it was because of Kitty, but he knew that was the reason. Kitty harangued him, challenged him, and utterly refused to let him live his own life.

"I was promised a pint," Mike said.

"And you'll get it." The two of them headed down the steps and into the sunshine of the early afternoon. The howling hysterical screams of the kids hawking newspapers filled the air.

"We'll be at war soon," Joe said solemnly. It had been building since March, when President Wilson ordered merchant ships armed in response to increased German U-boat activity.

"A lot of people are angry that we haven't put more pressure on Britain over Ireland—if we're going to save their hides, they ought to do something."

Mike's all-consuming interest in politics delighted Joe. "You don't write compositions or study your math, but you were born understanding politics, right?"

Mike laughed and stuffed his hands in his pockets.

Joe's mind wandered back to his father's words: "Take care of Mike, love him and watch over him, be a father to him, because you're all he has. Remember, he's only seven, you're twenty-two." Joe Scanlon made a silent vow to keep his brother out of uniform.

"You don't think America should enter the war?" Joe asked Mike.

"I think first we should make a deal to get our brothers in Dublin out of jail."

Joe leaned toward Mike. "I have it on good authority they'll be getting out."

"Really?" Mike's eyes were large and brown. "You didn't demonstrate. I didn't think you cared."

Joe smiled. "I'm Irish, I care." He slapped Mike on the back again. "A little political pull . . . sometimes it goes further than demonstrations."

"How do you know?" Mike pressed.

"I have friends. I've heard all the prisoners will be released by June, maybe sooner. But listen, that's not for publication."

"Tough secret to keep," Mike admitted.

"Try," Joe asked.

"How's Kitty today?" Mike asked the question more out of

form than real desire to know, Joe thought. Certainly there were no secrets; they all lived under one roof.

"Depressed," Joe answered honestly.

"I won't ask why," Mike commented as they rounded the corner and the great green awning of Dooley's greeted them.

"You don't have to," Joe answered. "She went somewhere and got royally snubbed."

"Party?"

"No, tea at the art gallery. She got an invitation because she made a generous donation. But an invitation doesn't mean she was welcome. She went, and the old biddies turned up their noses."

"Why do you keep letting her go?"

Joe shrugged again. "I guess I hope she'll learn or fight. She either stays away from them or she develops a tougher skin."

Mike fell silent and Joe knew it was because Mike didn't want to say anything about Kitty's drinking. He didn't want to ask: "Is she home drunk?"

From outside, Dooley's didn't appear open. Its green shades were drawn and its front doors barred. It was Sunday in good, godly Boston. The fine people of Beacon Hill firmly believed that a pious man didn't drink on Sunday. This was the first and greatest difference between Protestant and Catholic, Joe Scanlon decided. For Protestants, all pleasure was sinful, while for the Catholics sin was more closely defined and even forgivable.

The two of them walked around to Dooley's rear entrance. Joe knocked on the door, and through a peephole an eye stared at them. Then the door opened. Inside, from the cellar drinking room came the noisy din of celebrants.

Joe Scanlon was ushered to his usual table, and as he passed by, arms reached out to clasp his or pat his hand in a gesture of recognition and friendliness.

The genteel denizens of Back Bay Boston on stately Brimmer Street were the people Joe Scanlon resided among, but Dooley's was where Joe Scanlon lived. It was the place from which his growing political influence emanated, and in some way, the friends he had here were a source of sustenance and comfort as Kitty grew ever more distant and more sullen.

"And will that be two more pints?" Birdie O'Toole, the buxom barmaid leaned over them. She was like the heroine of an Irish song; a smiling, healthy, robust young woman with fine short legs and a full drooping bosom. More Irishmen had pinched

Birdie's ass than fought for freedom, the men at Dooley's joked.

"Two pints indeed," Joe answered with a wink. He did not pinch Birdie's ass. His position dictated a somewhat more dignified behavior.

4

April 4, 1917

Dublin

Colonel Jenkins rounded the corner and turned toward Emerald's flat. He checked his watch. Yes, Mrs. O'Shea would be gone by now.

His mouth felt a little dry and he reluctantly admitted to himself that he was anxious. "Like a young schoolboy," he mumbled aloud as he climbed the stairs. A man my age ought to have more sophistication. But the fact was, he yearned for Emerald Hughes, yearned like a young man over his first love. Emerald was twenty-two years old and had that special kind of Irish beauty—red-gold hair, deep green eyes. She was well built, with a small waist, gentle rounded hips, a full bosom. Her skin was creamy, and when she had been outside, her cheeks grew pink. She had a few pale freckles, and when she smiled, she always looked as if she were on the verge of laughing. It was as if Emerald Hughes knew a secret the rest of the world didn't. But beyond her physical characteristics, she had a strong character and was filled with energy. He couldn't help thinking that her feminine figure hid a raw physical strength, that she was, he concluded, the product of generations of people who had barely survived, and as a result of having survived, grew stronger with every generation.

She's all any man could want, he told himself. She's beautiful and brave; intelligent and vivacious; charming and every bit a lady.

He stood outside her door and hesitated. Then he knocked lightly.

Emerald opened the door. Her red-gold hair fell from beneath her green straw bonnet.

"I just got home." She smiled. "You're early."

He stepped into the room, and Tom ran over, sure on his

strong little legs. He hugged Jenkins, grasping him about the knees. He uttered a sound which was his word for hello.

Jenkins bent down and lifted the lad up, holding the delighted youngster over his head. "And how old are you?" Jenkins beamed. Tom's eyes were clear and his dark hair wavy. Jenkins smiled and felt a wave of affection. I could easily rear you as my own, he thought. And it was true that Tom Hughes, who would be two in a month, was another reason why he felt so strongly attracted to Emerald.

He set Tom down and withdrew a neatly wrapped chocolate. "May I give it to him?"

Emerald frowned. But Tom's eyes were already bright as he looked at the gold paper in which the chocolate was wrapped.

"It would have been better to wait till after dinner," she replied in a voice that slightly scolded him. "But it's too late now, he's already seen it."

Jenkins unwrapped the candy. "Here you go, lad."

Tom took the chocolate and ran off to the other room, laughing happily.

"He'll either eat it straightaway, or squirrel it away. You know, at two they're little pack rats. You wouldn't believe the things I find. Shipping bags packed with treasures!" Emerald laughed.

Jenkins reached out and grasped her hands. "You haven't changed your mind, have you? You're still coming?"

Emerald didn't pull away, but instead allowed him to take her into his arms and kiss her lips. She kissed him back, unable to resist him, but still wary of her inner turmoil.

"I'm not sure it's right," she said after a moment. "So I have to find out . . . No, I haven't changed my mind."

Jenkins beamed and was suddenly aware that a mantle of worry had been lifted from his shoulders. In Parliament Sir Edward Carson was mounting a campaign against David Lloyd George, the prime minister—all over the Home Rule Bill. In the Atlantic over 250,000 tons of shipping had been sunk in the first few days of April. And everywhere on the war front things were going badly. The English were suffering massive defeats. For his part, keeping the peace in Ireland and enforcing British law seemed a superfluous duty—no, an unpleasant duty. But none of it mattered! He was going away to Wales with Emerald.

"Tom will love the ponies," Jenkins said as the youngster came back into the room.

"He ate the chocolate," Emerald observed, shaking her head at the dab of chocolate on the end of her son's nose and his

rather sticky little fingers. "Come on, you little devil!" She
coaxed Tom over to the sink, and taking a damp cloth, washed
his hands and nose while he giggled at the feel of the cool water
and struggled to get loose of his mother's grasp.

"I planned to leave Saturday," Jenkins said. "Is that all right
with you two?"

"Yes, Albert, it's fine."

"I suppose you haven't told anyone where you're going?"

"No. I told them I was taking Tom and going down to County
Cork for a few days. I admit I don't know how to explain you."
Emerald looked at him steadily. She felt a little underhanded,
less than truthful certainly. I ought to be able to tell people how
different he is, she thought. But I can't.

"*If* you decided to marry me, you'd have to tell people. Does
it bother you so much?"

"I don't know," she replied truthfully. "Please, Albert, don't
press me. I know it's hard for you to understand . . . you, you're
in a different position altogether." Emerald sank down into the
chair. "Go play in your room," she said kindly to her son. "I'll
call you when dinner's ready."

He toddled off, and Emerald undid her bonnet, hanging it
casually over the corner of the armchair.

"Albert, if you married me, your friends would say you'd
made a mistake and they'd forgive you. My friends would say
I'm a traitor, and there would be no forgiveness. I'd be forever
alienated from my own people. I couldn't in a million years
explain the compromise, the mental leap even being your friend
has been for me. You understand some of the problems, but you
can't reach the depth of emotion, you can't get inside the Irish
mind, so you can't understand all the difficulties."

"But I favor home rule," he protested. "I've grown to understand and to sympathize. Dammit! I'm on the same side as your
friends."

Emerald shook her head. "No, Albert. First, no colonized
people want sympathy—they want freedom. Second, you only
believe in home rule for us—not for the counties of Ulster.
Third, my dearest, home rule is not what we want—we want an
Irish free state and we want it to be whole."

"I suppose I could support that," he said slowly.

Emerald shook her head. "You can say you do now, and I
believe you. But you don't deep down inside. No, Albert, you
couldn't hold to that view."

He shifted uncomfortably because she was right. Ulster would
never accept home rule, and an Irish free state was out of the

question. Ulster would pressure Parliament, and all the history would come into play. Sooner or later he'd get an order to put down a rebellion or a civil war or something. Sooner or later he'd be back killing the relatives and friends of the woman he loved.

"I'll resign my commission," he said, thinking out loud.

Emerald studied his face. It was a mask of conflicting emotions and thoughts.

"I couldn't let you," she said in a near-whisper. "Albert, let me take one step at a time. Please."

5

April 6, 1917

Boston

A breeze swept through Scollay Square, and the new, small green leaves on the trees shuddered. They had only just popped out of the branches, and like magic, they seemed to grow larger and stronger in the afternoon sunlight. It was Good Friday and Joe Scanlon and his brother had just had a long talk and a good lunch at Dooley's.

"I ate too much," Joe said, patting his stomach.

"I drank too much," Mike answered.

"Hey! Hey! Read all about it! Hey! U.S. enters war!"

Joe and Mike Scanlon stopped short and listened to the paper boy on the far corner as he hawked his papers. A crowd had gathered around him and they pressed in on the boy, holding out their coins.

"Shit!" Joe Scanlon breathed. Not that he and everyone else hadn't expected it. Wilson was known to be going to Congress. No one in his right mind could have thought that the die was not already cast. Still, he found there was shock in the reality of the dark, black-inked headlines in the *Boston Globe*'s special edition.

"Damned if I'm going off to fight the Germans before Ireland's free," Mike muttered. "If I go anywhere, it will be with Eamon de Valera!"

Joe Scanlon smiled indulgently. Eamon de Valera was known personally to neither of them. But he was a legend in the Irish community, and Mike worshipped that legend. Joe almost said: "You're not going to fight anywhere," but he didn't. Michael, he decided, was committed to a dream, not a reality. To begin an argument about de Valera, Ireland, or the war would be a waste of time and energy.

Mike paid for the paper, and reaching across a man's shoulder, took it from the waving hand of the paper boy, who looked up at him with excited eyes. The child wore coarse brown knickers and a threadbare argyle sweater. Over his unruly red hair he wore a cap. "Going to join up?" he asked Mike. "I'm going to join up, I'm going to fight the kaiser!"

Mike shook his head and unfolded the paper. The headline was nearly four inches high. "April 6—Good Friday."

"Happy Easter," Joe returned bitterly.

Mike laughed. The two of them shared a black humor, a tendency toward sarcasm.

"Yesterday we were singing 'I Didn't Raise My Son to be a Soldier,' now we'll start singing war songs and marching along in double time." Joe glanced at the paper as he spoke. It was already full of war news.

"They'll have conscription," Mike observed. "Probably I'd be smarter if I did join up."

"Smarter would be not to join up *or* be conscripted," Joe snapped quickly. "Being a part of the war effort is one thing, fighting is another. I can tell you, I have no intention of being conscripted."

"You're too old anyway," Mike said playfully.

Joe stood and faced his younger brother. "I can still tan your hide," he joked back.

"Aren't we sensitive," Mike teased. "But are you fit for one of the lady wrestlers—can you still handle an armful?"

"Yes, but I've developed better taste."

They stopped on the corner and looked at one another. "Coming home?" Joe asked.

Mike shook his head. "Got to go see a friend."

Joe nodded. "Don't join anything," he warned.

Mike turned and waved as he bounded on down the street in the April sunshine.

Joe shoved his hands in his pockets and started walking toward home. The coming of war had certain profound implications. First, he thought, the Irish community will be torn apart. Some would engage in a patriotic fervor, others would sulk and complain because American was entering the war on the side of the British before the Irish question was settled, even before the bulk of Irish political prisoners were released from British jails. The kind of divisions that would result in the Irish-controlled wards in Boston, New York, and Philadelphia were divisions that could reduce political influence, divide voting blocks, and ruin a careless political organizer.

There was, he thought, a tightrope to be walked, and it would take a careful man to walk it. He would have to support the war effort and he would have to use his influence to bring about changes in American policy toward Ireland. To survive, he would have to be seen as exerting pressure on the American government, even while performing his duty by fulfilling government contracts.

Joe glanced at his watch. It was after four o'clock, and even if it was late, he could imagine his phone ringing wildly. His connections would guarantee him and his various firms a number of contracts. There would be barracks to be built, housing . . . a hundred electrical jobs. Certainly his electrical contracts had proved extraordinarily lucrative in the last year. Boston Navy Yard was in full swing, and there were ships to be wired. Well, contracts would mean more jobs, and as the man who gave the jobs, his hand would be strong. He smiled to himself and turned another corner. There was no time to go home; the office was more important.

16

1

April 8, 1917

Boston

"It's Easter!" Joe Scanlon could hear the anger in his own voice, but he couldn't cover it.

Kitty was propped up in the center of the four-poster bed. Her hair hung in a tangled mass, and her nightdress had slipped off one shoulder, leaving her small white breast partially exposed. It looks limp, like the rest of her, he concluded.

The early-morning sunlight was flooding through the front windows of the room, and it shone on Kitty almost as if she were under a spotlight; it left her vulnerable to scrutinization. The tiny lines around Kitty's mouth all pointed downward, contributing to her perpetual expression of misery. She looked older than she was, much older, and on the edge of an emotional abyss.

The room looked vaguely like the lair of some wild animal. Clothes were strewn about untidily, face powder coated the top of the dressing table, and jewelry which ought to have been locked away was scattered about as if each and every tiny box had been opened and all tokens rejected in a fit of agony. Near the bed were used tissues which had been tossed into a nearby wastebasket inaccurately, and on the bedside table there was a glass of tomato juice that had already begun to grow a series of little islands composed of green mold. Joe couldn't see the bottles. They were the one item Kitty picked up, hiding them away like a squirrel hides nuts for winter. But he didn't have to see them to know they were there. The room, he noted, reeked of their contents, as did Kitty, whose appearance revealed her condition.

Ours was close to being an arranged marriage, he thought. I never loved her, but dammit, I was good to her and I've been faithful and given her everything.

"It's Easter!" he repeated angrily. "I'm going to mass, and you ought to be with me! Dammit! It's important for you to be with me!"

Kitty expelled air through her mouth and sounded like a horse. "Why? So you can display me, show all your political cronies you're really happily married?" Her words were slurred and her eyes were already filled with tears of self-pity.

"I don't ask you to get out of bed more than twice a year! Christmas and Easter!" He spat out the words sarcastically. "I know now that's too much to ask!"

"I'm sick!" She wailed out the words, and then, as if to punctuate the comment, began coughing, a deep miserable cough caused by chain smoking. "You don't care that I'm sick!" she sobbed as soon as the coughing fit passed.

"This room is disgusting! It's a pigsty!"

"It's what our good neighbors expect us to live in! I wouldn't want to disappoint them! When I die, they'll come and clean it out and they'll say, 'See, they hung white lace curtains in the windows, but they lived like the pigs we always knew they were.' I'm surprised you want to disappoint the neighbors, Joe. We ought to keep coal in the bathtub to make them happy. That's what they say we do! They say we don't know what a tub is for, and that we keep our coal in it!" Her tears were coming heavily now.

"I don't give a shit what our neighbors say or think! I do care about the mess! I do care about what our people say about you!" Joe's fists were clenched and he took an ominous step toward the bed, vaguely aware that he wanted to strike her, to slap her face and hear the sound of the slap as he hit her. He thought that the look of sheer shock on her face would be a reward. But he only took one step, and he knew he would not take another.

"Do you know what the neighbors say about me?" Her eyes were wide, her pupils mere pinpoints.

"I don't know what they say, I don't care. My friends are my only concern."

"I don't have any friends. You have friends!"

He gripped the side of the dresser and looked at her. Goddammit! She'd done it again, she'd trapped him. If he said, yes, you're right, you have no friends, she would go on crying and then pull the covers over her head and retreat into a trancelike escape. If he argued that she did have friends, she'd fight with him to prove him wrong. Reluctantly, he was willing to concede the point—it was true, she had no friends, but that was because she had alienated them.

He forced himself to think clearly, to lower his voice. After a moment he looked across at her, and sounding a little more calm, told her, "You don't want friends, Kitty. You make enemies of people who would be your friends."

It was a new tack, and it took her a moment to recover.

"People use me," she retorted in a small little-girl voice that dripped with sympathy for herself. "Even you've used me!"

He closed his eyes for an instant to block out the sight of her. This was the beginning of her most destructive phase. He'd been through it before, he'd played out the whole scene *ad nauseam*. Now, he thought, she would have a tirade about being used sexually, she would complain of her barrenness and finally slip into a deep depression. She would complain that he didn't use her enough and she would beg him to hit her, to punish her, to hate her with the same fury she felt for the world.

Joe turned and put his hand on the doorknob. "I'm going to mass," he said flatly as he turned the knob and walked out into the hallway. I can't take another repetition of this play, he conceded to himself. Then he congratulated himself that after so long he had finally become sufficiently hardened to leave, to break the pattern and sequence of events.

"I'm used!" Kitty shouted after him, half-sobbing.

Joe passed the white marble bust of Venus in the upper hallway, and he doffed his hat dramatically, bowing to her quiet, still loveliness.

"Don't wait up for me," he called loudly. "I'll be late."

He walked down the stairs and at the front door put on his overcoat. He opened the door. It was nearly eleven o'clock and the church bells were already ringing.

The weather was crisp, but the smell of spring was in the air. The image of Dooley's robust barmaid filled his mind, and Joe knew he would not remain faithful to Kitty much longer. "Soon," he said aloud to himself.

2

April 9, 1917

Colonel Albert Jenkins' estate was large and included stables, a pond, and a small river. The house itself looked like an English manor house; it was sedate and aloof, surrounded by formal gardens and furnished elegantly.

Parts of it, Emerald learned, were closed off. But the main section was fully open and consisted of a huge kitchen, a large foyer, a formal dining room, a large spacious living room, and a smaller cozy den with a great stone fireplace. Upstairs were four bedrooms.

The only servants were an elderly couple. The woman, Mrs. Foster, had prepared and served dinner; her husband laid the fire and was in charge of general upkeep. In addition, Jenkins told

Emerald, there was a gamekeeper and two stable hands to look after the horses.

"If I lived here . . . I mean, really lived here, I'd take on more servants," he explained to Emerald. "But the house is partially boarded up, and what with no one here, I keep only a skeleton staff." He sighed. "The Fosters have been with the family forever. It's almost as if they came with the house."

Emerald tucked her dress around her. She was sitting like a contented kitten in front of the blazing fire. "I wouldn't know what to do with servants," she said abstractedly.

"You'd know what to do with them as soon as you had them. It's never difficult stepping up in the world, it's when you have to step down that there's trouble."

"You sound so class-oriented," she chided.

He leaned over and handed her a large brandy snifter. "The English are all class-oriented. None more so than the working class, who really won't be called anything else. In a way, I come out of that class—on my mother's side. Her family made money in industry, practically a dirty word. When I was a child, we used to have wonderful parties here. Mother would invite all her friends, and my father would be shocked by them. The house was alive then. I'd like to see it alive again—alive with people, with children, with arguments and with love. Emerald . . ."

Emerald sipped her brandy and looked up. "We had a marvelous day, Albert." She wanted to change the subject, to keep at arm's length for a while. My emotions are too close to the surface, she thought. I'm too vulnerable.

"Tom loved the horses. I've never seen him so intrigued."

"You've a bit of the child left in you too. Wading barefoot in a pond. You'll probably catch cold. It's hardly summer, you know."

An image of her flashed across his mind. She had taken off her shoes and stockings and lifted her skirts, revealing shapely white legs. She had dangled her feet in the cool water, then waded all the way across to the green carpet of grass on the other side. She had looked incredibly beautiful then. She looked even lovelier now.

He sat down beside her, and she was silent. He put his arms around her, and she allowed herself to lean against his shoulder. "Happy?" he dared ask, kissing the back of her long graceful neck.

"I don't know," Emerald answered. "I'm . . . peaceful, contented. Is that happiness?"

"Some people would say that's all one can expect."

He kissed her neck again. "You know it could always be like this, Emerald. Tom could always be upstairs sleeping, you could always be in my arms in front of the fire. You'd have whatever you wanted." He kissed her neck and ears. Emerald shivered and turned her face toward his; the last of her resolve melted as she looked into his gray eyes.

There were no words, only their lips pressing together and the feel of his hand as it slipped over her breast, pressing her gently and rousing in her a long-felt desire.

Emerald closed her eyes and gave in to her sensations. She could feel the tenderness and gentleness of his touch; she understood the poignant, almost boyish way in which he clung to her.

The warm hand on her thigh sent another shiver through her, and the feel of her dress being opened filled her with a lonely hunger. The feel of his lips, the pleasant roughness of his male cheek against her tender, white, unexposed skin . . . his lips pressing, moving over her, and covering her like the morning mist . . . He was urgent and sensual.

Emerald moaned with pleasure as he kissed her nipples, then slipped her dress away and opened her legs. She lifted herself to him, though she was hardly aware of him. He rocked her in his arms and she yielded completely to the motion, feeling the heat from the fire on her bare legs. He filled her, and Emerald moved against him. She felt him as he throbbed into her; she herself experienced a brief spasm of fulfillment.

Their two heartbeats raced in unison, and Emerald opened her eyes to see Albert Jenkins' loving, almost worshipful face above her own.

"You are an angel," he whispered. "My beautiful, soft, lovely angel."

Emerald met his gaze and felt the wave of guilt sweep over her. He loved her! He loved her the way she loved Tom Hughes! He had said it, but only now did the revelation fill her with remorse. It was not Alfred Jenkins she had just made love with; it was rather a memory aroused, a ghost stirred. Yet she lay in his arms, allowing Albert Jenkins to hold her, to fall deeper in love with her, to believe she cared for him as he cared for her.

Emerald felt paralyzed. She could not spring from beneath him and tell him the horrid truth, that his loving, romantic act had been nothing for her but the reliving of another moment. Oh, it would be simple if I despised you, she thought. But I don't. I love you as a friend, I respect you as a man. It makes it all so difficult, it's all so unfair. But now I know, she decided. I know

I couldn't live a lie of loving you, because you care too passionately, too deeply.

I hope you will forgive me, Emerald thought as he kissed her. I hope you will understand; I hope I don't hurt you as much as I'm afraid of hurting you. . . .

"You will marry me," he pressed.

Emerald fought the desire to beg: Don't ask me now. Somehow I want you to enjoy this moment; you must enjoy it, because it's all I can ever give you. If I answer your question, it will be over, tonight will be lost. I don't want to hurt you now.

"Say you will. We can be married in the summer. . . ."

Numbly, Emerald shook her head. "I can't, Albert, I can't."

His face became a mask of disbelief wrapped in an expression of pain. "But just now, I felt you . . . you wanted me . . ."

"Don't," she replied in a whisper.

"Emerald, I love you. I felt you love me back. I know you do, I know you can."

. Tears flooded her green eyes and she shook her head. "I wanted someone. You're gentle and loving. But, Albert, it wasn't you. I like you, I'm fond of you. But I couldn't live a lie of love with you and know how you feel. My God, I'd hurt you every time we . . ."

"Made love," he finished.

She sank back. "I love it here, but I can't live here. Albert, I beg you to understand."

More pain filled his expression; then, with all the discipline he could muster, he mastered his emotions and sat up. "I understand," he said with a cool formality. "I wouldn't dream of forcing myself on you."

"You didn't," Emerald replied. "Don't respond that way. I wanted you, I enjoyed you. But, Albert, I don't love you."

He nodded silently.

"Please try to understand."

"I'll try," he answered after a long while. He turned and reached for his brandy, gulping it all down. Emerald let out a long-held breath and pulled herself up. Now I've hurt a fine man. I should not have allowed myself to come here, to get in so deep. I've caused him nothing but misery.

Jenkins pulled himself up into the easy chair in front of the fire. He sipped on his brandy and stared into the fire while Emerald dressed. He fought to think of something else, of something besides this woman to whom he was so drawn.

"I was going to tell you that all the prisoners being held in England will be released. Indeed, all the prisoners, period."

"The countess too?" Emerald asked.

"The lot."

"To make conscription more palatable," Emerald observed.

He didn't answer. A month ago he would have argued. Of course, she was quite right. Tit for tat.

"I trust you won't forbid me the pleasure of calling on you."

"Is it such a pleasure? I'm a very difficult woman, you said so yourself."

"It's such a pleasure . . . even if you are stubborn." He tried to smile.

"Albert, you're a military man, not a doctor. But in some ways military men and doctors are alike. I work with doctors. When a surgeon has to cut, he cuts. It has to be swift and clean. If it's not, the pain is prolonged. Albert, you have something to do—make it swift and clean."

His gray eyes met her eyes and he nodded. "Perhaps I enjoy pain."

Emerald reached up from her sitting position on the floor and touched his cheek. "I don't enjoy being the instrument of pain, Albert. Especially yours."

3

May 10, 1917

Dublin

The crowded hall was filled with smoke and the smell of beer. It was packed to overflowing, and Emerald had to hold her breath to cross the room.

When at last she reached the election boards, where the results of the election would be posted, she was breathless and felt both disheveled and excited.

"Ah, there you are, my pretty." Michael Collins embraced her warmly and sat her down on a wooden bench near the platform. He passed her a glass of brew and winked at her.

"I can't wait," Emerald enthused. "I was excited when Count Plunkett won in February, but this is even more exciting. It's harder, you know. South Langford isn't as easy a constituency as Rosscommon."

Michael Collins grinned. He had been working nonstop for days, but in spite of his weariness, he seemed alert and as excited as she. But of course, Emerald reflected, this whole election had been his idea.

The candidate was Joseph MacGuiness, a member of the Irish Republican Brotherhood who at this very moment was serving a term in Lewes Gaol for his part in the rising. Needless to say, MacGuiness wanted no part in conventional politics, and there was no question about his loyalties and views.

It was Sinn Fein's National Council that was running Mac-Guiness, and in this election they had taken a new approach. Naturally their program denied the right of any foreign parliament to make laws for Ireland, but now Sinn Fein added to its program by demanding that Ireland be given a seat at the Peace Conference, when and if it took place.

"When are you going to run away with me?" Michael Collins asked. He smiled mischievously. "Don't you think we deserve some recreation after working so hard?"

"I think you should stop teasing me," Emerald answered. Collins was an exceptional-looking man, she noted. He had straight white teeth, thick wavy hair; he was tall and well-built. Some complained that he was inconsistent and given to wild temper tantrums, but she herself never saw that side of him. His only problem, she concluded, was that he was too good-looking and had more than slight personal conceit. She smiled at him in spite of his constant bold teasing. He had been with her when Seamus died, he had respect for her, and no matter what he said to her, their relationship was nothing more than friendship.

"Politics excites you," he whispered. "You have the look of a woman in love; by God, your eyes are sensuous."

Emerald laughed. She ignored his flattery, but admitted he was correct on one score: politics did excite her. She liked it, she liked people, and it was a rare game. Perhaps, she pondered, it was because of her isolated childhood that she reveled in the crowds and camaraderie of political involvement. It made her feel a part of a group and it gave her a sense of positive accomplishment to be working peacefully toward what she prayed would be Ireland's independence.

"Don't just smile at me, you wicked woman, I know excitement when I see it." Collins laughed.

"I'm just anxious to know if we've won, that's all."

Michael winked again at her. He pointed to her glass of beer. "Have a drink, woman, and relax. We won't know for a while yet. Are you easier to seduce when you're drunk?"

"You're too full of yourself, Michael Collins, to be seducing me or anyone else."

"One day I'll surprise you," he retorted confidently.

"Save your energy to fight for Ireland," Emerald advised him.

"Tell me, Emerald Hughes, are you going to be like the countess? Are you going to take a man's job and stand for office yourself?" He laughed, and his dark eyes twinkled. "Think of all the Sinn Fein candidates who could ride in on your petticoats!"

"You're outrageous," Emerald said, scowling at him. "I hadn't thought of standing for election, but now that you mention it . . ."

Michael was convulsed with laughter, and Emerald straightened up. "It's not funny," she said in a dignified tone.

"God knows it's not! When we get rid of the British, we'll have no one to fight with but ourselves! We'll surely need a good nurse in our Parliament!" He bent over and slapped his knee once again, unable to control his laughter at his own joke.

"If you don't stop your laughing, Michael Collins, you'll be needing a nurse a lot sooner!" Emerald hissed, looking at him angrily. "You go right ahead and make fun of women in politics! We'll show you, all of you!"

He stopped laughing and wiped a tear off his cheek. "Dear God in heaven, I didn't mean it!"

"Of course you did," Emerald snapped. "Englishwomen have time to fight for their rights, but we Irishwomen are too busy fighting for Ireland to take up our own position. Well, Michael Collins, as soon as Ireland is free, you're going to see some changes, because we women are going to take up another fight. It'll be against the likes of men who don't think a woman can run a country as well as she runs her kitchen."

"Oh, dear, you did spend too long with the countess, who spent too long with that old biddy Mrs. Pankhurst! I mean, politics is all right for Pankhurst . . . have you seen her? Built like a British fortress, she is. But it's not all right for the likes of you! You should have a husband and more children!" He grinned and slapped her across the thigh. "My God, you were built to keep a man's bed warm and bear children!"

Emerald stood up and shook her dress out. She narrowed her eyes and stared at Michael Collins. "I'm not breeding stock, Mr. Collins. I have a mind. As many women have minds as do men. And, Mr. Collins, I should like to remind you that but for the training given by your good mother, you might still be peeing in your pants!"

"It's official! It's official!" A loud voice boomed across the Union Hall, and an almost instant silence fell on the rowdy gathering. "We've won! We've won! We've taken South Langford by thirty-seven votes! But, by God, we've taken it!"

The assembled people roared and clapped. Almost instantly there was music, and people began to square off and dance, joining hands and singing.

"Another Sinn Fein man elected! Another seat that won't be taken!" Michael Collins shouted and turned and hugged Emerald, picking her up off the floor, though she was still incensed.

"If you have a mind, woman, then smile!"

Emerald's frown faded and she returned his grin. Theirs was an argument that would keep. He set her down and then embraced her around the waist and began whirling her in time with the music.

"By heaven, we did it!" Emerald said breathlessly. "We've elected an IRB man to the bloody British Parliament!"

4

July 4, 1917

"Over there, over there, send the word, send the word, over there, that the Yanks are coming, the Yanks are coming, and we won't be back till it's over, over there. . . ."

The parade down Broadway was impressive, and in a way, it was sad. The voices of the singing troops, the blare of the trumpets, and the sound of martial music rang in Joe Scanlon's ears, but the image of the soldiers' faces remained in his mind. The soldiers were boot-clad, wore broad-brimmed hats, but they were only boys in stiff uniforms; fresh young faces without lines of worry; lads with pimples and freckles, with peeling sunburned noses and hands barely callused by hard work.

Dammit! They were an army of children being sent off to sniff chlorine gas and come back with twisted, shrunken lungs or with mutilated bodies blown to bits by grenades or flying pieces of artillery shells. Joe didn't like it; he felt resentful that so many would die for so little.

He'd come to New York with Mike on business, and when it was finished, he sent Mike on a short vacation to Florida, reasoning that three weeks away from the house and from Kitty's ravings would do Mike good.

He himself had decided to remain in New York for a few days and then steal away alone down to Virginia Beach for a bit. He admitted to himself that he needed to get away, needed time to think. And toward that end of guaranteeing himself complete privacy, he hadn't bothered to tell anyone where he was going.

Joe expelled his breath and again took in his surroundings. The hotel was on Sixth Avenue; the room was plain and cheap. In a sense, it suited his frame of mind.

The paint was peeling off the far wall, and clearly the numerous occupants of the room had taken up the widening of the decay as a hobby, because the paint had been peeled off in a neat circle, the edges loose and inviting to casual destruction.

The window was open and a warm July breeze stirred the gray-white curtains. In one corner there was an easy chair with a hole through which cream-colored stuffing could be seen. It was a chair with a gaping wound, Joe thought.

The wood dresser, directly opposite the bed, had lost all pretense of sheen and its mirror was warped so that the image it revealed was akin to that in the fun house, a wavery reflection of reality.

The sheets on the bed were as gray as the curtains at the window, but the curtains hung straight, while the sheets were rumpled. Joe was sprawled out and clad only in his shorts. He had propped himself up and was smoking a cigarette, reveling in the squalor of his surroundings, enjoying the charm of his purchased poverty.

The woman beside him was asleep. Her long naked legs were crossed one over the other and her flat white belly moved with the rhythm of her breathing. Her breasts fell to either side, their long dark nipples looking a bit like the ends of well-sucked cigars. Her pubic hair was dark and curly, but the hair on her head was blond, white-blond with dark roots. He'd pumped his frustration into her four times, but she had no name, even though he could still hear her itsy-bitsy voice and her strong New York accent.

He remembered he had poured out his feelings concerning the young boys marching off to war and she had frowned as if every word he spoke was in some foreign language.

She told him, "Gee, you're talking like some old man or something. How old are you? Twenty-five? Thirty? Gee."

It was true that he was only thirty-two, but he felt older and he was certain he seemed older. After all, he was self-educated, he'd been working in his father's business since he was fourteen. And he had reared his brother; that had given him maturity—perhaps too soon, he reflected.

But what had aged him was Kitty. Kitty, who had grown old and diseased and was dying before his eyes. Kitty, who appeared to reach out for him with clawlike fingers; Kitty, who grasped at him, trying as desperately as she could to take him with her, to draw him into her own personal hell.

"You're acting older than you are," the girl with no name commented. Then, weary from her role in their activities, she had rolled over on her back, crossed her legs, and fallen asleep.

This morning, Joe thought, I picked up a lucrative contract to build seven barracks in Quincy to hold naval personnel assigned to the Boston Navy Yard. Then he had watched the parade and after that had gone walking through the Irish neighborhood around Fourth and Sixth. Then he drank enough to overcome his inhibitions and he hired the woman who was sleeping beside him. It was the third time he had committed adultery in three months. They had all been prostitutes. He took them for the day and he even tried to talk to them; tried to make it more intimate, more satisfying. Physically there was no problem; there never was. But the women always left him feeling empty, as if there ought to be more. He wanted them to respond in some special way; he needed some special response.

Joe drew on the cigarette and expelled the smoke slowly, blowing a large ring of smoke into the room. He watched as the breeze from the open window attacked it and turned it into a lopsided, fading circle that evaporated and disappeared like magic.

Kitty had been dead drunk and asleep when he left, taking the train from Boston to Grand Central with Mike. The memory depressed him; the young marching men who looked so much like Mike depressed him. The girl with no name began snoring softly. She depressed him too, but somehow he didn't feel as if he deserved better.

He checked his pocket watch, which he had put on the bedside table. It was four o'clock. Small wonder the afternoon sun was so hot and the room so stale and wretched. He was supposed to go to a political meeting at six. He glanced at the girl, and almost on cue, her blue eyes blinked open. Her full lips puckered and she looked like a startled cat. He swung his long muscular legs over the side of the iron bed.

"Oh . . ." She half-spoke the word and half-moaned it. Then, like the trained actress he was sure she was, she reached out and touched his bare back. "Gee, are we finished? It's only four."

He didn't turn around. "So, you'll get off early today."

There was a moment of silence and he knew without turning around that she had a pouty expression on her face.

"Didn't you like me?"

Lord, why did they always have to ask questions like that?

Briefly he wondered if there were any mute prostitutes in New York, but he decided the odds were against it.

"I like you," he answered without emotion. Then he reflected: I don't know your name, but it won't hurt me to say I like you, even if your hair is the wrong color and your mind is nonexistent. I suppose you have feelings, everybody has feelings, and I'm tired of hurting people's feelings. . . . no, I'm tired of hurting Kitty's feelings. But there isn't any way not to hurt them. She puts them right out there in front and demands that I hurt them. She says "Hurt them" and I do.

"Sure you don't want to do it again?" She was standing up now, and she walked over to the wounded easy chair. Her butt was small and absolutely round and tight. It had a line of tiny red pimples down one side of the crack. She bent over to put on her undergarments, which she had shed on the floor. Her legs were apart, and through them he could see her pink labia. It hung like a half-open door, inviting him in. He felt the swelling and he stood up and walked over to her, seizing her buttocks as she bent over. "All right, one more time," he said, taking a deep breath.

5

July 7, 1917

Dublin

"We're not at war with Germany!" Eamon de Valera shouted. "You have no enemy but England!"

He'll be elected, she predicted to herself. Eamon de Valera had been returned with the other prisoners on the eighteenth of June, and Sinn Fein had immediately nominated him to run in East Clare, the constituency held by the late Willie Redmond, John Redmond's brother. It's the beginning of the end for the Redmonites, Emerald thought. Oh, they were nationalists of sorts, but time had tarnished their image in the eyes of the Irish voters. They were good men who supported home rule, but the Redmonites all believed in conventional politics; they all went to Westminster when elected. Then, not surprisingly, they were sucked into political coalitions in order to have some small influence in the Parliament. If their influence in Parliament grew stronger, then it grew weaker at home. Only if they had stood alone against every one of the traditional political parties in England could they have been popular at home. But that was not what was happening. Sinn Fein was electing members, and the members weren't taking their seats. The Redmonites were losing their elections; the voice of the Irish nation was louder in its absence from Parliament than it ever was when it was present in Westminster.

I don't agree with everything Eamon de Valera says, Emerald admitted. But still she was working for his election because she knew and remembered Seamus' fondness for him. And then too, she knew that in spite of his words, de Valera had mellowed some. He was, like the others, going the political route, and though he wouldn't take his seat either, it was the route she approved of.

The crowd roared its approval when he commented that he didn't care if the British Empire were blown to bits. He climbed down off the makeshift platform and was at once surrounded by his admirers—Eoin MacNeill, one-time head of the Irish Volunteers, among them.

De Valera looked across the sea of faces that pressed in on him. "Mrs. Hughes!" He walked to her side and took her hands in his. "I know you've been working for my election, but this is the first time I've seen you since . . . that day . . ." He looked her up and down slowly. "Let me say, you look much better today. The last time I saw you, you were a bit worn and grubby." The men standing about laughed, and Emerald herself smiled.

"I was that, Mr. De Valera," she replied.

"And Seamus? He's been released too, I suppose."

There was an awkward silence, and Emerald looked down, hardly able to look up. "He was killed during the rising," she said softly. "I thought you knew."

Eamon de Valera patted her hand, then let it drop. "No," he answered. "Those of us who were held in England didn't get full reports . . . I'm sorry."

Emerald lifted her eyes. "You don't have to be. He died doing what he thought was right, he died fighting for what he believed in."

"And your other brother? You have a brother in America, don't you?"

Emerald nodded. "Padraic. He's with the American forces now, being sent to Europe next month."

De Valera wisely didn't repeat the remarks he had made from the platform, nor did he launch into a speech about Irish-Americans fighting the kaiser. Emerald suspected that Eamon de Valera was not pro-German at all. In fact, he was simply anti-English.

"Will you be nursing us during the next rising?" he asked.

"If there are enough elections, there might be no need for another rising," Emerald returned.

De Valera didn't answer, but the expression on his face was answer enough. If Ireland was granted her freedom, he would be there to take full advantage of that freedom, but he did not believe that would happen. He believed there would be fighting; he believed the only thing the British would understand was force.

The next few days passed quickly. Emerald was working the night shift at the hospital and spending part of the day working on Mr. de Valera's campaign for Parliament.

On July 12 the results of the election were announced: Eamon de Valera received 5,110 votes; his opponent, Patrick Lynch, received 2,035 votes. It was yet another victory for Sinn Fein and a blow to constitutionalism—British constitutionalism.

6

July 12, 1917

Colonel Albert Jenkins felt a hundred years old. He hadn't seen Emerald since Easter. Staying away was harder than he had imagined, and he often came close to giving in and visiting her.

At first he told himself that he was merely obsessed with her beauty and that his feeling toward her was sexual and not to be confused with the mature kind of love a man of his age ought to be experiencing. But that was a deception. As the days grew in number, his memory of her physical appearance faded and she became a disembodied voice, the sound of gentle laughter, the shimmering reflection on still water. The total of her being settled over him like a soft covering, and it was then that Albert Jenkins admitted that his love for Emerald Hughes went far beyond mere physical attraction. Her eyes haunted him and her ideas and experiences became a part of him. There were times when he succeeded in putting her entirely out of his mind, and he was not a man given to public weeping or even private tears. He was, however, a man given to melancholy. And as memories and present events combined to reinforce his feelings for Emerald Hughes, he gave in to his melancholy, allowing it to take him over. The result was inaction and lethargy.

Albert Jenkins had requested a transfer, hoping that a change of scene might help break the spell that hung over him. But the

War Office simply told him he could not be transferred immediately and that he would have to wait, while they, in turn, would keep his request under advisement.

"Oh, his majesty's this and his majesty's that . . ." Jenkins sighed as he put the official letter aside. It was nine A.M., but he didn't feel like moving. He put his feet up on the plump footstool and leaned back, adjusting his brocade red smoking jacket. It was an elegant jacket with black velvet trim.

This morning he was not a busy officer, but rather a gentleman relaxing at home. He reached over and opened his black leather briefcase. He had brought it home the night before, and it rested, beckoning him to do some work, on the table near his favorite chair. He looked at the large pile of reports and shook his head in disgust. The government was losing its war with paper.

The report on top was from the chief secretary and it was marked "URGENT." Albert Jenkins skimmed it rapidly. It declared that Eamon de Valera and a small group of Sinn Feiners had advanced their claims. "At first they wanted only a seat at the Peace Conference," the report indicated, "but now they advocate physical force." And the report went on to say, "Since few Irishmen have emigrated due to the war, there is a young, militant, able-bodied core which is willing to fight for Irish independence."

Jenkins went on reading. "I urge you to take note: Sinn Fein will resort to military force. Even without arms, there are now sufficient numbers to overtake government offices and police barracks."

Hysteria, Jenkins said to himself. The report, which had already been sent to the War Cabinet, indicated a situation far more grave than the one which actually existed. He himself did not believe there would be another rising—at least not until after the war. The only issue that would cause one was conscription. Still, he decided, he was out of touch. He no longer knew what people were thinking or what people might do. He was sitting out the war in Ireland protecting the British from an internal powder keg. Sadly he admitted he no longer cared for his position.

7

July 15, 1917

Boston

Joe Scanlon climbed out of the cab while the driver carried his suitcase up the front steps. Joe followed and paid the driver, who doffed his cap and hurried back to his vehicle. Joe fumbled for his keys. It was nearly three-thirty in the afternoon and the sunlight reflecting off the window was blinding. He finally found the right key and inserted it in the lock, opening the door and letting himself in.

He'd been gone since June 29 and though he was tired, he had enjoyed his trip. It was the longest time he had spent alone since his marriage to Kitty ten years ago. He'd gone down to New York, where he had spent some time relieving his frustrations and acquiring a new baggage of guilt. After that, he headed down to Virginia Beach and stayed at a hotel near the seashore. The air was warm and clear; the salt water was invigorating, and now his fair skin was slightly sunburned and his nose was peeling.

It was the first vacation he'd taken in three years, and it felt good. Oh, he'd asked Kitty, but she wouldn't go anywhere. "We won't tell a soul where we're going," he had promised her. "Let's be like gypsies, just traveling here and there." But she scoffed at him and hid in her bed, claiming to be too ill to travel.

"Then goddammit, I'll go alone!" It was another fight in a chain of fights; another no-win battle. But proudly he had gone, and he hadn't called or even said where he was after he left New York. So for one glorious week he was a runaway boy again; he was fishing and swimming, sunning and sleeping.

He set his suitcase down in the front hall. The house smelled strangely musty, and it was too warm, as if the windows had not been opened for several days.

"Aggie!" Joe called out. Only silence greeted him. Well, he thought, the housekeeper must be out shopping. Mystified, Joe climbed the narrow winding staircase to the second floor. "Aggie!" It wasn't her day to shop. Near the top of the staircase he called for his wife. "Kitty!" But still there was no answer.

He paused before her door and then turned the handle. It

swung open and he saw that the bed was stripped of all its
linens, leaving only the vertical stripes of the blue mattress to
stare at him. His eyes moved around the room quickly, taking
everything in. The clothes that usually bedecked the floor were
all hung up, and the closet doors, always open, were closed. The
floor was clean; even the trashcan was empty. Kitty's jewelry
was put away too, and the dresser was neat, with all its tiny
exquisite bottles row on row like little misshapen soldiers.

Joe scratched his head. His first thought was that his wife had
left him. But Kitty wouldn't do that. Catholics did not divorce,
nor did women as lonely and frightened as Kitty run away. In
any case, there was no place for her to run. She had no money;
she didn't even have access to his money. He walked to the
closet as if to confirm his thoughts. He opened the door and
breathed a sigh of relief. Her clothes were still there, just as he
imagined them. No, Kitty had not left.

He returned to the parlor downstairs and sat down in the large
overstuffed chair. He lit a cigarette, and after a time went to the
liquor cabinet and made himself a drink. It was now nearly five.
Aggie ought to be home, and certainly Kitty would be returning
at any moment.

He had a second drink, and when he finished it, it was
five-thirty. He had been traveling since early morning, and
weariness overcame him with the third scotch. When he finished
his fourth, he fell fast asleep in the chair, an unread magazine in
his lap.

His eyes snapped open at the sound of a piercing scream.
They snapped open to a semidark room, a room lit only by the
streetlamp outside the front window.

Before him, Aggie stood with her mouth half-open, a bag of
groceries spilled on the floor.

"What the hell is the matter!" He wasn't at his best when
awakened from a sound sleep, and the Scotch had muddled his
mind. He must have been sleeping soundly, but not for too long,
because he felt irritable and totally unrested.

"I didn't know you were home, sir," Aggie stammered.
"You startled me, sitting in the dark. I thought you were an
intruder, sir."

"Obviously not," he said gruffly. "Where's Mrs. Scanlon?"
Aggie didn't answer; instead, she let out a little moan.

"What's the matter? Can't you say anything?"

He could actually hear the girl breathing. He turned and
snapped on the light near his easy chair. He blinked, and he saw

that Aggie was pale and shaking; she looked upset and terribly frightened.

"I'm sorry I gave you a start," he apologized. "Now, tell me, where is Mrs. Scanlon?"

Aggie blinked; then, crossing herself, she mumbled, "Dead."

Her answer hung between them for what seemed a century; they were like two statues in a pose. Aggie's face was contorted and her hand rested near her right shoulder just where she had finished her gesture of making the cross. He faced her with his mouth partially open and his eyes still adjusting to the light. One foot was in front of the other, one hand in midair. A partial fragment of memory passed across his thoughts—he had gone to Italy one summer, and there in Pompeii he had seen some ancient bodies, petrified by the lava flow. Two were turned into stone while in mutual orgasm, their bodies welded together for all time, their expressions of pain and pleasure turned to granite. Another was caught in mid-step; still another was running—one leg lifted, the other on toe with fine muscles visible. It was the way he and Aggie stood now. Had it been a second since she had said the word "dead"; had it been a minute or an hour?

"When . . . how?" he managed to blurt out. Again there was a time lapse, but finally Aggie managed to say something.

"Three days ago. We tried to get in touch with you. Father Adare tried and tried. No one knew where you were, not even Michael, whom we found in Florida. He said you'd left New York and just gone off for a week." Aggie was blinking back tears, and she sniffed. "Oh, I didn't want to be the one to tell you!"

Joe closed his eyes and saw the bed upstairs stripped of all its linens. Aggie had cleaned up after Kitty; she had removed all the telltale signs of Kitty's self-destruction. He looked again at poor Aggie; her distress was evident.

"Here, sit down." He turned to the liquor cabinet and fixed two drinks this time. He handed Aggie one, and she took it, her small, shaking hand closing around the glass.

"How did she die, from what?" he finally asked.

Aggie took a sip of her drink. "In her sleep, sir. She didn't suffer at all, nor even cry out. I found her the next day, sleeping. The look on her face was so peaceful." She took a longer sip. "She'd taken some sleeping powders and . . . and had a bit too much to drink, sir. The doctor said it was an accident, she just didn't wake up, her heart stopped."

Joe finished his own drink. Aggie was tactful. "Too much to drink" could have meant three bottles or more. The ruling of

accident was kind too. Suicides couldn't be buried in consecrated
ground. Through the fog of his own guilt, however, he certainly
considered Kitty a suicide. Albeit she had done it slowly, lacking
the wherewithal to do it quickly.

"Go get some rest," he told Aggie. "I'll call Father Adare."

Aggie bent down quietly and retrieved the groceries. She
stuffed them back into her satchel and then padded off toward
her room behind the kitchen.

Joe stood up and walked to the telephone. He felt as if he were
sleepwalking. Abstractedly he dialed Father Adare's number.

17

1

March 1918

London

David Lloyd George looked out the window at the damnable rain. "Drat!" he mumbled. It was still raining, a cold wretched rain that threatened to turn the cobbled street below into a river. The rain and the dark clouds depressed him; the war depressed him; Ireland depressed him; and Parliament . . . Parliament was unbearable!

"You're all distracted again. I can tell when you're distracted." Magda had a deep voice, a sensual voice. And, he thought, she had many other things to commend her as well: extraordinarily long legs, a bushy triangle of chestnut-colored pubic hair, hazel eyes that were huge and luminous, and nice firm buttocks. She also had the high cheekbones of her Magyar ancestors and a slight Hungarian accent which was, for purposes of seduction, preserved.

In addition to her physical qualities, Magda was also a free spirit, one of those wonderfully modern women who spoke of Havelock Ellis and who read D. H. Lawrence in spite of the fact that poor old Lawrence was holed up in Cornwall with his German wife and suspected of being a spy. Of course, he wasn't a spy; he was too abstract to be a spy. There had been talk of interning him and Frieda, but that was rejected. Instead, his passport was withheld and he and his harpy of a wife were left to their own ends, but surrounded by suspicious villagers.

He smiled a bit at the thought of Lawrence and Frieda—he supposed that Magda could be suspect as well. After all, Hungary was part of the Austro-Hugarian Empire and allied with Germany. But then, he reflected with joy, prime ministers could get away with more than writers, and besides, Magda had been reared in England and had not in fact lived in Hungary since the age of five. Or so her Scotland Yard file indicated.

"Are you really going to spend the rest of the afternoon looking at the rain? It's March, you know, it always rains a lot in March."

"If it weren't for the blasted war, I could be in the South of

France and quite away from this inclement weather," he complained.

"And would I be with you in the South of France?"

"I imagine," he rejected saying, "you or someone else." He relished his reputation momentarily. He was called a rogue—and a handsome rogue. In spite of being married, his affairs with lovely young women were legend. He didn't bother to discourage the talk.

His wife, Margaret, was a splendid woman, but no one woman could satisfy his appetites, and Margaret seemed to understand that. At least she seldom said anything to him unless he had been terribly indiscreet; then she mildly rebuked him, reminding him that she too had to live with the gossip.

Currently he was seeing four women. But Magda was one of his favorites. For one thing, she didn't mind if he discussed politics in bed, and at times he even rehearsed some of his speeches. Not, of course, while making love, but afterward, when he could be certain of her full attention.

"So what are you going to do? Are you going to allow conscription in Ireland?" They had been talking when he had gotten up and walked to the window to look out. For some reason, he was particularly restless today.

"I suppose I shall have to promise to support it, at least in order to get the Ulster nationalists to give in to home rule for the southern counties. Damn! I hate having my hand forced."

"The papers say we lost over seven hundred thousand men last year and over a hundred and fifty thousand since the first of the year. They complain because they say only good Englishmen are dying, while the able-bodied Irish do nothing."

"You sound like the members of my cabinet." He turned toward her. She was bedecked in clinging silk and smelled of lavender perfume which permeated the entire room. Her nightdress had slipped provocatively off one white shoulder, and the curve of her fine small breast was revealed.

"I'm only repeating what the papers say."

"You repeat it more politely." He walked to the table and picked up his pipe; he tapped it against the ashtray and then filled it with fresh tobacco from the humidor. He was wearing a dark silk robe which fell below his knees, meeting the tops of his black silk hose. On the chair nearby, his dark suit was laid out neatly, and with it were his heavy coat trimmed in lamb's wool and his smart bowler hat. His trusty umbrella was open wide and drying in one corner. He lit his pipe and billows of smoke circled his head.

"God knows what's happening in Russia. The reports that come in are unbelievable. All I can say is that events there have released sufficient German troops from the Russian front to make their spring offensive rather more successful than we'd like." It was one of his understatements, and he would not have dared make it in Parliament. Magda was right. The Ludendorff offensive had caused losses in excess of 150,000 in three months. The war! The Russians! Ireland! Ireland was like a tiny pimple and the rest of the world was like a great festering boil. But there were plenty of people who were terrified of what would happen in Ireland. Another rising, they predicted. Rifles had been confiscated, U-boats sighted . . . rumors fell nearly as hard as the spring rain. It was 1916 all over.

He sucked on his pipe and then laid it down, allowing it to smolder till it went out. He walked over to the bed, sitting down next to Magda, whose long legs were stretched out and whose head rested against a pile of pillows. He bent down and kissed the exposed area of her breast. She wiggled about delightfully and slithered beneath him, putting her arms around his neck.

When she moved, she reminded him of a snake. It was as if she moved all in one motion, and he knew from experience that in a moment she would wrap her legs around his midsection, drawing him into her and constricting like a great lovely boa. He felt his robe part, and she touched him with a sigh of appreciation for both his length and breadth.

David Lloyd George plunged into the depths and found his greatest pleasure. It was lovely, warm and moist; it was comforting, and she closed about him and the pressures of his day vanished; even the rain stopped, and he basked in the temporary warmth of her body heat. Gone were the memories of his early poverty-stricken childhood, gone were the fears that possessed him night and day, fears of returning to poverty, fears of not being able to afford the pleasures hard work and a good mind had bestowed on him.

Her movements, sinuous, slithering, and skillful, seduced his mind till it went blank and he was aware of nothing save the sensations of the constrictor as her body squeezed pleasure from his.

He groaned in the instant of his spasm and fought to be free of the legs which held him; then, at long last, she groaned and released him, still panting from her role of snake in his garden of Eden.

"You're agonizingly delightful," he said at length.

"And you are much too well-endowed for your own good," she countered. "A man should be less perfect."

David Lloyd George smiled at her compliment. "It doesn't matter how much they want it, it won't work."

"Do you make all your decisions in bed?" she said, rolling over.

"Most of them," he answered truthfully. There was something about sexual activity. It cleared his mind.

2

May 12, 1918

"Oh, I'm coming!" Emerald pulled the covers over Tom. He was sleeping in a full-sized bed now and he looked up at her wide-eyed. "It's just someone at the door. Now, you be good and go to sleep." He nodded and held his rag doll close. Emerald smiled indulgently and backed away, closing the door behind her.

She wiped her hands on her apron just as the second knock pounded on the door. "I'm coming!" She flung open the door and looked into the face of Albert Jenkins.

"Are you going to ask me in?" He smiled and took off his hat, looking for all the world like a penitent schoolboy, come cap in hand, Emerald thought.

"Of course, Albert." She ushered him into the flat, her mind muddled at the sight of him. It had been a little over a year, and reluctantly she admitted to herself that she had missed him. "I wasn't sure you were still in Dublin," she said with a little hesitation.

"I asked for a transfer. It will be coming through within the next two months."

"Do you know where to?"

He shook his head. "How's Tom, how are you?"

"He's grown so much you wouldn't know him . . . he'll be three on the eighteenth." She paused. "I've been fine."

"I can't stay long, Emerald. Do you suppose we might have a drink for old times' sake?"

"I was going to offer. I don't know what I'm doing standing in the middle of the room asking and answering questions. Please, sit down." She went to the sideboard and got out two glasses and some whiskey.

"I hear they're trying to prohibit whiskey in the United States."

"If they do, my brother Padraic will be home on the first boat after the war," Emerald answered.

Jenkins laughed nervously, and Emerald caught his mood of agitation.

"You didn't come to make small talk, did you?"

"No. I came to talk seriously to you. Emerald, you're still involved with de Valera, with the countess, and with Michael Collins, aren't you?"

"They're my friends. I wouldn't say we all agree on everything, but, yes, they're still my friends." She leaned forward and knew the excitement she felt must surely be evident in her eyes. "I've been working on the elections. I enjoy it, I enjoy politics."

Colonel Jenkins took a sip of his drink. "Major Price and his cohorts are nervous. I have reason to believe there will be arrests."

"Arrests? My God, they all just got out! What do you mean, arrests?"

"I mean the leaders of Sinn Fein, the Irish Volunteers, and the Irish Republican Brotherhood—their leaders. The British are going to crack down again. Price sees agitators under his bed."

Emerald leaned back in her chair. "Why are you telling me this?"

"Because I'm worried about you and your son. Because I'm leaving in two months and I can't protect you. Emerald, I don't want you back in prison with the rest of them. My God, woman, listen to me. You're in danger, and dammit, I still love you."

Emerald felt her face grow hot as she blushed at his declaration. When she had opened the door she had half-expected it, but she had not expected his warning, nor was she unaware of what giving her that warning meant to him.

"You seem very sure. I just don't see how the British could do this!"

He shook his head. "I've seen the list—over seventy leaders and you, my dear. Look, the British may have to conscript. They want to avoid a rising against it, so they'll intern the leaders."

"That's the most absurd thing I've ever heard. We'll gain a hundred times our current strength if de Valera and the countess and Michael are rearrested. We'll multiply a hundredfold overnight."

"I agree, we've made one mistake after another here. We're digging ourselves a hole five hundred feet deep. But don't you see, it's a trade-off. David Lloyd George is shrewd. He had to get Carson to accept the idea of home rule for the southern counties. He can get Carson to accept it, if conscription is allowed first."

"You know we won't accept a separate Ulster! Ireland is one

nation! Besides, conscription will cause a rising, I can tell you that!''

"That's why the arrests will be made. Soon.''

Emerald looked at him intently. "You can't expect me to keep this secret.''

Colonel Jenkins looked at the floor. "I expect you to do whatever you have to do.''

Giving her advance information of this sort could only be considered treasonous by the British, yet Alfred Jenkins, because of his love for her, had decided to go this far.

He stood up and drained his glass. "I can't stay,'' he said, brushing off his coat. "I have a lot of reading to do tonight. Reports and things . . .''

Emerald walked behind him to the door. She took his hand and gently squeezed it. "Thank you, Albert.'' She hoped she sounded as sincere as she felt. She wanted to reach out to him, to make certain he knew she understood.

His hands were soft as he patted her hand. "Take care, Emerald.''

She kissed his hand and touched his cheek. "I know what this meant to you,'' she told him.

He didn't respond. He turned and quietly left.

3

May 13, 1918

Dublin

Emerald spent much of the night packing her belongings. She and Mrs. O'Shea boxed them carefully and sent them to Mrs. O'Shea's daughter in Larne for safekeeping. That done, Emerald packed one box each for her and Tom.

"Holy Mary," Mrs. O'Shea kept saying, "you'd think they'd leave peaceful law-abiding people alone."

Finally, in the early hours of the morning, there had been a tearful farewell. Emerald promised to get in touch as soon as it was safe. And Mrs. O'Shea kept assuring Emerald that no one would bother her. "I'm too old to waste time on," she said over and over. "But where will you be going and what will you be doing?"

In truth, Emerald didn't know the answer. Her immediate plan was to take her personal belongings and put them in a locker at the railroad station; then, she decided, she would have to wait till afternoon and try to contact either the countess, or Eamon de Valera, or Michael Collins.

By noon, Emerald had left the things at the station, and she took Tom to St. Stephen's Green to wait till two P.M., when she hoped she would find Eamon de Valera in his flat.

While Tom played happily with a group of other youngsters, Emerald sat on the park bench, her mind reviewing the events that had led to her present position.

In July 1917 Eamon de Valera had been given a place on the Sinn Fein National Council and in the provisional executive of the Irish Volunteers. The Sinn Fein was the political arm of the nationalist movement, while the Volunteers were the military arm—an arm Emerald hoped would never be needed.

De Valera's first tactic was to defeat the British at the polls, and, failing that, he made no secret of the fact that he would then support the use of force.

Eamon de Valera was a tall, thin man whose glasses, when he wore them, slid down to the middle of his nose and rested there precariously, giving him the appearance of a thin owl.

De Valera's face always seemed to reflect his mood, Emerald had observed. When things were going well, he looked youthful, bright in appearance; when they went badly, he looked older than his thirty-six years. If she considered it, Emerald could not think of two people more unalike than de Valera and Michael Collins, yet both were leaders and both had large followings.

Michael Collins seemed to Emerald to be a dreamy-poet revolutionary given to derring-do; de Valera was a former mathematics professor with an eye for detail, a man who kept his own counsel.

Earlier in the morning, Emerald had ruled out approaching the countess. As it turned out, one phone call confirmed the fact that she was out of Dublin in any case. And I can't go to Michael Collins because I don't know where he lives, Emerald conceded. That left her only one choice: she had to see Eamon de Valera.

In any case, Emerald decided, she would not go to Collins even if she found him. In the Sinn Fein elections, de Valera was elected president, while Arthur Griffith and Father O'Flanagan were elected vice-presidents. When Eoin MacNeill was placed on the Executive Committee, the Countess Markievicz had been truly angry. She held MacNeill responsible for the failure of the rising in 1916 because it was he who had published the statement to the Volunteers that the rising was called off. Not surprisingly, the countess and de Valera fought both publicly and privately about MacNeill's appointment. In part, it was that argument that further endeared de Valera to Emerald. He treated the countess' views with the utmost respect, and at no time was he condescending because she was a woman.

Michael Collins, on the other hand, would no doubt have been kissing and flirting with her in public! But none of that for Eamon de Valera. He treated the countess as he would have treated a man, and the countess lost her argument, if not with good humor, then with a begrudging silence.

Tom was running toward her, and Emerald got up to meet him. She swept her son into her arms and hugged him. "We have to go now," she told him.

Emerald inhaled deeply. The smell of spring was everywhere on Saint Stephen's Green. The trees were all sporting brand-new light green leaves, the flowers were heavy with buds, and the lilac were in bloom.

"We have to go and see Mr. de Valera," Emerald told Tom. "I've decided he's the one we have to see."

"Potato! Potato!" Tom pointed to an old man with a pushcart who sold hot baked potatoes on a stick. He was surrounded by children, each paying sixpence for a hot potato.

"Not a bad idea." Emerald smiled as she ran her hands

through her son's unruly hair. "Are you really hungry now? You wouldn't be trying to fool me?"

"Mama, I want a potato."

"All right, come along, but then we're going to see Mr. de Valera."

Emerald paid for the two piping-hot potatoes and she and Tom sat down on a nearby bench to eat them. They were mildly salted, and when she bit into hers, steam came out from beneath the roasted skin. "Oh, be careful," she cautioned Tom. "They really are hot!"

When they were finished, Emerald put Tom in his pushcart and began walking. "Now," she said. "we'll go to Mr. de Valera."

"Mrs. Hughes, it's a pleasure to see you." Eamon de Valera smiled at her warmly and ushered her into his flat. It was untidy, cluttered with newspapers and books. "I hope you've come to tell me that you'll stand for election. You'd be a great asset, having been in the post office and all."

"I don't think I'm quite ready for that." Emerald smiled.

"And this must be Tom." De Valera lifted him out of the pushcart and held him up over his head. "Now, what will it be, lad? Some hot cocoa? Some tea? Or how about some cookies?"

"He just ate," Emerald put in. "But tea would be nice, though I suppose he would prefer cocoa."

"Then tea for you and me and cocoa for him."

De Valera disappeared into the kitchen for a few minutes and soon returned with a tray of tea, one cup of cocoa, and a plate of tea biscuits. "Even we who lead a bachelor's life can make do." He smiled.

"That's nice," Emerald said.

"Now, let's see, lad. Let's put you up on this chair to drink your cocoa and eat your cookies. Now, when you finish, here are some pencils and papers—draw me some pictures, can you?"

Tom nodded his head enthusiastically. He seemed in awe of Eamon de Valera.

"You're very good with children," Emerald told him.

"Oh, my dear, a politician must be good with children. Now, tell me, have you come to discuss being a candidate? And what more do you need to know about the issues? I've talked to you, and it seems to me you know more than most people."

Emerald blushed. "I'm afraid a politician has to make statements and take firm positions with a special kind of confidence.

I always see several sides to every argument. It makes it difficult for me to take a position."

De Valera's eyes twinkled. "My, I think you may be too honest to be a politician."

"It's not a question of honesty, it's a question of political skill. I've listened to you. When you're among moderate nationalists like myself, you take radical positions; when you're among radicals, you take moderate positions. You keep a balance, and you're sincere and honest in wanting to keep the balance, as opposed to being sincere and honest about what you're saying all the time."

De Valera grinned. "Why, Mrs. Hughes, you're very insightful, very clever indeed!"

"But I like politics, and maybe one day I'll develop the technique . . . I think there is a technique."

"It's a game, a very serious game, and as you well know, it can have serious consequences. I'll admit it to you, Mrs. Hughes, I would truly prefer to defeat the British at the political game."

"I too," Emerald answered.

"Mind you," de Valera revealed, "I do take a certain perverse enjoyment in being pitted against David Lloyd George. And there's a double pleasure in it when England is ravished by war."

"From what I know of Lloyd George, he's Welsh, and, I read, a social reformer."

De Valera laughed. "Ah, the central issue. If his words didn't come out of his mouth, we might get on quite well. But the man is prime minister of England—though I admit that gives him ample opportunity to be a reformer." De Valera chuckled. "Our time is coming, Emerald. It's so close I can almost taste success; this time, this time we'll be free, by God!"

His eyes glowed with the fire of his own vision, and Emerald was briefly reminded of the pictures of saints and martyrs in the textbooks. Eamon de Valera had the fiery vision of the saint, but not the temperament of the martyr, she decided.

"I will say one thing for David Lloyd George. His government threats of conscription for Ireland have done more to unite the leaders of this country than I could have done in the next one hundred years."

Emerald saw her opening, and she didn't hesitate. "Too much," she said carefully. "The leaders are now so united that they pose a threat. You, Michael Collins, and the countess . . . myself, for reasons best understood by God, and about seventy other people

are scheduled to be arrested in the next few days. All the leaders
of Sinn Fein and many of the party organizers.''

"Well, you're one of our best organizers.''

"I don't want to go back to prison," Emerald admitted.

"Nor need you. Collins won't go either. But for myself and at
least some of the others, we'll go. Mind you, we have to meet,
but I think definitely our strategy should be to go back to prison.
You need not go. You are not visible enough to create a public
outcry.''

"Mama, I'm sleepy." Tom was rubbing his eyes.

"Put him down in the bedroom," Eamon de Valera suggested.
"We need to discuss your information further.''

Emerald took his suggestion, and then, when Tom was curled
up on Eamon de Valera's unmade bed, she returned to the main
room of the flat.

"How did you come by this information?''

In her mind, Emerald had rehearsed her answer. I'm not a
good liar, she admitted. But let me be one now. I must never
implicate Albert in any way.

"When I surrendered," Emerald told de Valera, "I met a
young British officer who works in Dublin Castle. Price, that's
his name. Well, ah, it's a little different, but he seemed to be
enamored of me; a crush, I guess. In any case, he showed me the
list and gave me warning.''

"Price! My, that is a coup. The man is an absolute paranoid.''
De Valera smiled wickedly. "But then, I suppose even paranoids
can have strong attractions or fall in love. Mind you, he shows
better taste than I would have thought he had.''

Emerald again blushed. "I didn't encourage him," she
murmured.

"Well, anytime you want to turn professional spy, let me
know.''

"I think not," Emerald answered. "Being a spy would
require far too much lying." And that, she thought as she said it,
was her first truthful statement in the last ten minutes.

De Valera poured Emerald a drink and handed it to her. "I
know your information is reliable because it cross-checks with
information obtained by Michael Collins. He says the arrests will
be made on the sixteenth or seventeenth. What we will need is a
safe place for you and your son to stay. And needless to say, you
can't go back to work.''

"What will we live on?''

"It will all be taken care of. . . . Now, let me just write down
an address here. What have you done with your things?''

"I packed some boxes and sent them off to a close friend's relatives. What I need is in a locker at the railroad station."

"You have foresight, Mrs. Hughes." De Valera turned to her and handed her a slip of paper. "This is the address of Dr. Gregory Gregory and his wife. Dr. Gregory will be needing a nurse for his clinic, and a small room goes with the position. They're with us, they're safe. Their names appear on no membership lists. Now, sit down with me and we'll have a drink or two. Then, when Tom wakes up, you can go over to the Gregorys'."

4

June 15, 1918

Boston

Joe Scanlon sat at a table in the Adams House. If Dooley's was his private political domain, the Adams House Tavern was the domain of every Irishman in Massachusetts, including their senator from Clinton, Senator David Walsh.

"Come to have a pint or fetch a two-bit bucket of beer?" the cheerful bartender asked.

"A pint for now," Joe answered. It was always the same at the Adams House. A good many Irish took a bucket of brew home with them, while others sent their wives or children to fetch an iron bucket full and bring it home. Of course women and children were not allowed in taverns, so they stood in line outside the back door, where their buckets were passed out to them as fast as the quarters were passed in.

"You know why the black Protestants of good old Boston town call us pig-shit Irish?" Terrance O'Rourke blustered cheerfully. "It's 'cause we keep our pig in the parlor and he's Irish too!"

There was a round of laughter, and Joe smiled. He was lace-curtain Irish—moneyed. The shanty Irish lived in the slums and worked long hours in the mills. The pig-shit Irish were the poorest of them all. And in Boston town, the Protestants were always called black—heretics with black, black souls.

"Did you hear the one about old Seamus O'Toole?" O'Rourke punched Joe in the ribs playfully. "Old Seamus, he was fornicating with Molly O'Hara, Mary Malone, and little Kathy Finney. And on Good Friday, right as rain, the three girls they up and went to the confession and told good old Father Murphy how it was they'd been fornicating with Seamus O'Toole. So the good father, he delivered them absolution and he told them: 'Say five "Hail Marys" and be putting five dollars in the collection plate every week for the next three weeks. Now, go home and sin no more.' Well, wouldn't you know it—next day Seamus O'Toole was walking down the street, and who should he run into, he ran right into Father Murphy. And Father Murphy said, 'Seamus O'Toole, I'll want to be talking to you about your fornicating with the girls of this parish.' 'And what did you say to the girls?' Seamus asked. 'Well,' said Father Murphy, 'I told them to put five dollars in the collection plate every week for the next three weeks and go home and sin no more, and what do you think Seamus O'Toole did? He burst out laughing and he said, 'You'd better not be telling me what to do, Father, or I'll be taking my prick right out of this parish! Then you'd be poor!' ''

A roar of laughter followed O'Rourke's story. When O'Rourke finished laughing himself, he took a long swig of beer. "Let's hope the Professor never signs prohibition into law!" They all called Woodrow Wilson "The Professor."

"Now, there's a way to get the Irish out of America!" someone called out, joining the free-for-all discussion.

"Hell, can't we make our own law here? More laws have been passed by the Irish politicians here than in the state legislature!" Again there was a roar of laughter.

"At least the Professor is trying to make peace," someone allowed.

"He's from a black Protestant Ulster family. What kind of peace can they make?" Terrance McCue slurred.

Joe took a gulp of beer. America had been at war for fourteen months, and her losses were substantial. Wilson had submitted a fourteen-point peace plan to Congress in January. It included the restoration of Alsace-Lorraine to France, independence for Poland and the Austrian minorities, freedom of the seas, and self-determination. It was the latter that appealed most to the Irish and to Irish-Americans, because self-determination is what Ireland wanted. Wilson's proposals also included a thorny issue: the setting up of some sort of international association of nations to guarantee the political and economic independence of all nations.

But proposals or no proposals, fighting was fierce in Europe. And in Ireland, the leaders of Sinn Fein had been rearrested even as American Sinn Fein followers stood on their soapboxes behind the iron fence on the south side of the Boston Common and gave rousing speeches urging the Boston Irish to support their brothers and sisters in Ireland. And outside the British consulate in New York City, angry Irish-American women carried signs of bitter protest and walked up and down calling for the release of the prisoners.

"And did you save me any beer?" Mike Scanlon eased onto a chair next to his brother.

"If they've run out, it's not me that's drunk it," Joe said. And he thought as he looked at Mike that his brother was a great comfort to him. In the months since Kitty's death, the days had seemed long, tedious, and lonely. Not that Kitty had been company; she was a responsibility, though, and her passing had left him with an empty void.

"What do you have in mind for the summer?" Joe asked. Michael's grades had picked up and it looked as if he might be the first Scanlon to receive a degree.

"I'll work, of course." Michael winked. "But I'll be raising money for the Irish Volunteers."

"Why not for Sinn Fein?"

"It's the Volunteers who are organizing quietly. They need arms, and to get arms, they need money."

"I've heard that before," Joe said in a near-whisper.

"It's not the same now," Michael argued. "Britain is at war and too weak to offer resistance to a real uprising. Things have changed. The Irish are united now."

"Oh, that will be the day," Joe replied.

Michael drained his mug. "Let me give you a sample," he said, standing up. "Listen to me, all of you!" Michael's voice was loud, and he banged on the bar to get everyone's attention. "Listen! I've only just come from a meeting where I've heard a man who's just come from Dublin. Smuggled out on a freighter, he was. Let me tell you all the latest news from Ireland!"

"You talk, we'll listen," a man called out.

Michael began speaking, and Joe leaned back. His younger brother had a flair; he spoke with some eloquence, Joe thought proudly. And his fine-featured good looks certainly gave an added edge to his well-chosen words.

Joe listened and found that even he was falling into a trance-like spell. His brother had what one might call a "golden tongue." He was a hotheaded, inspiring revolutionary incarnate, born again in Boston, but still very much a son of Ireland.

"I'll donate right now!" Finney called out.

"Me too," O'Rourke slurred. "And after that, I'll tell another story, I will."

In a few minutes the hat was being passed around and all the boys were talking about what fine rifles would be bought.

"And England's troubles are our advantage!" Mike called out, paraphrasing an old battle cry. The hat came to Joe Scanlon, and a hush fell over the room. Joe smiled and winked at Mike then, to the roar of applause and good-natured curses, he took out his checkbook and started writing.

"It's a mean way to get a donation out of your own brother," Joe chided after the noise had died down. "Tell me, have you been taking lessons in the fine art of oration?"

"It comes naturally," Mike confided. He added the check to the rest of the money and transferred it to a small bag. "It was you who taught me always to get a man in a position where he can't refuse—in front of his friends. You would have donated anyway."

"Maybe," he allowed. "But mind you, I'd rather give to Irish orphans—somehow it seems a better use than buying the weapons to make more orphans."

"A free Ireland is more important."

Joe finished his beer. "You'd better go to the bank before it closes."

"I'll do just that," Mike replied, quickly gulping the remainder of his second brew.

5

November 11, 1918

Alison Gregory was in her early forties, a bustling, busy woman who tended her house, kept a nice garden, reared her five children, and managed to find time to assist in her husband's clinic as well as maintain an interest in the political situation.

"I wish Gregory would get home," she complained.

"He only just left," Emerald answered. She wiped her hands on her apron and sat down at the kitchen table. Her life since last May was all too reminiscent of her childhood—a confined world that comprised Dr. Gregory Gregory's clinic, which was in the lower part of the house; the house itself; and the occasional shopping foray. Michael Collins had forbidden her to attend political meetings: "They're watched, and since the police may still be looking for you, I want you to stay away."

Reluctantly Emerald had agreed, and the result was isolation from most of her friends and considerable loneliness in spite of the Gregorys' kindness.

The door slammed shut, and both women jumped. "Alison! Emerald!" The doctor's voice boomed through the house. "The war's over! There's been an armistice!"

Alison hurried to the parlor to see the newspaper brought home by the doctor. Emerald followed in her wake; her first thought was that now letters from Padraic would be more frequent.

Alison peered over her husband's shoulder to read the news. "All our good Irish boys will be coming home now," she sighed.

"And they'll have been trained as soldiers and ready to help press our demands," the doctor added.

"Well, look at that, will you?" Alison pointed to the election story that helped fill the front page. "The hell our elections are free!" She shook her head in disgust.

"How can the British have the nerve to tell the world we're going to have free elections when we have censorship, when over a hundred of our leaders are in jail, and when Sinn Fein is officially banned?" Greggie shouted.

"Now, Greggie, you're going to have an attack," Alison warned. "Settle down."

The doctor slumped into his chair on his wife's suggestion, letting the paper fall into his lap. His face was quite fuchsia, and in point of fact, it always got fuchsia when he read an English newspaper.

"Why did you buy an English paper?" she asked, shaking her head.

"Because they were all out of ours," he replied tersely. "There isn't an armistice every day, you know."

Emerald turned away and looked at a section of the paper that had slipped to the floor. The Gregorys had a good marriage, but they bickered a bit from time to time.

"They're going to be historic elections even if they aren't free," Emerald commented. "It'll be the first time all of Great Britain has voted at once."

"And hopefully the last," Dr. Gregory mumbled. "Sometime I'd like to vote in an Irish election for our own Parliament!"

"We're going to bury the Irish Parliamentary party," Emerald predicted. "We're going to elect a Parliament full of Sinn Fein!"

"None of whom will go to Westminster and all of whom will form a national Parliament right here in Dublin!" Alison finished off. She clapped her hands like a delighted child.

"If those elected get out of prison," the doctor added. "But the bloody bastards won't let us go that easily . . . no, now that they're rid of the Germans, it'll be us they come after, and we'll have to fight them; it won't be just an uprising, it'll be a war.''

"I hope not," Emerald said sadly. "I want us to win by political force.''

"Don't we all," retorted the doctor. "But, Emerald, look at how bright and intelligent the British are! They've imprisoned every moderate leader in Ireland and left the real revolutionaries free. You and I know that the most rebellious feature de Valera has is his rhetoric. He wants to force Lloyd George's political hand. And by heaven, he might—though I still think the British will fight rather than lose Ireland.''

Emerald nodded. Eamon de Valera might want a political settlement; she wasn't sure anymore. But she was sure that Michael Collins wouldn't wait too long. His power was growing daily.

18

1

January 21, 1919

The results of the December 14 election were finally announced on December 28, and considering the British clampdown before the elections, Emerald considered it a small miracle that the results were even announced—though if they hadn't been, there would have been instant war in Ireland. Prior to the election, there were more arrests, including the arrest of the Sinn Fein's director of elections, who was hustled off to jail in November.

And for days before the election, planes bombed Ireland with leaflets containing strong warnings about the consequences of supporting the Sinn Fein cause. "And after the elections," Dr. Gregory warned, "they'll be dropping bombs!"

As Emerald remembered his comment, she looked up in the sky. No, there were no planes, and so far, no bombs. Perhaps, she hoped, Lloyd George was too stunned; and stunned he should be, she thought.

Sinn Fein, in spite of everything, had won seventy-three out of one hundred and five Irish seats. The Parliamentary party of John Redmond had won only six seats, and the Ulster Unionists— the party of Protestant leader Edward Carson—had won twenty-six, all quite naturally in the northern counties of Ulster. But Sinn Fein had the rest! And surprisingly, even in Ulster the Unionists had a popular majority in only four, and in the other six northeast counties, the Nationalist minority was larger than the Unionist majority was, in comparison with the rest of Ireland.

" 'Tis a poor, poor case for the exclusion of the six counties from an independent Ireland," Dr. Gregory warned. "And if that's what Lloyd George tries to do, Ulster will fester like a sore on the soft underbelly of England. Future generations will have David Lloyd George to thank for their ensuing misery."

Emerald knew that the doctor was right. But I won't think about future complications today; today I will only listen and feel proud.

Emerald pulled her shawl around her. The cold January wind whipped around the building, and the small group who had invitations to the day's events shuddered en masse while they waited to enter.

Count Plunkett walked past her and up three steps before he turned around and paused. "Emerald Hughes?" He squinted at her and smiled.

"Good morning," Emerald returned. She felt like a butterfly newly let out of her cocoon. After being so careful for so many months, she was afraid that no one would remember her.

"Good morning indeed! And a wonderful morning it is— historic, happy, proud! You do have an invitation?"

"Yes, thank you," Emerald replied.

"Good, good, good. You of all people, you worked so hard! You shouldn't miss this day, I'll tell you." He retreated down the three steps and squeezed her arm. "History needs its witnesses, you know. Ha! I'm an old man and feel like a boy!" He leaned over conspiratorially. "I'm so excited that I've had to go to the loo three times already. Do you think I'm getting senile?"

"It's only the excitement," Emerald assured him.

"Good! I shouldn't want to be senile at sixty-five, nor mentally impaired, that I should miss this day. Are you sure you don't want to come in with me?" Count Plunkett added as he started again up the stairs.

"No, we'll be let in when everyone arrives," she explained.

"Well, then, my dear, I must go inside to meet my destiny." He made the comment in such a way that it revealed his flair for the dramatic.

Emerald waved at him as he passed through the large doors. And in a few minutes the rest of them were allowed in. Emerald hurried to find a good seat—today was to be the first historic meeting of Dail Eireann, the Assembly of Ireland.

Of the seventy-three members of Sinn Fein who had been elected to Westminster, only twenty-seven were able to attend. Eight were absent for other reasons, but the remainder, thirty-eight in all, were in prison in England.

At promptly three-thirty P.M. the meeting was called to order, with Cathal Brugha in the chair. As each of the names of the imprisoned elected M.P.'s was called out by the clerk, the answer was read out in Gaelic: "*Fe ghlas ag gallibh!*" The words meant "Imprisoned by a foreign enemy."

Next the Declaration of Independence for Ireland was read, and midway through the first section, the clerk proclaimed: "Whereas the Irish Republic was proclaimed in Dublin on Easter Monday, 1916, by the Irish Republican Army, acting on behalf of the Irish people . . ."

Emerald blinked back tears as thoughts of Seamus flooded into her mind. It was Seamus O'Hearn that had fought and died for this moment. It was to Seamus and the others like him that this victory belonged . . . and because of Seamus and those who died in 1916, our political fight today has more power, Emerald acknowledged. She ran her hands over the coarse material of her skirt. And maybe, she hoped, Tom could grow up in a free Ireland. Perhaps no more like Seamus would have to die. But in her heart, she knew the battle had only just begun. To declare independence was not the same as having it, and by allowing the Dail Eireann to meet today, the British were, in a sense, calling the bluff of Sinn Fein. How, Emerald pondered, could this hard-fought, theoretical independence be made a reality?

She studied the earnest faces of the Dail and wondered if the American president, Mr. Wilson, might be of some help. After all, he was going on and on about the rights of small nations.

This was the first meeting of the Dail, and outside, American flags fluttered along next to Irish flags. They were intended as a silent blessing on the Peace Conference now in progress, but they also called out to America across the sea.

Emerald folded her hands tightly in a gesture of determination. I shall speak to Michael Collins tomorrow, she promised herself.

2

January 22, 1919

Emerald paused two buildings away from the tearoom and looked into a glass window to adjust her bonnet. I have to be at my most dignified, she told herself. Michael Collins is a difficult man—totally immersed in himself.

She looked at her image and approved it. Then she wondered why she really cared how she looked, apart from the aspect of dignity. Michael Collins was an enigma, she admitted. Over the course of time they had known one another, he had comforted her, worked with her, flirted with her, and argued with her. Sometimes his attitudes—especially his attitude toward women—made her furious; at other times, he was capable of making her laugh. But, she allowed, between them, no matter what else there was, was an unspoken bond. In April 1916 they had shared and survived hell together, and during that week, time had eclipsed and all relationships had intensified.

Emerald considered herself to be in the moderate wing of Sinn Fein, and since she had become involved with politics, Michael had teased her. She resented the teasing and often found herself responding with sarcasm. But the simple truth was that if it had been someone else, the teasing would have had no meaning and she would simply have walked away. The difficulty was that their shared nightmare made it impossible for her to ignore his opinions and even more difficult to walk away.

Their last exchange filled her mind as she entered the tearoom. She glanced around, and Michael stood up and motioned her to a chair. It was midafternoon, and Michael assured her the tearoom was safe, though he assured her, "You are not in much danger anymore—it is I who have to be careful."

"You're looking especially prim today." He had a slightly wicked grin.

"And how should I look?" Emerald retorted, arching one eyebrow.

"Given your exceptional figure, I think a lower neckline would be in order. Frankly, it's a pity to hide all that ravishing hair under so dull a bonnet."

Emerald sighed. "You're such a flatterer," she replied dryly.

"Now, now. I've told you before: but for my all consuming passion to free Ireland, I'd be courting you. Your eyes are the eyes of Ireland. Ah, Emerald I adore you."

"I doubt I would let you court me," she said crisply.

"Doubt—I have no doubt. I really don't think you would say no."

"You have a swelled head and much too fine an opinion of yourself, Michael Collins. You're much too in love with your image in the mirror to be courting me."

"I do like my women with a sharp tongue and a bit of spirit."

"I am not your woman, not by a long shot. I did ask you to meet me for a reason."

"Seeing you is reason enough," he said playfully.

"Well, seeing you is not reason enough for me. Please listen, Michael. Seriously, I do have something important to say."

He sighed and picked up his teacup. "Lord save me from serious beautiful women! They're my fate." He set down the tea. "And Lord save me from tea, too."

Emerald suppressed a smile. "I've read that Mr. Wilson is receiving the delegations of small countries in Paris."

"Versailles," Michael corrected.

"I know where Versailles is. What I thought was . . . well, I thought we ought to go. I think a representation ought to be made."

"I can't court you, but you're willing to go off to Paris with

me!'' He burst into laughter and slapped his knee. "Oh, Emerald,
I'm touched! And by God, while it's true that I can't give you
my life, I'd certainly be willing to give you a weekend in Paris!''

Emerald scowled at him from across the table. "I ought to
have had better sense than to even discuss this with you. I didn't
mean me when I said 'we'—I meant the Dail ought to send a
representation.''

His dark handsome face clouded over with mock disbelief.
"You mean you don't want to spend a weekend in Paris with
me?''

"Certainly not,'' she replied coldly.

"How about England, then, say London?''

"Oh, why can't you be serious?''

"I am serious, Lady Ireland. I've never been more serious in
my life. I think your idea is splendid! But Paris is not the place.
President Wilson is coming to London next week, and I think we
ought to see him . . . yes, you and I. I as minister of the Dail,
you as a fine representative of Irish womanhood! Gad, what an
example, as the British would say! There you are, Lady Ireland,
beautiful and kind, intelligent and literate, widow of a man who
fought in the late great war, mother of a male Irish infant! Rebel,
nurse, and healer of mankind! Ah, not even the professorial
American president could resist your rebel's green eyes and your
pacifist profession and inner thoughts. And all of it wrapped in
the fine figure of a Gibson Girl!''

Suddenly Michael Collins' facial expression changed completely.
The look of amusement fled his face, and instead he leaned over,
looking at her seriously.

"I have to go to London with a woman who's been active in
politics. The countess is in jail, so, dear Emerald, I choose you.
Now, I would be terribly pleased if you got up ever so naturally,
and without drawing attention to us, moved closely by my side
and walked, covering my face if at all possible, right out of this
charming tearoom. See if you can look warmly affectionate,
rather as if we had just enjoyed love in the afternoon. Call me
'dearest' and smile a lot, cuddle up.''

Emerald opened her mouth to respond, but he smiled, leaned
over the table, and kissed her on the lips. Then he whispered in
her ear, "A member of the Royal Irish Constabulary just came
in, and he's a bugger if there ever was one. Get up slowly, now.
God, you have wonderful ears!''

Emerald reached across the table and stroked his cheek. "Shall
we go, my darling?'' She almost breathed the words out, loud
enough for the RIC man to hear, softly enough to make it all

sound private. She leaned over Michael Collins, partially obscuring his face. "Let's go to my flat." She smiled, squeezing his arm and allowing her shawl to fall across him.

Together they moved toward the door, and Emerald caught the filthy expression of amusement on the RIC man's face.

"He wishes he was me," Michael Collins whispered. Then, pinching her, he added, "I wish I was me."

Outside, a cold blast of wind hit Emerald in the face and she pulled her shawl away from Michael and wrapped it around herself. "You're truly impossible, Michael Collins!"

"But you'll come to London, won't you?"

Emerald nodded.

They stopped, and Michael looked down on her, his expression as serious as she had ever seen it. "You can't really get angry with me, Emerald. You see, we've bled together, you and I. It's a rare experience for a man and woman. Emerald, blood binds."

Emerald nodded and felt suddenly numb at the same time. It was in that instant that she had the first real premonition she had ever felt. As she looked into Michael Collins' handsome young face, she knew he wouldn't live to grow old.

3

January 27, 1919

London

Michael Collins acknowledged himself as an effective revolutionary, and that might have been considered personal ego if, in fact, so many of his colleagues had not agreed with the assessment. At the same time, he realized that to some extent fate had played a large role in his present position.

He had been born in West Cork in 1890, and like many young men, he left when he was sixteen and went to England. There he worked for the post office, and finally, through Irish connections, he obtained a position in the London branch of an American bank, Guaranty Trust Company of New York. Early in 1916 he returned to Ireland and there had taken part in the rising of 1916. Afterward, he was arrested and interned in North Wales in a camp called Frongoch.

Next to his banking experience, he considered his time in Frongoch the most important learning time of his life. In London he had learned to manipulate bank accounts and move money secretly. This talent he fully intended to use now. As Irish minister for finance in the Dail, he fervently hoped to allow the British banks to finance the new Irish republic by using fraudulent accounts to obtain large loans for the new nation.

At Frongoch he had learned to organize, and more important, he had learned how to recruit men and make them beholden to him. In short, he had come to recognize his own talents of leadership. At Frongoch he had set up an efficient Irish Republican Brotherhood network, seeing to it that those in charge of the various huts in which the prisoners were held, as well as the chief administrative duties in the camp, were all sworn IRB men. He further used the British prison to organize educational and military classes.

Further, because the prisoners at Frongoch were from all over Ireland, he was able to form a nationwide intelligence network.

Outside Frongoch, a skeleton organization was able to operate through bogus branches of the Gaelic League, one of the only organizations not outlawed. Thus, while the rebels who entered Frongoch and other British prisons were undisciplined and disorganized, they came out hardened and prepared for a long fight. For the first time in the history of Ireland, there was an effective communications system and strong leadership, as well as a leader dedicated to collecting intelligence information in order to beat the British at their own game. Michael Collins had, in his files, records of friendly members of the Royal Irish Constabulary as well of long lists of those he intended to eliminate. The once disorganized members of the Irish Republican Brotherhood were now welded into an army, and more and more they were being called the IRA—the Irish Republican Army.

"It's important for a man to understand himself," Father Flanagan had once told Michael Collins. And Michael did understand himself. He understood that he could laugh and enjoy laughing; he understood that he had what it took to lead men, and he relished in his leadership; he knew he was handsome and could pleasure himself with nearly any woman he chose—with few exceptions; but most important, he knew he had to be utterly ruthless in his aims. He aimed, after all, at nothing less than a free Ireland.

"More wine?" Tonight Michael Collins was dressed like a real gentleman. He had insisted they stay in London's finest hotel so as not to look like the stereotypical Irish the British conjured up. And he had insisted they dine in the hotel dining room, dressed formally, playing their proper roles as diplomats from a soon-to-be-free Ireland.

He leaned across the crisp white linen tablecloth and smiled at Emerald. She was wearing a long dark green dress that rustled when she walked. It made her green eyes look huge and hypnotic. Her red-gold hair was pulled back and wrapped up, but small curls escaped, giving her a warm, soft, feminine appearance.

"A little more, thank you. It's nice. I don't usually drink wine."

"It's not an Irish drink," he whispered. "You know, you really are the most beautiful woman in this hotel. And I say that truthfully. There are a lot of elegant women here, but you are both elegant and stunning."

Emerald smiled and ignored his flattery.

"You're right to be careful of the wine," he continued. "It wouldn't do if I had to carry you out of the dining room. This is England, so you'll have to act a lady."

"I hardly think I'll get drunk. What's happened to your accent?"

"I lived here for ten formative years. Listen, I do a passable Oxbridge accent, and if I didn't use it, the waiters would be even ruder than British waiters usually are."

"Are they usually rude?"

"Oh, indeed. It's all too good for them, you know. They think such work ought to be done by natives from the colonies. Waiting table is not for the superior British mind! No, no."

Emerald looked across the thick maroon carpet of the dining room to the well-polished shoes of the waiter who stood like a sentry, guarding a tray of food which he didn't deign to serve because they hadn't finished their appetizer. She lifted her eyes to his craggy face, which had all the human passion of a rock.

"He does look a bit prissy," she said with an uncharacteristic giggle.

" 'Prissy' isn't the word." He leaned over. "The RIC have to use bullets to kill Irishmen; an English waiter can do it with a single look."

"Michael, you're making me laugh."

"About time. I thought all you thought about was politics. My God, your teeth are straight too! Is there no end to your perfection?"

"I have a vile temper," she returned.

"Speaking of that, have you an impassioned plea for Mr. Wilson tomorrow?"

"I think that, properly put, the truth is impassioned enough."

He smiled warmly at her. "Emerald, I shouldn't like you to be disappointed. We're here more for form than for content . . . if I may say so."

"I'm not certain I understand what you mean."

"No one would like it better than I if Mr. Wilson and his League of Nations would press for Irish freedom, but I'm a born skeptic. I think that Americans of Irish descent care about Ireland, but other Americans don't give a damn. What's more, Mr. Wilson wants peace, and he wants peace badly enough not to say boo to Lloyd George, whose government, I'm sure I don't have to remind you, is a coalition, and part of that coalition are the Ulster Unionists. Now, David Lloyd George is not going to risk his government to make Ireland free. He's going to leave us alone so he can be a big actor on the world stage, and Mr. Wilson is going to leave Ireland alone, so Lloyd George can be left alone."

"I don't doubt you're right," Emerald said, leaning back against the velvet cushion of the Queen Anne chair. "First, Wilson comes from Protestant Ulster stock. Second, we have to make this representation so that Irish-Americans who support the cause of Irish freedom will see that we cared enough to try."

Michael Collins' face broke into a wide grin. "You learn fast, Emerald Hughes. I may have to revise my opinion of women in politics."

"And you, Michael Collins, are your mother's son."

"Well put, my dear."

The waiter removed the appetizers and brought the main course. The whitefish fillet floated in a sea of milk and fresh butter topped with sprigs of parsley. To one side, little fresh carrots surrounded a pile of potatoes. Silently, almost belligerently, the waiter refilled their wineglasses.

"And bring another bottle, my good man." Michael spoke in his very best upper-class English accent.

Emerald giggled again. "I shan't be disappointed," she said earnestly.

They ate their dinner in leisure, and then, having finished two bottles of wine, partook of an after-dinner brandy, and after that they went out into the damp London air for a short sobering walk.

"I ate too much," Emerald complained. "And I think I drank too much too."

"Much to my surprise, you seem sober enough." His accent had returned fully, and owing to the amount he had drunk, he slurred his words a bit.

"I think we should go back to the hotel. I'd like my wits about me tomorrow," Emerald suggested.

"I'm certain you'll have them." He took her arm and propelled her around, heading back toward the hotel, the rooms of which waited in red-velvet splendor.

"I've never spent a night in a hotel—a small inn, but not a hotel."

"Does that mean you want company?"

"No, that is not what it means."

"Do you like London? Personally, I like London, or I would like it if it weren't peopled with Londoners."

"It's too big and too dirty," Emerald said.

"And everyone is just too damn English!" he added with a robust laugh. "And all of them caught up in the euphoria of peace and world government. Hell, it'll never happen, not in five million years!"

"I like the idea," Emerald said thoughtfully. "Just because something isn't entirely practical doesn't mean the ideal isn't worth anything."

"I don't have time for ideals. I have too many practical aims. You can't have world government overnight. Hell! It's taken Ireland seven hundred years just to get organized enough to declare our goddamned independence!"

They traveled up to the third floor trapped in a tiny brass cage of a lift. Michael escorted Emerald to her room, and they paused outside the door in the long silent corridor.

"Your language deteriorates when you drink," she teased.

"Not as much as my thoughts," he slurred, leaning over her. He pressed his lips to hers and encircled her waist. With his second kiss, he pressed his body flat against hers. Then he released her. "Don't invite me in for a drink unless you're going to let me sleep with you," he advised.

"Oh, Michael," Emerald sighed. She would have to be dead not to find him attractive; she would have to be unconscious not to recognize the feeling of desire that his lips moving on hers had aroused. And by the same token, she was almost certain that if she allowed him to make love to her, she would think of Thomas Hughes, and who could guess who Michael Collins would think of. But, she admitted, there was a *quid pro quo* in this relationship. Michael Collins didn't love her as Albert Jenkins had, so there was no need for guilt. She didn't love him, so there was no need to carry on a long affair.

"Would you like a drink?" Emerald asked softly as she turned the great brass key in the lock.

Michael's arms went around her from behind. "My God, woman, you are a rebel!"

Michael opened the door and removed the key. In one motion he swept Emerald into his arms and carried her to the large double bed, setting her down gently. He sat himself down on the edge and removed his shoes, socks, and shirt. Then he stood up and removed his trousers.

Emerald began to undo her dress, but he reached out and stopped her with a restraining hand. "I'd like to do that," he requested, running his hand along her neck.

"Somehow you seem to be more sober," she suggested.

Michael kissed her. "You're a sobering woman," he told her as he silently began to undo the buttons on her dress. "I've often thought of making love to you. Once I dreamed about it. But I must say, I'm pleasantly surprised to find you agreeable."

He parted the material of her dress, pulling it away and off her. Then he undid her snow-white camisole and sighed as he bent to kiss her breasts.

Emerald moved beneath him and lifted her arms to encircle his neck. She could feel the rippling muscles in his arms and shoulders; he was well-built, strong; he was young and virile and only five years older than she.

He caressed her thigh and ran his hand over her. She felt a chill of anticipation followed by the warmth of her desire.

"You're exquisite," he breathed in her ear. "Not even my fertile imagination conjured up the reality of you, though I knew the tips of your breasts would be like rosebuds. . . ."

His words were close to the ones Thomas Hughes had used and his body had the same weight and the same proportions. But Emerald did not close her eyes as she had when Albert Jenkins made love to her. Instead, she found herself looking into the eyes of Michael Collins and being excited by the glint of pure animal desire she saw in them. She sensed that she was the first woman he had known in some time, just as he was the first man she had known since her one night with Albert Jenkins over a year ago.

"Oh, Lady Ireland, you're seducing me and I love it!" He buried his face in her breasts and pulled her on top of him. His hands massaged her back lovingly and then moved across her buttocks. Beneath her, Emerald could feel him, and she instinctively parted her long legs to straddle him.

He smiled up at her slyly and pushed himself up, taking both her breasts in his hands as he did so. Emerald moved slowly

above him, amazed at the expression on his face and ecstatic
with the sensations he caused her to feel.

In this position, his hands seemed everywhere, and he filled
her and caressed her in what seemed a single motion. Her face
grew warm and flushed and she began to shiver. She groaned
slightly and then shook with satisfaction as she felt him reach his
height of pleasure. Finally, still breathless, she collapsed against
him and he nuzzled into her neck, laughing softly.

"Not so many men like being on the bottom," he joked. "But
I rather like seeing a woman and being able to reach her."

Emerald pressed against him. "I rather liked it myself," she
admitted.

"Brazen hussy, that's what you are."

"I am not. Where is it written that a woman shouldn't enjoy
coupling as much as a man?"

"Happily, it is not written anywhere. And if you think I
would want to . . . ah . . . yes, couple with any woman who
didn't enjoy it, you're wrong."

"Well, I enjoyed it."

"I know you did, Lady Ireland." He leaned over and kissed
her damp forehead. "But don't expect more tonight. I've had far
too much to drink."

"And tomorrow is an important day." She snuggled down
next to him and marveled at the warmth of his body heat and the
male odor which exuded from him. She sighed to herself and
thought that she must be careful with her emotions. Michael's
love was for Ireland, and he would only be faithful to Ireland.

Emerald touched his large hand which covered her breast, and
she felt content nestled in his arms. He had begun to snore, and
again the sadness of her vision of his death came over her. She
fell asleep saying a silent prayer for his life.

"You look stunning and every inch a lady," Michael said, his
voice full of admiration. "I doubt Mr. Wilson will listen to us,
but if he doesn't notice you, we'll know the silly old crock has
had his eyes removed."

Emerald looked up at him, a vague memory of pleasure from
the night before sweeping over her. "There are a lot of people
here," she observed. Her eyes traveled the room. It was a long
antechamber, and along the walls were tall straight-backed chairs.
In them, dressed according to protocol, were various delegations
waiting to see Mr. Wilson. Directly across from Emerald was an
oriental gentleman in a morning coat. He was small and thin,
with a skeletal face and deep-set eyes. Still, she thought, he

didn't look much more than Michael's age. Perhaps, she concluded, they were the same age. In fact, most of the people waiting to make representations seemed young, or so it appeared to Emerald.

"Who's that?" Emerald whispered to Michael, indicating the man across from her.

"A man of many names," Michael replied in a whisper. "Currently he's called Nguyen Ai Quoc, which I'm told means 'Nguyen the Patriot.' But I've heard, round about, from a member of Scotland Yard, that he's been called Ba, Ho Chi Minh, and that his real name is Nguyen That Thanh. He's from Indochina via the world and he's been in Paris organizing Vietnamese students and workers living there. He's a socialist and he wants freedom for Indochina."

"Where's Indochina and where is Vietnam?"

"Near Siam, below China. You know, the British and the French carved up Africa, Asia, and the Middle East. They learned how to divide and conquer in Ireland."

"Oh, Michael, I've so much to learn."

"Not that much." He winked.

"Oh, dear. He's coming over. I do hope he didn't hear us talking about him."

The oriental man came and stood in front of Emerald and Michael and bowed from the waist. "Good day," he said; then, pausing, "You do speak English, yes?"

They both nodded.

"And may I be so bold as to inquire what country you come from?"

"Ireland," Michael replied.

"Ah, Ireland. I am Nguyen Ai Quoc from Indochina, at your service." He bowed again and then straightened up. "Ireland has had many years of difficulty with the British colonials . . . yes, yes. But you are most fortunate, most fortunate. There are many Irish in America. I have been to Boston—not so many years ago, when I was a hand on a French steamer, I went to Boston and New York. It's all Irish! All of it! I love the Irish. I wish America had an Irish president!"

"Perhaps one day they will," Michael said with a broad smile.

"Then I would want to deal with him."

The chief secretary opened the double doors and called their names. Emerald stood up and looked at the man whose name— any of them—she couldn't pronounce. "It's been a pleasure meeting you."

The little man bowed again. "Good day," he said solemnly.

*   *   *

In the rear of the large room, President Woodrow Wilson sat behind a desk which dwarfed him. He looked small and impotent, and Michael whispered in Emerald's ear, "Hell, he even looks like Edward Carson!"

Michael spoke first, then Emerald.

"We are a nation," she emphasized. "We have boundaries which are clearly defined; a culture, a heritage; a language which is not English. And while we accept freedom of religion, we are predominantly Catholic."

President Wilson looked up, peering at her through his thick glasses. He appeared utterly myopic.

"And wouldn't the Catholics of Ireland treat the Protestant minority—majority in Ulster—as badly as you claim the Protestants have treated the Catholics?"

Emerald frowned at him. There was a hint of prejudice in his choice of words and she felt her temper a little on edge. "We have learned how to treat people from our teachers," she said evenly. "But I believe we have also learned how not to treat them. A little trust, Mr. President. It's needed all around."

President Wilson's face flushed and he fumbled with the papers in front of him. "Ah, yes, well . . . I think there are ramifications here . . . . ah, well, I'll read your papers carefully." He stood up. "It's been nice chatting with you," he said awkwardly.

Emerald forced herself to smile. "I wish it had been a fruitful use of our time." She turned away and took Michael's arm. They walked to the door and Emerald whispered, "Get me out of here before I throw something at him."

"My heavens, you do have a temper." He looked to be on the verge of laughter as they walked briskly down the hall.

"What a waste of time," Emerald mumbled.

"Well, now we have a date at our hotel with the American press. We'll be telling them that we made our representation and that Mr. Wilson is considering it."

"And that will put political pressure on him at home?"

"Yes, my darling, exactly." Michael whisked her out of the hotel where President Wilson was holding court. He kissed her cheek as soon as they were outside. "At least we'll make the American president and dear David Lloyd George uncomfortable."

4

January 29, 1919

London

"What in the world do you suppose he wants?" Emerald was pinning up her hair and Michael Collins was watching her hungrily.

"He must want something, to be coming to our hotel in what I might describe as secrecy. My, my, the prime minister himself."

"Well, I guess I'm ready, as ready as I'll ever be."

Michael laughed at her. "I don't think, with Mr. Lloyd George's reputation with women, that I'd want you any readier."

"And what does that mean?"

"It means he's a bounder—bounds from one bed to another. He's got the worst reputation in England for being a womanizer!"

"Look who's talking about being a womanizer." Emerald walked across the room and put her arms around his neck, kissing him on the mouth.

"Oh, not now, woman. I'm an M.P. and the bloody prime minister's coming! How will I look if I'm hot and bothered and sporting a bulge in my pants? Have you no mercy?" He backed away from her and his dark eyes twinkled with mischief. "When he's gone, I'll take you to bed and make love to you till you're so tired you can't stand another moment of pleasure."

Emerald knew as she gazed at him that her feelings of both fondness and desire were perfectly evident in her eyes. I must not fall in love with him, she reminded herself. But it was of little use. He aroused her, and she felt wonderful when he held her. Perhaps it wasn't love, perhaps it was only loneliness and the fact that they were both hungry for one another. Then again, who could know? For the moment, Emerald put it all aside.

"Won't you sit down," Michael invited. He looked at David Lloyd George coldly, but he sounded polite enough.

Lloyd George returned Michael's expression. "I prefer to stand," the prime minister announced. He allowed his eyes to stray to Emerald for the first time. She felt them travel from her face to her toes, and so brazen was his look that she felt herself blush.

"On the very day your so-called Dail met in Dublin, an act of wanton terrorism was committed in County Tipperary."

"It's a long way to Tipperary," Michael said with a casual laugh.

The prime minister did not smile.

Emerald leaned forward a bit so as not to miss anything. She had not heard anything about Tipperary, and if Michael knew anything, his face did not reveal it.

"Two constables of the Royal Irish Constabulary were escorting a cart of gelignite to a quarry at Soloheadbeg. They were set on by two masked men—so-called Irish volunteers, an organization I think you know something about. They were shot in the face at point-blank range. Needless to say, the gelignite hasn't been seen since."

"Gelignite is a valuable and useful commodity." Michael's voice had taken on an icy quality Emerald had not heard for many days. In the warmth that had grown between them, she had forgotten how single-minded he could be.

"Force will be met with force," Lloyd George warned.

"I had nothing to do with this killing," Michael said, looking the prime minister right in the eyes. "Nor do I have proof any volunteer was involved. Not that I control them, either."

Lloyd George grunted. "I have important business. We have a duty to orchestrate peace in the world. When the time is right, negotiations will be held regarding Ireland. Good Lord, man, you know I'm committed to home rule. But you also know I'm head of a coalition government."

"With a murdering bastard named Edward Carson!" Michael's voice was suddenly no longer cold and detached. It was filled with emotion, and Emerald saw his dark eyes flash.

But the prime minister didn't react at all. "I shall be releasing the prisoners soon," he said in a conciliatory tone.

This time it was Michael who did not react. They stood looking at one another stonily.

"I feel negotiations would be warmer with the lady." The prime minister took a step toward Emerald. He smiled at her and took her hand.

Michael Collins stepped between them, and the prime minister dropped her hand.

"Don't touch her," he said angrily. "She's a rebel's woman."

"They have a way of becoming widows," the prime minister returned.

Emerald wanted to cry out that she wished they wouldn't discuss her as if she were not present. But in this instance, she held her tongue.

"Well, I came to give warning, and I have given it." The

prime minister turned and opened the door; stepping through it, he closed it behind him with a thud.

For a moment Emerald stood silently.

"Did you order the attack on the constables?"

"No," Michael answered, looking into her eyes. "But I have ordered other actions . . . it's my job." He walked over to her and embraced her. "When friendship catches fire, it's a powerful kind of love. I called you a rebel's woman. I'm the rebel, Emerald Hughes. Be my woman." He leaned over and kissed her deeply.

Emerald, folded in his arms, barely felt her feet on the floor. She couldn't resist him, and she felt their two hearts beat in unison as he held her. She discarded thoughts of violence and struggle and gave in to Michael Collins.

"I have to send you back to Ireland alone," he whispered. "But I'll be back by the tenth of February. I'm sorry, darling, but I have a small matter to attend to here in London."

He touched her hair and ran his fingers over her neck. Emerald nodded, but she hardly heard his words as he began making love to her. Michael Collins was as intense in his passion as he was in his activities as a rebel. Love and violence consumed him by turns.

19

1

February 5, 1919

London

Eamon de Valera downed his third whiskey, set the glass down on the table with satisfaction, and confronted Michael Collins with a bemused expression.

"I got damn thirsty in Lincoln Gaol," he admitted with a slight grin. "I must say you've outdone yourself!"

Collins didn't blush. "Well, we can't have the speaker of the Dail rotting away in Lincoln Gaol, can we? It doesn't seem right that the prime minister of England can wander about being magnanimous with other people's countries while the new speaker of the Irish Dail languishes in a British prison."

"They would have let us out. You didn't have to be so dramatic—rushing in and breaking me out! You son of a bitch! I know your type, you just want the boys singing songs about you! You fancy yourself a latter-day Willie Brennan on the moor!"

"I wouldn't mind a song, as long as you don't sing it. I tell you, Eamon, for an Irishman you've got the worst tenor I ever heard."

"I don't sing," de Valera answered seriously.

"You're telling me," Collins retorted with a wink. He tapped his fingers on the table and thought for a few minutes.

"You'll have to stay in England for a few weeks. It's not quite safe for you to travel back to Dublin right now."

"You might as well have left me in prison."

"You're no fun there," Collins answered.

"I'd say you were secretly proud of yourself, but you're not making much of a secret of it."

Collings laughed. "It was derring-do, man. I got you out of an English prison without a single casualty, and now I have you ensconced—at the expense of English banks—right here in London in a fine hotel not five doors away from the prime minister's residence. Look, you'll have to watch it in the halls. They say this is where he brings his lady friends in the afternoon. Now, if you run into him, be sure to tip your hat."

De Valera smirked. "I'll try to remember my manners. What are you doing in Dublin, Michael?"

"You don't want to know, Eamon. Yours is a political role, so frankly, it would be better if you didn't know."

"I didn't ask for specifics."

"Then let me answer you this way. The more disorder I can create, the sooner I can force the British hand, the better for the country. It's a game of action and reaction. We have to goad the British into coming down hard; it's the only way to weld every man, woman, and child in the country into one massive independence movement—otherwise we go back to the mere discontent caused by having no representation. The majority of people are complacent. I have to create an atmosphere that makes complacency impossible. Toward that end, I've begun to eliminate the informers within the Royal Irish Constabulary—men known for their brutality."

"Is your information that accurate—you know who these people are?"

"Oh, I've been through the files at the police station myself. I have a fine list and I'm simply running down it."

De Valera shook his head in disbelief. Collins was a mass of contradictions; he had boyish charm; he was full of energy and enthusiasm; he was good-looking in the extreme; he had a fine-tuned sense of humor. At the same time, he was single-minded, he could be utterly ruthless, and he was a cold-blooded killer. But was he indispensable? de Valera thought. He's the best organizer in all of Ireland, a man whose intelligence network is so good that he need not even go into hiding.

"How do you run down the list?" de Valera asked after a minute.

"Oh, I send them a polite letter telling them to resign their jobs. If they don't, I send one of the boys to eliminate them."

"Are you trying to make yourself the most wanted man in the United Kingdom?"

"No, I told you. I want to create an atmosphere that will create a free Ireland. When I turn around, Eamon, I want to see the whole nation behind me. In 1916 when I turned around, no one was there."

De Valera nodded. "I'm planning a trip to America," he confided. "We need funds."

"I can't smuggle you out just now," Michael answered. "Come back to Ireland first, then go to America the duly elected president of the Dail."

"Elected by all twenty-seven members who are not in prison?"

"The rest will doubtless be out by then." Collins smiled mysteriously.

"You can't break them all out. I know you'd like to try, but it's impractical"

"I don't have to break them out. You're an exception, Eamon. A lesson to David Lloyd George. But as far as the others are concerned, I have his word they'll be released soon."

De Valera studied Collins skeptically. Sometimes it was impossible to tell when he was joking and when he was serious. "Really?" he asked.

"Really," Michael confirmed.

"Lesson or no lesson, why did you go to the trouble to break me out, then?"

"To make the bastard mad," Michael replied.

De Valera raised an eyebrow and then smiled. He reached over for the bottle and poured himself another whiskey. Michael Collins' answer was too simple to be a lie.

2

April 7, 1919

Dublin

"I wish you'd be more careful." Emerald held Michael's arm as they walked along together. It was a warm, lovely spring afternoon and St. Stephen's green was alive with color and the sound of birds in the trees.

A week ago, on the first of April, Eamon de Valera was unanimously elected president of the Republic of Ireland. His ministers were Arthur Griffith, handling home affairs; Cathal Brugha, in charge of defense; Michael Collins, in charge of finance; Count Plunkett, heading foreign affairs; W. T. Cosgrove as the minister of local government; the Countess Markievicz handling the labor portfolio; Eoin MacNeill in charge of industry; and Laurence Ginnell in charge of propaganda.

"We ought to have called Mr. Ginnell's post the Office of Information," Emerald told Michael. " 'Propaganda' sounds as if we aren't telling the truth."

Michael stroked her long hair with his hand. It was loose the way he liked it.

"The truth can always be made to sound better," he joked. "Let's go sit by the pond."

"Oh, Michael, I worry about you. You're careless. It's broad daylight and we're wandering around in a park."

"And we're watched and protected. If I'm not safe, you're not safe. I wouldn't endanger you." He sat down on a slab of rock by the pond and pulled Emerald down next to him, encircling her with his arm. "I don't spend enough time with my woman." He kissed her neck and gently bit her ear. "Do you miss me?"

"Of course I do."

"I'd move in with you and warm your bed every night if I could." His eyes caressed her lovingly, and she leaned against him.

All my resolve has weakened, Emerald thought. I've given in to him completely. She cursed herself for loving him, but she couldn't withdraw. Sometimes he made her angry, but most of their hours together were blissful. When he left her in the morning after one of their rare nights together, she could feel the impression of his body on hers all day; she could feel him as if he were still with her. And standing in Michael's shadow, she felt loved and protected. But she admitted: This is no ordinary love; this is wild and dangerous. And somehow the danger of being with a wanted man made their relationship more intense, more thrilling.

Emerald looked into his eyes. They were soft now, but she knew they could be hard.

"We're sending Eamon to America," he told her casually. "To raise funds and to gather political support."

"I'm selfish—I just want it to be over and done. I want peace and I want normalcy."

"Emerald, we're long past settling for home rule. We must have self-determination, total freedom."

"I understand, but I hate the bloodshed . . . all the killings. Only three nights ago two policemen were killed."

Michael's eyes flashed and the softness was gone. "Perhaps they deserved to be killed."

Emerald tensed. She hated it when he suddenly changed moods.

"There's repression, you know. You of all people should be aware of the crimes committed against our own people."

"In a way, they're all our own people—I only wish that the killings would stop. They kill one of us, we kill one of them. . . . I worry about what kind of country this will be when we do get our freedom. Maybe we can't turn off the violence so easily. I don't want a free Ireland to drown in her own blood."

"It's not always necessary to kill," he said, returning to a softer voice. "Emerald, don't blame me personally. I don't order the killings. Sometimes the men take action on their own—if they're successful, we take the credit; if they're not, we deny involvement. But, my darling, the IRA doesn't do all it is blamed for." He cupped her chin in his hand and lifted her face to his. "Love me, Lady Ireland. Don't ask me so many questions."

Emerald stood up, and he stood too. She put her arms around his neck and stood on her tiptoes to kiss him. He circled her waist with his arm, and again they began to walk.

Emerald didn't have to look behind her because she knew that somewhere eyes watched wherever she and Michael went. Michael knew everything; he had a remarkable intelligence network. She knew he had placed a guard on her; she was watched over night and day.

Emerald did not feel as vulnerable as Michael thought she was. I'm getting used to it, she admitted. I'm getting used to the killing and the sound of gunfire in the night. I'm getting used to blood and vengeance and hate. She shivered. What would Tom be like when he grew up? How used to the sound of gunfire would he be?

3

June 30, 1919

New York

First America witnessed the Mexican Revolution, then the Russian Revolution. In Greenwich Village an electrifying creativity fed on the rebellions and emerged fat and happy, having spewed forth new playwrights, novelists, musicians, journalists, and lovely and not so lovely hangers-on.

"It's amazing," Mike Scanlon commented. "The cries of *'Viva Villa!'* and *'Viva Zapata!'* rallied Americans and made them pay attention. And when the Russians overthrew the czar, the anarchists hurried off with their hopes in woolen satchels. For the Mexicans and the Russians, wealthy Americans had dollars to burn. Ah, but let the Irish, who build their houses, and unload their ships, and put money into their stinking banks—let the Irish rebel, and the society snobs turn up their noses and slam shut their pocketbooks!"

"What the hell do you expect?" Joe Scanlon retorted. "The Russian Revolution is the all-consuming passion of this country's intellectual elite. But we have the truck drivers, the stevedores, and not a few good old-fashioned hoodlums."

Mike drained his stein of beer. "There's one intellectual who's with us." He motioned toward the end of the long bar. "Hey, Gene, buy you another?"

From the other end of the bar the gaunt, morose, mustached man looked up. His eyes did not flicker with recognition. "Do I know you?" He squinted in the half-light.

Mike leaned over, extending his hand. "Mike Scanlon. We met here the last time I was in New York. This is my brother, Joe."

The man got off the bar stool, and steadying himself on the bar, made his way to their side. He held out his hand to Joe Scanlon. "Pleased to meet you. I'm Gene O'Neill."

"He writes plays," Mike said by way of explanation.

"And he drinks a lot and sleeps with as many women as he's up to." O'Neill slurred his words and spoke of himself as another would.

Joe grinned. "Another round," he shouted as the weary, blurry-eyed bartender passed by.

They were in a saloon called the Golden Swan, though it was far from golden and the nearest swan was uptown in Central Park. The Golden Swan was on the corner of Fourth Street and Sixth Avenue; it was as typical an Irish saloon as one could hope to find. The floors were sawdust-covered, and beneath the scattered wood chips, spit, urine, and blood were evidence of the patrons' habits. The saloon smelled to high heaven of perspiration and of men who'd spent the night in a flophouse and carried its special odor. All the various smells combined with the reek of beer and raw whiskey.

"We who frequent this divine dispensary of medicinal magic call this dump 'the hellhole,' " O'Neill told them, as if he had guessed what Joe Scanlon was thinking.

"A good name for a typical Irish saloon," Joe said as he drained his own stein of beer.

"Where else can a drunken Irishman feel comfortable?" O'Neill asked. "But I hear a Boston accent—Dorchester or Scollay Square, my ears tell me. And what brings you to New York? Come to have a sentimental look at the detention centers where they stacked our good forebears on top of one another?"

Joe laughed wryly. "We've come to meet the new president of the Irish Republic, Eamon de Valera." The revelation, given their surroundings, sounded foolish even to him.

But O'Neill didn't laugh. "I'll drink to that," he said solemnly. "Now, there's a good Irish name, de Valera!"

"It's Spanish. His mother was Irish," Mike explained.

"Hot-blooded people, the Spanish. God knows, when the Spanish and the Irish get together, they must reproduce like rabbits. I was in Spain once. Shipped out on a rotten freighter and landed in a whorehouse in Barcelona. All I fucking remember is sour red wine, piles of paella, and gobs of black fuzzy cunt." He guffawed and took another belt of whiskey, which he washed down with a gulp of beer.

"He's got a lot of stories," Mike said knowledgeably. "Before he started writing, he was a seaman, a dockworker, and a truck driver."

The man was at least in touch with reality, Joe conceded. That gave them something in common. He prided himself on the fact that regardless of his own money and self-education, he still felt at home in a saloon like the "hellhole." And what's more, he didn't stand out. His fellow Irish accepted him.

Mike checked his watch. "It's time we got going. It's time to meet de Valera."

"He's going to cause me to part with half the money in my pocket," Joe surmised.

"It's for a good cause."

Joe slipped off the bar stool, reminding himself of how much this meeting meant to his brother. Mike was going to escort Eamon de Valera around America, and together they intended to raise money for the new Republic of Ireland. Well, Joe decided, this was one of the first commitments Mike had ever stuck with; he seemed truly dedicated to the cause. By heaven, the boy was actually trying to learn Gaelic and he had immersed himself in Irish history. Joe recognized that one road to discipline and learning was as good as another, and certainly Mike's contacts among militant Irish-Americans were only helping his own political aims. He always gave to the right causes anyway, but Mike's activities were different. He had now joined an American branch of the Irish Republican Army.

4

November 1919

Dublin

Emerald leaned over and filled Maggie O'Shea's teacup. "Are you certain you're all right?" She hadn't seen Maggie for some months, since Maggie lived on one side of Dublin and the Gregorys, with whom she now lived, resided on the other side.

There was no denying that Maggie O'Shea had aged. Ever since Emerald had known her, Maggie's hair had been gray and her skin wrinkled. But her wrinkles were deeper now and her eyes, covered with the white film of cataracts, seemed more sunken.

"I'm quite all right. Who'd bother an old lady like me? I'm in no danger."

"You could come and stay with me. There's room, and Tom misses you."

Maggie smiled. "He's getting to be a big boy—four now, time goes by so quickly."

Emerald nodded.

"You're better off where you are." Maggie's expression and tone were somber. "Tom's safer too. It's not the kind of neighborhood where they come looking. This block of flats is a hotbed, you know that. There isn't a family here without a son or father in the IRA. And every time a policeman is shot, they storm through here looking for suspects, roughing up old people, threatening the little ones in front of their parents."

"Then how can you say you're all right?" Emerald leaned over, her face filled with concern.

"My sons are gone, and that's that. They don't come to my flat."

Maggie took some more tea and shook her head. "Emerald, I know I'm old and foolish, but I sense the coming of the apocalypse. Either Ireland will be free or they'll kill us all. Emerald, send little Tom away—get him out of Ireland."

Maggie's hand was shaking, and Emerald felt a chill at her grim prediction. It was more than just the fear of an elderly woman growing senile. Maggie wasn't senile; her mind was still sharp and she sensed the atmosphere far better than she understood it.

"I've lived to see my sons murdered," she continued sadly. "Emerald, I brought Tom into this world, and you and I are like family now. Please listen to me, please."

Emerald took Maggie's hand in hers. They were like family.

"I know about you and Michael Collins. And I'm not saying a word about it. You deserve to be loved. But, Emerald, loving Michael puts you in special danger. It puts Tom in danger too."

Emerald looked away and stared at the floor. The floorboards were old and warped; the cracks between them left room for insects to come and go, passing from the dark world beneath the floor into the light of the room, into another world. She herself felt as if she had passed from one world to another.

Finally Emerald lifted her eyes. "Michael takes care of us. There are special guards."

"Michael Collins is a shrewd man. He's head of our army, he's head of the IRA. They say he's responsible for the killing of the policemen. Emerald, he's smart, but there are things he can't protect you from."

"He doesn't order them killed," Emerald protested. But behind her protest was her own doubt, and she knew, even as she spoke, that her words lacked conviction.

Maggie pressed her lips together. "If you're in love, you're entitled to believe what you want. My concern is Tom. Emerald, send him to your brother in America so he can grow up in peace. Send him to the land of promise, where he'll be safe. Then, when it's all over . . ."

Emerald's mouth opened in surprise. "I can't send him away. I'd die without him, I'm his mother. I can't send my baby away."

Maggie O'Shea let out her breath. "When it's over, he can come back, or you can go to America. Emerald, if you don't send him away, you might find yourself carrying the guilt of a tragedy for the rest of your life. What kind of place is Ireland for a child, Emerald? You know what's happening, you must know what's going to happen. Certainly Michael Collins knows—he's planning it."

Emerald started to protest, but her argument died on her lips. She had tried to put it all out of her mind. She knew full well that the man she shared her bed with was the man in charge of gaining freedom for Ireland. She believed that Michael was good and just. She admitted, however, that she had refused until this moment to think of the details of his plan. *I've concentrated on the man*, she admitted, *rather than on Michael's role as an organizer and a participant in the violence she was so sickened with*.

"Michael loves Ireland," Emerald said weakly. "He can't bring us disaster."

"Emerald, you're smarter than that. Michael gets us to support the Republicans by having us backed into a corner by British soldiers. Men have gone into British prisons favoring peace compromises; they don't return with that belief. Your Michael knows that, and so do you. Emerald, send Tom to America for a year, maybe two." Maggie held Emerald's arm fast, and she pressed it. "If you can't do it for him, do it for me. Do it so I'll know he's safe. You and Michael can face danger because you're both grown people, but Tom is too small to make that kind of choice."

"You're saying I deserve what I get into, but Tom doesn't."

"I'm saying you know what you're getting into and Tom doesn't. I'm saying he could be an innocent victim."

Emerald bit her lower lip and remained silent.

"Promise me you'll think about it," Maggie pressed.

Emerald only nodded.

5

December 1, 1919

Boston

"Shit! You're just a snotty-nosed brat! I've been trying to see to it that you got an education for the last ten years. Now you stand there and tell me you've volunteered to go off to Ireland and get your empty head blown off!"

Joe Scanlon was sweating, and he was shaking with anger. It was one thing to send money to Ireland; it was another for Mike to want to go off and fight.

"You think you're going to walk into Dublin? Do you have any idea what's going on in Ireland? How the fuck do you suppose you're going to smuggle yourself and de Valera back into the country? He's probably still wanted, and I suppose you soon will be!"

Mike Scanlon shuffled his feet on the carpet. "Gene O'Neill arranged for us to ship out on the S.S. *Celtic*. We'll just be two old sailor boys."

"Sailor boys! You get sick in the bathtub!"

Mike laughed. "Nothing is going to happen to me. Stop ranting and raving like an old woman and take me out to dinner.

Hell, it's liable to be the last decent meal I have in months—
according to you, the last meal I'll have, period.''

"This is not something to joke about.''

"I'm going. I believe in this. Look, there are things you
believe in. I don't expect anything from you—I just want you to
wish me well." Mike broke into a boyish smile.

It was the same smile he gave Joe the time Joe found him lost,
when he was only five; the same smile that had been the thank-
you for his first catcher's mitt. It was the smile that always
weakened Joe's resolve. When his father had died, the authorities had wanted to take Mike away. "I'll be looking after my
own brother," he had announced. "I'm old enough." And he
had fulfilled that pledge. There was fifteen years between them,
and Joe Scanlon was both brother and father.

"I'm going," Mike repeated. "Our ship leaves in the morning."

"I could stop you," Joe threatened.

"Sure, you could have me kidnapped till the ship left. But
there are other ships. Eventually you'd have to let me go, and
then I'd beat it on my own. Look, I'm nineteen, stop protecting
me! I can't live forever in Big Joe Scanlon's shadow.''

Joe eyed Mike and thought that he had a kind of frailty, rather
like their mother. And of course that was it; Mike had just said
it—he had to prove himself. He had to prove to himself that he
was as tough as his brother. He had to test, test, test.

I could stand here and argue, he thought, but it's destructive. I
could rant all night, and it wouldn't change a thing. He didn't
want to point out Mike's weaknesses; it was cruel. Instead, he
tried to hedge.

"Are you sure you're up to this?" he asked after a minute.
"It's not a game. The British are tough. They've shot enough
Irishmen to populate half of England. We're dogs to them.
Besides, fighting takes discipline. There'll be times when you're
hungry, maybe hurt. Have you really thought about this?''

"I've thought about it. It's no use, Joe. My mind is made up
and I'm going.''

Joe's expression grew less harsh as he gave in to the realization that he wasn't going to change Mike's mind. Finally, after a
long moment of quiet, he reached across the space between them
and grasped Mike's arm. "Buy you a farewell steak?" he offered.

6

December 23, 1919

Emerald stared into the darkness and thought about Padraic's last letter. The armistice had been November 11, 1918, but Padraic had not gotten out of the army till May 1919. It was another six months before he was reinstated as a New York City policeman. Now, six months later, he wrote cheerful, warming letters:

> I have a nice two-room flat, Emmy, and the window overlooks a playground. Every morning I see mothers with their children and I think of you and Tom.
> I know you won't come to America, my darling sister, but how I wish you would!
> I've discovered a new food. It's called a bagel. It's a kind of bread made by the Jews—the priest serves them at church socials, so I guess it's all right to eat them. I mean, they're not sacred or anything. Ah, but, Emmy, would they make fine weapons. You could render a British soldier unconscious if he was hit right smack on the head with one. Tasty, but hard like rocks they are.
> There's snow on the ground now, and men on corners dressed like Santa Claus ringing bells and collecting money for the poor. I've sent a package for Christmas. I hope it arrives.
> Emmy, be careful. Write soon.

Emerald blinked into the darkness. Padraic seemed happy, America seemed peaceful. In her mind's eye she tried to imagine his flat and the playground beneath the windows. Carefree mothers with happy, fat, carefree children. Maggie's words kept haunting her. Restlessly Emerald turned over on her stomach.

Michael stirred beside her, and then, propping himself up on one elbow, swatted her playfully across the bottom; the sound of his smack on her naked flesh echoed in the quiet room.

"Ouch! You're not so gentle."

"Well, it's a lovely tempting white ass. Maybe the nicest in all Dublin."

"Flatterer," she replied.

"You seem distracted. Is something troubling you?"

"I was just thinking."

"How revealing. Are you going to tell me what about?"

"Last month I went to visit Maggie . . ."

"I know," he replied. "Bad neighborhood. I wish you'd agree to meet her somewhere else. You gave my men a fit."

Emerald ignored him. "Michael, she thinks things will get much worse than they are now. She thinks . . . well, she suggested, that I ought to send Tom to stay with Padraic in New York. Michael, how much worse are things going to get?"

He reached across the bed and dropped his hand onto her breast. "A lot worse, I hope. The British are training auxiliary troops in England to send here. I expect them to be sufficiently ruthless to ensure the people of Ireland will be willing to respond in kind."

Emerald closed her eyes. The calm cruelty of his words upset her; they were out of character for the Michael Collins she knew and loved. But the warmth of his fingers on her flesh still caused her pulse to quicken, and once again her physical desire, emotions, and common sense all went to war with one another.

He moved his hand abstractedly and she responded because his hands always made her respond. She drew in her breath. "Then you agree? You think I ought to send him to America? I know a family who would take him by ship—I know Padraic would be glad to have him. What do you really think?"

He leaned over and took her nipple into his mouth, flicking his tongue over it till it was hard like a pink stone. Then he removed his mouth and leaned over her. "I think it would uncomplicate our lives at a dangerous time." He ran his hand over her stomach.

"Michael, you're distracting me. This is a very important decision for me, the most important I've ever made."

"All right, yes, there's going to be more violence, a lot of violence. It's easier for me to protect you than to protect you and a child. Yes, children make good instruments for finding out information—what would you tell the British, Emerald, if they had Tom?"

Emerald shuddered. "They would use little children." It wasn't a question, but a statement. She groaned as horrible images flitted across her imagination.

"Send him to your brother," Michael urged.

Emerald nodded her head, and he pressed her gently. She moved into his arms automatically.

"You're quite ready again," he said, pulling her flat against him.

She didn't answer because her desire erased the images. His

hands were large and rough on her skin, but he aroused her skillfully and all thoughts vanished as his lips caressed her, and she shivered in his arms, giving way to him completely, losing herself as his fingers turned her into a pliable being which sought to both please and be pleased.

"Be one with me," he whispered.

Emerald moved with him as she acquiesed to his will.

20

1

April 1, 1920

Dublin

Emerald looked at four-year-old Thomas Hughes, Jr. He looked grown-up in his little tweed suit and hat. But there was something pitiful about the tag that identified him and gave Padraic's address. He wasn't, after all, a little package, but a little person. Emerald fought back a sob. The tag was a formality; he wasn't traveling alone. Jenny Reilly would take good care of him; she had to keep saying it to herself.

"We'll treat him as if he were our own," Jenny said, as if she read Emerald's mind.

"This is Padraic's picture. He sent it last month. You have the address . . . but I know he'll be at the docks. He promised in his telegram, and he has your picture and Tom's. God, it's such a long voyage!" Emerald bit her lip and fought the desire to call it all off and take Tom home with her.

"Now, you mustn't cry," Emerald advised her young son, even though it was she who was crying. Tom was too distracted with the sight of the ship and the thought of going on it. In fact, he seemed quite caught up in the adventure.

Emerald leaned over and hugged him, holding him to her tightly. "Promise me you'll be good and do whatever Uncle Padraic tells you. And you understand, you'll come home as soon as possible."

"Yes, Mama." Tom hugged her around the neck tightly.

Emerald pressed a package into his arms. "This is for you when you're on the ship at sea. It's a surprise."

"I love you, Mama."

"Be good," Emerald murmured.

"How does it float on the water, Mama?" Tom's bright eyes had already turned to the vessel.

"I don't know," Emerald admitted. "When you're on it, maybe Mr. Reilly can tell you. Tom, you must do as Mrs. Reilly tells you. Do Mama proud and be a good boy."

Tom kissed her cheek and patted her face. "Don't cry, Mama."

Emerald sniffed back her tears. She stood up and looked at

Jenny Reilly "I hope I'm doing the right thing," she finally said.

"I'll make sure Padraic wires you when we arrive. I'll tell him all about the voyage, and he can write. I'd write, but I can't. Emerald, don't worry."

"Do you think I'm doing the right thing?"

Jenny thought for a moment; at last she replied, "Yes. I hate to admit it, but I think it is right. Things are getting worse and worse."

"That's not why you're leaving."

"We're leaving because we want a new start in life. We have relatives who write us about the opportunities. But I can't say I'm sorry to be going."

In the distance a whistle blew. Emerald bent down and kissed and hugged Tom again. Inside, she felt as if she were being torn apart; still, she felt it was right.

"God be with you," she said to Jenny.

"And with you," Jenny replied.

Tim Reilly turned and kissed Emerald on the cheek. "You held my brother Tom Reilly in your arms when he died in the post office in 1916, Emerald. You did something for my Tom, now we'll do something for your Tom. No fears, Emerald, he'll be safe, we'll look after him."

Emerald nodded, unable to say anything. She stood stock-still and watched as they climbed the gangplank of the ship. She closed her eyes and held herself rigid, lest she fly up the gangplank after them. She closed her eyes when sometime later the ship pulled out of dock. She opened them when Jenny, Tim, and Tom were specks on the deck, waving at her. Emerald waved back.

She waved till her arm ached and until she could see them no more. Then, heartsick, she left the dock.

2

October 1, 1920

Twice Michael Collins had Emerald move. "It makes you harder to find," he told her. "It's safer."

The first of the auxiliary police had come in March, just before Jenny and Tim Reilly took Tom to America. The new auxiliary police were noncommissioned soldiers; many had survived the worst of trench warfare in Europe. They joked to one another about making Ireland a hell for rebels to live in; they were rude, threatening, and truly dangerous. Augmenting the Royal Irish Constabulary, they were outfitted in dull tan uniforms and became known as "Black and Tans" for their outfits. Most Irish felt they had been sent to oppress them, to break the will of the nation. They had been sent because Michael Collins was so successful at killing the members of the Royal Irish Constabulary.

Emerald climbed the stairs to the third floor of the rooming house where she was currently staying. It was a lonely room, but all things considered, she felt more at ease than she had in some time.

She unlocked the door to her room and looked around. It was a bare undecorated room; all her things were packed and stored away. The only picture she had was one of Padraic and Tom; Padraic had taken it on Tom's fifth birthday, a short time after his arrival in New York.

Emerald kicked off her shoes and sat down on the edge of the bed. She lifted the picture and kissed Tom's image. Then she put it back on the table and looked at the cracked ceiling of her room.

Three days after Tom had left with the Reillys, the IRA attacked and destroyed the British tax offices throughout Ireland. Thomas McCurtain, lord mayor of Cork, was murdered in his home and over three hundred British barracks were attacked and burned.

In July, during the Orange Day celebrations in Belfast and Derry, Protestant mobs ransacked and pillaged through Catholic areas of both cities. And when the Catholics, led by the IRA, defended themselves, the police opened fire on them.

Some nights, Emerald lay in bed and listened all night to the sound of gunfire; she no longer jumped at the occasional explosion; she learned to move quickly, to avoid parcels, to keep her own counsel, and to be wary.

She sat up when she heard the knock on the door. It was Michael; he had a special knock.

Emerald opened the door a crack and looked into his face.

"It is me," he said, pushing the door open.

"You told me I couldn't be too careful," Emerald replied.

"Brought you two presents." He set a brown paper bag down on the table. "Apples," he announced, withdrawing one. "Here, catch!" He tossed her another. Emerald wiped it on the side of her dress and bit into it. "Oh, it's delicious."

"Still love me?" His eyes twinkled and he winked at her.

"Would I be here waiting for you if I didn't?"

"Here, then, the other present." He handed her a letter. "Had one of the boys pick it up this morning."

Emerald grabbed it hungrily, as if it were food and she hadn't eaten in a week. Padraic had to write to her under another name. Michael had to have someone collect the letters.

> Darling Emerald,
>
> I feel absurd addressing this to Mrs. Molly Flynn in care of general delivery. I can't think of you as a Molly Flynn, but if you say it's necessary, I believe you. I know—or I've read—what it's like. I wish you were safe here with us.
>
> Tom is fine and healthy. He's grown a whole inch. You know, I think he'll be tall like his father. He's a smart lad. We have a holiday here, it's called Thanksgiving. There's a parade then. I'm going to take him to it. And to the P. T. Barnum Circus—I got special tickets, all the policemen in New York did. We got the tickets so we wouldn't arrest the hooch drinkers in the crowd and spoil the show. But of course we'll have our brown paper bags too.
>
> I took Tom to Central Park on Saturday and he loved it. We bought a helium balloon, but he let go of the string and it may have floated to Ireland by now. I have a housekeeper now and she loves Tom and Tom loves her. He's fine, Emerald.
>
> We both love you. Be safe.
>
> Padraic

"Do you cry every time you get a letter?"

"Yes," she answered with resignation.

"You miss him a lot, don't you?"

Emerald sat down on the edge of the bed and looked across at him. He was sprawled out in the easy chair in the corner.

"Yes, I do." She didn't feel like belaboring it. He must know how I feel, she thought.

"A fine lad," Michael commented. But Emerald sensed his real lack of concern and it troubled her. Michael, unlike Albert Jenkins, had never shown much interest in Tom. Michael's interest was clearly in her, and she suspected sometimes that she was the only human he did care about. That too worried her. But she always told herself he had many things on his mind, and when it was all over, he would be like other men. He would want children, he would want to marry her, he would want to settle down to normalcy.

"Did you come on your bicycle?" she asked. He usually rode it around Dublin as calm as could be. He acted as if he weren't the most wanted man in the country, but he insisted on incredible security for her.

Now, she surmised, their routine would continue. They would talk, they would make love, they would talk. Then he would leave and she wouldn't see him for a week, or perhaps two. She wouldn't know if he was dead or alive. But their relationship never lost its intensity, perhaps, she thought, because his life was always in danger.

"Michael, I want to go back to work. I can't stay here all the time waiting for you—I'm a nurse, let me work."

He took a bite out of the apple. "I'd planned to speak to you about that. We've set up a sort of hospital in a house on a street near Saint Stephen's Green. Dr. Gregory will be there on duty. Would you like to work there? Naturally, you'll both be guarded, but it's no more dangerous than if you stayed here."

"Oh, please! In the name of heaven, I have to do something, Michael."

He got up out of his chair and came over to her. He kissed her cheek and brushed a wisp of hair out of her face. "You're a rare specimen, you are."

"You're rather unusual yourself," she replied.

3

November 21, 1920

Dublin

Dear Emerald,

A friend is writing this letter for me. America is a wonderful place, and even though the streets are not paved with gold, there are luxuries you can't imagine.

Tim hasn't been too well lately, but he has a job with a construction company and he's been working on a building that will house the electric company. Next he will be working on some barracks in the Charleston Navy Yard across the way from Boston, where we have moved.

Padraic likes New York, but it is too big for us.

I am writing because I have met a man named Joseph Scanlon. He is a kind man and has a much younger brother named Mike. The young one went off to Ireland with Mr. de Valera. Mr. Scanlon hasn't had a letter from him in five months. He frets all the time, and I hate to see such a nice man worrying. Do you think you might be able to find this Mike Scanlon and ask him to write his brother? His last address was the Wynn's Hotel, room 611. Please try. I am sorry if this letter sounds strange, but you know, you can't sound like yourself when someone else does the writing.

Love
Jenny Reilly

Emerald refolded Jenny's letter. She had taken it out of her purse to check the room number. "Six-eleven," she repeated aloud. I'm terrible with numbers; they always go right out of my head.

Mercifully, the hotel lobby—such as it was—was quiet. Of course, that was the reason why she had chosen to come on a Sunday morning just before mass.

Emerald looked about warily. The desk clerk seemed to have retreated to a small room behind the desk. He was not in sight. Emerald followed the sign that indicated the stairs. She headed down the long dark dingy corridor, noting that there were stairs at either end.

Emerald paused on the landing as she completed the fourth flight of stairs. She had phoned the hotel earlier and ascertained that Michael Scanlon was still there. But she had decided that it would be better to come rather than to leave a message or have him called to the phone.

I should have just asked Michael, she thought. If he came to Ireland to fight, he's probably with the IRA. But no, she decided. This was a personal favor for Jenny. She would leave Michael out of it. He seemed most distracted lately anyway. If she asked, he'd probably forget to look the young man up.

Emerald reached the sixth floor. She opened the door that led into the semidark corridor. She walked down the hall, squinting at the rusty numbers on the doors.

The sudden burst from the Thompson gun broke through the silence, and Emerald, terror-stricken, stopped dead, flattening herself against the wall. "Holy Mother!" she exclaimed under her breath.

The next sound was the piercing scream of a woman and the

haunting, shattering cry of a young boy. Emerald turned and saw
that down the hall the door had swung open.

"Don't kill my baby!" the woman screamed. "Don't kill
him!" It was half-scream, half-plea.

"Do it!" a male voice commanded. Two men edged out the
door into the hall. They pointed their gun inside the room, and
Emerald could hear the woman begging.

Emerald could see them clearly now, and with horror, she
recognized the masks of the IRA. She grasped her skirts and ran
down the hall toward them.

"Don't you dare shoot that child!" Emerald's voice startled
both of them and they turned toward her in unison, their guns
pointed directly at her. Emerald stopped and stood looking at
them, still grasping her skirt. Her green eyes were wide and her
lips parted.

"It's Mrs. Hughes," one of the men said in an amazed voice.

Emerald moved forward a step. She didn't know their voices,
but clearly they knew her, and that gave her courage. She came
even with them and looked into the room.

"Holy Mother of God!" she whispered, crossing herself.

Across the bed, the lifeless body of a half-dressed man lay
crumpled like a rag doll, blood oozing from half a dozen wounds.
In the center of the room a small dark-haired woman in a white
slip cringed, holding a little boy to her. The child's face was
ashen and the woman's was a study in terror. The little boy with
the huge frightened eyes could not have been more than five.

"What have you done? Who are you?" Emerald demanded.
But she knew; and she also knew she sounded like a naive
schoolgirl or a voice floating down from the stage in the playhouse.
Their masks told her everything. They were IRA; they were sent
by Michael.

"Get out of here, Mrs. Hughes. We have work to finish!" His
voice sounded young, petulant, and annoyed.

Emerald stood up straight. "You're not going to kill that
woman or that child. We don't need our freedom so badly we
need to go about killing women and children in cold blood!"

"It's orders, Mrs. Hughes! That man was a member of the
Cairo Gang—that's his wife and kid. Do you know what the
Cairo Gang is, Mrs. Hughes? They're a crack section of British
Intelligence. They've stormed into plenty of Irish homes and left
no witnesses. None, Mrs. Hughes. Not even the babies. In one
house they skinned a little boy's dog alive in front of him, then
shot his parents and left him blind. We've been ordered to kill

the child as an example. That's the orders, Mrs. Hughes. Now, get the hell out of the way."

"Clearly you know who I am," Emerald countered. She struggled for control of her voice; perspiration began to form on her brow in spite of the cold dampness. "I won't have you kill them," she said with all the calm she could muster.

"It's our orders," one of them protested. But he sounded less certain now.

"And just who gave you the orders to kill a woman and a small boy?"

"Michael Collins ordered us. He planned this raid, and he told us personally whom to kill. I told you, they're to be an example."

However prepared her subconscious was for their answer, the reality filled her with a cold numbness. She knew when she saw them that they came from Michael; she had hoped against hope the idea of killing the woman and boy was their idea alone.

"You'll not kill them," she said evenly. "Orders or no orders. I'll take the responsibility myself. You go back to Michael Collins and tell him that. You either accept that, or you kill me too!"

There was silence. "We can't do that," the younger one finally said. Emerald knew he was the younger—his voice was boyishly high. She concentrated on trying to imagine what he looked like.

The older one lowered his gun.

"And you had better get out of here," Emerald said.

They both turned and within a moment had disappeared through a door at the far end of the corridor. Emerald stood for a second till she could hear their footsteps no more.

She looked up and down the hall. No door was open, and she prayed that no one was behind any of the doors. She turned quickly and ran back the way she had come. Behind her she left the woman and child, still standing like statues.

She hurried down the stairs, one flight after another. Then, on the ground floor, she paused. Somewhere in the distance she heard the distinct beeps of the police vans; they half-wailed, half-honked.

Out of sheer instinct, Emerald did not stop on the ground floor. She went down one more flight and emerged into the damp, almost dark basement. It was obviously a storage room, and she looked around and saw that the only light came from the far corner, where there was a half-flight of stairs and a door. She hurried across the room, lifting her dress. A rat skittered in front of her, and Emerald froze in fright; but equally distressed, the rat ran under a great box. She reached the door and opened it. Blessed daylight flooded into the basement, and Emerald slipped into the alley.

She began her flight vaguely aware of the danger she herself was in, but as she moved on and her mind cleared, the reality of her peril came into focus.

The woman and child had clearly heard her name. What's more, they had both seen her. They had heard Michael's name too, but Michael was already wanted.

Emerald reached the end of the alley. Cautiously she rounded the corner. The police vans had stopped in front of the hotel. Walk, she commanded herself. Don't run, walk.

Her heart beat faster and faster; in moments they would have her name and description. I need a change of clothes, she thought. And my hair. I'll have to cut it.

Emerald turned onto a side street. I have to get off the streets, I have to be inside, a crowd . . . I need to be in a crowd.

Emerald hurried toward the nearest church. It was the only refuge she could think of. They'd be watching the crowds that came out of mass, but they wouldn't come in. "And I won't come out," she said under her breath. Home, she decided, was out of the question. Now all she could think of was how grateful she was that Tom was safe in America with Padraic.

Emerald hurried into the church. She pulled her scarf over her hair and sat up front, close to the altar. She slipped her suit jacket off, just in case.

When mass was over and the people had finally all filtered out of the church, Emerald lingered in the shadows near one of the alcoves that housed one of the stations of the cross. She waited for what seemed an eternity. Her mind flooded with conflicting thoughts and questions. How could Michael order a child killed? How many others had he ordered killed? Tears started to flow down her face, and she began to shake. Inside, she felt betrayed and deceived, but there was no denying her other emotions—she felt fear and the will to survive.

Emerald knelt down and stared at the cross. She hadn't felt like this since the night she had fled across Belfast, running from Mr. McArthur. She buried her head in her arms and began to sob. All Ireland is dying around me, she thought.

4

November 21, 1920

5 P.M., *Dublin*

Michael Collins stared at the circle on his calendar. November 21. They were already calling it "Bloody Sunday," and bloody it had been.

Seventeen of his execution squads had wiped out the Cairo Gang, a team of British intelligence specialists who had been imported directly from England to put down the rebellion. But he had cracked the gang with the help of his informers in the Dublin metropolitan police; he had located the places the gang lived, he had planned the action carefully, and it had been, save one unexpected incident, a total success. Eleven members of the Cairo Gang had been killed in their hotel rooms, two in front of their wives, and four were severely wounded.

He had planned for one of the wives and a child to be eliminated as well. He regarded it as strictly a terrorist action; he felt the need to set a frightening example in order to let the British know they were in a situation where their enemies would stop at nothing. It was his intention to begin by shooting one child; if that did not succeed, there would be others. They would be selected at random and killed brutally. Random selection was, of course, the key to terror. If his plans for this day had come off, the British would have wondered: Why this wife and child? Why not the others? That was terror; it let the enemy know that no one was safe, least of all the innocent. Then the innocent brought pressure on the guilty, and soon, he reasoned, Ireland would be free.

But today's highly planned action had run amok. With irritation, Michael Collins spit into the trashcan and fumed over the situation. He was in a foul rage when the unhappy twosome who were death squad number six were ushered into his office.

He listened to their story about encountering Mrs. Hughes, who like an avenging angel challenged them and took full responsibility.

Though he had already heard the story through one of his lieutenants, it angered him even more from the lips of these sniveling bastards. As he listened, his fingers gripped the edge of the table, while small red blotches appeared at his throat and around his temples. The vein that transected his forehead throbbed and stood out; it was visible proof of his tension.

"And who the hell do you take orders from?" he bellowed back at them.

They stood before him with their mouths open, fearful and upset.

"We take orders from you," the younger one of the two finally mumbled.

"And am I Mrs. Hughes?"

They shook their heads. "But we know Mrs. Hughes. You had us guarding her once."

I can't run an army with this sort of discipline. Then the significance of their words hit him like a bullet. "Did you call her 'Mrs. Hughes'?" His tone was demanding.

They nodded their heads in unison.

"You called her 'Mrs. Hughes' in front of living witnesses!" With terror-filled eyes, they both nodded again.

"Ain't that her name?" the younger one asked.

"You stupid, worthless, fucking sons of bitches!" His voice was low and mean, his eyes narrowed, his lips pressed together. He felt his fingers tighten around his own pistol, but he controlled himself.

"Discipline demands you have a trial," he mumbled. "Paddy! Joseph! Get the hell in here!" His two lieutenants came running.

Michael Collins stood up and walked around the table. "It seems we have a discipline problem here—one coupled with stupidity!" He laid out the facts of the situation. Then he finished, "Mrs. Hughes will be dealt with, but at least she's not in the IRA! These two are! I think they should be shot. How do you find them?"

"Guilty," Paddy answered without blinking an eyelash.

"Guilty," Joe Duggan agreed.

The two stood like statues. But Michael Collins didn't care to wait any longer. He drew his pistol and fired two shots. He shot the older one first, point-blank. He crumpled, falling like an accordion on the wooden floor. The younger one started to say something, and Michael Collins fired the second shot. He shot him in the face, as if he were a clay pigeon in a shooting gallery.

"Get these two traitors out of here!" He waved his gun at the lifeless bodies. "And clean up in here!"

He paused momentarily in the doorway. "Find Mrs. Hughes," he ordered. "Find her before the police do; don't harm a hair on her head. She's not a member of the IRA, and I'll personally deal with her. This sort of thing won't happen again."

Michael came back an hour later and sat down. There was no word from Emerald, save a report that the police were seeking her.

"Fuck!" he muttered. She was in mortal danger from the Dublin metropolitan police, from British Intelligence, and from the Black and Tans. As for himself, he hadn't decided what to do about Emerald Hughes, whom he reluctantly admitted he loved.

At the very least, she would have to be reprimanded. It's because her son's the same age, he reasoned. Silly, sentimental woman. But what could he expect? He was furious with Emerald because she had interfered where no woman had a right to interfere, and her interference had prevented him from setting a necessary example. And two lives—he mentally added the two men he had recently shot.

No one since Brian Boru had succeeded in welding the Irish nation together the way he had. I have succeeded where others failed, he thought. And, by God, no one is going to change that! He brought his fist down on the desk. But where the hell is she?

A moment passed and there was a knock on his door.

"Sir?" Paddy sounded hesitant.

"Come in," Michael shouted. He looked up into Paddy's watery blue eyes. "Have they found her yet?" And if they had, he honestly didn't know if he was going to kiss her in relief or rage in anger, telling her the exact cost of her small humanitarian gesture.

Paddy shook his head. He looked nervous, and Michael sensed he was bringing more bad news.

"A group of the Royal Irish Constabulary and some Black and Tans that were with them opened fire on a crowd at the football match just outside Dublin."

Michael steepled his fingers as if he were saying a short prayer. "Dear God," he said softly.

"Twelve people were killed and sixty wounded," he finished.

Michael stared at the floor, but Paddy remained. That could only mean more bad news.

"The two men—the ones arrested last night—were shot in Dublin Castle."

Michael didn't say any more. He lifted his hand and waved Paddy out of the room.

Across town, Emerald remained in the church. She alternately cried and prayed.

"Can I help you with your troubles, daughter?"

Emerald looked up into the eyes of a priest. It was nearly dark, and Emerald had been crying. She squinted, and suddenly the face came into focus.

"Father Doyle!" Emerald practically fell into the arms of the elderly priest who had been working at the hospital when she had run away from the McArthurs' house at the age of fifteen—it seemed like a million years ago.

"Emerald?"

"Oh, Father . . . help me!"

"Now, now, what is it? Still looking for the Catholics?"

She nodded. "In a way. Father, what are you doing in Dublin? I didn't know you were here."

"Well, my darling, I didn't know you were here." He smiled warmly at her. "I'm on leave, visiting my old friend whose parish this is—makes a change from the hospital. Come along, come into the chancellery and sit down. I think I can find a spot of brandy. Tell me all about it, tell me everything."

It was after seven when Emerald finished her story.

"Is that all of it?"

"I've sinned," Emerald said, looking at the floor. "And I've been a fool, Father."

He folded his hands and looked at her. "Oh, Emerald, we live in troubled times, times when choices are not so easy. It's not the sinning that troubles you," he observed. "You can confess your sins and do your penance. No, what bothers you is pride. You've been guilty of bad judgment, and now you're angry with yourself."

"When you love someone, you don't think they can do something so terrible; you only see their soft side." Emerald could hear that her voice was steadier, and her hands had stopped shaking. She felt for the first time in the whole nightmare of the day that she was gaining some self-control.

"You did the right thing to stop the killings. God put you in this position, Emerald, for that reason. You did not fail him. We're no better than our enemies if we must kill small children and innocent people. War can sometimes be justified. But not murder. No, that's different."

"Father, I'm in grave difficulty." Emerald looked at her old friend. She had told him everything save Michael's name. She knew she had to see Michael, and in spite of everything, she didn't fear him. Like a shade being lifted in the early-morning light, the truth of Michael's true personality had been revealed to her. And as surely as if he had put a knife through her heart, her love for him had died with the revelation. She would have to see him, and she knew they would have a scene that would end their relationship forever.

"The authorities are looking for you," Father Doyle surmised. He frowned. "Stand up, Emerald. I think I have a solution. Sister Patricia is about your size, I'll go find her."

He left the room and returned shortly. "I think this will fit you," he announced, handing Emerald a nun's habit.

"I'm not sure I'm cut out for running about disguised as a nun," Emerald protested.

"Put it on. Do you have someplace to go?"

"I have to go to him, Father. I have to confront him. I have to end it."

"I agree, you must close old doors before you open new ones."

Emerald went into a small antechamber and put on the habit. It fully covered her hair, and with only the heavy black veils surrounding her face, she looked even paler than before.

She folded her own clothes neatly and carried them back to Father Doyle. "What shall I do with these?"

"They'll have to be burned. I'll take care of it." He opened a drawer and fumbled about. "I remember seeing something in here . . . Ah, yes!" He withdrew a small pair of wire-framed glasses. "This should complete your disguise."

Emerald put them on.

"Ah, you look very different, Mrs. Hughes, very different."

"I don't know how to thank you," she murmured. "This is the second time . . ."

"Let's go hear your confession, my darling. It will make you feel better. You know, Emerald, bad judgment is a human trait. Even Jesus chose Judas as his disciple."

Emerald followed her old friend into the sanctuary. He disappeared into the confessional, and Emerald entered the other half of it.

She said the general confession.

"And is there more?" he asked softly as a matter of form.

"Yes, Father." Emerald took a deep breath. "I have committed sins of the flesh, Father."

"More than once?"

"Yes, Father."

"As Jesus Christ, in the name of the Father, forgave Mary Magdalene, he will forgive you also, my daughter. Do five 'Hail Marys' and one 'Our Father' nightly, and devote yourself, till this terrible fighting comes to an end, to healing the sick and tending the wounded. Go now in peace, and God be with you.''

Emerald read the rest of the confession when Father Doyle finished his absolution. She said a short silent prayer and left the confessional. Father Doyle was gone before her; the church, her refuge, was silent and empty.

5

November 21, 1920

9 P.M., *Dublin*

Michael Collins tilted his chair back on two legs. "For God's sake, woman, take off those ridiculous glasses. You look like a nearsighted penguin.''

In spite of his earlier anger, he smiled at her. He had been terrified that she had been arrested. Then, too, he had had time to cool off, and now he had to admit that the sight of the beautiful Emerald Hughes dressed as a severe nun made him laugh. And the glasses were the final touch.

Emerald stared at him stonily. She was shocked at her own lack of emotion. "I don't think this is a moment for flippancy.''

"I have to give credit where credit is due, Emerald Hughes. I've had the IRA out looking for you since noon, and now you waltz in here unrecognized, all on your own. My God! I hardly recognized you myself. You are resourceful!''

"Michael, we have to talk. Now.''

"Damn right we do! Tell me, woman, why are you so solemn-looking—like a stone! It's I who am angry!'' He narrowed his eyes and looked at her meanly. "I gave orders which you countermanded! Never mind what you were doing in a sleazy Dublin hotel at eleven o'clock on a Sunday morning! Countermanded, Emerald! No one countermands my orders! No one!''

His voice reached a crescendo. "I've trained these men to walk in front of bullets if I tell them to, I've taught them to kill their own flesh and blood if necessary. And here you come, Mrs. Emerald Hughes, you dance into something you don't understand, and you countermand my orders! Well, you'll be happy to know that the two men who listened to you instead of me have been shot. I shot them! And, Mrs. Hughes, if you ever try to countermand one of my orders again, it'll be you who's killed. I may love you, woman, and I do, but I'll not have you interfering with my army's discipline!''

Emerald thought for a moment of Albert Jenkins. He had Bowen-Colthurst arrested; he had disciplined his men to be soldiers, not animals. He was a man of honor. And if the Black and Tans were exactly like Michael, she knew that not all the British were like the Black and Tans.

''I'll do as I damn please, Michael Collins. I'll do what I want, when I want. But I'll not be asking for your protection any longer. I can't love a man who orders little children murdered. Oh, I've made mistakes in my life, but you're the biggest I've ever made.''

For a moment they stood and looked at each other. He looked stunned, wounded. Then his face broke into a smile. ''That's what I love about you! Look at the way you counterattack! Come on, Emerald, let's have a kiss. Let's call it a day and go home to our bed.''

Emerald shook her head. ''No, Michael. It's over, we're over. I meant what I said.''

The color had drained from his face and he stood looking at her, half-hurt, half-angry. Emerald waited.

''It had to be done to set an example.''

''An example of what? Barbarism? That child was the same age as my son. That's not an example, that's murder. Michael, you're a murderer.''

''So are they!''

Emerald expelled her breath. ''Well, I don't have to be a murderer, and I will not love a man who is.'' She turned her back on him and took a step toward the door.

''Stop!'' His voice was full of rage, and Emerald turned and saw that he had his pistol pointed at her. It was cold black steel and it glinted in the soft lamplight.

''Oh, Michael. Do you think I'm afraid you're going to shoot me in the back?''

''No woman has ever walked out on me.'' His voice was strangely high-pitched, as if he were on the verge of tears. He was tense and tired; he was still in a rage, like a small child having a temper tantrum.

''Then let me be the first, Michael.''

Emerald lifted the long skirts of her nun's habit and turned away from him. She took three steps toward the door, putting her hand on the knob. She could feel his eyes burning through her.

''Wait. Please wait . . .''

Emerald was at the door; she turned around and faced him again. He had put the gun down.

"I do love you," he said softly.

"I know you think you do," Emerald replied. His anger seemed gone now, dissipated in seconds. Only weariness was left.

"You need help. Emerald, listen to me. The police have your name and description. You need my help."

"I know that," she answered simply.

"I'll have someone take you to a safe house. I'll have your clothes and things delivered to you."

"I still want to work in the hospital," she returned.

He nodded silently.

"And you won't try to see me?"

Michael mumbled, "No, I'm a busy man. A very busy man."

"I have the address, Mrs. Hughes, but I still don't know my way around all that well."

The young man was quite good-looking. He's not more than twenty, she thought. Five years younger than I, but much younger in terms of experience.

"You're not Irish. Are you American?" The car rounded a corner.

"Irish-American, returned to Ireland to help Mr. Eamon de Valera."

Emerald didn't answer. "Where are we going?" she finally asked.

He reached over and handed her a piece of paper that had the address Michael had written on it. They passed under a streetlamp and Emerald read it. "Ah, you'd better turn at the next corner and go down that street in order to avoid the roadblock."

"Thank you," he replied.

"What's your name?" Emerald inquired.

"Mike Scanlon."

"Michael Scanlon." Emerald repeated the name, the very name that had begun this nightmare day. The day which to her now seemed a hundred years long.

"I know that name," she told him. "Do you have a brother in Boston?"

"You know him?" Mike asked incredulously.

"No, no. I have a friend who knows him, a friend in America. She wrote and asked me to try to find you. Your brother is quite worried."

"I was waiting till I had something positive to write."

His answer was open and honest, and he sounded so idealistic that Emerald wanted to cry.

"In Ireland, that could be a long time. Why don't you just write and say hello. I think he'd be glad enough to hear that."

"I will," he promised her.

Emerald leaned back in the seat.

"Is it far along this road?"

"Another few miles," she answered. "Are you in the IRA?"

He nodded. "But they don't let me get too heavily involved because I'm American. I do stuff like this, like take you to a safe place, because if I were stopped, they can hear I'm not Irish from Ireland."

"Count yourself lucky," Emerald answered.

"I don't understand. Aren't you an IRA supporter?"

"Not exactly," Emerald replied. Her head was throbbing and she longed to lie down, to close her eyes. She looked over at his profile. "Come and see me in a few days," she said. "I'll tell you about Ireland . . . all about it. You tell me about America."

"I'd like that," he said enthusiastically.

"In a way, you saved my life," Emerald said. She thought to herself: If I hadn't been looking for you, I wouldn't have found out . . .

"By driving you to a safe place?"

"No," Emerald answered.

"Will you explain that?"

"In a few days," Emerald replied. "In a few days."

21

1

October 1921

Dublin

"Ah, have another drink, Emerald, my love. Mrs. O'Shea would have wanted her wake to be memorable! She was a good woman, she was!"

Emerald allowed old Johnny Flannegan to fill her glass.

"These are all her children," he said with a wave of his arm. "Thirty years a midwife, she was, and now her sons and daughters all come to pay her tribute!"

The wake was being held in the home of Katherine Grady, one of the many children Maggie O'Shea had brought into the world. A good thing, too, Emerald thought. Mrs. O'Shea's small flat would never hold all these people.

Along one wall a table had been set up, and on it were brimming pots of Irish stew, boiled cabbages, baked potatoes, and sweet cakes. On the other side of the room another table held rows of bottles and glasses. Not one of the fifty people had come empty-handed; each brought some food and drink to share in the memory of Mrs. O'Shea, whose body was displayed standing upright in her coffin against the wall at the far end of the room.

In front of the coffin four fiddlers turned out a merry tune, and in the center of the room ten couples stomped out a traditional Irish dance.

Mike Scanlon's face was flushed with whiskey. "I'm glad you brought me." He grinned. "It would be sad to say that I'd been in Ireland for nearly two years and not attended a real Irish wake!"

"And don't the Boston Irish have wakes?" Emerald was also a bit flushed. It was the first time in a long while she had gone out, the first time in nearly a year that she'd seen old friends.

"Oh, do we have wakes! Sometimes they last for days and not a soul is sober enough to move—hard to tell the celebrants from the corpse!"

"Your Gaelic has really improved," Emerald said. "Look at you, drunk, and you can still speak it!"

"It's your lessons." He grinned. "You're a good teacher."

"I enjoy giving them to you—and anyway, how else could I be spending my evenings in hiding?"

"It looks as if that's over," he said cheerfully.

"I hope you're right," Emerald replied.

Mike Scanlon had been visiting Emerald twice a week since Bloody Sunday and she enjoyed his company as well as his curiosity about all things Irish. She taught him Gaelic and Irish history; he told her about America, and somehow his tales made her feel closer to her son.

Their relationship was that of young man and older sister. She was his guide and his instructor; he was her friend and made her feel less lonely.

"Oh! There's a song I know!" Mike Scanlon walked across the room and joined a group of four fine tenors who now serenaded Mrs. O'Shea's corpse with an old Irish song called "The Parting Glass."

> Oh, all the comrades e'er I had,
> They're sorry for my going away,
> And all the sweethearts e'er I had,
> They'd wish me one day more to stay,
> But since it falls unto my lot,
> That I should rise and you should not,
> I gently rise and softly call,
> Good night and joy be with you all!

Ah, the wake, Emerald reflected. It was the "night watch," for no body could be properly buried till all attempts to wake it had been made. And those attempts were made with loud music, stomping dances, and general rowdiness. But there was a love in it all, a love that reached out to the spirit of the departed and begged it to return for one more toast.

Emerald stood in the corner listening to Mike Scanlon sing, and her mind traveled back to May 1915, when little Tom had been brought into the world by Maggie O'Shea.

"Now, you begone!" Maggie O'Shea shouted at Seamus. "It's a good thing your brother is in America! Dealing with one helpless man is quite enough! Two is a burden no woman should have to put up with!"

And Emerald remembered watching as Seamus, mumbling under his breath, backed out of the bedroom and finally left the flat.

Then Maggie had returned to Emerald's side. "Now, don't fight the pains, my girl. Move with them, give in, and bless the fact that you're an Irish lass. You have fine wide hipbones."

Gently Maggie applied cool cloths to Emerald's forehead. "Here, now, let me examine you and see what the little devil is up to."

Maggie propped up Emerald's legs. "That's it, bend them at the knees. Mmm, I see your vagina is well dilated. Soon, Emerald Hughes, your child will be bursting out to join this fine world! Although, if you asked me, I couldn't tell you just why."

She paused and straightened up, her hand on her back. "All this bending," she complained. "I know why this child wants to come into the world, it's because he has such a pretty mother. Yes, that must be the reason."

"How can you be so sure it's a boy?" As she asked the question, the thought made her tremble a little. She wanted a son for Thomas Hughes's memory. All that had sustained her in the six weeks since Thomas' death was the vibrant kicking of the baby inside her womb.

"I'm certain it's a boy." Mrs. O'Shea smiled mysteriously. "I can tell by the look in your eyes; you want a son, and if there's a God in heaven, and there certainly is, it's a son you'll be getting. It's just like it was back in 1908 when Rose Dougherty was on labor, bless her sweet soul. Anyway—"

Mrs. O'Shea was cut short by Emerald's scream, and she bent over. "Ah ha! It's ready, my girl. Now, when the next pain comes, push a little and don't breathe so hard. Let your breath come in short little pants, like a dog on a warm summer's day. Like this . . . ha, ha, ha . . . Can you do that?"

Emerald nodded and grasped the iron headboard in order to brace herself.

"It would be good if we had a proper Irish birthing bed. Not so many homes have them now. They were fine, made it all much easier. You know, the more advanced we get, the harder it is to do things. It's all you can do to get the milk wagon down the street these days; the streets are too cluttered up with all those contraptions. But cars won't last, let me tell you. After all, they're not horses, and you can't eat a car if there's a famine!"

Emerald cried out again, and she panted as Mrs. O'Shea ordered. It was not a sharp pain; rather it started in her back and seemed to wrap itself around her body—a long internal contraction.

"Ah, there's his wee head now . . . gently . . . gently . . . let nature do her work too, don't push too hard the next time . . . pant, come on, girl . . . pant . . ."

The next pain came before the former one finished.

"There it is! There he is! Darling . . . and just dangling there is his manhood! It's a boy, all right! See, I told you!"

Emerald suddenly felt cold, and she was aware she was bathed in sweat. Then another pain swept through her. It was like the others, but not so severe.

"Just the afterbirth," Maggie explained. "My you're a fine strong woman, you can have lots of babies. And you don't shriek much either, not like Rose Dougherty!"

A few minutes later, Mrs. O'Shea handed little Tom to a tearful Emerald.

"Oh, you're crying . . . oh, it's because I said you could have lots of babies. I forgot about your dear departed husband. Ah, Emerald, I'm an old lady, a prattler. Can you forgive me?"

"It's all right." Emerald tried to smile through her tears as she looked into the eyes of her son. "He's a rare gift."

Then Emerald had slept, and when she awoke, Seamus had returned.

"Are you drunk?" Mrs. O'Shea questioned him. "I can abide with a little celebrating, but not with drunkenness."

"I'm not drunk," Seamus protested. "Now, out with it, woman, is it a wee boy or a wee girl?"

"A wee boy, of course! And you *are* drunk!"

They both came into the bedroom, and Emerald showed Seamus little Tom.

"He's drunk," Mrs. O'Shea said. Then she burst into gales of laughter. "Well, Seamus O'Hearn, seeing as you're already drunk, I suggest you get out the John Jameson and let me catch up with you!"

Emerald lifted her eyes to look at Mrs. O'Shea's coffin. She lifted her glass. "One more toast," she said under her breath. "I'll miss you, Maggie, really miss you." Then she thought silently: Say hello to Seamus and give him a kiss for me.

It was after one in the morning when Mike Scanlon dropped Emerald off at her flat.

She opened the door and went in and lit the lamp. The friendly warm room greeted her, and she sat down in a chair and looked around.

From November 21, 1920, to late August 1921, she had lived in a bare room with only little Tom's picture. She wore her hair short, lived under an assumed name, and carried false identity papers. She also continued to work in the first-aid station for wounded IRA men.

On July 9 the fighting abruptly stopped; before that it seemed as if all Ireland dripped with blood. Before July 9 the IRA dug holes in the roads to trap military transport, and when the hapless occupants struggled out of their vehicles, which looked like turtles on their backs, they were mowed down with Thompson guns. In reprisal, the Black and Tans would burn houses, driving the occupants outside and making them watch while their meager possessions went up in flames. They had burned the whole town of Balbriggan.

In Dublin, whole streets were cordoned off, and there were police checks everywhere. Sean Tracy, one of two IRA men who had fired the first shots in this undeclared war against England, was captured at a police checkpoint on Talbot Street. It was an irony that he was caught in an ordinary blockade, when he had escaped for so long. "British justice" was performed on the spot. Sean Tracy was shot, his bullet-riddled body was tossed on top of an army lorry like a side of beef so that the schoolchildren might see the gory sight and learn a lesson on the perils of terrorism.

And Terrance MacSwiney, the chubby mayor of Cork, was arrested and went on a hunger strike. He died after a dreadful seventy-four days in prison. He was a pitiful bundle of bones when buried.

"Oh, dear God," Emerald prayed as she looked around the room, "don't let this be false hope. Let the wounding, maiming, and killing really be at an end."

Abstractedly she touched the short red-gold curls that surrounded her face. She was letting her hair grow now, she had gone back to her own name, she had moved, and she once again had the pictures of Padraic, Tom, her brother Seamus, and her wedding photos around her.

Toward the end of August she had been notified that her name was no longer on the wanted lists, and last month she had returned to work in the hospital.

So far, the truce was holding, and there was to be a peace conference. I'll save money and go to America, she decided. But of course she couldn't go yet—there were no documents, and had she tried to leave, her name might turn up on some list.

She leaned back in the chair and closed her eyes. Eamon de Valera had not gone to London for the peace conference, and indeed, he would not go. He had told Emerald that if the treaty were unsatisfactory, he would deny it and claim he had nothing to do with the capitulation. "We've fought too hard," he kept saying, "to settle for only half of what we've fought for."

It was a well-known fact that Michael Collins had lost many men and that while the IRA was still dominant in the countryside, they were weak in the cities. There was also a general shortage of arms. The British had made it quite clear to Collins that after the truce was signed, they would talk.

Well, let them talk, she thought to herself, but please let them settle this reasonably. Let Seamus have died for something worthwhile; let all the dead have died for a truly free Ireland.

2

January 1922

Emerald cleared the dishes off the table. Mike Scanlon was sitting in the big easy chair, his feet up on a footstool, a glass of whiskey in his hand.

"I'm glad I came tonight," he said. "I need to talk to you. I swear to God on high, I don't know what's going on."

"Nor am I sure I can explain," Emerald answered.

"What the hell does it mean?" He wiped a shock of his hair off his forehead and looked up at Emerald, waiting for her answer.

On the ninth of December, a month ago, Michael Collins had signed the peace treaty. When Eamon de Valera read it, he denounced it and in the Dail it was hotly debated.

Arthur Griffith, who had founded Sinn Fein, and William T. Cosgrove supported the treaty along with Collins. Collins said he signed it because he was tired of fighting and killing. Emerald found his pronouncement hard to believe, but she recognized that her personal experiences with him had prejudiced her view of him. The treaty, Collins insisted, "gives us not the ultimate freedom all nations aspire and develop to, but the freedom to achieve that ultimate freedom."

Against the treaty were the Countess Markievicz and the widows and mothers of the martyrs of 1916.

The problem, Emerald decided, was that everyone had a different reason for either accepting or rejecting it. She herself had grave concerns over the clauses that pertained to Ulster. Under the treaty, Ulster had the option of voting on whether to join a new country called Ireland, under the commonwealth arrangement, whereby the Parliament of Ireland would be sovereign, but the Constitution could only be amended in Westminster and the crown would still sign all legislation as a matter of form. "It's the same arrangement Canada has," Emerald was told. But she thought: Canada is not as close to England as Ireland is. Distance tended to make independence rather more real.

In any case, there was no hope of Ulster taking the option and joining Ireland—even though Lloyd George urged them to.

Emerald sat Mike Scanlon down and explained all her thoughts.

"It will divide Ireland," she concluded. "That's what I can't accept. I know the division will cause more fighting and more bloodshed in the long run. We'll cut off the Catholics in Ulster, they'll be victims of the Protestant majority."

"That's not the same reason de Valera won't accept the treaty. Though I think he's opposed to that clause too. He's concerned with the wording and definition of commonwealth—he says we'll still be under British rule."

"That's it, don't you see. We all have different ideas because we're being asked to compromise, and we can't agree on what can be negotiated and what can't. I don't approve of negotiating away Ulster; Eamon doesn't approve of negotiating away absolute independence."

"Are you worried?" He leaned forward a bit in his chair.

Emerald nodded. "I've always feared we couldn't turn the violence off."

"We're more united in America than in Ireland." He smiled. "We have lace-curtain Irish, shanty Irish, and pig-shit Irish. But we're all just Irish."

"I'd like to be " 'just Irish.' " Emerald smiled back. Then, more seriously, "Mike, why don't you go back to America? You don't talk much about your brother, don't you get on with him?"

"Oh, we get on well. It's just that he's much older. I know it's hard for you to understand, since you're separated from your little boy, but I have to be on my own, I have to be doing something that's just mine. I can't live in my brother's shadow, that's all."

Emerald nodded. "I couldn't live in Michael Collins' shadow, either. I understand. Living in a shadow keeps out the sun, it keeps you from being your own person, from doing what you want and accomplishing what you want."

"In Boston," Mike said, "I'm Big Joe Scanlon's brother. Here I'm just Mike Scanlon." He finished his drink. "I think I'll stick with Eamon de Valera, even if it means trouble. What about you?"

"I don't know," Emerald answered. "Sometimes I feel like a leaf in the wind. I seem to go where it blows me. I'll keep on nursing till I can go to America . . . till I can be with Tom."

"You may have to choose, Emerald."

"You mean choose whose first-aid station I work in, whose bullets I take out of which bodies?" She shook her head. "I'm not sure who's right. But I know I can't support an isolated Ulster. So I guess I too choose Mr. de Valera and one Ireland."

3

July 4, 1922

Emerald hurried along the street toward home. The warm July sun shone down from the sky and a mild breeze blew off the river.

Her thoughts were mainly on her son, Tom. He was seven now and had started school last year. She tried to picture him in his dark school uniform as he headed off to St. Patrick's school.

But he was on summer vacation now, and the letter she had just received from Padraic talked about the Fourth of July parade he was going to take Tom to. Today is the fourth, Emerald thought. Today Tom stood by his uncle's side and watched the brass bands march down Fifth Avenue.

Emerald stopped short, and the cyclist rode up over the curb and came to an abrupt halt directly in front of her, cutting her off.

"Emerald!" She opened her mouth in surprise as the familiar voice spoke her name.

"Michael," she replied, looking into the handsome face of Michael Collins.

He drew his lower lip into his mouth and looked down at the sidewalk. "I know you don't want to see me, but I saw you walking down the street—the temptation was too much." He lifted his eyes and met hers.

"It's all right," she answered. It was awkward. What was she to say: How have you been?

"Have a coffee with me," he asked before she could say anything. He motioned toward a small coffee house on the other side of the street. "Just to talk for a few minutes."

Emerald nodded and followed him across the street. He parked his bicycle and they went into the coffee shop and sat down. Michael ordered.

"How long has it been, Emerald?" He looked across at her, seemingly less nervous now.

"A year and a half," she answered. "You don't seem any different. Have you been well?"

He looked at her almost shyly. "I've been busy," he answered. "Things are not going as well as they might."

It was an understatement, Emerald thought. When the Dail had finally approved the treaty, Eamon de Valera had resigned. There had already been some nasty incidents between pro-treaty and antitreaty forces.

"There's a great deal of division," Emerald said, not knowing what else to say to the man who had negotiated and signed the treaty.

"I know you won't believe this, but I am tired of the fighting. I think it's as good as we could have gotten. It gives us a chance."

"Did you stop me on the street to approve the treaty?" Emerald came close to smiling at him.

He shook his head. "I stopped you to say hello; I stopped you because when I saw those curls bouncing up and down, I knew it was you."

Emerald blushed. "It hasn't grown out yet."

"I like it short. It's cute." He winked at her.

Emerald looked at the tablecloth. "I've heard you're engaged," she said distantly.

"I am. She's a nice girl who'll make a good wife—if I live long enough to marry her." He paused. "But she's no Emerald Hughes."

Emerald lifted her eyes to his, meeting his gaze eye to eye for the first time. "I'm glad you've found someone," she said softly. "I wish you wouldn't talk about dying. . . ."

He leaned over the table and took her hand. "That's why I stopped you, Emerald. I stopped you to say good-bye. Our last good-bye wasn't satisfactory. Believe it or not, I've changed. But change or no, the military force I trained is ripped by division. My own men are gunning for me, Emerald. The IRA is divided right down the center."

Emerald let his hand squeeze hers, and she looked at him blinking back tears.

"Don't say anything," he asked. "I haven't much time. You know that since the treaty was signed I've had to enforce it. That means using British guns and it means arresting people I've worked with and known for years. Emerald, I loved this country with all my heart. Now I'm the most hated person in it. And I can stand that, but I can't stand your hating me. I know you have a new young man—Michael Scanlon, is it? And I have another woman. But, Emerald, I still love you. I'll carry my love for you to my grave, but I don't want to die bearing your hatred."

"Michael, I don't hate you, I don't. And I don't have a new young man. He's only my friend. I've been teaching him Gaelic." Tears started to run down her face. "I don't hate you," she said softly.

Michael drained his coffee cup and looked at her. His hand still covered hers, and she could feel it large and warm. "I have to go now. It's a bit dangerous to be seen with me, more dangerous than before, because I don't know whom I can trust and whom I can't.''

He stood up and leaned over the table, gently kissing her on the forehead. ''Good-bye, Emerald, my love. Keep well.''

4

August 1922

Emerald covered her eyes with her hand, but not even the darkness could blot out the evil headline.

Michael Collins had been killed outside Limerick, gunned down in cold blood in a maneuver he strangely enough had designed. He'd been driving in an open motor car when he was assassinated by IRA men, men he trained himself.

Some said it was his friend Emmet Dalton, and there were other theories as well. Some even said it was planned by de Valera, but that Emerald doubted. De Valera was not involved militarily.

Emerald sighed. Her short talk with Michael Collins came back to her. The divisions of the politicians were not as important as the divisions within the IRA; they were tearing the country apart; they were the divisions that had resulted in murders, killings, and arrests.

And what was it in the end, this civil war? It was anesthetic for the pain of cutting off Ulster. The southern counties—the Irish Free State—was asleep in its own nightmare of civil war; and meanwhile, Northern Ireland—Ulster—was allowed to slip away, to remain a part of England, thus isolating the Catholics of Ulster from the Catholics in Ireland and splitting Ireland in two. She bled from the wound.

The boundary was going to be established, and it would bisect Ireland, forever making it a divided nation. ''Divide and conquer''—a wise saying, Emerald thought.

She opened her eyes and looked at the newspaper again. There was going to be a short truce so both sides could attend Michael Collins' funeral. ''You're a hero,'' Emerald said aloud to herself. She shook her head. ''I hope you did change, Michael. I hope you came to understand. I'd like to think you did.''

She brushed a tear off her cheek. ''Good-bye,'' she said under her breath.

5

April 1923

"How did it happen?" Emerald stared at Mike Scanlon. He looked lost in the big bed; his face was ashen. He was dying.

"He saw a little child, not more than three. The child had run off into a field, and there were mines in the field. He went after the child, and she ran away, free as a lark, but he stepped on the mine and it exploded."

Emerald turned away from the man who had brought Mike to the hospital. She sat down by Mike's bed and looked into his face. She lifted his limp hand and pressed it in hers. How many men had she seen die this way? Too many . . . but it was all but over, the parties in the civil war had called a truce. It was almost over and it wasn't fair that Mike was dying. Another day, another week . . .

"Emerald?" Mike's voice seemed far away; he labored over the syllables in her name. His lips were dry and coated with salt.

Emerald wiped a trickle of blood from his nose. "I'm right here," she answered, pressing his hand in hers. "Can you feel my hand?"

He shook his head. "Can't feel anything," he breathed. "God, Emerald, don't go away and leave me, stay here, please."

Emerald fought back her tears. Goddammit! If only she could stop crying! He was going to see her crying and he was going to know. He must not know; he might be frightened. I ought to be used to death! My brother died in front of me, men have died in my arms. I'm a nurse and I've seen more than my share of violent death. I ought to be hard, I ought to be immune.

"Emerald, tell Joe I loved him . . . tell him I always wanted to make him proud, tell him I really tried."

"You'll tell him yourself," she lied. She pressed his hand harder, even though she knew his spinal cord had been severed and he couldn't feel anything. It was a mercy, because beneath the blanket that covered him, his young body was mangled beyond recognition. Even if he lived, he would be paralyzed from the neck down.

She wanted to throw her arms around him and hold him to her and sob: Why? Why are all the people I love taken away? But she didn't move and she didn't say anything. She held his hand and looked at the boyish face with the shock of unruly hair that always fell over his eyebrow.

Mike opened his mouth and gasped for air, then painfully exhaled. Emerald leaned over and kissed his cheek; as she did so, she smelled his breath. He breathed the odor all experienced medical personnel knew was the smell of death. The decay of the internal organs as they ground to a halt, dying one by one, bringing his young life to a rapid end.

He would gasp one or two more times. If God was merciful, he would live a few more minutes; if not, he might linger on for several hours, comatose, awaking now and again, aware of his dying.

Emerald lifted her free hand and motioned the priest to her side. "Now," she said, biting her own lip and fighting for control.

The priest began the sacrament of extreme unction, and Emerald mouthed the prayers. Mike opened his eyes once more and blinked. The priest anointed him, and Emerald crossed herself and again kissed his cheek. He opened his eyes once more and looked directly into hers. His eyes seemed full of a new kind of wonder; they were wide and childlike, innocent, but still sad.

Michael gasped again, but this time he exhaled and his chest rattled and his hand fell limp from hers. She waited and silently counted, feeling with her fingers as the last pulsebeat faded away.

"He's gone," she whispered to the priest. She let her tears flow freely now. "He's gone," she repeated.

Emerald watched numbly as the priest pulled the white sheet over young Mike Scanlon's face. She sat for a moment longer, then walked to the window and looked out. It was spring, and on the branch of a nearby tree a bird warbled out its mating song. She watched it for a long while, trying to remember when she had last heard the song of a bird.

After a long while she gathered up her things. I'll go home and write to his brother, she thought. She wanted to write: "He was a good man, he loved little children." But was that what a brother wanted to hear? No, she decided, I shall write: "He was very brave, and he loved Ireland dearly."

22

1

May 1923

Joe Scanlon reread the letter. The handwriting was neat and even, but something in the phraseology seemed to convey more than formal condolences or mere friendship. The Mrs. Hughes who wrote the letter seemed genuinely fond of Mike, and her feeling showed in the warmth of her words and in her talent for not trying to say too much.

He knew a little about Mrs. Hughes from Mrs. Reilly, who was now his housekeeper. He knew a little more from Mike's letters.

He knew that Emerald Hughes had sent her young son with Mrs. Reilly to her only relative in America, Padraic O'Hearn of New York. He knew that Mrs. Hughes was a widow and that by profession she was a nurse. He also knew she was involved with politics and had been teaching Mike Irish history and Gaelic. He wondered briefly if there was more to their relationship, but he discarded that thought. Somehow, he pictured Emerald Hughes as being middle-aged, motherly, and more intellectual than most Irishwomen.

He glanced again at the fine hand in which the letter was written. Mrs. Hughes was certainly not illiterate like Mrs. Reilly or her husband, Tim, who worked in the mill. Both of them were hardworking, God-fearing Irish who had saved to travel to America and start a new life.

He leaned back and closed his eyes. There really wasn't enough in the letter. He wanted to know how Mike had spent the last four years of his life, where he had lived, who his friends were.

When Mike had first left, Joe had taken it all as a burst of youthful adventurism. But then, when he didn't hear for many months, he began to worry. Mrs. Reilly had written to Mrs. Hughes, who found Mike, and since then Mike had at least written, though his letters were far from illuminating.

He tried to bury his worries for his younger brother, even though he knew full well that Ireland was aflame. God knew, enough of his friends had relatives who were killed.

It wasn't that he didn't intellectually understand the passions involved. He himself had supported politicians like Eamon de

Valera. But during the civil war the Irish community in Boston was as split as Ireland. Keeping politics cool was a job for a master tightrope walker, and Joe Scanlon was just that, a master tightrope walker.

Through it all, Joe waited for Mike to come home, to apply his newfound political idealism and knowledge to the Irish political aspirations in America. But now Mike would not come home.

Joe had first known of his brother's death in a telegram from Eamon de Valera that had arrived two weeks ago. Today he had received the letter from Mrs. Hughes.

He stood up and went to the corner bar and fixed himself a drink. It was strange, but his responsibilities and obligations had all been taken away; he felt empty and alone.

First he had looked after his mother when he was a child. His father was seldom home. Then, after his parents died, he reared his younger brother and looked after him. Later, he married Kitty, and she was weak, ill, and mentally disturbed. Kitty was dead, Mike was dead. He felt robbed of his obligations, empty because no one was there to be taken care of.

Sadly he realized that since he and Kitty had no children, he had come to think of Mike in the same way other men thought of their sons—someone to live for, someone to work for.

He was thirty-eight years old and he felt sixty emotionally, though physically he was in prime condition.

"I haven't one damn relative in the whole world!" he said, feeling sorry for himself.

He had wept for Mike and prayed for Mike; now, two weeks after the initial shock, he was starting to feel a lonely guilt and he was facing the reality of his own loneliness.

"Did you call me?" Jenny Reilly poked her head into the sitting room. Her white dust cap was tilted slightly.

"Just mumbling to myself," he said, looking up. "I guess as you get older you do that."

She laughed. "I've been doing it since I was twelve! Besides, you're not old! You're young and the most eligible Catholic widower in all of Boston!"

Joe blushed. Jenny was short, round, and forever jolly. In the first few days after Mike's death, she had been incredible. She had taken care of everything, and she was there like a solid Irish rock.

"I was just thinking about my brother, wondering where he lived, who he knew . . . wondering why he stayed in Ireland instead of coming home."

"Most of us do go in the other direction," she answered. "I guess the Irish have exported more people than potatoes."

Joe smiled in spite of his mood.

"Why don't you go to Ireland?" she asked, fixing her dust cap. "You ought to know . . . you ought to go and feel the place. After all, you were raised here. If you went and visited his grave, found out about the country . . . well, you'd feel better. Besides, I always said you work, work, work. You need a vacation, Mr. Scanlon."

Joe looked at her steadily. It was as if she had picked an idea from the back of his own head and formulated it for him. But he hesitated. "I really do have a lot to do."

"You haven't anything that can't wait. That's the whole trouble with you. You haven't a soul to look after."

Joe smiled slightly. She was damn right—that was his whole trouble. "I'm going to take your advice," he said after a minute. "I'm going to go to Ireland."

2

June 1923

Emerald studied her bankbook earnestly. Together with the money Padraic had sent, she would have enough for passage to America in another two months.

She bit her lip. Another two months! As the reality of her dream grew closer, time seemed to pass more and more slowly.

Emerald gathered up her budget and bankbooks and put them back into the large brown envelope where she kept them. Another two months seemed like an eternity; it seemed unbearable. She closed the drawer where she kept the envelope.

Midway back to her chair, there was a knock on the door. She glanced at the clock; it was past seven-thirty.

"Just a minute!" she called out.

Emerald opened the door, half-expecting one of the neighbors. But instead, a tall, broad-shouldered stranger stood looking at her. He smiled. "Does a Mrs. Hughes live here?"

"I'm Mrs. Hughes," Emerald replied, brushing a loose piece of hair from her brow.

"You are?" he stumbled. He looked decidedly confused. "Mrs. Emerald Hughes?"

"The same." Emerald suppressed a smile and the desire to ask just what he was expecting, he looked so surprised.

Awkwardly he extended his hand. "I'm Joe Scanlon, Mike's brother from America."

Emerald was aware that her mouth opened slightly in surprise.

If Mr. Joe Scanlon was shocked by the sight of her, she was
doubly surprised at the sight of him. He was young! Younger
than her first husband. He was also extraordinarily good-looking.

"I tried to call, but I was told you had no phone. Your address
was on the letter. Perhaps I should come back at a more convenient time . . . I know it's after seven-thirty. I got lost getting
here from the hotel. I don't know Dublin all that well."

Emerald laughed and extended her hand. He had the same
crooked smile as Mike, the same unruly lock of hair, the same
accent. "Oh, please come in, Mr. Scanlon. It's quite all right,
really it is. I have the day off tomorrow in any case. Please."

Emerald motioned him into her sitting room. "Please take a
chair." She held out her arm for his coat, and he took it off.

Joe looked around the flat. It was small and cozy. The table
was filled with pictures, and a bookcase bore evidence that Mrs.
Hughes read a great deal. It was, in reality, a two-room flat. But
the main room had been divided up, so that behind the chairs and
sofa there was a dining table and behind that a small kitchen.

"May I offer you something?"

She had a lilting Irish accent; when she spoke, it was almost as
if she were singing, Joe thought. And, my God, she was beautiful!

"A little whiskey, if you have any."

Emerald went to the cupboard and got the bottle of whiskey
and two glasses. She handed him one and took the other herself.

He smiled at her mischievously. "I thought you were older,"
he admitted. "When you opened the door, you surprised me."
He took a gulp of whiskey and blushed. "I thought you were
much older. Mike was twenty-three. I guess for me he was
always sixteen. He wrote about you. I don't know, I thought
from his letters you were middle-aged."

Emerald laughed and looked across at him. "I'm twenty-
eight," she answered. "Well, almost twenty-eight. Only five
years older than Mike in age, but, Mr. Scanlon, in terms of
experiences, much older. In Ireland you grow up quickly."

Joe nodded. She was stunning, warm and so obviously bright.
Now he knew why Mike's letters were full of what she said, but
never, never did he mention her looks. He frowned as it crossed
his mind that they might have been lovers. In a way, he almost
wished they had been. He would like to have thought the kind of
happiness this woman could probably offer had been Mike's.

"What's the matter?" Emerald asked.

"You were close to Mike . . ." He didn't know what to say;
he didn't want to ask the question that now, for some reason,
seemed to surface.

Emerald caught the look in Joe Scanlon's eye. "No, Mr. Scanlon, we were not lovers. Is that what you wanted to ask?"

"No . . . I mean, yes. I mean, I'm sorry. You're more direct than I bargained for."

Emerald leaned back: "You know, I thought you were older, too. Mike always spoke of you as if you were his father. I thought you were fifty."

Joe smiled, and it was a beguiling, boyish, crooked smile. "A mere thirty-eight, Mrs. Hughes. Though, like you, I suppose I grew up sooner because of my experiences and responsibilities."

For a long moment they were silent, studying each other. Emerald took a sip from her glass. "You've come to Ireland because of Mike."

Joe nodded. "To see his grave. To find out more about what he died for. I guess to meet you. Of course, Mrs. Reilly told me a little about you. She told me you were a widow with a little boy she'd delivered to New York for you . . . to your brother, I believe."

"Yes. My son just had his eighth birthday. He's with my brother, Padraic. Padraic is a policeman. I'm going to be joining them in two months' time when I have saved enough money."

"You'll immigrate to America?"

"I don't think so. I've been part of the struggle here. But I have to go and get my son, and I'd like to see America, it sounds like such a grand land!"

"You've made up your mind to come back, then."

"If I can . . . I think so. But I'll have to stay awhile. It takes time to save, you know. There's no such thing as a rich Irishman."

Emerald lifted the bottle and held it out. "More," she offered.

"A drop."

"A drop. What kind of Irishman are you?"

He laughed and held out his glass while she refilled it.

"Yes," she continued, "there's poverty for the Irish here, and in spite of the stories, I know there's poverty in America too."

"There is indeed," Joe agreed. No need to tell her he was the exception, her so-called rich Irishman. To do so might place a barrier between them. That was something he didn't want.

"It's nice to have company," Emerald confessed.

Joe tilted his head. "I find it hard to imagine you alone." He said it a bit too flirtatiously. Then, realizing he might have embarrassed her, he took a gulp of whiskey and leaned toward her. "I'd like to talk about Mike. I want to talk to you because you were his friend."

Emerald lifted her legs and curled them under her in the chair. Perhaps because this man was Mike's brother, perhaps because he was a stranger from America with a warm smile, she felt instantly at ease with Joe Scanlon. In fact, she felt as if she wanted to talk to him, talk as she hadn't since Mike's death.

"Of course. I'll tell you everything I can. . . ."

An hour passed and Emerald found that as she talked about Mike and the way he died, she couldn't help but cry. In a sense, his death summed up all the deaths. . . .

Emerald looked up at him with her huge green tear-filled eyes. She let out her breath. "Your brother's death was no more useless than all deaths caused by war. But that's not what matters, Mr. Scanlon. What matters is how he lived and what he lived for. Your brother was a rare breed, an idealist. He lived and fought for what he believed, and he did it with honor. He died saving a life, not taking one."

Joe felt his own eyes fill with tears too as he listened to her finish, her voice trailing off. He finished his drink and set the glass down. "Thank you," he said, though the words were inadequate. "Emerald . . . may I call you Emerald?"

"Yes," she murmured. She seemed still lost in thought, still reliving moments he had caused her to recall all too vividly.

"Emerald, I have the use of a friend's motor car. Would you go to the countryside with me tomorrow? Would you spend the day with me, perhaps we could have a picnic. Please, I'd like to talk to you more. I'd like to know more about you because you were Mike's friend."

"I'd like that," she answered. "I'll fix something."

"Let me see to that, you be my guide." He stood up and looked at his watch. "How rude of me, it's nearly midnight."

"I didn't mind," she answered.

"Can I come for you around eleven?"

"That's fine." She looked up into his face and tried to smile. "Till tomorrow," she said.

Emerald looked at the car suspiciously. "I hope you're a good driver," she teased.

"I'm a very good driver. Once I drove a truck." Not for a living, he might have added, and when he said "once," he meant once. He opened the door.

He followed Emerald's directions out of Dublin and soon they were on a winding road, making their way through gentle hills.

"Tell me about yourself, Emerald Hughes." He gripped the steering wheel and watched the curves in the road.

"That's a long story, Mr. Scanlon."

"You're supposed to call me Joe. Tell me. I'm a good listener."

"I was orphaned at the age of five," she began. She told him about her strange childhood, about Tom Hughes and about the rising of 1916 and her brother's death. She even told him about Michael Collins and said, "But I was wrong about him. He wasn't the kind of person I thought he was. I was deceived."

"In what way?" Joe asked.

"He ordered children killed because their fathers were British spies . . . he did it so the people would react. I couldn't condone that." Emerald paused. "I miss my own baby."

Joe stole a look at her pretty, sad face and wondered how many details lay between the lines of her short painful biography. Surely, if he told her about his life with Kitty, he too would leave out the horrible details.

"I'm sorry, Mr. Scanlon . . . I mean, Joe. I'm babbling and I'm boring you. Forgive me. I think I must be feeling sorry for myself. Try to understand. It's as if everyone I cared about is dead. Except for Padraic and Tom, and they're so far away. I've missed so many years of my baby's childhood . . . but I was so afraid that he'd be killed too."

Joe was silent for a time. She had just expressed the very thought he had been living with for months. Finally he half-turned to her. "We're a good pair, you and I. I feel much the same way. And please, you were not boring me in the slightest. I told you I wanted to know about you too. Please don't be embarrassed."

He drove on for a while in silence and then asked, "Were you in favor of the treaty?" He supposed she wasn't, because she was Mike's friend and he was against it.

"I objected to it because of Ulster. Ulster is part of Ireland, not part of England. I objected because the results of the election that first brought Eamon de Valera to power showed that our strong support in those counties made it unjust to separate them. Ulster is an industrial heartland, Joe, and the rest of Ireland is rural, nothing but tiny farms. You can't separate one from the other; a divided nation is no nation. It can't be strong economically; it can't be strong politically; it can't survive without hatred for its own severed parts."

"You are quite the politician," Joe observed. "And quite a lady."

"I talk too much." She laughed softly. "There, Joe, take the next turning. There's a nice stream on the other side of that low hill."

"I'll be hiking for my lunch," he said, turning to her with a grin.

He parked the car and carried the picnic basket he had asked the hotel to prepare. Over one arm he carried a large blanket.

He went ahead of Emerald, checking the footholds and following a winding steep path upward. He stood on a rock four feet above her. His long muscular legs were wide apart for balance, and his hair blew in the afternoon breeze. He was wearing tweed trousers and a white shirt that was open at the collar, revealing the curls on his tanned chest. His hair was brown, lighter on top than underneath; his eyes were brown too, and his smile was nice.

He leaned over and offered Emerald his hand. "Come up to our summit," he invited.

Beneath them was a valley carpeted in green and dotted with shrubs which were thicker down by the meandering stream. Here and there, huge boulders stood together in piles.

"We used to say the giants used these rocks for playthings," Emerald told him.

"It looks like a playground," he admitted. "How about having our lunch down there—that looks inviting." He pointed across an expanse of green to a lovely old gnarled tree by the stream.

"That's a good place," Emerald agreed. "Be careful going down, sometimes the rocks give way."

"I'll go first," he volunteered. Surefooted, Joe started down the rock-strewn hillside, glancing back now and again to see if Emerald was all right.

"You're doing well," she called.

"Oh, it's not rougher than the cliffs on the Maine coast. I like to climb."

Emerald stopped short. "Oh, look, Joe!"

He turned and stopped. It was a few steps back up to where she stood. He climbed back up.

He paused for a minute and looked into her hypnotic green eyes. "Emerald," he said. "God, what an appropriate name for you." He realized then that he wanted to kiss her, but he hardly knew her, even though he felt they had known each other for a hundred years. But no matter how many lovers she had had, Emerald Hughes was a lady, and one he already respected and felt drawn to. Ladies were treated in certain ways; happily, he suspected she was also every bit a woman.

"Yes," he responded. "What am I to look at?"

"There, look over there."

Joe followed the motion of her arm, noting that it was lovely, long, and graceful. He saw a number of large boulders that seemed to form a cave. But it was not deep, nor was it dark. At the end of it, backed up against a large stone that was planted in the hillside, there were smaller stones. But the smaller stones were not casually placed. They were piled neatly, and one slatelike stone served as a flat-topped table.

"What is it? It looks like a table."

"It's a rock altar," Emerald replied. "A true symbol of Irish history, Joe. You know, we were denied our religion. Our churches were burned, the mass was forbidden. But we didn't let our faith die. The people built outdoor rock altars like this one, hidden away. And the priest, dressed as a shepherd, would come and perform the mass."

Joe squeezed her arm. "I didn't know that," he admitted. "It's stupid, really. I took night class after night class to learn about American history. I can name every president, but apart from the famine which my father used to talk about, I know almost nothing of Irish history. Having grown up in America, I'm pitifully ignorant of Irish history."

She smiled up at him. "How about folk tales?"

He winked at her. "Oh, my mother told me those."

"Good." Emerald smiled. They walked down the hillside together and across the meadow. Joe spread out the blanket. "Do sit down," he invited, bowing from the waist.

Emerald sat down and folded her skirt about her. Joe opened the great basket and spread out a white cloth.

"Now, let me see. We have ham, fruit, bread, and three kinds of cheese. And"—he smiled and pulled a bottle of champagne from the basket—"champagne to celebrate our meeting." He then pulled out a bottle of Irish whiskey. "And this is whiskey in case the champagne runs out."

Emerald looked at the feast. "Oh, you shouldn't have spent so much money! This must have cost a fortune!"

Joe made a mock pout. "I'm staying with rich friends. They won't let me go anywhere without a bottle of champagne." Again he reached in the basket and withdrew two elegant crystal glasses.

"Oh, really!" Emerald laughed.

"Really." He set them down and undid the wire on the bottle. With his thumbs he forced up the cork, which flew into the air with a bang.

"Oh!" Emerald almost screamed, she was so startled.

He looked at her, raising one eyebrow. "You've never had champagne before?"

"No, never," she admitted as he poured the liquid into the two glasses.

"To a free Ireland," he said, raising his glass. "What would you drink to, Emerald?"

"To peace, to a peaceful childhood for all children. Protestant and Catholic, all of them."

Joe drank his champagne and stretched out on the blanket, leaning on one elbow.

"Oh, it tickles my nose."

"That's what champagne does, my lady."

"And it makes me light-headed, too."

"Careful," he joked. "I try to be honorable, but sometimes when I'm with a beautiful woman, it's difficult."

Emerald blushed. "You're embarrassing me."

He laughed. "I'm sorry. It's only that it seems I've known you longer. Tell me, how much do you charge to teach Gaelic?"

"Oh, it's my pleasure to teach Gaelic. I don't charge."

He rolled over on his back, holding his glass over his head and staring into its base. "Ah, woman, you'll never get rich doing things for nothing."

"Well, I couldn't charge. Especially you."

"Ah, especially me!" He rolled over again, and propping himself up, looked into her heart-shaped face. It was a near-perfect face. Pale with wondrous great green eyes. Her shoulder-length red-gold hair glistened in the sun. "I like being 'especially me.' Emerald, I do feel as if I've known you forever."

"Because of Mike's letters. It's the same with me. He used to speak of you all the time. He loved you a great deal. He respected you and wanted to be like you."

Joe nodded. "Did he tell you I was opposed to him coming here?"

"No, he only said he had to do it and that you would understand."

"I'm beginning to," Joe said thoughtfully. He reached for her hand and covered it with his. "Emerald, I want to see more of you. I'm going to stay in Ireland for a while."

She didn't move her hand, but let it remain motionless beneath his. She amazed herself, and wondered about the feeling of warmth she felt toward him. "You can see me whenever you want," she finally answered.

3

August 5, 1923

"Good heavens, what is all this?"

"While you've been at the hospital healing the sick, I have been doing the marketing."

"It looks like you bought out the whole store. Joe, I keep worrying about all the money you spend. You'll not have enough to get back to America."

He laughed, and it occurred to him that he ought to tell her what his brother obviously hadn't and what Mrs. Reilly had omitted. Of course, Jenny couldn't write and she had had only two letters sent to Emerald in any case. But on the other hand, he decided, it would be more fun to surprise her.

"I told you not to worry. I have a friend in New York who can arrange anything. I'll work passage back if necessary. Now, concentrate on what I've brought."

Emerald opened a square box. "Joe!" It was a huge cake and on it were the words "Happy Birthday, Emerald!"

"I've never seen such a thing! It's beautiful. You shouldn't have."

"We take birthdays very seriously in America. Children have parties and everyone has to bring a present."

"I like that." She smiled.

He came around the table. She was still in her nurse's uniform and she looked all starched and white. He took off her cap and then undid the ribbon that held her hair back. It fell in ringlets and framed her face. She stood stock-still and just looked at him, but it was a look of wonder and warmth. He cupped her chin in his hand and kissed her full on the lips. When she responded, he wrapped his arms around her and kissed her harder. It was the first time he'd kissed her since he'd come to her house in mid-June. He'd come nearly every other day since.

"God, I wanted to do that," he breathed in her ear.

Emerald leaned against him, and she shivered. His body was warm against hers and his arms were strong as he held her lovingly. There was something about this man, something she couldn't say to him, but somehow wanted him to know. He was more attractive to her than Michael Collins, and in just a little over six weeks she had learned that he was kind, generous, warm, and loving. He was lonely like she was. She sensed in Joe Scanlon a great strength, the kind of strength that didn't need the barrel of a gun. And there was animal magnetism too; that she couldn't deny.

But I am lonely, she considered. Being lonely makes you careless, it makes you vulnerable, it makes you willing to risk your emotions. She stood arguing with herself for a moment, but she couldn't pull away; her logic couldn't fight her feeling for him.

He moved his large hands gently over her back, and his lips kissed her neck. "I dreamed about this moment."

"I think I wanted you too," she confessed. "But, Joe, it frightens me. We're moving too fast. I'm unsure. I don't trust my own judgment anymore."

Joe drew back and looked down into her face. "Be honest, Emerald. Do you like my lips on yours?"

"Yes, too much perhaps."

"And my hands . . ."

She nodded silently.

"Do you want me to hold you?"

Again Emerald nodded.

"I've known you six weeks. It seems like a lifetime. I love your laugh, Emerald. I love the sound of your musical, lilting Irish accent. I like your mind and the way your hands move when you talk. I like your cool head, the fire that I know burns beneath the calm. And hardly will I deny I like the way you move your hips when you walk, the shape of your breasts, your face. I see you as a whole woman, the woman I want to spend the rest of my life with, and, God willing, the woman I want to be the mother of my children."

Emerald opened her mouth to say something, but Joe lifted his finger to his lips. "I know I'm lonely and vulnerable. So are you. But, woman, I'd have wanted you if that weren't so. I wanted you the first minute I laid my eyes on you. We'll go to America, Emerald, and I'll be a father to your son. Emerald, you've taken chances before . . . take one more. This one is right."

His eyes held her and she could see the mist in them. She didn't answer, and he pulled her into his arms, holding her against him and rocking her slowly while he caressed her hair with his hand. "I love you," he said.

Emerald lifted her face to his and sobbed, "I don't know what I'm doing, but I think I love you too!"

Joe picked her up off the floor and held her above him as if she were a doll. "You'll marry me!" he shouted like an eager schoolboy.

"Oh, not if you drop me, Joe Scanlon!"

"Drop you . . . you're as light as a feather!" He set her down and Emerald lifted her arms and put them around his neck. "I do love you. It's a miracle we've found each other."

He kissed her passionately and held her. "Next week," he said. "At the rock altar, that's where I want to marry you. It has to be next week. I've already made our steamship reservations!"

"Did you have enough money?"

He looked down at her with merry eyes that danced with amusement. "You'll love steerage!"

4

August 21, 1923

As the two cars wound their way through the rolling hills, Joe Scanlon mentally congratulated himself for having phoned Eamon de Valera and told him: "You're not to tell Emerald about me, not about my background, my money, or my position. I want to surprise her."

"I've kept more important secrets," de Valera replied dryly.

"Well, keep this one if you expect future donations," Joe joked, and de Valera promised.

The wedding party consisted of six in all: Joe and Emerald, Eamon de Valera, Father Doyle, Katherine Grady, and Sister Celeste, who had come from Belfast with Father Doyle.

"I daresay this would have been more sensible in a proper church," de Valera complained from the backseat. "On the other hand, I suppose it does have more symbolism this way."

"And heaven knows, we're all taken with symbolism," Emerald added, half-turning.

"It's going to rain. Look at those clouds. I know it's going to rain." De Valera shook his head.

"I've ordered it not to rain," Joe said cheerfully. "Now, Eamon, I'm only letting you give the bride away because you've assured me that you're going to be the future president of Ireland."

"And why would a poor Irishman from Boston want a president as part of his wedding party?" Eamon smirked only slightly, and Joe stared at the road in order to maintain a straight face.

The cars came to an abrupt halt and pulled over to the side of the road. Resolutely they walked across the grass and began the climb up the hill. A brisk breeze blew out of the west, and de Valera stopped now and again to eye the ominous clouds.

Joe's eyes followed Emerald lovingly. She was wearing a deep green summer suit with a full skirt that fell to her trim ankles. She carried her fashionable hat in one hand so it wouldn't blow off her head, and her hair fell loose, gently moving with the breeze.

The little group made its way to the rock altar and Father Doyle unpacked the sacred objects for the altar, which he carried in a square black case. He went about his work quickly, laying down the altar cloth, setting out the cross, and preparing for the sacrament.

"Good thing it's sheltered," de Valera grumbled.

"You're the typical dour Irishman, Eamon. We come in two kinds—cheerful optimists and dour melancholy poets of emotional depression. You are the latter."

De Valera smiled a little. "Not always," he answered. "But it *is* going to rain."

"Now, my children," Father Doyle said, beckoning them to kneel down.

Father Doyle blessed them and they took their vows of marriage. Then, mindful of the threatening clouds, he said an abbreviated version of the wedding mass.

When the mass was completed and everyone had taken the sacrament, Joe kissed Emerald and everyone clapped.

"It is raining!" Eamon declared with triumph.

"Then may I suggest we make for the cars." Joe laughed.

Father Doyle quickly gathered up his things and packed them away. They all hurried back down the hill to the shelter of the motor cars.

"We're going to luncheon at the hotel," Joe explained.

Emerald turned and frowned at him. "You know, now that we're married, I ought to have something to say about how you waste money."

"It's all paid for, and so is our passage. And so is the hotel room where we'll be spending our last night in Dublin."

"We could have stayed with friends."

"I like hotels," he replied, winking at Eamon. And then he thought: Neither of us is a virgin, but I feel like one. I feel like a man who's about to have his first woman.

Emerald shook her head. "I'll be scrubbing floors in Boston to help pay for all this."

"Never," Joe replied. Then, more seriously, "Emerald, you only live once."

"The Royal Hibernia?" Emerald said with surprise. "This is the most expensive hotel in all Dublin!"

"Really? It seemed quite reasonable to me. Perhaps they gave me a cheaper rate because I'm American."

Emerald looked at the luncheon table, all set with pure white linen. She touched the cloth almost reverently, and her mind strayed momentarily to Seamus, who had worked in the linen mills. But she was soon distracted by the opening and pouring of champagne.

"A gift from your mysterious friends?" she asked.

"Indeed," Joe replied. Then, looking very solemn, "They wanted to be here so much, pity they were called away on business."

"It's terrible," Emerald replied seriously. "I wanted to thank them for all they've done."

Eamon raised one eyebrow and sighed. Then he stood up, raising his glass. "To the bride and groom, to a free Ireland, and to the Irish in America!"

"Always the politician," Joe whispered. "Never forget any of your constituencies."

Before the food came, three bottles of champagne had disappeared and even Father Doyle was laughing heartily and telling slightly off-color stories, while Sister Celeste merely giggled.

Finally the waiters brought rack of lamb, salad, vegetables, and potatoes. And there was more to drink, much more. By the time the late luncheon was finished and the guests had staggered off, it was nearly six o'clock.

"Our ship leaves early," Joe said as they took the highly polished brass lift to the third floor. "We have to board at nine."

"Oh, a week of packing, and then today! I feel that it's all so sudden. It's all so sudden!"

"You're slurring your words. Are you drunk?" he teased.

Emerald tilted her head and smiled drowsily up at him. "Not really drunk. It's that champagne. It makes me light headed and giddy."

"How about sexy?" he whispered in her ear.

"Oh, that too," she admitted, smiling. "Yes, that too."

Joe opened the door to their suite. He swept her into his arms and carried her over the threshold. "Old American custom," he said, taking her to the bed and bouncing her down on the huge feather mattress.

Emerald looked around. "It's beautiful! This room is lovely! I'll be washing floors for sure!"

"Will you stop worrying about money!" He was certainly on

the verge of telling her that he had money, but then he thought it would spoil tomorrow's surprise.

Emerald kicked off her shoes. "I suppose we deserve one night of luxury before two weeks in steerage. I hope I'm not going to be seasick."

Joe laughed and chucked her under her pretty chin. "I hope not." He pulled off his shirt and then his undershirt.

Emerald rolled over on her back and made a deep moaning sound. "You have such a nice chest, so big and broad." She stretched herself out, thinking about him covering her; when she opened her eyes, he was leaning over her, looking down on her with hungry eyes.

"Champagne makes me very lecherous." He began undoing her dress.

"Me too," Emerald agreed. She lifted her arms and put them around him, letting her hands drop down over his chest. His dark hair was tinted with a touch of silver, and the touch of his skin made her feel alive with desire.

Joe looked at her breasts. "I didn't think anyone could have skin like yours, it's like rare ivory. My God, you're beautiful." He bent and tenderly kissed her nipples. He did it almost reverently; then, burying his face in her flesh, he kissed her again and again before he removed her clothes.

When she was completely naked, he spread out next to her and drew her into his arms so they could lie side by side for a few moments.

Emerald sighed in his huge arms; he made her feel small and delicate, tiny and vulnerable. And even as he held her, she could feel him growing large with his own desire. The very sensation of his rising passion made her tremble with her own wantonness.

She moaned and moved against him, and again he covered her with kisses. He was gentle yet strong, loving yet persistent. His kisses sent chills through her, and when he touched her intimately, she felt she would do anything for him. But more than her body cried out for this man; he aroused her whole being and spoke to every facet of her own personality. She knew that just as he had the skill of the perfect lover to bring her to pleasure, he also had the ability to make her cry or laugh, to interest her and keep her interested in ideas. He can seduce my mind as well as my body, she thought, and that made him the best of all the men she'd known. And when she responded to him, she found she was partaking in more than response; she was making love back to him, moving her hands on his body, exploring him and caressing him even as he caressed her.

"Oh, Joe," she breathed in his ear. "I love you so, please don't ever leave me. Almost everyone I ever loved was taken from me."

He pressed her harder. "I know," he said tenderly. "I'll never leave you, my darling. I found you by accident half a world away . . . we were meant to be."

He kissed her again and parted her legs so gently that she was hardly aware of it. He slipped into her moist depths and they were joined.

Emerald felt that all-consuming passion building as he moved within her, and she moved with him until they both felt the sudden joy of release, the tumultuous descent into the valley of pleasure.

It was Joe who woke first and began their lovemaking anew. When Emerald opened her eyes, she found him wrapped around her curved form, his hands on her breasts, his manhood pressed against her. She moved against him. "You feel good," she said, starting to turn.

"Don't," he whispered. He pulled her up on her stomach and touched her breasts from behind, fondling her while she knelt. He aroused her slowly, till she swayed with anticipation and glowed with desire. He entered her from behind, moving into her passageway with ease while Emerald shivered with pleasure and moved with a lovely rhythm.

After a time, they lay quietly.

"I've never had a woman like you," Joe Scanlon said with admiration. She was, as he had anticipated, every inch a woman, a fine hot-blooded woman with a mind as perfect as her body.

Emerald smiled. "And what kind of woman am I?"

"An intelligent one; a perfect lady on the outside, a perfect whore in bed."

"Joe!" Emerald exclaimed in a tone of mock surprise. "Are you shocked?"

He grabbed for her and she eluded him. "Shocked? It's more than a man has a right to ask."

"Oh, there's someone at the door!" Emerald pulled up the covers. "Who would come so late?"

"Not who, but what." He got up and put on his dressing gown and opened the door.

Emerald stared out from over her quilt while the waiter wheeled in a cart and uncovered it with a flourish. Joe tipped him and he left instantly, a wicked smile on his young face.

"Our midnight supper," Joe announced. "Your gown, my lady." Emerald slipped into her nightdress.

"It looks good," she admitted. "I didn't realize I was so hungry."

"It's all that exercise," he joked as he poured the wine.

"You know; Joe Scanlon, for all the money you've spent, we could have gone to America second class instead of steerage."

"Sh!" he commanded, handing her a glass. "Let me spend my wedding night the way I see fit."

It was early Saturday morning and the nine-o'clock bells were still ringing across the city of Dublin.

Emerald wore her same wedding suit and carried her purse and a new little wicker suitcase Joe had given her. Their trunk had been loaded in the hold. Joe was all dressed up too; he wore a fine tweed suit and had his raincoat slung casually over one hand.

"We look as different from the other passengers as night from day," she whispered. "I think we should have dressed more casually. I mean, steerage is steerage."

Joe shrugged. "Come along." He guided her toward the gangplank.

"Not this one!" Emerald protested. "This one is for first- and second-class."

"Don't argue, woman. I'll say good-bye to Ireland from the first-class deck and then we'll go where we belong." He gave her a nudge and she began to climb upward reluctantly.

"We're going to get into trouble," she warned.

"Just act as if you're rich," he whispered. "Let me handle the officer up top. Just put your lovely head in the air and walk on past."

"We're not supposed to be on that deck."

"Sh! For once do as you're told," he said good-naturedly.

At the top of the gangplank Emerald did as Joe said, almost afraid to look behind her as he paused briefly to speak to the deck officer.

When Joe caught up with her, he took her arm. "See, it's all right."

"We'll be found out eventually."

"Well, you can't say good-bye to Ireland from steerage. Here, let's stand by this rail."

"For goodness' sake, we're right outside the first-class cabins!"

"Good," he said, smiling. "Be bold, be brazen. I know you have it in you." He winked.

Emerald sighed and set down her suitcase.

They waited for a time and watched as the great gangplanks were raised. The ship slid easily out of its berth, and as the tugs escorted it out of the harbor, Joe held her around the waist.

"Leaving is hard," she confessed as Dublin faded into the distance and the smell of salt air became even stronger.

"We'll come back one day," he promised her.

She smiled up at him as Ireland disappeared, submerged in a low summer fog. "We can go now," she told him. "If we don't, I'll cry."

He looped his arm through hers and guided her down the deck.

"We're going in the wrong direction," she protested. "Steerage is that way."

Joe laughed and opened the door to one of the cabins.

"You can't go in there!"

"Yes, I can."

He turned and pulled her inside. The room was large and filled with baskets of flowers and fresh fruit. It had its own window that looked out on the promenade deck.

"Welcome to our accommodation, my lady." With that he picked her up and set her down on the bed.

He stood over her with a bemused expression. Her mouth had opened and closed. Her eyes took in the sumptuous room and the forest of flowers and the bottles of champagne.

"Joe Scanlon," she breathed, "what have you done?"

He grinned boyishly and took out a cigarette, lighting it with a gold lighter Emerald had never seen before. He blew the smoke into the air. "I'm afraid you've done something quite unusual. I'm afraid you've fallen in love with one of the few rich Irishmen in America."

He bent over and grinned at her. "Do you think you can live with that?"

She had been frowning, but she suddenly fell back on the bed and burst into musical laughter, shaking her head. "If this is a joke, Joe Scanlon, I'll not forgive you till you've made a million dollars."

He collapsed and kissed her hair. "I've already made it, honest. This is no joke."

She sat up, cradling her chin in her hand; then impulsively she kissed the end of his nose. "You led me on," she said in mock anger. "You led me on. I thought you were poor like me. I don't know if I can live with money. I'm a rebel, remember."

"One of the things I love about you . . . you rebel, you!"

He pulled her into his arms. "We have a little poem we say in Boston. 'Saint Patrick's in Ireland, the shamrocks and you, I love with a heart that's both Irish and true!' "

"Oh, I love you," she breathed.

He kissed her passionately, moving his lips on hers and feeling her respond in his arms.

"Joe, the door's not closed," she whispered.

He released her and glanced over his shoulder. "I'll close it," he said. "And we won't come out till we get to America!"

Book IV

23

1

November 8, 1932

The Ancient Order of Hibernians had a fraternal name somewhat grander than their hall. But on this night, the second Tuesday of November 1932, only the dimensions of the hall actually mattered. The decaying paint, the loose floorboards, and the ever-present cockroaches could not be seen for the number of people who milled about expectantly.

The most overpowering odor was stale beer. In spite of Prohibition, an election without beer was not an election. In any case, the Honorable James Curley, mayor of Boston, was present, and the police were all Irish.

Up near the front of the hall, on a platform, there was a blackboard which indicated the various Boston wards, a blaring radio, and a long table peopled by Irish Boston's political leaders.

As he moved toward the platform, Joe Scanlon could see Emerald, who sat at one end of the long table while Mayor Curley sat at the other.

Beneath her broad-brimmed hat, her red-gold hair was done up in a mass of cascading ringlets which was the current style. Joe thought that her hairstyle suited her far better than the current vogue in clothes. He hated the loose belted blouses and the baggy skirts, though he admitted he loved the embroidered silk stockings.

At thirty-seven, Emerald had a mature ripe beauty, a flawless complexion, and a lilting Irish accent.

"It's Joe Scanlon!" Colin McBride slurred drunkenly. "Oh, Joe, do I have a story for you! Have you heard the one about poor Mrs. McSwinney, now?"

Joe paused and slapped Colin on the back. "No, that's a new one."

"Well, it seems that old Terrance McSwinney, he up and died, and when the undertaker got the body, he saw that the poor man's prick was standing straight out like a stick. And the undertaker's assistant said, 'Oh, dear me, now, we'll not be getting the coffin closed, and I can't get it to lie down. Do you think we should cut it off and lay it by his side?'

"The undertaker shook his head. 'Now, we can't be mutilating the dead without the permission of the next of kin, so I better call the poor distressed widow.' So he up and called dear Mrs. McSwinney and she wept and sobbed—oh, dear me, did that woman weep and sob. So the undertaker, he explained the problem, and he asked, 'Shall I cut it off and lay it beside him?' Well, the dear widow, she thought for a minute, and then, don't you see, she realized just how good old Terrance died. So she said, 'By all means cut it off, but don't be laying it by his side. Roll him over and stick it up his arse! It's the only arse in town it's not been in!' "

Colin McBride broke into gales of laughter and stomped his foot on the floor. Joe too laughed and again slapped Colin on the back.

"Well worth the telling," he said cheerfully. Then with a wave of his hand he continued to fight his way to the platform.

He bent over and kissed Emerald on the cheek.

"What are you smirking about?"

"Just a good story, much too raunchy to repeat right now." He winked and then lifted his hand to wave at James Curley.

"Emerald!" Jim Curley called out. "Come here and speak with this good woman. I told her you could help her."

Joe watched as Emerald walked across the platform. The depression had hit the Irish hard, and Emerald had been working with orphans, the hospital auxiliary, and was a member of the mayor's Committee on Housing. She was one of the party's greatest assets.

Standing next to the poorly dressed woman, the two appeared to come from different worlds. But in reality they came from the same world, and Emerald knew how to talk to the woman.

Emerald knew poverty from her youth, and while she was wide-eyed and innocent-looking, she had an honest gut understanding of politics. She understood image and she was shrewd. Unlike his first wife, Kitty, Emerald had no difficulty coping with her Brahmin neighbors; she outdignified them at every turn. She never flaunted money or wasted it; she was respected by the Brahmin establishment for her reserve, her intellect, and her style. Among the Irish, she was loved for her hard work and genuine interest in the community. Emerald was a true chameleon who knew when to be what; she was at home in all worlds.

In a few minutes Emerald returned and sat down. "Poor woman. She's been turned out of her flat."

"And did you solve her problem?"

"Temporarily," Emerald replied. "But I'll have to see to a permanent solution on Thursday." She sighed. "We need a hostel or a place of that nature. I really must give that some thought.''

Joe's eyes dropped to her ankles. "Are the tops of your stockings embroidered too?'' he asked playfully.

"Shame on you,'' Emerald said, shaking her head.

Joe winked again at her and pinched her gently under the table. He was filled with admiration for her, and she looked incredible.

Joe thought about the children who were at home listening to the election returns. In the morning they would all have breakfast together, and if Roosevelt was elected, they would go to Washington for the inauguration together.

Tom Hughes, Joe's stepson, was involved in the election because he was older than the other children. He was working down in one of the South Boston wards. Sometimes Tom Hughes reminded Joe of his own brother, Mike. Tom had the same kind of raw political interests, a similiar temperament, and certain revolutionary tendencies that Joe hoped would be curbed by higher education and a good job. But like Mike, Tom showed little interest in academic pursuits.

Tom also had more disturbing aspects to his personality. He seemed to feel himself an outsider in the Scanlon clan, and there was no doubt he felt some bitterness over his early separation from his mother. That too, Joe hoped, Tom would overcome. Tom was a big, strapping seventeen-year-old, a good-looking boy whose potential was as yet undeveloped.

The children would be going to bed now, Joe thought. Katie and J.J.—Joe Junior—were eight-year-old twins; young Seamus was six; and Edward was four. For a man who thought he'd never have children, Joe congratulated himself for doing so well. Yes, he admitted, I'd almost written myself off when I met Emerald. And now he believed he had the perfect marriage, if such a state existed. He and Emerald shared interests and values and in the ten years of their marriage their passion for one another hadn't waned.

"Here comes Tom." Emerald nudged him and pointed off across the hall.

Doubtless, Joe thought, he carried the results from South Boston. He was a tall dark-haired boy with deep-set brown eyes. Emerald said he looked like his father. He waved at them and grinned.

"We've taken wards six and seven! All the South Boston wards! Everything! Boston's a landslide for Roosevelt!''

Tom Hughes wiped his brow and handed the figures to the

secretary, who wrote them on the blackboard. Those near the front of the hall began cheering, and the cheer spread like a wave, till it became a roar of approval.

Of course, South Boston was a foregone conclusion, but everyone always cheered. This was home territory, the base of Irish political power.

"We won't know about the state till the upstate vote comes in, and it won't come in for a while. I doubt Lexington and Concord will go Democratic!" Joe said, smiling.

Emerald tilted her head. "Roosevelt has middle-class vote-pulling power. I think a lot of people will cross political lines in this election. People's politics are in their pocketbooks. Children going hungry, men and women out of work. There are still bread lines in this rich country. We need the New Deal. I believe in Roosevelt and the humanity of his politics."

"You don't have to convince me! I've been working my butt off for the man," Joe replied good-naturedly. He hugged her. Damn, she was intense! A real crusader.

"Sorry, don't get me started. You know how much I like Mrs. Roosevelt. She's going to have a lot of influence."

Joe smiled. Yes, he knew how much Emerald liked Mrs. Roosevelt. When the Roosevelts had come to Boston pounding the campaign trail, Emerald had been virtually closeted with Mrs. Roosevelt, who was a former social worker. They found common ground.

The next time they had met, FDR had cornered Joe and laughed heartily. "I'll tell you, we better keep those two apart, because if I'm elected, Emerald and Eleanor are going to cost the taxpayers plenty!"

Emerald stood up to embrace Padraic. "I don't see enough of you. It seems like I only see you at election parties—and when you come, you come to see Joe instead of me," she chastised him mildly, but hugged him tightly. And she was right; the last two months had been utterly hectic between business and the election.

"As party bagman, I've got to do my duty," Padraic answered. "You know, I do believe the results of this election are going to be one of the best birthday presents I ever had!"

"And are we going to have a celebration! Forty-eight years old! Padraic O'Hearn."

"Stop reminding me!"

"It's nothing to hide from—after all, with age comes wisdom."

"And a bald head." Padraic patted his shiny dome.

In ten years Padraic had developed a considerable paunch,

which made him look shorter than his five-foot-ten-inch frame.
His brown hair was almost gone except for a straight fringe. And
even though his demeanor was jolly, his eyes were still intense
and brooding. Within Padraic the passion of the poet still burned,
and although he had become literate, it was functional literacy
that did not offer him the power of a Yeats.

At Joe's urging, Padraic had moved from New York to Boston
nine years ago. It hadn't taken much urging, because Padraic
missed Tom so. It was an easy move because Padraic had never
married, so there was no wife to uproot and no adopted family to
leave behind. Emerald and Tom were his family, and Joe had
adopted him as a brother.

As bagman for the party, Padraic collected funds for political
campaigns. He also worked for Joe Scanlon. In fact, Joe was
more than willing to admit—though not publicly—that it was
Padraic who almost accidentally tumbled on a facet of Joe's
business that helped see the Scanlon fortune through the worst
years of the depression.

Padraic had begun with a division of Scanlon Electric and his
first job was in security, since his background was that of a
police officer. First Padraic began with simple alarm systems for
the firm; then he urged Joe to sell the systems to wealthy
homeowners. Next, Padraic discovered that the systems provided
excellent warning of impending raids on hooch parlors. Thus
Scanlon Electric had made a small fortune during Prohibition,
outfitting illegal pubs with simple alarm systems. The device
was sold as the Scanlon burglary alarm, but in every bar on the
East Coast it was known as the Scanlon Screamer.

"Joe, look at these votes from upstate! Look at the votes for
Roosevelt and look at the votes for Hoover! They won't be able
to offset the Boston vote! Joe, I think we're going to be able to
take the state!" Emerald's eyes were glimmering with sheer
delight. She clapped as the entries were made on the big board,
and again a rippling roar of approval swept the Hibernian Hall.

Padraic reached under the table for the brown paper bag that
contained the bottle of fine Irish whiskey. He gripped it by the
neck and lifted it to his lips, taking a quick swig. "Ah, decent
whiskey," he announced gratefully. Joe Scanlon always had the
best, and as Padraic well knew, he imported it himself.

"They say another state will ratify the amendment to repeal
Prohibition by the end of next year. I'll be damn glad when it's
over!"

Joe laughed. "Has it inhibited your drinking?"

"Not likely, but it's damn expensive. Hell, I think I drink

more now than when I went to the pub every day. Forbidden fruits and all that.''

"Everybody does. Hell, those do-good women got Prohibition passed for the good of little children who didn't have milk because their fathers spent it all on booze. So what happened? The fathers went out and had to pay through the nose for homemade brew that hadn't been tested, and now the kids have blind fathers.''

Padraic eyed the bottle under the table suspiciously.

"That's good stuff, brought down from Canada," Joe assured him in a whisper. "You know I only import and sell the best. I wouldn't deal in rotgut, it's immoral. Emerald told me that thirty thousand people went blind last year from homemade hooch. Damn, what a waste!"

He looked around, but Emerald was engaged with someone else and wasn't listening. He always whispered about his dealings in whiskey because he wasn't sure if she knew he imported and sold it. Well, he thought, she knows I import because it's in the house. It was the scale of his business she didn't know about. Or at least he didn't think she did.

"Do-gooders," Padraic said with a tone of disgust as he took another swig while he vowed silently to drink only Joe's whiskey until Prohibition was repealed.

"Ah, me boys, we're going to do it tonight! We're going to send Hoover packing and we're going to have a New Deal for the whole of America!" It was Mayor Curley and he was dead drunk. And why not? He had been dealing with the depression for years now and he saw the first ray of light in Roosevelt's election program, indeed in Roosevelt himself.

"He's a real man of the minorities," Curley claimed. "For the first time, if he's elected, we'll have a place in the government. You'll see an Irishman—you'll see Jim Farley in the cabinet!"

Joe pumped Curley's outstretched hand. Curley was a strange man. He was certainly not without faults, but he did good things too. In many ways the two of them thought alike, though Curley had a reputation for corruption in the Brahmin homes of fine old Boston. Joe had escaped that; he dealt clean. But they agreed on one thing. They were both sick to death of Hoover's inaction, his unwillingness to commit himself to social programs, programs that would feed and house people, programs that would get men back to work and off the public dole.

The depression was devastating, though it hit Boston unevenly. Those hit hardest were the areas which were already disadvantaged—the coloreds in the South End and Roxbury, who were largely illiterate and more than seventy percent unskilled. There the tuberculosis death rate was four times higher than in lily-white Boston and the unemployment rate was fifteen to eighteen percent higher than elsewhere.

Last August, Mayor Curley had grown tired of waiting for federal funds and had instituted four-cent suppers and penny lunches. He announced that he had no intention of waiting for Mr. Hoover, because Mr. Hoover didn't give a damn.

Nowhere in Boston was the depression more evident than on Mile End Road. It was lined with shacks where men paid no rent at all and lived like animals from one free meal to another. In the heart of the slum there were acres of ugly wooden tenements where the rent was ten dollars a month and a family's co-tenants were large, ugly wharf rats. There was no heat, no running water, no indoor toilets.

Boston was a city divided by its ethnic origins, a city waiting to be made whole again by full employment. The North End was filled with poverty-stricken Italians, the poor Irish were in Charlestown and South Boston, the coloreds in the South End and Roxbury. Here and there were Russian and Polish Jews—people who seemed to live nowhere, but who with pushcarts seemed to live everywhere.

But through it all, Mayor Curley reigned supreme. He took from the rich and distributed the money as best he could to the poor. He did it because he cared and because it yielded political support. His problem was, he didn't bother keeping very good books.

Emerald, on the other hand, became involved in social programs only because there was a need for them. She was primarily concerned with the welfare of children—she was a nurse turned social worker. But, Joe thought, regardless of her real reasons for working so hard, the political benefits were obvious and her activities had endeared her both to the mayor and to Eleanor Roosevelt.

Emerald had helped establish a lunch program for colored children and she herself had seen to it that a clinic was set up to diagnose tuberculosis.

And, he reflected, she had changed his views, or more accurately, she was responsible for him having views in the first place. He, like most of the Irish, had always been caught up in the struggle of the Irish and had never given any thoughts to the city's coloreds. Some Irish, not a few in fact, thought the coloreds were inferior.

"They're no different than we are," Emerald insisted. "They

were denied literacy and education, they've been oppressed. They've been denied the opportunity to show they're equal. Home of the abolitionists indeed!'' she raged. ''Oh, it's fashionable to have a Negro butler, but a Negro banker is unthinkable.''

It was Emerald's work in the colored community that had come to the attention of Mrs. Roosevelt, and it was the main reason they had become instant friends.

''We've taken the whole city!'' someone cried as the next set of figures was put up on the board.

Joe snapped out of his thoughts. He got up and walked over to Emerald and hugged her. ''A lot of work went into this election,'' he observed.

''A lot,'' Emerald agreed. ''Look at the mayor, Joe. He looks as if he could dance a jig.''

''And next the whole damn state!'' Curley was saying. ''Holy Mother, I hope the nation follows suit!''

The Scanlon house on Brimmer Street was a lovely old brownstone with a large window that faced the narrow cobbled street. It was four stories high and had long narrow rooms with highbeamed ceilings and beautiful inlaid hardwood floors.

Joe had thought Emerald might want to sell the house and move out of the city, but she would have none of it. ''I can walk to the Common and the public garden from here; we're only blocks from the summer outdoor Pops concerts, and everything I want to do is downtown. Don't you try to take me away from the bookstores on Tremont!''

And so they had kept the house and Emerald had redecorated it, making it her own.

The main floor held the living room, the small study, the dining room, the kitchen, and the housekeeper's room off the kitchen.

The second floor had two bedrooms and a sewing room, the third floor had two more bedrooms and a storage room, and the fourth floor was all one huge room shared by Joe and Emerald.

''Our retreat,'' she told him.

''And big enough to chase you around,'' he remembered joking.

The dining-room table was massive and made of oak; the chairs around it were also oak and upholstered with red velvet cushions. On the walls were paintings of Ireland, pictorial scenes with rolling green hills and winding dirt roads.

"Aren't you tired?" Joe asked. They had just finished breakfast and were lingering over a second cup of tea.

"No, but I will be," Emerald confessed. She picked up the morning Boston *Globe* and looked one more time at the election results. The final tally in the state of Massachusetts was 800,000 for Roosevelt, 700,000 for Hoover, and 34,000 for the Socialist Norman Thomas.

"Great election," Joe commented. "A lot of Socialists voted Democratic. There really will be changes."

"It was still close," Emerald said, laying down the paper.

"Not that close." Joe beamed. Frankly, he liked cliff-hangers. It made winning more exciting.

"I'm glad for the country and the Roosevelts," Emerald said.

"Are we really going to Washington?" eight-year-old J.J. asked.

"Really," Emerald answered. "And Mrs. Reilly's going to take you to the Lincoln Memorial, the Washington Monument, and the Smithsonian."

"I want to cross the Delaware like Washington," J.J. announced.

"That's not in Washington," Joe corrected. J.J. was notoriously bad in geography. "Will a boat ride down the Potomac do?"

"He wanted to throw a dollar across like Washington did," Katie popped up.

"A dollar won't go that far these days," six-year-old Seamus put in. "Everybody says so."

Emerald laughed, and Joe smiled. Seamus was so serious-looking. He was at the age where he took everything everyone said literally.

Edward looked up from his cereal and smiled because he thought something must be funny, but he was too young to understand what.

Emerald craned her neck so she could see the old grandfather clock in the living room. "You better hurry," she told the children, "or you'll be late for school."

"It ought to be a holiday," J.J. said, pouting. "We ought to get a day off to celebrate!"

"Well, you don't," Emerald said firmly. "Come on, now, off with you!"

The children left the table together, running into the hall to put on their coats and hats.

"Better wear your scarves too!" Emerald called out. "The weather's getting quite cold."

Joe stood up and stretched. "Damn, I'm getting too old to stay up all night." He yawned. "How about an after-breakfast brandy, then an all-day nap?"

"Sounds good," Emerald said, following him into the living room.

Joe poured her some brandy and handed her the snifter. Then he poured his own.

"A toast. To the New Deal!" Their glasses touched and the crystal tinkled in the silence of the high-ceilinged room.

Emerald sighed. "Perhaps we *should* celebrate. J.J.'s right. You know, I mean really celebrate."

Joe pulled Emerald into his arms. "The last time we really celebrated, you got pregnant with Edward!"

Emerald blushed and nuzzled into his arms. "That isn't what I meant. I meant we should go somewhere, take a trip."

"We're going to Washington for the inauguration. Isn't that far enough?"

"Well, I did have something else in mind."

"Europe," he guessed. "You want me to take you to Europe."

Emerald smiled. "After the inauguration in the spring. I always wanted to go to Paris. . . ." She delighted in the thought of being in Paris with Joe, and she thought: I can keep a promise and take Tom to his father's grave.

Joe's face took on a slightly mischievous expression.

"Joe Scanlon! I know that look. It's the same look you had on your face just before you confessed you were one of the only rich Irishmen in America! Every time you do something to surprise me, you get that look on your face. Have you already got the tickets? What are you keeping from me?"

She had her hands on her hips and was trying to look severe, but she couldn't erase the look of delight on her face and the amusement in her green eyes. "Well?" she questioned, half-laughing.

"France and Italy with the children." He smiled. "Then they'll have to come back to school. The rest of Europe alone . . . just the two of us."

Emerald threw her arms around his neck. "Oh, Joe! It sounds wonderful!"

"There is something else," he said. "Something we ought to discuss."

"Oh, you sound serious."

"Here, sit down a minute."

"Is it so serious I have to sit down?"

"Well, it's something I want you to keep in mind, think about."

Emerald sat down on the sofa, and he sat down across from her.

"Mayor Curley wants to remain mayor. But there are political favors to be paid off to the party in Boston. Well, there is the hint of an appointment in the air . . . maybe an ambassadorship, something like that."

"For you!" Emerald exclaimed. "Oh, Joe, what an honor!"

"Well, it's a big decision. Not one we have to make now, mind you. But something we ought to think about, because it might well materialize."

"I think it would be wonderful, Joe."

"Well, time will tell. Now, let's go up and get some rest before I fall asleep in this chair."

Emerald got up. "Good idea."

They started up the stairs toward their room.

"Tom missed our traditional after-the-election breakfast."

"He's getting older," Emerald said as they reached the fourth-floor landing. "He's got his own friends now."

"I suppose," Joe replied, opening the door to their bedroom.

Emerald turned and hugged him. "Don't worry about him," she said, looking up into her husband's face.

Joe bent down and kissed her on the neck. "I'm not, I just thought you might be."

2

March 4, 1933

"It was a wonderful speech," Emerald commented, "moving. 'The only thing we have to fear is fear itself.' He's going to move quickly, very quickly."

"With so many banks closed, he has no choice."

Emerald kicked off her shoes and sank onto the chaise longue. Their suite in the new Embassy Hotel was sumptuous. The bedroom was huge and airy, with a large four-poster bed, a long dressing table, and a full-length mirror. The reception room outside had several tapestried couches, five chairs, and a table for small supper parties. There was one bathroom off the bedroom, and two others off the long hall which led to the two smaller bedrooms the children occupied.

"Lord, I thought my hair was going to blow off, never mind my hat!"

"Well, it is March. It's always windy in March." Joe snickered. "In fact, it's always windy in Washington—all those politicians!"

Emerald laughed and looked at her toes. She wiggled them. "I'm numb, it was cold. The fathers of this country are certainly guilty of bad planning. They ought to have had the election in June and the inauguration in July."

"Then people would faint from the heat."

"I suppose. My God, it was impressive. Even Edward didn't move. He listened to the whole speech. I thought I was going to cry."

"It takes very little to make you cry. You cry when you laugh too hard, every time you're feeling patriotic, and when you're unhappy. You cry in sympathy, you even cry at the movies—especially at the movies!"

"I'm Irish. We laugh easily and we cry easily. But it was moving, wasn't it?"

"It was indeed. I'm glad the children were there."

"I ought not to be lying here, I ought to be soaking in a hot bath. I have a lot to do before the reception."

"When will the children be back?"

"Oh, not for hours. They're at the Smithsonian with Mrs. Reilly. They'll be exhausted when they get back, and so will she. I do wish Tom had come. He really missed something."

"You said yourself he has his own friends." Joe sat down on the side of the chaise longue. "We must get one of these for our bedroom. You look like a Turkish harem girl spread out on it." He put his hand on her ankle and then ran it up the side of her leg, over her silk stockings to the top, where he stopped and playfully snapped her garter belt.

"Ouch!"

"Oh, ouch yourself. Come here, we're alone."

Emerald giggled as he nuzzled her. "You're tickling me. Oh! My goodness, stop!" She burst into gales of laughter, then moaned slightly as she relaxed in his arms, allowing him to caress her.

"Oh, you always touch me in the right places," she whispered. "Aren't we going over to the bed?"

"No, I like this thing, whatever it is."

"A chaise longue," she answered.

"Lounge?"

"No, longue—it's French."

"Should we make love like the French, then?"

"How do the French make love?"

"Ah, madam, allow me to remove your undergarments and illustrate."

"Such diplomacy." Emerald put her arms around his neck. "Do with me what you will . . . Oh, my," she breathed heavily.Then she was lost in sensations, and so was he. They melted onto one another, moving and touching each other till they seemed to be traveling in space, then plummeting back down to earth.

"My God, that was good," he said, kissing her again.

Emerald wiggled out from beneath him. He had completely undressed her except for her stockings and garter belt. "I feel indecent." She laughed.

"You look sexy as hell," he said, rolling over on his back and lighting a cigarette. "I damn well hope I come down before the reception!"

The reception was simple in the extreme and reflected the view of the new president that a lavish inauguration would be out of place in the atmosphere of severe depression.

"I hear you're going to be traveling," Roosevelt said as he shook Joe's hand.

"I feel I need to see a bit more of the world," Joe admitted. "Reading can't compensate for seeing, for getting a feel for the international situation."

Roosevelt nodded. "You know, there may be an ambassadorial post opening up in the future—I'd say within a year. I'm considering you for the appointment."

"I'm deeply grateful," Joe replied. "And all the more reason why I should do some traveling and get a feel for the diplomatic role."

Roosevelt grinned. "Damn, I wish all my appointees cared so much! I'll be honest," the president said with candor, "some of them aren't too bright, but of course I've tried to keep them out of sensitive positions."

Joe laughed. FDR was honest, and among those he trusted there was no attempt at political subterfuge.

"Where will you be traveling?"

"France, Italy, Spain . . . Emerald wants to go to Africa too. She keeps reading Hemingway, mostly because he's banned in Boston."

"What an excellent criterion for picking fine books!"

"Books—you're discussing books at the inaugural reception?" Emerald took Joe's arm. She had broken away from Jim Farley and come to join Joe and the president.

"Lean down here," the president requested. He was sitting in his wheelchair, and he craned his neck upward.

Both Joe and Emerald leaned down.

"This isn't quite the moment," FDR said in a near-whisper, "but while you're traveling, how would you like to go to the Soviet Union?"

"The Soviet Union?" Joe looked surprised. "I'm a staunch capitalist."

"They will be too, in time. I'm thinking of according them diplomatic recognition. I'm sending different people off to visit there. I want as many opinions as possible. I don't have to tell you, it's a political bombshell—hell, the Daughters of the American Revolution will go to war!"

Joe laughed. No one had to tell an Irish Bostonian about the DAR.

"Anyway, I want opinions apart from those emanating from Foggy Bottom. How about it? Good way to get part of your fare paid for by the government." The president winked and nudged Joe in the ribs.

"I think it would be fascinating," Emerald said.

"Oh, you just want a new fur coat," the president joked. "Make him buy you a good one, white sable perhaps. Yes, you were definitely meant for white sable."

"I accept your offer." Joe smiled. "But only because I want to see dancing bears. I always associate them with Moscow."

"Good, good!" The president beckoned Joe with his finger. "I want to thank you for the whiskey," he whispered. "We enjoyed every last contraband drop of it!"

3

April 24, 1933

Boston

"Bloody British! Goddamned Protestant bastards! Did you read about the murders in Belfast? You, your mother's from Belfast, isn't she? If the British don't get the hell out of Northern Ireland, there'll be hell to pay!"

"Damn right!" Tom Hughes lifted his glass of beer and then drained it.

The basement room of the hooch parlor was a trifle damp and the candles on the tables provided only dim light. It was a typical drinking hole, off a back street, hidden and below street level, down a flight of rickety stairs.

Inside, the tables were covered with stained red-and-white tablecloths and under each table there were brown paper bags that contained bottles of liquor. If the place was raided, the illegal brew wasn't on the table—it belonged to no one. But raids were not of much concern. The alarms were good, the lookouts experienced. In any case, since Roosevelt's election, the Treasury Department had backed off a bit. It was well known that Prohibition and its enforcement was not one of the president's priorities; in fact, it wasn't even on his list.

"Well, here's to the anniversary of the rising! Here's to Padraic Pearse and his brother Willie and all the blessed martyrs of 1916!" Paddy Murphy raised his glass and he too drained it in one long gulp.

"My uncle died in the post office," Tom Hughes said proudly.

"And your mother surrendered it!" Paddy said meanly.

Tom Hughes felt a bitter anger deep inside. He wanted to shout: You weren't there, you don't know anything about it! But he didn't. He gave his standard answer instead: "On James Connolly's order, that's all! She did it because James Connolly told her to!"

"Ah, don't be getting all hot under your rich white starched collar, there. Can't you take a little joke?"

Tom gritted his teeth. He felt all tight inside; he wanted to smash Paddy Murphy's fat face in. "I can take a joke," he answered sullenly.

Tom refilled his glass and blessed Paddy's momentary silence. When he was with Paddy and the boys he always had a dreaded fear that someone would discover his father had died wearing a British uniform; he dreaded that more than the comments that were sometimes made about his mother. But then, he told himself, no one would find out; how could they?

"Well, since your uncle died for a free Ireland and your mother was in the General Post Office, don't you think you ought to be doing something about the British in Ulster?"

Paddy was bellicose and he knew how to get to Tom's sensitivities.

"I'll do something," Tom blustered.

"No you won't. You won't do a damned thing because you're not like us. You're not shanty Irish or pig-shit Irish, you're lace-curtain Irish—you're a Scanlon, you have money."

"I'm a Hughes!" Tom retorted.

"No you're not. You're Joe Scanlon's stepson."

"I'm a Hughes," Tom repeated. Paddy had done it again; he'd struck a raw nerve. Tom liked Joe Scanlon; God knew, the man was nice enough to him. But Joe Scanlon wasn't his father. And who the hell was his father? How had he lived? Why did he join the British Army? No, Tom thought. J.J. and Katie are Scanlons. Seamus and Edward are Scanlons. I'm not. I'm nobody; a nobody whose mother shipped him out of Ireland and away from her; a nobody who was nothing more than an appendage to the Scanlon name and reputation.

"Well what? What are you going to do? My guess is you'll go to Notre Dame! Joe Scanlon will set you up in business, and while the Irish die in occupied Belfast, you'll be making money and drinking hooch!"

"I will not!" Tom Hughes retorted. "I'm not taking anything from Joe Scanlon! I'm going to Ireland, I am. I'm going to Belfast. I'm a Hughes."

Paddy pounded the table with his little fat fist. "Hear that, will you! Tom Hughes is going to Belfast! First thing you know, he'll be in the IRA!"

24

1

May 1, 1933

"I don't understand," Emerald confessed. Joe stood on the edge of this family discussion, ready to support Emerald, but unsure himself of just how. Tom Hughes was, after all, eighteen—or would be in a few weeks.

"I'm only coming as far as France with you," Tom repeated. "Then I'm going to Belfast."

"But this trip is a marvelous opportunity! And you'd be back in time to start school after Labor Day. Think of it, darling, Paris, Madrid, Rome . . ."

Tom stood up restlessly; Joe could see he was as agitated as Emerald was mystified.

"You know we're all packed, the ship leaves day after tomorrow, and all the hotel reservations have been made. You might have said something sooner." Joe kept his voice even. He was more exasperated than angry at his stepson. The boy, he decided, was only attempting to exercise his newfound independence. *Or perhaps he has wild oats to sow, as the saying goes. Maybe,* Joe rationalized, *I would not want to have traveled with my parents at his age either.*

Emerald was sitting on the edge of the sofa. Her hands were clasped tightly. Tom, Joe thought, was throwing a spanner into the works. Emerald had looked forward to spending time with Tom on this trip. "He's older than the others, just the right age to appreciate everything."

"I'm sorry," Tom stumbled. "I want to go to France, I want to visit my father's grave. But then I want to leave and go to Belfast on my own. Is that so hard to understand?"

"But why?" Emerald asked.

Tom's face muscles tensed. He almost looked as if he might be on the verge of tears. Beyond the surface of this discussion was something deeper, Joe decided. Tom seemed to be troubled, deeply troubled.

"Because I'm eighteen! Because there are things I have to find out about! Because my father came from Belfast!"

"So do I," Emerald replied. "We could take you, I could show you where your father and I lived. We could take a side trip to Ireland, couldn't we, Joe?''

"Of course." Joe looked steadily at Tom, and beneath the surface he could see the lad was clearly at war with himself. Something was eating at the boy's gut, and Emerald couldn't quite see it.

"That's not what I want, it's not even what I mean! Why can't you understand? I don't want you for a guide. I want to stay there . . . I might even want to live there!"

"Lower your voice," Joe said sharply. "Neither your mother nor I are deaf!"

"But we're a family," Emerald protested. Her voice was strained and her face pale. Tom's sudden outburst, his rejection of her, had wounded her deeply, and Joe glared at Tom, silently warning him to go no further.

"The Scanlons are a family," Tom said in a lower but somewhat bitter tone. "I'm a Hughes. I want to be on my own."

"Tom . . ." Emerald's voice was faint, and Joe felt the next of Tom's comments coming.

"You were happy enough to leave me when I was four. Now that I'm eighteen, you want me tied to your apron strings! Years, Mother, it was years, and you just weren't there. Well, you can't make up for it now. I want to be on my own!"

Tears flooded Emerald's eyes. Tom could hurt her as no one else could, and Joe was only too aware of the terrible guilt she felt about her son's childhood.

"Go to Belfast," Joe said evenly. He walked to the sofa and sat down beside Emerald. He was fighting to control his own fury with Tom, knowing all the time that to vent it would cause Emerald further pain; it would twist the knife her son had just so skillfully thrust.

Tom stepped back. Then he suddenly came and stood directly in front of his mother. "I'm sorry," he said softly. "I didn't mean it, I didn't mean to hurt you. God, I'm sorry!"

Emerald looked up at him. She just nodded silently.

"Please understand, I just want to be on my own for a while. I want to find myself, explore where I came from . . . find out about things."

Tom knelt down in front of his mother. "I didn't mean what I just said. I love you, Mother . . . I do, I really do."

Emerald touched her son's head. "It's all right. I guess I just have to realize you're grown." She tried to smile. "I'm just selfish, I wanted to be with you."

"I know . . . but let me straighten myself out. Please."

Words spoken in anger are hard to take back, Joe thought. He remained unforgiving that Tom had just caused Emerald pain. But he was glad Tom had apologized and he found himself agreeing that Tom needed to be on his own. The lad just needed a fight of his own. A little struggling wouldn't hurt Tom Hughes at all. He glanced at Emerald. She was strong, and though her son had just hurt her, she was fighting back with understanding rather than with raw hurtful emotions.

"What will you do in Belfast?" she finally asked.

"Work, live for a while . . . I want a taste of it."

Emerald nodded. "I guess I understand," she allowed.

"I think it will do him good," Joe announced. He squeezed Emerald's hand. "We were both on our own at that age, it didn't hurt us. I believe Tom should explore his Irish heritage."

"You're right," Emerald agreed. She managed a smile.

Tom stood up. "Thanks," he said. He held out his hand to Joe and Joe shook it, though not with a great deal of warmth.

"We'll all be together in Paris," Emerald said. "That's better than nothing."

Tom smiled at her. "I am sorry," he repeated.

2

June 21, 1933

"Oh, I've never had a day like this! I think my feet are going to drop off!" Emerald flounced onto the bed wearily. "I feel as if I've been through acres of museums! Acres and acres!"

"It's Seamus and his five iron replicas of the Eiffel Tower. My God, those things weigh a ton!" Joe sat down beside her. "Here, let me rub your back, it'll make you feel better."

He unbuttoned her dress and began to massage her.

"Oh, I like that," she said in a satisfied tone.

"We have time for a nap before dinner. I like the continental dining hour. The children are all in bed, and I can have you all to myself."

"When Mrs. Reilly takes them home in August, you'll have me all to yourself all the time."

"After ten years of marriage, I deserve a month with you alone. Anyway, I don't think they'd enjoy the Soviet Union. It's rather austere, I think."

"Oh, yes . . . right there, mmm, that feels good. I think I've got a stiff neck from looking at all those paintings on the ceiling." She laughed lightly and Joe was relieved that in spite of the fact that Tom was leaving day after tomorrow, she seemed to be in good spirits.

"Are you sure you don't want me to come with you tomorrow?"

"I think it's something Tom and I have to do alone. Do you mind terribly?"

"Of course not. Besides, I'm fully booked. In the morning I'm taking the children to the Bastille, in the afternoon we're going on a boat ride down the Seine, and when they're safely tucked away, I personally am going to the Folies Bergère."

"To see all those scantily clad beautiful women?"

"You bet!" He finished up massaging her back.

"That felt good."

"Want me to do the front?"

"You're terrible!"

"Think how I'll be after the Folies Bergère. Frustrated as hell!"

Emerald laughed and rolled over. Joe was wonderful. He knew when she needed to talk and when she couldn't. Tomorrow she and Tom were going to take the train out of Paris and go to visit the grave of Tom's father. It would be an emotional day, a day she both looked forward to and dreaded. And the next day Tom was leaving for Belfast. *I don't want him to go,* she had admitted to Joe. *But I have to try to understand what motivates him.*

He leaned over and kissed her lips. "If I were you, I'd take care to wear me out before I'm tempted by the sight of bare-breasted dancers."

Emerald reached over and touched him, fondling him gently. "I'll take care of you," she said in a low seductive voice.

3

June 22, 1933

The sky above was overcast, but the rolling fields were lush and green and wildflowers seemed to grow everywhere.

Emerald swallowed hard when the rows of white crosses came into view; it was a profound sight and it conjured up memories from the deep recesses of her mind.

Tom Hughes and she walking along a lonely stretch of beach; Tom Hughes paying for a picture of her in her nurse's uniform; Tom Hughes dancing happily with her; Tom Hughes going off to war in his British uniform.

"What would it have been like if he hadn't been killed?" Her son's piercing question broke through Emerald's veil of memories. They were standing in front of a simple white cross in Ypres. It looked like all the other simple white crosses; what lay beneath them were thousands of complicated lives.

"We'd have stayed in Dublin. You'd have grown up in Ireland. I don't know, it's a very hard question to answer."

"What would have happened to my father in his British uniform during the war with England? Tell me that."

Emerald tried to see Tom's face. He was standing next to her and his head was turned away. He had asked the question in a near-whisper.

"I don't know," she answered honestly. "I think I once asked the same question myself during the rising. I asked my brother Seamus what would happen if Tom Hughes were alive and if the British used Irish troops—if they'd brought them back from France—I asked Seamus if he could kill Irish troops in British uniforms."

"And how did he answer."

"He didn't. But, Tom, the answer came during the civil war. Once you start killing, you have no trouble killing your own. That's why I'm a pacifist."

"You can't always be a pacifist. There are things you have to fight for."

"I know that. I mean I try to be a pacifist, I believe in trying everything else first, in exhausting every possibility in negotiation. I know that tyrants have to be toppled, but war is a last resort, not a first resort. Tom, you haven't seen what I've seen. . . ."

"And I can't live through your experiences. I have to have my own." He kicked a small pebble with the toe of his shoe and stared downward at the ground.

"It's little children, Tom. They grow up hating. It's wrong."

"Our people are being murdered every day in Ulster. That's wrong too."

Emerald nodded. "And our people murder too. Tom, once the IRA were just a group of young men fighting for their country's freedom. During the civil war they split apart; today the IRA is different. It's not an army anymore, it's a lot of bitter, brutal men who terrorize in retaliation for being terrorized. It has to end somewhere."

"Then let the other side end it! Let the British get out of Ulster!"

Emerald fell silent. There was no argument she hadn't heard before, but it was strange hearing the same argument from her son that she had heard from her dead brother, Seamus. The same arguments she had once heard from Michael Collins . . . from everyone she knew.

"I don't understand how he could have done it!" Tom kicked the earth hard.

She bit her lip and frowned. Tom's voice was strange, distant and cold. Inside, something was eating at him.

"He believed the kaiser had to be stopped. He believed in the rights of small nations."

"He put on a British uniform and he was a traitor to Ireland!" Tom's emotions finally burst forth, and he raised his voice.

Emerald stood rigid. She felt as if she were rooted in the ground like the white cross in front of her. What was wrong with Tom? Where have I gone wrong, why does he feel this way? Lord, he doesn't even have to face these questions the way I had to face them. He's full of some kind of secondhand hatred. She began to wonder about his friends, about his early formative years, but certainly he didn't get his ideas from Padraic.

"That's a terrible thing to say in front of your father's grave," she said sadly. Emerald bent over and placed the flowers she was carrying on the grave. She straightened up and faced her son.

"It may be terrible, but it's the truth!" His voice rang with a terrible bitterness, a bitterness Emerald couldn't account for. But again she chastised herself silently for having sent him away.

"Look at me!" she demanded.

Tom turned to face her. He lifted his eyes slowly to meet hers.

"Your father was a wonderful, kind man. He was a hardworking good man. He loved Ireland as much as, if not more than, those who fought the British. If he and others like him had come home, the whole civil war might not have happened. Maybe the whole rebellion. Maybe the British would have seen that the Irish were loyal and they would have negotiated. Perhaps they wouldn't have. Perhaps you'll even think I'm a traitor to suggest that things might have been settled differently, perhaps you think it would have been a sin for the Irish to accept British gratitude. Frankly, I don't know what's right and what's wrong. I don't know what might have happened, I only know what did happen. And what did happen was that many people died here because they believed in the rights of others, and a lot of people died in Ireland because the frustration and anger boiled over. What might have been is only a discussion for academics. Tom, don't call your father a traitor, don't ever do that again." She held his eyes with hers and spoke evenly. She tried to tell herself that he was too young to understand, that he hadn't had the experience . . .

Emerald wiped her cheek, almost unaware that she was crying.

"I always wanted to come here with you," she said softly. "I never expected to hear you say what you just said."

"You can never explain it, Mother. You just keep saying he was a good, kind man. That's all you ever say about my father! I didn't know him!"

Emerald looked at her son in amazement. "I didn't either," she returned. "He died here before I knew him. I was young, we had so short a time . . . I haven't told you more because Tom Hughes and I hardly lived together. There were days and hours of our love, not even months!"

Suddenly Tom reached out and pulled Emerald to him. He held her tightly and began to sob violently. "I've hurt you again. . . . I didn't mean it, God, I'm so mixed up!"

Emerald closed her eyes. "Oh, Tom. I'm so sorry."

After a time he let her go. "I'll be all right," he promised. "I just have to work it out for myself."

4

June 23, 1933

"You're picking at your food. I didn't bring you to the most expensive restaurant in Paris to watch you pick at quail. I know you're depressed about Tom's leaving, but I've known and loved you too long to think that's all of it." Joe laid his fork down and looked at his wife.

"I'm sorry, I guess I haven't been exactly cheerful all day."

"That's something of an understatement. Want to talk about it, or should I ignore you?"

Emerald tried to smile at him. "Oh, Joe, I want to talk about it, I'm just not sure I can. I mean, I don't know how to put it."

"For a woman who can analyze complicated world situations, talk with presidents, and be at home in palaces, I find that a bit hard to believe."

"It's easy to be objective about things that aren't close to you."

Joe poured some more wine into her glass. "Something happened yesterday when you went off with Tom—mind you, I knew your visit to Tom Hughes's grave wasn't going to be easy for you, but I suspect something else happened too."

"I wish you weren't so damned perceptive."

"It doesn't take a hell of a lot of perception to see something's wrong with you. Christ, you usually eat like a horse—I'll never know how you keep your figure—and tonight you've hardly touched anything.''

"I know, and it's very good, too.''

He sipped some wine, sensing that she was getting ready to say something.

"Going to Tom's grave ought to have been different. I knew it would make me sad, but it ought to have been a time of remembrance . . . good memories. I wanted Tom to understand that, I wanted to share those good memories with him.''

"And you didn't?''

"I tried, but he wouldn't let me. Oh, Joe, Tom is so troubled. I just don't know what to do about him.''

Joe nodded. "What happened, specifically?''

"He thinks his father was a traitor because he died wearing a British uniform. I tried to explain, I tried to tell him what it was like. Then he said some awful things and I got angry and tried to explain more—I did that badly—then he just broke down and sobbed and sobbed. It made me feel terrible, and worse, it made me feel helpless. I just couldn't reach him. I feel as if I really did fail him as a child. I never should have sent him away.''

"Emerald, stop blaming yourself. Look, you know so many Irish felt strongly about those who joined the army and fought in the war. You always hear them being called traitors. Tom's young, he only looks like a man; he has to find himself. He has to sort out on his own those conflicts we all have to sort out. Emerald, he can't come to terms with his conflicts on the basis of your experiences; he has to have his own experiences.''

"But if I'd been there when he was a child . . .''

"He'd still be a troubled teenager. Christ, it's the time for trouble. Let that boy sow his own wild oats, flirt with his own political ideas, and get his own experiences. Let him sort himself out. In fact, 'let' doesn't enter into it; he's going to do it anyway. Stop worrying about him.''

"You're in favor of him going off to Belfast? Joe, you know how violent it can be there.''

He smiled at her and reached across the table to pat her hand. "It can be violent in Boston. When Mike died, you told me how he died wasn't as important as how he lived. Let Tom find his own way, Emerald. Let him find a way to live, and something to live for. That's not a gift we can give any of our children, darling. Once they're out there in the world, they're out there on their own.''

"Oh, Joe. I don't know what I'd do without you. That sounds trite, but there aren't words to say how I feel.''

He laughed. " 'I love you' is trite too. But I do.''

5

September 3, 1933

Moscow

"And this is Uspensky Sobor—the Cathedral of the Assumption—built in 1475 by Aristotele Fioravanti. It is in the Italianate-Byzantine style. Note the white stone and the elegant arches. It is the oldest of the cathedrals in the Kremlin. It is now a museum for the people," their guide concluded. He was short and round, his crumpled suit was out of fashion, and his English was slow and stilted. He walked with his hands in his pockets, and instead of using them to point at this or that, he used his chin, expressively extending and withdrawing his neck like a turtle.

"I think all the tour guides in Europe go to the same school," Joe whispered to Emerald. "They're all equally boring."

"It's particularly bad here because they won't let us walk about alone. But, Joe, this is stunning. I wouldn't have missed seeing it for the world. Still, I have to admit I'm appalled at the denial of religion. All these empty cathedrals turned into museums gives me a displaced feeling."

The guide had stopped talking to listen to them. He looked annoyed. "I thought you were American, from the American president. Why aren't you speaking English? What is that language you're speaking?" He scowled at Emerald.

"Gaelic," she answered brightly.

"But you speak English?"

"Of course, but I prefer Gaelic."

"I don't prefer it. Speak English so I can understand whether you like what I show you or not."

"I like what you show me," Emerald replied with irritation. She felt like adding that the Kremlin and its history were far more interesting to her than the endless mornings they had spent touring factories. She had told Joe she would scream if another Russian showed her another tractor.

"When I have a comment on what you show me, I'll speak English. When I want to say something else, I'll speak Gaelic."

"No." The guide looked at her and shook his head vigorously. He glanced around nervously. "No, please," he said in a more conciliatory tone. "I am ordered to understand you, and I don't understand the . . . what is it again?"

"Gaelic."

The guide withdrew a small worn book from his pocket and quickly leafed through it, mumbling all the while under his breath. Emerald felt certain he was swearing.

"How do you spell it?"

"G-a-e-l-i-c."

He continued to frown. Then, triumphantly, he closed the book and stared at her. "We do not list that language, therefore it does not exist. We do not recognize it."

Emerald burst into laughter. "Neither did the English till we had our glorious revolution in 1916!"

The guide looked horrified. "What revolution?"

"The Irish Revolution." Emerald smiled brightly.

"You're confusing him," Joe said in halting Gaelic.

"It's fun, isn't it?" Emerald replied with a wink. Her Gaelic was better than Joe's; she almost seemed to be singing the language.

The guide stomped his foot and looked truly hurt. "You'll get me in trouble! Please speak English! Please!"

Emerald looked at him and felt a twinge of pity. Doubtless he was under orders. "You've never heard of our revolution?" she asked.

He shook his head. "What was its purpose?"

"To achieve our independence, to ensure religious freedom, to establish a true democracy."

"Is it a capitalist state?"

"Very, though there isn't much capital."

"The poor will rise up," the guide predicted.

"They did. Yours is not the only revolution, you know."

"It's the only true one," he announced in the same annoying tone of authority he had been using most of the day. "But we must hurry along now. There are two more factories on your list. We can't waste time here."

Emerald folded her arms defiantly. "Comrade Dubinskii, I want to see every art gallery, museum, and cathedral in the Kremlin. I want to study the history of this place. I do not want to go to another factory, nor do I want to see another tractor. Ever. And if you do not allow us to properly see the Kremlin, I shall speak nothing but Gaelic for the rest of today."

Comrade Dubinskii frowned at her and seemed to be considering the alternatives. At last he said, "I shall have to consult my superiors. I shall have to make a phone call."

"There's a telephone over there." Emerald pointed off across the square.

"The phones don't always work," he confessed. "If I leave you here, will you stay? I mean, don't wander about. It's not allowed."

"We'll stay," Emerald agreed as he turned and with his hands still thrust in his pockets tromped off across Red Square.

"You're really terrible." Joe smirked. "I think you've given poor Comrade Dubinskii a first-class headache."

Emerald laughed. "Dear me, I always thought the Irish were dour till I met the Slavs!"

"Tell me, what do you think of the United States recognizing them? I will have to write my report to the president tonight."

Emerald's eyes followed Comrade Dubinskii as he entered the phone booth on the far side of the square. "I can't approve of the ungodliness of this government, but it would be wrong to isolate the Russians. It would only make things worse; it's a big country, a strong country. Mind you, I'll speak against recognition if they show me another tractor."

Joe hugged her. "Me too," he whispered.

6

December 1, 1933

London

"This hotel is the cat's meow," Emerald joked, doing her mock Jean Harlow imitation. "And so British, my de-ah!"

Joe lit a cigarette and put his feet up on the plush blue velvet footstool. "Well, glad to be going home tomorrow?"

"Yes, I've missed the children. And let me tell you, after France, Spain, Italy, Russia, and North Africa, I've had enough traveling for a while. I just want peace, quiet, and drinkable water."

"And if I go home to find Franklin has a diplomatic posting for me?"

"Then we'll pack up everything and go. Mind you, I hope it's not to Russia!"

"What did Tom say in his letter?" Joe pointed to the open letter on the table.

"You can read it. I must say, it's not very illuminating. He says he's well, he's got a flat, and he's working. But he doesn't say at what. He also said he's met a nice girl."

"Well, that's something. Maybe a nice girl is what he needs."

Emerald nodded. "I was hoping he'd come and meet us here, but he says he can't leave his job."

"Want to go to him?"

Emerald shook her head. "I want to, but I'm not going to. I think you're right about him needing to be on his own."

"I think a little distance between you might be good. The boy's just confused."

"And I'm part of his confusion." Emerald leaned over and looked at a section of the *Times*. "The news isn't good, is it?" she said after a few moments.

"Mixed. Now that Germany has quit the League of Nations, I'd say it was all over for the dream of international government. Mind you, the organization had no teeth; you can't expect sovereign nations to give up their sovereignty."

"It's ironic. The last time I was in London, the League was just being born; now it's dying. Oh, Joe, there was such hope for it. All those people from small countries, all hoping for peace and security."

"Isn't that why you were here?"

"Yes, we had dreams too. But we were also jaded. I think we knew it wouldn't work."

"There is some good news. Prohibition has been repealed."

"I'll drink to that!" Emerald joked.

"I'll drink with you." Joe got up and walked over to the champagne bucket. "Are you glad that Roosevelt has accorded recognition to the Soviet Union?"

"I'm glad. Oh! Don't point that bottle at me! You know I hate popping corks!"

He laughed and turned around. "I hear the Daughters of the American Revolution are calling Eleanor a Communist and they're mad as hell about recognizing Russia. They're all talking about 'the Red Menace in America.' "

Emerald took a sip of the champagne he had poured, and she giggled girlishly. "Red Menace? Sounds like a bad epidemic of measles to me—Red Menace, really? Is that what they call it? Oh, dear God. The lace-curtain Irish, the Yellow Peril, now the Red Menace. What next? Our Brahmin neighbors are circling their wagons, Joe."

"You didn't like Russia."

"No, I didn't. But I don't think America is in any danger of becoming like Russia. And I think the Russians are too busy loving their tractors to be interested in taking over America. I think the so-called 'Red Menace' is a ploy to discredit Roosevelt. He's put too many immigrants in high positions, he's insulted the Eastern establishment, he's too egalitarian. You know why they're really mad? It's because he's one of them. He's a white, Protestant American who comes from a moneyed family, and he cares about the Irish, the Chinese, and the Negroes. He's betrayed the WASPS. While they're circling their wagons, he's out rounding up the Indians."

"Very astute analysis. I think I'll keep you around, maybe for another fifty years. Here, let's toast the great state of Utah! The thirty-sixth state to ratify the glorious amendment to repeal Prohibition!"

7

December 10, 1933

Belfast

Colleen O'Mara is an orphan like my mother, Tom Hughes thought as he watched her making tea. Her flat was off Falls Road in a decaying, wretched building. It consisted of one bleak room on the fifth floor; it had neither running water nor indoor plumbing. The furniture—a table, two chairs, and a bed—were all relics, and the flat and its furnishings were ample testimony of Colleen's circumstances.

He watched silently as she poured the tea into the chipped china cups. She was a beautiful girl and she seemed out of place in her drab surroundings. She was small, a mere five feet, two inches in height. When he stood next to her, he towered over her and she seemed all the more in need of his protection. Her hair was long and raven black; her eyes were the bluest eyes he'd ever seen. She had a nice figure, but of all her physical charms, Tom liked her smile the best.

He had actually met her in the market, and he was so taken with her that he followed her home. But she would have none of it, and it had taken him days of persistence to overcome her reserve, to make friends with her.

But now they were friends, and in fact they were more than friends. They were drawn together by loneliness and, he thought, physical attraction as well. But, he reflected, they were not yet lovers, nor was it likely that they would be unless they married. Colleen had been reared in a convent; she was shy, quiet, and had high moral standards.

He had kissed her, though, and when he had kissed her he had felt the warmth of her moist lips and knew she desired him, but he also knew she was not a tease and would not allow him to go further.

Some girls were teases, he thought. He remembered a girl he had taken out in Boston. Her name was Muriel Myers and he had taken her out because she was Jewish and all the Catholic boys said she "put out" because Jews didn't have to go to confession.

He'd borrowed his father's Ford and picked her up. They went to the Tremont Street Theater and saw Fredric March in *Dr. Jekyll and Mr. Hyde*. She had sat very close to him during the film, and when the film was scary, she had almost crawled into his lap. He put his arm around her and she hadn't objected, and after the film he drove out to Revere Beach and parked. He kissed her and she responded with her mouth open and her hands running all over his back, her fingers like little spiders. She even *touched* him, and he had gotten so hard he thought he would burst. She let him put his hand down her dress, and he felt her soft, full teats go hard and firm. But when he tried to lift her dress, she objected, and when he persisted, she doubled her fist and hit him square in the jaw. He pulled himself up, with considerable dignity given his swollen condition, and told her, "You don't have to hit and scream, I'm certainly not going to force myself on you!" Then he drove her home in angry silence, aware all the time that he was still hard as a rock and that he ached with frustration. The next day at school, he didn't say anything about his failure. After all, it was a known fact that she was Jewish and that she "put out" to the other boys. So he lied even though he knew that with him she'd been nothing but a tease.

But Colleen wasn't like that. She was careful that she didn't let him kiss her too passionately, she moved if he began to feel her plump little breasts. It wasn't Colleen's fault if he mentally undressed her, and it wasn't her fault that he allowed his imagination to run wild.

"Can we spend Christmas together?" he asked as she handed him his tea. "I'll bring a feast of food."

She smiled shyly. "I'd like that," she replied softly. "You're very good to me, Tom."

"You're easy to be good too. You're beautiful."

She blushed and looked at the table, her magnificent blue eyes veiled by long thick lashes. "Christmas is a hard time," she confessed. "It's a time for families."

His eyes caressed her and his strong sense of desire was mixed with sympathy. Colleen's mother had died in childbirth, her father had been a member of the IRA and was killed in a retaliatory raid by the Ulster Volunteers. Her brother had died in a rail accident. "We'll have a good Christmas," he promised her. "We'll be our own family."

8

December 25, 1933

Boston

"It'll be a happy new year, this year!" Padraic announced. "The first year in many without Prohibition!"

Emerald sank into the chair and put her feet up. "I feel glutted," she announced.

"Too much turkey and trimmings," Joe agreed, leaning back.

Emerald yawned. "It's a disgrace—it's only four in the afternoon, and I feel like it's midnight."

"Busy day, Christmas. Up at seven for mass, home to open presents, big dinner."

The children came hurtling down the stairs. "We're going to the Commons!" J.J. announced. "Edward wants to use his new sled!"

"And we want to skate!" Seamus beamed.

"Is the pond frozen over?" Emerald asked.

"Of course it is!" Katie was all dolled up in her new skating outfit and she tossed her scarf over her shoulder dramatically.

"She just wants everyone to see her," J.J. said with some disgust. "She'll just put on her skates and sit on the bench showing off."

"I will not!" Katie retorted. "But I do love it, it's all soft!" She caressed her own face with the rabbit-skin tassel on her scarf.

"You're to be careful," Emerald instructed. "You look and make certain the 'Safe Skating' sign is up."

"We wouldn't want Katie to get her rabbit skin wet," J.J. sang, doing a fine imitation of his twin sister.

"She told everyone it was ermine." Seamus laughed.

"I did not! Oh, it's a curse to have nothing but brothers! You're all boorish!"

Emerald laughed. Her daughter's imitation of Katharine Hepburn was improving. "Off with you, and stop fighting."

Skates and sleds; scarves, hats, and coats—the children hurried out the door and headed toward Boyleston Street on the short trek to the Common.

Joe set down his whiskey and leaned forward. "Peace and relative quiet." He smiled. "Now we can talk."

"That sounds serious." Emerald smiled.

"A Christmas surpise I didn't give you this morning."

"Oh, I like surprises . . . better when they go on all day long."

"Well, I waited till now because this one involves Padraic as well."

Padraic laughed and gulped down some of his drink. "I haven't been surprised in a long while!"

Joe took a deep breath. "The president called yesterday. He has asked me to take up an ambassadorial post in the spring."

"Oh, Joe! That's wonderful!" Emerald's eyes glistened with the pride she felt for her husband and his success.

"If I accept, I'll have to ask you, Padraic, to look after the businesses—I couldn't trust anyone but you, you're family."

"You know I'll do anything I can." Padraic beamed.

"Don't keep me in suspense! Where are we going?" Emerald said eagerly.

"Ireland." Joe smiled. "To Dublin."

"Ireland! Oh, Joe! Ireland!" She ran across the room and embraced her husband. "Ireland, I can't believe it!"

"I'm afraid as an ambassador's wife you can't be occupying any post offices!"

Emerald giggled. "For how long?" she prodded.

"Two or three years."

"Oh, Joe, it's wonderful! But what a nasty thing to do to the British! Sending an Irish-American to Ireland!"

"I think he knows how funny it is. He made me promise you'd be good."

Emerald hugged him. "Very good," she promised. And she thought happily to herself: And I'll be near Tom, too.

25

1

June 1934

"This is a rather grand reception," Emerald said, looking around. "Never in my wildest dreams did I think I'd be returning to Ireland under these circumstances."

"An ambassador has certain social obligations, my darling."

Emerald squeezed Joe's arm. The reception line had seemed endless, as if half of Ireland had come to welcome them.

Eamon de Valera was overjoyed, to say the least. And he insisted on holding the reception for the new ambassador in the regal charm of Dublin Castle—"The one objective we didn't take in 1916! Well, Emerald, you shall occupy Dublin Castle today!" he had told her.

De Valera strolled toward them, a rare grin on his narrow face. "A fine turnout," he observed. Nineteen-thirty-two was a good year! I was elected prime minister, and your Mr. Roosevelt was elected president. And as a special gift, he sent me the Scanlons of Boston to represent his government."

"It's wonderful to be back in Dublin," Joe replied.

"And even nicer to be in Dublin Castle," Emerald joked.

"Ah, my dear, I'm so relieved that ten years in America has not changed your Irish lilt."

Emerald blushed. She felt alive with happiness and anticipation. Not only was she home in Dublin, but she'd had a letter from Tom. He wanted her to come to Belfast, he wanted her to meet the girl he was going to marry.

"Joe will be a fine ambassador," Emerald said proudly. "But frankly, Eamon, I'm at a loss. I don't think I can just sit around being an ambassador's wife."

"I've heard about you. There's a lot of traffic between Dublin and Boston. I heard about Emerald Scanlon's work with orphans and on Jim Curley's committees. Last year one of Jim's boys was here on a little visit and I asked after you, and he said, 'Emerald Scanlon! The mayor wouldn't set up a committee without her! Because, the praise goes, other committees meet, Emerald's committees work.' "

"That's a bit of an exaggeration."

"No, it's not," Joe corrected.

Eamon scratched his cheek and looked at her thoughtfully. "I don't think an ambassador's wife can go back to working on hospital wards, but it's not unheard-of to be involved with social work. My dear Emerald, I don't think you need be idle."

Emerald smiled. "I should like to work with orphans," she said almost wistfully.

"I'm certain it can be arranged. Tell me, how is little Tom?"

Emerald laughed. "Oh, dear, Eamon, 'little' Tom is six feet tall."

De Valera blushed himself. "I don't like to think of time passing so quickly. Did he come to Ireland with you?"

"He's been in Belfast for the last year."

"Finding himself, as we Americans say," Joe added.

"And has he?" Eamon asked.

"He's found a girl. I suppose that might be almost as good."

"I think we should mingle with the guests," Emerald suggested.

"You mingle. I have a few more things to discuss with Eamon."

"And a woman gets in the way . . ." Emerald looked lovingly at Joe and walked across the room, stopping here and there to speak to people.

"Ah, Mrs. Scanlon . . ."

Emerald turned to face a short round man. He held a drink in one hand and the left side of his face twitched ever so slightly. He had a hard face, but, Emerald thought, a familiar face. "Do I know you?" she asked.

"I think you do. I was in the post office back in 1916 when you were just a slip of a young girl, a pretty little nurse."

Emerald leaned forward a bit. The post office . . . His face was older, and he was fatter. The incident came back to her in a rush. She had asked the postmaster where the first-aid supplies were; the man had insulted her. And the man that stood across from her now was the man who had rushed up and broken the postmaster's nose, nearly killing the man in savage retaliation. Emerald remembered it all; she remembered the glint of pure hatred in her defender's eyes . . . she remembered having begged him to stop.

"I remember you," she said coolly.

"It's nice to have you back in Ireland," he announced. "You're a woman of influence . . . that's nice too." He leaned over to her conspiringly. "It's even nicer since your son is one of us."

"One of us?" Emerald said even as the feeling of apprehension swept over her.

"IRA," the man whispered. "Working for us in Belfast, I hear tell." He made a face. "You can't be too careful. De Valera's against us, you know."

Emerald felt rooted to the floor. A chill ran right through her. IRA . . . She repeated the man's words to herself and he babbled on, assuming she knew, assuming she approved of what the IRA had become.

She took a deep breath, forcing herself to recover. "We shouldn't discuss this in public," she returned.

The man—Paddy, that was his name—glanced to the far side of the room at de Valera and Joe, who were still talking. "You're dead right," he allowed. "Still, I wanted to say something. It's nice to have you back in Ireland."

2

July 1, 1934

Belfast

Emerald walked up the steps of the church, turned, and stood a moment looking out on the deserted churchyard. A warm July breeze rustled through the old tree and the crocuses quivered on their long stems.

She clutched her purse. The steps of this church brought back a hundred memories, memories of a horror-filled night almost twenty-five years ago when she had run terrified through the streets of Belfast in search of "Catholics." And here, on these very steps, they had found her the next morning: a soaking-wet, frightened young woman, a young woman deprived of her culture and ignorant of the world.

The church bells pealed out the hour of noon, and instinctively Emerald checked her small gold watch. Joe had wanted to come with her to talk to Tom, but Emerald had insisted that she must come alone. "I can travel incognito and meet him privately. You must not get involved with this. Even the hint that Tom is involved with the IRA could ruin your career as an ambassador. No, Joe, just this once I must do something alone." And she had added, "This is between mother and son. I understand what he's gotten himself into. Force won't bring him back; he's infected with the romance of the IRA, he doesn't understand."

She turned and opened the heavy doors of the church. The foyer was empty. She put a few coins in the offering box and

anointed herself with holy water; then she genuflected and walked
down the aisle, slipping into a darkened pew.

She took out her rosary and said it a few times. Then, as if he
materialized out of the shadows, Tom slipped into the pew next
to her.

"Mother . . ." He leaned over and kissed her cheek. "What's
all this mystery? Why did you insist I meet you here? I want you
to meet Colleen."

Emerald shook her head. "Not yet, not now."

"What is it?" he pressed. "You're acting very strange."

"Tom, I am an ambassador's wife, your stepfather is an
ambassador. It's a delicate position. A hint of . . . Tom, I know
what you're involved in. How could you have become involved
with the IRA?"

"The IRA?"

He's trying to sound naive, Emerald thought. But his voice
doesn't ring true. "Don't try to deny it. Don't lie to me!" She
turned and faced him, catching the look of guilt in his eyes.

"They're killing Catholics here! Ulster belongs to Ireland,
you can only fight their hatred and murder with force."

"You're fighting it with more hatred and murder."

"You don't believe that Ulster belongs to Ireland?" His whisper sounded angrier.

"Of course I do. But murdering people won't achieve a united
Ireland. I'll not have you turn into another Michael Collins, killing
little children to teach their parents a lesson. Don't tell me about
the IRA! Once they were a real army of young men fighting for
Ireland, but during our civil war they were torn apart, and what
survives today are brutal terrorists." Emerald realized that even
though she was whispering, she was angry and her whisper was
loud. She looked around; then, realizing the church was quite
empty, she leaned back and tried to regain her control in spite
of the fact that she was tense all over.

Tom didn't answer immediately. He folded his hands and
leaned forward, studying the red-velvet kneeling bench. It was
faded and worn. "I'm going to stay in Belfast, Mother. I'm
going to get on by myself. I've met a girl, as I wrote you. I'm
going to marry her, as I wrote you. I love you all, but I'm not
really a Scanlon. I'm a Hughes. I'm cut from another cloth."

"And does this girl know about the IRA?"

Tom shook his head. "No," he replied. "But she's an orphan,
her father was killed by the Ulster Volunteers."

"That doesn't mean she would favor a husband in the IRA."

"She probably wouldn't—she's rather like you, actually."

Emerald inhaled. "I don't understand you," she admitted. "You may be Joe's stepson, but he's always treated you as a son. You're very much a part of the family. I don't know what happened that made you feel otherwise."

He shrugged. "I'm not sure."

"You've always resented it because I sent you to America?"

"I suppose. I don't know. It was a long time ago. I suppose I didn't understand."

"Do you understand now?"

"I'm not sure. I only know I'd never leave my child if I had one."

"Oh, Tom! You don't understand how it was. But if you look, you'll see it here. You'll see how the children are . . . you'll see their little faces twisted with hatred; you'll see the fearful memories . . . their children, Tom. Children of Ireland's troubles."

"Maybe I'll understand one day. I just don't understand now. And I don't understand my father, either. I keep trying, but I don't."

"The IRA isn't going to help you understand it either. Tom, listen to me . . . I beg you to listen to me. Get out of the IRA, please."

"I'll have to think about it."

"Tom, when you decide to leave them, you bring your girl to Dublin to get married. I want to know her, I want her to know us. But, Tom, don't come till you've left the IRA."

"Are you cutting me off, is that what you're saying?"

"I'm saying I feel strongly about this. I'm saying I don't want to see you until you sever your relationship with them."

"You'd do anything to protect Joe, wouldn't you?" He said it meanly and turned to look at his mother.

Emerald's eyes flashed with her own sudden anger and exasperation. She lifted her hand and slapped him hard. The sound of the slap against his flesh echoed through the deserted church. "I'd do anything to protect you," she said, tears welling in her eyes.

Tom's hand went to his face, and he stroked the slap with his hand. "You've never hit me before," he said in a shocked tone.

Emerald blinked at him. It was true, she had never hit any of her children. "You pushed too far, Tom." She said it sadly. Then she stood up. "I'm leaving. Write if you change your mind."

3

July 2, 1934

Belfast

Tom Hughes sat at Colleen's table and stared into a glass of porter.

"You're very sullen," she said, sitting down. "Your mother doesn't like the idea of our getting married, does she? I knew she wouldn't, that's why she didn't come here. Mind you, it would have been embarrassing to have her see how I live, and I can't blame her. She probably thinks I'm after your money—"

"Stop it!" Tom looked up, his face etched in pain. "Stop degrading yourself, it has nothing to do with you. Besides, my mother wouldn't care if you were a char girl or a princess, she's not like that."

Colleen reached across the table; her warm hand covered his. "I'm sorry, but you're so sad, I thought that must be it."

Tom shook his head. "No, that's not it. It's something else."

"I love you," Colleen said softly. "Can't you confide in me? Tom, what kind of marriage can we have if you don't trust me? Please . . ."

He looked across at her. Her intense blue eyes bored through him; she looked hurt and she looked worried.

He nodded silently. "I've been involved with the IRA. All these many months, didn't you ever wonder where I went, where I disappeared to?"

Colleen let out a little gasp of surprise, but the expression on her face said far more than words. She looked stricken.

"I was going to tell you . . . I didn't know how you'd feel."

Colleen was shaking her head. "No, no . . . why didn't you tell me? Oh, Tom, that's a terrible secret to keep."

"I wanted to tell you, I really did."

"Tom, you couldn't do what those people do, you're not the type. . . . Please . . . I love you. Please give it up."

"Your father was a member." He paused.

"My father died as a result. Oh, no, Tom, that's not the way, it's not."

"That's what my mother says."

"Your mother's right."

"If I leave them, will you still marry me?"

Colleen nodded. "I love you, I told you that."

"I'll leave them," he answered slowly. But he thought to himself, the IRA was not the easiest organization to leave.

4

July 10, 1934

Dublin

Dear Mother,

I've been thinking over our talk . . . no, I've been talking to Colleen about our talk. She does feel as you do and so I have decided to leave the IRA and come to live in Dublin for a time. We will be arriving in a few weeks' time. Dear Mother, I'm sorry for everything . . . I always am. But I know you will love Colleen—this is one thing I've gotten myself into that won't disappoint you.

Love,
Tom

"Well, I've had a lot of letters from Tom. This is one of the few that's made me truly happy."

"Sounds as if he's finally growing up."

"I hope so, if he's going to get married." Emerald folded the letter and put it away.

"Married is safer than the IRA." Joe smiled. "My God, you do look as if you've had the weight of the world taken from you. Good! Next month is a month to end all months!"

"Well, it's an expensive month."

Joe grinned. "It's your birthday, Seamus' birthday, and the twins' birthday, and, by God, our eleventh wedding anniversary!"

"That's what I said, it's an expensive month."

"I'll manage to get through it financially."

Emerald lay down on the bed. "It's been a day and a half," she said casually.

"I'll have to go home for consultations in September. You want to come, or stay here?"

"September's an inconvenient time, the children are going back to school then."

"Mrs. Reilly can well take care of them for a few weeks. You know I love ocean voyages with you."

She smiled up at him and sat down on the edge of the bed. "Too tired to make love?"

"Never."

"Good. We'll practice for the trip." He laughed and bent down to her. "You make love to me tonight," he suggested.

"I might," she said, touching him lightly.

Joe discarded his dressing gown and rolled over. "I guess you won't have too much trouble arousing me. It's that slip . . . I like you in slips."

"You're quite a wonder," she replied playfully.

"Oh, my dear, I like that," he answered.

5

August 21, 1934

The ambassadorial home was on the outskirts of Dublin, surrounded by rolling hills and parkland. It was a huge old mansion with twelve bedrooms, a spacious drawing room, a cozy parlor, a study, and downstairs, a billiards room.

The Scanlon clan had finished their dinner—a special anniversary dinner of squab and fresh asparagus, candied sweet potatoes, and a huge cake.

"I'm glad we didn't go out alone," Emerald announced. "This is such a celebration—we're all under one roof again! Oh, Joe . . . a big family means so much to me, because I didn't have any family as a child, I guess."

"Well, we certainly have made up for it."

Katie danced into the room, humming a song. She and J.J. had just turned ten, and Katie was feeling especially grown-up.

"Where are your brothers?" Emerald asked.

"Seamus is playing upstairs—he's teaching Edward Monopoly. They wanted me to be banker, but I didn't want to be banker."

"Don't you like money?" Joe asked.

"Not play money," Katie replied quickly.

"A child after my own heart," Joe joked.

"I haven't told you where Tom is. Tom is in the billiards room with what's-her-name. When they get married, will Tom go and live with her?"

"She has a name, and you know it quite well. Her name is Colleen, not what's-her-name. And, yes, when they get married, they'll live alone together."

"Why can't he live with us?" Katie pouted.

"Because he's older, and they need to have a home of their own."

"I'm not sure I like her all that much."

"She's a lovely girl. I'm surprised at you!"

"She's all right, I suppose . . ." Katie whirled around. "I think I'll go talk to Cook," she announced as she pranced out of the room.

Emerald turned to Joe with a knowing look. "I think she's a wee bit jealous. She always had a crush on her older brother."

"She'll get over it. Come here, I've been trying to be alone all day with you. It's not easy with four children and a happily engaged couple around."

Emerald went and sat by her husband's side. "And why do you want to be alone?"

He smiled lovingly at her. "I have a trinket for you." He withdrew a small box from his pocket. "Rightfully, I should have given you this last year, but we were traveling. Happy eleventh wedding anniversary, my darling." He reached over and drew her into his arms, kissing her on the mouth. "And may we have many more."

"Oh, Joe . . . what is it?"

"Open it and find out."

"Oh, Joe . . . it's truly beautiful! It's exquisite! A diamond bracelet—oh, you shouldn't have spent so much money!"

He burst out laughing. "Damned if you didn't say the same thing exactly eleven years ago!"

She laughed and leaned against him. "And now Tom is getting married. Time does pass too quickly."

"He better get married, they both have that look."

"What look?"

"The look that says they're either sleeping together or will be soon."

"I think they can wait another ten days for the wedding."

"I hope so. A solemn high mass! God, what an ordeal!"

"Now, now . . . just because we got married outdoors in a near-rainstorm doesn't mean they have to."

"Out of the question anyway. When you talked Eamon into giving the bride away, I distinctly remember that he agreed only if the wedding was to be indoors."

Emerald snapped the bracelet on her arm. "Oh, it's so beautiful."

"I agree. It's the most beautiful arm in Dublin."

"Sh." Emerald smiled. "Sh! And let me tell you how much I adore you and how glad I am we found each other."

6

September 1, 1934

Tom Hughes lay on the bed and watched Colleen as she brushed her long, thick, jet-black hair. She was wearing a long white nightdress; she was all dark hair and milk-white skin, and he surmised, she was nervous as well as tired.

"I thought I'd die during the wedding," she told him. "I've never seen so many people, I never believed a solemn high mass could last so long! All those people staring and staring . . ."

"You were something to stare at," he said admiringly. "This is the inn where my father brought my mother on their wedding night . . . my real father."

Colleen put down the brush and came over to him. "It's very nice here, peaceful."

"You're very nice." He reached up and drew her down to him. "Don't be nervous, please."

"I can't help it."

"Sh, come here."

He could feel himself ready, but he continued to caress her. He pulled down her nightdress and rubbed his face against her soft white skin, and she shivered in his arms.

A man should move slowly, he thought. A woman, especially a virgin, had to be aroused. He toyed with her awhile longer but he felt he was going to burst. He began to move more quickly, more roughly. Unable to hold back, he parted her legs and entered her. She cried out and tensed beneath him.

"I hurt you, I'm sorry." He blurted out the words, but he couldn't stop himself. "I'm clumsy," he said after a while. " I love you so much, I waited so long . . ."

She moved next to him silently, moaning a little.

"I wanted you too much." He pulled her back into his arms. "I'm a terrible lover."

"No you're not. I'm all right now."

He rocked her in his arms and felt her damp, lovely, sweet smelling body next to his. Slowly he moved his hands on her back, rubbing her gently, feeling her rounded buttocks, touching her softly.

She moaned again, but this time he knew it was in pleasure and he gently turned her on her back so he could kiss her lovely breasts. She put her arms around him and moved his hands over her front as he had her back until she was glowing warm in his arms, and returning his kisses with a hot passion, a passion he had always suspected lay beneath the surface of her shyness.

Slowly he entered her again, and this time he was able to control himself till he felt her shaking in his arms, quivering with pleasure.

Then they lay quietly for a long while, half-asleep, half-awake.

"It's better the second time," he told her.

She nodded her head against his chest. "Tom, how long will we stay in Dublin?"

He shrugged. "A year maybe, then we'll go back to Belfast."

He pressed her more tightly to him, but the face of Jim Brody clouded his mind. "You don't leave the IRA," Brody had warned. "It's not as easy as hello and good-bye. You know too much, you poor stupid son of a bitch. Nobody just up and leaves."

"A year seems like a long time." Colleen sighed.

"We can be close to my family . . . . they'll be going back to the States by then anyway. At least I think so."

He hadn't told her about the threats. He hadn't told anyone.

7

July 15, 1935

The train station was filled to overflowing with summer travelers who brushed past Emerald, Joe, Tom, and Colleen.

Emerald still carried the baby in her arms; Tom carried the empty basket in which little Emmy would sleep.

"You're taking my baby away," Emerald said reproachfully. "And to think that I was there when you were born, my very first grandchild. Oh, she's so lovely."

"That's why we named her after you." Colleen beamed.

Emerald smiled warmly at her daughter-in-law. She was a different girl now; she had come out of herself and she was more lively and happier. And what a difference marriage had made in Tom, Emerald thought. He seemed responsible, settled, calm for the first time in his life.

"Belfast is only a few hours on the train," Colleen said. "You'll come often."

"As often as I can—oh, I won't make a pest of myself. But we will be going back to America in six months, and then, unless we can persuade you and Tom to come, I'll be a lot farther away than a few hours!"

"The train's loading." Tom took Colleen's arm. "We better be going."

Emerald handed Colleen the baby. "I do this reluctantly," she told her. "But I'm putting her in good hands." She leaned over and embraced Colleen. "You're like a second daughter, you know."

Colleen's lovely eyes were misty. "You've been a mother to me, too. Oh, I've learned so much from you."

Emerald kissed her again; then she hugged Tom. "Take care of them," she said.

Joe kissed Colleen and bear-hugged Tom. "Take care." He waved as the three of them headed off for the train. "Our car is waiting." He took Emerald's arm.

"I really do hate to see them go. Damn, I wish he weren't so stubborn. I want him to bring them home, back to Boston when we go."

"And you wish he weren't going back to Belfast."

"That too," she said, shaking her head. "What's happening in Germany is making me uneasy. All I see and read is militarization. All those people marching around. I've felt uneasy since Hitler renounced the Versailles Treaty. I keep getting this uneasy feeling that Germany is on the move again, or will be soon."

"You're not the only one who feels that way. But you have to remember what the Versailles Treaty did to Germany. It destroyed the country economically."

"I know, it's just that I wish they'd come home to America with us."

"With an ocean in between America and Europe's troubles."

"Yes," Emerald said thoughtfully, "with an ocean between."

"Mind if we don't go home?" Joe asked as their chauffeur-driven black limousine pulled away from Heuston Station.

"Not go home?" Emerald questioned.

"It's Sunday, it's ten in the morning, and we have the whole glorious day. Let's go for a ride out in the country."

"I'd like that. Let's start with our rock altar."

"I'd like that," Joe smiled.

"The Irish countryside is so peaceful . . .it's such a marked difference to its history." Emerald gazed out the window as they wound through the hills.

"Why do you really want them to come back to America?"

Joe asked when they were standing near the altar and looking out into the valley below.

"Because I don't want my grandchild raised in Ulster, Joe. I've seen too much of the casual brutality there, too much of what it does to the little ones."

"I knew that was it, I knew it wasn't Hitler and Germany."

"That's a side worry," she answered, trying to smile. "When I was working at the orphanage, I met a twelve-year-old boy whose parents were killed in our civil war. He's been without a soul in this world since he was two months old. He doesn't know what to make of it all, he doesn't know whom to blame. One day he'll be good material for the IRA—he's twelve years old and he's filled with nameless, faceless hate. And that's here in Dublin, that's our legacy from the Irish civil war. Eamon will outlaw the IRA . . . but that won't stop them. All that will stop them is an end to the hate."

"You're a strange mixture of woman, Emerald Scanlon."

"I suppose I am."

He reached across the distance between them and playfully slapped her behind. "Enough of this. Do you remember when we brought the children here?"

"I don't think Katie was very impressed." Emerald laughed.

"Seamus liked it."

"Because there are fish in the stream, not because this is the spot we were married."

"We have good children, Emerald."

She turned and kissed him. "We have a good life," she replied.

26

1

February 12, 1936

Belfast

Tom Hughes crouched in the shadows and stared at the building across the street—his building, the place where he lived.

Confused thoughts filled his mind and he fought to keep from vomiting again. "For want of a nail, the kingdom was lost. . . ." He spoke the words to himself; it was an old nursery rhyme, one he used to read to his little daughter, though she was too young to understand and only giggled at the sound of his voice.

That thought was chased away by the image of Colleen on their wedding night. The milk-white skin, the soft pliable body, the perfect sweet face, her always loving ways . . . He choked on a sob and shook himself.

Days . . . a matter of days, and they would have been safe! For want of a nail . . . No, because of my pride, he confessed. My stupid goddamned pride!

The first six months in Belfast had been peaceful, idyllic. Then, right after his mother's last visit a month ago, it had all begun to crumble and fall apart.

His mother had begged him to come to America with them when they left in January, but he had rejected the idea. "Life is hard here," he told her. "But it's our life. I can't live off Joe. I have to make my own way."

That was the sin of pride, and now it had cost him everything.

A week after his mother's visit he met Brody, whom he hadn't seen in a year. "They know you're back in Belfast, my boy, they hear you've been chummy with de Valera . . . you know too much, boy. You're in real trouble with Eoin McDuffy. He's a mean one. I'd hightail it out of Belfast if I was you. In fact, if I was you, I'd hightail it right out of Ireland and back where you came from."

Tom took Brody seriously and began to make plans to take Colleen and little Emmy to America. But still, pride intervened and he didn't wire Joe for money. He waited, he wasted a precious week before he wired his Uncle Padraic. But Padraic didn't get the wire immediately because he was away on business— another week of time lost. Then today . . . today the money for passage and expenses had arrived. Tom had it in his pocket, but it was too late.

He stomped his foot on the sidewalk and he pounded his bare fist against the side of the brick building he was standing beside. Blood trickled from his knuckles, and in sheer anguish he looked again at the pile of rubble that had been his home. His flat was dead center of the explosion—dead center for seven sticks of dynamite.

The fireman had found a baby's arm clutching a teddy bear, tiny fingers holding fast to the bear's arm. No other part of little Emmy was found. Teeth, a few bones, and a finger with a plain gold wedding band had given evidence that Colleen too was blown to bits.

Tom felt the vomit rising in his throat again, and uncontrollably he retched on the sidewalk. They were dead because of him, because of his former connections with the bellicose Eoin McDuffy, whose particuliar IRA cell was highly militant, highly fascist. In fact, they now called themselves the Blue Shirts.

Tears welled in Tom's eyes, and he wiped his cheek with his bloodied hand. "I'll get you, you son of a bitch," he mumbled. "If it's the last thing I ever do on this earth!"

2

February 27, 1936

Emerald picked up the teacups and they rattled in her hand because she was still shaking uncontrollably.

"I wish you could stop working," Joe looked at her pleadingly. She was nothing short of manic and had been since the first telegram telling them about Colleen and the baby. Then yesterday there was a letter from Tom—a long guilt-ridden miserable letter. And, he thought, it made it no better that they didn't know where Tom was, only that he was wandering around Europe lost and alone.

"I can't stop working. I have to keep moving. Joe, I can't give my mind time to think, to conjure up images. My God! I can't, I just can't!" She hurried off to the kitchen with the cups. Her eyes were puffy from crying, she hadn't taken more than tea and toast for two weeks, and she looked haggard and deathly pale.

He poured himself a drink and gulped it down; then he poured another. She's a strong woman, he thought. She's dealing with her grief in the only way she knows how, by driving herself to physical exhaustion so she can sleep.

He wanted to be able to reach out to her, to hold her and to protect her. But there was no protection for what she saw in her mind's eye.

In her grief, Joe admitted he found something else to admire about his wife. She wouldn't take the pills the doctor offered her. "I don't want them," she had insisted. "I'm not sick. I have to work this out in my own way."

And work Emerald had. She sent the servants away and she washed every floor in the house. Now she was working on the windows while their curious neighbor, Mrs. Clapp, hung her head out the window next door in amazement.

At night Emerald insisted on making dinner, on doing the dishes, on leaving every room in the house spotless. He had watched her polishing furniture until her face appeared in the fine wood; he had seen the look of dogged determination on her face and the anger she applied to scratches.

"Can you sit down for a minute?" he asked softly in a tone that implied he would understand if she couldn't.

Emerald nodded and slipped into one of the high-backed chairs behind the massive dining-room table.

"How about a drink?"

She hesitated, and he understood. Emerald didn't drink when she needed to.

"One," she gave in. "Make it weak."

He poured the drink and handed it to her. "You look exhausted."

She shook her head and let out her breath. "Not yet, but I'm trying."

"Emerald, you can't go on like this much longer."

"If only Tom would come back. It's bad enough to think about . . ." She couldn't even say their names. ". . . without worrying about Tom. Oh, Joe, he must be torn apart. He tried to break with them—that's what his letter said."

"Tom will be all right. You have your way of working these things out, he has his. Let him wander around a bit, let him find his own way."

He waited and let his words settle on her mind. "Emerald, why don't you go to the retreat? It's quiet, it's peaceful, and Mother Superior is a good woman, she can help you."

"It'll give me too much time to think," Emerald protested.

"I feel you're ready to think. In fact, I'm certain you have to face what you keep running from." He reached out and took her hand. "You have to confront the images that haunt you."

She lifted her hands to her face and began to sob. "She was only a little baby, a sweet little baby! And Colleen was a sweet, good girl. Joe, how could anyone . . .? How could they!"

Joe leaned across the table and kissed her forehead. "Please go to the retreat, Emerald. Please."

Emerald nodded.

Joe let out his breath. "I'll drive you up there tomorrow."

3

March 15, 1936

The retreat, run by the sisters of Saint Mary's, was nestled in the rolling Massachusetts hills, several miles from Amherst.

The room in which Emerald stayed was a tiny cell with an iron bed, a small table with a washbasin, and a black ebony crucifix hanging on the wall.

Outside, among the trees, were the stations of the cross, and each morning and evening, no matter what the weather, Emerald followed the path of Christ, saying prayers and relishing the sheer beauty of the surroundings.

The ground was snow-covered and the trees bare. The wind rustled through them, and only a few birds risked the winter snows.

Every day Emerald had long talks with Mother Superior, who quietly counseled her and made her face the images she so feared, the faces of her dead grandchild and her young vibrant daughter-in-law. Finally Emerald mourned openly, releasing her grief and finding strength where she always had, in her church.

Emerald completed the last station of the cross and walked slowly through the snow toward the great iron gates that separated the nunnery from the rest of the world.

Outside, Joe would be waiting to take her home. She had already shed her long plain garments for her dress and coat; she had bid the nuns good-bye.

She skirted the chapel and walked beside it, heading for the gate, where she could see the car parked on the other side. Joe was leaning against it, and she waved to him and quickened her step.

She reached the gate, and Joe picked up her suitcase, which was already there. He put it in the trunk and opened the door. He leaned over and kissed her when she got into the car. "You look wonderful, you look rested."

"You were right to suggest I come here," Emerald told him as she settled back against the seat and he backed down the winding driveway. "It was so peaceful."

"Ready to rejoin the world?"

"Yes. I missed you."

He stole a glance at her. She wasn't wearing any makeup, but her complexion was beautiful and placid. Her hair was pulled back, her lovely eyes clear.

"I'm having most unreligious thoughts," he admitted.

"So am I," she whispered back.

They drove on for a while in silence, and Emerald thought how unnecessary it was for them to talk. They always seemed to be in communication even when they were silent. As if to prove what she had been thinking, she sensed he was keeping something from her. She was about to frame the question, but Joe spoke first.

"There's been a letter from Tom."

"Did you open it?"

"Yes. It's in the glove compartment. Read it."

Emerald opened the compartment and took out the letter. She unfolded it, and her son's writing stared up at her from the blue writing paper.

> Dear Mother and Joe,
> I'm in France. I've been wandering around for a month, but I think I'll stay here in the south for a while. I'm living in Nice, in a pleasant little hotel. I can see the ocean from my window. I still have no clarity, but I'm feeling less suicidal—I shouldn't say that to you, but I have to.
> I'd like to stay here for a while. Maybe in the summer I'll go up to the wine country and tramp grapes—I still feel like tramping. Don't worry. I'll come home when I can, this time I promise.
> Tell Uncle Padraic I'll pay him back. Tell him I love him. And, mother, I love you.
>
>   Tom

Emerald let out a long sigh. "He's going to be all right," she said confidently.

Joe nodded. "He'll be fine."

4

November 1936

Nice

Tom Hughes set down the Belfast paper on the table. He had come by it through sheer accident; a tourist had left it behind.

"More wine?" the fat waiter in the strained apron asked. He spoke in the peculiar Niçois accent, part Italian, part French.

Tom nodded. The wine cellar was down two flights of stairs. It was dark, cool, and damp. It smelled of red wine, garlic, and cheese. Not ordinary cheese, but potent, well-aged French cheese. And every bottle of home-brewed wine came with a plate of the cheese, half a loaf of heavy French bread, and a branch of red grapes. "You drink here, you don't have to eat," the waiter always joked.

"Yes, more wine," Tom answered. He'd spent a hundred days in this place, or so it seemed. The rest of the time he spent on the beach or wandering through the hilly town.

And true to his letter, he had spent the summer in the wine country earning a bit of money. But now he had returned to Nice, where at least the roly-poly waiter was his friend.

"It's not been a wasted year," he wrote to his mother. "I've learned to speak passable French, always an asset in Back Bay Boston." And he had promised to come home in April.

Tom flipped through the Belfast newspaper and suddenly his eyes fell on the name Eoin McDuffy. He closed his eyes and mentally envisaged his enemy's face, the face of the man he held personally responsible for the death of his wife and child. He bit his lower lip and took another sip of wine.

Tom moved the flickering candle on the table closer and began to read the article. Eoin McDuffy had taken his fascist Blue Shirts, as his followers were now known, and announced they would be fighting in Spain for the Nationalists. "Many others in the illegal IRA," the article commented, "have gone to fight for the Republicans. Good riddance to them all, let Spain have them."

The paper was an Ulster Protestant publication; it was Conservative in the extreme and viewed all those fighting in Spain dubiously with the view "a plague on both your houses."

"Fucking fascist bastard," Tom mumbled under his breath.

Spain—Spain was on fire and Germany was fanning the flames with arms. It was, he surmised, a situation much like Ireland. Spain was a poor oppressed country; Spain and the Spanish Republicans were fighting for freedom and independence. People from all over the world were coming to Spain; they were coming to fight for freedom, though some, like Eoin McDuffy, were fighting for oppression.

"Seldom does a man have both personal and idealistic reasons for fighting," Tom said aloud to himself. He doubled his fist and closed his eyes. "I'm sorry, Mother," he murmured, "but I can't let the Eoin McDuffys win. I can't."

Tom Hughes finished his wine and paid his bill. He walked slowly through the winding narrow streets back to his hotel. Once there, he took pen to paper to write home:

> Dear Mother and Joe,
>   I know you will not approve what I am about to do. I can only hope and pray that you understand the reasons. I know (especially you, Mother) you do not approve of war. But there is a time for war, a time when a man cannot stand by, cannot negotiate with his enemy. For me, that time has come.
>   Colleen and Emmy were murdered by a section of the IRA, an especially murderous section, a group of men who now call themselves the Blue Shirts. They were murdered because I knew too much, because I tried to leave. Let me say in passing that I was never involved in killing during my short relationship with these people. I was an errand boy, one who just found out too much. Then too, and I don't have to tell you this, when the IRA was outlawed in the Republic of Ireland, this group and others turned against their own. The rifts caused within the IRA during the Irish civil war have never been healed. Perhaps they never will be.
>   Now I have read that Eoin McDuffy and his Blue Shirts have gone to Spain to fight for the fascists. Other Irish—some from other sections of the IRA—have and are going to fight for the Republic.
>   Oh, I do not delude myself. This is not a war to end all wars (is there such a thing?), but it is a war that will ask the world one question: should the Eoin McDuffys and their ilk be allowed to pillage, kill, and ultimately rule the lives of people?

I cannot deny my personal reasons for going to Spain to fight for the Republicans, but the question raised above is also very much on my mind, Mother.

I know I wrote I was coming home in April. But now I can't. Please, Mother, forgive me. Try to understand that I am older now and I know what I'm doing.

And, Mother, one last thing. I understand why my father died in a British uniform. I understand that he believed the German advance through Europe was more threatening than the British. If you think I'm too idealistic, Mother, then know this—it's a different kind of idealism. There are some things a man has to do. If I didn't go to fight against Eoin McDuffy and his kind, I couldn't live with myself.

I love you, Mother,
And, Joe, thanks,

Tom

5

February 1937

Spain

Tom Hughes lay absolutely flat. His face was in the dirt, his fingers dug in, clawing at the ground. He knew there were tears in his eyes: tears of anger and tears of fright as the hand grenades exploded around him. He jumped with each noise; he shook and wanted to scream. His whole body cried out in pain; he couldn't remember when he'd felt a bed, had a bath, eaten his last hot meal. All he remembered was the sounds of ceaseless gunfire, the sudden whistle and then the burst of the shells, and now cannon—thundering cannon which grew closer and closer, louder and louder, till now, with his face in the dirt and his ear to the ground, he could feel the earth shake in near-unison with his own pounding heart.

He had arrived in Spain on February 7, and while the Lincoln Brigade, to which he and other Irish fighting for the Republicans were assigned, was supposed to be the offensive, they found themselves instead thrust into a retreat confused by the large numbers of newcomers in the ranks and by a surprise attack by Nationalist forces which began on February 6.

Tom had joined the battle at the junction of the Manzanares and Jarama rivers, in the Jarama Valley. Originally he was supposed to have been a part of the government's new offensive led by Largo Caballero, but instead he and the others had faced a Nationalist offensive and were thrown into a battle the likes of which Tom Hughes could not even have imagined.

The Nationalist weaponry was vastly superior to the Republicans', on whose side he fought. The Nationalists had 155-mm batteries and 88-mm guns. Their intent seemed to be to cut the Madrid-Valencia high road, and toward that end they had undertaken their attack along a nine-mile front running north to south from a line to the east of the Madrid and Andalusia high road.

That, Tom Hughes thought, was the last bit of official news he had received. Since then he had seen seven of his comrades blown to bits and he himself had only barely escaped a direct hit into the gully in which he and two others had taken refuge.

Then, after a twenty-two-hour nightmare, the eleventh International Brigade—the Thaelmann Brigade—composed largely of German Communists, had arrived to fight. On the ninth of February he and the others were reorganized into a new line of defense along the heights of the east bank of the Jarama River. The Italian Garibaldi Brigade was placed in the rear as a reserve in order to prevent a major breakthrough.

It crossed Tom's mind that he couldn't see the face of his enemy—it was a face he wanted to see, the face of a fascist, and, more specifically, he wanted to see the face of Eoin McDuffy. But behind the murderous explosives there were no faces. There were only the blown-up faces of men blinded and wandering aimlessly as a living target of a more deadly shot. There were men with their arms and legs blown off; there were those who bled to death; and those who were obliterated.

Face in the dirt, trembling, Tom couldn't count the men who were dead around him, though he could smell them as they lay in the warm Spanish sun. Dried blood, crusted on gaping wounds; screams, curses, fear. Tom gripped his gun; his fingers were numb from gripping it.

"It vas the Moroccans," a seventeen-year-old German Jew told him in broken English. He was fighting with the Thaelmann Brigade.

"The Moroccans came last night in the dark and they knifed every sentry on Pindoque Bridge—one by one—ya, silently all the Frenchmen died. They were all French from the Fourteenth Brigade." He wiped some spittle off his mouth. His beard was thick, black, and curly. His skin was deeply tanned. "Why are you here?" the man asked Tom.

"To fight for the Republic—to fight against the fascists. I believe—"

"Ya, I know, you believe in democracy."

"Why are you here?"

The man shrugged. "I'm a Jew. The Communists are the only German party to oppose the fascists. I'm here because I'm a Jew. Because my mother sent me."

"What's your name?" Tom asked.

"Franz Friedenburg," the man replied, offering Tom a cigarette.

Tom took it and lit it. For a moment, his mind wandered to the Jewish girl he had once taken out, it seemed like a million years ago. A tussle in a car parked on Revere Beach—a youthful exploration and an attempt at sex.

Tom drew on the cigarette and watched the face of his compatriot. "Catholics and Jews—strange we should be here together."

Franz nodded. "Religion doesn't enter into this—it has to die under the jackboots of the fascists. There's too much good in it, too many questions."

Tom frowned. He didn't quite understand. Then another shell whistled through the air and conversation came to an end.

Ear to the ground. There were trampling feet! A charge on the gully, men screaming; Tom gripped his gun. He heard a wild war cry in Gaelic. It ripped through him and he stood up. Charging the gully was a mixed group of men, bayonets extended. Tom leaped forward and charged into the bloody fray, vaguely aware that Franz was at his side. He saw the face of a Blue Shirt, and though it wasn't Eoin McDuffy's face, it became so, and Tom plunged his bayonet into the man's soft fleshy stomach.

Almost simultaneously, he felt the bullet rip through his back, and he stumbled, falling face forward in the dirt. What went on above and around him, he didn't know. He saw only his mother's face and he felt her soft hands caressing his cheeks.

He was suddenly a child of nine and his mother was running toward him on the dock in New York City.

She was beautiful, and she embraced him and sobbed. "We're together again . . . oh, my darling, we'll never be apart again."

Soft hands, a lilting voice, a kind laugh—he remembered burying his face in her coat and crying.

Painfully Tom opened his eyes. Wafts of smoke floated overhead, and there was an eerie silence. He forced himself up and began to crawl; he left behind him a great puddle of his own blood.

He reached Franz's crumpled dead body and with great effort pulled the German Jew into his arms. Tears flowed down Tom's face; then he too fell backward onto the dirt, pulling the dead German with him, still holding the man. He died that way.

6

February 1937

Boston

"He's dead!" Emerald's scream rang through the peaceful darkness of their bedroom, and Joe Scanlon bolted upright in bed.

"He's dead! I know he's dead!" He could feel her shaking in the darkness and she stared across the black room as if she could see, as if she did see.

"Emerald, wake up, you're dreaming! Wake up!"

He reached over and turned on the bedside lamp.

Emerald blinked as light flooded their bedroom, and he saw that tears were streaming down her face.

"Emerald, you had a bad dream."

She shook her head. "He's dead. I know he's dead. I saw him."

"What did you see?" Joe prodded.

"I just saw him dead, I know he's dead, I feel it. It's as if something in me died too."

"Emerald, sweetheart." He drew her into his arms and rocked her gently, stroking her hair. She was cold and she trembled against him.

"You've been upset since you got his letter, your fear has become your reality. You don't know it, you don't know if anything's happened or not."

"No, no," she murmured. "I know."

"Emerald, I can't argue with what you feel. All I can say is what you said to me so many years ago. How a man lives is more important than how a man dies. . . . Emerald, you read his letter. Tom was—maybe is—a good boy."

Her face was buried in his chest, and he felt her nodding in agreement.

"We had too short a time," she finally said. It was what she had said when Tom's father had been killed, and she felt as if she were reliving that moment as well.

Joe waited and continued to hold her, rock her in his arms. Emerald had great good luck and happiness in one part of her life, but tragedy seemed to stalk her. It was as if she could not have happiness without tragedy, as if some higher power had ordained she should endure both.

"Downstairs you have four children. Kathleen, J.J., Seamus, and Edward need you, Emerald. If Tom is dead—and I'm not saying he is—it's a chapter of your life that's over, a tragic chapter. You'll never forget Tom or Colleen or Emmy, but you have four children to live for and four children to raise. I loved Tom too, but I suppose he did what he believed he had to do; I suppose, in the final analysis, I might have done the same. Emerald, if anything has happened to him, you have to cherish his memory, you have to remember that he did what he thought was right."

"Oh, Joe, I'm so certain . . . call it what you will, but I'm sure."

"I know you are. Look, I'll call Washington in the morning. I'll go through diplomatic channels, find out what I can."

Emerald nodded. "Thank you. You're so good to me, you're always there when I need you."

Joe switched off the light and pulled her down against him, holding her tightly. "I could say the same to you," he answered.

27

1

August 20, 1938

Emerald hurried along toward home on Brimmer Street. She had cut through the Common and now walked through the public gardens. She carried packages in both arms, fresh fruits and vegetables from the Farmers' Market, fresh seafood from the wharf. It was true that Cook could have done the shopping, but Emerald always found she enjoyed it too much to give it up. There was something about the Farmers' Market that always reminded her of the markets in Ireland; besides, she really admitted, I like to haggle.

It's a beautiful day, she thought. Warm sun shone down on the always perfect, uniform flowerbeds of the gardens, and the trees blew in a gentle breeze. Children gathered to dip their feet into the great stone fountain, and everywhere women walked their children in prams.

Tomorrow, Emerald thought, is a special day. Our fifteenth wedding anniversary. And for you, Joe Scanlon, a real New England clambake! Fifteen years—it hardly seemed like fifteen years. But so much had happened in their lives—so much had happened in the world. Joe was traveling to Washington more and more and serving on various government committees; Padraic was absorbed in running Joe's various enterprises; Tom had died over a year ago in Spain, buried in an unmarked grave.

Emerald walked on, more slowly now because she was going uphill. And the children were getting older, more and more grown-up every day. Katie and J.J. had just turned fourteen, Seamus was twelve, and Edward was ten. Emerald inhaled and let out her breath, savoring the sweet smell of the flowers. Ah, Katie, my beautiful Katie. Katie at fourteen was ravishing with her long red-gold hair and her deep-set green eyes. "She looks like you," Joe always said. But Emerald thought Katie was prettier.

It might all be perfect, Emerald reflected, if it weren't for the threat of war. Poor Eamon de Valera, he was president of a crumbling League of Nations; he presided over its death with calm dignity.

Emerald saw an empty bench and sat down. It's too nice a day to be hurrying so, she told herself. She unloaded her various bags from her arms and put them next to her. She half-slipped her feet out of her shoes.

"You dirty little black Protestant bastard!"

Emerald straightened up as out of the bushes on her left a frightened young boy ran. His nose was bleeding, and tears ran down his dirty face, causing white lines amid the dirt.

Emerald jumped to her feet just as an older boy appeared in chase. He was much bigger. "Dirty little black Protestant!" He shook his fist in anger and grabbed the younger child by his shirt collar, pulling him down. He lifted his foot to kick.

"Stop that!" Emerald shouted with an authority in her voice she hadn't realized existed.

The older boy turned, a mean look on his face. Not more than twelve, Emerald surmised. And the other one eight or nine.

"What do you think you're doing?" she demanded as she ran over to them. She lost one of her shoes in the grass and cursed under her breath.

The older boy looked at her quizzically. "You're Irish," he said, hearing her accent. "This little bastard called me a pig-shit Irish! I'm going to kick his putrid little black Protestant face in!"

Emerald grabbed the older boy and jerked him away from his intended victim, who lay sobbing in the grass.

"You'll do no such thing! And stop using such foul language, you little brat!"

"What business is it of yours! You're Irish! Do you like being called pig shit?" He narrowed his eyes.

"Sh! Or I'll smack you! That child is smaller than you by a long shot. Names! You can't go around hitting small children just because they call you names—no matter how terrible the names!"

The older boy wiggled in her arms, and Emerald shook him. "If you don't want to be called pig shit, stop acting like pig shit!" She surprised both herself and the boy, who stood still and kicked the grass with his foot.

"And you," Emerald said, turning on the other youngster. "You watch your tongue. You pick yourself up and go home. And wash your face!" She turned back to the older boy. "You certainly do your Irish proud when you beat up younger boys!" Emerald said. "Shameful!"

"You don't know how it is . . . what do you know?" The boy looked intently at the grass. Judging from their dress, Emerald decided, they both came out of the South Boston tenements.

"I know more and I've seen more than you're liable to see and learn in a lifetime."

"They hate us! They have older boys! I've been beaten by the black Protestants . . . black little heathens, they've got no souls."

"And if that's what you think, you've got no mind."

"If you were any kind of Irish, you'd of let me bash him a good one!"

"I'm any kind of Irish," Emerald said, straightening up. "But being Irish and being Catholic don't mean having hate."

"They hate us, we hate them."

Emerald closed her eyes for a second. "Not here," she whispered. "Not here."

"What did you say?" the boy demanded.

"I said we don't have to hate here. We don't have to hate anywhere."

"You don't know what they're like!"

"No," Emerald corrected, "*you* don't know what they're like. Not everybody is a *they*. They, as you call them, have names and faces. Some of them are prejudiced and some of them aren't. Some of us are prejudiced and some aren't."

"I guess you're one of them, huh?"

"One of who?"

"One of us who aren't prejudiced, or whatever you said."

Emerald, in spite of herself, laughed. "Them" and "us" were getting to be a bit much to handle.

"What's funny?" The lad scowled at her.

Emerald ignored him. "Where do you live?" she asked.

"Down on the South Side. Took the subway up here for the day."

Emerald smiled at him and let go of his shirt. He stood in front of her, shifting restlessly from one foot to the other. "Come here, sit down a minute."

He hesitated.

"What's the matter, am I keeping you from beating someone else up, or can you hardly wait to find someone else to call you a name?"

The boy grinned sheepishly and followed her to the bench.

"What does your father do?" Emerald asked.

"He's dead."

"Oh, I'm sorry. And your mother?"

"Works. Scrubs floors in that building over there. But she's not there now. She works nights."

Emerald nodded. "Listen, have you ever had a chocolate-fudge sundae?"

He shook his head. "I had some ice cream once."

"Did your mother buy it for you?"

He shook his head. "Naw, I stole it."

Emerald suppressed a smile. "What's your name?"

"Sean—Sean Casey."

"Well, Sean Casey, there's a nice ice-cream parlor between here and where I live. If you carry my parcels for me, I'll buy you a hot-fudge sundae and give you subway fare home. Fair?"

He broke into a wide grin. "Fair," he answered.

2

August 21, 1938

"Happy anniversary," Joe said, rolling over and looking at Emerald, who sat in front of her dressing table combing out her hair. She was half-dressed in a pure white slip. Her hair was just a bit shorter than shoulder length and fell in deep waves. It was graying now, but in a splendid way. In the front a nearly gray shock of hair contrasted to the rest. It gave her a dignified appearance. Her complexion was still flawless, though there were tiny lines around her eyes. Her figure, as always, was perfect. Emerald at forty-three was more than beautiful, she was stunning.

She turned from the dresser. "Happy anniversary to you," she said brightly. Her face absolutely glowed.

"You look wonderful! You look happy. I haven't seen you look this happy since . . ." He stopped short. "For a while."

"I feel wonderful! I had a . . . a miraculous day!"

"Such adjectives! It must have been good."

Emerald pressed her lips together and her eyes danced with sheer glee. "It was inspirational, that's what it was."

"Well, I hope today is as good. I confess I haven't bought you anything yet. I thought we'd go to the jeweler's and you'd pick out something you really want."

Emerald smiled and walked over to the bed. She sat down next to him, running her hand through his thick gray hair. "I have a sable coat, diamonds, a ruby, and two emeralds. Joe, I love you and I love everything you've ever given me. But I don't want jewels."

He smiled indulgently at her. "What do you want?"

"A building," Emerald said brightly. "A large building with a gym and a playground. And free ice cream."

"What?"

"Joe, I met a little boy yesterday. His name is Sean Casey. He was beating up a little Protestant boy . . ."

"And that made your wonderful day and that's why you want a building? Slow down, you're going too fast for my elderly, distracted mind."

Emerald laughed and fairly bounced on the bed. "Yes," she answered. "I stopped him, of course. He was fighting because the younger one called him names. We had a talk about that. Joe, his father's dead and his mother works nights as a scrubwoman."

"That's not so unusual."

"That's just it. It's not at all unusual. Do you know how many women in Boston work to support fatherless children? They can't spend time with their children and so their children— Catholic and Protestant, Irish, Italian, Portuguese, all of them— they run around all day like ragamuffins. They're playing at hating, Joe. And one day it won't be a game anymore."

She had grown more serious. She leaned over. "Joe, I want my building near Scollay Square, near the melting pot where they all come together. I want to build an interdenominational recreation center and I intend to raise money from everyone in Boston—even our good neighbors, even the people on Beacon Hill. I've been thinking about . . . You give me the building, and I'll raise the funds to run it!"

"I see a look of determination in your eyes that I wouldn't take on for the whole world. But I'm more of a pushover than the inhabitants of Beacon Hill will be."

Emerald grinned. "Can I have my building?"

"Of course. Anyway, it wouldn't do for me to say no."

"Good. I'm going to see Eugenia Monteith."

"Eugenia Monteith! Senator Frederick Monteith's wife? Emerald!"

She smiled and leaned over and kissed his cheek. "Now, now, there's an election soon, and you know how many Democrats there are in Boston."

Joe burst out laughing. "You're priceless!"

Emerald moved seductively in his arms. "And wanton. It *is* our anniversary."

He rolled on top of her and tickled her neck. "So it is," he said playfully.

3

September 1, 1938

Emerald paused and looked out on the little lake where the swan boats had just begun to sail crazily around in wide circles while their small passengers squealed with delight.

She smiled to herself. They were called swan boats because the front and sides of them were carved to look like swans—to her they looked like a bit of moving scenery from a Wagnerian opera. But the children loved them and they were an institution: like the Common itself, a giant park for commoners.

There was something about Boston, and something about the Common specifically. Its history, albeit a Puritan history, was everywhere. On Beacon Hill the gold dome of the garish State House reflected a blinding light in the midafternoon sun. On the far side of the Common that faced Tremont Street, Filene's was doing a brisk afternoon business, while Stearns and Company catered to the carriage trade.

Emerald checked on the time. Yes, time to climb Beacon Hill and assault the High Brahmin herself, Madam Eugenia Monteith.

Eugenia Monteith was nine generations out of Protestant Ulster, and reputedly as prejudiced as if she had left there yesterday.

Only nine generations! Emerald laughed to herself. "I come from dear old Boston, the land of the bean and the cod, where Lowells speak only to Cabots, and the Cabots speak only to God." She whispered the words to the children's rhyme under her breath—they were delightful, they were true. Briefly she wondered why no one ever mentioned that John Cabot was originally called Caboto and came from Venice. Eugenia Monteith would probably say, "Just another foreigner."

Eugenia Monteith was a tall woman, tall and straight like a Salem clipper. She was a year younger than Emerald and the mother of two sons. One was at Annapolis, the naval academy; the other, young Philip, was at the Boston Conservatory of Music.

Emerald had met Eugenia once or twice casually at the art gallery, and, as she recalled, Eugenia was quite a striking woman with her prematurely white hair and her youngish face. She also recalled that Eugenia had a biting sense of humor, sarcastic and droll.

Emerald paused midway up the near-vertical hill. It was indeed an assault, she thought. But it was a lovely day, and

Boston was a city for walkers, which was why she hadn't taken the car or a taxi.

As she trudged on, she congratulated herself on her own strategy. She had purposely let Eugenia Monteith win the first round.

Emerald had written and invited Eugenia to her home, saying that she must see her on an urgent matter. And Eugenia Monteith was caught in her own net of manners versus prejudice. Eugenia couldn't refuse the politically influential Mrs. Scanlon, but neither could she, or would she, be seen going to the home of the Scanlons—even if it was in respectable Back Bay.

Thus Eugenia had broken her own rule and invited Emerald to her house for tea. Never, to Emerald's knowledge, had an Irish Catholic, other than servants, been inside the home of Eugenia Monteith, the wife of Senator Frederick Monteith.

Clearly Eugenia had chosen between two evils: one, to go to Emerald; the other, to see what Emerald wanted while remaining like a ruling lioness in her own cave. Eugenia opted for the latter, where no doubt she felt more in control.

Emerald stepped in front of the house. Then she walked up and knocked with the huge brass knocker. Sweet New England, she thought. The object was to have money and station and to show neither. The dictum of the Lowells and the Cabots and those who followed slavishly in their footsteps was to live beneath your means in understated elegance, breathing the same dust that made the Founding Fathers sneeze.

"Madam . . ." The tall bald butler opened the door and ushered Emerald into the foyer. "Madam Monteith is expecting you." He looked down his long nose. No, Emerald thought. Not even the butler is Irish.

Emerald smiled sweetly. "Thank you," she whispered, conscious of the fact that one always whispered in the houses of Brahmins.

Eugenia swept into the sitting room dressed in a plain russet dress trimmed with white lace. She wore a small hand-carved cameo brooch which bore the face of a delicate, exquisite woman. Her gray hair was perfectly coiffed and brushed back away from her fine-featured face.

"Mrs. Scanlon, how nice to see you. Please, do sit down."

Rule two, Emerald thought. Never call a Brahmin by her first name. Not until you're asked, and you may never be asked. People who have known each other for twenty years don't use first names, and one woman Emerald knew always referred to her own husband as "Mr. Clifton."

"Mrs. Monteith, I'm charmed. It's nice to see you again. When did I see you last? Was it at the benefit for the Boston Pops? Or was it the afternoon the Metropolitan Opera had its last matinee?"

"I think the benefit for the Pops." Eugenia looked her over without being one bit obvious. "Please, do have a pastry. Jasper will serve tea soon. It has to steep, you know, it's not good unless it steeps. I always buy my tea from S. S. Pierce, they have the finest English tea. But here I am telling you about tea when you come from the British Isles. . . . I do hope the Munich conference works out. It would be dreadful to have the importation of good British tea cut off, wouldn't it?"

"Indeed," Emerald answered patiently, ignoring Eugenia's barb about coming from the British Isles.

"I'm such a chatterbox," Eugenia gushed girlishly.

Much too girlishly, Emerald thought. I'm making her nervous. She must be wondering if I have some special Irish disease.

"When I got your note, I did want to come to your home. But you know, I have this bad back, and it's sometimes difficult for me to get about."

Especially to the home of an Irish Catholic, Emerald thought, filling in the blanks. She suppressed her smile. "I understand perfectly," Emerald replied.

Jasper entered the room and set down a silver tray with silver teapot, creamer, and sugar bowl. On it were two delicate Royal Doulton cups and saucers.

"Will that be all, madam?" He looked at the floor and sounded for all the world as if he had just stepped out of the Brighton amusement park.

"Mrs. Monteith, I've come to you because you are the most influential lady in Boston. And to say that you are known for your good works is no doubt an understatement."

Eugenia blushed. "You're too kind. I've heard of your generosity as well."

"I'm never *too* kind," Emerald said pointedly. "I've come to offer you an opportunity to do something truly unique, to do something that, while being the ultimate in good works, perhaps especially for you, will also serve to endear your husband to a larger segment of his voting constituency. Perhaps, with my help and your cooperation, it might even help him to survive the next election."

Eugenia's eyes widened considerably. "You're being a trifle blatant, my dear."

"A trifle, my dear. But you and I both know he's finished as senator if he doesn't do something about, shall I say, his image. The upstate vote can no longer overcome the Irish, Italian, and Portuguese vote in Boston.''

"You really are being crass, Mrs. Scanlon."

"All in good cause, Mrs. Monteith. When you're crass, can you say the same thing?''

Eugenia stiffened. "I'm not used to the kind of approach your kind makes.''

"Then hear me out, Mrs. Monteith. I'm not going to ask you to do anything crass. I want your help in establishing an interdenominational foundation for children; specifically, a recreation center which my husband will build. To run and maintain such a community service needs funds—but because it's interdenominational, it also needs support from you and your kind. I cannot get that support, Mrs. Monteith. I need you.''

Eugenia gazed at Emerald thoughtfully. "Interdenominational? Surely you know my family originates from Loyalist Ulster, from Protestants.''

Emerald smiled. "And mine originates from Catholic Ulster,'' she said. "Precisely why I am here, Mrs. Monteith, precisely. First, even though your family connections are quite far removed, and even though you live and prosper in a city that rose up against loyalism to the British crown—''

"But that was a long time ago,'' Eugenia protested.

"So was Oliver Cromwell, Mrs. Monteith. And I am quite willing to forgive you.'' Emerald smiled warmly. "You see, it's the hatred. I have experienced that hatred, but more, I have seen children experiencing it. I have seen small children growing up ready to kill, not even understanding the arguments and names they call one another. Mrs. Monteith, no male in my family has died a natural death in three generations. In those same three generations, countless British soldiers died killing them and the others like them. I have been in England. I do not hate the British, because I know there are many fine British people. I do not hate Protestant Bostonians, because I know among them there are many fine people. But I see it happening here, I see the children who are Catholic and Protestant fighting; I see the Italians and the Irish at each other's throats, I see them at the throats of children who are white Protestant Bostonians. Do you want to live in an Ulster?''

Emerald paused and leaned over. "What I suggest is a small beginning, but it's a beginning. Hundreds and hundreds of children in this city come from fatherless or near-fatherless homes. They need a place to go when their mothers are working to feed them; they need a place where they can play together and learn each other's ways, a place where they can learn not to hate.''

"And where do you intend to do this?''

"Near Scollay Square, where the groups come together. It's the melting pot of the city. Mrs. Monteith, they can grow up liking each other, or they can grow up hating. Help me. Help me, and I'll help your husband.''

Eugenia rubbed her small hands together. "Will we have publicity?'' She stood up and walked to the window and looked out.

"I daresay our alliance would be . . . well, front-page news.''

"Could we call it the Scanlon-Monteith Recreation Center?''

Emerald grinned, though Eugenia could not see the look of delighted self-satisfaction. "It seems like a good name.''

"And you will help my husband to be reelected.''

"I shall work night and day on his campaign.''

Slowly Eugenia turned around. Underneath, she's a good woman, Emerald thought. Shrewd, too.

"It's not just for Frederick, you understand. I am not . . . how shall I say it . . . I am not without feeling for the things you speak of. I must say . . . well, I'm shocked. You're different than I thought you would be.''

"And I,'' Emerald said, "am pleasantly surprised.''

"Don't exaggerate, dear. You're *mildly* surprised. Well, Mrs. Scanlon, why don't you call me Eugenia.''

"Only if you'll call me Emerald.''

4

September 1, 1939

The brick building was two stories high and surrounded by green grass with a playground in the back. Its main floor had two large gymnasiums which could be converted into one large auditorium. Upstairs there were a lunchroom and crafts rooms; in the basement, pool and Ping-Pong tables.

"I must say I'm impressed,'' Eugenia said as she leaned over to sip some water from a small fountain in the hallway. She laughed lightly. "Even the drinking fountains are child-sized. My God, when I bent over I heard my back crack.''

"Eugenia, I'm the one who's impressed. You're really quite the fund-raiser.''

"Well, you have to know how to get money out of the old skinflints, but it's an idiotic vocation. Oh, it's rewarding enough when something like this comes to fruition, but you know, it's not exactly what I had in mind. As a matter of fact, I didn't really want to get married."

Emerald looked at Eugenia in surprise. First because in the entire year they had been working together Eugenia had never said much of anything personal, second because she was confiding in Emerald as if they were true friends.

"Yes, I really envy you," Eugenia murmured as she turned to walk down the hall. Emerald fell into pace beside her.

"You had a career as a nurse, you were part of a . . . well, rebellion I guess I have to call it. You've traveled a great deal . . . I don't know. I feel wasted. You seem to have been living while I've just been existing."

"Eugenia, you've left your mark on this city—the art gallery, the shell for concerts in the summer, and now this center."

"Oh, I only went out and got money, but you were no slouch either. Anyway, it was your idea, Emerald Scanlon. You are the mover behind this enterprise. I only did what the Boston Brahmins are supposed to do—that *is* what you call us, isn't it?"

"That and less flattering names," Emerald answered candidly.

Eugenia laughed sardonically. "My God, you don't understand what I'm saying. I've lived my whole life in a Royal Doulton teacup! I'm like a hothouse plant. I wear white gloves in the summer and kid gloves in the winter. I only go to the right places! Frankly, I'm up to here with all of it!" She leaned over mischievously. "I wanted to be a dancer, to kick up my heels," she confessed.

Emerald eyed Eugenia. "You certainly have long enough legs. Eugenia, you're really quite a woman."

Eugenia turned and looked Emerald in the face. "And so are you, Emerald Scanlon. I hate to admit it, but I like you. Really like you."

Emerald hugged Eugenia. Then she smiled at her. The woman she saw beneath the surface had interests not unlike her own.

"And I like you," she told Eugenia. "You know, Protestants are not the only ones who are prejudiced. People have to get to know one another, to find out what's underneath."

Eugenia reached out and looped her arm through Emerald's. "Why, my dear, some of my best friends are Irish!" They both laughed.

It took an hour through heavy traffic before Eugenia's chauffeur-driven sleek black Buick pulled up in front of the Scanlon house.

"Tea?" Emerald asked.

Eugenia looked a trifle wicked. "I'd prefer bourbon," she whispered.

"Oh, I think that can be arranged."

"I shall be staying for a while," Eugenia told the chauffeur. He nodded and climbed out of the car, opening the door for them.

Eugenia looked up and caught sight of old Mrs. Clapp, whose window was open and whose head was only too visible. "Mrs. Clapp, dear, how nice to see you!" Eugenia called out. She waved gaily. "Would you like to come and join us?"

The old woman immediately covered her face with her hands and let out an almost anguished cry. She pulled down her shade so hard it broke and fell, crumpled on the sill. Mrs. Clapp disappeared.

Eugenia turned to Emerald and grinned. "You can't win them all, as Philip would say."

Emerald burst into laughter. "Oh, you shouldn't have!"

"Well, it's all right for the old girl to stare at you day in and day out, but not at me!"

"I doubt I shall ever see her old gray head again." Emerald giggled.

Mrs. Reilly opened the door. She eyed Eugenia with suspicion, but Emerald noted there was more than that. She actually looked quite distressed.

"Is something the matter? Are the children all right?"

"The children are all right. It's the news."

"What news?"

"It's the Germans, they've broken the Munich treaty. They've invaded Poland."

"Oh," Emerald said, shaking her head. She slipped off her coat and Eugenia slipped off hers as well.

"Well, now I need a bourbon," she announced.

"Yes," Emerald agreed. "It's terrible."

"Mind you, I never thought those silly idiots marching up and down in shiny boots were to be trusted. I knew it would come to this."

"England will go to war," Emerald said sadly.

"As long as they don't drag us into it," Eugenia replied.

5

November 20, 1939

"If I knew how long you were going to be in Washington, I'd know what to pack." Emerald was making steady trips between the great maple chest of drawers and the open suitcase on the bed. "I've put in four shirts, four pairs of socks, four sets of underwear, and your navy sweater. I think you ought to take two suits, what do you think?"

"Two should do it. Hey, I'm going to Washington, not to Dublin. It's only an overnight train ride. If I forget my toothbrush, I'll come home and get it."

"If you're gone more than a week, I'll come and get you."

"That's not much of a threat."

"It was a promise." She stopped and kissed him on the cheek.

"And they called it the war to end all wars. . . . Roosevelt's right, you know. The Germans have to be stopped."

Emerald nodded. Germany had invaded Poland on September 1, England had declared war on Germany September 3, and so had Australia and New Zealand. Canada declared war on September 10. Somehow the involvement of Canada made it seem closer and more real. Hitler was on the march; of that there could be no doubt. The man signed treaties and he tore them up.

"The peace movement is very strong," Emerald observed. "Americans don't want to be part of another European war." She sat down on the edge of the bed. "I guess that's everything you need."

"You're a pacifist of sorts—how do you feel about it?"

She looked at him and shook her head. "I doubt I'm a barometer of public opinion."

"I want to hear what you think."

"I have an abhorrence of violence, but, Joe, I believe Hitler is evil. He's built a militaristic state. I don't believe in that. He's invaded his neighbors. I don't believe in that. He's caused repressive laws, and I don't believe in the purity of any race." Emerald sighed. "The British drew a line, the Germans stepped over it. I hate war and the idea of war, but sometimes . . . sometimes you can't negotiate because of the pure evil of those who force you to defend yourself."

"I agree." Joe looked into her eyes. "You may not believe in the master race, but the Bund is making converts—right here in Boston, and dammit, among the Irish.''

Emerald swung her legs onto the bed and lay back, her head on the pillow. "It's not because they believe in Hitler. It's because they still hate the English. When the chips are down, you'll see Irish-Americans as ready to be Americans as anyone. Someone has to tell them what Hitler's doing and what he stands for. When they understand, they won't like it.''

"Why don't you tell them?'' Joe asked, smiling.

"Me?''

"As the wife of a former ambassador, I think some talks could be arranged. Go out speaking to Irish communities. I'll arrange it.''

"I can't get up and talk to people in public, in front of crowds!''

Joe leaned across the bed and nuzzled her neck. "Bet you can! Bet you'll kill them in Philadelphia!''

"Joe, be serious.''

"I am serious. Do it, Emerald. I want you to.''

"My voice isn't loud enough.''

"You'll have a mike. Ah, my darling, your Irish lilt will hypnotize the crowds.''

She turned and looked at him quizzically. "You really are serious, aren't you?''

'You bet I am. Will you do it?''

"If you want me to, I'll certainly try. But don't blame me if I'm terrible.''

Joe hugged her and held her close. "You won't be,'' he said confidently.

Emerald nestled comfortably in his arms. "Make love to me, Joe. You're going away for a whole week. I don't like that.''

"I'll miss you too,'' he said, pulling her closer and kissing her ear. "Front, back, or sideways?'' he asked, winking at her.

"All three,'' she answered.

28

1

December 22, 1939

"And in 1916, when Padraic Pearse stood on the steps of the General Post Office, he delivered a proclamation on behalf of the provisional government of the Republic of Ireland. . . . He said in part, 'We declare the right of the people of Ireland to the ownership of Ireland, and to the unfettered control of Irish destinies, to be sovereign and indefeasible. . . .'

"And did we of Ireland ask for the kind of freedom we would deny other nations? Now that the Republic of Ireland exists—albeit without Ulster—are we content to see the principle of independence and people's destiny trampled? If we are, we fought in vain.

"Ladies and gentlemen of the Ancient Order of Hibernians, do not be lulled by the words of the Bund. No man is superior to another—the English told us they were superior! And we proved them wrong!"

A round of spontaneous applause broke out, and Emerald paused.

"Hitler breaks his treaties, but when we finally got a settlement from England, at least they kept to it! Hitler has denied the rights of Poland and other nations; he threatens peace in Europe. We must know where we stand. We must stand for the rights of all people and for the rights of independent nations. When the Bund comes to you and tells you to hate the English and to remember what the English did to you I say no! I say look at what Hitler is doing to Poland and know he would do the same to Ireland. To believe in independence is the heritage of our oppression; we cannot deny the right of independence to others and remain true to our own history."

There was another round of applause; this time both the men and women in the hall stood and clapped.

Emerald sat down. "I'm shaking all over," she whispered to Dennis O'Sullivan, who had arranged her talk.

"Hush, woman, I've got to wipe my tears. I don't think you've left a dry eye in the house."

"Oh, begone." Emerald laughed, relaxing for the first time all day. The crowd was up now, and the folding chairs were being put away and the refreshments laid out on the paper-covered tables on the far side of the room.

"Faith and if it isn't Emerald O'Hearn!"

Emerald turned abruptly at the sound of her maiden name. The woman was plumper and older-looking by far. But the face was unmistakable. "Maureen!" Emerald cried. "Maureen Malone! Whatever are you doing in Philadelphia?"

"Whatever are you doing making me cry and feeling so patriotic! And your name's not the same . . . what was your husband's name . . . ah, yes, Hughes. What happened to Mr. Hughes?"

Emerald embraced Maureen warmly. "He was killed in the war," she acknowledged. "You remember, he told us all at the wedding that he was enlisting."

"Oh, I remember. There was a terrible row! Oh, so many didn't come back from that war. I'm sorry, Emerald. He was a nice man, a good man." She paused and studied Emerald's face. "I missed you after you went to Dublin."

"And I missed you, but whatever are you doing here?"

"Oh, we emigrated—way back in 1925, it was. It's a lot better. A lot better."

"It is that," Emerald agreed, wiping a tear from her cheek. Seeing Maureen caused a hundred memories to flood her mind—good memories, bad memories. "Come over here so we can talk."

Emerald guided Maureen to a far corner, away from the laughing, talking, drinking Irishmen and women.

"Did you remarry, then?"

"Yes," Emerald said. "To a wonderful, wonderful man. We live in Boston."

"I almost died when I saw you. The leaflet said you were the wife of the former ambassador to Ireland. I thought you'd be all fancy and cool. And I said, 'That's Emerald O'Hearn! The very Emerald O'Hearn who taught reading and who lived with me.' And my neighbor Mrs. Reardon didn't believe me."

Maureen paused and reached out and touched Emerald's cheek. "You were right, you were. Education is for girls. My girl Rose, she wasn't born when you lived with us, she's learned to read, and now she's a proper teacher."

Emerald hugged her again. "You come along, Maureen. You take me to your neighbor Mrs. Reardon so I can tell her I am the very one who lived with you."

"Would you?"

"That and anything else. Let's go and have a long talk, a really long talk."

"Would you come to my house, then, would you see the children all grown-up?"

"Try to stop me," Emerald said cheerfully. "You just try to stop me."

Maureen grinned. "Oh, nothing can stop you. I always knew that."

2

December 24, 1939

Emerald stepped back and admired the giant Christmas tree. They had to trim off its top to get it into the living room.

"We'll decorate it after supper."

Joe was sitting in the large easy chair, his feet propped up, his pipe in his mouth. The *Boston Globe* was folded neatly in his lap. Its front page featured a large picture of three tall columns draped in Nazi flags with huge swastikas in their middle. On the platform in front of the columns was a gathering of unnamed Nazi leaders; presumably Hitler was in their center. In front of the platform were rows of helmeted German troops. Their heads reminded Emerald of mushrooms growing in the dark.

"Fungi," she said, examining the picture.

"Deadly fungi," Joe added. "Who'd have thought the Russians would join them?"

"I doubt that will last long." Emerald straightened up and stretched. "And the Italians. My God, what do they think they're doing?"

"Creating a massive war."

Joe ran his hand through his hair. "You know, I'll have to go to Washington again after the holidays."

"Can you talk about it, or is it all hush-hush?"

"I can talk to you about it. Otherwise it's a secret—hush-hush, as you say."

"We can talk now. Mrs. Reilly is out doing some last-minute shopping and the children aren't home from skating."

Joe laughed. "I think you'll have to stop calling the twins 'children.' J.J.'s only two inches shorter than I am, and Katie's starting to look like the vamp of Savannah!"

"You're right," Emerald conceded. "But they'll always be children to me. Now, tell me about your trip."

"I can't tell you everything. But you already know we're in

full production—war materials. You also know we can't send those materials to England . . . well, legally, because technically we're neutral.''

Emerald nodded.

Joe took a deep breath. "The president says we'll be in it eventually, says there's no way to avoid it. He says the British have to be able to hold out. In a sense, I suppose, England is buying us time. Personally, I think he's right. I'd say that Germany, Italy, Russia, and Japan have to be stopped, before they can't be stopped.''

Emerald shook her head in sadness. "Poland, Hungary, Czechoslovakia, Finland . . . it's terrible. They've lost their independence and their freedom. It sickens me.''

She folded her legs and sat down on the floor near his feet. He leaned over and patted her hair. It looked lovely with the white shock in front and the silver gray mixed with the gold. Emerald, at forty-four, was astounding. "I hear you did kill them in Philadelphia,'' he acknowledged.

"It was a good turnout. Good enough that the German-American Bund picketed outside. Scary people, those. Mostly young men in love with their uniforms.'' Emerald bit her lip. "My brother Seamus used to be in love with his uniform. Sorry, my mind is wandering. Tell me more about your mysterious trip.''

"Not so mysterious. It's only that we can't send arms to Britain, but Canada can. So I guess we'll have to arrange a little hanky-panky at the border, arrange for the Canadians to wake up one morning and find some tanks.''

"You better be careful. They say there are spies everywhere.''

"I assure you Franklin and J. Edgar know where they all are.''

Emerald giggled. "And just how do you keep a straight face around J. Edgar? You who smuggled more hooch into Boston right under his nose than any bootlegger around?''

Joe roared with laughter and leaned back in his chair. "I really didn't know you knew about that!''

She arched her eyebrow. "Joe Scanlon, there's not much I don't know about you. Anyway, Padraic told me . . . accidentally.''

"Talk about spies everywhere. God, I better be careful,'' he joked.

"Oh, you better,'' she teased.

"In any case,'' he told her, "I'll have to make some arrangements with the Canadians.''

"Why you?'' Her lovely green eyes were wide with both curiosity and amusement.

"Well, it goes back to the hooch. I have contacts in Canada. Some of them are in high places now. Made their money selling me good Irish whiskey and used it to get themselves into Parliament."

Emerald laughed. "That's a wonderful story. Small wonder it's a secret."

The front door opened and then slammed. Emerald frowned. "Fifteen years old, and J.J. can't close a door without slamming it."

"How do you know it was J.J.?"

Emerald laughed. "Because it always is—he comes in last."

"Well, our lively brood is home." Joe smiled. "And one day when they're all gone, you'll miss the slamming door."

"How was skating?" Emerald asked. "Did you have hot chocolate at the park?" They were a gaily dressed crew. Eleven-year-old Edward, soon to be twelve, sported a two-foot-long orange scarf which was blindingly bright. Dressed in his winter togs, he looked twice his actual size.

Thirteen-year-old Seamus was dressed from head to toe in green. He looked like a mischievous elf. Fifteen-year-old J.J. was the giant of the group. He was tall like his father, and gangly. He might easily have been eighteen. He wore mute brown with a long brightly colored argyle scarf and hat.

Kathleen—Katie—was tall like her twin brother, and Emerald knew that beneath her fur coat she had a fine figure, and no one could deny her face was also beautiful. She, too, looked older, and Emerald admitted her misgivings on that score readily.

"We were late getting to the park to skate," Edward complained. "Katie wouldn't leave the film. She wanted to sit through it again just so she could watch Rory O'Hara kiss that girl again! Ich!"

"Girls are yuk," Seamus agreed without hesitation.

"Let me show you how Rory O'Hara acts," J.J. said, moving to the center of the room and confronting his sister. "Ah, my darling! Have no fear! I shall rescue you from your wicked uncle! Let me draw my sword!" J.J. danced about the room in mock imitation of Rory O'Hara in a sword fight. He leaped to the sofa. "*En Garde!*"

"Enough, you'll knock over the Christmas tree!" Joe said in a deep voice. Emerald laughed. J.J.'s imitation wasn't far off the swashbuckling character Rory O'Hara portrayed in most of his films.

Katie lifted her chin proudly in the air and tossed back her hair dramatically. "Rory O'Hara is a man," she intoned in her best

Katharine Hepburn imitation. "You're all just little boys—*very* little boys—and you're jealous!" With that, Katie slung her scarf over her shoulder and marched out of the room.

"She's so dramatic," Joe whispered to Emerald.

"It's a phase." Emerald smiled. "She'll outgrow it."

"I hope you're right," Joe said.

"Listen, you all go upstairs and get out of your skating clothes. This tree has to be decorated, you know, and I'm certainly not doing it alone."

The three boys raced up the stairs.

"They sound like a herd of bull elephants," Joe commented.

"That's the way happy, healthy young people ought to sound."

"I agree. Tell me, have you had a talk with Katie?"

"A talk? We talk all the time."

"No, I mean about personal things, women things."

Emerald laughed and patted his knee. "Really, Joe! Considering what a lovely, lecherous man you are, you're certainly skirting what you want to say. Yes, we've talked about 'women things,' as you say."

"Good. Look, only a really lecherous man knows enough to worry about a beautiful daughter."

"I'm sure."

"It's just that she's so infected with the movies and fantasy."

"All the young girls are."

"I suppose. I just want her to have enough sense not to . . ."

"Get pregnant," Emerald finished. "Well, your wife the nurse told her how it happens; the nuns have told her about morality; and frankly, there's not much one can do but trust. She's only fifteen. You can't expect judgment at fifteen."

"I'll bet you had judgment at fifteen."

"Oh, Joe . . . I was never fifteen the way Katie is fifteen. At fifteen I didn't know what was beyond the street I lived on. I had the sense to run away from a man who was attacking me, yes, I had that much sense. And that was mostly instinct. But Katie? Katie's whole life is as different from mine as night from day. In a way, I'm living the years of a carefree young life with her and through her. In a way, it's as new to me as it is to her."

Joe gazed at her indulgently. "I love seeing you happy."

"And I am happy," she confirmed. "Things are going wonderfully at the center. We're having our first interdenominational basketball game in January. The Boston Streakers versus the Saint Christophers." Emerald laughed her lovely musical laugh. "They called themselves the Saint Christophers because he's the saint of travelers and they said they were going to really travel with the ball!''

"I hope I'm back from Washington. I wouldn't want to miss that. Nice to see kids pounding a basketball instead of each other."

Emerald stood up and stretched. "Shall we have a drink, Mr. Scanlon? Shall we drink to Christmas 1939?"

"Yes. Let's hope the worst doesn't happen."

Emerald nodded. "To a better year for the world."

Joe kissed her on the cheek. "To the impossible peace," he added with resignation.

3

February 11, 1940

Joe Scanlon looked out the window of the railway carriage as his train sped along, covering the distance between Detroit and Ottawa.

He had spent the day before in Detroit with various industrial leaders discussing production quotas and making the final arrangements with the American half of the transaction he was about to finalize.

He had crossed the Canadian border early in the morning, entering the country in Windsor and boarding the Canadian National Railway there.

He had passed through Toronto an hour ago. It wasn't a large city, but it was virtually the only center of real habitation he had seen, save scattered villages.

He had specifically chosen to take the train rather than fly. First, because he didn't really like planes; second, because it was February and the weather was not the best for flying; and third, because he wanted to see Canada, which he had not visited previously.

Joe shook his head in amazement. Canada was empty. It hardly seemed possible that it was so close to the teeming masses of the Eastern United States; it wasn't just another country; it was another world. He had to remind himself that he was only an hour out of the huge nation's second-largest city and on his way to the nation's capital.

Joe leaned back. The train was now moving straight along through dense woods. The trip between Windsor and Toronto had been through cleared farmland which consisted of rolling hills and low brush. The scattered farmhouses were few and far between, and the largest population was not human, but rather the placid cows and sheep which dotted the hillsides.

Trees, trees, Joe thought after another two hours. Canada was second in size only to Russia; but there were no people. Only trees. He smiled to himself and made a mental note to buy some land here. A man with interests in construction and paper needed trees.

He leaned back and contemplated his businesses and his wealth. People always said he had foresight, but in a way, he regarded the accumulation of his fortune to be largely luck.

He had inherited the construction business from his father, but its great burst had come after he took it over. He has been sitting in Dooley's when he overheard a drunken customer saying, "A man ought to be able to build his own house—like a child plays with blocks. Ought to be able to open a package and take a hammer and nails and put it together!"

Joe even remembered the chill that ran through him as he listened to the idle conversation. He had gotten up, gulped down the rest of his beer, and run all the way to the Boston Public Library.

There, with the help of an old prune of a librarian, who seemed to regard him as insane, he had read all there was to read about prefabrication. Hell, even the Egyptians had precut and prefitted the stones of the pyramids.

After that, Joe had hired an architect, and together they worked out the details. Of course others were using limited prefabrication already, but not on exterior walls.

Thus when America entered the war in 1917, Scanlon Construction received huge government contracts for its prefab barracks. After the war the need for such rapid construction evaporated, but Joe had invested his money in Scanlon Electronics. Now the government was ordering again, and this time Scanlon prefab buildings came wired and completely ready for electricity. Now, Joe reasoned, there would be needed barracks, plane hangars, storage facilities . . . endless structures that would comprise mobile military bases. And, he thought with considerable pleasure, Scanlon Structures, Inc., was ready and more than willing to take up the challenge. After the war, and he didn't doubt there would be one, Scanlon Structures might well turn to prefab residential housing. He thought again of the drunken man at Dooley's who had made him rich. Yes, he decided, a man ought to be able to build his own house with only a hammer and a bag of nails.

Yes, he thought, returning to the present. He would invest in some Canadian trees, maybe even a branch plant.

After a time, Joe opened his briefcase and began to go over some papers. C. D. Howe was the man he was off to see, and he and Franklin had enjoyed a chuckle over the irony of the meeting.

"He's one of ours," the president had announced. "From an old New England Brahmin family . . . the Howes go back a bit."

"He's younger than I am," Joe had observed as he studied the dossier compiled by J. Edgar on C. D. Howe. J. Edgar wasn't too kind. He regarded anyone who gave up his American citizenship as . . . well, insane at best, and guilty of treason at worst.

"But still an old Brahmin. Men like C.D. are born old. He's from Waltham, Mass. I think his people owned the mills there and worked their Irish labor to the bone. You ought to get on well with him."

Joe Scanlon took a gulp of Scotch. It was Franklin's favorite drink. "Sounds like we were meant for each other," he joked.

Franklin laughed heartily. "It should be fun for you. You have something he wants. Dicker a little, have a good time. I've heard from Churchill that C.D. is shrewd. But just between you and me, it's a good thing the Canadians have C.D. Their prime minister is an absentminded fuddy-duddy. Without C.D., he'd probably forget Canada's at war!"

"William Lyon Mackenzie King? He certainly has a strong name. I know politicians who would kill for a name like that!"

"Ah, quite so. In England, Canada, and Australia, names are the key to being elected. But in America what counts is money and nicknames. Mostly money. Americans trust rich men; rich men don't need to steal. Every time Americans elect a poor president, he turns out to be either incompetent or a thief, or both. And we like nicknames, makes people feel at home with their leaders."

"Yes, sir, FDR," Joe said, beaming.

The train took a turn and Joe again looked out the window. The scenery was really quite pleasant. Snow-covered hills, more trees. But it was barren, still unpopulated. Well, it wasn't going to be difficult to smuggle arms into the country. Hell, the border was largely unguarded bush. Presumably they could drive the tanks right out of Detroit and into a nice secluded area, and just sort of set them there so the Canadians could slip over and "steal" them. He laughed; the idea amused him.

* * *

The sun had nearly set when the train pulled into the Ottawa station. Joe Scanlon turned his luggage over to a porter, stuffed his gloved hands in his overcoat, and walked out of the station. He took a deep breath, and when he exhaled, his breath hung in front of him. "February in Ottawa," he said aloud. He pulled his scarf over his nose. Damn, it was cold!

As promised in his advance information, the station was right smack in the middle of downtown and directly across from Ottawa's pride and joy, the Château Laurier Hotel. Its green-copper roof glistened with ice and snow in the sunset.

He looked around. Just to its left on a rolling hill were the Parliament Buildings—Westminster on the Rideau—a miniature version of London, complete with red-coated, fur-helmeted guardsmen.

Joe scurried across the street, vaguely aware that his unannounced appearance was going to cause a problem. Most emissaries would have been met, then wined and dined, he assumed. But he had chosen to slip into Ottawa unknown and to leave the details of his visit a mystery to his hosts. In any case, wartime was no time for lavish protocol. As he looked at Ottawa—a town of fewer than fifty thousand souls—he decided his hosts might not have the wherewithal for lavish affairs in any case.

"Scanlon," Joe said to the desk clerk in the ornate and surprisingly elegant lobby of the Château Laurier. "I have a reservation."

Once in his room, Joe opened his suitcase. Emerald had packed it, and as if by some miracle, nothing was wrinkled. He hung his shirts, put his shoes in the closet, hung his dress suit. He was taking his toilet kit out when there was a knock on the door.

Assuming it was the bellboy, Joe called out from the bathroom, "Come on in, it's open."

He turned, bathroom door still ajar, and pissed into the toilet. He looked up to see a shorter man in a crumpled gray suit staring at him.

"Mr. Scanlon, I presume?"

Joe cocked an eyebrow. The man wore plain glasses with light wire frames; they hung over his nose, and his cool blue eyes studied Joe curiously. He spoke with an unmistakable clipped New England accent, an accent that always gave strangers the impression of incredible efficiency.

"Mr. Howe, I take it?"

C. D. Howe nodded and stepped into the bathroom. He unzipped his pants and he too pissed into the toilet. "It's damn cold outside," he said by way of explanation. "Besides, I've always believed that two men who piss together can do business together. Do you agree with that?"

"It seems a decent start for negotiations." Joe grinned. The man had style. "Does this place have a bar?"

"Mr. Scanlon. It's Sunday. We do not sell spirits on Sunday in the province of Ontario, which unfortunately is where we happen to be."

"If I'd known, I'd have come up Monday."

It was C. D.'s turn to grin. "No need to worry. We're only a short drive from Hull, which happily is in good Catholic Quebec. They drink on Sunday."

Joe smiled. "We're off to a good start."

"Mr. Scanlon, you have me at an advantage. I have to be nice."

"So you do." Joe winked. "And now, shall we drive to Hull?"

4

October 4, 1940

It was autumn, Emerald's favorite time of year. The leaves of the giant old trees on the Boston Common had gone all red and gold; fallen leaves blew in the brisk autumn wind.

Emerald and Eugenia walked across the Common together. They had just lunched at the Carlton and then gone to a newsreel.

"You're truly fortunate," Eugenia proclaimed as she adjusted her hat. "I think that every time I see a newsreel. My God, it's getting worse every day, every second! And I just hate it when that man comes on the radio—Gabrial Heatter—he always starts off with that voice, 'Ah, yes, there's a bright spot on the dark horizon *to . . . night!*' "

Emerald laughed. Eugenia's inflection was just right. "Edward R. Murrow isn't too cheerful either. 'This is London'—just to let us all know it's still there."

"Must be terrible, having bombs falling out of the sky, not knowing where they're going to land. I can't imagine it."

"It's terrible," Emerald replied, not elaborating. Eugenia knew about 1916 and the Irish civil war, she knew Emerald had experienced warfare. "But why am I fortunate?"

"Because your children are younger than mine. If we do get into it, they won't have to fight."

"If you consider Spain the beginning of this, I've already lost a son," she said sadly.

"Was Spain the start of it?"

"They say Hitler tested his weapons there." Emerald paused. "The swan boats are put away for the season," she said abstractedly. They were covered with canvas and stood alone like great bird ghosts. Now, she thought, only the persistent pigeons are left. A few yards away, an old man sat feeding them, and hundreds of the bold creatures flocked to him; some sat on his shoulder, and one, like a masthead, posed atop his head.

"I doubt I will ever have to worry about Philip. He's my artistic child. He's been offered a position with the Boston Pops—Mr. Fiedler says he has real potential. Of course, Frederick wants him to take over Monteith Mills, he says there's no money in being a classical cellist. Mind you, Philip doesn't care about the money and he certainly doesn't want to run Monteith Mills and sell carpets!"

Emerald nodded knowingly. Frederick Monteith was a senator, but he came out of, and had inherited, his family's business.

"Frederick doesn't seem to want to run it either—he went into politics. Philip plays beautifully. I think children should follow their talents," Emerald said.

"Well, both Philip and I will give Frederick an argument. In any case, if there's a war, the one I'll have to worry about is James. He's already in the service! Oh, I wish he hadn't gotten into Annapolis! If only his grandfather hadn't been an admiral."

"If we enter the war, James will have lots of company."

"Do you think we will? Frederick's against it. He's voted against any kind of involvement. The Senate makes these decisions, and Frederick says the Senate will never declare war!"

Emerald thought of Frederick Monteith. He was getting on, he hardly knew where Germany was. And as far as France was concerned, he was probably only sorry that he couldn't go to the Riviera this year. Still, he was a good man with consideration for his constituents. Even Joe said that Frederick had seen to it that numerous public-works programs had come to New England.

"Most of the Senate is pacifist," Emerald agreed.

Eugenia tossed her fur over her shoulder. "Those RKO newsreel films of Paris were devastating. Do you realize what will become of the fashion industry? Saks will go out of business!"

"And half of Fifth Avenue with them. Eugenia, never mind Frederick, what do you think? Do you think the Germans will stop where they are? Would you want them here, could you live under that sort of regime?"

"My God, no! But of course I'm not French or German—thank heaven! But no, I certainly couldn't. All those dismal soldiers in their idiotic boots, walking like wind-up dolls and saluting like little machines. No individuality. You know how big we Bostonians are on that! Besides, I simply can't stand the smell of sauerkraut. No, I couldn't live under Hitler. All that regimentation goes against my grain."

"People have a right to their independence. We ought to be helping the British and the French."

"Aren't we?" Eugenia raised her eyebrow and leaned closer to Emerald. "Frederick says we are, Frederick says Joe knows all about it, and Frederick says it's illegal."

Emerald giggled. At times Eugenia was out-and-out funny. Frederick Monteith was twenty years his wife's senior. Most of the time she spoke of him as if he were her father and not her husband.

"Maybe," Emerald hedged. "But is rampaging through Europe with tanks and killing people legal? Good heavens, Eugenia, Hitler lied at Munich and now he's invaded Finland, his own ally. Do we have to play by the rules for this man Hitler? The hell with him and his fascist followers."

"My goodness. When you're upset, your language becomes undignified."

"That's not half of what I'd like to say about Hitler!" Emerald said with a smirk. "Come along, Eugenia, in the quiet of my living room I'll let you know how unladylike an Irish rebel can be!"

"Sounds entertaining and educational. Gawd! I've led such a sheltered life! Can you teach me to swear with feeling?"

"I daresay," Emerald answered. "But for real feeling, you'll have to think about all the children being killed by Hitler's bombs. That makes it simple to swear."

29

1

January 15, 1941

Joe walked along Brimmer Street. He was half a block from home and he still didn't know what he was going to say or how he was going to say it. If asked, he would have confessed that he himself felt like shit. In the last eight years, Padraic O'Hearn had been like his brother. Padraic had worked for him, helped run the companies, invented and marketed the Scanlon Screamer, and been the world's most wonderful uncle. "Damn!" Joe mumbled under his breath. "Damn!" He could feel the tears in his own eyes. He was going to walk in the door, and the minute Emerald saw him, she would know something terrible had happened.

Joe inhaled and mustered all the strength he had. He climbed the steps to his house and opened the front door. Emerald sailed down the hall, arms outstretched. There wasn't going to be a second's reprieve.

"Emerald."

She stopped short and looked at him. "Something's wrong . . . Joe, what's wrong?"

He reached for her and led her into the living room. "It's Padraic," he said forthrightly. "He had a heart attack . . . he died—Emerald, it was instant. He didn't suffer at all."

She stood for a long moment and stared at him. "Padraic?" she said dumbly. "Dead?"

Joe nodded. "Behind his desk . . . his secretary came in, and there he was. She thought he was asleep."

"Oh, Joe . . ."

He pulled her into his arms and held her. There weren't any words, nothing more he could say, nothing he could do.

Finally, after a long while, she looked up at him, silent tears running down her face. "He was so young—only a year older than you."

Joe nodded. "I know," he said quietly.

"Padraic was the one Father Doyle found first . . . he came to the nunnery, and he was sitting at a table. He looked across at me and he said, 'I'm your brother . . . I'm Padraic.' He gave me a present . . . he brought me that picture. . . ." She pointed to the faded tintype on the mantel; now it was protected by glass and was in a wood frame. "My parents," she said abstractedly. "I remembered my mother's face, but I'd never seen my father till Padraic gave me that picture. Then he took me home with him, and later I met Seamus."

Emerald brushed her cheek. She looked dazed.

"I loved him too," Joe said.

Emerald looked across at her husband. She could see the tears in his eyes too. "Of course you did," she replied.

Joe got up silently and made them both a drink. He handed Emerald the glass, and she accepted it, sipping it slowly, not saying anything.

"I think we should have a wake," Joe finally suggested.

Emerald looked up. "Padraic would have liked that," she answered. "He has so many friends here."

"In the Hibernian Hall?"

"Yes. Do you realize that Padraic is the first male in my family to die a natural death in living memory? Seamus told me our grandfather was killed in a riot protesting the corn laws, my father was killed in South Africa, Seamus died in the rising of 1916 . . . Tom died in Spain. . . ."

Joe nodded. It was a profound thought, four generations of violent deaths. "Emerald, when I die, I hope I die like Padraic. It's every man's dream to die painlessly and quickly."

"Don't talk about your dying."

"I'm very healthy."

Emerald leaned back in the chair. "Will you tell the children? I can't, at least I don't think I can." She sighed, "I don't want them to develop a fear of death. They would if I told them."

"I'll tell them. The hardest thing was telling you."

"I'll be all right. I'm numb now, but I'll be all right."

Joe walked over to her chair and kissed her. "I know you will."

2

January 20, 1941

"I've never seen so many people, all stomping, drinking, and dancing about. I think Padraic had more friends than almost any Irishman in Boston."

"It makes me happy that there are so many," Emerald answered.

"I'm glad you invited me," Eugenia put in. "It's certainly an interesting custom . . . I think I like it. I think I'd like to be sent off with this kind of farewell, everyone drinking and dancing. Certainly is an improvement on weeping and wailing. Let me tell you, Protestant funerals are positively dismal."

Joe eyed Eugenia and then broke into a wide grin.

"And what are you smirking at, Mr. Joe Scanlon?"

"I was thinking of Padraic over there in his coffin, his spirit looking down from on high . . . I was thinking what pleasure it would give him if I danced with the lord-high Lady Brahmin of Boston at his wake."

"Darling, if you're going to ask me to dance, just ask. Don't make a religious experience out of it. And try to remember, I do still have some of my Brahmin reserve."

"Not much." Joe laughed. "Well, come along, Eugenia, religious experience or no, I insist."

"Frederick would be appalled," Eugenia announced as Joe whirled off with her.

Joe laughed. "Ah, Eugenia . . . we've corrupted you."

"Well, not really. It's just another kind of corruption."

She smiled sweetly, and people actually cleared away and clapped as Joe and Eugenia became the center of attention.

"See, everyone is pleased," Joe told her.

"I'm always the center of attention—wherever I go. I make a point of it, you know."

Emerald watched them and smiled broadly. "I can't believe what I'm seeing!"

"No one else can either," someone quipped.

At that moment a devastating siren ripped through the hall and the room became utterly silent as the dancers froze in motion and the fiddlers stopped playing.

"Good heavens," Emerald exclaimed.

Then Dooley of Dooley's bar stood up on a table and roared with laughter. "To my friend Padraic O'Hearn, a great tribute! Why, it's only his greatest accomplishment, the Scanlon Screamer! And every one of you know its fine sound! It saved you all from the police during Prohibition, it did! And if the Scanlon Screamer doesn't wake the corpse, nothing will!"

A round of laughter and applause filled the room, and even Emerald managed to smile.

3

March 8, 1941

"Am I going to have a coming-out party on my eighteenth birthday?" Katie asked as she smoothed out her dress. Of late she had been totally preoccupied with her appearance and with movies, which were her passion.

"You're not even seventeen yet. Isn't it a bit early to be concerned about your social position?"

"All the other rich girls in Boston have coming-out parties."

Emerald watched her daughter. Katie was standing in front of a full-length mirror; she couldn't take her eyes off her own image. "Do you think I'm pretty?" Katie whirled around, her long red hair flying.

"Yes, I think you're pretty, but pretty has to come from inside, too."

Katie didn't answer, but instead turned back to her mirror. "I'm sixteen, you know. I want to start wearing stockings."

"None of the girls your age wear stockings."

Katie made a pouty expression. "It's not easy being feminine in this house full of boys." She uttered the word "boys" with superiority.

"That's got nothing to do with stockings."

"Well, anyway, I look older than I am."

It was Emerald's turn not to reply. She certainly couldn't argue with that. Katie was fully developed and had high, full firm breasts, a tiny waist, and round hips. But her most outstanding feature was her legs. They were long and shapely; the gangly girl had turned into a poised charmer and something of a young flirt. When they went out together, Emerald noted, men turned to look at Katie and their eyes revealed both admiration and lust.

Only recently Joe had commented, "Thank God she's in a good Catholic girls' school. At least in her uniform she looks modest." Emerald had agreed, though she knew only too well how much Katie despised the blue serge suit, the white blouse, and the long, scratchy wool socks.

"Well, think about it, Mother. I really want a coming-out party. After all, Daddy's an important man, so why can't I? Why can't we have it at the Copley Plaza. Oh, I can see myself dancing now under the crystal chandelier."

"I'll think about it," Emerald allowed. "I only have a year and five months."

She took another long look at her daughter and sighed inwardly. Then she left the pink-and-white bedroom and walked down the hall. J.J. was at basketball practice and Seamus was with him; Edward had gone to the Boston Museum of Natural History to see the new dinosaur exhibit. For a Saturday afternoon in March, the house was extraordinarily quiet.

"Emerald!"

"Joe? What are you doing home this time of day?"

She hurried to the top of the stairs and down them. It was only two P.M. and she hadn't expected Joe till at least six.

He had just slung his coat over the rack in the hall, and he held out his arms to her, a crooked, mischievous smile on his face. "Mark this day! March 8, 1941! It's important."

"What's happened?" Emerald studied his face; it certainly couldn't be bad news, he looked far too cheerful and she knew that twinkle in his eyes. "Joe Scanlon, what have you done?"

"Done?" He feigned complete innocence. "What makes you think I've done anything?"

"I know you, I know that look!"

He pulled her to him. "I have a surprise for you!" He kissed her and hugged her. Then he glanced at his watch. "Will the children be home by six?"

"I imagine. Are you really going to keep me in suspense that long?"

"Longer. I want everyone in bed early tonight, because tomorrow we're going up to the Cape!"

Emerald eyed him suspiciously. "It's only March, nothing is open. And as much as I'd like to get away for a few days, this is hardly the time of year to be going to Cape Cod."

"Do not question me, madam. I am the master of this household, and if you do not do as you are bid, I shall turn you over my knee and spank you." He was pretending to be a nineteenth-century autocrat.

Emerald burst out laughing and kissed his neck. "I'm not sure that doesn't sound like fun," she said submissively.

Joe picked her up in his arms. "Well, woman, if that's the mood you're in, I'll damn well oblige you."

"Oh, Joe, put me down."

"I will, on the bed, in our room, as soon as the door is locked."

"What?"

"I'm going to make love to you, my darling. On a Saturday afternoon. I'm going to make love to you till you beg me to stop."

"Oh, I'd never do that. . . ."

4

March 9, 1941

"It's raining," Edward complained. "I won't even be able to fly my kite if it's raining." He was slumped in the back of the long black Cadillac, his gay red-and-orange kite firmly tucked between his legs. He had refused to surrender it to the trunk of the car with the luggage.

Katie stared out the window as the large drops of rain began to splash against it. "There isn't a single movie theater around! We'll be gone for a whole week! I'll miss Rory's new picture, it just opened at Loew's!"

"There is too a movie theater," Joe insisted. He was driving instead of the chauffeur. He liked driving, he liked to watch the big Cadillac eat up the miles as it moved along the road smoothly, taking the curves in stride.

"You mean the Bijou? They don't have films, all they have is Hopalong Cassidy! They never have real films, they never have romances."

Joe laughed. "I can live with that," he said under his breath.

"In the summer there's lots of live theater," Emerald said. "Of course, it isn't summer. Really, Joe, where are we going to stay? None of the hotels are open yet."

"Allow me to be in charge." He reached over and patted her knee. "Trust, just a little trust."

J.J. sat uncomfortably between Edward and Katie; his long legs were folded up like a closed accordion. A shock of unruly hair fell over his handsome young face.

J.J. stole a furtive glance at Katie. Her dress had ridden up when she squirmed around; it now rested somewhat indecently just above her rounded knees. He couldn't help but stare; Katie had pretty knees—almost as pretty as her teats, which he had accidentally seen when she was on her way from the bathroom to her room and had casually draped a towel too loosely around her. He always thought she had revealed herself on purpose, because when he stopped short, gawking at her, she had gone red and burst into giggles.

Since that moment—which was almost a year ago—he had thought about Katie now and again while he was soothing himself, as he chose to call his frequent efforts at self-gratification. But of course, it was not really right to think of Katie, so he always imagined Katie's body with someone else's face. Usually Peggy Faraday. She had a nice face.

"Move your foot," Seamus said irritably. He had been relegated to the jump seat and felt like a piece of meat between two slices of bread. He too was mildly irritated with this sudden trip, this uprooting from his usual schedule. It was unfair, decidedly unfair. He was almost exactly two years younger than J.J., and shorter than J.J. was two years ago. Much shorter. He lifted weights, he exercised daily. But all to no avail. He seemed to have stopped growing entirely.

Joe wheeled the car off the main road and proceeded up a long winding driveway lined with cedar trees. They were bent from the wind that battered the cape; they looked like lonely misshapen sentinels.

There, at the end of the drive, was a rambling three-story white Victorian house with a wide veranda on its left side. In front was a large expanse of lawn, and behind the house, a grove of woods. On the beach side there was a long stretch of white sand leading down to the now turbulent surf. It was marked off by giant boulders on either end. Near the far end of the swimming beach was a long dock, and tied to it was a fair-sized yacht.

"How do you like the outside?" Joe asked.

"The house? It's beautiful, it's a mansion! The whole place is beautiful."

"It's got nine bedrooms and five baths. It's got a real billiards room and a bar—I mean a big one! It's got a library, a giant kitchen, and a huge living and dining room. It's truly spacious, you'll love it."

Emerald turned to him, her mouth open slightly as a look of enlightenment spread over her face. "Joe, you didn't? It . . . isn't, is it?"

"Ours," he said proudly. "All ours, for the summers left in our lives."

"All summer, every summer?" Katie interjected. "Oh, God, I'll miss all Rory's films!"

"Is the boat ours?" J.J. asked with enthusiasm.

"Yup, comes with," his father replied.

J.J. immediately envisaged himself at sea with two beautiful girls—girls in bathing suits . . . no, girls without bathing suits—alone, all alone!

"Wow!" said Seamus, beaming. "Look at that beach!"

Edward peered out the window. "I wonder if there are any Indian artifacts in the woods." Edward was consumed by interest in archaeology and dinosaurs. He spent all his time at the museum and always used big words.

"Allow me to give you a guided tour," Joe said. "Look, I'm a man who makes preparations. Even the beds are made, there's toilet paper in all nine bathrooms." He led them to the front door and opened it. "The furniture came with." He smiled. "Feel free to decorate at will."

"It's really quite nice as it is—needs a few pictures. Oh, I love the clock!" Emerald stopped to admire the great grandfather clock in the hall.

The children were little interested in the downstairs. J.J. and Seamus headed for the billiards room. Edward went right out the back door to the woods.

"Which bedroom is mine?" Katie called.

"The one with the mirrors!" Joe shouted back.

"Well, what do you think? Look, I even have the bar stocked with champagne."

"Let's christen our house," Emerald suggested. "Oh, Joe, it really is a wonderful surprise."

5

August 15, 1941

"This is a brilliant idea," Joe praised. "Setting aside the exact middle of the month and having all our celebrations at once, together! Our anniversary, your birthday, and Seamus', Katie's, and J.J.'s birthdays."

"I'm the only one who doesn't have something to celebrate," Edward complained.

"And have we ever short-changed you on your birthday?" Joe asked.

"No."

"Besides, my birthday is in March."

"Yeah, but you got your anniversary in August."

Joe laughed. "Can't win, can I?"

"Nope."

"Ah, there's Eugenia now, and Frederick is with her. I'm glad they could both come."

"Eugenia is entertainment, Frederick is . . . well, to be endured."

Emerald laughed. "Sh!" she said, smiling. "Eugenia, Frederick!" Emerald embraced Eugenia and she shook hands with Frederick, who grunted, albeit more pleasantly than usual.

"Well, what's on the agenda?" Eugenia asked. "Besides a delightful week of sun, surf, and sailing."

"An old-fashioned clambake—this one on our own beach!"

"Sounds fantastic. And what about the boat, is no one going to take me out?"

"J.J. will," Emerald volunteered.

J.J. looked at Eugenia. She was a nice lady, but not quite what he had had in mind when he imagined himself alone at sea with a woman, or women. "Sure," he said, "anytime."

"Sure. Anytime. That's what I like. A young man with a large vocabulary."

J.J. blushed. "I'll be happy to take you out in the boat."

"Good grief. A complete sentence. You're the first person under twenty I've heard speak a complete sentence in three years. Even Philip and James go about saying 'Yeah,' 'Okay,' and 'Sure' all the time."

"Frankly, the Senate sessions would be much shorter if everyone spoke like Joseph Junior," Frederick guffawed at his own little joke. Everyone smiled at him indulgently except Eugenia. She made a face.

"He's called J.J. and not Joseph Junior—an attempt to keep him from being confused with his father—one of the few attempts in this world to prevent confusion. Of course, you spend so much time in Washington, you're used to confusion."

Frederick grunted.

"Excuse me," J.J. said as he left the room.

"Would you care to see a genuine Soricidae perfectly preserved in a jar of formaldehyde?" Edward asked.

Eugenia frowned at him. "What's that?" she queried.

"A dead shrew," Edward said with all the pride a thirteen-year-old scientist can muster.

Poor Edward didn't understand the pun, but Emerald had to put her hand over her mouth, and Joe laughed out loud. Even poor Frederick could not suppress a smile.

"Well!" Eugenia said, but even she couldn't keep a straight face.

"It's all right," Joe roared. "It's tamed!"

"So am I," Eugenia retorted.

"Let's have a drink," Emerald suggested.

"Good idea," Eugenia put in.

Edward shrugged and followed J.J.'s exit. "Nobody wants to see my collection," he mumbled.

"What's happening in Congress?" Joe knew perfectly well, but he always enjoyed feeling out Frederick.

"Oh, the same old pressures—to increase aid to Britain, to take some sort of position. But I say the hell with Europe! There's an ocean between us and the Germans. There's another ocean between us and Japan. The Germans won't come here, and a bunch of disorganized, half-assed orientals won't either. Hell, those people only know how to imitate—their ships are all made out of paper, they don't know one damn thing about modern technology, and I suppose their gunpowder is made out of fireworks!"

"No, dear," Eugenia corrected. "Fireworks are made out of gunpowder."

Frederick didn't acknowledge her. "Anyway, I say we fought a revolution to get Europe off this continent, and we've got the Monroe Doctrine to keep Europe out of this hemisphere! We got sucked in once. Well, I say we ought to mind our own business!"

Joe didn't respond. He had known when he asked the question that he would get Frederick's last Senate speech for an answer. Frederick was an isolationist supreme. But that wasn't a hard fight, because the mood of the country was isolationist.

Emerald sipped her drink. "Last month the American Bund held a meeting in Soldier Field in Chicago. They filled it, Frederick. There are Nazis right here in America."

"Well, let J. Edgar Hoover take care of them. Damn good men in the FBI, damn good!"

"You voted against their last appropriation," Eugenia said on a note of triumph.

"That's because they wanted too much," Frederick grumbled.

"I imagine our feast is almost ready," Emerald said brightly. "I'm afraid you'll have to endure our gift-giving. We chose to celebrate everything that falls in this month on one day smack in the middle."

"I don't mind how many gifts you give, as long as Congress doesn't have to pay for them!" Frederick guffawed again.

Joe thought of the huge contract Scanlon Structures had just been awarded to construct prefab housing on the Norfolk naval base, and he smiled. "Well, they do," he admitted. "But not directly."

6

August 20, 1941

Joe and Emerald walked along the sand beach holding hands. "Sometimes I think the tide is higher in summer because the island sinks a little with its added inhabitants," she joked.

Joe laughed and squeezed her hand. "Do you like it here? Are you glad I bought the house? We can come here in the spring too, maybe even for long weekends in the winter. The house has a perfectly good heating system."

"I love it. It's so roomy, really quite suitable for our brood and their army of friends. Besides, you know I'm at home with the sea—I come from an island, a bigger island than this, of course."

"Emerald from the Emerald Isle. You ought to be happy that Ireland has declared and maintained its neutrality."

"It's a bit idealistic under the circumstances, but we're an idealistic lot—most of us, anyway."

"You look rested," he observed. Her hair wasn't short, but it was cut in a wavy bob. It blew in the breeze, and she walked barefoot in the sand, allowing it to ooze through her toes.

"I feel rested, but I miss Boston, too. And even though Eugenia only left this morning, I miss her."

"But not Frederick?" Joe teased.

"No, not Frederick," Emerald allowed with a grin.

She looked off across the sea. "It's hard to think there's a war over there." She stared at the Atlantic. "German subs—do you think they might be out there?"

"We're not at war," he reminded her.

"Neither was Poland," she answered. "And London. My heavens, all those little children being evacuated, torn from their mothers. The bombs, the destruction—it reminds me of . . ."

"When you sent Tom away."

Emerald nodded. She stopped walking and sat down on the sand; then she lay down, folding her arms under her head. "Oh, the sand is warm, it feels nice. I wish this summer would never end—ocean or no ocean—I feel it all coming."

Joe sucked on the last of his cigarette and sat down beside her. "Here comes Katie. She's running like the devil's chasing her."

"Mother, Father!" Katie collapsed breathlessly on the sand next to them. "Guess what! Guess who's coming here for the last play of the season! Guess! Guess! It's my dream come true, it's stupendous!'' Her huge green eyes were aglow, and she waved her hand in the air with excitement.

"Tyrone Power," Emerald guessed. "My, I do hope so, he's so handsome."

"Personally, I would prefer Vivien Leigh," Joe said.

"It's Rory O'Hara! He's coming here, he's coming in person. Of course, I'll go to the play, I'll go every night! Do you think if I did, he'd notice me? Mother, can we have him to dinner? No, can we have a party for the whole cast? That's less obvious. Can we? Can we?''

Emerald groaned.

"You might as well give in," Joe suggested. "It'll be easier." He turned to Katie. "They look different in person, you know. He probably wears a girdle, and I'm sure he couldn't slice his way out of a paper bag with a sword. You, my dear, are star-struck."

"He's gorgeous and he does not wear a girdle! You're terrible. I love Rory, I really do."

Emerald groaned again. "You have a crush on him," she corrected, knowing it was no use whatsoever. "All right, we'll have a party for the cast. But you, my dear, will plan it and do all the work."

"I will, I will, I will!" Katie scrambled to her feet. "Oh, I have to phone everyone! Rory O'Hara is coming to my house! I can't wait!"

Emerald sat up and shook her head. She bent down and touched her toes, wiggling them as she did so. "That girl is impossible."

"You said she'd outgrow it."

"She's too privileged," Emerald concluded.

"You wouldn't want her to be poor. You wouldn't want her to be like the children who come to your recreation center. Emerald, there's no way to avoid the fact that money makes her different. She's not really impossible, she's just a very pretty girl who's a little vain and still very young emotionally. Our children are a new experience for us," he continued, "because we didn't have what they have."

"You're right," Emerald answered. "But I think I'll talk to her anyway, calm her down a bit."

"Good."

30

1

September 1, 1941

Katie sat on the end of her bed wrapped in her blue nightdress, the morning paper spread out before her. The story that filled the society column was her story, and she reread it avidly, devouring each word and reliving each ecstactic moment.

> The large stone patio was lit by the subdued colored light of over one hundred Japanese lanterns. The long white-clothed tables were laden with fresh salads, meats, breads, and delightful desserts. The party, held after the opening night of Eugene O'Neill's *Desire Under the Elms*, was attended by the elite of Cape Cod's youth.
>
> Miss Kathleen Scanlon (Katie to her many friends) was radiant in pink chiffon, while Gloria Barton (Barton, Gross and Henderson, Inc.) wore light green silk. Present were: Jack Madison, Jr., Loretta Swift, William Adams, Martha Gibson, and Jason Quincey III, among others. The entire group, which included the full cast of the play, was entertained by Tom Appleby's band. They danced till dawn.

Katie put down the paper and giggled to herself. She put her arms around herself and rocked back and forth on the giant canopied bed, humming and singing. The world was a wonderful place, and Rory himself had danced with her and held her close. "Glorious" was not the word! "Stupendous" was the word! Rory had kissed her!

Katie jumped from the bed and ran to her full-length mirror. She smiled at herself and turned, assessing the curves of her body. Then she ripped off her nightdress and looked at herself nude. She pinched her breasts until the little pink nipples stood up, erect. She smiled at her own long thighs, at the tuft of red-gold hair that covered her plump pubis. She moved this way and that, posing outrageously.

And tonight, tonight, Rory O'Hara had promised to meet her near the great rock pile that all the young people called Stonehenge, after the performance.

Katie planned it all out in her mind; the play wouldn't be over till ten-thirty, so she would have to sneak out of the house, but that, she reasoned, would be a simple matter.

What matters, what really matters, is that Rory wants to see me again!

Down the long hall, behind the large white double doors, Emerald and Joe still lazed in bed.

Emerald turned in Joe's arms. "I'm getting old," she confessed. "I thought all those young people would never go home—Lord, it must have been five in the morning."

Joe leaned on his elbow and looked down at her. He kissed the tip of her breast. "I thought we'd never get to bed," he agreed. "You know, you're truly beautiful."

"Forty-seven-year-old women are not beautiful."

"You are." He leaned back, flopping down, but still allowing his hand to rest on her bare skin. He had only just finished making love to her, but her disheveled appearance and state of half-dress excited him. It excited him almost as much as feeling her move with him, press against him, and finally yield herself in pleasurable abandon. When he made love to her, he felt younger; it was as if neither of them had aged a single year since their wedding night.

But they had, he admitted, and in spite of his excitement, he knew he could not make love to her again—at least not right away.

"What did you think of Rory?" Joe asked, almost laughing. "You know, it's hard for a man to watch his only daughter have a crush on a person like that. I thought girls were supposed to fall in love with men like their fathers."

Emerald laughed. "You're jealous."

"No, just mystified."

"I'm sure she'll eventually fall in love with someone just like you, when she develops some maturity and good sense. She's only seventeen, and he is a film star!"

"He's wet behind the ears, a young tyrant who's got too much for his own good."

Emerald didn't ask "Too much of what?" because she had seen him in swimming trunks. He had a fine build; even she had to admit that. He looked like all those men who devote themselves to the male body beautiful. But besides his body, Rory was blessed with a boyish face, with sandy hair that hung loose with a spoiled little pout of the sort that often appealed to young women. And he was rich.

"Katie's seventeen and Rory's twenty-five. She's still a child and he's a movie star. I really wouldn't worry about it."

"My dear Mrs. Scanlon, when you were fifteen, I was twenty-five. The age difference between us is greater than it is between Katie and Rory. And by the way, had I met you at a younger age, I would have fallen in love with you anyway. Of course, I would have had to wait for you to grow up a bit, but I'm a patient man."

"Are you suggesting we should be concerned? Joe, this is the first of September and school starts on the fifteenth. We'll be going back to Boston on the tenth, and Rory's play will close and he'll be going back to Hollywood."

"I suppose you're right. But that young man has no character."

"Does he need character for Katie to clip his picture out of *Silver Screen* and put it on her wall?"

"No." Joe laughed. "But he's no picture right now. He's here and he's talking, walking, and dancing with my daughter."

"Time is on our side," she assured him.

He moved his hand over her silky flesh.

"Joe, don't tease me, you're driving me crazy."

He sat up again and loomed over her. "Let's give it a whirl." He pulled her closer.

2

December 5, 1941

Katie paused outside the theater and looked at the pictures of coming attractions. She pressed her lips together when she saw Rory's face peering at her from the poster advertising *The Rose and the Blade*. Then wordlessly she reached up and touched the life-sized picture of his face, transferring the kiss from her fingertips to the poster.

Katie then whirled around and with mist-filled eyes darted across Tremont Street and into the Common. Beneath her winter coat, her pleated skirt was becoming uncomfortably tight. Her once-slender waist was thickening. She fought back tears, which would surely freeze right on her face.

Katie paused and looked across the street at Schrafft's. On a sudden impulse she changed directions and ran toward it, seeking warmth and refuge in a leather-lined booth, surrounded by the smell of candies and hot chocolate.

"May I help you?" The waitress hovered over her, dressed in black with a crisp white apron. She held a pad and pencil.

"A wet walnut sundae," Katie ordered. "And a glass of milk."

The woman disappeared, and Katie leaned back. She couldn't go on much longer. God knew that every time J.J. said she was getting fat, she almost cracked.

She took a deep breath and momentarily wished she were dead. She leaned back and closed her eyes, but the scene of her downfall always returned to her; it returned vividly, and with it, its exciting horror.

After the play ended the night after the stunning party so dutifully reported in the society column of the local newspaper, Katie had gone to meet Rory at the place called Stonehenge.

"You came." Rory devoured her with his eyes and spread out a blanket on the sand in a secluded area behind a huge boulder. "I wasn't sure you'd come."

"Not come! Oh, Rory, how could you think such a thing!" She had gushed out the words and then felt embarrassed, thinking that she ought to hide her feelings and not let him know how passionately she cared. That's what all the magazines advised: play hard-to-get. But it was difficult advice to follow, and she only wanted to throw herself into his arms and cry out, "I'd follow you to the ends of the earth, my darling. You are my sun, my moon, my stars." Vaguely she had remembered Ronald Colman saying that too, or was it Bette Davis? She couldn't quite recall.

"Sit down," Rory invited. "Kathleen . . . Katie, what a lovely Irish name."

She looked up at him and was unable to speak; she was paralyzed by the sound of his voice.

"And you're a real Irish beauty, too." He brushed the shock of sandy hair off his forehead and with the same hand reached out and brushed her cheek. "I think I'm in love," he told her. "I know we've only just met, but you're breathtaking, more breathtaking than any woman I've ever known. Do you believe in love at first sight, Katie?"

Katie flushed. "There must be lots of beautiful women in Hollywood."

"But not like you. Not innocent, not brave, not so lovely." He pulled her into his arms, and she went limp with desire.

His hand wandered to her full breast, and she allowed it to remain before she tried to remove it.

"It's all right," he said authoritatively. "I have to touch a lot of women in films . . . I've seen hundreds of naked breasts, I've touched many . . . it's no more to me than taking your hand or stroking your hair.''

"Oh," she responded, feeling dumb and unsophisticated.

He continued to press her breast till he felt her nipples harden beneath the thin material of her dress. Then Rory kissed her; forcing her mouth open, he moved his tongue around.

Katie felt damp between her legs in that place; she protested weakly, but his hands were everywhere, now underneath her dress. He undid her bra strap and caressed her naked flesh; then he kissed the tips of her breasts, moving his other hand up her thigh.

"Oh, I love you," he whispered in her ear. He pulled at her cotton panties and forced her long legs apart.

"No, no," Katie protested.

"If you love me, prove it. . . . Love like ours has to be . . . it can't be stopped, my darling."

Katie gasped and let out a small cry, and he penetrated her. But Rory played with her, toyed with her till she was a bundle of raw nerves, till she moved with him, wiggling and moaning.

After that, Katie had gone to meet Rory every night until she and her parents left for Boston. They made love over and over and they made plans, they talked of a future together.

"I have a snow-white house with a red-tile roof," he told her. "It's high in the hills and from the window you can see all of the city; it looks like a million stars at night. And there's a swimming pool. You'll love it, Katie, you'll love it!"

"I know I will," she murmured. "When . . . when can I come?"

"When I finish my next picture," he promised. "But, Katie, I'll write to you and you'll write to me."

The waitress set down the wet walnut sundae and Katie jumped, jolted back to reality from her reverie. The sundae sat in a cold steel dish: three scoops of ice cream covered with walnuts soaked in maple syrup, oodles of whipped cream, more nuts, and a huge bright red cherry. Dismally Katie lifted her spoon and began eating. She had written twenty letters to Rory O'Hara, and not one of them had been answered. It was Friday, December 5, 1941, and Katie knew she was a little more than three months pregnant.

3

Sunday, December 7, 1941

The dining-room table was covered with papers, folders, and cost estimates for the coming year's operation of the recreation center.

Emerald and Eugenia went through the folders attempting to assess what new programs might be offered. In the background, the Atwater Kent radio played soft music—Sunday fare after the broadcast of various church services.

"That was a delicious lunch," Eugenia said. "And this is delightful red wine. My, it has a charming bouquet. It's hard to get decent wine now, not to mention French soap."

"It's left over," Emerald answered. "We have a case of it in the cellar. We brought it back from our trip in thirty-three, just put it away and forgot about it."

"Lucky you and damn the Germans!" Eugenia raised her glass. "It's a good idea to do this on Sunday afternoon. It's such a sleepy day; one always gets more done because there are no interruptions."

"That's why I suggested it."

"Where are the children? Has Joe spirited them away? I always expect Edward to be here, forcing me to look at dead things in jars."

"Joe's at a community meeting." She avoided saying he was down at Dooley's with his cronies who delivered votes in the various South Boston wards. "And J.J. took Seamus and Edward skating. Katie's up in her room suffering from the sweet-seventeen blues or some related disease."

"Maybe she's about to get the curse. Girls are always so absurd just before it strikes. You say good morning and they burst into tears . . . at least my younger sister did. I've always preferred not to know too much about these things."

"I don't think it's that. She's been this way for weeks, yea, months."

Eugenia picked up her wineglass. "Well . . ."

". . . . interrupt this program to bring you an important announcement. Early this morning, at seven A.M. Pacific time, United States military installations at Pearl Harbor were attacked by Japanese fighter aircraft. First reports indicate damage to be heavy, especially to those ships in port. Ladies and gentlemen, reports are flooding into the Mutual Network. Please stay tuned for further details. We will interrupt this program to bring you bulletins as they arrive."

Eugenia gripped her glass so hard it shattered.

Emerald turned quickly away from the radio. Eugenia's face was contorted—a mask of apprehension. Her hand hovered in midair, bleeding from the broken glass.

"Eugenia!"

She blinked her eyes as if she were coming back to life. "James is on the *Oklahoma*! He's in Pearl Harbor!"

Emerald ran to her. "It'll be all right, Eugenia." Emerald took a white linen napkin and wrapped Eugenia's hand in it. "This doesn't look too bad."

"He's dead. I know he's dead."

Emerald remembered with horror her own premonition of Tom's death. She pushed it aside. "Stop it, Eugenia. Wait until you know . . . come on, come over to the sofa. Let me make you a drink."

Emerald sat Eugenia down and fixed the drink.

"We interrupt this program. . . . we have just learned that today at two-fifteen P.M., eastern standard time, the Japanese ambassador passed a note to Secretary of State Cordell Hull. The contents of that note are not yet available. . . . More news of the attack: The Japanese are said to have utilized fifty-one bombs, eighty-nine torpedo planes, and forty-three fighters in the first of two waves of attack. In the second wave, unconfirmed reports suggest the use of seventy-eight bombers, fifty-four torpedo planes, and thirty-five fighters. As a result of this dastardly surprise attack, the battleships *Arizona, California, Oklahoma,* and *West Virginia* are sunk or sinking."

Eugenia let out a long agonized moan.

"The battleships *Maryland, Nevada, Pennsylvania,* and *Tennessee* are badly damaged and burning. The target ship *Utah* has just sunk. The light cruisers *Raleigh* and *Helena* are burning. . . . That is all we have for now."

The music came on; it played two bars.

"We interrupt this program to bring you further news on the Japanese attack on Pearl Harbor. All U.S. military personnel have been placed on war alert. Congress had been recalled and will meet tomorrow, at which time the president will ask for a declaration of war against Japan and the Axis powers. . . . We will repeat this broadcast in twenty minutes' time."

"He's dead," Eugenia said again. "The *Oklahoma*'s been sunk . . ."

"Pearl Harbor." Emerald repeated the name. It seemed light-years away from the comfortable house on Brimmer Street, yet it was here, because of Eugenia.

"Frederick will be headed back to Washington, Eugenia. Stay here with us. I'll call Philip."

Eugenia nodded dumbly. "I know he's dead," she repeated again. "I feel it."

The radio droned on, and Eugenia sat like a turtle drawn up in its shell. She listened to every word, though each new piece of information brought her only more torturous thoughts.

"He's worse than dead!" Eugenia said incoherently. "He's sealed up below the water line in the darkness and he's dying slowly. Oh, God! I didn't want him to go to Annapolis! I wanted him to go to Harvard!"

Emerald wrapped Eugenia in a blanket and called the doctor as well as Philip.

When the doctor came, Eugenia took the medication, but she still did not sleep. Instead, she sat quietly staring at the radio as the announcer went on and on.

The reports of ships sunk varied; first it was said there were civilian casualties, then it was said there were none. There was a report that a Japanese gardener in California had been lynched by a gang of boys; there was talk of burning Japanese farms, and the Chinese were warned to wear identification tags.

Hickam Field had been destroyed. Planes were destroyed before they got off the ground, the fleet was devastated. All the news, Emerald thought, was contradictory, confused, and unclear—except for the fact that the *Oklahoma*, among others, was sunk and now rested at the bottom of Pearl Harbor.

One bulletin after another flooded into the living room, each bulletin interspersed with solemn music or Kate Smith singing "God Bless America."

At seven Philip finally returned her call. He said he'd been at the music conservatory all day and hadn't heard the news till he got out on the street. Once home, he found Emerald's message and phoned right away.

"Your mother is terribly worried about your brother," Emerald told him, trying to avoid details.

There was silence for a moment on the other end of the phone and Emerald knew she need not have avoided those details; Philip, she thought, sounded as if he might be crying too.

"Come over," Emerald urged. "Your mother's staying here. Why don't you come too."

"Thanks, I will," was his slow answer. Emerald hung up the phone.

"Philip is coming, Eugenia. I've tried both his office and your house—where is Frederick?"

"Somewhere, I don't know."

At nine the phone rang again. It was Joe. "Emerald, you know, of course."

"Yes." She glanced over at Eugenia. Her eyes had finally closed and she breathed heavily. She still clung to the blanket as if she were a child in a crib.

"I'm on my way to Washington," Joe said. "I'm at the train station now."

"Without packing?"

"I'll buy something up there. I won't be gone long."

"We'll be all right," she assured him. "Joe, Eugenia's here . . . I've tried and tried to reach Frederick. James is at Pearl Harbor, he's on the *Oklahoma*. Eugenia's sick with worry."

There was silence; then, "I've been trying to get him all afternoon."

"Maybe he's on his way to Washington, but damn! He should have called Eugenia first."

"I'll find him."

"Thank you. Joe, I love you."

"And I love you."

The phone clicked and Emerald looked at it. Then she put it back in its cradle. Where are the boys? It was getting dark.

As if in answer, they burst through the door.

"We're at war!" Edward screamed. "The Japs attacked us. Are they really yellow?"

"Where have you been?" Emerald said it half out of habit. It was an absurd response.

"In front of the RKO, watching the news bulletins," J.J. answered for all of them.

"Buzzzz . . ." Seamus spread his arms like wings and took off up the stairs. "I'm going to be a pilot! Bzzz, rat-tat-tat!"

"Stop that!" Emerald screamed, and Seamus stopped dead in his tracks, Edward and J.J. stared at her in shock. She had never screamed at them before.

"Eugenia's here. She's sleeping. Her son . . . her son is at Pearl Harbor. Please . . ." Emerald spoke more softly now. "Get something to eat from Cook and go to your rooms."

They looked at her sheepishly, except for J.J. He nodded and literally turned the other two around. "Can we listen to our radios?" he asked.

"Of course," Emerald answered. She took his hand and squeezed it. "Thank you, J.J. And tell Katie to come down and get something to eat too. She hasn't been out of her room all day. . . . I suppose she had the radio on."

"She doesn't need to eat, she's getting fat."

The comment went past Emerald. "I'm going to put Eugenia in the guest room, and Philip's coming too."

The boys disappeared into the kitchen. J.J. went upstairs after his sister.

"Why are you lying around mooning like a sick cat?"

Katie sat up, closed her favorite movie magazine, and looked dutifully at her twin brother.

"I suppose you know we're at war? They'll probably stop making movies. Rory will have to go off and fight the Japs. Guess he'll have to use a gun, though. I don't think he'll do well with a sword."

Katie blinked uncomprehendingly. "What? Japanese?"

"We're at war, the Japanese bombed Pearl Harbor. Hell, you stupid cow, half of Boston is in the streets. Mrs. Monteith is downstairs, she thinks her son's been killed. Our fleet's been sunk! Look at you, sitting up here mooning over a dumb movie magazine."

Katie sucked her lip. "I'm not mooning," she said defensively. "No, I didn't know, I don't care! I have more important things to worry about than some dumb war! Go away!" Symbolically she threw the magazine on the floor, and large tears filled her eyes.

"Hey, bubblehead, what's the matter with you? You're no fun anymore." He strode across the floor and looked down at her.

"I have problems," Katie sniffed.

"Mother said you should get some dinner from Cook. Of course, maybe if you went without eating, your problem would go away. You know, you really are putting on weight. Pretty soon we'll all be calling you 'Old Thick Waist.' "

Katie narrowed her eyes and glared at him. "Shut up! Just shut up, J.J. Scanlon!" Then the tears began to flow and she dissolved into deep wrenching sobs.

J.J. frowned and sat down, noting that her knees, which were showing, were as pretty as ever. A wave of deep affection passed over him. "Hey, want to tell me about it?"

"No."

"Is it your beloved Rory? What's the matter, hasn't he answered your fan letters?"

"They're not fan letters," she said coldly. "They're personal, between the two of us."

Joe laughed. "Come on, sis, he's a movie star, you're a kid."

Katie wiped her cheek. "You're the kid. I'm not a kid anymore!"

He studied her and admitted to himself that he totally adored her flair for the dramatic, even if it was corny. "I like being a kid. No responsibilities. Come on, tell me what's eating you. I won't tell anyone, honest."

Katie covered her face with her hands. "I'm pregnant! I'm going to have a baby! It's Rory's and he won't answer my letters!" Her words were incoherent at first because of her sobs, but she kept repeating them over and over.

J.J. sat frozen next to his sister, then slowly stood up. He reached down and pulled her hand away from her face. She dropped the other and stared wide-eyed at him.

"You're a slut!" he said meanly, yanking her to her feet. He felt consumed with love for her, with jealousy, with hate. His emotions warred with one another and he shook her roughly. "You'd better tell Mother!"

Katie started to shake. "I can't! I can't!"

He lifted his hand and slapped her, bringing instant silence. "You brought this on yourself! You're a disgrace to this family!"

Katie threw herself on the bed facedown, sobbing. "I know it! I just don't know what to do!"

J.J. looked at her. "I'm going to tell Mother to come upstairs. You're going to tell her, or I will!"

"You promised!" She twisted around and looked at him horrified.

"You tell her," he insisted. Then, still shaking with his own anger, he left the room. "God, I loved you, Katie! How could you!" he muttered halfway down the stairs. He felt betrayed; he felt lousy.

Emerald looked at Katie in astonishment; then she sank into the chair, totally stunned. "Pregnant," she said numbly.

"He hasn't answered my letters. I hate him . . . no, I love him. He promised me . . . he lied to me . . . he said we'd be married . . . he lied!"

"That much seems apparent," Emerald said wearily. Joe had just called again. He had heard that almost everyone on the Oklahoma was dead. In the next room Eugenia slept fitfully, mercifully drugged. Philip hadn't yet arrived. Now, like some sort of bad melodrama, Katie sat explaining her affair . . . could one call it that? One child dead or missing, another pregnant.

God giveth and God taketh away—it was a phrase she had repeated often.

"What are we going to do?" Katie's voice sounded no older. The question was as weakly childish as the one she had asked when she was five years old and had thrown her new Raggedy Ann doll in the lake. "Raggedy Ann is drowned. What shall we do?" In that case Joe had bought her a new doll. This time it all seemed more complicated.

"Obviously I have to talk to your father."

"Does he have to know?" Katie's eyes were utterly wild with terror.

"I daresay he does."

"He'll kill me! No, he'll kill Rory!"

"I doubt he will kill anyone. I do expect he will be deeply hurt . . . as I am."

Katie hung her head.

"You have committed a sin, Kathleen. You have done something very stupid. You're immature and silly, but I'm afraid you're going to grow up rather quickly." Emerald got up, feeling totally drained. "Get some rest," she advised.

Emerald walked down the stairs. The Japanese weren't the only ones to drop bombs today, she thought. And where was Frederick?

She went back into the parlor. Cook had cleared the table; the room looked neat, clean, and untouched. Everything was in place. Emerald made herself a drink and sat down. The radio still droned on; there was no end to the bad news.

At ten-thirty she answered the door. It was a weary-looking Philip Monteith.

Philip was tall like his mother, and his face had the sensitivity of a fine musician. He had deep dark brown eyes and he stood on the threshold looking in. Philip, as Emerald knew, was a quiet, shy young man of twenty-two.

"Come in, Philip. I've been waiting for you."

"Thank you."

She ushered him into the living room. "I still haven't been able to reach your father."

"Nor I, and his Washington office phoned twice. They don't know where he is either."

"Please sit down, Philip. Would you like something?"

"Scotch," he answered. "With water."

"Your mother's upstairs. She's finally gone to sleep."

Philip reached out and accepted the drink. He stared at the rug. "Nobody knows anything about James."

Emerald inhaled. "We'll find out," she said. "We'll find out as soon as possible."

4

December 8, 1941

Emerald got up and stretched. A pale December sun had risen in the sky over Boston. It flooded her bedroom with light and she looked out on the snow-covered back courtyard.

Emerald had slept fitfully herself, though finally around one she had dropped off into a deeper sleep. She sat down at the dresser and abstractedly picked up her parents' wedding picture. "I wonder what you'd have done?" she asked, studying her mother's face, which was so much like Katie's.

At seventeen I was studying nursing, at twenty-one I was married and in a rebellion . . . but I've committed sins of the flesh too. . . . Emerald could not quite bring herself to total condemnation of her daughter.

She picked up the brush and pulled it through her hair. Damn! Too much was happening at once! Eugenia was in the guest room, Philip was in the bed in the study . . . Her mind was filled with problems both real and imaginary.

Joe will call today, she told herself. Then she rejected the idea of telling him about Katie on the phone. God! What would he say, what would he do?

Abortion was out of the question. That left only a few limited possibilities. Katie could go away for her confinement and come back in a year and a half with the baby, they could say she was married to a serviceman who was killed. A convenient war!

Or Katie could go away only while she was pregnant and the baby could be put up for adoption. . . . No! Emerald thought. No matter what, it's our grandchild and I want it kept in the family.

Of course, Rory might be made to marry Katie . . . but did she want to marry him, and would Rory do it? Terrible to be stuck in a loveless marriage, Emerald thought. She sighed inwardly and vowed to talk to Katie more today. At least she ought to try to find out Katie's wishes before she talked to Joe.

The phone on the bedside table rang and Emerald hurried to it; it was only eight o'clock. I hope it didn't wake Eugenia, she thought.

"Yes?"

"It's Joe." His voice sounded tired and down.

"I didn't expect to hear from you till later." She resisted saying, "God, I need you," because she knew he had more important things to do than rush home into her arms. "I'm glad you called," she told him. "It's good just to hear your voice."

"Is Eugenia still there?"

"Yes, do you have some news about James?"

There was a momentary silence. "Not yet. I'm working on it. The figures are bad—over two thousand dead, more than that wounded. It was Sunday, and nobody knows who was where. They can't make accurate identifications because the duty rosters haven't been gone over yet and the wires are jammed. Emerald, I didn't call about James."

Emerald didn't answer, but her heart raced. His tone indicated bad news.

"It's Frederick Monteith."

"Where is he?"

"He must have heard the news broadcast when he was out in his car. He started driving to Washington . . . the roads were icy . . ."

"Oh, no, no . . ."

"He skidded off the road about twenty miles outside of New Haven and the car rolled over in a gully. They couldn't identify him till this morning. I told his office and the authorities I'd notify his wife."

"Oh, Joe, how am I going to tell her? She's so upset about James. Now Frederick . . . it's a tragedy."

"Can you handle it?"

Emerald inhaled. "I'll have to," she said in a resigned tone. "But, God, poor Eugenia, poor Philip. It's so unfair."

"Yesterday wasn't a fair day," he answered. "Anywhere."

Emerald first told Philip, who wept silently for a time and went upstairs to the guest room where his mother was staying.

Emerald waited downstairs, half-expecting to hear an agonized shriek from the bedroom, but it was not forthcoming. She stared into her tea, almost unaware of what was going on as Cook prepared breakfast.

J.J. came into the kitchen. He pulled up a chair and sat down. "How's Mrs. Monteith?" he asked dully.

"Frederick was killed in an auto crash last night. Philip's talking to her now."

J.J. shook his head. "Katie all right?" he asked after a time.

"I don't know," Emerald answered truthfully.

"She's up in her room. Says she's not going back to school."

"I'll talk to her later. Have Edward and Seamus left?"

J.J. nodded and ate his second piece of toast. "Where's Dad?"

"In Washington. I guess I forgot to tell you."

"The president is speaking to Congress today."

"I know."

"See you later." J.J. stood up; then he bent over and kissed his mother's cheek. "It'll be okay," he told her.

An hour passed, and Emerald turned on the radio. They were still talking about Pearl Harbor.

Philip came in and sat down. Cook poured him some tea, then silently disappeared, mumbling, "I think I'll make a cake, I feel like beating something."

"How's your mother?"

Philip stirred the tea and took a sip. "I think she'll be all right," he answered. "In time."

"And you, Philip?"

"I'm in shock," he answered truthfully. "I don't know how I am, I can't feel right now."

Emerald reached out and took his hand. "I'll pray for your brother," she said quietly.

5

December 29, 1941

Emerald and Joe were in their bedroom on the top floor of their house on Brimmer Street. Emerald stood at the window; Joe sat poised on the corner of the bed, his hands together, in a position that indicated his internal anger.

He had gone through several stages. First stunned shock, then anger, now cold reason. "He'll have to marry her," he finally said in a resigned tone. "That's the long and short of it."

"He doesn't answer her letters."

"I imagine I can take care of that."

"What? Avenging father holds shotgun to groom's head."

"Nothing so crude. Joe Kennedy owns the studio that has Rory's contract."

"I've talked to Katie," Emerald said. "Of course she wants to marry him"

"She's pregnant," Joe said again. "Listen, don't think I'm

crazy about the idea of marriage. There just isn't any alternative. Two parents are better than one.''

She looked at him and knew he was talking about himself—his mother had died when Mike was born. "I guess you're right."

"I'll give Kennedy a call."

"What if he won't marry her?" Emerald asked.

"He'll marry her or he'll spend the war as the rudder on Admiral Nimitz's flagship. Which is a nice way of saying that Rory O'Hara can have a front seat in a heavy combat zone or give himself over to holy matrimony."

Emerald looked at Joe. He was even more tired than she, but his sense of humor had not fled, and even in the face of Katie's condition, he was strong and decisive.

"I need you to do something else for me before you go back to running three companies and winning the war."

"Eugenia?"

"She's going out of her mind. She keeps having this nightmare that James is . . . *did* die slowly, trapped in an air pocket below deck. You've heard those reports . . . about the man who was gotten out after nine days, whose hair had turned white with fear. They keep reporting divers hearing pounding on the hull, but they can't penetrate it."

"I'm afraid they're more than stories."

"Don't tell me any more. Joe, can you pull some strings . . . get the War Department to send her a letter saying he died on deck or something?"

"You know it's probably not true."

"It's a kind lie, Joe. Eugenia can't live with the truth."

"I'll see what I can do," he promised. "And I'll take care of Rory. I have something to tell you now."

"Good or bad?"

"Good, I think . . .''

"I could stand to hear something good."

"Emerald, the governor has approached me, he wants me to fill Frederick's seat."

"Oh, Joe! What an honor! But can he get it through the state legislature?"

"He says he has the votes. He even called Eugenia, who said she'd lobby for it."

Emerald smiled. "Eugenia's a fine person. She's going to come through this."

"How do you feel about it?"

"What about me? My past, I mean—I was once on a British arrest list, you know."

He smiled. "I know. But there's no record of it. I asked the governor to check into it. I didn't want anything to come up at the hearings. You know what he said? He said he'd called J. Edgar Hoover, and Hoover personally approved of you. The FBI has picked up about two hundred Bund members in the past few weeks, ones who are spies. J. Edgar followed your career when you were out speaking to Irish groups and telling them not to become involved with the Bund. The governor says when your name is mentioned, J. Edgar Hoover's eyes twinkle with American flags. He said if you weren't a good American, he didn't know any."

"My, what a compliment."

"Well, given all that, do I have your approval to accept?"

"You don't even need to ask."

"I always ask you everything." He held out his arms to her. "Come give me a kiss."

31

1

April 7, 1945

Washington

Emerald hurried through the lobby of the Embassy Hotel. It was packed with young officers and a variety of women. It was Friday, and the students from Annapolis frequently came to Washington for the weekend, as it was considered an ideal place to find young women among the thousands who worked as secretaries in the government.

"Just my luck! Not a damn taxi in sight!" She spoke a little breathlessly to the doorman. He was black, with snow-white hair and a mouthful of gleaming teeth. He was at least sixty-five. Every man in Washington was either sixteen, or over fifty, or in uniform.

"I'll try to get you someone to share with, madam. Where are you headed?"

"The Red Cross," Emerald answered. She glanced nervously at her watch. Gas rationing limited the number of cars and taxis on the road, and the rubber shortage made new tires worth a small fortune. It was unthinkable to take a taxi alone; everyone had to share.

A gust of April breeze blew her skirt, and she cursed under her breath. "Damn material!" All the clothes available were skimpy and short. She felt six feet tall in her platform shoes.

But Joe liked the styles dictated by wartime austerity. "Thank heaven I have a woman with good legs and a slim figure. I love the short skirts and the heels. Hell, when you sit down, I can see the tops of your stockings."

"When I wear stockings, which I only do when I can get them," she had retorted.

"Sorry, we need the silk for parachutes."

Emerald smiled as she remembered the conversation. She pushed a bit of stray hair back in place. She always wondered how Joan Crawford kept her hair in such perfect rolls. Surely it wouldn't even blow around in a blizzard, never mind a lovely warm April day in Washington.

A long black limousine pulled up. It flew the diplomatic flag of Great Britain. A tall distinguished gray-haired officer climbed out. He was wearing his dress uniform, and his chest was filled with medals. He stepped in front of her and stopped dead. "Emerald?"

A warm smile lit up his face, and Emerald smiled back. "Albert? Albert Jenkins?" He was fifteen years older than she—that would make him sixty-five. But he looked more than five years older than Joe who was sixty. Still, Albert Jenkins was a handsome man. He was tall, and as a result of years in the army, he stood unusually straight, having a dignified military bearing.

"I'd know you anywhere, even after all these years. My, my, you're still ravishing."

Emerald blushed.

"I have a taxi here," the doorman interrupted.

"Do you need a lift?" Albert asked. "Please, get in my car, I'll take you wherever you're going." He didn't wait for her answer. "The lady's coming with me," he told the waiting doorman.

Emerald hesitated but then got into the car, leaning back against the rich leather upholstery.

"Where to?" He climbed in beside her, still smiling.

"The Red Cross."

He leaned forward and gave the driver the order, then sat back and looked at her. Her hair was long and pulled up into a large thick roll. It was gray, but her complexion was lovely and there were only a few lines around her magnificent eyes. Her voice was still low and lovely; she still had her Irish lilt.

"What are you doing in Washington? I always pictured you happily retired in Wales."

His smile faded slightly. "I couldn't have been happy without you, so I didn't retire. I went on to fulfill that blasted family tradition of becoming a general."

"But what are you doing in Washington?" She smiled warmly—that smile that still made him feel strangely sentimental and soft.

"I'm too old to fight. They sent me off to serve as military attaché at the embassy. Plenty of parties, certainly no shortage of wanton women in Washington—even for an old warhorse like me—there's good food, what more could I ask?"

"I'm really glad to see you."

"And what are you doing in Washington, Emerald Hughes? Somehow I thought you'd be in the Irish Parliament, where you could continue, albeit peacefully, to be a thorn in the side of Mother England." He laughed. "You're not occupying the post office, are you?"

Emerald laughed at his good humor and shook her head. "Not

me, though it's in the hands of the Irish. Roosevelt saw to that when he appointed an Irish postmaster general.''

"Very wise.''

"Yes, as you know, we know a lot about post offices.''

"I take it you're married?'' His eyes fell on her huge diamond. "Well, I would say.''

"To Joe Scanlon. Senator Joe Scanlon.'' Emerald loved to say it. After taking over Frederick's seat, he had been elected in November 1942.

"Senator Scanlon. I've heard of him. A very influential man! A businessman too—Scanlon Structures, is it?''

"The firm's in trust till he retires from the Senate.''

"Of course. But let me assure you, there are few army men, British or American, who haven't spent a night in a Scanlon Structure. He's also known in England as the man who pushed the tanks across the Canadian border.''

"And so he did. Well, he's my husband and we have four children. J.J.'s almost twenty-one, he's at Harvard . . . well, now he's in officers' training.''

"They're called ninety-day wonders,'' Albert commented.

"What a lovely name.''

"That's what the old navy men call them. You don't seem old enough to have a boy that age.''

"Well, I assure you I am.''

"You're radiant. You know, maturity has given you an interesting look. Of course, you were always interesting.'' He smiled a wry smile.

The car purred to a stop in front of the Red Cross. Emerald moved toward the door, and the chauffeur opened it.

"I'm sorry, Albert, I have a meeting.''

He nodded, but restrained her with his hand. "Have lunch with me,'' he suggested. "I'd really like to talk with you.''

"I'd be pleased,'' she replied.

"On the twelfth? How's that, can you make it?''

Emerald thought for a moment. "Yes, that will be fine.''

"How about the Carlton? Shall I pick you up or meet you?''

"We live far out, I'll meet you.''

"Perfect.''

Emerald climbed out and stood for a moment on the curb as the long car pulled away and rejoined the traffic. Then she turned and hurried up the steps of the Red Cross Building, her mind immediately filled with thoughts of war orphans and all the work to be done.

2

April 12, 1945

Boston

The Falcon's Head didn't quite classify as a hotel, nor, J. J. Scanlon decided, was it a house either. It was something in between; a building that had seen far better days.

The main floor of the Falcon's Head housed a raunchy tavern peopled mostly by young men and a few women of dubious vocation. Upstairs, there were rooms for rent, seedy rooms with peeling wallpaper and worn tasteless furniture.

J.J. stretched. His head ached and his throat was absolutely dry. "Shit! My mouth feels like the inside of an outhouse!" He kicked off the gray sheet and stood up.

Louisa Rossini, waitress and Harvard whore supreme, was still curled on the mattress. Her huge breasts were limp, her dark brown nipples at ease. He looked for a moment at her heavy buttocks and decided they were not totally uninviting, though she had looked better after seven whiskeys than she looked now.

She was like all the Italian girls he had ever screwed. She had mops of hair everywhere. Her head was overflowing with dark tresses, her underarms were rich dark forests, and he had to virtually fight his way into her past a jungle of pubic hair. He smiled; he was at least the hundredth man in officers' training to have her—Louisa was an institution for those approaching the course's end.

He walked into the bathroom and rinsed out a foggy glass. He waited because the water in the tap came out yellowed with rust. He watched it till it finally turned clear. Then he filled the glass and gulped down the liquid. After three glasses full, he felt bloated but no longer dehydrated.

He contemplated a shower, but a large dead cockroach near the drain deterred him. He went back into the bedroom and dressed. He hated mornings, especially "mornings after."

Louisa unfolded her voluptuous form and sat up; swinging her legs over the side of the bed, she stood. She looked overweight and untidy. She didn't have nice knees—she had fat knees and heavy, hairy thighs that looked like unplucked ham hocks.

Still, she had a kind of earthy sexiness about her, and he

vaguely remembered a blow job that had left him practically crying for another.

"Hey, where you going? You don't like Louisa?" She made a pouty expression with her full red-lipped mouth. Her breasts flopped as she attempted to thrust them forward. She picked up her bright red imitation Chinese red satin robe; with its purple embroidered dragon, it looked like something Kid Malloy would wear into the wrestling ring.

"I like you." He reached in his pocket and pulled out a ten. It was more than she was worth, but what the hell? "Here . . ." He held it out to her, and without saying anything, she took it.

Half an hour later, J.J. was half-running, half-walking across the campus when he saw Adele Jameson walking ahead of him—alone for once, he noted.

He slowed his pace and followed her for a few minutes, relishing the swing of her perfect little round butt and the bounce of her flaxen hair. He couldn't see her face, but he knew she had deep sea-blue eyes and a round, pouty mouth. He liked to imagine that mouth around him.

The rest of Adele's anatomy was a mystery to him. Like all the Radcliffe girls' clothes, hers seemed too big as if they had been handed down, though in fact they were always new and expensive.

"Adele?"

She turned around and smiled without showing her teeth. Her knees were cute—he caught a glimpse of them as the breeze blew her skirt. He concluded that a girl with cute knees and a perfect little round butt could not be flat-chested, though it was hard to tell because of her loose blouse.

"Going to the library?" he asked, trying to sound casual.

"No, for a coffee," she replied coolly.

"May I join you?" He had been trying to get to know her since last year. He hadn't gotten far, largely because he had dropped his senior classes to enter the officers' training program, the course he was just finishing.

"If you wish." Her layer of arctic frost melted slightly. "You look as if you've been up all night."

"I'm on a fire-fighting course, it's murder. Been studying sonar, too, been cramming all night," he lied.

She looked mildly sympathetic and he mentally scored a point in his favor. He always did that when he was trying to pick up a girl. He envisaged two columns: one in his favor, one against. When he felt he had more points in the favorable column than in the unfavorable column, he asked for a date. Right now, the unfavorable column consisted of the mental note that Adele was of good, conservative Protestant upstate New England stock and he was lace-curtain Irish out of Boston. The favorable column now listed "hard worker."

They reached the Claridge Coffee Shop, which had already set out little tables with umbrellas on the sidewalk. J.J. pulled out the rickety iron chair for her. A cool breeze blew off the Charles River, and Adele nestled down in her tweed jacket.

He ordered coffee. "Yup, I'll be finished with the course next week and be commissioned an ensign in the U.S. Navy. Then I'll be shipped out."

"The war in Europe is almost over," she said as her eyes watched one of the ever-present pigeons as it searched vainly for doughnut crumbs.

"I imagine I'll be sent to the Pacific theater to fight the Japs. They'll take another year or two, barbaric fighters." He shook his head gravely. "If they defend Japan the way they fought in the Philippines, there'll be huge losses of life."

She seemed nonplussed. He subtracted the point he had scored himself before. The I'm-going-off-to-fight-in-the-war-and-might-be-killed ploy usually made women softer, but not Adele.

He smiled and imagined she had no blouse or jacket on. He imagined her with white skin and nice firm little pink-tipped breasts. "Sugar?" He held out the bowl.

"Roosevelt! Roosevelt! The president's dead!" The shouts came from a student who literally streaked by the outdoor coffee shop, screaming out the news. "It's on the radio! He died of a heart attack in Warm Springs!"

J.J. set down his coffee with a force that sent most of it splattering over the side of the cup. "Shit!" he exclaimed, forgetting Adele.

"It's the best thing for the country," he heard her saying in an emotional, somewhat bitter tone.

He looked at her in amazement. She looked totally unmoved and utterly calm and satisfied, even though everyone around them was going inside the shop to listen to the radio or heading back to the dormitories. Some people, he noted, were even crying.

"Four terms! Disgusting! He was on his way to being a dictator. My father hated him, and so do I. I'm glad he's dead, really, really glad!" Her voice was low and cool, her eyes narrowed and mean. "Now we'll get rid of his Commie nigger-loving wife too! Did you know the old bag was having an affair with that left-wing writer . . . what's his name?"

J.J. stood up shaking with rage as Adele spewed out her DAR propaganda line. At least, that's how he regarded it. He leaned over Adele menacingly and whispered, "Shut your filthy mouth, you little cunt!" Then he turned and stomped off. What the hell? Cute knees weren't everything!

3

April 12, 1945

Washington

The dining room of the Carlton managed to retain its prewar elegance in spite of rationing, a lack of decent wine, and the impossibility of refurbishing during wartime.

Its inlaid oak floor was carpeted with a luxurious Persian carpet with intricate designs in soft blue and muted magenta. Its tall windows had long white curtains, and on either side, floor-to-ceiling blue velvet draperies added a feeling of warmth and intimacy to the large room.

The tables were well spaced and had damask tablecloths. Owing to the shortage of light bulbs, the small copper lamps had been replaced with pewter candlesticks.

Emerald Scanlon and General Albert Jenkins sat quietly in one corner. They dined on steak, since Albert was in the diplomatic corps and didn't require rationing stamps.

"I've never really been convinced there was a need for rationing in the United States," he confessed. "It's not like England."

"We have a few real shortages," Emerald told him. "Mostly toilet paper. But essentially, I think you're right. There are advantages, though. Rationing makes people feel as if they're doing their share, that while young Americans are fighting and dying, they're at least giving up something."

Albert smiled gently and ran his hand through his thin hair. "Frankly, after thirty-five years in the British Army, many of them spent in godforsaken places where there was nothing to eat except hardtack and nothing to drink but raw whiskey and tinned coffee, I feel I have already done my share." He leaned over and whispered, "I feel I'm entitled to a good piece of rare steak."

"Just between us, I'm enjoying it too." Emerald smacked her lips symbolically and took a sip from her highball. "What's the worst duty you ever had?"

"Burma," he answered without hesitation. "I'm afraid all us

white folks—the British and the Americans—underestimated the Japanese. They're highly intelligent people, they're shrewd, and they fight like devils."

"The papers keep saying they have no regard for human life, things like the Bataan Death March—"

"Hogwash. It makes good propaganda, but it's not true. Look, the Japanese culture, their code of living if you like, I mean the military, it rules out surrender. It's not that they don't have regard for life, it's that they have a great deal of regard for death. They were stunned on Bataan, and everywhere else for that matter, because they didn't expect to take prisoners and they never made provisions for prisoners. I'm afraid they don't understand us any better than we understand them."

"You're a strange man, Albert Jenkins. You fight like hell, then hold out a velvet glove to the vanquished. Even in Ireland, you tried to understand."

"Strategy is the key to war, understanding is the key to peace. The seeds of this war were laid in the Versailles Treaty. Germany was left devastated and impoverished. As a military man, I can tell you I hope we don't make the same mistake this time around. Tell that to your husband."

"I doubt Joe would disagree with you."

"Say, is he jealous that you're having lunch with an old admirer?"

"No, I think he's pretty sure of me."

"Should he be?"

"Yes."

"Too bad for me." He smiled.

"Tell me about yourself, Albert."

"There's not much to tell. I won't be absurd or obnoxious. Don't take it the wrong way, but I'd be lying if I said I hadn't always loved you, Emerald. There just couldn't have been anyone else."

Emerald blushed and looked away. "Albert . . ."

"It's all right, I've said it. I won't say it again. I've had a good life. I'm not morose. Say, where's that son of yours . . . Tom? I used to like to bounce him off my knee."

"He went to fight in the Spanish Civil War . . . he died at Jarama."

"Oh, I'm so sorry . . ."

"It was a long time ago. He died for what he believed in."

Albert took a sip of his gin and tonic. "You said you had a son who's a ninety-day wonder—what about the rest?"

"Well, my daughter Katie is married to Rory O'Hara and

lives in Los Angeles. She has a little boy who will be three next month."

"You're a grandmother!"

"I'm afraid so."

"And the others?" Albert pressed.

"Seamus, he's nineteen, is at Princeton studying to become an architect. And Edward, who's seventeen, has been admitted to MIT." Emerald half-sighed and half-smiled. "He's going to become a biochemist. I don't even know what that is, outside of the fact that it obviously involves biology and chemistry."

"How about the ninety-day wonder? The war won't last forever."

"I think he'll end up a politician, though I think he has a way to go. No tact, and he hates kissing babies."

At that moment the headwaiter tapped a crystal glass and spoke loudly. "Ladies and gentlemen, may I request your silence for one moment . . ."

A hush fell over the crowded dining room. People looked up apprehensively.

"I have just been informed that the president of the United States, Franklin Delano Roosevelt, succumbed to a heart attack while in Warm Springs, Georgia. Any member of Congress, members of the cabinet, or government officials present are requested to return to their posts immediately. Thank you."

For a moment shocked silence filled the room. Then there was a wave of voices whispering, the sound of chairs being pushed back as the government clientele of the Carlton prepared to leave, and the sound of crying as one woman sitting near them wept openly.

"That is bad news," Albert finally said.

"Oh, poor Eleanor. And the war in Europe is so close to an end and we're finally winning in the Pacific. It's so unfair that he couldn't have lived to see that victory."

Albert nodded his agreement. "England might have been defeated without Roosevelt. He certainly has his place in British history."

Emerald took another few bites of steak. "I'm afraid I don't have much of an appetite," she finally admitted.

Albert looked at his steak and signaled the waiter. "Put them in a bag," he whispered. "And bring me the check."

Emerald reached across the table to pat his hand. "I'm sorry," she said earnestly.

"I'm not. It was wonderful seeing you. Emerald, I'm going back to England in a week's time. I want you to know I still care

or you, that I'm glad you're well, that I'm even glad you're
happily married. From what I know of him, Senator Scanlon is
an unusually bright and very good man.''

Emerald did not withdraw her hand. "Thank you, Albert, for
loving me. Few women are privileged to have had one fine man
love them. I've had three: Tom Hughes, Joe Scanlon, and you.
You're a good man, Albert Jenkins, your love is a great
compliment.''

4

May 1, 1945

Los Angeles

Los Angeles' Union Station was packed, and the May heat
added to the stuffiness. Katie Scanlon O'Hara wiped her brow
and then resumed her position on tiptoe. At last, and only
because he was so tall, she caught sight of her brother disembark-
ing from the troop train, which disgorged white-uniformed men
as if it were a magician's hat and they were all white rabbits.

"J.J.! J.J.! Over here! Here I am, J.J.!" Katie waved and
called out, then pushed her way through the surging crowd of
men. She felt someone pinch her bottom and she jumped, but the
offender, one of the three hundred milling marines no doubt, was
only one of the crowd.

"J.J.!" She stood as tall as she could, and was rewarded by
his wave of acknowledgment and the certainty that in a moment
he would be on her brother's arm.

"Katie!" He picked her up and kissed her cheek.

She leaned against his snow-white ensign's uniform, feeling
the cold gold buttons against her. "God, it's good to see you!
God! Jimmy will love your uniform! God, I'm glad you're here!
How's Mother? How's Daddy? What's Eddie doing? And
Seamus?"

"Halt! One question at a time." He looked at her and grinned.
Her hair was lovely and loose, her skin was tanned, and her eyes
were as lovely as ever. She was dressed in bright yellow, her
skirt well above the knees—her knees were as cute as ever.

"I'm afraid Jimmy will have to wait. I only have two hours
before I have to take the train down the coast to San Diego and
the Eleventh Naval District. I'm shipping out in the morning.''

"Oh, God! Damn! After three years I only get two hours!''

"You could have come East, Dad would have gotten you travel vouchers. Mother keeps complaining about not seeing her grandson."

"Oh, J.J., it's terribly hard. All the trains are moving troops, and Jimmy's only three. Even with vouchers, you can get stranded in Chicago."

J.J. nodded. She was right. The train he had come on had forty-three cars. It was slow, hot, and there was not enough food in the dining car to feed even the troops. A woman traveling with a small child wouldn't even be able to get a Pullman—even if her father was a senator.

"God, only two hours, really?"

"God is playing a big role in your vocabulary these days. Katie, can we go somewhere out of this crowd? Where can we go and just sit and talk?"

"Are you hungry?"

"Yeah, I could eat a horse. Troops trains are the shits. Five days across the continent, and I've had cold food. The line for the dining car takes two hours, and when you get there, the food's all gone. The USO ladies board the train in every little station and pass out coffee, popcorn, and doughnuts—that's damn near all I've had for five days. Shit, if I never see another doughnut again, it'll be too soon."

Katie laughed. "Harvard hasn't changed you, nor has a uniform." She paused. "Do you like Mexican?"

"Mexican what? Women? I'll take three."

"Stop that!" She pressed her lips together. "I get enough of that at home. Mexican food."

He looked at her sheepishly. "Sorry. And I don't know if I like Mexican because I've never had any."

"It's time you did, then. We'll go up to Olvera Street and find a café. We'll eat and just talk."

J.J. followed her as she led the way out of the station. It was hot and dry, the sun reflected off the white buildings.

"It's not far, just up that hill."

"That hill?" He pointed to a near-vertical hill.

"No, silly. Not the one with the cable car . . . just over there." She pointed off to the side.

"That's a relief. Hey, I thought all the cable cars were in San Francisco."

"No, we have one. It's called 'Angel's Flight.' "

He laughed. "If the cable ever breaks, the passengers will be angels."

They walked along together arm in arm. Then they turned

down a street and were soon lost in a maze, finally ending up on
the one called Olvera Street. It was lined with open-air shops and
sidewalk cafés. The complexion of the people had changed when
they rounded the first corner; suddenly they were among swarthy
faces and Joe was aware of hearing Spanish more than English.

"Here," Katie suggested. "It's as good as anyplace." It was
a small patio restaurant with red awnings and a low wrought-iron
railing that fenced it off from the street, which was in any case a
mall not open to traffic. The sign, burned into a plank of wood,
read "Los Pollos."

"Los Pollos." J.J. smiled. "Sounds romantic."

Katie giggled. "It means 'the chickens'—they serve chicken
dishes."

They sat down and J.J. let Katie order; his was an easy
decision, he explained: "I can't read the menu . . . How's it
been Katie? How's Rory? Your letters leave something to be
desired. Mind you, Mother is happy enough with Jimmy's pictures,
but you never really say anything."

She shook her head, red-blond curls glimmering in the sunlight.
"Three years of living hell, J.J."

He gulped down some cold beer. It tasted good; the dry heat
of L.A. was different from the moist heat he was used to.

"He doesn't hurt you? I mean, well, physically?"

She shook her head. "No, he's very polite. He's even good to
Jimmy. But he doesn't love me, J.J., and I don't love him. I
honestly don't think Rory could love anyone but himself."

"He married you."

"I don't know for sure, but I have a sneaking suspicion he
was forced into it. Mind you, he's never said. I'm not sure I
even want to know."

"You never wrote you were having trouble."

"It wasn't so bad till Rory's career went into a tailspin. Now
all he does is drink and chase women."

Joe blushed. Rory didn't sound all that different from him.
"Men are like that," he said a little too defensively.

"Father isn't. I don't think he's ever looked at another woman."

J.J. nodded. She was probably right. But then, he himself
might not either after he found the right woman. That was
undoubtedly his problem. He hadn't found the right woman.

"Isn't there anything between you two?"

Katie laughed sarcastically. "There's everything between us: a
whiskey bottle, a blond floozy named Deborah Jean Mann, a
redhead named Kim Case, a brunette named Jodie Ann Lodd . . .

all starlets, don't you know? That's it, we're not together because there's too much between us.''

Katie seemed intense to him, and she had changed more than he thought possible. But she still had her flair for the dramatic. She was quick with her tongue, and her face had grown a little less soft. She seemed older than he, though they were twins.

"What are you going to do?"

"I don't know. I guess I'll have to leave him . . . eventually."

"You can't get a divorce." He said it flat out. He said it in the same tone his father would have said it. An Irish senator standing for reelection didn't need a divorced daughter, especially one divorced from a movie star. The publicity would be wicked.

And she won't do *me* any good either, he thought selfishly. He did have his own plans. The war with the Japanese would go on for maybe two years; then he'd take his last year at Harvard and go on to law school. He'd likely be ready at twenty-six; he'd have the education and his war record; he'd have his father's political reputation to glide in on; and he intended to do just that. First he'd work for the party, then run for the House of Representatives, later the Senate, then . . .

Katie stared at the red-and-white-checked tablecloth and at the chicken tacos the waitress had put in front of her. The glob of redfried beans steamed up. "I don't know," she said softly. "But, J.J., I can't take much more. I can't stand living with him." Tears flooded her eyes. "He brings them home, J.J. He . . ." Her voice trailed off.

"Separate, then. Nothing formal. Christ, Katie, if I weren't shipping out, I'd talk to him."

"I know you would." She ignored the tacos and drank some beer. Then, with resolution, she let out her breath. "Maybe I'll try again to reason with him."

J.J. grinned. "Do that," he suggested. "Try again."

Katie nodded. "These are tacos—try one."

J.J. bid his sister good-bye at the train station and climbed aboard the train to San Diego. He slept the first two hours of the stop-and-go trip down the coast.

When he woke up, it was nearly five, but the sun was still bright, or would have been had it not been blocked.

On either side of the tracks were war plants—Convair, Ryan, Rore, were the names he saw. Across the top of the railroad tracks for perhaps as much as five miles, netting had been strung so that it covered the top of the tracks and the buildings on either

side. In the netting, visible from underneath, mock clumps of
greenery had been stuck in and secured, and of course, the
buildings were all painted green and wheat brown, splotchy
fashion, so that from the air the whole scene must have looked
like a rural farm area instead of a heavily industrialized center.

When the train emerged from its net tunnel, J.J. caught a
glimpse of San Diego Bay. He burst out laughing with delight.
The entire bay was filled with floating barrage balloons painted
different colors. It looked like a huge playground of blue water
with a fleet of toy ships beneath. But of course, in spite of how
comical it looked, it had served a purpose. No one had forgotten
Pearl Harbor, and San Diego with the Eleventh Naval District
and Camp Pendleton nearby constituted a major target. At no
time, he had been told, were there fewer than a million men in
the area; men, ships, war plants.

The train came to a jerky halt, spewing steam and unloading
what seemed to be the next million. J.J. shouldered his duffel
bag and climbed off the train.

"Headed out for the Pacific?" an older man asked.

"Yeah, what the hell?" J.J. answered.

32

1

May 8, 1945

Washington

"Oh, when the lights go on again, all over the world . . ." Joe Scanlon's deep Irish baritone sang out the words melodically. "Are you dressed, Emerald? This is going to be one hell of a celebration! They'll be dancing on the Boston Common, singing in Times Square, and right here the Republicans, Democrats, and idle bureaucrats will hug, kiss, dance, and get roaring drunk together. I for one intend to get roaring drunk while dancing with Washington's most desirable matron. Then I intend to bring her home and make love till dawn! Don't primp so much! You look ravishing in everything you own!"

Emerald came out of the bathroom. Her three-quarter-length russet taffeta dress clung to her body; her hair was piled up in front and hung loose behind. "The party doesn't start till ten," she said.

"And it all ended just three hours ago, six P.M. eastern War Time. You're a vision!" He took her in his arms and began singing again, while waltzing her around the bedroom.

"I think you're already drunk." She laughed and they finished the waltz. Then he lifted her in the air, a full two feet off the ground, brought her down, and kissed her.

"Victory in Europe—V-E Day! Damn, I wish FDR had lived to see it . . . only a month." He shook his head. "But he certainly would have wanted us to celebrate. In fact, I think he would have wanted us to have a few drinks for him."

Emerald sat down and emptied her purse. She had another beside her, and began shifting the contents to the smaller evening purse. "What's Truman like, Joe?"

"Hard to make an assessment yet. Damn different from FDR. He's sort of down-home Midwestern, he's full of homely homilies, some of which don't go over with the Eastern establishment."

"I can imagine." Her thoughts fell on Frederick Monteith. He definitely would not have liked homely homilies. Emerald sighed. She was looking forward to going to Boston for a few weeks to see Eugenia.

"But he drinks a lot," Joe said, interrupting her thoughts of Eugenia. "I guess that's in his favor." Joe laughed.

"You would think so," Emerald agreed.

"Truman's a good machine politician. Tom Pendergast put Harry in the Senate, and Harry paid him back by getting Missouri's share of the pork barrel dumped in Kansas City." Joe sat down on the edge of the bed. Emerald had finished with her purse and now sat at the dressing table putting the final touches on her makeup.

"Funniest damn Truman story on the Hill is 'Brush Creek.' "

"What's Brush Creek?"

"It's a nice long concrete riverbed into which sewage can be taken on a lovely, winding trip right through the best neighborhood in Kansas City. It's open, there's parkland on both sides of it. It's a multimillion-dollar open sewer and it runs right down millionaire road."

"What?" Emerald laughed.

"Pendergast couldn't get establishment support for his candidates, so he got federal funds to build a sewer past their homes."

Emerald giggled. "Too bad Beacon Hill is so steep."

"All the shit runs downhill."

"Please, make an exception for Eugenia."

"There's always an exception, mind you. I think a lot of establishment are coming around. Even Lodge has an Irish wife. . . . Anyway, Harry Truman can't be all bad. I mean, he didn't waste his years in the Senate, not with projects like Brush Creek."

Emerald stood up. "Ready," she announced.

"Let's go celebrate," Joe answered.

"I wish we were all together," Emerald told him.

Joe nodded. J.J. was on his way to the Pacific. He'd already been shipped out. Katie was with Rory and her small son—she didn't write often enough. Seamus and Edward were in school. They'd come to Washington in June when classes were finished.

"We're probably all celebrating, though," he said.

"I hope J.J. is all right," Emerald answered. "It'll be more of a celebration when it's all over."

2

June 20–June 25, 1945

The Pacific

The U.S. Carrier *Kersarge* had looked like a floating hotel when J. J. Scanlon first saw her in San Diego Bay, anchored placidly off Coronado Island. But he soon discovered that the *Kersarge* was a light carrier, considerably smaller than fleet carriers like the *Lexington*.

He had left San Diego nearly seven weeks ago; now the U.S. *Kersarge* was in convoy off the coast of Okinawa.

Rumor had it that the Japanese on Okinawa were beginning to surrender; everyone hoped it was true. Okinawa was a nightmare. Already nearly ten thousand U.S. soldiers and marines had been killed, and they said the number of Japanese was ten times higher. J.J. thanked God he was in the Navy—somehow it seemed safer, cleaner.

His eyes scanned the sky diligently, though he continued to think of home. His brothers were both well, his mother and father had bought a home outside Washington, but of course they kept the house in Boston and the summer house at the cape. Thoughts of home were pleasant; what wasn't pleasant was the fact that there were no women at sea, that the war might end before he saw real action, and that Katie might mess up everybody's political life by getting a divorce—a messy divorce.

Katie's manner of living made him uneasy. She had been stupid when she was seventeen; now she was the wife of a fading movie star living in Hollywood, and Hollywood hardly had the best reputation around. Movie people were unstable and scandal-ridden, and Katie appeared unpredictable. Christ! A divorce!

A distant roar penetrated J.J.'s thoughts before his eyes found the speck in the blue sky above. He leaned on the alarm, and all the men on deck scrambled into instant battle stations. In a split second one of the big guns was fired and a deafening noise sent a tremor across the deck.

"It's a fucking kamikaze at two o'clock!" J.J. yelled out the warning as he himself hit the deck, clawing at the rivets beneath his hands, automatically trying to dig a trench in the unyielding steel. On the other side of his eyelids, which were closed, he saw the orange of the blinding flash; his ears recorded the blast of a direct hit; his body felt the impact as the metal beneath him momentarily heated up as the deck was awash with the fireball. Then he felt the shock of sudden pain; blackness and silence settled over him and his fear was replaced by a dark void.

J. J. Scanlon woke once and found himself strapped on a stretcher in a small coffinlike compartment. He moaned and called, "I'm not dead!" He felt motion, he heard the sound of a loud droning engine.

"You wouldn't be here if you were dead," a sharp male voice returned. Then J.J. felt his arm punctured by a needle and soon again it was black and he was left dreamless.

The next time he opened his eyes, he saw a muddy mustard-colored ceiling above him, a ceiling that matched the walls that rose to meet it. He groaned; then he screamed. His legs were numb and he felt nothing.

"Will you be quiet, Ensign Scanlon!"

He blinked into the face of a middle-aged woman whose cold blue eyes studied him without either emotion or compassion. She wore the uniform of a Navy nurse. It crossed his mind that when John Payne was in the hospital, he got Alice Faye to nurse him back to health, usually with a song and a fifty-piece orchestra.

"My legs," he moaned.

"Are quite intact, but we have given you a local anesthetic. We removed shrapnel fragments from both of them, fortunately not too serious."

He smiled at the information and moved the top half of his body a little. "Where am I?"

"Naval Hospital, Honolulu, Hawaii. You were flown here in a B-17 hospital plane along with other casualties."

"It was a kamikaze attack," Joe explained.

She nodded knowingly. "Your ship wasn't sunk. But there were a lot of injuries. We've had over two thousand from kamikazes alone." She looked at his chart.

"Let's see, it's June 25. By the way, Okinawa surrendered while you were under. I think you'll be back on duty in about eight weeks."

"Really?"

"You'll have no limp, probably only minor scars, and no pain. I imagine you can go back to your ship."

"Good."

"I suppose you'll qualify for a Purple Heart, too."

She said it as if she didn't think he deserved it. But he didn't answer. "Will I be in the hospital for the whole eight weeks?"

"Good heavens, no. We need the beds for injuries more serious than yours. You'll be here for a week; then the remaining weeks are for rest and recuperation—R and R. That's standard when you're wounded."

"R and R," J.J. repeated. She might call it rest and recuperation; everyone else called it rape and run.

"Have my parents been notified?"

"They have," she answered crisply. "And just because your father's a senator, don't expect any favors, son. This is the Navy!"

J.J. frowned at her, but she was up and away.

"Wounded, he returned to action undaunted!" Good public-relations material, he thought. Good political stuff, really fine.

3

June 26, 1945

"He sounded chipper," Joe said, putting the telephone receiver back in its cradle.

"Even with all that static on the line," Emerald agreed. "I know the telegram said he had only minor injuries, but I just didn't believe it till I heard his voice. It sounds absurd to say you're glad your son's in the hospital!"

"I understand," Joe told her.

"But he'll be sent back into action . . . God, it's so nerve-racking."

"Well, he won't be going back for at least six weeks."

"A reprieve from worry." Emerald sighed.

"At least it's only one. The others are both exempted."

"They're in the reserve, they could be called up."

"Not as long as they keep up their grades."

"Joe, I keep hearing that the chiefs of staff say an invasion of Japan will cost half a million American lives."

"That's what they say; personally, I doubt it."

"Albert Jenkins told me the Japanese don't surrender, or at least it's not in the military code of ethics."

Joe smiled. "That's officers, and it's true that the Japanese commander on Okinawa committed hara-kiri, but plenty of ordinary soldiers surrendered."

"They'll fight hard to protect their homeland."

"You're probably right—people usually do fight hard to protect their homes."

She sank into the easy chair in the corner of the living room. She thought of Ireland, of the way the Irish fought. "It will mean a terrible loss of life," she said sadly. "I somehow wish we wouldn't keep insisting on unconditional surrender."

"So do I, but the public wants vengeance for Pearl Harbor."

Emerald nodded sadly. "I know a lot about vengeance."

"Why don't you go up to Boston for a few weeks, take some time off and really rest?"

"I'd like that," Emerald said. "But I don't like leaving without you."

"I'm not alone. Edward and Seamus are here. Hell, I can spend some time with them."

"It would be good to see Eugenia."

"Why don't you go?"

"All right, I will," she answered. "But not till the fifteenth of July. I have a meeting I can't miss on the fourteenth."

"You and your war orphans. You're busier than I am, and I'm in Congress."

4

September 1, 1945

Washington

It was the first of September and the first films of the mushroom clouds that had engulfed Hiroshima and Nagasaki were playing in newsreel theaters everywhere. They were censored: Emerald knew that, she knew the real films were so horrible they might never be released; she knew there was a new terror.

A month ago, she thought, the front rows of the RKO newsreel theater were filled with youngsters who waved their fists and shouted their approval as blind diving kamikazes missed their targets and crashed into the sea, great balls of all-consuming fire. And the cheers continued when the long-held censored films of the fighting in Okinawa were released.

But tonight it was different; the atmosphere had changed; there was no cheering. The audience sat in hushed silence as they realized something profound had happened; the atomic bomb would change the world forever.

The films that were released were bad enough; not horrible in the extreme, but moving and frightening in a less obvious way. The one that kept reappearing before her eyes was the one taken on one of the bridges leading into Hiroshima. Its steel rails bore the images of small Japanese children. But the images weren't shadows or mere outlines; they were the children themselves, burned into the steel in one second of white-hot light, a light they said rivaled the sun in heat and intensity.

And program after program attempted to explain in lay language what the new weapon was. Calm voices, one after another, told people why they didn't need to be frightened of the new atomic power. But calm voices, Emerald thought, could not erase the bridge at Hiroshima.

Joe thrust his hands in his pockets as he and Emerald came out of the theater in downtown Washington.

"It's staggering," Emerald said, and she trembled slightly.

"I'm sure it was a difficult decision to make, but I still think Congress ought to have been consulted. Even a select committee . . ."

"No, I'm glad you didn't have a part in that decision." ·

"Those who did will forever have to weigh their own wisdom."

"God, how could anyone make that decision and sleep a night?"

"Easily, I suppose. They looked at the casualty reports all day long. Emerald, over a hundred thousand Japanese died on Okinawa over twelve thousand Americans. I suppose if Okinawa is the example, they decided that the loss of life on both sides would be less if they used their super weapon."

Emerald was silent. She felt that since the sixth of August when the American people first learned about the bomb, she had heard every conceivable argument on the merits and demerits of having used it.

"I have to admit I'm glad J.J. will be coming home instead of going back to fight. I doubt I'm different from any other American mother on that point. But, Joe, I'll never forget those little figures burned into that bridge. We have something horrible . . we've invented something dreadful."

"Somebody must have said that about gunpowder."

"Maybe."

"The war's over, Emerald. Be glad of that."

"I am," she said thoughtfully.

5

October 2, 1945

Rory O'Hara still had a boyish style, loose unkempt hair, a well-worked-out body, penetrating eyes. But on closer examination, J.J. could see that his brother-in-law had wrinkles burned into his tanned skin by the constant and unkind California sun. And if Rory's body still showed the benefits of exercise and weight lifting, of good food and constant grooming, his eyes did not. They were a network of red lines that looked like a road map of New York City. And beneath his eyes, concealed most of the time by dark glasses, there was a puffiness that made Rory look more than thirty-five.

J.J. insisted that Rory meet him in the bar of the Garden of Allah on Sunset Boulevard. It was a typically California motel-hotel that had low white stucco guest houses with red tile roofs; it boasted a tangled garden with tethered parrots squawking from tree branches; it was a little tacky, a fake harem peopled by Hollywood sheiks. But it had a reputation. F. Scott Fitzgerald had lived there; so had Robert Benchley. J.J. liked the place; the bar was intimate, the tables secluded.

"You're making her fucking miserable," J.J. said.

Rory took a gulp of his gin and tonic. The lime floated on the top; the ice cubes had holes in the center.

"I didn't exactly volunteer to marry your sister," he replied in a deadly tone. "What the hell, it wouldn't have mattered who I married. I can't be faithful. Can you? I'm not making her miserable, she's making herself miserable."

"She's my sister, you son of a bitch. I want her to be happy. You can make her happy."

"Fuck you! I can't even make myself happy. I haven't had a decent role in two years! I even tried to join the service, but I'm 4-F! Yeah, with this body I'm 4-F. Bad kidney."

"Well, I'm sure sitting out the war left you in big demand," J.J. said sarcastically.

"Easy come, easy go. The town's full of flesh. It's my career I'm worried about. It's bad publicity not to have been in the service—the war effort and all that. 'Course, Payne and all those jerks got leave to make films. Hell, Flynn took all my roles. He and Victor Mature. Look at that profile." Rory turned sideways. "Is that a profile? Don't you think it's better than Mature's—fucking wop."

"I don't give a damn about your profile. What are you going to do about my sister?"

Rory rubbed his chin thoughtfully. "Look, I may not have made a picture recently, but I still got drag. Every dingbat stacked tomato in Hollywood thinks I can help her get into films. I'm faced with constant temptation." He smiled and took more of his drink. "I really don't think you could forbear either. Sister or no sister."

"What I could or couldn't do has got nothing to do with you." J.J. shifted around in the booth. Rory was right, of course, he probably couldn't forbear. Even now, he was contemplating Rory's excesses with some mental enthusiasm and, though he hated to admit it, jealousy as well.

Rory slipped his sunglasses down over his nose and stared at J.J. intensely. "I'll make you a bet," he offered. "I'll take you out on the town and I'll fix you up. If you don't succumb to temptation, I won't either."

"What the hell are you suggesting?" J.J. asked. He was already more than a little drunk.

"I'm suggesting you forget about your sister and come on out and enjoy yourself with me." He laughed. "Go on, tell me what you like. Blonds? Redheads? Brunettes? Flat-chested or inflated balloons? Tall or short, one or two? Come on, J.J., you've been gone a long time. I can get you an unbelievable piece of ass. Stop worrying about Katie. She's just young and naive."

J.J. took another gulp of his drink. Rory was a bastard, but at this second he didn't care as much as he should have.

The Andrews Sisters—Patti, La Verne, and Maxine—singing the song that went "She's a real sad tomato, she's a busted valentine," kept running through J.J.'s head. The girl Rory provided was long-legged with vulgar swinging hips, a wasp waist, big full breasts, and a mouth that could . . . well, a mouth that could.

Her hair was so blond it was white, but she was a natural blond, because her pubic hair was light too and her skin was like tissue paper.

Her name was Toddy and she danced nude and then fell on him playfully and mouthed him till he nearly burst. He fondled her, played with her, and wore himself out, knowing that in the next room his brother-in-law, Rory O'Hara, was doing similar things with Rose Marie Something-or-other.

It was a weekend J.J. would never forget; it culminated in near-tragedy.

They headed home, he and Rory. Home was up a winding road off Laurel Canyon to a house perched on the edge of a cliff overlooking Sunset Boulevard.

"Katie!" J.J. called out drunkenly. Rory had gone immediately to the bar in the sunken living room. J.J. went in search of his sister, his guilt obvious in his facial expression.

"Katie! Where are you?" He still hadn't decided if he should 'e or not. "We spent the whole weekend talking, I think I've brought Rory around," came to mind. Yes, he decided, a lie 'ould be kinder than the truth. She didn't need to know that he had been party to yet another of Rory's adulterous weekends. She didn't have to know that he was no better than Rory. Katie's my sister, not my wife, he told himself. He pumped himself up with that thought. He managed an air of self-righteousness.

"Katie!" He knocked on the door of the cavernous room Katie and Rory called their bedroom, and he gasped.

Across the bed lay his sister. She was fully dressed, her makeup was on, her hair combed. She was as pale as the sheets; her arms hung over the side of the bed, her wrists were slit, and she was bleeding neatly into the trashcan she had put by the side of the bed.

"Katie! My God!" He ran to the bed and shrieked for Rory, who came running. They wrapped her wrists with strips of the sheets to stop the bleeding, and Rory called an ambulance.

Katie lay motionless, her breathing labored, her skin white.

J.J. held Jimmy in his arms and sat in the waiting room of Cedars of Lebanon Hospital for what seemed an absolute eternity.

Jimmy, his eyes closed in sleep, snored peacefully.

"Mr. Scanlon?" J.J. looked up and nodded. The white-coated doctor held out his hand. "Dr. Cohen," he intoned.

J.J. extended his hand. "J. J. Scanlon."

"Your sister can see you now. Here, leave the little one, I'll have a nurse keep an eye on him."

J.J. nodded and laid Jimmy on the couch.

"You know there are police reports to fill out?"

J.J. nodded.

"All right, you go talk to her, but don't be too long, she's still pretty weak."

J.J. followed the doctor down the hall and was ushered into Katie's room.

She looked small and vulnerable in the middle of the bed, with

her arms all attached to bottles. But they had given her four
transfusions and her color was better.

"Katie . . ." He looked down at her and felt sick.

"Take me home to Boston," she murmured. "Just take me
home."

"Jimmy's outside, Katie. Yes, yes, I'll take you home."

6

October 29, 1945

Boston

Emerald bent down and kissed her grandson, three-year-old
Jimmy O'Hara. "I think if you go out in the kitchen, Cook will
have some chocolate milk and cookies for you."

His small mischievous face broke into an instant grin and he
was off like a shot.

"You've certainly taken to being a mother again," Eugenia
quipped. She unpinned her floppy hat and took it off. "How is
Katie?" she asked with real concern.

"It's hard to tell," Emerald replied. In truth, she herself
wasn't sure. She and Joe had placed Katie in a small private
hospital near Rockport. There she received psychiatric care and
plenty of rest.

"She's distant and uncommunicative," Emerald answered.
"J.J. took her attempt to kill herself very hard—for some reason,
he feels he's to blame."

"And what about her useless husband?" Eugenia's voice
was heavy with cattiness. It was a persona that suited her,
though in fact she was genuinely kind in spite of her verbal
assaults.

Emerald shrugged. "He's certainly not remorseful. It was a
mistake, Eugenia, her marriage was a horrible mistake."

Eugenia obviously agreed, but chose to change the subject.
"How are Edward and Seamus?"

"They're both doing wonderfully well."

"I've always loved your Edward best," Eugenia admitted.
"In spite of all those dead things in jars. Of course, you'd be a
terrible mother if you played favorites, but I can." Eugenia got
up and helped herself to a drink. "Is J.J. going back to finish at
Harvard?"

"Yes. You know, I think he'll go into politics and give his father some competition."

"I take it Joe will definitely run in forty-eight for reelection."

"Yes, in spite of the fact he thinks Harry may be a liability."

"It's Harry's mouth that's a liability, my dear."

33

1

March 1948

Washington

The Scanlon house on Birchmont Hill, outside Washington, was overflowing with guests. Emerald called it "an auxiliary inauguration party" especially for some of Joe's constituents.

"It's quite a party," Eugenia proclaimed. "I think it deserves my stamp of approval."

"I'm so glad you brought Philip." Emerald stole a glance at Philip Monteith and Katie. They were sitting alone, talking intensely.

"They look good together," Eugenia said. Her comment was full of meaning.

Katie looked relaxed. No, Emerald thought, she actually looked happy, and heaven knew, poor Katie deserved some happiness. She had spent nearly a year in treatment for depression; then, just as she began to come out of it and build a new life for herself and her small son, Rory had died of kidney disease.

I was a single mother at the same age, Emerald thought. But at least I had a happy, if brief, marriage. Katie hadn't had that, and the result was that she suffered remorse and guilt; happily she seemed to be getting better, and that, Emerald surmised, had something to do with Eugenia's sensitive and talented son, Philip.

"Katie's shy," Emerald whispered.

"*Katie's* shy! What on earth do they find to talk about? Philip is painfully shy. It comes from being artistic. I never thought I'd have a shy son."

"It's unbelievable," Emerald teased. "You of all people!"

Eugenia smiled and drained her martini glass. "I wish it weren't considered gauche to go after the olives. I do like them so."

"I have a whole bottle in the refrigerator. After everyone is gone, Eugenia, you can have them all."

Eugenia's eyes darted around the room. "Everyone who is anyone is here, simply the lot! My Gawd, I never thought I'd live to see the day when Irish ward bosses were drinking with Brahmin bears. Just look at Thomas Henderson of Finchly, Hinchly, and Wescott, will you? The old snob's drunker than a skunk and standing there listening to all those delightful filthy stories that Jim Kelly tells."

"Snob? He's one of yours."

She shrugged. "My family have been snobs longer than his. I can say what I please."

When Eugenia was in good form, no one could outdo her, Emerald mentally conceded.

"I'm a little worried about J.J. He's off with Kelly's daughter and he's something of a womanizer. I think I'll have to speak to him, or have his father speak to him."

"It's Joe who should speak to him. Emerald, dear, a moment of truth. J.J. is not a mere womanizer, he's an out-and-out Don Juan."

"I know," Emerald admitted.

"Emerald! You look sumptuous, you look desirable."

"Oh, Governor, you're such a flatterer. I know you. That's how you keep getting elected. You kiss babies and tell old ladies how pretty they are."

"Old? You're not a day over forty!"

"I'm fifty-two and proud of it."

The governor blushed. "But you'll never lose your Irish lilt. It's so soothing."

Emerald laughed, and the governor hugged her. "Let me tell you, the election of 1948 is going to be one to remember! The New York papers will never live it down!"

"Nor will the pollsters," Eugenia said sweetly.

The governor belched. He's drunk, Emerald decided. "I have something special for you, Governor." She took his arm. "Over there, just waiting, are some rare roast-beef sandwiches."

"Oh, they do look delicious. Is this a hint?"

Emerald smiled. "Just a little hint. Eat a little, drink a little."

He winked at her. "You're a practical and tactful woman, Emerald."

Emerald kissed him on the cheek and then glided away, peering for one second onto the wide veranda. J.J. and Mary Kelly were deep in conversation.

"There goes your mother, J.J." Mary smiled coquettishly. She vaguely reminded J.J. of a Radcliffe girl he had once pursued and given up the moment he discovered her right-wing leanings. But Mary Kelly was a good Democrat, and her father, like his, was one of Boston's most influential Irishmen. She's prettier, he thought, remembering the Radcliffe girl's actual appearance.

Mary's eyes were bluer and her hair was not white blond, but a deep gold blond. She had a good figure, too. But she was not without drawbacks. The first was that she was a good Catholic girl; the second was that her father was a close friend of his father. This, he reasoned, ruled out a casual sexual liaison.

"Want to talk? It's not so cold for March. I'll go inside and get your jacket."

She shook her head. "I'm working," she announced impishly.

"Working?"

"Sure. I do a column for the Boston *Globe*. One day, if I'm very good, I might get to the news desk. I'm getting awfully tired of writing 'and they served pinwheel sandwiches and wine punch with tropical flowers floating on the top.' It's boring, darling, terribly boring!" She waltzed about, and she had lowered her voice to do a good imitation of Tallulah Bankhead.

J.J. laughed and lit a cigarette. "Have one," he offered.

"Camels? No, I only smoke English Ovals."

J.J. raised an eyebrow. He was never sure when she was putting him on and when she wasn't.

"Sure you don't want to walk? How about a ride?"

"Not on your life, J.J. Scanlon. A girl could ruin her reputation by disappearing with you."

"Is my reputation that bad?"

"It's worse. Personally, I wouldn't go out with you unless my mother came along."

He smiled but didn't answer. He felt she liked him, and she was interesting. And, he admitted, I've always been a sucker for the hard-to-get ones. "I have a thought. You know my sister?"

"Of course I know your sister." Mary sipped her drink. It was something long and cool. So's she, he decided.

"How about double-dating or something? Go up to the cape for a couple of days."

Mary ran her tongue around her full lips. "I'm not sure," she answered. "I'll have to think about it."

2

August 1, 1948

Washington

Joe Scanlon's Senate office was warm and cluttered. On the left-hand corner of his desk, an ashtray overflowed with half-smoked cigarettes; on the other corner were piles of letters from constituents; and in the center were reports from his foreign-relations committee, reports on the rebuilding of the German and Japanese economies, on aid programs, and on forthcoming appointments to be made by the president.

In front of the desk, J.J. stood with his hands in his pockets. Joe lit a cigarette and leaned back in his blue leather swivel chair.

"Aren't you going to put your feet up on the desk?" J.J. asked.

"Why?"

"Well, you'd certainly look the consummate politician if you did."

Joe didn't smile. "You're almost twenty-four years old," he observed. "You've graduated from Harvard, not with the best grades, but nonetheless you did manage a degree."

"Edward's doing better."

"Edward is not my concern at the moment. You are my concern."

J.J. shifted from one foot to the other restlessly. "Are you asking what my plans are?"

"For starters."

"Obviously I want to go into politics."

"You're too young. You can't legally run for the House until you're twenty-five, and if you run then, you won't be elected. You're still wet behind the ears and living off my money. Frankly, I wouldn't support you in a political race. People deserve decent representatives, not playboys."

J.J. looked at the floor. He glanced around, unconsciously looking for an escape route. His father didn't seem angry, he seemed resolute, and as J.J. knew, resolution meant something that might be worse than anger. "Well, I guess I'll have to do something first, you know, till I'm ready to run . . . till you think I'm ready to run."

"I might never think you're ready. Let me give you some options. First, you could go back and get a law degree, though, in my humble opinion, with your grades I don't think you'll get into law school."

J.J. reached in his jacket pocket and took out his cigarettes. He tapped one on the side of the desk and lit it. Finally, sensing this was going to be a longer conversation than he had originally thought, he sat down dejectedly. It was at least tactful of his father not to mention that Seamus and Edward were both outstanding students.

"I have a good war record," J.J. protested. "That ought to help in politics."

"There were nearly seven hundred thousand men wounded in World War II. They all have good records—some of them better than yours. Frankly, J.J., a little shrapnel in your butt isn't sufficient."

J.J. took a puff, and the smoke circled around in the stillness of the office.

"Option two is that you go to work. Though, let me say, I'm not sure what you work at when you have a degree in pre-law, without the grades to go further."

J.J. let out his breath. "I could manage one of your—"

"Shit! Managers are trained. What gives you the idea that just because I have money, you can start at the top without lifting as much as your pinky? As for politics, well, getting elected is something you earn. You haven't earned one damn thing!"

"But—"

"But nothing. Shut up! Your third option is going back into the Navy."

"Oh, hell!" J.J. started to stand.

"That's far enough. Sit down!"

His father's voice was cool and commanding. J.J. sat down.

"I take it you would rather work. I am therefore in a position to offer you a job you don't deserve. It is my hope that within six months of taking this position, you will have proven yourself worthy—not only of the position, but what comes with it."

"What?" J.J. shook slightly and hoped his father didn't notice.

"You will begin as manager in training at Jim Kelly's electrical-contracting firm."

"Radiant Electric?"

"That's what it's called. Fortunately, the starting salary is quite good, but then, you'll have a wife to support."

"What?"

"You've said that twice now. Haven't you been seeing Miss Kelly? Let's see, for about three months—"

"We've never! I didn't! I wouldn't! Jesus, I'm not stupid. I know the Kellys are good friends and supporters. If Mary's pregnant, dammit, I'm not the father!"

"Pregnant? Did I say she was pregnant?" Joe Scanlon's face broke into a grin. "You're awfully self-righteous for a boy who's probably got twelve illegitimate kids wandering around from San Diego to Boston. I know about you and that Italian girl, and while I have nothing against the Italian community, your idea of integration and mine seem to be quite different."

"Mary's not pregnant?"

Joe raised a bushy eyebrow. "Should she be?"

"No! I already told you that, at least not by me."

"You love her?"

"I think so? I mean, I think more about her than other girls. She's different, and I've never . . . never . . ."

"Well, she loves you. Damned if I know why, but she does. Damn pretty woman, that one, and lucky for you her father thinks more of you than I do, so he's prepared to give you a decent job. Frankly, I'd jump at the chance if I were you. You never know, you might end up in politics, and then you'll need a wife like Mary Kelly." Joe's tone changed and he smirked at his son in a way that indicated affection beneath his gruffness.

"I'm not marrying her for the job," J.J. announced. "But I will marry her. Hell, I didn't know that's what she wanted."

Joe stood up and walked around the desk. He slapped J.J. on the back and laughed. "Guess she wants to make an honest man out of you, son."

3

August 5, 1948

Boston

The sun was just setting and the magnificent sunset illuminated the Charles River, turning it into a rainbow of blue, green, and reflected pinks and oranges. The park on the banks of the Charles was long and narrow and punctuated by the stone bridges that led to the little island that was also a small park.

Near Emerson College, the park grew wider, and where it was widest, the Hatch Memorial Shell had been built between Beacon Street and the winding river with its island refuges. Across the Charles, the buildings of MIT could be seen clearly.

In front of the shell were rows and rows of folding chairs, and on the surrounding grass, families had spread out blankets for their picnic suppers. Beer, popcorn, and roasted chestnuts were sold by vendors who kept their silence when the music played and who, while giving change, tapped their feet keeping time.

The summer Boston Pops were a tradition—free concerts in the open air on summer evenings. At the moment, Arthur Fiedler was conducting the last piece, a rousing version of "Pop Goes the Weasel," arranged into a symphonic fugue, with each group of instruments chasing away the melody of the former group. The musicians relished their task, playing with delight and enthusiasm while children clapped, vendors tapped, and the audience smiled with glee.

When the piece came to its resounding conclusion, the Pops Orchestra took its bows. From the front row, Katie smiled at Philip and waved.

She waited patiently while he put away his instrument; then he joined her amidst the milling crowd.

"Did you enjoy it?" He smiled and kissed her on the cheek, brushing the skin lightly.

"I love the Pops. I think they're the best thing in all Boston. Mr. Fiedler's brought fine music to everyone, not just those who can afford the winter concert series."

"That's his aim. It's thrilling to see the audience respond like that. It's something a musician seldom experiences. Roaring crowds are usually for a guy like Ted Williams, not for musicians."

"Kind of makes you proud," Katie said, beaming, "that in Boston, the symphony gets the same treatment as the Red Sox."

"Nowhere else," Philip agreed. "What's the West Coast like in that respect?"

Katie scowled. "I don't know about San Francisco, but Los Angeles is gruesome. The whole city is one long billboard advertising mile-long hot dogs, spiritualists, and inner-spring mattresses. Culture in any form doesn't exist."

"Film is an art form," Philip argued.

"It can be," Katie agreed.

"Hey, let's walk over the bridge to the island, then I'll take you for dinner."

"Sounds good."

Philip and Katie crossed Storrow Lagoon on the footbridge. The island was cooler because the trees were taller and the grass was neatly trimmed except down by the shore, where the calm waters of the Charles lapped into reeds. All along the shore, families of ducks nested peacefully, unconcerned with either children or passing lovers.

"Oh, here, I have some popcorn left." Katie bent down, and two ducks waddled over, eating out of her hand, eyeing her suspiciously.

When she had gotten rid of the popcorn, she stood up and Philip took her hand. They walked silently to the far edge of the island and stared across the Charles at Harvard and MIT.

Philip touched her hair. He let his hand rest on her shoulder. "Katie, we've been seeing each other forever."

"Not quite forever." She smiled.

"I don't know how to say this . . ."

"Say what?"

"I . . . I think we ought to get married."

Katie turned and looked into his face. He was blushing. "Is that a proposal?" She lifted her arms and put them around his neck. "Oh, Philip, if it is, I'll be so grateful. I thought you'd never ask."

His face broke into a wide smile. "You will marry me?"

"Of course I'll marry you. I love you. . . . I didn't used to know what that meant. I do now."

"Oh, I love you too. I think I always have—ever since the first time I saw you."

"You never even asked me out till last March."

"I didn't think you'd come."

Katie fell into his arms, and he embraced her, his hands moving up and down, his lips seeking hers.

"Look at the two lovebirds!" a small child called out.

Philip let go of Katie, still blushing. "Let's go somewhere more private."

Katie laughed, the same musical laugh her mother had. "Let's have dinner and then go somewhere more private."

He nodded. "How about the Union Oyster House for a lobster? We ought to celebrate."

"Perfect," Katie answered. And perfect was how she felt.

4

August 10, 1948

Boston

J.J. paced up and down in front of the Tremont Theater. He turned, and as if she had appeared out of nowhere, Mary Kelly stood beaming. "Good evening," he said with a slight bow.

He took her arm and began guiding her along the street through the crowds that were headed for the subway. It was five-thirty; Boston was emptying. "I've found a cozy little restaurant, unique and really quiet."

"In an alley?"

J.J. guided her down the narrow alley. They entered a blue door, and Mary inhaled. "Smells scrumptious."

"It's called Olga's and it's got the best Scandinavian food this side of Norway."

"It's quaint."

The room was tiny and filled with little tables.

"This way." He guided her out of the dining room and into the courtyard. It was entirely surrounded by brick buildings and the tables were wrought iron, each with a flickering candle protected by a hurricane lamp.

"I love it," she whispered when they sat down.

They ordered drinks and the waitress brought them plates and directed them to the smorgasbord. They filled the plates with salads and cold fish dishes.

"After this, we get hot Swedish meatballs."

"I doubt I can eat that much."

J.J. ordered wine, and Mary began eating slowly. "It is good."

"I have wonderful taste. Will you marry me?" He filled her glass with red wine.

"That's not a very romantic proposal."

"It's not very romantic to be summoned to Washington to be told you're a blooming failure at twenty-three. It's not nice to be told you can have a decent job if you marry the boss's daughter—whom I was told comes with the job."

"You're twenty-four and you're exaggerating." She looked away.

J.J. leaned across the table. "When my father spoke to me, I was twenty-three. I just had a birthday. Write it down. I'll expect a party every year. And I'm not exaggerating."

"I'm sorry you were embarrassed."

"Dammit! I want to marry you, I don't want your father's job. I have a job. I know that fact will surprise my own father as well as yours—and yes, dammit, I've wanted to make out with you since I met you. But I haven't because you're different."

She grinned at him, though her lips were pressed together and she was obviously suppressing a smile. "Where's the job?" she asked when she could without laughing.

"WKJ. I'm going to be a newswriter. Of course you'll have to lower your standard of living, and so will I. We'll have the wedding presents, though, and if we're lucky, we won't have to buy any sheets."

"I'd have thought we'd wear those out first," she said with a deadpan expression.

He laughed. "Well?"

Mary put down her fork and reached across the table. Sh

covered his hand with hers. "What is it you always say—'Oh, what the hell?' I guess I'll marry you. At least we have my salary too." She shrugged and went back to eating.

"One more thing—my sister's getting married too. How would you feel about a double wedding?"

"I've already discussed it with Katie."

"You're pretty sure of yourself, aren't you?"

"Yes."

"What did you and Katie decide?"

"We decided to have separate honeymoons."

J.J. smiled.

34

1

January 2, 1949

Boston

The reception room of the Statler was decorated with great pots of red poinsettias and large graceful ferns. In the middle of the long table along one wall were a huge punch bowl and trays and trays of meats, sandwiches, and delicate hors d'oeuvres.

All around the room people mingled in small groups of three and four. Irish accents mixed with old New England.

"My, my. Some clichés are really in. 'Still waters do run deep.' " Eugenia laughed sarcastically. "The day you climbed Beacon Hill, who'd have thought it would ever come to this? And who'd have dreamed that dear, quiet, artistic Philip would ever get up the courage to ask Katie to marry him. You know, I'd all but given up on that boy."

"I feel like hugging you. You're like a sister now," Emerald said.

"Mind you, it went against my grain when Philip told me he'd converted. Then I said, what the hell difference does it make? Do you remember Clarence Barton, Elispeth's son? Well, he told his mother he'd converted. But he meant into a woman! The poor boy—or whatever you call him—is as queer as can be. And Elispeth took a fit, I'll tell you. So I said to myself, at least Catholics are normal . . . at least most of them are. At least Philip is marrying a woman. And then too, I don't have to run around saying, 'Some of my best friends are Catholic,' I can say, 'Hell, not only are some of my best friends Catholic, so is my son!' "

"Eugenia, you're outrageous," Emerald chided.

"I know, but isn't it fun? I love the champagne punch. It's so elegant."

"The cost is split between the two families of the brides. I'm so pleased they wanted a double wedding. It seems so suitable for twins," Emerald told her.

"It's staggering! And so politic! My dear, it certainly won't hurt Joe! Press, press, press—this wedding is front-page news."

"The Scanlons and the Kellys, the Monteiths and the Scanlons . . . well, it seems now as if it were meant to be."

"And having the governor as best man was a real coup. The cathedral was packed! Like a royal wedding or something. That's all we lack, you know. Tell Seamus to marry a princess or something. I'd like that."

Emerald nodded. "I'll tell him. But no English princesses, or come to think of it, no German or Austrian princesses either. How about a French or Spanish princess?"

"French, I think. They dress well."

"Seamus looks nice," Emerald said proudly.

"Edward is no slouch either. God, he looks so much like Joe when Joe was younger."

Joe walked over and handed Emerald another cup of punch. His arm circled her slim waist. "Glad they decided on separate honeymoons. I wouldn't want their togetherness carried too far."

"I feel like hugging you, Joe." Emerald looked up into her husband's face.

"Don't let me stop you," he joked. "Eugenia will forgive us."

Emerald turned and squeezed him. "Everything that was wrong is right again. Katie's married to a fine man who's the son of my best friend. J.J.'s settling down with a fine girl."

"And soon our mutual houses will be crawling with more grandchildren."

2

March 1950

Boston

Dr. Paul Rosen's office was filled with textbooks and diagrams. Joe Scanlon abstractedly studied one; it depicted the heart and the veins and arteries leading to it.

"How long have I known you, Joe?" Dr. Rosen didn't look up, but shuffled some papers on his desk. He had been the Scanlon-family doctor since 1925. He was near retirement now and he reminded Joe of an old woman.

"Twenty-five years," Joe answered.

Dr. Rosen looked up now. "Listen, Joe, you can go to another doctor, and by the way, I urge you to." Dr. Rosen's glasses slipped down over his nose; they were steel-rimmed and they caught the light. "You have to slow down. Tell me, exactly ow do you feel?"

Joe shrugged uncomfortably. "I feel okay. I mean, if I felt really shipshape, I wouldn't be here."

"Exactly. Look, you're a strong man physically and your weight's fine, but your blood pressure is way up, and as far as I know, you've been under pressure since Pearl Harbor. Lately you don't know how to relax, do you? You haven't got the foggiest idea."

"It was you who organized the lobby for Israel and kept me up half the night with phone calls back in forty-eight. Do you know how many lobby and pressure groups I have to deal with?"

"Guilty!" Dr. Rosen admitted, throwing up his hands. "But that's why I know what you're going through. Look, you have to take it easier, Joe. Really."

"How serious is it?"

"Not too serious if you learn to relax. If you don't, I suggest you get your worldly affairs in order and tell Emerald she's going to be a widow."

"That's blunt."

"You ask, I tell. Listen, you're a big boy now. Too big that I should lie to you." He shrugged. "You go home, you take the pills I give you, you learn not to answer the phone . . . except when I call." He tried to wink, but instead blinked.

Joe stood up. "You won't tell Emerald, will you?"

"You don't want me too, I won't. But I think you should."

Joe bit his lip. "I will, but not right now." Then he silently promised himself he wouldn't tell her at all. Sixty-five, he thought. Hell, my father got my mother pregnant at that age!

3

June 1950

Washington

"I love it out here." Emerald threw open the double doors that led to the garden and inhaled. Birchmont Hill was twenty miles outside Washington proper, nestled in the rolling Virginia countryside. "It's not Cape Cod, but I do like it, especially in June."

Joe rolled over and kicked off the sheets. "What is so rare as a day in June?" he quoted. "Mmm, what time is it?"

"Seven," Emerald answered. "Oh, it is a rare day, it's lovely and warm out.'' She looked lovingly at her garden. Many of the flowers were in bloom, and the occasional butterfly flitted about.

"Coffee time," Joe announced as he stood up. "Hell, I ought to get up to the Hill early today. I don't think I have time for a proper breakfast.''

Emerald turned to him. She put her arms around his neck and kissed him. "I insist on sharing coffee with you. Then I think I'll ask you for a drive into town. I have things to do too.''

"At the new Washington Interracial, Interdenominational Center, no doubt. That's the second building you've had the company construct.''

Emerald smiled and winked. "Seamus runs the companies, and he gave it to me for my birthday.''

"That's not till August.''

"Well, now he won't have to give me anything.''

"You're quite an operator, lady," Joe joked.

"I learned how from watching you. Anyway, I have shopping to do too. I have to get a christening present for Angie.''

"That baby is the spitting image of her mother," Joe remarked.

"And Mary has had a remarkable influence on J.J.''

Joe agreed silently. J.J was now all one could wish for. He had been promoted to head of the news department, he showed all the signs of maturity Joe had always hoped for, and Mary was the only woman in his life. As for Kathleen, she was blissful. Philip was clearly her perfect mate.

Emerald giggled. "You know, we've been married for twenty-seven years this August and I've never understood why you put on your shirt and then go into the bathroom to shave and take it right off again.''

"Habit." He kissed her. "Like loving you.''

"Don't start, or neither of us will get into town on time.''

He laughed. They had made love last night, and he wondered how many people were so passionate after twenty-seven years. Not too many, he decided.

Emerald pulled on her dress and ran the brush through her hair. It took her only a minute to adroitly pin it up. Next, she sparingly applied makeup.

"Senator Austin asked me if you'd had a face lift," he told her.

"And what did you tell him?''

"I told him your face hadn't fallen.''

Emerald laughed, and Joe went to shave.

* * *

The coffee was already hot in the breakfast room. They sat down and the maid bustled in. "Breakfast?"

"Not this morning. Just coffee and some rolls."

"Time for the news," Joe announced officiously. "You never know, maybe J.J. wrote it."

They both listened. The newsman was solemn: "Sixty thousand North Korean troops have crossed the forty-seventh parallel to invade South Korea. They were spearheaded by over one hundred Russian tanks."

Emerald set her coffee cup down. "What does it mean?"

Joe scowled into his cup. "It might mean nothing, were it not for the Russians." He shook his head. "I'm not sure, but I don't like the sound of it."

"Nor do I," she agreed.

"The cold war seems to be heating up."

Emerald closed her eyes; memories of the newsreels of Hiroshima sped into her mind. She saw the images of the children on the bridge, she saw the mushroom cloud. She looked across the room to the mantel. Her parents' faded wedding picture, the picture of her and Joe at the rock altar, the pictures from Katie and J.J.'s wedding, the photographs of her grandchildren . . .

When she was a child, her family was lost to her. Now she looked at the pictures and shook her head. "It can't happen," Emerald said. "We can't destroy the earth."

Joe saw the look in her eyes and knew what she was thinking. "No," he answered simply. "That we can't."

4

July 10, 1950

Washington

"I don't care if he *is* the president! I don't care if he *is* a Democrat. I don't give a shit! The right to declare war rests with the Congress of the United States of America, not with the president!"

Joe Scanlon was aware that his face was beet red and he was shaking with anger. But he found his fellow senators infuriating; they seemed to have no sense of history and no sense of the checks and balances that were designed to keep the country free.

Joe took a deep breath and tried to assess the political mood of his companions. They were in a bar, a bar where more deals were struck than had ever been struck on the floor of the Senate. And the outcome of this conversation that had become an argument would not only set the tone of the debate on the Senate floor but would indicate the outcome, since those gathered together over bourbon, Scotch, and Irish whiskey were representative of the factions that actually existed.

Hayden Richards leaned back in the leather chair, and when he did, his tiny short legs went out nearly straight. Emerald always called Richards, who was the esteemed senator from Virginia, "Humpty Dumpty Richards." Her description was quite accurate. He looked like an egg with legs.

"Hell, I was an isolationist in thirty-nine! Ah said 'Let the Europeans have their wars and let the Japanese take over the orient—one damn little yellow bastard ain't no different from another!' But Ah was wrong! You gotta get out there and protect what's yours. And Ah always recognized the Red menace—sons of bitches—we ought to have taken out the Russians right after Hiroshima!"

Joe squirmed slightly and fought the desire to smash Humpty Dumpty Richards' face in. Prejudiced, Bible-thumping little fucker.

"I was against our joining the UN in the first place. I knew it would eventually lead to an abrogation of our own Constitution. See what's happened? The UN has declared a police action and our president has committed troops without consulting Congress. I'm with Joe on this one."

The speaker was Senator Barkley Neilson, the senator from Wisconsin; he came out of the farm-labor party and his ideas often reflected a certain muddled thinking—at least that's what Joe thought.

"It's not the short term I'm concerned with," Joe said slowly. "It's not even the right or wrong of the action. It's the precedent it sets. If the president is allowed the power this precedent gives him, then the Congress may well have to face a knockdown, drag-out fight with some other president in the future. Say what you want, but it wasn't some foreign power that got the UN to vote the police action in the first place, it was our own government. We're responsible for the police action, and therefore it's a matter of our policy too. Congress might well agree to commit troops to Korea, but we have to be asked. Dammit! The authorization for that rests with the Congress!" Joe set his glass down on the table. His hand trembled, and he was vaguely aware of a tightness in his chest.

"Maybe McCarthy is right. Maybe the State Department is full of Commies," Hayden Richards said

Richards was incredibly stupid, Joe decided. And McCarthy, fellow Irishman or no, was dumber yet. "I think you're missing the point, Hayden." Joe tried to sound conciliatory, and it crossed his mind that the trouble with democracy was that Hayden's vote counted too, and in order to make even minimal progress, one had to constantly seek the support of dolts like Hayden.

"Look, we can support the president. We can authorize the funds for the police action, or war, or whatever name we decide to call it. We can approve the whole thing. In fact, I'm in favor of that. But we have to come on strong with some initiative, or it will look like the White House is running the country instead of the Congress. What we're talking about here is public relations and precedents. We have to let people know the President can only do this if we approve it."

"Do we?" Hayden's eyes were blurry

"I'm not sure," Barkley Neilson said thoughtfully.

Joe closed his eyes. His arm hurt and a sharp pain filled his chest with a sudden agony. He opened his eyes and stood up, bracing himself on the arm of the chair; the red velvet wallpaper behind the bar looked like a distant fire; the ornate mirror in front of which hundreds of bottles were stacked revealed the sudden image of his own face. He let out a groan.

"I certainly have to think about authorizing an arms buildup . . . Joe! Joe, what the matter?"

Barkley's question was the last word Joe heard. His mouth seemed to fill with liquid, all the blood in his body seemed to have gone to his head, which felt like a pounding, pain-filled balloon. "Emerald . . ." he blurted out. Then he staggered and fell to the floor.

5

August 1, 1950

Cape Cod

Outside the Scanlon house on Cape Cod, the misshapen trees bent to the summer breeze. In the woods behind the house, wildflowers bloomed in the sunny areas, while graceful ferns covered the ground beneath the tall trees. All across the eastern horizon, dark cloud banks threatened a summer thunderstorm.

Inside the house, Emerald sat curled in her favorite chair, listening to the turbulent waves as they crashed on the beach outside. She glanced up at the clock. The governor had asked to see her around five; it was ten past the hour now. Another ten minutes passed; then Emerald heard the big car as it came up the long driveway. She stood up and shook out her dress, then went to the door to greet the governor of the Commonwealth of Massachusetts.

"How are you, Emerald?" The governor pressed his lips together and kissed her on the cheek. His snow-white hair blew in the breeze, and he lifted his hand, smoothing it down.

"Come in before you blow away," Emerald invited. She took his coat and ushered him into the living room.

"Now, what I need is a little brandy," he said as he sat down.

"That can be arranged." Emerald poured some brandy into two snifters. "I think we're in for a storm."

"There's certainly a wind coming up," he agreed. "You look well," he commented truthfully. Her lovely eyes still held a deep sadness, he thought. But the worst was over; her expression was placid, her manner outgoing.

"I'm all right. Lonely, a little lost, but I'm all right. Joe left me a letter. He'd written it over a year ago when he'd been to see a doctor. He knew he had a bad heart. But he said he couldn't change his whole life and become an invalid, he said he wanted to live his life fully, no matter how short a time there might be." She paused and blinked back tears.

"It's all right, Governor, I'm not going to dissolve into tears. It's just thinking about his letter that makes me a little sad. Joe had such a full legislative program—the school-lunch program, the housing program, urban renewal . . . those bills were Joe's dreams, and he told me that few people have the opportunity to make their dreams reality; he said he couldn't give up that opportunity. He asked me to forgive him, to know he was doing what he wanted, to know he wanted to die quickly and not live his life monitoring every breath and every activity."

Emerald sipped some brandy. "I miss him terribly," she added, "but I think I understand."

"Your husband was a fine man. We all miss him . . . his constituents will miss him most of all. Now, tell me, Emerald, what are you doing to keep busy?"

"Oh, there are lots of papers to go through. Of course, Seamus is looking after all the business interests. And I have my children and grandchildren." She smiled as she thought of them.

Mary was pregnant again, and Katie and Philip were expecting their first. Jimmy, Katie's son by her first husband, was eight.

Edward was in his last year of medical school, and J.J. was writing a book that threatened to become the "in" Washington book of the season. But it was the little ones who sustained her, and Eugenia, who came offering no wisdom and no clichés, but only the experience of her own losses.

"Are your grandchildren enough to keep you busy, Emerald?" He paused and lit a cigarette. "You're terribly intelligent, you know politics, and you know the party. I don't doubt your talents as a grandmother, but, woman, I know you, and it's not enough."

Emerald tried to smile. "You're still an old flatterer, aren't you?"

He shook his head. "The truth is no idle compliment."

"Well, I have the recreation centers, too."

"They seem to run quite well on their own," he replied.

Emerald nodded her agreement. Both centers were well-staffed.

The governor leaned forward in his chair. "I'd like to make you an offer on behalf of the party. We want you to run in November, to fill Joe's seat. I can appoint you now, you'll run, and there's no question in my mind that you'll be elected. I want you, Emerald, the party wants you."

Emerald looked at him in near-disbelief.

"You're surprised! I never thought I'd succeed in surprising you."

Emerald ran her hand across her skirt nervously, searching for the right words, indeed for the right response. "I'm shocked," she finally managed.

"And I'm serious. We don't have time to find a candidate. We've been meeting since Joe's death. You're our first choice."

"If I join Margaret Chase Smith, both women in Congress will be from New England."

"And as it should be," the governor joked. "We're very progressive. Emerald, it will give you the opportunity to fulfil Joe's legislative program."

"I ought to think about this."

"The election is only three months away. You don't have time to think about it. I need to know now."

Joe's letter came back into her mind. "I'll do it," she said after a minute. "I don't know if I can, or if I should, but I'll try it. After all, I might be defeated."

The governor smiled. "Not likely."

"Governor, can you wait a week to announce this?"

"Will you change your mind?"

"No, it's just that the children are coming up. I want to tell them myself."

He smiled warmly. "I understand. I know it's a big step for you."

"It's just that it's so soon after . . ." She hesitated. "Our twenty-seventh anniversary would have been this month."

The governor nodded. "Joe would have wanted you to do this. In a way, it's an anniversary present. Emerald, you can fulfill his dreams, his aspirations."

Emerald took a breath. "That's why I have agreed," she said honestly.

"I'll wait a week. But no longer, just a week. You have campaigning to do. We're going to keep you very busy indeed."

"Good," Emerald replied.

Emerald waved good-bye to the governor as his big car eased down the driveway toward the main highway. Then she put her hands in her pockets and headed down to the shore. She sat down, leaning against a rock—*their* rock was how she thought of it. How often had they sat on the beach together, watching the sea, listening to the waves?

A wind came up, and on the horizon lightning flashed across the sky. "I miss you, Joe," Emerald said out loud. It was as if he were somehow with her; the house, the beach, had been so much a part of their lives.

"Have I done the right thing?" she asked. "I made the decision quickly. Is it what you would have wanted?" She closed her eyes; the words of his letter again occupied her thoughts. Yes, she decided. He would have wanted her to finish what he had begun.

6

August 6, 1950

J.J. had his feet up, and he smoked his cigarette as if he were pasha in a harem. Mary did not sit at his feet, however. She stood by the window and looked out at the ocean.

Katie and Philip were in the kitchen talking; Seamus and Edward had gone for a walk, announcing that they needed the exercise after having eaten so large a meal.

Eugenia Monteith, casually dressed in Bermuda shorts, was draped over a chair, a copy of *Vogue* in her hands.

"Where is everyone?" Emerald asked as she entered the room with a bottle of champagne and a tray full of glasses.

"What's this, champagne?" J.J. looked puzzled.

"Is there something to celebrate?" Eugenia asked, putting down her *Vogue*.

Emerald smiled mysteriously. "Maybe. But I want everyone together."

J.J. stood up. "Seamus and Edward are out walking. They can't have gotten too far, though. I'll call them back."

"Does this mean there's an announcement to be made?" Eugenia said dryly, eyeing the champagne. "Is that why I was summoned to come up here? Do you realize I missed the opening play of the summer theater season?"

"Oh, Eugenia, I'm sorry, darling. I sent your tickets to Willard Anderson from the NAACP."

"My theater box is being occupied by a Negro? Gawd! How perfectly fashionable!"

"Mother knows what's best for you, Eugenia," Katie said as she stood in the doorway with Philip just behind her. "Now you'll get gold points in heaven."

"And the Ku Klux Klan on my lawn the next time I vacation in Alabama."

From outside, J.J.'s voice calling Edward and Seamus could be heard clearly.

"Is something the matter?" Katie asked.

"I'm just trying to round everyone up. Feed this group, and they run off in all directions. I should have made my little speech at the dinner table."

"A speech, is it?" Eugenia cocked her head.

"A sort of speech," Emerald hedged.

"Well, I must say you're looking mysterious, and mystery becomes you."

"I haven't done that in a long while!" Edward collapsed against the door jamb panting. "Raced Seamus all the way up the beach."

"You beat me!" Seamus exclaimed. "Of course, it's because you've got longer legs. I protest!" Seamus burst into the room J.J. followed. He strolled at a pleasant pace, hands in his pockets the inevitable cigarette in his mouth. He was, Emerald noted even beginning to look like a writer.

"Sit down, I have something to tell you."

"How dramatic." Eugenia slipped into her chair and crossed her long legs.

Katie and Philip sat on the sofa. J.J. sat down, Mary on the edge of his chair. Seamus and Edward sat down on the floor.

Emerald remained standing, the champagne tray in front of her on the table. "I have a surprise," she began. In truth, she didn't know how to begin. She was a little afraid of how they would all take it.

"You're joining a Catholic group to liberate Ulster peacefully," Eugenia joked. She churned her glass of gin and tonic about. "I must try Catholicism sometime. Now that Clare Boothe Luce has converted—Gawd, if its good enough for her, it must be good enough for me."

"You're being sacrilegious," Mary said somewhat sharply. Mary didn't quite approve of Eugenia.

"Posh! I don't think the Catholics would have me anyway. I'm not as pure as Clare Boothe Luce and I'm not married to the owner of *Time* magazine."

Emerald cleared her throat and they all turned to look at her. "I'm assuming Joe's Senate seat," she announced. "And running in November to keep it."

Not unexpectedly, Eugenia spoke first. "It is practically the same thing as joining a Catholic group to bring peace to Ulster. My Gawd, Emerald, you'll become one of the Holy Trinity!"

J.J., Edward, and Seamus laughed. It was said that at all times there were at least three Irish-American senators who pressed the Irish cause in American policy, bringing pressure on Great Britain at critical moments in history. At present, they were Fitzgerald Larkin, Hy O'Malley, and Eugene Duggan Pearce. None of them counted Joe McCarthy—he belonged to a cause of his own making and his existence enabled Eugenia to breathe deeply and mutter, "Now, there's an Irishman I can really hate."

"It won't be a trinity if there are four of us." Emerald laughed. "In any case, my priority will be your father's legislative program. Well, tell me what you think."

"I think it will enable me to sell an article to *Harper's*: 'My Mother the Senator.' " J.J. winked. "I've been taking Clifton Webb lessons from Eugenia, but I'll never be as good as she is."

Eugenia hissed, "I should think not." Then she turned back to Emerald warmly. "I approve. It's brought you back to life, it's what you need, and God knows the country needs you."

"Are you sure it won't be too much, Mother?" Katie looked at her mother with concern.

"Not at all! I refuse to sit here and rot. Do you know how many bills your father had ready to introduce? No, for thirty years I've been standing on the edge of politics. Well, I'm diving in.''

''Bravo!'' Seamus clapped his hands and walked across the room and kissed his mother. ''Good for you!''

Edward hugged her too, and she looked up at him lovingly. ''I'm proud of you,'' Edward whispered.

''You're not the only one,'' J.J. added.

''Oh, begone with you,'' Emerald answered playfully, her Irish lilt still evident.

''I do think I'll come to Washington with you,'' Eugenia announced. ''You'll need a fashion adviser. Perhaps I can write something too—for *Vogue*: 'What the Well-Dressed Senator Will Be Wearing in 1951'!''

''Oh, Eugenia! Would you come to Washington with me?''

''Of course. Anyway, now that you've given my box at the theater to the NAACP, I might as well leave, there's simply nothing to keep me here.''

35

1

January 15, 1954

Washington

Emerald sat in a corner of the Senate dining room. As she ate, she leafed through her notes. The dining room was usually a quiet place to dine; it was where senators who wanted to do a little work during lunch often retreated, spreading out their papers before them while lunch was served by unobtrusive waiters.

"Emerald!" Senator McCarthy called out from two tables away. He raised a pudgy finger and motioned her over to him.

Emerald didn't turn her head to acknowledge him; instead, she cultivated her newly discovered deafness.

But deafness was not sufficient. She looked up when a warm finger prodded her shoulder.

"Emerald, are you going deaf?"

Emerald looked up stonily. "Good afternoon, Senator."

He ran his hand through his thinning black hair. It's greasy, Emerald noticed, and he smelled of whiskey. He eyed her with his little dark shoe-button eyes.

"May I help you, Senator?" She pointedly didn't call him Joe—it was unthinkable to call this creature Joe; Joe was a special name for her.

He cleared his throat. His face was pinkish. "I want to talk to you, Emerald. May I sit down?"

"Mrs. Scanlon," she corrected coldly. "Or Senator Scanlon if you prefer."

He grinned stupidly. "I can't think of women as senators."

"There was a time, Senator, when the public couldn't think of the Irish as Senators. You make their prejudice frightfully easy to understand." She felt suddenly proud of herself. I have learned something from Eugenia, she admitted.

But Senator McCarthy was not so easily put off, nor did he wait for her permission to sit down. Undaunted by her blatant sarcasm, he flopped down and his grossly shiny shoes caught her eye. There was something sloppy about Senator McCarthy, and there was, she noted, a catsup stain on his coat.

"I'm worried about you," he confided in a hushed voice.

"Really, whatever for?" she replied brightly.

"I've been studying your voting record since you were appointed in August 1950. I must say, you've displayed a decidedly left-of-center stance."

"Left of center! Saints preserve us!" Emerald burst into peals of laughter. "It's a wonder you haven't called Our Blessed Savior and the Twelve Holy Apostles in front of your committee—and I am being ladylike calling it a committee."

"You're being frivolous," he grumbled.

"Frivolous, am I? Well, when you call my position on child welfare, on social security, and on school-lunch programs left of center, you're being more than frivolous, you're being absurd!"

"And what about your position on loyalty oaths?" he hissed meanly.

"Let me tell you something, Senator McCarthy. I know your kind of Irishman. You're just small-minded and mean. You're dangerous, too, because small-minded, mean people are always dangerous. Do you know that last week my son and his wife went to get their passports, and the little one, the eighteen-month old, had to have her little right hand held up so she could pledge that she wouldn't overthrow the U.S. government?" Emerald laughed. "Tell me, Senator, if that baby wets on you—and I wish she would—would you have her prosecuted for perjury?"

"The loyalty oath is a legal instrument—"

"To keep a baby from overthrowing the government? Oh, you're in terrible shape, you are. God knows what will become of you when you find out the men who make your whiskey are Communists!"

"They're good Irishmen!" he blustered.

"Like Jim Connolly, who commanded the General Post Office in 1916. Oh, I was there, Senator, and Jim Connolly was socialist—I think you'd call him a pinko. Senator, you see things—wee things that go boo in the night! Now, we Irish are fine tellers of tales, but your tales are hurtful lies."

"You had better watch yourself," he threatened. "Do you know what kind of fight you're getting into?"

Emerald laughed. "Oh, Senator! In 1916 when I agreed to stay in the General Post Office, I didn't know what kind of fight I was getting into. Since then, I've always known!"

"You're un-American!"

"You've surpassed being un-American," she mumbled. "Go away. Being seen with you may harm my reputation—or yours."

Suddenly, on impulse, Emerald stood up and tapped on her glass with her knife. In her loudest voice, she addressed the twelve senators in the room. "Gentlemen! Behold! Senator McCarthy speaking with a woman! Does this mean he is now, was, or ever might have been a woman? I give you the evidence: his mother was a woman, he was seen with her often, she even wore skirts!" The laughter began as a twitter, but Kal Kemper from California burst into uproarious laughter.

Joe McCarthy stood up, his face beet red.

Emerald scowled at him and craned her long neck upward. 'In the words of my late husband, Senator, 'piss on you,' '' she whispered.

He turned his back on her and retreated not only back to his own table but also right out of the Senate dining room.

Emerald smiled at the apprehensive waiter. "I'll have my lunch now." She smiled sweetly.

2

August 21, 1954

Cape Cod

Emerald walked across the living room to the mantel. She smiled thoughtfully at her collection of pictures. They spanned three generations. Her parents' wedding tintype; her father in South Africa; her own wedding pictures; pictures of Tom Hughes and their son; pictures of her dead brothers, Seamus and Padraic. And there, by the rock altar, she and Joe taking their wedding vows. But there were more: there were the smiling happy faces of Katie and Philip and their children; of J.J. and Mary and their three youngsters; of Edward graduating from medical school; of Seamus on the yacht out in the bay.

"God has been good to me," Emerald murmured. She opened the mother-of-pearl keepsake box on the center of the mantel and took out Joe's last letter, the one he had left with Dr. Rosen to be given to her.

Today, she thought, would be our thirty-first anniversary. She kissed the letter; then, returning to her chair, she reread it:

> My darling Emerald:
>   When you read this letter, I will no longer be with you, though I will always be at your side in spirit.
>   Last week I went to Dr. Rosen; this week I consulted a specialist who confirmed his diagnosis. I have high blood pressure and a weak heart. I was given a choice,

Emerald. I was told I could slow down—retire from the Senate—and live another ten years, or I could keep up my pace and take my chances. You will know I made the latter choice. I want you to understand why.

First, I cannot become an invalid living in fear, waiting for my last breath. Second, I have not yet fulfilled my aspirations of shepherding through the new social-welfare package: the school-lunch program, the urban-renewal bill, and the new child-welfare act. To leave the Senate without seeing these measures come to fruition would be to deny the dream I have held for so long—a dream we have held for so long.

My darling, I hope you can forgive me, but I would not be the man you love if I were different. Emerald, you have given me the happiest years of my life. You have given me wonderful children, you have given me the kind of love few men know. I love you.

Mourn for me, but do not mourn long . . . to fulfill a dream, Emerald, I have that opportunity.

Love,
Joe

Emerald wiped a tear from her eye and refolded the letter "Happy anniversary," she said out loud.

She put the letter back in the keepsake box and went out to walk along the beach, to visit "their" rock.

She sat down and leaned against the great gaunt rock. It was warm from the afternoon sun, and she watched as the giant breakers pounded onto the sandy shore.

She closed her eyes and remembered her nightmare run through Belfast over forty years ago; she remembered dear Mrs. Higgins who showed her pictures of Boston; she remembered Father Doyle; and she thought about Tom and his wife and child.

She smiled to herself when she remembered the little boy in the Boston public gardens who had inspired her to open the recreational center: it helped to fight hate in Boston, she thought.

"Ireland suffers from too much history . . ." The words written by Yeats went through her mind. "Too much history, but the history is a history of hate, of action, and of reaction," she said talking to herself. "And it's the children, the children of the troubles, the children of Belfast who nurture the hate, carrying from one generation to another. . . .

"Oh, Joe, I miss you," she sighed. "I've fulfilled your dream

wish you were here . . . the legislation has all been passed . . .
we did it, Joe, we did it.

Emerald picked up a handful of sand and let it run through her
fingers. I have a dream too, she admitted. Joe, it's time I got on
with it. Understand, my darling, I have to go home. . . .
Emerald closed her eyes; quietly, she made a decision.

3

August 29, 1954

Cape Cod

The whole family was spread out around the living room; it
was reminiscent of the scene four years ago when Emerald had
told them she was accepting the appointment to the Senate.

They all sat primly except J.J. He lolled over a chair, his feet
draped over its arms.

Emerald smiled. Mary was pregnant again; J.J. insisted he
wanted his own basketball team.

Katie and Philip huddled together, while Seamus sat in a
straight-backed chair expectantly.

Edward was with his fiancée, Miriam Cohen. He said that
since he wasn't a Jewish doctor, it was best to have a Jewish
wife. But he was joking; one had only to look at Edward and
Miriam to know how much in love they were. Eugenia had
quipped that the whole clan was becoming a melting pot.

"I've told the governor and the party I will not stand for
election this coming November," Emerald told them.

"Why?" Katie asked in a surprised tone.

"Oh, hell, Mother, you're such good press." J.J. sat up,
swinging his long legs to the floor.

Emerald sighed. "I want to read you all something . . ."

She walked to the mantel and opened the mother-of-pearl
keepsake box. She carefully unfolded Joe's letter and read it
aloud to them.

When she finished, she refolded it and replaced it.

"You see, when I accepted the appointment and then when I
was elected to fill out the four years of your father's term, I did
so fulfill his dream."

Emerald paused. They were all quiet and thoughtful. Edward's
eyes were misty. Katie was crying.

"Don't cry," Emerald said kindly. "It's a joy to have a

dream." She took a breath. "I've been through the Korean peace negotiations, through McCarthyism, and I've spirited through the programs your father held so dear and thought were so very important."

"You could do more," J.J. said. "There's more that needs doing."

"There's always more that needs doing," Emerald agreed "Oh, my darlings . . . don't you see, I have a dream of my own." She shook her head. "I'm fifty-nine years old, next August I'll be sixty, and I don't have so many years left to fulfill my dream . . . so I'm going to start now. I'm going back to Belfast and I'm going to begin something I've had in the back of my mind for years."

"Belfast?" J.J. repeated.

"Oh, what I want to do won't change the world or unite Ireland, but it's a step, and I believe you have to take small steps to cover long distances . . . so I'm going to take that step."

"What are you going to do, Mother?" Katie asked.

"Well, when I opened the first interdenominational center in Boston it was because I had met a small child who needed some place to go, someplace where he could learn not to hate. For years I have known that the troubles in Ulster would never end until the people of Ulster could stop hating one another. For years I have believed that the children of Ulster carried the seeds of hatred that it was the children with whom the new beginning must be made."

Emerald smiled. "Oh, I know I sound idealistic, and perhaps I am. But the world was never hurt by ideals . . . by dreamers. I was fortunate in one way. When I was a child, there was an old woman who befriended me. I lived with unfeeling people, but I learned from Mrs. Higgins that not all Protestants are alike, that there is good and bad everywhere. It is that lesson I have to to pass on to the children of the troubles."

"But Belfast is so far away," Katie persisted.

"Oh, my darlings, I am going home to my past. I can do this because I'm leaving behind a happy present. You are all settled, you're happy and able to look after yourselves."

"And if they get into trouble, I'm here," Eugenia quipped.

J.J. laughed. "I think that's a threat," he joked.

4

April 16, 1956

Emerald turned the corner onto Falls Road; it was the dividing
ne between the Protestant and Catholic areas of Belfast.

On the east side of the street loomed a large three-story
uilding. It contained a gym and a variety of recreation rooms; it
as surrounded by a large playground filled with children.

Emerald walked closer, and little Timothy McCall rushed to
eet her. "Good morning, Mrs. Scanlon," he said politely.

Emerald beamed down at him. His red hair fell in his face and
boasted a freckle on the end of his nose. He was an orphan and
lived on the top floor of the Scanlon Interdenominational Center.

"Good morning to you," she responded.

"We had a fine soccer match," he said, grinning. "We tied
: Catholics!"

"Oh, a tie, was it?"

He nodded. "Are we having ice cream for lunch today?"

"I'm not sure." She smiled. "But I hope so."

They passed the playground, and Emerald and Timothy stopped
watch. Emerald sighed a sigh of satisfaction. The children,
otestant and Catholic, were all playing happily.

"The beginning of the end of hate," Emerald said under her
ath. "Let it be a real beginning."

"Did you say something, Mrs. Scanlon?"

"Yes, I was just making a wish." Emerald sighed.

"About what?"

"Oh, it won't come true if I tell you."

"I make wishes," he confided. "But I always tell them."

"Since you've already told, you might as well tell me—what
you wish?"

"I wish I would grow up," he replied.

Emerald bent down and looked into his face. She touched the
:kle on the end of his nose. "You'll be grown up when your
:kle disappears—that's what my mother told me."

"Really?"

"Really," Emerald answered.

He suddenly put his hand over his mouth. "Oh, I forgot!
re's a man in your office—an old man," he whispered.

"Thank you. I'll go along and see who it is."

"I'll go and ask the cook if we're having ice cream."

"You do that," Emerald suggested.

She hurried to her small office and opened the door.

Patiently sitting in a chair was a distinguished elderly gentle man smoking a pipe. A gold-tipped cane rested by the side of th chair. He looked up as she entered. Emerald stopped short.

The man stood up, tall and straight. His hair was still thic and snow-white, his face was a network of lines, but qui recognizable.

"Emerald . . ." He held out his withered hand.

"Albert . . ." Emerald took the hand of seventy-five-year-o Albert Jenkins.

He smiled warmly at her. "I came to see your dream," said slowly, almost painfully. "No," he said, shaking his hea "I came to share your dream."

Emerald continued to hold his hand.

"My dear, I have little time left. I've come to make a donatio if I might call it that." His eyes were watery and he lifted h hand to touch her cheek. "You're still beautiful, Emerald. . . .

"Oh, Albert, I don't know what to say to you."

He withdrew his hand and reached into his inside coat poc and withdrew a check. "I'm not well," he confessed.

"I'm sorry . . ."

"Oh, don't be sorry. I've had a splendid life. In any case, I sold my estate and made peace with my maker." He handed the check.

"Oh, Albert, that is for an enormous amount of money."

He touched her cheek. "You chose not to let me share y life . . . let me have the pure pleasure of sharing your dream

Emerald nodded. Then she kissed his hand. "You're a wond ful man. It's a dream I should like all Ulster to share."

"You have begun in one small corner of Ulster. I know have faith, have patience too."

"Thank you, Albert."

He turned to leave, and Emerald touched his sleeve. "Can stay for lunch?" she asked. Then added, "I think we're hav ice cream."